BLOOD MERCY

BLOOD GRACE BOOK I

VELA ROTH

FIVE THORNS PRESS

ISBN 978-1-957040-00-4 (Ebook)
ISBN 978-1-957040-01-1 (Paperback)
ISBN 978-1-957040-02-8 (Hardcover)

Edited by Brittany Cicirello, Suncroft Editing

Cover art by Patcas Illustration
www.instagram.com/patcas_illustration

Book design by Vela Roth

Map by Vela Roth using Inkarnate
inkarnate.com

Published by Five Thorns Press
www.fivethorns.com

Visit www.velaroth.com

CONTENTS

Content Note ix

Map x

Winter Solstice.. 1

    The Cloak... 3

42 Days Until Spring Equinox 13

    Anthros's Fire and Sunsword 15

    Dusk Rites..23

    Blood in the Night...28

    Trespassing 36

    Blood Union 41

    Apparition...43

    Opening Remarks 46

    The End of an Era...52

    Test of Will..62

41 Days Until Spring Equinox 69

    Lady Cassia's Garden 71

    Diplomat Errant 83

    Negotiations 96

40 Days Until Spring Equinox 107

    War Games 109

    The King's Feast 113

    Wallflower...121

    Invitation..126

    New Terms 129

    Proof of Honor 136

36 Days Until Spring Equinox 143

    Change of Plans 145

    Risks Reckoned 152

    Peace Offering...157

28 Days Until Spring Equinox 171

    Threads 173

    Hespera's Rose 177

    Affinity...184

    Free with Words 190

    Forbidden 195

    Frost Fever 207

    A Place at the Table..215

27 Days Until Spring Equinox 223

    Summons...225

    Cassia's Seat 228

    Anger 232

26 Days Until Spring Equinox 239

    Dirty Hands..241

    Cassia Speaks 246

    Victory...252

25 Days Until Spring Equinox 265

    Intermediary...267

24 Days Until Spring Equinox 271

    Sacred Ruins...273

    A Heretic in the Temple...283

23 Days Until Spring Equinox 295

    The Drink..297

    Trust..302

    Anointing..306

    Silence 309

    Catapults...313

    Mercy..316

    Light..325

22 Days Until Spring Equinox 331

    Day Terrors...333

Offering of Blood 342

21 Days Until Spring Equinox 347

Day of Mourning 349

Flint and Steel 355

Vigil 358

20 Days Until Spring Equinox 363

More 365

19 Days Until Spring Equinox 369

Snowfall...371

Wanting 375

Pleasure 382

Cassia's Blood 388

18 Days Until Spring Equinox 389

Touch 391

17 Days Until Spring Equinox 403

Lio's Mission...405

Cassia's Choice..409

Falling 419

First Tryst..423

The Feast 434

Natural Union 441

Hours Before Dawn 444

16 Days Until Spring Equinox 449

A Stranger to Trust 451

Across the Pavilion..455

Nothing to Do with Wisdom 459

A Necessary Monster...465

Happiness 470

15 Days Until Spring Equinox 481

The Laws of Men 483

The Way of Things...486

The Western Wing...496

Kindness...500

Life Price 502

Beauty 508

One Fortnight 515
14 Days Until Spring Equinox 519
What Dead Men See...521
Solia's Secret 530
Cassia's Treason 542
Saplings 555
Siege 559
Through the Veil 565
An Impossible Dream...568
Deukalion's Address...579
To the Gallows 591
Fire and Light..594
The Heretic and the Bastard...598
For All of Time...602
The Truth 605
Lio's Solace 608
The King's Noose 621
Spring Equinox 625
Last Call 627
Equinox Oath...632
Glossary 635
Blood Grace Book 2...649
Free Book...650
Acknowledgements 651
About the Author..653

For Emery

CONTENT NOTE

BLOOD MERCY portrays occasional medieval fantasy violence, an emotionally abusive father, and conversations about attempted sexual assault.

In particular, the main character has difficult encounters with her father in "The Cloak," "Change of Plans," and "Day of Mourning."

"The Way of Things" is an emotional, but not graphic chapter in which one woman confides in another that a man tried to assault her.

The novel confronts these topics to show women supporting each other, healing from trauma, and seeking justice.

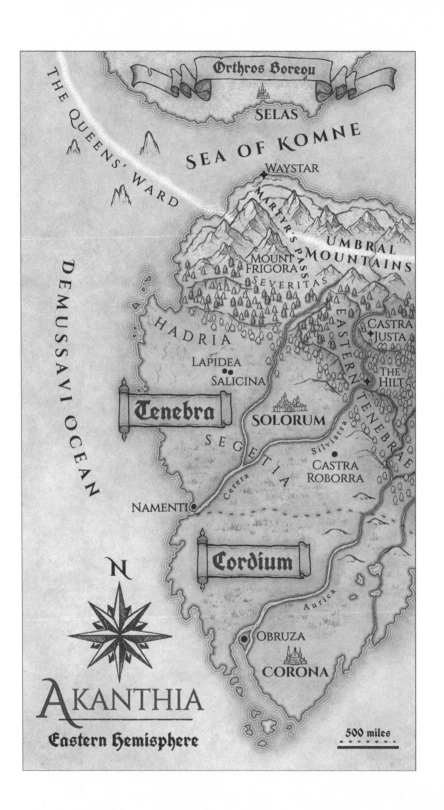

WINTER SOLSTICE

THE CLOAK

CASSIA WAS ALWAYS ONE maneuver away from her last breath. Every day was like a siege. Each decision she made, no matter how small, must fortify her defenses. She excelled at the practice of protecting herself. She lived by it.

One wrong move, and the king would destroy her.

Challenging him was always the wrong move. She hoped she lived to regret what she was about to do.

Today, she would cast aside all her hard-won defenses and place herself within death's reach. The king's reach.

She sat utterly still in her chair, but her breath wanted to rush in and out of her lungs. She forced herself to inhale deeply. Then a slow exhale.

She rearranged the cloak upon her lap, the better to display the hole in the otherwise flawless lambskin. Such a simple thing, but it would cause a chain of events that would accomplish her purpose.

Heat flashed under her skin and broke through in a sweat. She must not dwell on the fact that this encounter with a servant would soon lead to an audience with the king.

She couldn't afford fear. She had to see her plan through.

The seamstress stood over her. A band of late afternoon light slanted in from the high slit of one window and gleamed in her narrowed eyes. With a single glower, she judged the plain brown gown Cassia wore.

The wizened craftswoman had taken her time getting here. Her message was clear: she had more important tasks than mending for the king's bastard daughter. Yet she had come to this back corner of the palace, though it was Winter Solstice, when she could be spending the holiday off her feet.

Cassia had been right. The woman could not resist finding out what was to be gained by granting the favor. Other people's ambitions were very useful.

Cassia knew better than to have ambitions. A king's bastard had few resources and less power. A daughter had none at all. So why was she sitting here with this cloak, ready to move the sun and moons to achieve her ends?

Her pulse hammered through her body. She thought back over each step of her plan. She had taken every precaution. Nothing she did today would seem out of the ordinary to the king or anyone who might report to him.

No one would question why she called upon the most skilled seamstress in the King of Tenebra's household rather than attempt to mend the cloak herself. No one would doubt she mourned the loss of the finest mantle she might ever have, which had cost her suitor Lord Adrogan a number of prize shearlings.

The king would not suspect her. Would he?

Cassia's expression felt brittle on her face, a thin mask over the alarms sounding inside her head. She ran a hand over the cloak, knitting her brows as if she actually cared about the hideous thing. "Please tell me you can save it, Mistress."

The seamstress eyed the hole as if assessing its size and jagged edges. Then she peered at Knight. Cassia's hound lifted his head from his favorite resting place, his lady's feet, and sniffed. Whatever he scented, and whatever his instincts beyond his nose told him, he parted his jaws in a dog smile, showing the old woman a lolling tongue and a mouthful of teeth.

The seamstress's mouth puckered as if she wished to spit upon the beast for ruining such a fine garment. Or perhaps the reason for her disgust was not Knight's lack of respect for her craft, but the odor of his feet, which he had given a thorough licking just before she entered. As unique as the scent of a horse, the musk of a liegehound inspired either love or hatred.

When the seamstress turned her gaze on Cassia again, the old woman's lips creased into what passed for a smile. She patted the pincushion she wore upon her sleeve, which sported an arsenal of long bone needles. "I can repair anything, Lady. Of course, it will take time."

"How long?" asked Cassia.

"I trust the wait will be no inconvenience while the court is wintering here in Namenti. This far south, a lady has no need of the warmest lambskin in the kingdom, especially not here on the coast."

Cassia took her lower lip between her teeth, then waited for an instant to convey a hint of hesitation. She allowed a suggestion of apology to enter her tone. "I shall need it quickly. Naturally your compensation shall match the speed with which you return the cloak to me."

The old woman's eyes narrowed, but her smile remained. "I've repaired everything from a knight's leathers between one battle and the next to a lady's underlinens the very morning of her wedding. Name the day you need the cloak, and I shall deliver."

"I must have it in three days' time."

The lines around the seamstress's smile deepened. "And so you shall."

"Such service shall not go unnoticed by the king."

Nothing escaped his notice. Would Cassia really get away with this act of resistance under his very roof?

If she handed over the cloak now, her plan would be in motion, and it would succeed. There would be no turning back.

For an instant, she sat frozen in her chair. Her awareness of the smooth hide under her palm faded. She no longer felt the sweat on her skin or the shivers of tension in her limbs.

Numbness came over her. She saw the seamstress staring at the composed lady in the chair. Saw the lady's arms reach out and offer the cloak to the old woman.

Air reached Cassia's legs. Sensation returned.

She had done it.

The seamstress gathered the garment to her with the tenderness of a mother, but as soon as she had it in her arms, she hesitated. The flare of her nostrils was so slight it might go unnoticed, but Cassia was watching for it.

The smell of the herbal treatment Cassia had worked into the hide didn't carry far, but right under one's nose, the odor was unmistakable. She had made sure of that. Her stock of dried flora had supplied her with half a dozen of the most potent plants well known to ward off rogue magic.

No one took such precautions under the king's roof, where the royal mage saw to it all magic was practiced with the favor of the gods and the approval of the Orders. However, no one would set foot in the kingdom's untamed eastern reaches without wearing the proper herbs to protect against the malign spells of fugitive apostates.

The seamstress's eyes watered, but the calculation in her gaze revealed she had drawn the conclusions that Cassia had intended. The old woman bowed over the redolent cloak as if Cassia had done her a great favor, then took her leave with a self-satisfied smile.

Cassia let a shaking hand fall to rest on Knight's head and scratched behind his ears. "Good dog." Her voice came out small. She took a deeper breath, then another. "Good dog." Better.

The door to the adjoining chamber swung open, and Cassia managed not to jump. Perita appeared, one hand on the latch, toes firmly on the other side of the threshold. Behind the handmaiden, the dressing room was in chaos, strewn with all that must be readied in secret for the long journey east.

"Shall I pack your scent oils next, Lady?" The girl sounded breathless, either because she dreaded asking a question Cassia hated, or because she was trying not to breathe so close to Knight.

"If you must." Cassia studied Perita's face.

It didn't take odorous herbs to reduce Perita to tears, only the traces of dog fur that clung to everything Cassia wore. The girl's eyes were already swollen and red from sorting through Cassia's things.

"For now, take some air," Cassia instructed.

"Thank you, Lady." Perita swiped at the moisture oozing from her eyes, then tucked an escaping tendril of her hair back under her kerchief. She darted out the door of the hearth room, letting in a draft from the corridor.

With any luck, she wouldn't return for a while. She took every opportunity to sneak off with a particular guard, who served none other than Lord Hadrian and was quickly rising in the ranks.

Cassia savored a rare moment with Knight as her only companion. "Mark my words, dearest. Perita will be unpacking those oils again by sundown. That cloak will see to it we don't get sent away."

Knight gazed up at her from under his shaggy brows.

"You never liked Lord Adrogan, did you? Even before he tried to buy my hand with that cloak. How unfortunate for him that he had to leave court in haste, after we made sure someone told him what his concubine and his brother were up to back home."

Knight yawned, giving her a view of his impressive maw.

"You are a marvelous co-conspirator, Sir Knight. Thank you for your assistance with the cloak."

He rested his head on her feet again.

"The seamstress will tell her son what she learned from my cloak, so he can trade the news to his lord to win favor. The king isn't the only one with a bastard, you see. The seamstress secretly gave up a boy child years ago, and she still concerns herself with his fate. Now he is a grown man trying to distinguish himself in service to Free Lord Ferus."

A growl rumbled in Knight's chest.

"I know, love. Lord Ferus is all too interested in news of me. He's even more persistent a suitor than Lord Adrogan. No telling what rewards he'll give the seamstress's son for this information. He will know exactly which keep he should ride to, for all the king's holdings that far east are only home to soldiers, except one, which might be made fit for a lady."

Knight huffed a deep dog sigh.

"True, whether it is 'fit' for anyone is arguable, but we've done all right with much worse, haven't we? No matter in any case, for we shall not be there."

The afternoon waned, and there came the moan of the door, followed by Perita's footsteps. Then her voice, "I'll return to the packing now, Lady."

"Very well." Cassia spared a glance for her handmaiden.

The girl's eyes were dry, her nose less red, but now the rest of her had gone pale. No rendezvous with her lover had detained her, then. It had been a summons from the king. The only information her report to him would yield today was that Cassia had called upon the seamstress to rescue a suitor's expensive gift.

If Cassia was fortunate.

After the sun had set, she still sweated and listened for any sound of a messenger's approach. She quit the confines of the chair and shut herself and her agitation in her bedchamber.

With only Knight to observe her lapse of control, she paced at the end of her bed, east then west, east then west. He padded faithfully beside her, although he barely had space to turn around in the small room. These chambers where the king kept her were an afterthought.

She buried a hand in Knight's ruff. The familiar feeling of his shaggy fur under her fingers kept her panic from vanquishing her.

Her heart pounded. Then at last she heard a pounding from without. A fist on the door of the hearth room.

That would be her summons from the king.

The floor seemed to disappear from under feet, as if she floated to the bedchamber door. She couldn't feel the handle. She observed some other, distant Cassia open the door.

The next thing she knew, she was in her chair by the empty fire pit, sitting with her back straight and her feet tucked under Knight.

Her handmaiden admitted the messenger. The young man bowed, and a drop of sweat splashed from his forehead onto the threadbare hearth rug.

He was a smart boy, if he already understood that even a simple task from the king was cause for fear. "Your father the king commands your presence in his hall."

Cassia nodded, and the boy fled. He had not expected a longer response. There was only one response to the king, and the messenger would deliver it regardless of any words Cassia did or did not say.

"Shall I accompany you, Lady?" Perita clutched her hands in front of her, her knuckles white.

"No. Knight and I shall go."

"As you wish, Lady."

Cassia stepped out into the corridor. A chill crept between her shoulder blades where her gown was damp with sweat. Somewhere in the shadow and light ahead of her, the messenger's footfalls echoed. It was not long before she couldn't hear them anymore.

As she made her own way toward the royal hall, she listened for any sign she was not the only one abroad at this hour. One never knew which members of the court were in their beds and which were not. There could be eyes or ears anywhere, and any of them could report to the king.

But all she encountered was the odor of drying piss one of the lords had left in a corner. She traded places with Knight so she could smell his paws instead.

The king's door came into sight ahead. It seemed to draw nearer at an unnatural speed. Two guards flanked the entrance, as still and hard-faced as statues. When Cassia approached, one sprang to life and opened the door. Golden candlelight spilled into the corridor, glinting on the swords at their belts.

The guards' bulk made the doorway narrow. Knight pressed closer to her, his body taut as they walked between the men. Hound and guards eyed one another.

Cassia blinked in the bright hall. The iron chandeliers seemed too close. The guards at their posts along the walls appeared too tall, and the room felt crowded, although they few were the only ones who attended the royal presence tonight.

At the head of the hall, the king sat alone in a haze of candlelight.

Cassia broke out in another sweat from her scalp to the bottom of her feet. She fixed her gaze on the polished floor tiles and put one foot in front of the other.

When the king's fine leather shoes came into view, she halted. With Knight's toes no longer clicking on the stone, the room seemed very quiet.

She lowered herself to her knees. Her belly rose into her throat. Her mind filled with the horrifying vision of her emptying her stomach on his shoes. What would he do to her for that transgression?

She held very still. When his voice echoed through the hall, not so much as her finger flinched.

"You will not go east three days from now."

She kept swallowing until she was sure it was safe to open her mouth. "As you wish, Your Majesty."

At the edge of her vision, his fingers tightened on the arm of his chair. "It seems nowhere is distant and forgotten enough to keep you out of Lord Ferus's reach. He departed this afternoon to inspect one of his frontier out-posts that happens to lie within a day's ride of my easternmost household."

Cassia gave the king the response he now desired, her silent attention. She could feel the weight of his gaze. The floor ground into her knees.

His tone did not change. He was not a man who need speak with any great emotion. His will or displeasure was always self-evident. "This is the third time I have attempted to relocate you discreetly. This is the third time Ferus has suddenly learned his presence is necessary at one of his holdings in the vicinity. I will discover who is informing him of your movements and silence that tongue."

Cassia swallowed again, but her guilty tongue was dry.

How many more attempts would it take before the king decided the only safe place for her was where she actually wanted to go?

"Until I discover who is responsible for this," he said, "it appears I must keep you within my sight. Contrary to my plans, you will remain here at Namenti with the court, then accompany us when we depart for Solorum."

She was headed for the capital. Her plan had worked. She had challenged him…and won.

Although she knelt before the king, something inside her rose up and stood tall. The feeling shocked through her, new and wild and much too dangerous.

The displeasure in his tone punished her. "You will remain at the capital on my sufferance. You may reside at Solorum, but you will conduct yourself as befits a bastard I have been generous enough to acknowledge. You will keep out of sight, except when I require your presence."

"As you wish, Your Majesty."

He leaned closer, looming over her. "It is time I kept a closer eye on you. Any man with ambitions would find my royal blood in your veins useful, regardless of your mother's shame. Occasionally it is necessary to remind all concerned your blood is mine to use as I see fit, and mine alone."

Her grand scheme had succeeded, and here was the stunning result. She was on her knees before the king. She had just sentenced herself to a whole season of moments like this. If she lived that long.

Outmaneuvering him was so much more dangerous than submitting to his will.

She pulled a quiet breath into the vice of her lungs. "Yes, Your Majesty."

"It is a very unfortunate inconvenience that I must keep you at the capital," he warned. "This means you will be there when the Hesperine embassy arrives from Orthros."

The Hesperines. The king spoke their name, but it sounded like an invocation of magic beyond his power to control.

Yes. "Yes, Your Majesty."

"Too much is at stake at the Equinox Summit for me to suffer distractions such as you. In your ignorance, you can have no notion of the significance of the events transpiring in the kingdom."

She understood better than anyone.

The immortals would descend from the north and appear in human lands. This was the first time in nearly four hundred years that Orthros had sent official representatives to Tenebra. It might be another four hundred before Hesperines and mortals convened for the Equinox Summit again.

A moment like this would never come again. She must carry out her plan now.

The Hesperines were her reason for everything.

"Do not disobey me, Cassia. Especially while the Hesperines are there."

The king's weathered hand lifted in an abrupt gesture of dismissal. His rings caught the candlelight and scattered it in Cassia's eyes. Blinking to clear her vision, she rose to her feet and backed away.

She managed to get back to her rooms without stopping in the corridor to heave. By the time she slipped into her chambers, the flashes of heat and chill had left her damp with sweat and blessedly cool, and the sickening tension in her belly had eased.

There was no sign of Perita. The girl would surely be spending the longest night of the year with her guardsman.

Cassia sank down in her chair and considered what she had just accomplished.

She would not be swallowed by the eastern forests, while in the northern mountains, two lights faced each other on either side of the border between Tenebra and Orthros.

Tenebra's Summit Beacon burned at the fortress on Mount Frigora to summon the Hesperines to the negotiations. A transient fire atop a pile of old stones, making demands of the immortals.

Orthros's beacon had ascended into the sky in reply, a promise of the Hesperines' arrival. Cassia had never seen it with her own eyes, but everyone said it was a spell light as large and bright as a star.

She would not pass the Equinox Summit in a distant tower, while the Hesperines were at the royal palace. She would be waiting for them at court.

She had thrown herself in the most dangerous position imaginable. Nothing could be worse than an entire season in the king's sights. Except a lifetime of knowing she had missed her chance.

She had just seized her only opportunity to get close to a Hesperine.

42

days until

SPRING EQUINOX

ANTHROS'S FIRE AND SUNSWORD

SOMETIME IN THE NIGHT, someone had decked the entrance to the royal crypt with flowers and boughs. The sacred plants' pungent smell filled the entire Temple of Anthros, and Cassia knew word of the display would soon spread throughout Solorum.

Blossoms of Anthros's fire in every shade from orange to gold, tongues of flame to halt the unholy, lay scattered on the threshold of the crypt. Branches of sunsword, bound into rod-shaped bundles and woven into flat circles, flanked the steps and stood sentinel over the door. Their scent burned as sharply as sun in the eyes to drive away the defilers, the blood drinkers, those who defied death. The Hesperines were coming.

The court had only arrived at the capital last night. But the king would know by day's end who was responsible for this silent outcry against his decision to treat with the Hesperines.

Like all who were assembling in the temple for dawn rites, Cassia could not avoid walking past the crypt on her way to her place. As she neared the steps that led down to the tombs under the temple, Knight sniffed and let out a whine.

She did not slow her pace. Most of all, she did not look toward the head of the gathering, where the king sat in state. She kept her head down and held her breath. Tears stung her eyes as she walked past the deep stone archway and the age-darkened wooden door of the crypt.

She ought to be able to control such foolish things as her watery eyes. It was entirely the fault of the odorous herbs that she came so close to weeping. With a hand on Knight's ruff, she mounted the stairs to the temple gallery and pushed herself upward. The whispers followed her.

"She does not pay her respects."

"Does not even pause to remember her sister."

"Half sister. Tainted blood can bring no honor to blessed bones."

Cassia attained the temple's gallery, and the words faded into the general murmurs of the lords and their ladies assembled below. The crypt slipped out of sight, although she knew its black door waited beneath her.

No one bore any love for the bones of the past kings and their kin who now ruled only the silent realm under the temple. The flowers were for her sister. Cassia could have told them it was much too late for that. She could have told them why she had never set foot in the crypt where the king had buried the princess. How many, many things she could have told them. But Lady Cassia told no one anything; Lady Cassia did not speak.

She took her place at the gallery railing with other women who were not to be seen except when they did their duty and appeared in the temple. Today Cassia found herself beside Free Lord Titus's concubine of twenty years. Some of the woman's golden curls were fading to silver, and her famous figure was becoming stout, but her mouth remained a subject of great renown. Her lips had a natural upturn at the corners, as if she were always on the verge of a smile or mockery.

On Cassia's other side was a girl about Perita's age. Cassia didn't recognize her face, only the gown and jewels the newcomer wore. The girl must be Free Lord Tyran's latest doll. A couple of fortnights from now, a different body would be wearing the same finery, and a different pair of eyes would briefly meet Cassia's before the two of them turned their gazes ahead in obedient silence.

Cassia counted herself fortunate to be relegated to the gallery. She could see everything clearly from here, and it was the best place to make oneself invisible to the king. She had not set foot in Solorum Temple in years, but he and his court presented a sight she understood well.

At the head of the temple loomed the sun disk, half embedded in the eastern horizon of the stone floor. The vast bronze circle captured what little light crept in through the temple's small windows. The free lords stood assembled before the disk, their swords also waiting to catch the gleam of dawn.

Their conversations provided a wealth of information for a lip reader like Cassia. Today their mouths moved in discussion of every matter but the stinking display at the crypt. The ladies in the women's court behind them never so much as glanced at the door of the tombs that loomed at their backs. No one wished for the king's perceptive gaze to fall upon them.

King Lucis of Tenebra watched the room with his sword, his liege-hounds, and his heir close at hand. Had twelve-year-old Prince Caelum paused to honor his fallen sister, who had been the heir before she died and he was born? Cassia saw that the royal chairs were positioned as she remembered, against the wall and facing inward, that His Majesty might observe the crowd and the disk at the same time. The king never turned his back to his subjects or the gods.

At the foot of the sun disk stood the king's new royal mage. Only he presented an unusual sight, an unfamiliar figure in the position his predecessor had occupied for decades. The late royal mage had been fond of marching out to greet the crowd with a flash of light and a clap of noise that made the sun disk reverberate. His bald pate sweating, he had brandished his power to lift the screeching, groaning disk. But his successor was already here, waiting quietly.

The sun's rays now penetrated the windows and advanced under the temple's rounded arches. As light expanded within the old hulk of stone, Cassia peered at the new mage. A man of medium height and build and moderate demeanor. This was the best glimpse she'd had of him since he had joined the court upon their departure from Namenti. The king's bastard was expected to stay out of the way of such exalted men during the court's progress from the winter palace to the capital, just as she was expected to make a show of piety by attending temple once they arrived.

Dawn's light struck the surface of the sun disk fully, and Cassia squinted. Now the mage smoothly raised his hands. In complete silence, the disk lifted from its trench in the floor and began its ascent. It reflected light upon the pillars of the temple, turning the pale, time-worn sandstone the color of sunlight.

The columns had once been the temple, twice-seven stone sun rods meant to welcome Anthros's power down from the sky, before grandiose kings had added walls and a roof over the course of centuries. Now only peasants observed dawn rites outside. Lucis himself had ordered the last of the royal temples in the kingdom roofed, as his engineers and architects were all too fond of reminding his subjects. Just in case they forgot that their king demanded the same fear and trembling as his god.

Now the mage dropped his hands, and the disk continued moving, set on its westward path. It would reach its zenith in the rafters at noon and then set over the crypt at sundown, as it did all three hundred and ninety-two days of the year. The mage began to recite the same old invocations of Anthros in the Divine Tongue, which none but those trained in the Mage Orders could understand.

Cassia, however, found any speech quite revealing about the orator who delivered it. The late mage's bombastic recitations had demonstrated that he possessed considerable lung capacity and little else. The new mage, on the other hand, spoke at no great volume, but his clear diction and the steady timbre of his voice carried to her ears in the gallery. His tone rose and fell as if he held a conversation with his god. Only the slightly nasal quality of his voice detracted from the effect.

Cassia recognized the sound of the words that were the closing supplication to Anthros. The new mage fell silent and folded his hands. Along with the crowd, Cassia recited the worshipers' response they all learned as soon as they could speak. She still wondered what it meant.

The hall was full of sun now. The mage's distant gaze focused again on the mortals before him, and he smiled. In that same pleasantly nasal, calmly expressive voice he began to speak in the vulgar tongue.

"Obedient sons and daughters of Anthros," he greeted them, opening his hands, "blessed and fearful subjects of Tenebra, I am honored to be welcomed among you by your king, whose victories by the sword have long-since pleased the god of war. I am Amachos, Honored Master in the Order of Anthros, recently of the Temple of Anthros at Namenti."

He performed dawn rites without dramatic displays of power designed to mystify, and now he gave a speech in Vulgus, which everyone in Tenebra and Cordium could understand. Amachos was indeed a departure from the sort of mages who usually presided over the king's temples. Cassia listened now to what the mage's voice and his words told her.

She deemed him a very safe choice. The Temple of Anthros at Namenti had always stood watch on Tenebra's southern border, where Cordium waited to stretch its influence farther north. Of all the temples of the Tenebran mages of Anthros, Namenti was the one powerful and prestigious enough to rebuff the Cordian Orders' ambitions.

Everyone knew the Mage Orders in Cordium were the supreme divine authority in the world and the true mouthpiece of the gods. That didn't mean Tenebrans wanted their interference. Tenebran mages had worked spells their own way since before there were Orders, and neither king nor free lord wished to meet the fate of the Cordian princes, who had become nothing more than dogs on leashes to the Orders. There was a reason everyone called Cordium the Magelands, and no one spoke of the Principalities or the City-States anymore.

Amachos was sure to please everyone, for they would see him as a defender of the one principle the king, the free lords, and even the peasants agreed on: Tenebrans should be their own masters.

The mage smiled again. "It is with great delight that I take up the sacred duty to which the god has called me, to serve as your master in all matters sacred, and devote my gods-given power to the good of King Lucis's people. Together, let us put the plow to the soil of Tenebra and do fruitful work.

"The first work we must do together is of utmost importance to the safety of the kingdom and the honor of the gods. This very night, Hesperine diplomats from Orthros arrive among us for the Equinox Summit, and I rejoice that I am here to act as your guide at this crucial time.

"The god of war has bestowed upon this kingdom a great honor: to stand as the world's shield against Orthros. Tenebra is Anthros's aegis, the bulwark of man, safeguarding all that is holy from the Hesperines.

"The weak kings of the past failed in this duty, for they neglected to convene the Summit and thus allowed the Equinox Oath to lapse for hundreds of years. But Anthros has now delivered Tenebra into the hands of a mighty ruler who will once more face the Hesperines and hold them to the age-old truce. Lucis Basileus has been bold enough to order the Summit Beacon lit.

"Rejoice, Tenebrans, for you are fortunate in your king! The Hesperines have seen the fire on the mountain! Thanks to your courageous monarch, they have lit their beacon in answer. They shall come forth and treat with your king.

"All know that great Anthros hates the disobedient and rejoices at their defeat. Let us not forget, however, the god also loves order. A king may lead his people to victory at the negotiation table as surely as on the field of battle. Let us dwell on this as we welcome your king's guests and invoke the god's blessings upon his endeavor."

Now the mage folded his hands in the belled sleeves of his red-gold robe. He did not even move as the sun god's glyph flared to life above the crowd. A disk was carved on the air in golden light, throwing one magical sun rod upward. The sign hung in the air a moment, then disappeared without Amachos making any grand gestures.

A slight ripple of movement passed through the crowd. They seemed to realize belatedly that the dawn invocation was at an end, and the mage intended to say no more. The glyph was graven, the blessing cast. The king's subjects had received the spell of Anthros they had come for, the protection they sought against the immortals who would arrive when the sun fell.

Diplomats from Orthros, Amachos had called the Hesperines, to be welcomed as the king's guests. Where was his condemnation of the heretics? His diatribe against the fallen goddess Hespera and her perverse followers? If he was going to speak in a tongue comprehensible to everyone, why not issue a warning about Hespera's vile spawn and their alluring powers or a call to prepare for the presence of the godsforsaken among the blessed?

His speech had been a call to the talks, not a call to arms. The mage and the king both appeared committed to pursuing a truce with Tenebra's feared nocturnal neighbors.

The mage's presence displeased Cassia. It would be so until she knew what he wanted.

Perhaps his aim was nothing more than power. His position as the royal mage afforded him plenty, and his influence would only increase the more he displayed public support for the king's politics. But Cassia could not say for certain. She had evidence neither for nor against.

There was little drama about his person. There was no passion in his speech. Amachos was dangerous.

Those who wanted too much were dangerous. Those who appeared not to want anything were much more so.

The crowd below filed out of the temple through the western doors. Cassia and the others waited above for the powerful and respected to leave. Eventually the women around her descended in the wake of their benefactors. Lord Titus's concubine departed with an amused smile. Lord Tyran's picked her way down the steps, holding her expensive skirts as if they might break. At last Cassia and Knight trailed down the stairs.

As she neared the door to the crypt again, her steps dragged. Everyone's backs were turned to her. But she never knew from what direction a watchful gaze might observe her. She refrained from looking at the flowers and passed them by once more. Her eyes began to water again. When she stepped outside, the bright morning only worsened her blindness.

She blinked until she could see, then tried to get her bearings. She would have expected the ancient capital to look smaller in reality than the massive specter it remained in her memories. But she felt as if she had stepped right back into the Solorum of her childhood.

The Temple of Anthros towered at her back on the eastern hill, casting a long shadow as the sun climbed behind it. On the southern slope loomed Solorum proper, the oldest palace in Tenebra, once home to the Mage King himself—if he had really existed. Across from it on the northern hill stood Solorum Fortress, which seven much later kings had built over the course of two centuries. There the Hesperines would stay.

The greensward cupped between the three hills had been newly cleared, but the groundskeepers had lost their battle with the ivy that clung to the Mage King's throne. The stone chair in the middle of the green had stood since long before living memory and even before the memory of minstrels, its four-sided seat ready to receive sunlight from all directions. Songs said its back had once thrust high into the air in the shape of the sun rod, but now its jagged, broken top stood only a little taller than a man. Just visible beneath the carpet of ivy at its foot was the circular dais, a stone sun on the ground.

Leaves and tendrils of ivy cradled the throne, as if they alone held it up, even as they split tiny fractures in its surface. The woods still clung close to the edges of the greensward and blanketed the slopes surrounding the complex of structures. The grounds beyond looked damp and dark, and the scent of last night's rain still wafted from the forest's green depths. Somewhere within the trees, a bird unleashed a wild cry.

Cassia felt a sense of pressure in her neck, a tension in her limbs. She swept her gaze all about her again, taking in the buildings, but also the warriors who stood on either side of the temple door. The king's men. They watched her.

She rested a hand on Knight and walked on.

DUSK RITES

WHEN CASSIA TROD BACK into the temple for dusk rites, she saw that the sunsword and Anthros's fire were gone from the doorway to the crypt. She suspected those who had placed the herbs and flowers were gone from court as well, one knew not where.

The king often made public examples of those who committed private misdeeds, while a public act of defiance, such as trying to drive away His Majesty's guests, would surely cause someone to simply disappear and no more to be said of it.

As the sun disk shuddered down over the crypt, Knight flattened his ears against his head, but Cassia could not hear the noise that disturbed him. The bronze sun came to rest at the western end of the temple. Amachos drew out the dusk invocation. At last his words faded, and the crowd responded. The day was over. The night had begun.

Cassia's heart pattered faster as she followed the court back out to the greensward. Not a trace of dusk light lingered on the open side of the valley, where the sun had sunk beneath the western horizon. The moons had yet to rise, but it wouldn't be long now.

The unease that had kept her on edge all afternoon now made her stomach knot painfully. She welcomed the tension nonetheless, for it kept her alert and sharpened her senses. She smelled the wild hawthorn, juniper, and spruce that grew beyond the green. She heard the birds deep in the woods calling back and forth. Their voices grew a little louder every moment.

King Lucis now occupied the Mage King's chair. He sat in the northern seat, facing distant Orthros, from whence the Hesperines would come. The golden glow around him seemed to come from everywhere and nowhere, but even magic could not gild a monster.

The royal mage's apprentice stood nearby, his hands fidgeting as he adjusted the spell lights. The young man twitched glances between his master and the king as if he feared execution should they dislike his display. He would do well here.

The only occupant of the dais younger than the apprentice was Caelum. He occupied his usual place befitting the king's heir, a chair set up to the throne's right. Cassia did not envy her half brother that seat. But that was the extent of sympathy she could feel for him, seeing his customary expression of indolent dissatisfaction.

She could make out the shape of the palace to the south. Torch flames dotted its ramparts and towers, tiny lights pushing back against the deep blue sky and its many pale stars. Figures slipped away from the crowd toward the black refuge of the king's house. What a singular night, when anyone regarded that place as a welcome escape. How those returning to the palace must pity all who were forced to remain on the green to greet the Hesperine embassy.

But Cassia had paid dearly so she could be here at this moment, and she would have paid an even higher price to trade places with the free lords, advisers, and mages who now took their positions behind the dais in order of precedence. This was indeed a singular night, when she coveted any precedence at all in the king's company. Forcing herself to go near him tonight would accomplish nothing, however.

This was not her opportunity to get near the Hesperines. For that she must wait.

The people in front of her stopped so suddenly she nearly ran into them. The crowd stilled. Then it shifted and parted. Knight pushed against her legs, and she trusted his instincts, stepping back with the others to make way.

Through the gap came dozens of men and women driving a bull in their midst. They were farming folk all, with drab, worn garments and bodies made hard by lifelong labor. The beast dug its heels in, thrashing its head, and the men strained at the ropes that bound it.

One of the women slapped it with a switch of sunsword. Red stained one white flank, and the bull began to bellow. The voices of the crowd rose to be heard over its outcries. The woman switched the beast again, and the other farmers with her took up a supplication, wailing a prayer of protection to Anthros over and over. An ancient prayer, words the Mage King might once have uttered.

These folk were beyond weaving circles of branches and not so easily removed as flowers. They came within arm's length of Cassia as they hauled the bull toward the temple, and she saw the stark lines of their faces, the sweat soaking through their clothes.

When they reached the steps, they forced the beast onto its side. The man in the lead knelt before the door of the temple and drew the sickle he carried on his back. He laid the blade before him on the steps and called above the wailing women, "Mage of Anthros, will you not come out? Will you not make even one offering? Our children need protection. Shield us from the creatures that are coming! Give the god of war blood, so our children will not be a blood sacrifice to the dark goddess—"

The rest of the man's words went unheard amid the pounding of boots and the whisk of swords leaping from scabbards. The king's men were up the stairs and upon the gathering before the man had time to fall silent. The women's laments gave way to screams.

"Children of Anthros, be still."

The mage's calm statement brought instant silence. The guards paused, swords raised, their hands still closed around the peasants' arms and collars. Only the bull continued to groan.

Amachos stood silhouetted in the doorway of the temple, where there had been nothing but night insects swarming about the spell lights. "These good people have brought a fine sacrifice to their god. How can Anthros not be pleased with such devotion?"

The kneeling man bowed his head, pushing the sickle forward, which earned him a knee in his side from one of the guards. The farmer grimaced, but found breath to speak. "Please, Honored Master."

"I will gladly dedicate your sacrifice. However, such an act should not be performed in the dark, but in the sunlight. On the morrow, bring the bull here once more for noon rites, and we shall honor the god."

The man jerked up his head. "But the monsters come tonight. We will not be safe until tomorrow. Since before our fathers' fathers' time, the Hesperines have roamed unseen in these lands with no Equinox Oath to bind them. Who knows what dark deeds they have committed? What more might they do to us tonight if they walk in unchallenged, with no sacrifice to keep their evil at bay?"

"Calm yourself, man. We mages have protected you these many centuries, even when the Oath lapsed. We have never allowed Hesperines to dishonor the gods within Tenebra, nor does your king invite harm into his land tonight."

"Will their vile acts go unpunished?" cried a man somewhere in the crowd. "Will you not drive out the monsters?"

"Drive them out," other men called in unison. "No treaty. Drive them out."

The women's wails split the night again.

"Silence," said the mage.

The cries ceased again, but not the murmurs. Cassia could hear them all around her, the words no one had dared speak since the Beacon had ignited.

"The Hesperines don't want peace, only our blood…"

"…invited them to a feast, not a negotiation. They'll tear out our throats and drink us dry before the night is through!"

"Thieving monsters. They come for our children! They'll take them… my little ones…"

"…and desecrate our dead…fornicate with corpses and then our women…"

"Beware their seduction. To lie beneath a Hesperine is to welcome your own death."

"If you're fortunate. They spill no seed inside you, only blood, and if you live through it, you'll turn into one of them."

"Silence!" Light flashed in the mage's upraised hands. "We should not perform the sacrifice here and now, not when the Hesperines may arrive any moment and behold a sacred act they are unfit to witness. We will perform the rite tomorrow."

"You do not protect us!" The farmer's voice broke. In one motion, he closed his hand around the sickle and leapt to his feet. "May Anthros accept our meager offering."

He spun on his heels and brought the sickle down. Inches above the bull's throat, the blade spun away and clattered to the stone. The man pitched forward onto the beast. The guard behind him planted a boot on his back and retrieved a sword from between his shoulders, releasing a rush of blood in the blade's wake. The bull let out one roar after another, and the crowd echoed it.

Cassia did not join in their useless raving. Were they really so shocked? Had they expected their disobedience to end any other way?

The guard moved his sword into position at the bull's throat, as if silencing it could silence the people too. But he halted before his blade touched the animal, his attention riveted on something beyond the crowd. The bull blinked, sighed, and lay quietly.

Cassia recognized its calm. Its sense of safety. She knew what she would see if she followed the guard's gaze.

She looked. The silhouette of the trees had changed. The branches were no longer bare, but covered in birds of every size and shape, the only heralds of the embassy's arrival.

The Hesperines stood on the slope above the greensward like natural shapes that had grown there over centuries and not merely appeared just now.

Cassia felt like she was a small child again, looking up at their tall figures to gaze upon their perfect faces. Their dark, flowing garments were just as she remembered, coated in embroidery that caught every shard of light. How could anything alive stand so still?

Something unbearable tore open inside of her, and she wanted to howl as the bull had. But she stood silent.

BLOOD IN THE NIGHT

L IO BREATHED THROUGH HIS mouth, but he could still taste it. Bloodshed. The smell threatened to gag him.

His Hesperine senses gave him no mercy. Odors flooded up from
the crowd of mortals below and crept into his mouth. The bull's terror.
Human sweat and anger. The blunt stink of cruelty.

One stench overpowered all the others. He had never smelled it before,
and yet some deep part of him understood what it meant. Something was
wrong that could never be righted. Something irreplaceable was broken,
which he could never mend. He could not shut out the stench, no matter
how it horrified him.

He could smell death.

Lio's heart pounded in unison with the bull's. Through the Blood
Union that flowed between Hesperines and all living beings, he felt the
animal's veins straining under the stress of terror. Strengthening the Union
with his own magic, he joined his mind with the bull's. The one creature
here whose suffering he could ease. That much was within his power.

For the animal's sake, Lio found the Will to summon a sense of calm,
which he wrapped about the bull's thoughts. The bovine mind responded,
and terror gave way to relief until the bull lay quiet and content, assured
of safety. As if Lio could really promise it to him.

Beyond the Union of his and the bull's minds, Lio sensed his uncle's
approval and a far stronger spell of reassurance. His mentor's power
reached across the crowd, and the angry mob of humans quieted without
even knowing a Hesperine mind mage was at work. Not a single person
charged forward to share in the farmer's irreversible fate.

Lio could give into his uncle's power, as if he too were merely a frightened animal. But he held himself back from the spell, held respite at bay.

He would withstand his first journey to Tenebra by relying on his own strength. What use was he to his people otherwise?

A man lay dead below. What right had he to feel anything but horror?

Lio's gut trembled. He swallowed and gripped his hands tighter behind his back as if that could keep him on his feet. He glanced at the sky for fortitude, but clouds were creeping across the stars, and the moons did not yet gaze over the horizon. A gust of wind disturbed the fetid air, sweeping in from the grounds beyond the palace and across the greensward. He braced himself for another wave of sickening odors.

A powerful fragrance struck him full in the face and warmed its way through his senses. Clean skin, human hair, and the natural aromas of a female body. Deep, rich notes of dignity and pride. Anger a hot top note, grief a bittersweet flourish throughout. His gut clenched again, but not from disgust this time.

Humans could be so beautiful. Here was one, somewhere among the desperate, ugly scene below, so lovely she pained the senses.

Tightness spread in Lio's throat. She was alive. The man on the temple steps was not.

Lio had volunteered for the embassy with full knowledge of what he might witness. He had arrived in Tenebra well educated, with realistic expectations. He was prepared for this. That should make this easier.

No. No, he hadn't been prepared for the embassy's mere arrival to cost a life.

The white-haired figure on the throne below sat amid his frightened subjects. At last the king spoke, leaning close to the ear of a scarred warrior who stood beside him. "Get them out of sight."

The warrior leaped off the dais, although there was more gray in his hair than brown, which marked him as being in the latter years of his mortal life. As he strode toward the temple, the crowd parted to let him onto the steps. The influence Lio's uncle had exerted on the mob had helped them see reason, not taken away their will to fight. That they made way for this man spoke of their fear—or their respect.

The grizzled, stocky warrior must be the Free Lord of Hadria, the king's best sword and right hand, commander of his armies and the strategist essential to all his campaigns. Lio suspected it was not only prowess in battle that had kept the commander alive for decades under King Lucis's rule and secured his reputation as the most loyal free lord in Tenebra. Even now the canny warrior said no words, which the Hesperines could have easily heard. Instead he gestured to the guards in what appeared to be a language of hand signs understandable to his fellow mortal soldiers.

The guards sprang into action, and Lio flinched. In Union with the supplicants, he felt their mortal terror of the unknown fate that awaited them at the soldiers' hands.

"Please." Lio's uncle spoke his appeal in Vulgus. "Do not refrain from your sacred practices on our account. We beg your forbearance for our interruption."

A true apology would have demanded the embassy retreat and return when the rite was at an end, but Lio knew his uncle would not offer that. The Hesperine presence that had sparked this violence now seemed the people's only hope for clemency. For the moment. Lio knew not what would become of those poor souls when the king's guests were no longer watching. Responsibility demanded that he consider it, but his sanity required otherwise.

Lord Hadrian did not even glance at Lio's uncle, only continued to signal to the guards. Lio dared not watch the spectacle draw to an end. The sounds were enough. The women wept, and the men grunted in pain as the guards dragged them down the steps. Military boots marched, while poorly shod feet stumbled in the grass in the direction of the palace. The steady thud of hooves told Lio the bull, at least, walked away.

It was the king who responded to Lio's uncle with a gesture toward the Hesperines. Another noble left his side, this one chestnut-haired and tall for a human. As he descended the dais, more soldiers fell into step behind him. They marched up the hill toward the embassy.

Lio felt his people brace themselves and each other through the Blood Union they shared. On the same currents, Lio's uncle made known his instructions. Wait.

Lio made an effort to compose himself. His career as a diplomat Abroad had now begun. From this moment on, he represented his people, his Queens, and his Goddess in a way he never had at home in Orthros. Even if his first foreign assignment came to a premature end when those soldiers made it up the hill.

The fourteen warriors in gleaming mail carried longswords with the blades resting on their shoulders. The same elaborate heraldry covered each of their tabards, the royal arms of Tenebra over and over. The solar imagery and symbols of violence matched the paintings in Lio's scrolls exactly, but they looked different on living men.

Lio realized the lord at the head of the company wore an elegant velvet tunic instead of armor, although the sword at his belt was no ceremonial decoration. This close, Lio could see the silver at the man's temples, the crows' feet around his eyes, and the sheen of sweat on his brow. He smelled of expensive scent oils, bravery, and fear. "On behalf of His Majesty King Lucis Basileus of Tenebra, Champion of Anthros..."

As the lord recited the king's epithets and honors, Lio let his intellect take over and focused on the analytical exercise of testing his knowledge of Tenebran politics. He heard his long study of Lucis's many conquests summarized in one list of titles. Lio had not skipped a chapter.

"...allow me to welcome you to Tenebra, here to our ancestral capital at Solorum, ever the seat of our greatest kings," the man concluded with a bow. A shallow but courteous gesture befitting an encounter between equals. "I am Titus, Free Lord of Segetia, and it is my honor to serve as the king's voice during this, the first Equinox Summit in countless generations."

So this man with the sharp blade, pleasant countenance, and larger vocabulary than most Tenebrans was Free Lord Titus, reputedly the closest the kingdom had to a diplomat. Lio hoped the man lived up to his reputation, such as it was. At least he and not the soldiers behind him had opened the negotiations.

Lio's uncle offered none of the personal compliments that were customary between foreign dignitaries who knew one another by reputation. It was better if the humans did not realize how aware Orthros was of current events in Tenebra. Lord Titus was more likely to feel threatened than flattered if he knew Hesperines had been following his career.

"Well met, Lord Titus." Lio's uncle bowed. "I am Argyros, the Queens' Master Ambassador. This is my lady, Hippolyta."

With the rest of the embassy, Lio held his breath.

Lord Titus gave Aunt Lyta a deep, courtly bow worthy of a lady immortalized in love ballads, not one whose unholy deeds minstrels decried in marching songs. "Welcome indeed."

Aunt Lyta took Uncle Argyros's arm and offered Lord Titus a benign smile. "We thank you for your gracious welcome, my lord."

Lio and his companions traded relief back and forth through the Blood Union. It seemed the names Argyros and Hippolyta did not mean anything to Lord Titus. He did not realize Silvertongue and the Guardian of Orthros had arrived at his king's negotiation table. After the span of centuries since the last Summit, it apparently did not occur to him that he had just met the same Hesperine ambassador who had treated with his ancestors. And the petite, poised female before him, with her dark auburn hair groomed smooth as silk, must not look to Lord Titus like a notorious abomination of her sex.

Humans' written records were pitiable, but minstrels never forgot the likes of Argyros and Hippolyta. Argyros was the diplomat the Queens had always sent to Tenebra for the Equinox Summit since the first one nearly sixteen centuries ago. Hippolyta's role in the Last War, which made her legendary among Hesperines, made her equally infamous among mortals.

Thankfully, it was their deeds and not their names that lived on in song here. It appeared the mere fact that they were Hesperines already pushed even the king's bold spokesman to his limits.

Another drop of sweat trickled down Lord Titus's temple. "His Majesty wishes me to deliver his sincerest apologies for the disorder of his house upon your arrival. We assure you, this is not indicative of the rest of your stay."

"It is our arrival that has proved inconsiderate," Uncle Argyros replied. "It grieves us that we have intruded upon a sacred hour."

Lord Titus shook his head, holding up his hands. "These misguided subjects who have disobeyed our king and disrespected the royal mage are unworthy of your concern. Please join us below upon His Majesty's dais, while the offenders are seen to and the palace guard ensures the safety of all gathered here."

Regret weighed heavy in the Blood Union as Lio's aunt and uncle

33

inclined their heads and followed the soldiers down the slope. Lio waited for Basir and Kumeta to follow them first, before he took his position behind and to the right. Kadi, with Javed at her side, brought up the rear so she could watch their backs.

Lio felt the others' empathy bolstering him as they all descended. It should have brought him comfort. But it only reminded him they had seen death before and he had not. He did not want a crutch. He must stand on his own two feet.

By the time they reached the bottom of the hill, most of the crowd had ordered themselves into an array of burnished armor and busy heraldic tabards behind the king's dais. Lio sensed that most of the Tenebrans were grateful to be there, with the breadth of the greensward between them and the Hesperines.

When the embassy approached the foot of the dais, the achingly lovely fragrance wrapped around Lio suddenly and drew his mind away from the victims of the king's justice. Lio almost halted in his tracks. Hespera's Grace. The Goddess made miraculous creatures everywhere, and Tenebra was no exception.

He sensed about him, wishing for a better impression of the beautiful woman, perhaps even a glimpse of her. She slipped around the edges of his senses, on the move. Behind the throng that attended the king, a second crowd stepped lightly, attempting to return to the palace without causing any further disturbance. The woman's fragrance drifted away from him in that direction. He could not catch sight of her. Then she was gone.

And Lio stood before Lucis Basileus, the most recent and perhaps most brutal King of Tenebra. Also one of the most capable who had ever held the throne.

Lio studied as much of the man as decorum allowed. He knew well that among Tenebrans, one gazed at a king's shoes, robes, and jeweled rings, not his face. Thinking of his own Queens' ready smiles and kind eyes, Lio felt just how far he was from home. A sense of foreignness overtook him. The familiar figures of his own people appeared strange and out of place. He even felt distant from himself.

Lio was grudgingly glad about the very thing that had so frustrated him when they set out—he was not called upon to speak publicly tonight. Now he understood why his uncle had gently insisted he only observe during their first nights here. If Lio were required to put two words together now, in front of this gathering, to make himself the center of their attention after all he had just witnessed, it might really cost him what little he'd drunk since they'd crossed the border.

Lio fought down the nausea and disorienting emotions. He must do better than this, if he was to prove himself worthy to be an ambassador in his own right. Worthy of his mentor. Argyros had never been in danger of vomiting his breakfast on a foreign monarch.

Uncle Argyros had embarked upon the exchange of presentations with Lord Titus, who appeared to be keeping up. King Lucis watched in silence, apparently accustomed to sitting on his throne while he ordered men to speak or kill for him.

So this was how things were done in Tenebra. The king twitched a finger, a person died, and then the negotiators carried on as if nothing had happened.

When Lio heard his uncle say his name, he came forward and gave a bow he had practiced for decades to the king whose reign had captivated and appalled him throughout his studies. This was his one opportunity when it was appropriate to meet the royal gaze.

Lucis's eyes were as blue as paintings Lio had seen of cloudless, sunny skies. The king's gaze was as dangerous as midday and as sharp as the sword resting across his knees. He was of average human height, squarely built, with large hands and a scar on his bearded jaw. A brute wrapped in velvet and jewels. He looked exactly like what Lio knew him to be. And stank of it, as well.

Lio had hoped the Blood Union would reveal King Lucis to him in a way chronicles and reports had not. This man who had united fractured Tenebra surely had complex motivations that made his deeds more understandable, even if nothing could ever justify his acts of cruelty. He who had brought order and stability to his people must possess hidden virtues that coexisted with the violence he practiced as a way of life.

But all of Lio's Hesperine power would not bring him into Union with the king. Everything within Lio recoiled.

Here was a king who presented no illusions and needed none. Lucis

Basileus wore his nature for all to see, and that was one of his greatest advantages. He was a brilliant strategist. A wholly pragmatic one who, if it served him, thought absolutely nothing of slaughtering a frightened father for trying to keep his children safe. Lucis did not love violence. He used it the way a farmer used a plow or a potter used clay, and he tolerated no delay of the harvest nor a single imperfection in the ceramics.

This was the man who had invited Orthros to make peace. But what would Lucis's peace resemble? Worse still, what would it cost Lio's people?

TRESPASSING

ASSIA HAD SEEN THEM. She had endured her first glimpse of the Hesperines. That must surely make the rest easier.

She stared into the darkness above her bed and listened to the fire crackling to sleep beyond her open door. At last she heard the swish of slippered feet. Perita shuffled through the hearth room, kicking aside rushes as loudly as possible on her way to the corridor.

Their unspoken bargain worked well. What the handmaiden was not present to learn, she could not report to the king or be punished for withholding. What the bastard daughter knew regarding the handmaiden and Lord Hadrian's guard, she kept to herself. Their sleeping arrangements accommodated their truce. Perita had a pallet in the dressing room, Cassia had her bedchamber to herself, and Knight provided the excuse they needed to dispense with the custom of handmaidens sleeping by their ladies.

Whenever Cassia was fortunate enough to have a disinterested handmaiden, she always hoped that one would last awhile. She had lost count of how many the king had assigned her, then replaced in the years since her nurse had died. Spying on the king's daughter was a taxing occupation.

Cassia got up, shivering in nothing but her underlinens and long woolen tunica. The bed creaked as Knight flopped down beside her, and she leaned close to him. She would take a warm dog over a fire any day.

Best of all, Knight's role as her bodyguard had always meant the king never put soldiers at her door. A liegehound to keep her alive and a handmaiden to observe her were all the resources the king deemed necessary to expend on Cassia.

By the faint light that shone through her doorway, Cassia tugged her practical green dress over her tunica and shouldered her oilcloth gardening satchel. She wrapped herself in her wool cloak, which was much simpler and more serviceable than Lord Adrogan's lambskin monstrosity. On instinct she hunted for a kerchief, but none came to hand. No matter. Who would be there to see her hair uncovered?

No one but the Hesperines.

Together she and Knight padded out of her bedchamber, through the hearth room and into the narrow corridor beyond. It was easy to recognize where she was. The king had put her in unfamiliar chambers suited, such as they were, to a young lady, but the rooms that had been hers as a girl were just in the next hallway.

It was strange how everything looked exactly as it had when she was seven. But the palace had not changed in over a thousand years. Why should it have done so in the years that had changed her from child to woman?

Despite how little time she had spent in her own rooms then, childhood memory came powerfully to her and served her well as she found her way through the high, remote wing of the palace where she had stayed, then as now. Her life right after her time here was a blur to her, but Solorum was graven deep in her memory. Emotion was a sharp chisel. A tool she no longer had use for.

Only once did she halt, when Knight came to an abrupt stop in front of her and straightened, his ears pricked. She withdrew into the dimness against one wall, and he leaned against her legs to stay her. In the adjacent corridor, a tall shadow reached into a pool of torchlight, and a man staggered in its wake. He was soon gone, along with the reek of ale and a woman's scent oils. A sure sign the festivities to welcome the embassy had drawn to a close—except for the private dinner the Hesperines would hold afterward.

Cassia found her way through side doors and servants' corridors until bare floors and stained brown rugs gave way to thick, plush blues and finally to intricately woven golds. She stood in the forbidden halls of the queen's wing. A name that meant little now, when there was no queen, nor the promise of one in a beloved princess.

Cassia could not afford to hesitate here in the corridor. She could not allow any thought of the past to distract her from her task. Nor would it serve her to dwell on what lay behind the door at the end of the hall. Why should she be so aware of the king's presence there and of his soldiers who watched through the night? The king should not seem like a hunter with his bow drawn, ready to let fly an arrow at any moment, just because she came so near the door that led to the king's wing. Now that she was at court, she must learn to endure being near him. She had chosen this, and she must face the consequences.

But once she began to move down the hallway away from that door, her walk hastened to a run. Knight lengthened his stride beside her. She made it around the shelter of a corner.

And there above her, up a short flight of stairs, was the door that had once always been open to her. A rounded arch, a mahogany panel whose sinuous carvings of flowers and birds tried to gleam in the blurry moonlight from the thick glass windows in the walls above. Solia's door.

The metal ring handle bit Cassia's hand with cold. Slowly, warily, she inched the door toward her. A brief groan hinted what noise she could expect once she opened it fully.

She reached into her gardening satchel, careful not to cut her hand on her spade, and felt around. Her fingers halted on smooth ridges of carved wood. No, she could not pause. She had work to do.

Cassia pulled out a rag and a bottle of expensive scent oil. She doused the cloth in the foul stuff and went to work on the hinges of the door. She oiled, then tried the door, listened, then oiled again. The bottle was half empty by the time the door swung open with nothing but a soft, low complaint.

Cassia stared into the dark.

Knight walked in ahead of her, disappearing into the gloom. When his sniffs quieted and his tail thumped the floor, she followed him in. She eased the door shut behind her and listened to it seal away the corridor outside.

Dust weighted her breaths. A wisp of blue in the dark ahead of her was moonlight, sneaking in beneath a wayward curtain. Using that to orient herself, she envisioned the layout of the room. Knight snuffled, and she followed the sounds, hands out before her.

She found him sitting on the rug where he had slept as a pup. She felt its familiar texture beneath her slippers. How many forbidden nights had they spent in these rooms, squatting like waifs in the temple on the benevolence of the golden-haired goddess who had dwelt here?

Cassia must think. Not feel. Ha. Never feel. She put out her hands again and groped her way through the cold, dark hearth room, from one familiar piece of fine furniture to the next, until she came to what she knew was the outside wall. The intruding moonlight was right at her feet. A heavy drape hung before her. She slid it aside, and the light shone on her through translucent blue birds and green glass leaves. The greatest luxury in the queen's wing was this window over the garden door, a stained glass roundel the size of a platter. Cassia tried the door handle. Not even locked. The king was deterrent enough.

It took the rest of the bottle of oil to undo some of what weather had wrought upon the door in the intervening years. Cassia held her breath and grimaced as it opened on whimpering hinges. It didn't matter. It could not matter. This was the princess's inner courtyard. No one could even see into it, except from these very rooms. No one could hear through the massive walls of the king's wing. Cold air welcomed her outside.

Cassia stood fixed and confronted the sight of what had become of Solia's garden. The princess's fountain was dry, reduced to cracked tiles, dirt, and nettles. The annuals were long gone, the perennials tangled remnants beneath rampant weeds and an army of king's wort that must have somehow invaded from the kitchen gardens. The few stalks that survived would never turn into flowers come spring. The bed she and Solia had planted together was just one casualty among many in that havoc.

Cassia knew no one could see her, but she kept to the edges of the courtyard where juniper trees badly in need of pruning stood between her and the palace looming above. The ivy still held sway on the walls, and its leaves brushed against her as she passed.

At last she spied the long fall of ivy nestled in the corner of two walls where wood peeked out between the leaves instead of stone. A sigh escaped Cassia.

With the flora as her only witness, she slid under and between years of vines. The ivy shivered around her as Knight forged through behind her.

She opened the hidden postern just enough for the two of them to slide through. As soon as they were inside, she shut the door securely behind them and hastened into blackness.

The low tunnel stretched ahead of them, through the depths of ring after ring of walls that stood between the royal chambers and the grounds beyond the palace. One hand on the crumbly wall was enough to guide her, and Knight's presence was enough to keep the rats scattering before them.

Her legs ached by the time they reached the end of the tunnel. Moisture trickled down the walls here, nursing a thick growth of moss that promised they neared the fertile outdoors. She reached forward and a little above her head. A slanted panel of moldering wood, bound together by rough iron, greeted her hands. She could see the door that led out in the torchlight of her memory.

As long as the Hesperines were guests, the human residents of the palace were not to walk the grounds after nightfall. The king had made himself clear. But walks on the grounds after dark, especially alone, had always been forbidden to Cassia. Hesperines were hardly a deterrent in comparison with the king's injunction. A stroll through the royal forest was the least of the transgressions she would commit before the night was through.

"Come, my Knight," she whispered, violating the silence within the walls. "Let us trespass."

She gave the door a great heave and let them out onto the Hesperines' feeding grounds.

BLOOD UNION

LIO WISHED MOONLIGHT AND sated thirst offered him some peace. But the generosity of the king's deer and a walk in the night were no antidote for the tragedy the embassy's arrival had caused.

Father had warned him he would function at less than his peak with only the contributions of animals to sustain him. Perhaps Lio could attribute some of his distress to that. But he doubted even a draught of a human's lifeblood would give him any respite tonight.

He could not banish the smell and sensation of the man's death from his mind. There was nowhere to hide from it, not even within himself. The voices clamored inside him. The wound reopened.

He leaned his forehead against the trunk of a tree and let the moonlight bathe his back. He could feel the Goddess's Eyes looking down. Both watched over him, wide open. He sensed the clear, white beacon of the Light Moon beginning to wane for the month, while the liquid pulse of the Blood Moon waxed toward its annual fullness.

But the light of her gaze felt far away, almost like a dream. The torchlight felt close. Real. The crimson stain on the sword blade. The sound of the man's blood slowing in his veins. Lio tried to push it away, but it pushed at him, struck him, and he relived it again.

His own blood ground to a halt. He shed his own body and stepped out of it. His soul made to follow the man's. But the human departed and left Lio standing on the hillside in his own Hesperine skin again.

Now Lio looked down at his trembling hands, turning them over under his scrutiny. He had never once in his existence regretted the Blood Union. Tonight he wondered if these feelings would stay with him forever, tainting the delight and pleasure the Goddess's Gift had always brought him. How fortunate the Tenebrans had been, not to feel their fellow mortal's death the way Lio had.

Fortunate? What was he thinking? They had been ready to slaughter an animal and rejoice. Many had watched the man die with unconcern.

Was that why they were able to live like this? Were their deadened senses what made it possible for them to endure such squalor and suffering? It was the Blood Union that taught Hesperines the Goddess's Will. It must be the lack thereof that made Tenebrans unthinking of her mercy.

But Lio had thought somehow that all living creatures sensed what the Union made clear to him. Did they not all have the Goddess's voice within them in some form? Did not humans live with a soft whisper of what Hesperines heard loud and beautiful?

A tendril of sensation teased Lio's nose, a tinge of flavor behind his tongue. There was a scent to be smelled if he were to breathe. He drew in a lungful of air and straightened in surprise.

It was her. The fragrance in the crowd, the reminder of beauty. She was somewhere on the grounds tonight.

Lio breathed more in the next moment than he had in the entire time since he'd crossed the border into this land of foul smells. There was another new scent among the forest beasts, too, musky animal flesh and contentment, but he hardly gave it thought. He shut his eyes, tuned out sound, and parted his mouth, scenting her.

Hespera's Mercy, what was she doing here? A woman wouldn't risk exposing herself to one of his kind for a shortcut home after a day of hard work or a secret tryst with a lover.

Lio was confident none of the Tenebrans would take exception to him availing himself of the royal game. That was the agreement King Lucis had established. As much as his subjects hated it, their fear of Hesperines and the king's displeasure was sure to outweigh their outrage. Yet Lio would have been less surprised to meet a hoard of angry farmers wielding pitchforks and sickles, bent on subjecting him to the same fate they had planned for the bull, than to encounter a woman out alone after dark.

Here in Tenebra, that was unthinkably dangerous. What would cause her to take such a risk? What had made her so desperate?

APPARITION

K NIGHT HALTED IN HIS tracks before the Font of the Changing
Queen. Cassia bumped into him and stood still. His side rose and
fell against her skirts as he sniffed the air.

She listened. She heard nothing but the wind. But then, she wouldn't
hear or see the Hesperines unless they so desired.

They would already know she was here, though.

She watched Knight for any sign of what he detected that she could
not. The wild groundcovers in the clearing rustled as he gave himself a
quick scratch, then resumed his alert stance. She glanced about them. It
appeared that only dark, verdurous yews and bare-branched ashes watched
them, but Knight knew they were not alone in the woods.

Clouds passed in front of the moons, then away, then covered them
again, turning the stone fountain from gray to silver to gray. The fountainhead looked like a scavenger bird one moment, a proud falcon the next.
The minstrels said the Font had run with blood the day the Mage King
died, but tonight the bird was silent, and the basin beneath held nothing
more than the remnants of yesterday's rain.

Cassia considered the possibility the Hesperines would avoid her to
protect their tenuous accord with the king. The embassy would be wary
that any blame fall on them, should some ill come of a human violating
the agreement tonight.

Which begged the question, what did one do to attract Hesperine
attention, when they were determined not to attend? She glanced at
Knight. For what must be the first time in his life, he was not a helpful
deterrent. She would have to find a way to coax any Hesperines who were

here tonight to appear to her, despite the presence of a liegehound bred to hunt them.

Why did the task seem even more monumental now, when she had already managed so much?

When she realized the smudge of moonlight across the clearing was in fact a face, her heart jumped in her chest.

Knight leapt a pace in front of her, and his warning growl rumbled through the night.

"*Hama!*" she called out.

Knight snarled and lowered his head, crouching to spring.

"*Haama!*" she commanded.

Growling and whining in continuous protest, Knight backed toward her, never taking his eyes off his prey. In the long-dead tongue used to train liegehounds, there was no command that meant "go against your nature."

When he came within reach, she put her hand on his head. "*Het!*"

Knight obeyed and sat, but kept growling at the dark-clad figure lost in shadow.

One of the Hesperines had found her.

Cassia made herself blink. Her eyes shut and opened, and he was still there. She waited. He neither disappeared nor stepped forward.

The clouds shifted again, and moonlight bathed the entire clearing. For the second time, the sight of the Hesperine took Cassia by surprise. She had caught a glimpse of him when the embassy had arrived, but that quick look from across the greensward had not prepared her to behold him up close.

She knew from personal experience how lovely they appeared. But he exceeded even the impossible beauty she had witnessed in others of his kind. He seemed wrought of night sky and moonlight. Both reflected in his dark, jewel-blue eyes, and they glowed brighter than a cat's. His hair fell across his forehead and twined around his collar, gleaming black. Had the sun ever touched his pale skin? High cheekbones and a fine jaw graced his lean face, which tapered to a narrow chin. His mouth was too elegant to exist anywhere but on a temple statue. A high-collared black robe fell straight and long from strong shoulders down his slender body, making his height hard to judge. Much taller than her, certainly.

She would have said he was recently out of his youth and into his full manhood. He looked perhaps a year or two younger than she. And all his lovely features expressed that he was quite startled. As he stared at her hound, he looked a great deal more unsettled than she felt.

That was how he *looked*. He might remember the death of the Mage King from personal experience, for all she knew. She must keep that in mind and not let his godlike face misguide her.

And yet he had stood near the back of the delegation. The other Hesperines had appeared older than he, and he had followed their lead. Perhaps he was young, or at least younger than they and less experienced with humans.

If that were the case, she might have attracted the attention of the most useful Hesperine in the embassy.

OPENING REMARKS

ERHAPS SHE HAD COME to sacrifice Lio to her gods.

An image out of Hesperine laments was alive before him, growling with each breath. Powerful jaws that could lock on limbs and shred flesh. Thick fur that defied the harshest cold over tough skin resistant to puncture. Most dangerous of all, a mind unlike any other animal's, armored against all attempts at Union.

The dog was indeed a Tenebran liegehound, bred to live far longer than other canines and to withstand poison and disease. But above all, to track, hunt, and slay Lio's kind.

The hound was as massive as the chronicles described. No doubt he could indeed leap high enough to ground a levitating Hesperine.

Irrational fascination mingled with Lio's alarm. The hound's markings matched the illustrations in the scrolls exactly: shades of brown ranging from near-black on his back and shoulders to tan on his underbelly...with a patch of reddish fur around his jaws. His distinctive smell certainly lived up to its reputation, incomparable to any creature Lio had encountered.

Goddess have Mercy on his good intentions. When he had first caught the scent, he should have paid more attention, but the young woman's powerful fragrance had overpowered the creature's odor. All Lio had been able to think of was a woman who might be in dire need of help, alone and vulnerable in this sunbound domain of human predators. At least the shreds of raw meat caught in the hound's back teeth had belonged to an animal. His recent dinner had been mutton, not Hesperine.

Lio reminded himself not all Tenebrans used the dogs for their original purpose. This was not the northern border, where the heart hunters roamed with packs of the beasts, looking to run down Hesperines. The nobility prized liegehounds as bodyguards because of their brute strength and loyalty to the death, as well as the difficulty assassins faced in poisoning them. No wonder the hound's mistress felt safe on the grounds tonight.

Lio and the lady stared at each other over her guardian's hackles. The light touch of her hand on the beast's head held a great weight of authority. She was no humble farmer with a pitchfork. She smelled of more soap than touched the skin of the king's entire court combined. A pity it was noxious tallow soap, which tainted her fragrance with the stink of animal fat. But it was likely the best available to her. Someone near her had bathed in scent oil, but she had not touched it. On her olive skin, she wore a generous coating of freckles and the sweat of a long walk in the cold.

Belatedly, Lio considered the young woman's appearance. The moons' light and his Hesperine sight revealed to him all the lovely colors that comprised her. Dusky pink cheeks and bewitching hazel eyes. A long, straight curtain of sandalwood hair, unbound. She was thin as if she were not well cared for, but clean as if she were. Her cloak and gown were simple in cut and devoid of adornment, but well made of fine green wool.

The wind blew past her, and her scent struck him anew. He resisted the urge to flare his nostrils and take another deep whiff of her. He had no desire to resemble her beast.

Her hand drifted under the hound's chin, right below all those teeth, and scratched his smear of red fur. She lowered her gaze to the animal. What better way to show Lio she did not fear him than to look away?

He did not smell a whiff of fear on her. It was her trek through the woods that had made her blood lively in her veins. Her heart beat a fast, undulating rhythm in the night, and he caught himself listening with rapt attention. Never had he heard music like this. Not even in Orthros.

He had the Blood Union and all the power the Gift afforded. She had a Hesperine-eating dog. Perhaps they were not entirely on uneven footing.

"You have nothing to fear from Knight," she informed him. "He only goes after monsters."

Her words could not have surprised Lio more if she had recited the *Discourses on Love* in perfect Divine Tongue. Lio offered her a tardy bow, a deep one to convey sincere respect. Best to err on the side of caution until he was certain of her rank. Despite her spare appearance, the lady was almost certainly important if someone had gone to the effort and expense of bonding a liegehound to her.

This encounter was simply waiting to become a diplomatic disaster. Hespera help him, he must not make a mess of things. It was not too late to salvage the situation, if the reassurance the lady had just offered was to be heeded: she did not regard Lio as a monster.

"It is a good thing you have such a dangerous protector, Lady." Lio adopted a tone of courtly banter, testing her. "I'm afraid vicious monsters do indeed stalk the grounds tonight, seeking to devour beautiful young maidens."

She took the bait, and he heard her laughter for the first time. That airy peal did not sound natural, but studied and wielded as a defense. She looked up from her hound, a faint smile on her lips. "If I happen upon any such creatures, I shall warn you of what they look like."

Lio bowed again. "Gracious thanks. Knight and I might be called upon to drive them away, to ensure they do not disturb any ladies taking the evening air."

"I appreciate your heroic offer. I am quite adept at dealing with monsters, however."

"I suspect you are. Are you called upon to deal with them often?"

She tilted her head. "Are not we all?"

"At the risk of damaging your confidence in me, I can't say I have a great deal of experience in monster slaying, myself."

"You have not been in Tenebra long."

Lio considered his next words. They sailed farther and farther from the safe waters of banter, which no one ruled. "I hold out hope no monster slaying will be necessary during our stay here."

"Of course. You and your company ride under a different banner than the warriors of this house. You are the sort who would rather solve conflicts with words than swords, are you not?"

"I hope so."

"Then there is a favor you can do for me. No monster slaying required."

He folded his hands behind his back. What could she possibly want of him? What could he possibly do for her—safely? "As you say, I ride under a different banner. But perhaps I may still serve you, Lady. What is it you would ask of me?"

"Answer me a question, nothing more." Her heartbeat jumped again in her chest, although her expression did not change. She continued smoothly, but the playfulness was gone from her voice. "Are there any among your party who perform the Mercy for the dying?"

He was sure every bit of his astonishment showed on his face. He did not answer right away, more on guard now than he had been when he'd first seen the hound. "I was not aware your people and mine used the same name for that Hesperine rite."

"We do not. I prefer yours."

"Then you are quite unusual among your kind."

"Indeed. I even know the way your people honor the dying does not involve feasting on their flesh...or even drinking their blood."

Lio discarded his assumptions about her then and there. "Then you must know I am hesitant to answer you, lest I implicate any of my companions in practices that are...difficult for most of your people to understand."

"Of course. It is best if we do not name names. I ask only for a yes or a no. Can I persuade you to give me that much? As a deed of chivalry?"

Lio sought answers in the Blood Union. He let it draw him into the russet tendrils of light that were the veins beneath her skin. He barely managed not to gasp.

Suddenly, at last, he was in this moment. Not on the greensward dying with a helpless man. He was in the living current of her blood.

Here was the greatest beauty she possessed—a will to survive unlike any Lio had ever felt. A Will so strong it could only have grown under constant threat.

Here was the reason his people spilled their own blood on behalf of her kind. Why the embassy had walked voluntarily into this den of predators and the Queens had allowed them to do so.

This woman the Goddess had given life must fight for every beat of her heart.

Lio unraveled himself from her, struggling to resist the music under her skin. "If you would have me be your knight champion, Lady, you must condescend to offer me at least some small token of yours."

Her smile did not reach her eyes or her blood. "Of course. You would want a flower to adorn your breast. A trophy to carry onto the field."

"Nay, I would beg of you a treasure that is beyond my power to possess. It is yours to share or withhold. But if you will allow me, I promise I shall carry it with honor…and keep it close." He put a hand over his heart. "Your name, Lady."

Her blood rushed faster. She hesitated. "I thought it was agreed no names should pass our lips."

"To protect those who might be endangered, should their names be known."

"Did you imagine that includes only your own people?"

He bowed his head in concession. Hound or no hound, she was still a woman in Tenebra. And she was still disobeying her king. "Forgive me. A knight intends his lady no harm."

"Only a knight can be trusted," she told him. The hound eyed him, tensing as if to stand. "*Het,* love," she soothed, and the beast stilled.

Lio met the dog's gaze. "I have no wish to trespass on my lady's generosity, but could I call myself honorable if I answered such a question, not knowing who asks?"

"Fair," she acknowledged. "Yet you ask a name in exchange for a mere yes or no."

"Not at all. For I shall give you my name as well."

"Unwilling to endanger your comrades, but ready to place yourself on the sacrificial altar?"

He tried not to let her metaphor concern him. "A confidence for a confidence. And if that concerns you so, let me ask you this: to whom might I betray you? What reason have I to reveal your secrets?"

She was silent for a long moment, and he began to think he had lost his gamble, and she would turn and leave. But at last she nodded. "Very well. Who offers himself as my champion tonight?"

"Deukalion Komnenos. But my lady must call me Lio, as my friends do."

"A pleasure to meet you…Lio. I am Cassia."

"Cassia." He smiled at her, remembering just in time to keep his lips shut. She was her name, through and through: a spice beloved among Hesperines for its fragrance and flavor. Bitter, unless sweetened.

"May I have the answer to my question, Lio?"

"The answer is no. None of us perform the Mercy. We enter Tenebra to fulfill other duties."

A sigh escaped her, whether of relief or disappointment, the Blood Union did not tell him. And that, he wondered at. For all he beheld in her, there was a great deal he could not discern.

She dipped her head in a deep nod. "Thank you."

He bowed again instead of asking her more questions. Nor did he offer further answers. There was much more he could have told her, of course, but their agreement was only for a yes or no. One did not reveal all one's bargaining power during the first negotiation. He suspected she knew that as well as he did. He had haggled for all she would reveal tonight.

Would he have an opportunity to bargain for more?

Her hand shifted slightly on the dog's head, and he got to his feet. He still watched Lio, but there was no sign of teeth now.

"I bid you good evening." She turned away. "And good meal."

If he had not suspected it already, that last remark convinced him. There was a great deal more about her that would surprise him.

She could not simply leave it at that. Her question, answered but unexplained, hung between them, an agreement reached, a warning that he may yet have misstepped. "Cassia."

She hesitated.

"I am still a student of your people's ways," he said, "but do not some Tenebrans have second names to indicate their family, descent, or land?"

She arched a brow at him over her shoulder.

"I have given you my name and that of my bloodline as well as the answer to your question," he reminded her. "If Cassia is not the only name you bear, will you not do me the honor of telling me the rest?"

She looked ahead. If he were not Hesperine, he might not have heard the word she whispered. "Basilis."

Too stunned to reply, Lio stood and watched her, heard her, smelled her walk away from him.

What had he done? How great a prize had he just bargained for and won?

THE END OF AN ERA

LIO CROSSED THE LENGTH of the grounds at a run. But tonight, motion did not bring meditation. The sensation of the wind ripping past him and the ground falling away beneath his feet yielded no insight. When he came to a halt at the edge of the trees, Lady Cassia was no less a mystery to him than she had been the moment he'd first scented her.

And it was *Lady* Cassia. Lady Cassia *Basilis*. No one bore that name except a woman of the Tenebran royal house who was not herself royal. He had just met King Lucis's only living daughter.

Lio strolled out of the woods at a more dignified pace and approached the main gate of Solorum Fortress. Guards scurried along the ramparts, their wide eyes glinting at him. Fear and disgust wafted down to him with the smells of leather, sweat, and steel. Lio gave the men a short bow by way of greeting. They scurried faster. Momentarily the portcullis uttered a groan, then screeched upward, warning even the dullest mortal ears that Initiate Ambassador Deukalion no longer stalked the grounds.

No chance of stepping quietly back to his rooms and avoiding a confrontation with his elders, not when he must keep the Tenebrans abreast of his movements. The more visible he made himself, the less reason he gave their hosts to imagine he lurked about feasting on beautiful maidens.

Or that he had committed the equally forbidden transgression of having a rational conversation with one.

As he entered the fortress, his heart pounded faster than it should after such an easy run. The portcullis clanged shut at his back, but he could still feel the Temple of Anthros on the next hill and the seven mages within.

The magical workings of untold centuries steeped the structure, glaring to Lio's senses. The temple held far greater power than the men who tended it. He knew Hesperine sucklings back in Orthros who had more powerful magical auras than Amachos and his lot. But Lio didn't doubt the royal mage would use every rudimentary skill he possessed to keep track of the embassy's movements.

As for the fortress, no spells augmented its gruesome fortifications. Lio passed through the gauntlet of murder holes and inner gates, down into the lower levels where their hosts had given them quarters. The tomb-like barracks said a great deal about the Tenebrans' understanding of his people—or lack thereof.

No moonlight reached down here. The bare torches that lined the corridor hurt Lio's eyes. Did the humans plan to use the brands to burn the heretics if things got out of hand?

Stooping so as not to bump his head on the ceiling, Lio headed straight for his own room. He had his hand on the door when a formidable aura intruded on his senses. Someone possessed of true power loomed at the end of the hall.

"Good veil, Uncle." Lio lifted a hand, then opened his door.

"Good veil?" Uncle Argyros questioned. "On your way to bed already?"

Lio paused with one foot in his room. "The Slumber does catch up to me much faster than it does to the rest of you."

"You seem awake enough to remain upright through our evening conference. Come."

Lio looked over his shoulder. Uncle Argyros disappeared through the open doorway to the common room, his pale blond braid swinging at his heels.

Lio let his door shut and followed without protest. He needed sleep, solitude, anything but six elders evaluating whether he would hold up after the night's shocking events, but there was no point insisting. Uncle Argyros would see through all Lio's best negotiation tactics, for his uncle had taught him every one.

But it was not the entire embassy who awaited Lio around the table in the common room. Uncle Argyros sat alone, garbed in his veil hours robe. The simple garment of silver silk suggested this was no meeting between the initiate ambassador and his mentor, but between Lio and his uncle.

The table's scarred surface had clearly seen the wrong end of soldiers' knives more often than luxuries like the one that occupied it now: Uncle Argyros's copper coffee service. The fragrance of the finest Midnight Roast filled the room. Lio's uncle had been waiting for him, brewing the powdery grounds to perfection on the geomagical warming plate.

The familiar scene was enough to bring a slight smile to Lio's face. "I see the coffee and travel warmer are exempt from your injunctions that we travel as light as possible and employ minimal spells."

"Of course. We must be prudent, not endure harrowing deprivation." Uncle Argyros lifted a hand to indicate the empty chair opposite him. "Please, join me. We could do with a taste of home."

No one but Aunt Lyta could claim to know Uncle Argyros's mind. No one else could read anything in his stillness. Lio could, however, imagine what might trouble Uncle Argyros's thoughts on his and Aunt Lyta's first return to Tenebra in over four hundred years. Memories. Strategies. Human kings who no longer lived and Hesperines who still should.

This was Argyros, the mind mage who had once held off an entire invading army through sheer force of Will. Silvertongue, the ambassador who had dealt with hostile Tenebrans for almost sixteen hundred years. And Lio's fiercely loving uncle.

Had he called Lio in thinking the youngest among them needed help coming to terms with what had happened tonight? Or because he wanted to have coffee with his nephew?

Lio sat down across from him for their ritual. He watched Uncle Argyros take up the coffee pot by its slender handle and fill two delicate cups. How many times during Lio's education had they marked the end of the night's work this way? How many times over these very cups had Lio envisioned their future diplomatic journeys together?

This would not be the night he confessed it was not all he had imagined. Nor would this night, the first real test of his skills, be when he failed.

He could almost hear Xandra. *You hate making mistakes even worse than the rest of us, Lio. But you're always the first one to confess.*

He would confess nothing until he was sure his conversation with Cassia Basilis had actually been a mistake.

As Uncle Argyros stirred the rich, dark brew with one filigreed spoon, Lio stirred his Gift within himself. When his uncle slid the cup across the table, Lio took it, while gathering another layer of power beneath the spell that always veiled his person.

It was no easy task to strengthen one's personal veil under the nose of a Hesperine mind mage, and there were only two thelemancers in existence whose power was thought to compare with Argyros's. But Lio had the good fortune of being one of them. He had learned both diplomacy and thelemancy well under his uncle's tutelage.

Uncle Argyros lifted his cup. "To your first embassy."

"To your return to Tenebra." Lio raised his own cup. Taking his first sip of coffee, he suppressed a pleasant shudder. "Mercy, this is good. You made it even stronger than usual."

"The better to melt all other flavors off your tongue. It's the least I can do to help cleanse the taste of deer blood from your palate."

Lio lifted his cup once more in gratitude.

Uncle Argyros sat back in his chair. "Company makes resorting to animals less of an ordeal. Javed would go with you, if you wished."

"Take the family physician with me? So he can keep an eye on how well I fare surviving on deer?"

"Take family with you, to make the time pass more pleasantly."

Surely his uncle would not press the issue. If anyone had been with Lio tonight, they would have discovered his breach of conduct. Or he might not have been bold enough to reveal himself to Lady Cassia at all. He was not sure which would have been worse. "I appreciate everyone's concern, sincerely. But you know I don't mind solitude."

"You are equally fond of good company."

Lio put on his most relaxed smile and wove his veil tighter. "But it is so much more enjoyable over coffee than deer."

"I cannot dispute that." Uncle Argyros glanced around them at the worn stone walls and a hearth grimy with the soot of long-dead fires. "Does the legendary Solorum look as you imagined?"

"No," Lio admitted, welcoming the change of subject. "When I read about the Mage King's complex in the histories, I imagined it…grander, I suppose. And yet the reality of Solorum does impress me in ways I had not expected." One astonishing mortal here held more power to captivate him than any monument.

"How so?"

Lady Cassia did credit to her ancestors, whom King Lucis shamed. Lucis Basileus. Her father. Whose retribution she dared risk, all so she could speak to a Hesperine…to Lio. "The feats the humans here accomplish are remarkable, given the limitations under which they struggle."

"Never underestimate humans."

"I'm not likely to forget that lesson, Uncle."

Uncle Argyros sighed. "Of course not. Forgive me if my thoughts turn in dire directions."

"How could they not?" Lio said softly.

Quiet fell between them. A moment of silence for the farmer who had not survived his king's welcoming ceremony for the embassy.

"This is the first Equinox Summit in nearly four centuries," Lio said at last. "Is it not still cause for hope that a king of Tenebra finally wishes to reopen diplomatic relations?"

"I don't know."

Lio almost started in his chair. He had never heard his uncle say those words. Not about a matter this significant. "How can we regard this as anything but a hopeful event? Despite what we know of Lucis, he is the first king in generations to honor his obligation to hold the Equinox Summit once in his reign. He has given us our chance to reaffirm the Oath so it once more protects our people who wander in Tenebra to perform the Mercy and give children Solace. If we succeed, we'll finally be able to continue our sacred practices here without being persecuted—and reassure mortals we respect them in return."

Uncle Argyros cast Lio a smile. "I rejoice to see your ideals remain unshaken."

"My convictions would not be very strong if they could not survive a single night in Tenebra. I know how imperative it is to approach this situation without any illusions, but also without sacrificing our ideals." Even as he said it, Lio felt dishonest. For it was no strength of his own that had revived and bolstered his faith in his people's cause tonight. It was one woman's fearless gaze, which she had not turned from him, despite what he was.

There were humans in Tenebra who were not blinded by hate. Lady Cassia was astonishing, living proof there was still hope.

"What is your impression of Lucis?" Uncle Argyros asked. "Is he as you expected?"

"Too much so." Lio breathed the heat rising from his coffee. "The king has neither ideals nor convictions."

"What drives him, then?"

"Only motivations, and those are anathema to our own."

"How so?"

The night Lio had requested to join the embassy, his uncle had grilled him with similar questions. Then it had been a test of his readiness. This time it was surely a test of his fortitude. But tonight had prepared him more thoroughly for this even than his years of study.

"Lucis sees the Summit as only one of many strategic moves," Lio answered, "no different from ensuring he has a male heir or bringing the feuds between his free lords under control. He has devoted his reign to broadening his own authority within his kingdom and increasing his prestige in the eyes of his neighbors. And besides Orthros, he has only one: the Magelands." Just saying the name left a bad taste in Lio's mouth. "The Mage Orders in Cordium have taken notice of his power. That leaves us."

"How could we possibly benefit his prestige?"

"He wants to be the king who restores the tradition of the Summit in the footsteps of the Mage King, the champion of Anthros who halts the Hesperine encroachment by restoring the Oath." Lio grimaced. "Lucis is not motivated by respect for our people and certainly not by a love for peace. He does not hate peace, either. He simply has no use for it."

Uncle Argyros gave a humorless laugh. "So we are here to ensure peace with a man who regards it as useless."

"Which means the only way we can succeed is to provide him with a use for it. He forged peace between the free lords because it strengthened his reign. It also had the side effect of ending a great deal of suffering. We must show him that peace with us benefits him in order to reap the resulting benefits to us, to which he gives no thought."

"What advantages could the Oath offer him?"

"Hesperines have a long history of cleaning up the problems Tenebran kings can't. When the common people cannot provide for their children, we do. When their lords fail to protect them from crime, we keep them safe. When the casualties of Tenebra's troubles are beyond mortal aid, we can yet help."

"Do you think Lucis, in his merciless authority and calculated warmongering, has any need of us?"

"Regardless, there could be no peace without conversation, and there could be no conversation without the Summit. Lucis has given us our opportunity."

"What do you think we will be able to make of this opportunity?"

"It will not be easy, and it may take us many Summits yet, but this can be the beginning of the end—the end of the ambiguity that has ruled our relationship with Tenebrans since their kings ceased to reaffirm the Oath with us. We may yet put this era behind us. No longer will we have to steal like thieves into Tenebra, the ancestral home of many of our own people. Nor will human lords and kings turn a blind eye to whatever violence their subjects and mages wish to perpetrate against us within their borders." Lio studied his uncle's face.

Uncle Argyros's furrowed brow said only that he was worried and grave, not whether Lio's words met with his mentor's expectations. "You see the end of an entire era somewhere in this dark pile of stones."

Stone walls were not deterrent enough for the Goddess's gaze. Moonlight shone beyond the fortress, out of sight, but not out of reach. Lio could not resist drawing the glow of the two moons near them. He wove red and white light between his fingers, and the room brightened.

"We are Hesperines," he said. "We cause light to grow."

The lines on Uncle Argyros's brow softened. "Hespera's Solace. What would we do without our young ones to keep us from moldering?"

Lio closed his hands, ending his foolish display. He needn't show off tricks every newblood light mage knew. He wrapped his fingers around his coffee cup.

Uncle Argyros smiled. "The last time I sat in this fortress, it was clear to me the tide had turned. Little matter negotiations with that king had failed; I knew he would not hold his throne long, and the warlord who supplanted him would be even more preoccupied with conflicts within

Tenebra at the cost of maintaining relations with Orthros. I turned to your aunt and said, 'My Grace, I suspect we shall be at home for the foreseeable future.' She replied with a smile I understood well. What better time to seek out a child to Solace? The rest of the embassy returned to Orthros ahead of us, and by the time we rejoined them, Kadi was a suckling in her mother's arms. Now Kadi is old enough to accompany us here for the Summit and nearly as formidable as Lyta. It is good to have both of them at my side this time."

Lio had heard all his elders' stories of the past many times before, but he smiled. "The Queens would never have let us set foot over the border without a proper guard."

"Goddess forbid that we must resort to violence, but I cannot deny we must be prepared for anything."

Lio strove for a light tone. "Well, it should suffice that between Aunt Lyta and Kadi, we have half of Orthros's warriors with us. If you count Rudhira as well—"

Uncle Argyros gave a huff. "The First Prince is not to be counted. He is to have no contact with the embassy."

"I mean only to say he is also this side of the border, and thus three of Orthros's vast army of five are now Abroad."

"Don't you mean three of six, son of Apollon?"

"You of all people know Father doesn't call himself a warrior anymore. Mak and Lyros must protect the home front all on their own." The thought of his friends made Lio grin.

Uncle Argyros scowled. "Now of all times, when my son has just avowed his Grace. Mak and Lyros barely finished their vows before half the family had to depart for Tenebra and leave them with the responsibility of Lyta's command."

"You might as well call that another avowal gift. You know they're thrilled at the opportunity. They are ready." As Lio was ready for the Summit, he liked to think.

"I did not plan to spend the beginning of your cousin's new life with his Grace in a foreign country. Mak needs me near at such an important time. And what a poor way to welcome Lyros into the family! We have loved him as our own for years, but even so. Now he is officially my Grace-son."

"Mak and Lyros understand, Uncle, and as I said, they are proud of the trust Aunt Lyta has placed in them." In the face of his uncle's disappointment, Lio refrained from pointing out how Mak and Lyros rejoiced to have fewer relatives hovering at a time when they only wanted each other's company. It was still strange for Lio to dwell on the fact that he was not there to hover, either. He had always imagined he would be near to lend his Trial brothers a hand as they began their eternity together.

But then, they had imagined supporting him as he embarked on his eternity with Xandra.

He had no word for what he and Xandra were now. He was not yet able to call her a friend. Now she was not even that, when once she had been so much more.

Thank the Goddess for this opportunity to embark on his first journey Abroad instead. He was not fleeing. He wasn't. He was serving his people and taking an opportunity he would never have wanted to miss, regardless of the circumstances.

But it was a relief to no longer be in Orthros, surrounded by all that had not turned out as he had hoped and planned.

"At least one of my Grace-sons is with us," Uncle Argyros said. "I am glad indeed for Javed. We are blessed that Kadi's Grace is a healer of such skill who can act as steward of Orthros's medicinal gifts to Tenebra."

"I know how grateful you are Basir and Kumeta also agreed to lend their expertise to this endeavor."

"As loathe as I am for them to risk direct contact with Tenebrans, we could not enter these negotiations without the insight they can provide into current affairs. The First Prince must do without the Master Envoys for an occasion such as this."

"Thank you for recommending me to the Queens for inclusion in such a company," Lio said, not for the first time. "You have my gratitude."

"Do I still?"

"Of course," Lio answered in surprise. He hesitated. "Are you still confident in your decision to bring me?"

"I always want you at my side, Nephew."

Lio relaxed. "You honor me, Uncle."

"I also want to watch my son and Grace-son establish their residence.

I want to convince Kadi and Javed that Lyta and I are ready for grandchildren. I want to spend this season at home and look forward to my next journey to a more hospitable court than Tenebra. But this is not about my wishes."

Lio's last sip of coffee was bitter on his tongue. He set his cup down carefully. The grounds that clung to the bottom could reveal one's future, it was said, but if any omen lay within, Lio had not the skill to read it. He must rely on his own power to determine his fate.

Surely his uncle could not be thinking of sending him home.

The violence that had broken out upon their arrival had been an unexpected tragedy. There was no doubt their presence here sparked conflict that could easily turn against them. But that didn't mean the embassy was in such great danger that Lio must be packed off home like a suckling.

Unless... Hespera's Mercy. Was Lio to be banished back to Orthros for another reason? He had no doubt that would be his uncle's response, if he discovered Lio had shown such blatant disregard for the fragile rules on which the success of the Summit depended.

He felt no probe from his uncle's mind. Just Uncle Argyros's piercing dark gaze. He might in all fairness help himself to what thoughts Lio left unguarded, but he would never trespass on the veiled depths of another's mind. Nor had he ever needed to, to discern what he wanted to know from his nephew.

But Lio had never kept a secret like this from his uncle.

Could Uncle Argyros know Lio had spoken with Lady Cassia?

TEST OF WILL

UNCLE ARGYROS SET DOWN his cup and looked across the table at Lio.

Lio did not look away. He knew how to withstand a thorough scrutiny from Argyros.

How could his uncle know? Lio was no uninitiated newblood. Surely he would have sensed his mentor's aura if Uncle Argyros had checked on him from afar or, worse, come out to the grounds and discovered him in Lady Cassia's company.

Lio felt the veil he wore as close as his own skin, weightless as light, strong as stone. There was not so much as a flutter of disturbance in his working.

He did not break his uncle's gaze, only the silence. "I know more is at stake than what any of us want. I know this journey has already proved to be even more dangerous than we expected, and no one of my youth has ever been allowed to participate in the Equinox Summit. I do not take for granted what an exception the Queens have made for me under these extraordinary circumstances."

"I have never known you to take anything for granted."

"The first Summit in four hundred years, Uncle! As long as I will live, as many embassies as I may yet have the honor to serve, there will never be another like this. *This* is what I have trained for. This is the history I have waited to be part of, the opportunity I have longed for to commit all my power to the benefit of our people."

"You have always worked diligently for our good. Your work at home has not been wasted."

"My work on Tenebran history and politics. At last I have a real opportunity to put it into practice. I would be of no use in Orthros at a time like this. It would do no good for me to spend the Equinox Summit tending your scrolls and awaiting your return."

"You're wrong, Lio."

Disappointment threatened to sink him. He braced himself. "Am I?"

"Someone much younger than you once participated in the Equinox Summit."

"What?" Lio frowned. "Who? I have read the transcripts of all the Summits. I would have remembered."

"I wasn't always this old, Nephew."

Lio stared at his uncle. "You're speaking of your first Summit. Forgive me—of course. I should have realized."

"No apologies necessary. Your generation is taught to think of us as elders. I cannot fault you for your education, when I am the one who gave it to you. I cannot blame you for not knowing what I do not have the heart to teach you."

"Uncle…" Lio leaned forward, closing some of the distance between them. He observed another moment of silence before he spoke further. "I know how it pains all of you to talk about the Last War. Even the first Equinox Summit that ended it. You needn't now, if you do not wish to."

"No. We must."

Uncle Argyros took up the coffee pot and poured himself another cup. He held out a hand, and Lio slid his own cup across the table. It was not until they had both taken one, two more sips of coffee that Uncle Argyros spoke.

"I had been Hesperine for fewer years than you, Lio, when I stood with the Queens at the first Equinox Summit, and they personally swore the Oath with the best king and queen Tenebra ever had. That was the only reason the Last War with Cordium ceased."

"It must have been terrible and wonderful to witness that moment," Lio said. "If the Mage King and the Changing Queen had not reached a truce with us and let the Queens take our people safely out of Tenebra, this place would still be a battleground in the Mage Orders' attempt to destroy us."

Uncle Argyros nodded gravely. "In the name of all we had lost and all we prayed would never happen again, I pledged myself to the preservation of the treaty before the Queens, and they bestowed upon me the duty of returning here to reenact the Equinox Summit with each successive ruler of Tenebra. Our Queens had forethought. They envisioned and built toward a future for us in a time when most of us could scarcely believe tomorrow would come. Hespera's temples lay in ruins. Her worshipers' villages had become their funeral pyres. Lyta…" Uncle Argyros, never at a loss for words, faltered. "She could still feel the blood of her vengeance on her hands. I could still feel the blood of all those my words and my magic were insufficient to save."

"I understand," Lio said for the first time.

"Do you?" Uncle Argyros let out a long breath. "Your father was young then, as well. We were both men in our prime…or perhaps a little past it… when we became Hesperines. Neither of us realized how young we were."

"I do understand, in a way I didn't before tonight."

That was all Lio could say. He had seen suffering he had no power to prevent. One life lost. It felt enormous. And yet it had been only a small taste of the catastrophic suffering the Last War had wrought.

"For the sake of all those you lost, Uncle, I wish to remain in Tenebra."

"That's precisely why I wish to send you home. That and the fact that your mother will certainly curtail my immortal existence, if I allow this place to scar you. Not to mention your father may set his mind on joining us, if things grow too dangerous—for your safety, he'll say. Then my dear brother *and* our restive prince will be together on this side of the border and free to tempt you, my initiate ambassador, into their undiplomatic ways, and any members of the embassy who survive your mother's ire may give up all hope of peaceful negotiations."

"I had no idea I might be such a detriment to the embassy."

"I never said *you* are. You are an invaluable asset. I need all our best assets, Lio, if I am to make anything of this disaster."

At last. Those were the words Lio had hoped to hear. The only response he could give felt insufficient. "Thank you, Uncle."

"As the Queens' Master Ambassador, I would have my initiate on hand to assist me in this impossible situation. As your mentor, I would not deny you this opportunity to advance your career. As your teacher, I would not deprive you of education by experience. As your friend, I would have your company over my evening coffee. But as your uncle, I regret asking this of you."

"You never asked. I volunteered. And I would do so again. I *will* do so again, should I be blessed with the opportunity."

Uncle Argyros's eyes gleamed, not with thelemancy, but with pride. "Very well, then. There will be no more talk of sending you home. For now."

A victorious laugh threatened to tear out of Lio, but he caught it just in time. Instead, he gave his uncle a bow of gratitude over their cups.

Uncle Argyros sighed. "Since our Queens have authorized me to take the youngest member of House Komnena, Apollon's only heir, out of their sight, I shall trust them to keep the consequences well in hand. I am sure Komnena will refrain from plotting my demise, Apollon will behave himself in Orthros, and the prince will show neither pale hide nor blood-red hair of himself during our entire stay in Tenebra."

Now Lio did laugh. He could scarcely contain his relief. "I should like to see Father and Rudhira try to sit through the Summit with the king and Council."

"Goddess preserve us. That is something I hope I never witness." Uncle Argyros drained his cup.

As he brought it to rest on the table, his gaze fixed on something over Lio's shoulder—no, someone. Lio hadn't even felt his aunt approach, but now her lively aura filled the room as she rounded the table and went to Uncle Argyros's side. She wrapped her arms around her Grace's shoulders, and with the ease of reflex, he reached up to rest a hand upon her sleeve.

She gazed across the table at Lio. "How is our nephew?"

"He is well," Uncle Argyros said firmly.

Aunt Lyta smiled, and Lio could easily sense her relief. She was not one to keep her feelings to herself, nor her opinions.

Uncle Argyros's hand had relaxed around his coffee cup, while the other tightened ever so slightly upon Aunt Lyta's arm. "You and Kadi have finished the ward?"

"Indeed. Our daughter does us proud. As does our nephew."

"Indeed." Uncle Argyros smiled.

Lio returned the smile, into his coffee cup. "Thank you."

"For my part, I am glad you are here, Lio. With you near, I miss Mak and Lyros a little less." A shadow crossed Aunt Lyta's aura. "And I have spent too much time missing my children."

Uncle Argyros raised his hand to his Grace's hair, fingering the braid of his own hair she wore across her brow. Whatever he said to her, it was not for anyone's ears but hers. In the privacy of their Grace Union, perhaps he reminded her that on this side of the border, they were that much closer to Nike, wherever she was in Tenebra. Or maybe they only shared a moment of silent grief for the long years since they had last seen their first child.

"Well, I dare any of the mages across yonder green to disturb our sleep." Aunt Lyta's smile reappeared, as swift and sharp as her reflexes. "It will not go well for them."

Now that Lio was no longer engaged in a contest of Will with his uncle, he could sense Aunt Lyta and Kadi's ward around the embassy's grim quarters. Their shield rang of Orthros. Home.

It felt discordant with the tight veil he carried over his heart.

"At least our hosts agreed we should sleep under protective magic," Lio remarked. "In fact, the Tenebrans seemed to expect us to take such a precaution. It troubles me to think what strange superstition we might be confirming."

"They must think what they will," Aunt Lyta said. "It is out of the question for us to surrender to the Dawn Slumber in this place without a proper ward to ensure our safety until we wake."

"Speaking of which, I believe it's time to excuse myself, if I may." Lio set his cup back on the tray of the coffee service and counted himself fortunate he didn't knock anything over.

Aunt Lyta gave him a smile he often saw directed at him and his cousins. "The sun draws nearer under the horizon. You must be sleepy."

At this moment, the weariness merely lapped at him, making his limbs feel sluggish and his fingers clumsy. But it wouldn't be long before the Slumber dragged him under and took the power of his Will with it.

Before that happened, he had to be out of his uncle's presence.

Fear Lio had not felt since his childhood now overtook him. The dread of losing control. His uncle would be wide awake until sunlight broke the horizon, while Lio's power waned and his veil slipped.

"Good veil," Uncle Argyros bade him, "and easy dreams."

"Thank you, Uncle." Lio stood. His legs felt heavier already. "Good veil, Aunt Lyta."

"Sleep well, Lio."

He escaped to his room at last. As soon as he shut the door, he leaned back against it, closed his eyes, and devoted all his concentration to weaving a veil over his chamber.

He did this every night, he told himself. What Hesperine didn't? Living in Blood Union, they all learned to draw a curtain between what they wished to share with others and what they didn't. And they learned to do it in their sleep. All newbloods mastered the art of weaving veils over their sleeping quarters that would persist without constant tending.

But this time Lio felt like a thief in the night, next door to his own people. He was not merely ensuring his privacy. He was hiding something that could change the course of the negotiations.

Or get him sent home. Which would mean he had no chance to discover precisely what it meant for his people that the king's own daughter spoke of Hesperines' sacred rites with respect.

Lio would be as good as his word to Lady Cassia. He would tell no one she had spoken to him. He would keep his own counsel. That would have to be enough as he tried to decide how to proceed.

But he could make no monumental decisions tonight. Lio shuffled toward his narrow bunk, shucking his formal robes on the way. He had the presence of mind to send them into his trunk with a wave of his hand. Any more power than that was too much effort. Without the aid of magic, he tossed back a wool blanket that had seen better days, then fell onto his pallet. At least it was stuffed with straw, and there were no furs.

Lio could feel it, a behemoth beneath the horizon, rising up to bury him. The sun. He'd be under before its light entered the sky.

Aunt Lyta and Kadi's ward would ensure all of them survived the day. Lio's veil would protect Lady Cassia's secrets...and his own.

41

days until

SPRING EQUINOX

LADY CASSIA'S GARDEN

No.

Was that answer worth what she had traded him?

Pushing herself out of bed seemed too difficult. Cassia felt as if she hadn't slept. Perhaps she hadn't, in the scant hours between that moonlit conversation and the dawn that now threatened through the crack under her door.

So. She had her answer. After all she had wrought and risked to be in the right place at the right moment to stand in the dark with a Hesperine and ask it of him.

The answer was *no*.

She had given in to her compulsion to ensure she was at Solorum during the Summit. She had indulged her preoccupation with the Hesperines. Now she must be satisfied—and stop making trouble for herself, when there was already enough. Time to raise her shield and face another day.

It wasn't until Knight wallowed out of bed that Cassia heeded her self-admonitions. He went to sit at attention by the door, clearly ready to maul any intruders, but especially his breakfast.

Cassia disentangled herself from her blankets and dragged herself to her feet. She set the bed to rights, as she always did. If Perita tended the place where Knight slept, her resulting illness would render her of no use at all. As Cassia pulled the linens tight, she caught sight of a black speck on the undyed fabric. The dark spot hopped. She sighed.

Once the blankets were tidy, she snatched the floral wreath off the wall above the bedstead. The charm had clearly reached the end of its life. That was another thing she could see to today, and not a day too soon.

In the hearth room, Perita had a fire burning and a lid on the pot to keep their porridge from going cold. One of the kennel masters had been here, for Knight's meal awaited in a dish just inside the door. Cassia saw her hound settled with the bloody hunk of venison, then settled herself by the fire. She noted only Knight had any energy this morning. She and Perita both shuffled about as if they had engaged in too much exercise the night before.

It was not hard to understand why Perita's lover was so attentive or why she had held his interest since the court's stay at Namenti. Perita was clever about what men liked. She took pains over her appearance with every tool allotted to a girl of her rank and exploited a few her proximity to Cassia afforded. She tied her apron just so to create a desirable shape and let as much of her wavy, light brown hair escape her kerchief as a woman might appropriately do. She invested considerable effort in combining Cassia's unwanted scent oils for the greatest effect.

Men committed many foolish deeds over women less pretty than Perita, and Perita was pretty. But inciting them to such acts was a dangerous game, one that could easily backfire. Cassia wondered how skilled Perita was at managing her lover.

Cassia remained grateful for her own dull brown hair, flat figure, and especially the freckles that marred her skin from scalp to toes. Her complexion was a prize that could not be bought, too brown to be fair like lovely Solia's, not brown enough to remind anyone of Cassia's beautiful Cordian mother. Being so plain made her half-royal blood the only threat she must deal with. For now she had some reprieve even from that, while domestic affairs occupied Lord Adrogan, and Lord Ferus rode east, discovered Cassia was not there, and then toiled the long way back.

Cassia set her spoon down in her empty porridge bowl and eyed the hearth room's single window, whose open shutters let in gray morning light. Her plants could not thrive in her windowless bedchamber, but they would not do badly out here. The small window in the dressing room was of no use, for she must keep herself and her hound's fur out of Perita's domain.

At the moment, Cassia's containers of evergreens and dormant perennials sat about where the pages had dropped them upon the court's arrival. The barn troughs she'd salvaged had shed a few nails, but at least none of the pots had cracked. It was harder to finagle replacements for ceramics. She could fill some hours moving her plants into optimal positions and helping them recover from the upset of the journey. But not all her hours.

Carefully installed in the path of the window's light, the loom threatened. Cassia must find a garden to work in immediately. She would not end this day without a hoe to occupy her in place of a shuttle.

"I laid out your sturdy green gown, Lady. The one you always wear for gardening." Perita hid a yawn behind one hand.

"I see that. After I work on my plants, I'll start in the kitchen gardens, then try the Temple of Kyria."

"Very good, Lady. I'll see to the rest of your unpacking and the mending we hadn't time to do before we left Namenti."

The constant repairs Cassia's few, well-worn belongings required certainly offered her handmaiden plenty of occupation. Cassia left Perita to her work and set about her own. The morning eased by, not in hours, but in the scrape of wood and ceramic across the stone floor, the seep of water into soil, and the snap of stems as Cassia sliced off lost causes with the sharp edge of her spade. She was rotating the same pot of sage a tiny amount for the fourth time when Perita interrupted her with a bowl of reheated porridge and the news that it was midday.

Cassia could dally no longer. She covered her hair and ventured out with Knight. As they entered busier parts of the palace, heads turned, but the gawkers quickly resumed their chores. Other people turned their backs instead and continued their conversations about gowns or horses. It wouldn't be long before these folk lost interest in the king's bastard, just like their fellow servants and courtiers who had been at Namenti. Cassia looked straight ahead and did not change her pace until she and Knight walked through the door of the main kitchen.

It would take more than her presence to halt the swell of activity here. She received glances only over sudsy pots and between stages of a carrot's dismemberment. The head cook closed in, issuing commands and a couple of swats on her way. She fixed Cassia with the same gaze she gave everyone, one that assured them she respected her betters and was the absolute divine authority this side of the kitchen threshold. The curtsy she gave, just deep enough but hardly deep at all, said much the same.

Cassia had never met her, but had certainly encountered her sort. After her experiences in many of the palaces to which her nomadic existence had brought her, Cassia already knew how this conversation would end.

She need not identify herself. Knight at her side was evidence of her blood, and her presence here among the servants was proof of her status. "Good day, Mistress. What a fine kitchen you keep. An equally fine garden is certain to lie without."

"Aye, the finest in Tenebra, Lady, make no mistake. This is Solorum. If it grows, we grow it here, and account for every stem and leaf. All requests go through the king's chamberlain."

"In such an impressive garden, there can never be enough hands to give it the attention it deserves. I have come to assist in the tending."

"How generous of you to offer, Lady," the cook said immediately. "We're honored by your interest, but we know your time is more valuable elsewhere."

They exchanged the remaining appropriate complements and farewells between a virtuous cook and a fallen woman's daughter, and Cassia led Knight out again.

She always started with the kitchen gardens, on the chance the cook might be like Agata at Paradum, who saw little enough of the king's household and had been grateful for the help. Cassia had spent a fine season up to her shoulders in pea plants as a result.

"I suspect they will be in greater need at the temple," Cassia remarked to Knight.

Time to try building her bridges with the mages of Kyria. It was just as well. Ladies of the household were to make themselves useful, and bastards were to make themselves unexceptionable. Performing good works at the temple, even more than lending a hand in the palace, was optimal to achieve both, while affording Cassia's thoughts ample time to do their own work.

Cassia made sure to catch plenty of gazes and snubs on her way out. At a minor gate on the east side of the palace, she spoke to the guards loudly enough that every man in the gatehouse would remember precisely when she had left.

The road to the temple proved well kept, certainly one that received frequent attention under the king's rigorous program of repairs. She walked against the modest traffic of wagons and riders who were joining the court a couple of days late. Sun shone down on all of them, for last night's clouds had blown out already, and the bare groves that lined the road offered no respite. With any luck, this weather would make Cassia's freckles even more unsightly. The outdoors enhanced her undesirable qualities to great advantage.

Today was a rare day for winter, the god of death's season. The frigid month of Hypnos's Shroud that descended at Solstice had now lifted, only for the land to feel the icy touch of Hypnos's Hand. Even when Hypnos's Dream came and went and spring arrived at last, the Mourning Goddess was certain to usher in the new year with rain in her first namesake month of Chera's Tears. But today it seemed Anthros rode the sun chariot across his celestial domain, determined to drive out Tenebra's usual wet weather and remind deities and mortals alike he remained lord of all he surveyed.

A large party of riders appeared ahead, traveling toward the palace. Cassia wove closer to the trees to make way, although not close enough to mire herself in the muck on the edges of the road. Knight positioned himself between her and the oncoming travelers. In a moment they were upon her, and as they passed by, she tucked her cloak closer about her to shield against the mud the horses' hooves flung about. Bridles and mail clinked, and sun glanced off swords and white drapes that protected the horse litter in the center of the party. A lady of high station was joining the court. Behind the unseen noblewoman's conveyance, a young lady, perhaps a daughter or sister, rode in the open air. Her palfrey was delicate and white, its legs encased in the filth of the road. The young woman's attendant rode alongside her, offering some murmured jest or gossip that made the lady laugh.

Cassia let them pass, then walked on with Knight, who needed no sword to defend her, nor expected her to laugh at cruel jokes. As soon as the two of them were out of sight of other travelers, Knight bounded a bit ahead, then behind, but never far enough that he was out of sight. A few times he pricked his ears and glanced away, surely at some small animal under the trees. But he never left her side to pursue them.

"Poor Knight," Cassia said. "Never free to go on such a merry chase. We'll have a game before the day is over, I promise."

A liegehound needed more than just frequent walks to stave off rest-lessness and keep his skills sharp. But she would see to his regimen later. For now he simply relished being outside, and that reassured Cassia she need not be on her guard for the moment.

She must now give thought to how, in the short term, she would pres-ent herself to the Prisma of the Temple of Kyria and, in the long term, give the king every reason to forget her presence at Solorum.

But her thoughts kept turning to a simple word delivered by a pair of marble lips polished with moonlight.

No.

Cassia had waited most of her life for that *no*. She might now go the rest of her life without ever again beholding a Hesperine.

She would certainly go the rest of the Summit out of sight at the palace, traipsing between her rooms and the temple, if the Kyrians would have her. Deukalion would see no more of her. This Lio, as he insisted she call him, would be left to wonder at her cryptic question, and no more would come of it.

As they had acknowledged openly, a Hesperine had nothing to gain by telling the king his daughter had transgressed. Knowledge of her mid-night whereabouts would be of great use to some, but not to Deukalion. Such a detail was worth nothing upon a negotiation table where the fate of Tenebra's children and the treatment of the human dead were at stake.

As Cassia approached the temple, she encountered some of the castoff children who would be a subject of debate at the Summit. Orphans worked the fields on either side of the road. These were the lucky ones whom the Kyrian mages sheltered, but it was not as if anyone wanted them except the Hesperines.

The children sang in the Divine Tongue while they broke the soil, send-ing up prayers or praises to Kyria in their clear, high voices. Cassia wondered how many would one day prove suited to magery and learn to understand the hymns. Would the other orphans, when they set out into the world to make their fortunes, still wonder what those words meant, which they had sung as children? Words that eluded even the king on his throne.

Bluestone walls stretched far to the left and right. The Temple of Kyria at Solorum shielded the children and the maiden women who reared them, as well as the women's magical secrets. Forbidding double doors of solid oak halted Cassia at the entrance. But a smaller panel in one door swung open right away, and a mage in robes the color of the clear sky welcomed Cassia inside.

"How can Kyria's handmaidens assist you this day, Lady?" Only the woman's cheerful eyes could be seen above her veil, a cloth of the palest blue that wrapped her hair and face. She even had a benevolent gaze for Knight, smelly paws and all.

"I have come to offer something to the goddess," Cassia replied. "These two hands."

"Praise our Mother of the Harvest for extra hands!"

"Mine are most useful in the garden, and they shall be available to you till sometime after the Spring Equinox, should you have use for them." Cassia patted the basket she carried over her arm. It never hurt to emphasize pleasing words with bribery. "I would also make a small offering of seeds and cuttings from the south, which might enrich your gardens. With faithful tending from your power, I know they will grow, even in Solorum's clime."

"Bless you for your generosity, Lady. Who shall I say is here to see the Prisma?"

"Cassia Basilis."

The light of interest, rather than censure, appeared in the woman's gaze. "If you will please follow me, Lady. I am Deutera, and I will show you the way."

Excellent. Cassia would go home with dirt under her fingernails today.

She and Knight followed Deutera across a courtyard, past archways through which came the scents of water and soil. The temple must have male guests today, for Deutera did not remove her veil.

The mage led Cassia to one of the structures built up against the inner wall, which towered above them, a bulwark within the bulwark of the outer walls. With any luck, Cassia would be allowed through that boundary today, where only women were permitted and the real work of the temple took place. For now, the mage ushered Cassia into an antechamber for strangers and visitors from all walks of life.

"Please make yourself comfortable, Lady." Deutera disappeared through a door that must lead to the Prisma's vestibule.

Cassia sat on a bench facing the vestibule door, and a beam of light fell on the crown of her head from a window near the ceiling. The panels were small, their glass thick and plain, but stained in shades of blue that made the room seem full of cool water. Knight relaxed beside her. She heard no voices on the other side of the door. If any conversation was in progress within, strong architecture and magic shielded it from listening ears.

It wasn't long before the door swung open, and Cassia stood, ready to present herself. She found herself face-to-face with the new royal mage.

He observed her with bland brown eyes. He had the olive complexion and dark hair that were common in Namenti. But there was nothing bland or common about his red-gold robe denoting his honored mastery in the Order of Anthros and the bronze chain of office around his neck, which every royal mage before him had worn. Cassia dropped him a curtsy. He folded his hands into his sleeves and nodded to her.

Amachos's lapdog stepped out behind him. Like his master, the apprentice appeared to hail from southern Tenebra, but there the similarities ended. The young man's sunny yellow robes turned his tawny face sallow, and his slouch made him look permanently abject. He dipped his head in a further gesture of deference, which made his apprentice cap slide forward and push his limp black hair into his eyes.

Deutera had escorted the men out of the Prisma's vestibule. "I am sure I need make no introductions."

Amachos's smile was like his voice—pleasant, except for the undertones. "Lady Cassia, I believe?"

Her name and identity were not beneath his notice? Perhaps the stain of shame never escaped his attention. "Indeed, Honored Master Amachos."

"To what do I owe the delight of seeing you in this holy place?"

"It is my custom to devote my time to Kyria whenever I am near one of her temples."

"What a worthy endeavor for a lady of your station." His nasal tones made the remark sound even more patronizing.

Bright gold light flashed in Cassia's eyes. The hair on the back of her arms stood on end, and a host of tiny pinpricks stung her skin. She glanced up to see a glyph of Anthros hovering over her head. The image faded as quickly as it had appeared.

"May Anthros make your efforts fruitful," Amachos intoned.

Cassia bowed her head and spared him her response. If he hoped to scrub the stain from her, it would take a great deal more than a glyph. She doubted Anthros cared about her parsley, but if his mage's tracings in the air could make it grow faster, so be it. She resisted the urge to fidget at the tingles that still ran over her, although the symbol was gone from the air.

Amachos spoke to Deutera with the air of concluding a discussion. "Rest assured, as I told the Prisma, should there be so much as a hint that Eriphites draw near, you shall not want for my assistance."

Deutera clasped her hands together. "I'm sure the children will rest easier tonight. We have heard the tales of the dissenters' violence against obedient temples. They seem bent on revenge upon all of us who would cleanse their corruption from the land."

Amachos lifted both hands in a gesture of reassurance. "No such thing shall befall this holy house while I am near. Fear not, for the Eriphites' wild, false cult dwindles to mere remnants. They are little more than bandits now. Had they gracefully accepted Anthros's rightful authority over their lesser god, they might have remained a proud and prosperous people." Amachos sighed. "Their misguided ways have been their own reward. We must pity what has become of them. But most of all, we must ensure their disobedience brings no harm to the faithful."

"What a relief to have you near, Honored Master Amachos, one of Tenebra's very own from Namenti. Our brothers and sisters in Cordium shall see how fortunate we are to have the strength of your magic to protect us."

Amachos exchanged a sympathetic look with her. A knowing look. "We certainly would not wish the supreme Cordian Orders to trouble themselves over our little problems, would we?"

"You have our thanks and our prayers."

"Do not hesitate to call upon me, should there be a need."

"Honored Master, Apprentice, allow me to see you out." Deutera nodded to Cassia again, holding open the door. "Lady, the Prisma will be glad to see you now."

Cassia entered the Prisma's vestibule with a new harvest of words. One never knew what fruit they might bear later.

The temple's watery light bathed the two occupants of the room, a votive bluestone statue of Kyria and a figure hooded and robed in white. When the door shut behind Cassia, the goddess's attendant rolled up her bell sleeves above ropy forearms and wrinkled elbows, then put back her cowl to reveal a gray head and a smile. "Welcome, child. How glad we are that you have come."

"Thank you, Prisma. I hope I can be of service to you."

"Of course! This is the place for any woman who wants to discover her gifts and enjoy the fruits of her labors. And escape the confusion of the outside world for a little while." The Prisma reached beneath the ceremonial drapery at the goddess's feet and retrieved a wad of fabric—an apron stained all shades of green, apparently stowed in haste, which she now donned over her immaculate robes of office. "Poor Lady Cassia, trapped at Solorum, surrounded by men's foibles and a pack of foreign heretics."

Cassia returned the Prisma's secret smile. It was good the mage did not know just how different their secrets were.

The Prisma was brazen to imply she disapproved of the king and his Hesperine guests. But it was no wonder she had the confidence to make her opinions clear, especially when very human Eriphite heretics among Lucis's own subjects raided about and threatened those in her care. The lives of her mages and the children depended on every single decision she made throughout the day.

"You have come to the right place," the Prisma promised.

Cassia spent the afternoon helping the mages ready their gardens for the coming spring. Knight lay about at the edges of the beds, accepting pats and accolades from the women while they worked and he lazed.

Cassia counted herself fortunate indeed. Her recent fraternization with a wicked heretic went unnoticed by all these mages. Even the powers in the temple could not detect whatever mark her conversation with Hespera's disciple had made on her.

But she felt it, as if Deukalion had left some magic on her, discordant with the persistent sensation of Amachos's blessing. More than once she smeared her hands and arms with more dirt than necessary, and she wasn't sure which she was trying to drive away.

Had she really expected a *yes*?

She had not known what the odds might be that one of the Hesperines in the delegation performed the Mercy. Her experience told her nothing so useful as how many Hesperines were usually at large in Tenebra, how many were responsible for that particular rite, and whether one of them was likely to offer the Mercy and also be an ambassador.

She was not sure what she had expected, and that alone was foreign and unsettling to her. She always knew what to expect from such occasions as giving a cloak to a seamstress. But when it came to negotiating with Deukalion, she didn't know nearly enough.

That *no* was not enough.

Cassia froze in the act of drawing and quartering a resistant winter weed. Knight saw her pause from the end of the row and lifted his head.

Was she really considering making another escape?

She applied herself to the weeds again before anyone noticed her hands shaking.

What a fool she was. She had gone through the forbidden door once already. How dare she attempt it a second time? It wasn't worth it. Not when all Deukalion might give her was another *no*.

She employed this reasoning on herself for the rest of the afternoon. But she knew too much to fall victim to her own manipulation.

She knew much more than a simple negative awaited her if she spoke with Deukalion again. Even if none of the Hesperine diplomats had ever performed the Mercy, it didn't matter. There was so much more at stake than that one word and the one question she had so far dared ask him.

He was a Hesperine. He had answers to all Cassia's questions.

Of course their encounter had been worth the risk. Worth so much that she did not even regret admitting the name she bore.

This was not a simple matter of a cloak she could use to rid herself of a bothersome suitor, no matter how much she had tried to justify it to herself thus. She would be a fool to fall for her own excuses in that regard as well.

This was the farthest leap she had taken beyond each day's careful steps to preserve herself. Ensuring the king brought her to Solorum contrary to his wishes was more dangerous than anything she had attempted since fourteen years ago.

Why had she ever allowed herself to walk away from the Hesperine with such a meaningless answer, after everything she had risked to get it?

It had been, in the end, so easy to meet with Deukalion. Much easier, in fact, than negotiating with her goal once she had reached him. And far easier than asking one of the questions she had harbored all this time. She was so accustomed to them being inside her, unanswered. They were thorns in her heart, but she was used to them.

What would it feel like to know the answers? Would they be sharper thorns? Or poison?

Or an antidote?

Just as Deukalion's answer had not been enough for her, her question had not satisfied him. She had clearly surprised him and piqued his curiosity. He would be a fool if he did not try to determine what she meant for his embassy: a threat or an opportunity. He would appear if she went to meet him again. If she could get away—if Perita did not stay in tonight to make up for lost sleep. Ah, but Cassia raced ahead of herself.

She returned to her rooms after dusk rites and a hearty, fresh meal with the Kyrian mages, her back aching and her basket full of cuttings they had given her in return. The syrupy stench of Perita's favorite scent oil filled the room. Cassia tried not to breathe and hoped her handmaiden would use up every drop so she didn't have to. She went straight to her bedchamber to hang a fresh and fragrant wreath the mages had newly bespelled to drive away vermin.

Knight flopped down on the opposite side of the room and began scouring his paws with his tongue, as if he could lick away the tingle of magic left over from the herbal bath he'd endured at the temple. Better a day of that than a miserable season scratching flea bites. Cassia told him again what a good dog he was. Soon she couldn't smell the oils over his paws.

But she could still hear them. A bottle clinked on the top of the dressing table, and there came the wet sucking sound of the girl rubbing the viscous liquid over her arms. She always took her time, obviously luxuriating in the activity with great delight. She would definitely be seeing her guard again tonight.

Cassia would have her chance.

Tonight she would press Deukalion for the full meaning of that one word, which was all he had given her, besides his name.

DIPLOMAT ERRANT

MEMORY AMBUSHED LIO'S FIRST coherent thoughts, while the Slumber still trapped his body. He lay with his eyes shut and limbs frozen and relived the scene again.

Torchlight. Silent, empty body. Blood slowing there, rushing faster in those around. Blood. On a furred flank, a homespun tunic, a glimmering length of steel.

At last Lio's eyelids responded to his frantic efforts. He forced them open to fill his sight with something, anything besides the visions in his mind's eye.

Rough stone blocks overhead. He dragged in his first breath of the night. Damp rock. Old wool.

Lio was in Tenebra.

A pang shot through his stomach, and he winced. He pried his tongue from the roof of his mouth. The Thirst was a powerful distraction from his thoughts, at least.

Thank the Goddess he had not dreamed. She had given him respite in the Dawn Slumber. If the rising sun hadn't banished him into sleep, he might have been haunted all day by what he had witnessed last night. How did humans ever rest, with so much to trouble their minds and no irresistible Slumber to give them relief?

Did Lady Cassia ever rest, or did she spend all her nights seeking forbidden company in the woods?

Now that was no mere distraction. Lio focused on the puzzle of Cassia Basilis to drive out all other thoughts of the night before. He must decide how best to proceed in regard to the lady.

When he tried again to move his unwieldy limbs, they finally complied. He succeeded in rising from his bunk and took the two steps necessary to cross the chamber to his washstand. The basic appointments of his room gave him no cause to complain. The gnawing pit in his stomach was another matter. Lio doused himself at the wash basin. The water's chill served to refresh him but did nothing to assuage the hot ache in his veins. Hespera's Mercy, but he thirsted. And he still had to get through tonight's negotiations before he could do anything about it.

He braced his hands on either side of the washstand and shook his head, letting the water drip from the ends of his hair. He was stronger than this. He could do this.

He could also see the logic in sending diplomats to Tenebra who were already Graced and could start the night with a thorough feast upon one another before they left their beds.

And that was truly useless thinking on his part. He had no time for a second cold bath, and he would need one if he kept thinking about how he might have started this night, if circumstances were different.

Lio grabbed the rag beside the basin and worked himself over, as if that could drive regrets from his mind. The purpose of this journey was to build on his successes as a diplomat. Not dwell on his utter failure in love.

Lady Cassia might prove to be his greatest diplomatic success yet. Or his most spectacular failure. It was up to him to determine which.

By the time he was dry and attired in his formal robes, his thoughts were clear. Lio could no longer deny what he must do.

He lifted his veil from the room and gathered the working about himself, adding yet another unseen layer to the power that cloaked him. The others would not notice he had strengthened his personal veil again. They would be too busy bolstering their own against the nearby mages, and Lio had been trained too well.

Lio went out into the corridor, narrowly escaping a knock on the head from the door frame. This time no unsettling flames blinded him. The torches had burned down to blackened, odorous shafts.

There was no doubt the whole embassy now awaited him in the common room. He felt their silent greetings through the Blood Union, from Javed's friendly warmth to Basir's brief acknowledgment of Lio's presence.

Even if it wasn't Lio's fault he was the youngest among them and last to escape the Slumber, he didn't want to arrive any later than necessary. He stepped to the common room on a bit of power.

He found the others already seated, as he had expected. The table, typical of hierarchical Tenebra, was a rectangle, but Lio's aunt and uncle had pulled both their chairs to the head of it. To their left, Basir and Kumeta sat with their shoulders touching, focused as ever on the work at hand. Lio couldn't remember the last time he had seen either of the Master Envoys smile.

"Lio." Uncle Argyros gestured to the empty chair nearest the door. "Please join us."

"Thank you, Uncle." Lio's veil felt heavier than ever as he took his place. It was the seat at his uncle's right hand.

"Don't look so apprehensive." On Lio's other side, Javed laughed. "I won't subject you to an examination here and now. We've no time before the negotiations for a proper evaluation of how your diet of deer is affecting your health."

Lio had not imagined an occasion when the Thirst would have its advantages. If the others detected any sign of tension in him, let them dismiss it as malnourishment. "I can spare you the time now and later. I've never felt better."

"I never said you could escape me later. I promised your mother I'd keep an eye on you." Despite his threatening words, Javed relaxed back in his chair, twining a hand in Kadi's.

"Don't be stubborn." Kadi leaned around Javed and subjected Lio to a brilliant smile. "I wouldn't like to have to coerce you."

"Of course you would, Cousin. But there is no need for violence." He put on a grin. "You may both take my word for it. I'm fine."

"Are you?" Uncle Argyros asked.

Lio met his uncle's gaze. "I am. I will have no difficulty waiting until after the negotiations are over to drink again."

Aunt Lyta fixed Lio with a warm but level gaze. "Are you sure? Now is the time to speak, if you feel the Thirst may give you difficulty during the Summit."

"I cannot say I approve of this schedule," Basir said to Uncle Argyros. "Now is not the time for such risks."

Kumeta frowned. "This is too rigorous a test of one so inexperienced. It would be better if Deukalion drank first and arrived late."

Join the negotiations late and miss the beginning of the proceedings? Certainly not. Lio gave a slight bow to Basir and Kumeta. "You can have confidence in me, Master Envoys. I will not allow my thirst to affect my performance."

Even as he said it, his belly knotted. Let it gnaw on all he left unsaid. His growling stomach was the least of what his veil would conceal tonight.

But it was not upon him that everyone turned their gazes. Under their scrutiny, Javed appeared amused. "His color is no worse than I would expect. Since he came out of his room, I've been listening to his pulse, and it remains steady and strong. You can all sense there is no confusion over his mind. I believe we may rest assured he is not in bad condition."

Aunt Lyta smiled at Lio, and his uncle nodded in satisfaction. Basir and Kumeta said no more.

Kadi narrowed her eyes at Lio. "Don't think this means you're excused from a thorough exam later."

"As long as I don't miss any of the negotiations, I shall submit to Javed's ministrations as docilely as a lamb. Sorry to disappoint you."

"Hmph."

Trust Kadi to be in good spirits, even after last night. Or at least to appear so and make an effort to lighten everyone's moods. She was so much like her younger brother. Not for the first time, Lio wished Mak were here to jest with him. And now more than ever he needed Lyros to give him an honest opinion.

What would they say if they knew what he had done?

Uncle Argyros cleared his throat. "Now then, let us continue. All of us know the terms of the ancient treaty established between our people and Tenebra over fifteen centuries ago. I suspect we dream the Oath's tenets in our Slumber. They are written on our hearts. Tonight we shall remind the humans who have, perhaps, forgotten. This is our last hour of preparation before the negotiations commence."

"We must make good use of this time," Kumeta cautioned.

Basir nodded. "The humans accept that we Slumber under a ward throughout the day, but now that night has come, it will alarm them."

"We must not maintain our shield much longer," Aunt Lyta agreed. "Kadi and I will bring down our protections as soon as we conclude our discussion."

"You can all feel it." Kadi gestured at the stones around them, no teasing in her voice now. "There isn't a scrap of magic on the fortress, unlike the temple and the palace. This is the domain of warriors, and there aren't centuries of leftover magic muddying the water. It will be easy even for a mage of Amachos's skill level to sense spells we cast here, especially those like wards that require a noticeable expense of power."

"And yet, not all magic is a spell," Basir reminded them. "Now is the time to take full advantage of that fact."

"We must rely almost solely on our innate Gift, rather than on active castings," Kumeta advised.

"As I need hardly remind everyone," Basir said, "one wrong move by any of us reflects on every one of our people. To the mortals here, we are a faceless force, a threat with only one name: Hesperines. If the embassy antagonizes the Tenebrans, we will put every Hesperine errant who walks Abroad in immediate danger of retribution from mages and warriors alike."

"On the other hand," said Kumeta, "making a good impression could make Tenebra safer for all our Hesperines errant."

"We are fortunate the Charge can spare you," Aunt Lyta said.

"Is willing to spare you, rather." Kadi frowned. "I don't think they really can."

"Rest assured the envoys in our service carry on our work in force," Kumeta replied. "They will keep our Hesperines errant well informed in our absence. Basir and I are prepared to give our undivided attention to making the Summit a success."

"Or at least mitigating the damage it could cause." Basir's frown deepened. He added to Uncle Argyros, "You know that is no reflection on my faith in you, my friend."

"And you know I have the greatest respect for your fears," Uncle Argyros replied.

Lio began to wonder just how much his uncle shared the Master Envoys' fears.

Kadi sat straighter in her chair. "Mother and I did not come Abroad to see it become more dangerous for our Hesperines errant. Whether at home in Orthros or here in Tenebra, the Stand keeps our people safe."

Lio sent up a silent prayer for Nike and for Kadi. Although Kadi seldom showed it, they all knew the toll her elder sister's absence took on her.

Javed squeezed Kadi's hand. "At last, we have our chance to do some good Abroad. I can only hope the king will not close his heart to my offers of medical aid for his people. The gifts we've brought could alleviate so much suffering."

Uncle Argyros arranged the documents in front of him. "Let us once more review how we will discuss our aims with King Lucis and what facts we shall present in favor of our terms."

As the conference proceeded, anxiety took hold of Lio anew. Or perhaps it was just the restlessness brought on by the Thirst. He had studied all of this, pored over it. The only thing he lacked was experience. All those nights he had spent in Orthros searching for answers to the dilemmas that compelled him had revealed to him the path he wanted to walk in his future. He was taking the first steps on it now.

He would prove to everyone their confidence in him was not misplaced.

It felt as if far less than an hour had passed when Kumeta warned, "The royal house will soon finish their evening meal. It is nearly time to join them on the greensward."

Hours were shorter in Tenebra, Lio reminded himself, and there were twenty-four of them instead of sixteen. Even the way humans counted the passage of the night was different from Orthros.

"Does anyone have any additional questions or points for us to discuss?" Uncle Argyros asked.

Perhaps Lio was mad. But he needed more information if he was to proceed with proper caution, and he possessed information he owed to the embassy.

Besides, one of the best ways to keep a secret was to wear it in plain sight, as if it were not a secret at all.

"I wish to present a fact for our consideration, if I may." Lio looked to his aunt and uncle.

"Something we neglected to discuss last night?" Uncle Argyros questioned.

"Our conversation turned to other subjects, Uncle. Also, I think we would benefit from Basir and Kumeta's counsel on this matter. Something came to my attention last night that may be of concern to us."

Aunt Lyta's gaze sharpened. "What is the matter, Lio?"

"As I'm sure everyone noted, one member of the king's family was not present at the welcoming ceremony."

Uncle Argyros raised his brows. "His son and heir, Prince Caelum, was much in evidence. There are no other surviving members of the royal family, as you know."

"Sadly, yes," Lio answered. "The king has already buried two queens and a princess. However—"

"He lost two wives and his daughter?" Kadi shook her head. "For the first time, I feel some sympathy for the man."

Javed's gaze was full of regret. "What befell them? If this subject ever arises, I would not wish to appear ignorant or disrespectful before our hosts."

Uncle Argyros held out a hand toward Lio. "You wrote your initiation treatise on King Lucis's reign."

Lio cleared his throat. "Lucis's first queen suffered a long series of disastrous pregnancies trying to birth a son, and she ultimately gave her life in the attempt. She had one healthy daughter, however: Princess Solia Basilinna, the king's only heir. When Princess Solia was seventeen, rebel free lords captured her and held her for ransom. Although Lucis fulfilled their demands, they did not honor their agreement to spare her life. Widowed and without a successor, Lucis had to remarry in haste. His second union produced the coveted male heir, Prince Caelum Basilarion, but the second queen did not survive her son's birth."

"So much tragedy in one family," said Kadi.

Lio nodded. "The kingdom still mourns Princess Solia especially. She was beloved among Tenebrans of every station. But Lucis has one surviving daughter. A member of the king's family who is not royal. She was not there last night."

"You are speaking of his daughter by his concubine," Uncle Argyros said.

"What do we know of her?" Lio asked.

"I confess to a preoccupation with the royal line." Uncle Argyros spread his hands. "It's possible you know more about her than I do."

A great deal more. Lio knew she had a wealth of freckles and enjoyed the bath. He tried to put those distracting details out of his mind. "The recent chronicles I was able to obtain provide little more than a confirmation of her existence. You know human historians. They write almost exclusively about children born within marriages and focus their accounts on the male line. We probably know more about Lucis's living daughter from rumor than records." Lio looked to Basir and Kumeta. "Have you heard talk of her?"

In Basir's gaze there was no evidence of suspicion or censure. He appeared interested. "We know the king did acknowledge her, which means he provides for her. How well, we can only guess."

"But that does not erase the stigma of her origins in the Tenebrans' eyes," Kumeta pointed out.

"One can imagine the prejudice the poor child faces here." Aunt Lyta shook her head. "Some things have not changed since we were human."

Uncle Argyros looked to the Master Envoys. "I can't say you have ever mentioned her name."

"She hardly seems to be a secret," Lio protested.

If she felt any regret over her status, she certainly didn't show it. Lio had seen how proud she was. How could her countrymen fail to respect her for it?

"I am sorry to say she is often spoken of simply as the king's bastard," Kumeta said.

"Cassia," Lio corrected. "I can tell you that much about her. Her name is Cassia."

"Cassia Basilis, I presume," Uncle Argyros added. "Befitting a female relative of the king outside the line of succession."

"From what I recall," Kumeta said, "the king constantly sends her from one residence to another and allows few to know her location. I would hazard a guess she is never where our reports say she is, and she is seldom in one place for long."

Basir let out the sigh of someone resigned to an old problem. "We are often fed the same 'common knowledge' as the free lords Lucis wishes to deceive."

"Where does common knowledge say she is right now?" Lio asked.

Kumeta paused to consider. "A remote household of the king's in the eastern Tenebrae, I believe."

Lio shook his head. "That's not where she is."

Basir's eyes narrowed. "How can you be certain?"

"I'm afraid I may have underestimated the Tenebrans' boldness. The grounds were not entirely deserted last night—no, don't worry. I had no disastrous encounters."

"Of course not," Uncle Argyros said mildly. "Considering who trained you in concealment."

And that training was serving him well even now as he concealed the truth from his fellow Hesperines. His own family. "In my discreet stroll across the grounds, I overheard a few things." Such as the growling of her hound. And the flutter of her heartbeat. "Namely that the king's daughter is here at Solorum."

Aunt Lyta thumped her hand on the table. "She is here, and yet we saw no sign of her when we arrived. That is an insult."

Uncle Argyros rested a hand upon hers. "Children born out of wedlock are not public figures. Lucis is certain to keep her out of sight."

"That does not change the fact that she must take part in the Summit," Aunt Lyta countered. "She carries the king's blood in her veins."

Lio hated where his logic had taken him. "The free lords would be mindful of this as well, wouldn't they?"

His uncle gave a nod. "Some would be tempted to overlook her origins, for a daughter of the king is still a daughter of the king. She may attract suitors."

"This is most likely why the king sends her away so often," Kumeta said. "To prevent her from becoming too great an advantage to one of his lords."

Lio really was not used to being this thirsty. He felt hot, within and without, and it gave him the urge to deal the table a blow as his aunt had. "That is all she amounts to in their eyes. A means to an end."

"Nearly everyone here is someone's means to an end and uses someone else as their own," Uncle Argyros said. "Tenebran society is mere hierarchy upon hierarchy, with each person at a greater level of power making what use he or she sees fit of those beneath."

"Except for Lucis," Lio said.

"He stands at the peak of this hierarchy, yes."

"He has misstepped," Aunt Lyta insisted. "The treaty has always been sworn between the Queens of Orthros and the King of Tenebra's family. *All* of his family."

"The circumstances of our arrival did not go as the king planned," Uncle Argyros reminded them. "There could have been many reasons why his daughter was not included in the welcoming ceremonies. He may have brought her to Solorum with the intention of introducing her at some point in the negotiations. Let us wait and see if she makes an appearance." He fixed one of his unreadable gazes upon Lio. "You could have told me this last night."

The heat in Lio's veins seemed to have reached his neck, even his cheeks. "As I said, other topics occupied us."

"Other topics besides information of immediate relevance to the Summit?"

Hespera help him, he should have said something to his uncle last night, if only to avoid this conversation before the entire embassy. His veil held steady. That did not make their scrutiny any less uncomfortable.

The best defense was always the truth. "I confess... I feared you would think I was not careful enough last night. To come close enough to mortals to discover such information... I would not wish you to think I showed disregard for the strict rules of conduct to which we must adhere while we are here."

Javed chuckled. "Disregard for the rules? You?"

Kadi laughed outright. "Lio, you probably inscribe a Ritual Circle to the rules in your bedchamber every morning before you Slumber."

Lio shot his cousin a sardonic look and placed a hand upon his chest. "Not in my bedchamber. I carve the Ritual Circle on my heart, Cousin."

Aunt Lyta appeared to be struggling not to grin. "As long as the Tenebrans who were on the grounds did not accost you, we have nothing to worry about. I take it this was no bull-driving mob."

"Not at all. Just a couple of Tenebrans trespassing on the king's grounds." One human Tenebran and one canine Tenebran.

"Poaching is a perennial problem for the nobility," Basir conceded.

Some of the bite went out of Kumeta's aura. "Apparently starvation is more frightening than we are."

"And the punishment they would face from their king," Javed murmured.

Lio corrected none of their assumptions.

"They did not see you," Uncle Argyros said. It was not a question. "It is of no concern. But I hope you will be more forthcoming next time, should you overhear anything else. This information may prove useful to us."

Basir studied Lio. "See that you come to Kumeta and me with anything you learn."

"I certainly will."

Kumeta looked to Aunt Lyta, who nodded.

"We are out of time," Lio's aunt told them.

"Well." Uncle Argyros rose from his chair. "Let us begin."

Lio took a deep breath as they stood and followed his uncle out. They walked through the fortress for the benefit of the guards, who stood at very visible intervals from the hallway outside their guest quarters all the way to the gatehouse. See, said the embassy's dignified walk. See how harmless and well-mannered we are?

Lio watched the portcullis of Solorum Fortress rise to let them out. Was all this show lost on the men who watched? Or were there those among the soldiers who shared Lady Cassia's balanced view of Hesperines, but feared to let on to their countrymen?

It seemed the embassy's so-called honor guard comprised only armed men and not of any workings by the royal mage. Lio had yet to feel a hint of magic at work in the fortress, as Kadi had said. It was from the temple and the palace that the strongest power emanated.

Lio could feel in the age of those spells that this had once been the capital of not just a king, but a Mage King and a queen wise in her own arcane traditions. The ghosts of magic that haunted Solorum stood testament to the royal couple's steadfastness against Cordium. It was easy to understand why it had not been until after their reign that the Order of Anthros had succeeded in forbidding monarchs and lords to wield magic.

But at last the mages had enforced their decree that men must choose to live by the sword or the spell, and any who hungered for the power of both went against the laws of Anthros. If Tenebra's finest king and queen lived now, the Order would strike them down as apostates.

The drawbridge unleashed the Hesperines from their prison into a cool, damp night. Mist crawled along the ground, promising a winter rain to come. Lio breathed deep and let his head clear, here in the Goddess's hours where she ruled. Tomorrow night would require a pavilion set up, he predicted, but for now, the king and his company occupied the dais and the greensward in the open air. A vast council table had been erected at the foot of the throne. Lio could still smell how recently the wood had been part of living trees.

The ward the Solorum temple mages had built around the council table shimmered in the air like a wall of heat, visible but much fainter to the senses than Aunt Lyta and Kadi's working. Five of the men were retreating across the greensward to the temple, their work complete. Through the barrier, Lio could make out the royal mage, who sat in an unassuming position near the back of the dais to the king's right, with his apprentice hovering at his elbow.

As the embassy set foot within, Lio struggled not to shudder. He had never before felt the magic of Anthros, certainly not on his very skin. Its acrid taste made him feel ill.

Lio took a deep breath, hoping for a powerful fragrance to banish the bitter magic. He looked around the entire gathering, even the chairs set out in rows beyond the table for those who were not on the Council.

Lady Cassia was nowhere to be found.

King Lucis sat on the Mage King's chair, towering above all present. Unfortunately for Prince Caelum, his apparent attempt to mimic his father's dignified expression only served to make him look petulant. Lord Titus commanded one end of the Summit table, while Lord Hadrian sat encamped on the opposite end. The men who held the chairs between comprised nearly the entire Council of Free Lords.

Lio was looking at the most powerful men in Tenebra, those who held the chains of fealty and power that bound the fractious kingdom together. Only one of them, Lord Hadrian, was considered loyal to the death to King Lucis. Lio counted off the others. Loyal for personal gain, loyal out of fear, on the verge of rebellion.

Seven empty chairs awaited on the nearest side of the table, facing the king, with a lengthy expanse of empty table on either side to protect the lords from the Hesperine lepers. As the embassy took their places, Amachos watched their every move from his place by the king.

Lio followed his people through the performance of greetings and contemplated what seat Lady Cassia might occupy in this informative display, were she here. An oppressed subject engaging in secret rebellion. A hopeful contender for a crown seeking weapons against her father. A neglected daughter fishing for information that might buy her father's approval. She might be any of these things.

Not for the first time, Lio wondered how anyone but a Hesperine engaged in diplomacy with any confidence. He was sure one more conversation with Cassia Basilis was all he needed. Another chance to truly communicate with her, to sense her, and he would know how dangerous their meeting had been for him and his embassy. Or how promising.

She had called one of their most sacred practices by its proper name, the Mercy, when the kindest terms humans normally used were desecration of the dead, corpse theft, or necrophilia. She knew the Mercy to be none of those things. Where had she learned the truth?

He *must* see her again. There was no other way to discover the source of her interest…and to what degree it inclined her toward his people.

He found it difficult to guess if she would give him the opportunity. Her status and the severity of the transgression made the odds seem slim. But the anticlimax of their discussion made him think she was not done with him yet. Such a question…was that really all? Didn't she want more answers than the one he had given her?

He could only hope she would make another appearance on the grounds for a private Summit.

NEGOTIATIONS

Lio breathed the wind that blew from deeper in the woods. He could smell the doe in the spruce thicket, who was sleeping off his draught from her, and the vestiges of magic on one of the ruins up the path. No chance of catching Lady Cassia's scent if she approached from the palace.

This time it was sound that revealed her first. He heard the distinctive blood flow not of an animal, but a human, one whose pulse beat quickly from exertion. The beat of a liegehound's heart was there too, along with the rustles of two feet and four paws moving around a great deal in the underbrush.

How fortunate that Lio was the one to discover their very obvious presence. Anyone else might end the night with his throat no longer intact. Then again, it might be too much for Lio to assume his throat was safe, either. He could only hope his truce with Lady Cassia still held, and she would once more persuade her hound not to indulge his natural inclination to make a meal out of any Hesperine he saw.

Lio found them in the clearing by the old stone fountain and paused just within the shelter of the trees, stilling his body and breath. Lady Cassia was engaged in a vigorous wrestling match with her hound. The dog had his teeth around some kind of training lure that appeared to consist of the combined remains of a sheep and an untold number of pheasants, tied together with rags purloined from the corpse of some unfortunate knave.

As Lio watched, the hound left off the mundane prey and swiveled to face precisely where he stood.

Lady Cassia did not startle, only grew very still, as if trying to make herself stone. With her hands on her dog, she glanced over her shoulder in Lio's direction.

His heart pounding, Lio held fast to his veil, but met the dog's gaze. A bark erupted from Knight's barrel chest. Lio realized he had no idea what body language to display to a dog to indicate he was not a threat. He should have let Mak and Lyros talk him into defense training after all. Didn't they have specific strategies for dealing with liegehounds?

Lady Cassia put her mouth near the dog's ear and murmured words in that language only he seemed to understand, which Lio had never encountered in any of his studies. Knight returned his attention to her. It appeared only one thing was stronger than the hound's blood-deep enmity with Hesperines: his devotion to his lady.

She leaped to her feet, brandishing the lure again. When Knight lunged, Lio jumped. But it was the lure that was the hound's target. He won the mess from Lady Cassia's grasp and vanquished it, shredding fleece and feathers. At last he sprawled with his now thoroughly dead prey trapped between his paws. He panted, casting saliva and tufts of down from his jaws, and looked to his lady for approval. She knelt down beside him and stroked his fur, praising him with more warmth than Lio had yet heard in her voice.

This time Lio cleared his throat to warn her of his approach. She looked his way again. Her eyes and smile were cool and composed in comparison to the emotion she had just displayed toward Knight.

Lio strode out to join her, dropping his veil. She stood as he approached. Her skirt was covered in grass stains and dog hair. The natural scents of animal and night air that clung to her made her smell like something that lived wild and thrived here. But her body was poised with wariness, as if she were accustomed to being hunted.

Lio slanted a gaze at Knight. The hound did not bare his teeth, but lowered his head to gnaw on the lure as if that served as enough of a warning.

"Now I see the reason for your nighttime expeditions," Lio said. "Only the woods are a large enough playground for Knight, here. I was not the reason you came out at all."

"Do not take it personally."

"Too late. I am already gravely wounded. But comforted by your mere presence." He gave her an overly artful bow. "Which I sorely missed at the negotiations."

"If you expected to see me there, then I fear you must have been disappointed indeed."

"Certainly I was. Who made the dreadful mistake of not inviting you?"

"If you think my name alone qualifies me for an invitation, you do not understand what that name means."

"No, Lady Cassia, I think I begin to."

She reached down and dusted a bit of fleece off her skirts. "You Hesperines know all sorts of things, don't you? It is said you read minds."

"We are perceptive. That doesn't mean we go around harvesting people's thoughts, any more than we steal their blood. But apparently we are not perceptive enough to know a great deal about you. Not even your name or that you were here at Solorum."

If that surprised her, she didn't show it. She did meet Lio's gaze again. He hoped that was a sign his confession put her more at ease. By admitting his people were one step behind where she was concerned, he might be able to reduce her sense of threat.

Her gaze darted about them. "It is said you walk unseen anywhere you please."

"No Hesperines walking about unseen tonight," he assured her. He gestured at himself. "Just your visible champion."

She studied him. Lio had been scrutinized a great deal tonight: by a king, dozens of free lords, the entire Hesperine embassy, and especially Uncle Argyros. Lady Cassia's gaze was the most unsettling and the most pleasant. He felt it from head to toe.

She tilted her head. "Your companions leave you to dine alone?"

"No matter, for I have discovered what fine company there is to be had on the grounds. Although I wasn't sure I would see you here again."

"Nor was I."

"I see."

"Now that we meet again, however, I am reminded of a few more questions I wanted to ask you."

He narrowed his eyes at her, smiling. "I thought you could hardly be satisfied with my answer."

"Were you with my question?"

"Of course not." He smiled still more, careful to keep his lips closed, then not to open them too wide when he spoke. "But I was unsure whether you trusted me enough to ask for more."

"Trust is not something I consider relevant to me. However, I don't believe you'll cause me harm. It is in both our interests that no one knows we ever spoke."

Now he studied her. Her brows were level, her chin set beneath thin lips. Her petite nose had a natural upturn to it. "I do believe you are becoming more and more honest with me, Lady Cassia."

"First trust, now honesty. Do Hesperines ascribe great importance to such things?"

"Do you not?"

"I think words need not be honest to be mutually beneficial, informative, or productive."

"I see you are indeed accustomed to battling monsters. Please remember, Lady—there are none here tonight."

She cast a glance in the direction of the palace, but said no more.

"You are right," he pressed on. "I would never let it reach your father's ears that you were here. And I trust you wouldn't expose a young Hesperine who first approached you thinking only that a woman alone after dark in such a place as this might need protection."

Her mouth quirked, suggesting she had a ready answer, but she did not give it.

Lio smoothed the silence. "After all, I am right where I am expected to be. We *have* been given leave to drink from the king's game while we're here."

Now came her remark, and it was all her smile had promised. "To protect the populace from your rampant bloodlust, naturally."

"You do not appear concerned about my bloodlust in the least, Lady Cassia. You wound me again. I thought I had such great powers of intimidation."

"I am sure the deer feel quite intimidated."

"Ah, I have no hope of recovering my image now…truth be told, they seem to have deemed me quite harmless. They've been very friendly."

She gave him a thoughtful glance. "You drink from their throats? Here?" She put a hand to her neck, right over her jugular.

Lio stared at her hand. An audacious hand, one that dared him and demanded a response. Just when he began to gain his footing with her, she challenged him again. It drove him to challenge her. "Does that disturb you?"

"No." She let her hand drop, but the sight of her bare, freckled throat was no less beckoning.

He made himself look at her face, but he was still too aware of the little shadow under her chin, the moonlight on her neck. Most of all, that brush of her fingers against her throat that demonstrated her curiosity so fearlessly.

What had given rise to her lack of prejudice? It might prove unwise to test the limits of her tolerance, but he could not let the question go.

Perhaps it was the deer blood that drove him to take risks. He must not let that cloud his judgment. But it would prove wise, he reasoned, to get to the heart of her curiosity about his kind. She might need help. Or she might prove helpful to his people. He would never know, unless he continued his effort to draw her out.

"It puts the animal most at ease when you drink from it where it can see you," he explained. "Some are calmer than others and don't object to a draught from the large vein here." He mimicked her, placing his hand on his own throat. "Other times we drink from the limbs. An important vein runs here…" He gestured down his arm. "…and carries blood from the heart."

"You've studied healing?"

"I am no healer as such. But all of us are required to study anatomy. How else would we know how to minimize the discomfort for those from whom we drink, while also gleaning sufficient nourishment?"

"You do not kill them."

"Absolutely not. It is a human notion that we drink creatures to their deaths. We are not predators."

"You do not even hunt them."

"Fear and suffering are abhorrent to us. Everything we do to those from whom we drink, we experience with them in Blood Union. Why would we want to make them suffer? Even if we did, our own power would exact justice on us for it."

"Some people take pleasure in others' suffering. But it is clear your kind do not."

Lio would have treasured such a declaration from any human. But he appreciated how much more it meant from she who had survived a lifetime as Lucis's daughter. She knew the meaning of the words she spoke. "I rejoice that you realize this, Lady Cassia."

"You do not drink from the fallen," she said. "I gather it is the blood of the living you prefer."

"Only living blood has any power to nourish us. Despite the myths about us raiding freshly dug graves, the fact is, we gain no sustenance from a person's remains. I cannot imagine tasting death in that way." Lio shuddered. Seeing and smelling death was enough.

"The rites the Order of Hypnos performs upon the dead to discourage you from disturbing them are a great deal of wasted effort."

"We are not the reason those spells are necessary. It is lawless necromancers who desecrate mortal remains to fashion the bloodless, the undead in whose veins nothing more flows."

A slight furrow appeared on her brow. "You do not relish death, and yet it would be so easy for you to cause it. It must be difficult for you. When you are drinking blood, is it hard to stop?"

It should not have been difficult for Lio to stay focused during their conversation, as extraordinary as it was. But his thoughts veered, taking her words entirely, inappropriately out of context. His instincts awoke to the more pleasant implications of her question.

There were situations when it was hard to stop, of course. But that had nothing to do with death and all to do with pleasure.

"That's not how it is at all," he said firmly. "It is physically impossible for a Hesperine to bleed someone to death. As we drink, our bodies' natural regenerative properties enter the mortal's bloodstream, assisting his or her body in replenishing itself. The healing process always keeps pace with the blood loss."

"Humans really are ignorant," Cassia said. "And yet you prefer our blood, such as we are. Or is that a myth as well?"

Heat spread through his veins. Thirst. Already. This should not be happening. "We never subject any human to the Drink who is not willing. It is against our most sacred laws."

"So it is the blood of willing humans that you prefer?"

What was wrong with him? The deer had already provided for him tonight. Although they might not be ideal, they should be adequate. But he was actually salivating.

He swallowed. "I will not deny humans who are generous enough to provide for us offer optimal sustenance. Animals are quite sufficient, however."

More composed than he, she listened to him describe the Drink.

"It truly does not disturb you," he said in wonder.

"No."

"Lady Cassia, how did you come to have such an unusual perspective?"

"Ah, you know answers to such questions come at the cost of an equal trade."

"I have answered all your questions."

"They were questions you wanted to answer."

He looked at her askance, resisting the urge to reach up and loosen the collar of his robe. "You are not wrong. It is a relief to discover any Tenebran who knows my people are not throat-ripping, child-stealing monsters."

"Bulls on the temple steps do not survive their encounters with the sickle, unlike the deer that meet with your teeth. I do not see that drinking the blood of a live deer is any more barbaric than hounding a boar into the ground, slaying it, and parading its roasted corpse to the banquet table."

He winced. "Prescient observations."

She shrugged. He sensed that shrug all the way to her blood. "Something must die for mortals to live. Even the animals. The deer will consume an entire crop and starve the farmer if given the chance. It is the way of things."

"Is that what your life here has taught you to believe?"

"I am hardly discussing matters of faith. Merely facts of existence."

"It need not be so."

She appeared unconcerned, but he caught the note of bitterness in her veins. "Is it so much easier for you?"

"No, it isn't easy at all." Lio sat on the edge of the fountain's basin.

Her gaze followed his every move. She knew so much, and yet still had unanswered questions. Still watched for the dangers of what was unknown to her.

"Our way of life is an ideal we strive to achieve every night," he said. "We do not always reach it, but I believe that in the striving, we still achieve much. Suffering only comes when there is a failure...a falling short. But it can always be changed. Even forces that seem the most fundamental can be overcome."

"Such philosophy! I feel you are about to initiate me into some kind of Hesperine secret."

"No secret. Just principles I hold close to my heart."

"Forgive me. I do not mean to make light of something so important to you. Please understand, philosophy has never done me any good."

"Certainly not when it is used against you."

"I feel you have another philosophical declaration waiting on the heels of that remark."

He was hardly fit to debate philosophy at the moment. His teeth ached in his gums, and the rush of his own pulse in his ears made his head pound. But he could not miss this opportunity. "Take philosophy in hand. Turn it to your advantage."

"Women are not philosophers."

He snorted. "You're having this conversation with me."

"A woman, armed with philosophy? If I entered a war tournament carrying the finest steel blade, the men would take one look at my weapon, call it a wooden practice sword, and laugh me off the field."

Lio almost didn't catch himself before he grinned. "With that insightful commentary, you have just proved that women can indeed be philosophers."

"Very well, then. I give you leave to imagine I am a philosopher and to answer me as such. Tell me more of your ideals. What is life like in Orthros?"

Such a vast request. Such a welcome invitation. He must endeavor not to accept too gladly.

"There are many questions within that single one, Lady Cassia. Do you have so much to bargain in return?"

"As I said, what is willingly given requires no compensation."

Lio shook his head. "I fear I must insist. I will answer your question…
if you will come here tomorrow night and ask it of me again."

Frustration heated her blood, held in check by caution. The Light
Moon cast her face in a spectrum of silvers, while the crescent of the Blood
Moon brought out the red on her cheeks. From exertion? From the pace of
their debate? The blood that flushed her face taunted him with the knowledge he had nothing more than deer to look forward to for weeks on end.

The realization struck Lio, heating him with thirst and denial. He had
actually just thought of Lady Cassia in that way.

He *must* not stay long enough to answer her question tonight. He
took a step back.

His unconscious gesture appeared to affect her like a signal that he
was leaving, or that he was giving ground. He heard the debate in her
blood and found himself guilty of listening too closely. She wrestled with
herself as if his step backward might make him disappear before she had a
chance to make her next move. He felt her dilemma as if it were his own,
the abrasion of struggle with oneself, of wariness of a mistake. Or perhaps
it was his own.

"You have time to think on it," he said. "Give me your answer tomorrow eve at the prince's festival. I am sure if I received an invitation to that,
then so did you."

"The embassy was invited to Caelum's temple day celebration?"

Lio nodded. "There are to be no negotiations. The feast and music
are both after nightfall. The king is apparently willing to risk us as dinner guests."

He might have smiled to remind her it was a jest, but he did not feel
at all like smiling, and least of all like giving her a glimpse of how far out
of his swollen gums his fangs had now unsheathed. Why could he not
utter the word feast without thinking of it in an entirely different context?

"Can you tolerate mortal fare?" she asked.

Lio cleared his throat, putting a hand to his mouth. When he was certain he would not indulge whatever curiosity she might entertain about
the length of Hesperine fangs, he answered her with facts. "We can eat
and drink most human food and beverages, provided nothing suffered and

died to produce them. Our bodies simply absorb them without gaining nourishment."

"Can you taste them?"

Lio's mouth watered. "Yes. Hesperines enjoy culinary experiences." He cleared his throat again. "At the celebration, you can verify my claims by observation."

"Agreed," she said. "I will give you my answer tomorrow eve."

Lio bowed, and this time it was he who walked away first. Just at the edge of the clearing, he concealed himself from her sight. The last thing he listened to was her gasp of surprise at his disappearance. He went to find another deer.

40

days until

SPRING EQUINOX

WAR GAMES

CASSIA SPENT THE AFTERNOON'S bloodletting tucked away in the temple gardens.

It proved more boon than curse that the palace cook had disdained her help. Cassia began the prince's thirteenth temple day among the mages of Kyria, instead of at the palace with the women of the royal household who must break their backs to ensure plenty of alcohol, food, wreaths, garlands, and candles were prepared and in their places. She avoided the madness of beating out and rehanging ancestral tapestries and laying down new rushes. Along with other women fortunate enough to be unattached to husbands or lovers, she was not called upon to endure the randiness of males excited over the war games. While the warriors beat away at each other on the tournament field and their women cheered at each tooth spat in the dirt, Cassia turned over new garden rows.

But that was all the devotion she could afford today. When the sun's descending arms barely reached over the temple walls, Cassia cleaned her spade in haste and trudged back to the palace. For once she envied the mages their rites, songs sung amid a haze of dusk light with dust dancing attendance about them, to be followed by the easy companionship of their evening meal. Caelum would feel little enthusiasm for the presence of his bastard sister at his temple day feast, if he paid attention to her presence at all. He would be too busy bragging about the challenges the knights had let him win. Unfortunately, the king expected everyone from his champions to the dung sweeper's mewling infant to appear for a show of loyalty to his heir.

The nearer Cassia got to Solorum, however, the easier it became to make herself walk back. The festivities would not be entirely useless to her tonight. There was one person who anticipated her arrival and, it would seem, desired it. If she could bargain her attendance at the festival to Deukalion for more information, it would not prove a wasted evening.

Cassia had pushed her luck staying at the temple so late. The moment she returned to her rooms, Perita descended upon her, divesting her of her tools and gardening dress with record efficiency. The girl had reinforcements, as well: the seamstress, standing by with the new festival attire the king had allotted Cassia. The old woman smiled, baring her crooked teeth, and gave Cassia a glare that burned with spite.

It appeared the seamstress did not anticipate a bright future for her son, once his lord finally made it back from eastern Tenebra, having discovered his information on the whereabouts of the king's daughter had been worthless. Knowing Lord Ferus, the young man's prospects were certainly ruined. It seemed the old woman would not forgive the king's bastard for dooming her own. The hatred in her eyes said she blamed Cassia for being the reason, even though she had no idea Cassia had been the cause.

Oh dear. Having the person who made your clothes for an enemy was an undesirable situation.

As the seamstress closed in, Cassia balanced potential pinpricks and faulty seams against meeting a Hesperine at the festival and felt satisfied with her ledger. But she resolved to be on the lookout for the old woman's revenge.

With a snap, the seamstress shook out a fine linen tunica. "Allow me, my lady."

"How kind of you to offer, but I'm sure the king's own seamstress has many more important tasks to occupy her."

"Not at all. I can't call any creation complete until I see it on the one I made it for. I need to know if any adjustments are necessary."

"I'll do the alterations," Perita insisted.

But the seamstress was already swaddling Cassia in the tunica. Next came a bronze gown that evoked the royal gold without really aspiring to it. As soon as the seamstress had Cassia trussed up, the old woman held her in place by the hair and stabbed a beaded headdress on her with a handful of pins.

Cassia blinked her watering eyes. She was still waiting for her scalp to stop stinging when she saw what else the seamstress had in store for her.

"No," Cassia said. "I do not wear scent oils."

"The right fragrance is part of the gown, as surely as the fabric and trim. You cannot go to a festival without scent." With wizened fingers, the seamstress opened the bottle she held.

The pop of the cork echoed through the bare chambers.

Heat flared under Cassia's clothes. "I. Do not. Wear scent oils."

The old woman took a step closer, brandishing the vial under Cassia's nose.

As Cassia reached a hand toward Knight, he was already advancing. His growl started low in his throat and erupted out of his bared teeth, drowning out the sound of that cork as if it had never been.

The seamstress jumped back, dribbling oil down her hands and the front of her clothes. Her smile turned into a grimace, but she could not match Knight's. As she sealed the bottle, her fingers fumbled. She drew herself up, but her face had gone paler than her bone needles. "When the court ridicules you for presenting yourself so poorly, it will not be my fault."

She left, taking the putrid fragrance of distilled flowers with her. The moment the door shut, Cassia peeled out of her gown.

"Lady!" Perita squawked. "What are you—!"

Cassia finally got down to the tunica and yanked it off. She threw it to the floor on her way to her bedchamber. "Don't touch that."

Knight growled at the heap of linen, then posted himself at Cassia's bedchamber door. She dumped a waiting pitcher of water into the washbasin, then grabbed up her tallow soap and rag and began to scour herself from head to toe.

"There's no time for washing, Lady!" Perita looked ready to charge into the bedchamber, if not for the large obstacle that sat on his haunches in her way. She kept her distance from Knight and settled for glaring through the doorway.

"Get me a clean tunica to wear under the gown," said Cassia.

Perita tossed up her hands and disappeared into the hearth room.

The soap and water began to ease the burning on Cassia's skin. It had taken her an extra moment to realize it was not just the heat of anger, but the first signs of a reaction to the seamstress's handiwork. If Cassia didn't know her plants, she might have dismissed the subtle irritation as the result of anxiety and sweat. But any gardener knew that within the course of an hour, that discomfort would turn into unbearable itching, then the misery of sores.

The old hag had rubbed stinglily all over the inside of the tunica. The resulting hives would have forced Cassia to depart early from the prince's temple day celebration. To excuse herself from the king's presence before the permitted time.

Her heart pounding, Cassia started over and washed herself again.

She dressed herself this time. She didn't care if the hem of her homespun wool tunica looked wrong under the embroidered festival gown, nor that it was too late to do anything with her hair beyond brushing it out around the obstacle of the headdress. With a frantic light in her eyes, Perita looked Cassia over as if trying to decide which bleeding wound to bind first. Before the girl could attempt anything more, Cassia called Knight to her side and marched out of her chambers.

She would not slam the door. She would not run. She let the door close of its own accord and set out for the Temple of Anthros at a brisk but composed walk.

She took her place in the gallery just as the sun disk settled at her back and the royal mage began his incantations. Not late. She let out a breath of relief and did not look at the king. She wasn't late. He could not be displeased.

Instead Cassia watched the triumphant warriors below, who stood in Anthros's house as they did on the field, masters of the war god's domain in the world. At least none of them would trouble her bed tonight, reliving his triumph by the sword.

THE KING'S FEAST

THE MOMENT THE HESPERINES set foot inside the front gate of Solorum Palace, they encountered the first limb of the Tenebrans' sprawling feast. The gate did not shut behind the embassy, for it stood open to receive the crown prince's guests and subjects. But Lio felt the magic that closed around them from wall to wall and foundation to tower. That and the silence.

Voices and clinking tableware hushed. Uncle Argyros and Aunt Lyta did not pause, only followed the king's chamberlain through the courtyard wearing tight-lipped, benevolent smiles. Lio did the same and kept his gaze on his own people. He feared if he so much as glanced at the mortals who sat at table all around him, they might advance from terrorized silence to screaming. They seemed to find no reassurance in the embassy's escort, a small army of their king's guards bearing halberds that appeared useful for performing decapitations. None of the diners moved, although the way their skin hung from their bones suggested they sat before their best meal of the year.

Lio didn't bother breathing as he made his way between the trestle tables, which stood in trampled mud. On the evidence of sight alone, he concluded the warhorses had paraded through here during the day on their way to the tournament. The scent of dung had to be as unpleasant to the humans as the carcasses on their plates were to him. But he regarded a harmless natural odor such as the manure of living horses infinitely preferable to the stink of the dead flesh that comprised the mortals' meal.

The fact remained, however, that excrement did not agree with silk shoes, and Lio's had been a gift. A slight bending of the rules now would spare him extensive cleaning spells later. He walked without letting his feet touch the ground. The long hem of his robes would hide the slight levitation from the easily alarmed mortals. He was so much taller than his fellow Hesperines, they wouldn't notice either. Especially if they were doing the same thing.

Even after Lio and the rest of the embassy went inside, the celebratory chatter did not resume behind them. Lio did hear ale sloshing in tankards and the breaking of bread, then a great many teeth tearing into flesh. Pity overcame his disgust. The lowest of the king's subjects would not let even the creatures they most feared deter them. They would pick the bones of the prince's temple day and get every scrap they could out of it.

The silence followed the Hesperines, stilling the raucous laughter of craftsmen and merchants and their families who feasted in the corridors of the palace. Only when the embassy reached the doors of the king's great hall did Lio's sensitive ears tell him conversation had resumed all the way out in the courtyard.

The royal herald announced them, then the chamberlain led them into the king's presence as the soldiers who had flanked them fell away and took their posts around the hall. Here conversation gave way not to silence, but more formal greetings, the grease that kept the wheels of the Summit from grinding to a halt. Tenebran courtiers were pretentious but not particularly subtle. Lio listened for the implications in their words, whether thinly disguised insults or allusions to what had been said at the negotiations the night before, while he took a breath.

She smelled like life. She had spent several hours close to living soil and growing things, then taken a bath. The mere scent of clean skin had never had this effect on Lio before. Did Cassia enjoy a soak in a tub by the hearth? Or did she lather herself on her feet at a washbasin? Lio clamped his mouth shut over teeth that would be the bane of him from now until he escaped the festival.

She was seated at a table at the very back of the room, as close to being relegated to the corridor as possible while still sitting in the great hall. If he were to turn his head a little to the right, he would find her sitting in a corner the fire pit's light didn't quite reach. He would be able to see her just fine. But he dared not look at her.

There and then, facing hours in which he must not show a mouthful of unsheathed canines to the king's dignitaries, Lio was forced to admit to himself the effect Lady Cassia had on him.

Goddess have Mercy.

It had been so all along. On the greensward his first night in Tenebra, he had philosophized she was an epitome of human nature. In the fortress on his second night, he had reasoned she was a political dilemma. Anything to deny she interested him for more natural reasons.

Why couldn't he have developed a taste for someone at home? He had all of Orthros in which to find anyone besides Xandra to thirst after. Yet the Drink had become a diplomatic arrangement to him, respectful but dispassionate. He had seen to the Thirst so he remained in able condition to perform his duties. He'd had no heart for anything more. Until he had traveled all the way to Tenebra and gotten foolish with hunger over the most forbidden woman there was.

He would not pretend it was merely thirst. No. This was the Hunger. If he had met Cassia in Orthros as a youngblood out for a night on the docks, he would not merely take a cordial drink and leave it at that. He could see himself inviting her…tempting her…to the Feast.

Goddess have Mercy.

This was not Orthros. This was Tenebra, and she was the sunbound king's daughter.

Lio had a nose. And eyes. He would not expect himself or anyone else to be immune to her. But letting his appreciation grow into a distraction was entirely uncalled for.

It was for the best that the table allotted to foreign guests was on the opposite side of the room from her, facing the royal table on the dais and the king's steely gaze. The chamberlain seated the embassy in order of precedence, then beat a hasty retreat. No mortals joined them. These would be a quiet few hours.

A small army of the king's servants filed in and out before the embassy's table, each offering each course of the meal. The mortals' hands were steady, their eyes hollow. Lio's aunt and uncle refused each graciously, as was expected.

Bits of dead creatures floated in the soup. Rigid slabs of bread served as plates. Couldn't the humans smell that the dry chunks were only one night away from molding? Soon the bread softened under gravies that ran with animal fat.

The ubiquitous wine was the only nonviolent fare. When his elders accepted some from the servers to show respect for their host, Lio followed suit. He must give Cassia the demonstration he had promised her.

An hour of the grotesque had passed when a great cheer went up throughout the hall. Heads turned toward the doors that led from the kitchens. Men marched in carrying a platter on their shoulders, bearing the corpse of a boar. The unfortunate creature Lady Cassia had mentioned the night before. Excited conversation filled the hall, retelling the events of the royal hunt that had felled the beast, which had been left in the fortnight since to become, they enthused, gamey. Lio had long since given up on breathing, but the taste of burnt corpse invaded his mouth and nose anyway. He swallowed.

He exchanged speaking glances with Kadi and Javed. But none of them spoke aloud. Griping to one another about what passed for food and concealing the conversation from the watching humans probably qualified as a superfluous use of power. Lio wasn't sure it would have been wise to open his mouth in any case.

At last he had mercy on himself and tried taking a breath. Just as Lady Cassia's scent had once made him fail to realize a deadly liegehound drew near, now she drowned out the odor of the royal hunt's victim.

Lio shifted in his chair. She ate this mess like the others, but he didn't get a whiff of her dinner on her breath. Why could he smell only the layers of her fragrance that always captivated his attention? He would do well not to build up any illusions about her. Appreciation was permissible, distraction inexcusable. Infatuation would be madness.

He began sorting through the smells of the other humans around him. Scent oils were indeed beloved here; soap was not beloved by anyone at all, with one notable exception. The warm, vibrant scent of living blood told Lio some busted lips and broken skin from that day's tournament still bled. The tang of healing herbs and magic said they had received attention from mages. They had received the greatest attention from their wives, however. In the absence of veils or cleaning spells, it was obvious when two individuals left their unique scents on each other and how much they enjoyed doing so. Lio noticed more than one warrior had celebrated privately with a comrade-in-arms who had fought beside him on the field, and more than one wife preferred the intimate company of her handmaiden to that of her husband.

Clearly, the humans seldom denied themselves the natural pleasures that were forbidden here. Lio concluded that people in Tenebra loved very much as people did in Orthros, despite the mortals' adamant claims to the contrary.

Not everyone here cared only for titles. Heady currents of genuine enjoyment ran between guests who were happy to see one another or who had watched those they loved win honor this day.

It was not his place to wonder if there was someone here tonight whom Lady Cassia loved. But as he traced the bonds of attraction and affection, lust and love in the room, none led him back to her. He had yet to sense any evidence she had a lover. She would regard such a relationship as unwise. But what one chose to do about one's desires and what desires one felt were two entirely different matters.

She was not the focus of many guests' attention. In a few ladies, he sensed pity. A few lords looked at her like bandits sizing up a merchant caravan. Was there no one here who was good to her, worthy of her?

Lio sought the current of her longings, the veins of her regard for others. What greeted his senses was the pulse of her universal wariness toward every person around her. Did her cautious life leave no room for desire? Were pride and anger all that thrived beneath her composed surface?

The Union that had drawn him to her all along now lured him closer. Sights, sounds, smells around him shifted. A flash of awareness transformed what he saw before his eyes. He beheld the room from a different angle, disorienting, yet crystal clear.

A lone, trusted source of comfort lay at her feet. An army of threats surrounded her. Amid their ranks lay a mystery, dark and beautiful, which filled her with equal parts distress and...hope.

She watched someone with black hair and a pale profile outlined against the candlelight. For reasons she could not fathom, her gaze followed a graceful neck partly hidden in a high collar, the silhouette of broad shoulders, and the length of an arm clad in black silk to linger on a long hand that cradled a goblet of wine.

The realization he was looking at himself shocked Lio back into his own mind.

Hespera's Grace. This went beyond anything he had ever experienced. The Blood Union, even enhanced with his thelemancy, had never actually allowed him to gaze through another's eyes.

He ought to feel a sense of shame for trespassing so thoroughly on Cassia. To his dismay, he did not. What he felt was gratitude.

That fleeting connection had not felt like a transgression. It had not even been intentional. Like an act of nature or the divine, that honest, miraculous moment had taken hold of him and entrusted her thoughts to him.

By the Goddess, he would be a worthy steward.

His blood raced as if after a long drink. And yet his thirst was worse than ever. Discomfort was a small price to pay for what he had learned. The loveliest woman in the room deemed him worthy of, at least, her notice.

What she felt toward him beyond that, he could not guess. The Union allowed him to feel what another felt. If that person did not allow herself to feel, she made the two of them equally numb. Lio somehow suspected he had a better idea of why she kept looking at him than she herself did.

The grim odors of the banquet hall descended upon him again, and he resigned himself to them. The redolence of the liegehounds who eyed him from under the tables. Their masters' weighty suspicion and sour ambition. Above all, the two smells that ruled here, such a shock to him on his arrival: cruelty and fear.

But a whiff of innocent contentment drew his attention to his right. On the edge of his vision, he spotted a small child. He had little experience judging young humans' ages, but the tiny girl's teeth appeared to be recent arrivals. She wore a dimpled smile of anticipation. As her nursemaid plucked a choice bite from the plate before them, the little girl bounced on the woman's lap. A hint of spices, human saliva, and dessicated flesh told Lio what the nurse lifted to the child's lips. A bit of meat the woman had chewed soft for baby teeth. As he watched the girl mouth the morsel, he could not smell death. Only the scent of a baby's scalp and the primal sense of safety that came from a full stomach. He caught himself before he turned his head too far to watch. He didn't want to ruin their dinner by frightening them with his notice.

Lio let the swell of his Gift within him rise higher and expand his awareness. The humans were much more worthy of attention than their repast, and he passed the rest of the dinner in study.

And what a long opportunity for study it provided. Humans and Hesperines alike enjoyed lingering over their feasts. But mortals did so in a public glorification of death rather than a private ritual of pleasure. At last the Tenebrans finished a syrupy after-course that did not appear to have anything dead in it, and little remained on the tables but the endlessly flowing alcohol.

The dinner guests began to come forward in order of rank and present their gifts to the prince. One mighty warrior and fine lady after another knelt before the dais, dragging behind them servants bearing rich gifts. Then they returned to their seats, making way for those farther down the tables.

At last, from the corner of his eye, Lio saw a short, slim figure approach. One of the last in line, she walked down the right-hand aisle and passed within arm's reach. Her scent washed over him.

Sweat. Pain. Bile in the back of her throat.

Her whole being was stricken with fear.

For once Lio could look at her, for everyone in the room followed her with their gazes, as they had each gift giver before. He had never seen Cassia in torchlight. The woman before him seemed an entirely different one from she who had spoken to him so boldly under the Goddess's moons.

Her limbs were rigid with self-discipline, her back straight. She wore a shapeless dress the color of bronze weaponry. A tight beaded headdress tamed her autumnal hair. The part left uncovered, he saw now, was ashen brown and broken on the ends, devoid of any healthy gloss. Her olive complexion had lost all vibrancy, and her freckles looked stark upon her clammy skin. Her hound plodded in her wake like a cowed shadow.

Cassia halted in the firelight before her father and dropped to her knees, lowering her forehead nearly to the floor. She held out a length of tapestry. All Lio could see in his mind's eye was a desperate farmer making the same gesture with a sickle on the temple steps, and emotion cracked like a whip inside him.

He had seen her trespass in a forest by night and wrestle with a beast. He had heard her ask him questions about his ways that challenged everything she had been taught to believe. He could smell her dignity even now. She did not belong on the ground, prostrating herself before that man.

"What have you come to offer Us, Cassia?"

"My love and devotion to Your Majesty."

"And what to your brother?"

"My prayers on Your Highness's temple day for another healthy and victorious year. I beg that you accept this humble work of my hands as a sign of my sisterly love."

The prince glanced over Cassia and her gift, then the crowd again. He fidgeted in his chair.

It was the king who answered. "We accept this gift to Our son and heir. You may rise."

Leaving her work at the king's feet, she stood and backed away. Not until she was in the aisle again did she turn to face her seat. As she slid past Lio, it was all he could do to stay his hand from reaching out to her.

Look at me, Cassia. Just one glance. I'll bargain that glance from you for one of mine, and I will look upon you as no one here ever has.

But she ignored him and returned to her shadowed corner.

WALLFLOWER

CASSIA HAD BEEN WISE to dine sparingly, for what little she had eaten out of obligation felt like a stone halfway between her throat and stomach. She could manage her body's reaction during a brief encounter with the king, followed by a retreat to her rooms. Here in front of all these onlookers, with hours to go before she could privately master herself, it was another matter.

As the guests quit their seats and the servants dragged the tables to the side of the great hall, Cassia wondered if there was any possible way for her to leave before the dancing began. But it was useless to imagine a way out. She must stay.

If the king ever decided to invent some treason she had committed, she would be the executioner's bride. She must not give him any transgression that he could elaborate into an act of disloyalty, even an insult to her half brother on his temple day.

She would settle for finding a quiet corner where she could stand with Knight until it was time to leave. Tenebran superstitions had their uses. The festivities must end before midnight to allow everyone time to get home before the forsaken hour. If Cassia could just stay on her feet despite her traitorous stomach, she would manage that long.

She could only hope none of the ladies would be in the mood to show the bastard a bit of generosity and engage her in conversation. Or worse, that Lord Adrogan's and Lord Ferus's absences might give some of her other would-be suitors ideas. Such men were most troublesome when the king was not in sight, but the gaze watching from the dais might not prove deterrent enough for the more foolish lords.

Or for a lackey looking out for Lord Ferus's interests. When Cassia spotted Lord Beccus, she concealed herself behind a knot of other guests and hastened to find a wall with which to spend the evening.

She positioned herself between two tapestries and leaned back against the wall for support. Knight braced himself against her, and she focused on his strong body holding her up. She managed to still the tremors in her limbs, although they continued in her belly. What a distraction her body was every time she was near the king. What a wasted opportunity her weakness made of this night, which she might have spent in keen observation of the court…and the embassy.

From whispers in near-deserted hallways and rumors that flew from one mouth to another in temple, Cassia had gleaned only enough to match the Hesperine emissaries' names with their faces. She had counted on this chance to better inform herself. She had been a fool to look forward to it and to think seeing the Hesperines again would make it worth her while to endure this.

The minstrels began to play, and lords and ladies formed up in the now-empty center of the hall to begin the dancing. The Hesperines stood out of the way. The watching crowd gathered in knots around anyone who had liegehounds. Except Cassia and the king.

She observed the hall from under her lashes, doing her best not to look at the head of the room. She didn't want to know if the king was watching her. She looked instead at the guests, sure to let her gaze dart across the whole crowd and not rest too long on anyone.

Where was Deukalion? His black silk hair and shoulders had been ahead of her the entire banquet. Nowhere to be seen now. Strange, as his considerable height should make him easy to spot. He was taller than anyone else in the room.

She did see Lord Beccus again, who roamed the edge of the room as if she were not his target. She watched out for him from the corner of her eye while studying the embassy.

All Hesperines had been human once. Was it their magic, then, which made them taller than mortals? Which made their hair grow so long? Were there spells in the various braids they wore or in the trails of embroidery on their robes? Surely only magic could produce that strange, impossibly soft fabric they called silk, whose origin was a mystery to everyone but them.

The Hesperine called Arkadia captured Cassia's attention. The lady had the posture of a battle-hardened warrior, a contrast to her soft curves. She was both dangerous and lovely. Everything a Hesperine should be. With a figure only the truly wealthy could afford, she was the full-bodied, womanly sort many men would slaughter to possess, but she was tall enough to look most males in the eye, including the Hesperine beside her.

With his athletic build, he looked as if he could slaughter for her, but his expression was too gentle for violence and held no possessive glint. Cassia identified him as Master Healer Javed. For someone whose skin never saw the sun, he was remarkably brown. As he spoke with Lady Arkadia, his lips danced in patterns utterly new to Cassia's eyes, and she longed to understand the language he spoke.

Lady Arkadia and Master Javed were clearly devoted to one another, although they never touched. He angled his body toward her. She moved when he did. Most conspicuous of all, they appeared to be wearing braids of one another's hair. A dark, curly braid was attached at her blond temple, and a golden lock was bound amid his mane of curls.

Lord Beccus drew nearer and nearer to Cassia, weaving his way through guests and greetings with the appearance of aimlessness. She debated abandoning her refuge for a different stretch of wall. But if he proved determined, they might keep this up all night. Her trembling legs and quivering belly wouldn't tolerate a chase around the room, no matter how circumspect. Cassia made a point not to meet his gaze, hoping her inattention would discourage him.

She made a covert study of the embassy's Master Envoys, Kumeta and Basir. She had never seen anyone with skin so dark. Was it the result of nocturnal sorcery or an unfortunate encounter with a war mage's fire spell? So the temple mages would say. The same mages argued that the Cordian complexion was a mark of Anthros's favor, the result of living in proximity to Corona, the Divine City. They also called Cassia's Cordian mother forsaken for being a concubine. Cassia refused to heed their illogical judgments upon her or Kumeta and Basir.

The longer she saw the Master Envoys, the more she noticed the beautiful variation between them, the different richnesses in tone that defined their faces. They were two shades of the night they shared. Their gazes, grave and unreadable, eased only when they looked at each other. They also wore one another's braids. Cassia could not say they looked older than Master Javed and Lady Arkadia, but she beheld in Master Basir and Master Kumeta an unmistakable weariness.

If Cassia kept looking at the Hesperines, perhaps she would grow accustomed to the sight of them. Perhaps their beauty and perilousness and kindness would cease to prod at the ache inside her.

Lord Beccus made his way unerringly to Cassia. She would have to endure the encounter.

He put a hand to his broad jaw and looked her up and down. "Well, well. Look who is not where she ought to be."

Cassia cast her gaze downward in a modest pose. "I beg your pardon, my lord?"

"As we speak, our mutual friend Ferus is exhausting his horse so he may join you for a dance in the east. You're at the wrong festival, girl."

"I am precisely where my father wishes for me to be."

"Oh, I don't doubt it." He made to take a step closer, then took one look at Knight and remained where he was. "That beast looks like a frightful dance partner. Say you jilt him and take a turn with me instead."

She kept a hand on Knight's shoulder. "You have not asked my father for permission to dance with me."

He smiled broadly, leaning toward her. "Come now. You won't ever get away from the wall thinking like that, mouse. Just a little dance. Ferus wouldn't want me to leave you lonely while he's away."

Indeed, he would want his friend to occupy her on his behalf, to advance his case and discourage other suitors. My, what a compelling advocate Lord Beccus made. "I must decline, my lord."

He hooked his thumbs in his belt, dangling hands callused from sword work at a girth swollen from too much ale. "A little less caution, and you can escape your father and have yourself a husband."

"The king's authority is absolute."

"I see how it is. Nothing like a challenge to keep Ferus wrapped around your little finger. You certainly know how to tempt a man." Lord Beccus chuckled low in his throat. "Well. You stay in your tower, my lady. You can count on Ferus knocking it down as soon as he returns."

At last he sauntered off and let her be. Knight growled at Lord Beccus's retreating buttocks, and it was a wonder the man walked away with both of them.

The ordeal was over. That should make it easier for Cassia to control her stomach. She distracted herself by returning her attention to the crowd.

The leaders of the embassy made her curious indeed. They were not of remarkable height, but undeniably of great stature. They appeared mature and in their prime all at once. Lady Hippolyta's dark auburn hair fell all the way to her ankles, adorned only by one braid of the palest blond that ran over her brow like an athlete's headband. Master Ambassador Argyros was equally elegant, but far more solemn. His gaze was dark, his hair clearly the source of the token Lady Hippolyta wore.

Like all the male Hesperines, his chin was shaven, but his hair was the longest. Bound in a single thick braid with a shot of dark auburn woven in, it nearly touched the floor. He wore a medallion of office and a mantle of silver silk embroidered with a tablion of white flowers Cassia could not name. He was too striking to be either handsome or beautiful. She would have called him for a mage, rather than a warrior, had she not known him to be neither. His stillness marked him as a Hesperine.

Perhaps the length of a Hesperine's hair was an indication of age. If so, Deukalion was indeed the youngest among the Hesperines, and the only one who wore no braid.

She scanned the crowd again. She was not mistaken. Deukalion was nowhere in sight. Had he issued such a bold invitation only to withdraw?

"Good evening, Lady Cassia."

Any other voice speaking so suddenly beside her would have made her startle and, given the state of her stomach, most likely gag. But Deukalion's words eased into her hearing so smoothly she did not jump.

She looked to her right. He stood but a pace away.

Then the velvet beauty of his voice wore off, and she realized two things. He had used his power to present himself without startling her, and what he was doing in this moment was sheer madness.

INVITATION

"**N**O ONE CAN SEE or hear me. Except you." Deukalion's voice enveloped Cassia, light as a feather, deep as an ocean. "Do give me some credit. I know better than to be seen speaking with you in public, especially in front of the king."

The breath rushed out of her, and she couldn't quite catch it again. In the face of the sudden Hesperine threat, Knight seemed to think the safest place for her was crushed between him and the wall. She dared not utter a word to call him off. Everyone was watching.

"No one can hear you two, either," Deukalion reassured her.

"*Het!*"

Whining, Knight took his weight off her, then continued to growl insults at Deukalion.

"A pleasure to see you again, as well, Knight," the Hesperine said amiably. "Don't worry. If anyone looks this way, they will see your lady idling against the wall with you as if all is well. They will notice no details and feel no urge to continue watching. If asked tomorrow what they saw you doing, they will realize they didn't notice, for they were too focused on something else."

"I credit you for such subtlety," Cassia replied when she had recovered her breath. Why was her heart still racing? "Will you not teach me this trick? I could certainly use it."

Deukalion chuckled, and finally she looked up and met his gaze. The well-lit room made his reflective eyes glow as brightly as they did in the black of night. She had never stood this close to him before.

"This is madness," she told him.

"Not at all. Although I do think it unwise to keep it up all night. Eventually my people will notice I am not, as I told them, on the grounds with the deer."

She glanced between the Hesperine beside her and his companions across the room. What had he to gain by making her believe this was their secret, which he kept even from his own people?

Her trust.

No...he must recognize by now her trust was not on the table. He was smart enough to know better. She did give him credit for that.

"I kept our agreement," he said. "I have not told anyone I spoke to you."

The other Hesperines seemed focused on each other and the crowd at large. They didn't appear to pay her any particular mind. But she could almost feel the king's gaze on her. She dared look at him.

He was looking everywhere but at her.

"How much time do we have?" she asked.

"Oh, a few dances before my companions wonder why they can still sense my power in the room, when I've supposedly left. But only a couple of dances before I'm too famished to think straight."

She stopped herself before she whipped her head around to look at him and instead turned her gaze slowly. She could not say whether he appeared famished, for she had no idea what a deprived Hesperine looked like. Now that he mentioned it, however, she thought that if he were human, she would suggest he pay a visit to the Kyrian infirmary. Despite the plentiful glow of the torches, his pupils were dilated, and he appeared even paler now than he had by the light of the moons when she had seen him last. All the color seemed to have drained from his face, even his lips.

But he did not look like someone who might devour the blood in her veins. Not with those large, soft eyes beneath long, dark lashes. That half-smile on his enviable mouth. And the power to stand here unseen across the room from the king's mage.

A shiver moved down Cassia's spine. She could have told the king he would never be able to understand, much less control, the Hesperines. But even she had not known just how true that was.

"It would be terribly inconsiderate of me to keep my champion from his evening meal, after he has so graciously sat through ours. I shall not detain you."

"Very well, my lady. You have had all day to consider your answer. Will you join me on the grounds?"

What a strange moment, to be speaking with him surrounded by the entire court, as if he were not the most condemned of heretics and she were not a concubine's bastard. As if he were a courtier who could offer a cordial invitation to escort her on a walk, and she were a lady of consequence at liberty to accept and enjoy his company with her attendant strolling behind.

What a strange pair they would make in truth, confronting each other by a crumbling fountain with Knight as her handmaiden. But she had always liked Knight better than Perita, in any case. And if Deukalion had been such a courtier, she would have said no.

"Yes. I will see you later tonight."

He smiled his close-lipped smile that looked genuine and enigmatic at the same time. "I look forward to it."

"Good meal," she wished him, as she had before.

When he disappeared again, she could not stifle a gasp.

Belatedly she realized her knees were no longer threatening to buckle, and the sweat that had soaked her was now dry. Her stomach had ceased its rebellion. Their conversation had proved more expedient than a retreat to her rooms to allay her response to the king.

Just a little longer now, and she would be able to escape. She rubbed Knight's back, and he blinked in contentment as he panted off the heat of the crowded room.

Was it her imagination, or for the rest of the evening, did the king not look at her at all?

NEW TERMS

IT SEEMED AN ETERNITY before the first casualties of the wine, too incapacitated to dance, broke the moratorium on leaving the festival. Cassia escaped with the drunkards and overtired ladies and made it back to her rooms before the halls became any more filthy.

Perita was gone. It would surely take her until dawn to congratulate her guard on his accomplishments in today's contests. Cassia stood by the remains of the fire and undressed herself. She freed her scalp from its pinching decoration and discarded the headdress on a chair in a heap of pins. The ugly bronze festival gown was next. Let her handmaiden serve her purpose and put them neatly away when she returned.

Cassia once more chose her green gardening dress for her venture. The gown was dark enough that it wouldn't stand out in the shadows. Even so, it was a greater challenge to reach the queen's wing tonight, for there were so many people about. But with an extra degree of patience, she made it without being seen by anyone sober enough to pay attention to which way a slip of a woman and a big dog were going.

By now Solia's door opened on silent hinges, and even the door out to the derelict garden had quieted. Cassia's pulse ran away with her, and goosebumps broke out on her skin, but not the unpleasant way they had earlier under the king's gaze. He was floors away in the great hall. He had no idea she was here. Knight bounded out into the garden as if he heartily approved their new nightly routine.

"Slow down," Cassia told him in the silence of the tunnel under the wall. "Don't get too excited, or you shall be disappointed when we aren't doing this any longer."

When she pushed open the hatch at the end of the tunnels, mist blew across her face. She sniffed as Knight climbed out ahead of her, then followed him. A full rain might hold off until dawn, but this was certain to be their last dry night for a while. If she could call a night dry, when its dampness crept through every seam of her clothes and into her bones.

At least the mist clung close to the ground, and the clouds overhead roiled in and out, never fully obscuring the moons. She could not risk a torch, and without the moonlight, she would be forced to give up her explorations.

"Don't get too excited," she reminded Knight.

He heeled, but his tail still wagged.

Through the trees ahead of them, the bright circle of the clearing came into view, awash in plenty of light, as if the figure waiting there drew the moons' glow to him like moths to flame. Perhaps he did. He sat on the rim of the basin, lounging with more ease than he had in his chair in the great hall.

"How did you enjoy the festivities?" she asked.

"I am disappointed I did not get to dance. Apparently we Hesperines are too alarming if we do anything except stand about looking dour."

"I have suffered through those dances on a number of occasions. I assure you, you were fortunate to escape the obligation."

"Was there no one there tonight with whom you would have enjoyed dancing?"

"The king's daughter does not enjoy anything."

"I see. Not even cheering for her favorite warriors on the battlefield?"

"I was not at the tournament."

His lips parted, and she heard him take a breath. "Ah. Another escaped obligation. You were gardening instead."

She smoothed her skirts. She hadn't realized any stains had sneaked under the apron she'd worn to the temple. Then she realized what his breath had meant. He could smell…

"Magic." His nostrils flared. He held up a hand. "I have it now. You give your time at the Kyrian temple that's near here."

"The maiden mages would be disappointed to learn the scent of their magic on me is no deterrent to Hesperines. I'm sure they imagine their holy aura would ward off creatures of the night such as yourself."

He sniffed again, smiling. "They smell pleasant. There is kindness in that place."

She subjected him to her shrewdest gaze. "Is all this information about my activities what you'd like in exchange for the answers you promised me?"

He crossed his arms over his chest. His limbs did not speak the same language as human ones. His natural grace made the messages his body sent her hard to understand. But his face said a great deal. Every word he spoke and his every reaction to hers were written in the tilt of his brows, the angle of his mouth.

Right now his mouth was relaxed and no longer devoid of color. It was harder to judge color in the moonlight, but his cheeks and lips that had been so pallid in the great hall now held the natural variations in hue she would expect to see in any healthy human face. He had transformed from solid marble to a fair-skinned, rosy-cheeked young man. Was that what a well-fed Hesperine looked like, as opposed to a thirsty one? So he was negotiating on a full stomach.

"I begin to think your terms are all in your own favor, Lady Cassia." He leaned forward, and the moonlight seemed dim in comparison with his eyes. "I demand new terms."

"Suggest them, and we shall see if I agree."

He gestured toward the lip of the basin. "Will you not join me at our negotiation table?"

Cassia felt much better standing. But to sit would be a good demonstration of confidence. And a sign of goodwill. She seated herself out of arm's reach of Deukalion. Knight draped himself over her feet, warming her through her slippers.

Deukalion smiled, that same smile that struck her as both friendly and closed. Mysterious. Given the overall expressiveness of his face, that was noticeable.

She put her finger on why. He never smiled with his mouth open. Well, well. He was hiding fangs.

She might do well to remember that.

He leaned back, as if relaxing on the fountain, and the lower half of his face disappeared into shadow. "I think we both grow weary of these small, hard-won exchanges. If we are to demand so many questions and answers of each other, why not establish a broad agreement that covers all eventualities?"

"Spoken like an ambassador."

"Initiate ambassador. I am not a master, nor even a full ambassador yet. I only just earned my cords." He touched a hand to the silver-and-white silk braid that hung around his neck, which appeared ready to receive a future medallion of office.

"Oh, you are ruining your image now."

"I thought it already beyond saving and that I have nothing to lose. Although, to be fair, my position as an initiate is rather more advanced than that of an apprentice in a temple or a craft."

"You are here for the next level of your training, then? What a crucible your master has chosen for a workshop."

"I jumped in of my own accord. I am not ashamed to admit I begged him to let me come. We are making history here. Participating in this embassy is the opportunity of a lifetime, even a Hesperine lifetime."

And how long was that, in his case? "You must forgive my lack of enthusiasm for history. I live in it every day."

"I can already tell our new agreement will be a success."

"And why is that?"

"Speaking openly is coming naturally to us already."

If he thought this was openness, he was more innocent than she had believed. Wasn't he?

"This is what I propose," Deukalion said. "Let us make our own Equinox Oath to ensure all is fair and equal in our dealings. I will promise to speak my mind, and you will promise to speak yours, with no one as our witnesses but…" He pointed upward. "My protector." He pointed at Knight. "And yours."

Cassia looked up at the moons. They were high overhead, one smooth white, one liquid red, perfectly matched in size but opposing in nature. "Mortals call the moons Anaklastia's Mirrors and imagine them to be made of steel. One is said to reflect her father Anthros's light and the other the blood he spills. The myths say the moons wane because Hespera seeks to wrestle the Mirrors from the grasp of Anthros's devoted scion. But I know better."

"Have you seen any real moonstones that have fallen from the sky? They shine even when no sun touches them."

"So I would imagine. I am certain the moons shed their own light and belong wholly to Hespera." She rested a hand on Knight. "You know where the loyalties of my protector lie. What about yours?"

"She is loyal to all those who seek Sanctuary under her gaze. The Goddess's Eyes see and keep secret all that passes under the shelter of night."

Cassia met his gaze, and this time she did not tease him about his philosophical nature.

He must have seen the challenge in her eyes, for he shook his head. "You have seen I am as good as my word. I concealed our conversation in the great hall from the embassy."

"You dared to use a spell in front of the royal mage."

Deukalion actually chuckled and shook his head. "That was hardly a spell. Walking unseen? For Hesperines, that's like…simply walking, or speaking, or singing. Something you do naturally without expending effort. Effort is what rouses a mage's curiosity."

"It required so little effort for you to befuddle the senses of those who tried to look at me?"

"Including a human in Hesperine magic is a more complex matter, but my little tricks in the great hall were not anything that would draw attention."

"Yet you said if you kept at it too long, the other Hesperines would eventually realize you were there. What will you do when they come looking for you here, hoping to share your evening meal? If we make a habit of this, how can you assure me they will not become witnesses to our conversations?"

"That is not a concern." Deukalion sighed. "Truth be told, I am the only member of the embassy who requires the deer."

"Is that so. You'd best not let Amachos find out, or he shall suspect your companions of feeding on the human populace instead."

"They don't require humans, either. But on that subject, I must say no more, unless we protect our mutual revelations with an Oath."

Cassia could let their conversations end here, the negotiation in balance. Or she could agree to spill words with him under the moons' shroud.

What did he hope to gain by luring her to speak, as he called it, openly?

Perhaps the best answer to that was, what did she hope to gain?

As long as they both gave themselves the same amount of rope, neither could hang the other without sending them both to the gallows. As always, they were even.

Cassia drew a deep breath. She saw Deukalion do the same. She suspected his was informative, while all hers served to do was brace her.

"If you need time to consider my suggestion," Deukalion said, "I'm happy to wait again for an answer. You can tell me tomorrow night."

She could spend another day deliberating, another night wondering whether she would be able to get away. That would be a wasted chance, a waste of risk. She should press her opportunity tonight and get closer to the answers she sought.

"No," she said. His face revealed his disappointment before she clarified, "No, I don't need more time. I find your terms satisfactory. We shall both lay our questions and answers on the table…freely." She fixed him with a gaze. "And there shall be no consequences."

He placed a hand upon his breast. "I do so swear."

She stood long enough to drop him a curtsy. "I do so swear."

"May this Oath stand till those who come after us stand here again." He spoke the words with the solemnity of ritual, but then his smile widened slowly. Kept widening, until she saw a row of clean, straight, white teeth. The tips of his canines descended beyond, hidden in his lower lip. "You won't regret it, Cassia."

She hoped he was right. And she hoped he wouldn't regret it either.

He was too eager to trust. He did not seem to realize how dangerous she was to him. If he were human, he would hang long before she did.

But he was not.

"I believe," he began, "I ought to answer your outstanding question from last night. What about life in Orthros would you like to—"

He was holding up his hand suddenly, his expression alert. Cassia had not seen him move.

"Stay here, and no one will find you." He had hardly said it before he was gone.

Cassia surged to her feet, glancing about her for any sign of him. Knight stood at attention, silent but with his lips peeled back from his teeth.

There was someone in the woods.

Someone Deukalion had heard—smelled—sensed?

Her mind raced through possibilities, even as she urged herself to make a decision, to act in her own defense.

She had no idea who was out there or where they were. If she moved now, she might run into them instead of away from them.

But if Deukalion thought their newfound bargain meant she would sit here and rely on him to protect her, he was gravely mistaken.

Cassia dropped to her knees and took Knight's face in her hands, gazing into his eyes. He was bred, born, and trained to attack a threat head-on and destroy it, not to sneak about in the dark. But she had never once made a request of him he did not understand. She might never know to what magic the breeders had subjected Knight's ancestors, but she had seen more than once the evidence of his intelligence, his perception beyond even her senses.

So quiet only he could hear, she murmured, *"Loma. Hoor."*

Home. Silence.

When Cassia turned to leave the clearing and hasten carefully into the trees, Knight followed without a growl or a rumble.

PROOF OF HONOR

THE MOMENT THE MAGE noticed Lio watching him, the man startled visibly. Lio had to admit it was satisfying to see Amachos jump at the sight of him. Cassia could have taught the king's new glyph scribbler a great deal about the art of not displaying reactions.

This was one encounter Lio could spare her. His veil spell kept her concealed and safe back at the fountain, and he had succeeded in intercepting the mage some distance from her. Concealing a human while a mage was on alert required what Lio had described to Cassia as making an effort, but it was a manageable risk for him to cloak her in moonlight while she sat still and he distracted Amachos. Even if the mage noticed anything, the Font of the Changing Queen had a magical aura more palpable than Lio's subtle weaving.

Amachos stood bedecked in the full three-robe ensemble that signified his rank as an honored master in the Order of Anthros. Here under the Goddess's Eyes, Lio tried to find it in himself to regard the mage justly. He must separate Amachos as an individual from the Order whose robes he wore and give the man a chance to show what truly lay within his heart.

But facing a mage alone for the first time, Lio discovered the limits of his fairness. He could think only of the names his people spoke with reverence and grief, the names of Hesperines he might have had the privilege of knowing if not for the cult of Amachos's violent god. Among them was Prometheus.

Lio made himself perform his most studied ambassador's bow.

Amachos, hands in his sleeves, gave him a shallow, stiff bow in return.

Lio reminded himself the man before him was not personally

responsible for the deaths of those Orthros mourned. This Tenebran temple sweeper had nothing to do with the Cordian war mages who had cut short so many Hesperine lives. In fact, Amachos's home temple at Namenti played a vital role in keeping Cordium out of Tenebra, and Amachos himself had been outspoken in favor of restoring the truce between his people and Lio's.

Lio resolved to address the mage with courtesy in Divine, the language they both held sacred, which Hesperines spoke as their mother tongue and human mages still used in all their rites. Lio had learned it on his father's knee, while Amachos would have had to study it for years. Lio told himself it was a peace offering. Or perhaps he couldn't resist testing Amachos's education.

Lio opened with a neutral greeting. "Good evening, Honored Master Amachos."

"Anthros shine upon you, Deukalion." Amachos's accent was different, but his words were perfectly understandable.

The mage's inflammatory statement dried up what little compassion Lio had managed to muster. He did not reply. He need not defend his presence here, where the king had authorized him to be. It was Amachos who was out of place at the moment, and they both knew why.

Apparently the mage had judged his apprentice capable enough to spy on the elder Hesperines while they were in plain sight, surrounded by liegehounds and warriors. But Lio was in the wind, and Amachos had come to keep an eye on him. The silence stretched between them as Lio waited to see what excuse the mage would give for harassing him.

Amachos's smile appeared forced. "The king saw that one of his guests had excused himself before the festival was at an end, and he grew concerned his hospitality might have been found lacking. I have come to inquire after your satisfaction."

"My satisfaction?" What a disingenuous way of saying he had come to breathe down Lio's neck. But Lio was not afraid of this undereducated superstition-monger. No…it was not Amachos Lio was worried about.

The most dangerous person here was Lio himself. It was Amachos who would have cause for concern, if Lio could not master the strange and powerful feelings now threatening to overcome his conciliatory nature.

Lio never had this much difficulty formulating a tactful response. He was still considering his words when he sensed a disturbance in the veil he had left over the fountain.

He felt Cassia exit his concealment, as if a rose and her thorns had fluttered from his grasp. She had not taken him at his word that he would keep her safe.

Lio had no time to indulge his disappointment. This was not the bright, crowded great hall, where he had fiddled with the candlelight and nudged minds eager for diversion. He must wrap a moving, mortal target in a veil so complete that a mage on the hunt would not notice a Hesperine had cast a spell under his very nose.

Lio lifted his veil from the fountain and tossed it around Cassia an instant before she passed beyond the furthest edge of the Font's aura.

He allowed all his knowledge of flowery discussion free rein and spoke in the way Xandra always referred to as his "infuriating pretensions." His perseverance in reading all those verbose discourses hadn't been a waste after all. "How infinitely kind of His Majesty to trouble his thoughts over each and every one of his grateful foreign guests, and how beneficent of you, Honored Master, to cleave yourself from the festivities and sacrifice the exalted company of Tenebra's magnanimous prince, tonight's cele-brant, in order to convey His Majesty's thoughtful concern for the lowest member of our embassy from distant Orthros."

While he chattered, he made sure his veil kept pace with Cassia. Each band of moonlight through which she passed strengthened his spell. As she trod through shadows, his magic made a safe path beneath her feet.

Meanwhile, Amachos glazed over in the eyes without Lio having to employ any mind magic directly. Ah, the power of words, especially in overwhelming quantity. The mage's smile thinned, and his eyes narrowed. It was plain the man could not make up his mind whether or not Lio was mocking him. Perfect. Amachos sucked in a breath through his nose, as if to speak.

Lio preempted him. "Upon your return to His Majesty the King, please express my thankfulness and say to His Majesty that Deukalion found the generosity of the royal table to be without compare and treasured the opportunity to observe such a truly grand display of human culture."

"Yet," the mage cut in, "we missed you at the dance."

Lio spread his hands in a classic gesture of admission. "As the evening progressed, I became overwhelmed with concern on behalf of the many Tenebrans who would be returning to home and hearth long after nightfall, and I thought to hasten and conclude my own evening meal here amid the bounty of the royal grounds, while my merry hosts still celebrated, so that I might be gone by the time the king's well-satisfied subjects embarked on their path homeward. I would not wish to remain at large once they depart the palace, lest my presence cause them undue alarm."

A branch snapped in the distance. Lio dared not turn his head, but Amachos did. The mage paused to listen. Lio kept his physical gaze on his adversary and cast his senses far into the trees.

Knight moved with the certainty of a hound on a trail, giving Amachos a wide berth, but an animal of that stature was not built to move quietly. Thorns. Lio couldn't do anything about Cassia's liegehound. Except keep talking.

"Ah, the aforementioned bounty of the royal grounds," he declared. "I must compliment His Majesty on the number and diversity of creatures thriving under his care."

There came a pulse of Amachos's power. Lio recognized the Anthrian seeking spell from descriptions in scrolls and the uncomfortable warmth on his senses. He held his veil over Cassia steady and let his power wax, as diffuse as the moons' glow, as pervasive as the darkness, that his spell might be one more natural shade of the night.

The mage's probe sputtered out. He turned his attention back to Lio. "Yes...just an animal of some sort."

Lio had seldom been so grateful for his superior education.

"May I ask if you have concluded your evening meal?" the mage inquired.

Lio showed Amachos a close-lipped smile, filling one more moment's pause with the gesture, stalling for that much more time. "I thank you. Indeed, I too have enjoyed the plentiful gifts His Majesty has so liberally bestowed tonight. As you see, I was just returning to the comfort and welcome of my guest quarters within Solorum Fortress. I thought to go directly to bed, rather than return to the festival, for I suspect I am too late and have already missed the best of the dancing."

"Yes, I fear the prince's temple day is concluding somewhat earlier than in past years. I can't imagine why."

"Even so, such a celebration could not have been a disappointment to him. He is a truly fortunate young man."

"Indeed he is." Amachos eyed Lio. "Well, I am relieved to hear all is well. When the royal groundskeepers found no evidence you had taken advantage of the king's provisions, Basileus was troubled that what he set aside for you might be…insufficient."

"Evidence, Honored Master Amachos?"

The mage put on a supercilious smile. "The remains of the deer, naturally."

"Only dead deer leave remains, Honored Master." Lio made an effort to conceal his disgust.

The mage subjected him to a piercing gaze. "I trust it is only venison for which you have a taste, honored guest?"

Lio abandoned empty words. Such an insinuation called for a real response. How dare Amachos demand such gruesome proof of Lio's honor? How dare the mage imply that the lack of a trail of deer carcasses behind Lio meant he was drinking from humans instead?

Lio sensed Cassia's presence disappear into the palace's magical aura. She was safely away. He let his veil spell unravel into the night.

He looked Amachos in the eye. "No Hesperine has a taste for flesh, much less death. Unlike my mortal hosts, I do not slaughter my dinner. I assure you, all those I have 'taken advantage of' on the king's grounds walked away from the encounter."

"How…forbearing. The king will marvel to learn of how you contain yourself on his behalf. I shall return and reassure him." The look in Amachos's eyes said he would be watching Lio long after they parted company.

Lio put a hand over his heart. "May the Goddess's Eyes watch your path."

The mage's smile twisted. Oh, so close to a sneer. A sudden flare of light broke the darkness, and when it cleared, Amachos was gone.

Lio cringed at the intangible sparks that spat at him in the aftermath of the mage's expense of power. He couldn't believe Amachos had just performed a traversal. A working of that magnitude could leave a man bedridden, if he wasn't careful. Moving from one place to another with magic might come naturally to Hesperines, but not to mortal mages. Apparently Amachos would not be outdone by an initiate heretic.

When Lio reentered the barracks, he bowed to the guards at every turn to leave an impression on them, securing still more witnesses to his good behavior. At last he made it to the embassy's guest quarters, where moonlight and darkness had taken over, and no guards dared tread to replenish the torches even when Aunt Lyta and Kadi's ward did not bar them from entry. Lio was relieved to sense none of his elders in their rooms. It seemed he still had a little time before they returned from the palace. He retreated to his own chamber and sank down on the edge of the bunk.

He looked down at his hands. Yes, they were shaking, and light pulsed around them.

He could not remember ever feeling so angry in his life.

Lio curled his hands into fists and shut his eyes. Behind his eyelids, the current of his own power shone bright white and blood red in his mind's eye. He drew upon it, urging it into himself. Tonight it was like trying to herd the moons. The calm and joy he always felt in this moment, when he withdrew into himself to that place where only he and the Goddess dwelt, would not come to him.

The Gift, his own Hesperine nature, had never felt this way to him before. As if he did not have the Gift. As if his Gift, cold and clear, heated and wild, had him.

He had thought himself more reasonable than this. More altruistic. He was not prone to anger, never had been. But tonight his temper had arrived unannounced and determined to outstay its welcome.

Lio must regain control of his emotions. It would be wrong to let the sun rise on his anger, and if only the Dawn Slumber proved enough to calm his ire, that would feel like defeat.

36

days until

SPRING EQUINOX

CHANGE OF PLANS

I T WAS STRANGE HOW sound carried, or sometimes didn't, within the inner walls of the Temple of Kyria. Cassia heard the hoofbeats in the outer court as clearly as she could hear her spade scraping the soil, but she couldn't make out the voice of whoever had arrived.

Her aches distracted her. The preceding winter months had left her gardening muscles out of practice and wrought calluses on her hands more suited to accommodate a shuttle than a spade. In a moment she might have to give in and straighten to rest her arms and rub her back. But her body had no cause to complain. It had been in its own bed for the past three nights, all night long. Never mind that she had slept poorly, thinking of what she had not done.

Curse Deukalion for keeping her awake with thoughts of how close they had come to disaster. Curse him for inviting her out to the Font. The king's own mage had nearly caught them together! She had felt Amachos brandishing his magic as she escaped.

Cassia hurled aside the stone she had pried out of the soil. She was wiser than the idealistic, overconfident Hesperine. She knew when risk outweighed the answers she would never get.

She would not venture into such dangerous territory again.

"Lady Cassia."

At the sound of her name, Cassia finally straightened, rising up on her knees and allowing her body to stretch.

Deutera stood at the end of the row. She wore her veil, and a line between her brows suggested worry. Or perhaps regret. "A messenger has come for you. He awaits you in the outer court."

The pain in Cassia's limbs worsened from sudden tension. She got to her feet. Knight moved restlessly at the edge of the garden but did not disobey her command to stay out of the bed. As soon as she made it to the end of the row, he twined around her legs, eager to offer comfort.

"We won't completely clean up," she told him. "We'll be back after we've heard what the messenger has to say." She paused only to set aside her tools. This could not be a summons.

She and Knight followed Deutera around the inner wheel of the temple, through the walls that divided it like spokes and the gardens nestled in between. Cassia was coming to understand the purpose of the different segments and the ways of the soil in each. Most remained chill and hard in the grasp of winter, while others turned into lakes of mud as they thawed, but come spring, all would become home to the seedlings now tended so carefully indoors.

Tendrils of Kyrian magery brushed Cassia's arms as Deutera led her past women who nurtured the dirt with tools and spells. A group of apprentices stood laughing at a well, trying to wash mud from their dark blue robes. Splashes echoed off the walls, and sounds played tricks on Cassia's ears again. Although the infirmary was in the outer temple, she heard a child moan.

The cacophony faded as she and Deutera emerged from the nest of walls and fertile soil. They halted in the outer court, where the messenger in royal livery confronted Cassia. She knotted her hands in her apron and waited for the man to speak.

He had a hard face that showed no expression. "His Majesty requires your presence."

That meant immediately. That meant the king was, for the first time, calling Cassia back from the temple in the middle of the day for all to see. What it meant beyond that she could not imagine, if she were to reach the palace on her feet.

Trying to ignore the twisting pangs in her stomach, Cassia glanced down at herself and gestured to indicate the smears of soil on her apron. "I will take a moment to make myself fit to appear before him."

She must hurry. It would take too long to retrieve her tools. She must leave them and wash up at the nearest well.

She turned to find one of the apprentices already standing near with the basket of tools in hand. Another young mage offered a damp cloth. Cassia breathed a grateful thank-you to both girls and tidied herself, then took off her soiled apron and made to fold it with the clean side facing outward. The result was a haphazard, wrinkled pile she stashed on top of her tools. She gripped the basket to her, made a courteous apology to Deutera that she forgot as soon as she said it, and turned back to the messenger.

He was holding his horse for her. Waiting to pack her onto the animal and deliver her to the king.

She wasted an extra instant rubbing away the moisture between her palms. Then she marched to the horse, and the messenger hoisted her into the saddle. He took the reins in hand and led her out of the temple.

Knight paced beside her the whole way, now on one side, then on the other. He could not stand still, as if he wished to attack something, but could not spot it. Cassia focused her gaze on the countryside so the motion of the horse did not worsen what was going on in her belly.

The ride felt interminable, and she wished it had lasted forever. The messenger deposited her in the main courtyard of the palace and informed her, "His Majesty awaits you in the solar."

The walk through the palace seemed too fast, although she walked slowly, swallowing at every step. Suddenly she found herself in the king's wing. The corridor was full of sunny afternoon light falling upon her from the windows far, far above her head. The double doors that led to the king's rooms stood open.

The antechamber was full of guards. As she passed between their ranks, they chatted with each other as if she were not there.

The solar door was closed. Would they make her ask for admittance? Would they make her open it herself?

The door popped open, and Cassia jumped. Red-gold robes, oiled dark hair and an unremarkable face met her in the doorway.

Amachos smiled at Cassia and held out his arm to invite her inside.

No, no. He couldn't know. He hadn't told the king.

Let it not be true that Amachos had seen her with Deukalion.

"Lady Cassia." The mage's voice seemed to resound around her. "How very interesting to see you again."

The sunbeams swam in her vision, and the sight of the mage blurred before her. She could only hear his clear, deep voice. She stood there as if his words tethered her to the spot.

No reprieve. No recourse. No escape.

"Won't you join us inside?" he commanded.

Cassia feared the guards might have to push her over the threshold. If they did, what passed within would be infinitely worse. She forced herself to step inside. She made herself walk past Amachos, although her every instinct screamed that she mustn't put her back to the enemy.

She tried to ignore everything inside that room except the legs of the desk, where she pinned her gaze as she knelt. But in her mind's eye, she saw each stick of rich furniture that cluttered the chamber. All fourteen of the swords on the walls. The arch of the great hearth, where a fire always burned, as in the kingdom's forges. Most of all, every line graven on the face of the man who sat behind the desk. His hair and beard had gone white while he occupied that chair, but his blue eyes were as keen and piercing as they had been since Cassia could remember.

"Well," said Amachos behind her. "Out of all our daily afternoon meetings, Basileus, few have been so revelatory. I will leave you to…settle your family matter."

The door swung and landed shut with a quiet, final impact that sounded like a catapult. Cassia's whole body jerked. The startle gave way to the slow burn of humiliation. She had betrayed her feelings.

"What do you have to say for yourself, daughter?"

Cassia swallowed again. He expected her to speak first?

"Forgive me." She hated the words and how broken each syllable sounded. "The messenger did not…that is, he had yet to tell me for what purpose you summoned me."

"Do you not already know?"

Cassia clenched her teeth, willing her back not to tremble.

Did the king know?

She supposed others might have prayed in that moment, but all she could do was try to think. He was baiting her. She knew this; that open-ended question was a classic threat, a trap. If he didn't know, she must not condemn herself.

She heard the king shift in his chair, a warning her silence had stretched on too long already.

"Forgive me," she said again, pushing the words out of her tight throat. "I do not know."

"Your wrongdoing does not weigh on your conscience at all? That offends me most deeply. Even your mother had a greater sense of propriety."

Cassia waited. The glare of the sun streaming in the windows behind the king made pain erupt in her head, which felt as if it were much too near the ceiling. The promised rain hadn't come yet. Knight shifted his body closer to her, and right in front of the king, she leaned on her dog to steady herself.

"Go ahead," the king commanded. "Ask me what you have done."

Cassia coaxed a breath into her nose and convinced it to form words. "What have I done? Your Majesty?"

"You have done your brother a grave insult. He was angered to see you leave the feast in his honor so early. For his own sister to be among the first to depart…what sort of message do you think that sent to others in Our court?"

Cassia felt the mad urge to laugh. So this was to be it. A boy's party, her undoing at last.

She had miscalculated. Over something so simple.

"What do you have to say for yourself?" the king asked.

"I saw Lady Hadrian leave, and I thought it acceptable to follow the example of one so esteemed."

"Lady Hadrian is not my daughter, nor is she the prince's last surviving sister."

The hopeless laughter inside Cassia was gone. Something much more dire rose and raged, striving to fight its way out of her.

She held it within herself with every ounce of will she had.

"I. Was ill."

"Did you not feed a sample of every dish on your plate to the dog first, to ensure none of it would make you ill?"

"Yes. It was not the food." She cleared her throat. "I…I did not want to humiliate my brother by fainting before his guests. I thought it better to return to my chambers and not display my weakness before Your Majesty."

"It disturbs me that you always seek to hide your shame. Is there anything else you wish to confess?"

"N—no."

"Is there anything else you ought to confess?"

Her heartbeat pounded in her ears, throbbing with the pain in her head. Her life, as always, depended on her answer.

What could she possibly do to make him believe her?

She lifted her head, inch by inch. She tilted her eyes upward.

His blue gaze burned into hers.

"I have done nothing else that would offend Your Majesty or my beloved brother. Forgive me for my failure on his day of honor. It was...a feminine weakness." The most convenient lie she could grasp at. She hadn't used it yet this month. Had she? No. Time to contrive bloody rags for Perita to launder so the ruse would remain convincing.

"So much time spent with the mages of Kyria, and yet their healing arts do nothing to assist you with womanly complaints."

"I shall consult with them...for a new remedy."

"See that you do. It is a hardship for Us for you to be unreliable."

"Yes, Your Majesty."

He tapped blunt fingertips on the surface of the desk. "Go back to your rooms. Do not embarrass Us in that way again."

"Yes, Your Majesty."

She struggled to get her legs under her. If not for Knight, she would never have made it to her feet. She backed away, and the carpet seemed to clutch at her slippers. The knowledge that she stumbled in front of the king made her skin burn from scalp to belly. She still faced those cold blue eyes. Only when she got out the door and it shut on his gaze was she released.

She turned and fled.

No reprieve in her rooms. Perita sat by the fire at her mending. Cassia rushed past her without a word and shut the door of her bedchamber.

She saw herself slamming it. Saw her hand reaching for her spade and throwing it against the wall so she could listen to it clang and echo on the stone. She heard all that in her mind only, for every real noise she made, whatever she did in this room, Perita would hear and report to the king.

Cassia took her basket of gardening tools in both hands and hurled them with all her might onto the bed.

Her spade rolled impotently on the soft bedclothes, scattering bits of soil. Packets of seeds landed all about and spilled their precious contents. Her apron fluttered over it all and landed with its unstained side up.

Cassia made it to the basin on the floor by her bed just in time to avoid vomiting on herself. Knight nudged his head under her elbow until she wrapped one arm around him. She clung to him while her body heaved, pushing out and emptying everything from within her.

When it was over, she crouched there and rested her forehead against Knight. She cleared her throat, then swallowed. Her voice was rough, but she managed a whisper for Knight's ears to hear. "Change of plans."

RISKS RECKONED

L IO PAUSED TO SIT on the lip of the old fountain. A shower had passed
through around midnight and filled the thirsty basin. He wasn't eager
to return to the catacombs of their guest quarters or the pall of dis-
couragement that hung over the embassy. Soon enough, he must go back
to his room and make use of the time before dawn to log the depressing
events of tonight's Summit.

But not until he was sure there was no chance Cassia would join him.
As resourceful as she was, he deemed it unlikely an obstacle had prevented
her from meeting with him these past three nights. She was avoiding him.
Even so, he couldn't bring himself to go back just yet. She felt closer to
him tonight, somehow.

He stood up and paced around the fountain. So restless, always, ever
since he'd come here. Well, that was not necessarily a bad sign. This cagey
feeling from improper nourishment was maddening, but he had yet to feel
the lethargy and listlessness that signaled true deprivation. He just wished
any amount of running would work off his tension.

If Cassia did not seek him out tonight, he must face the fact she had no
intention of doing so again. What then? Their conversations might have
accomplished so much. Was he really willing to let Amachos's interruption
bring that to a premature end?

No, Cassia's interest in Lio's people was too rare. She was too rare.
Too important.

He must find a way to come in contact with her again, as he had at
the king's feast, and persuade her it was safe to continue their midnight
discussions.

Just then the vague sense of her closeness became the distant sound of fabric brushing against leaves and a hint of her scent on the wind.

It had *not* been all in his thoughts. She was closer indeed—on the grounds tonight. And headed for him.

She hadn't let the mage frighten her away. He'd been sure Cassia was the kind of person who let nothing stand in her way once she judged a goal worthy of pursuit. What he had not been certain of was whether he passed that test. But apparently she had decided he did, at least for one more night. Now was his chance to make his case for why they should remain in contact.

It was a good thing she was still some distance away. That gave him time to collect himself. He rubbed a hand over his mouth. Goddess have Mercy on him. After a lifetime of Hesperine teachings and training in self-discipline, a few nights of deer were all it took for his fangs to betray him at the first suggestion of a desirable human. His teeth didn't seem to understand what was so clear to the rest of him: the line between noticing and wanting.

That line had never been a problem for him before. His long fidelity to Xandra had acquainted him with it well, and he had never crossed it. Orthros was a land full of females worthy of notice, and notice he did, while wanting only one. But none of those noticeable females had affected him the way Cassia did.

Hespera's Grace. He had never wanted *Xandra* like this.

Lio felt of his fangs as if he had just grown them for the first time. He hadn't even touched Cassia. Hadn't stood closer to her than the space it took to keep him out of her liegehound's reach. Yet he wanted her in a way he had never wanted anyone, not even the Hesperine he had once planned to avow. He had never felt such a confluence of thirst and desire as he felt here, now, for this human who was so far beyond his reach she might as well dwell on the sun.

What had come over him?

Conversing with Cassia was enough of a breach of conduct, but one he had good reason to commit. He could never justify anything beyond talking with her. And even if he could, in spite of politics, it wouldn't matter.

Cassia had gazed upon him as he had upon her. That was all. She had never given him leave to want her, and she never would. Not circumspect Cassia. What would she think, if she had any idea where his thoughts wandered when she was near?

He had meant that to be a sobering thought. Imagining her censure ought to be enough to ruin the most voracious appetite.

So why could he only think of how she had touched her hand to her throat? Of the boldness he had seen in her eyes as she asked him about his ways with curiosity…almost fascination…

When she finally emerged from between the trees with her bodyguard at her side, her presence was what proved enough to silence Lio's inner wrestling with himself. She was so astonishing to his senses, from the sound of her heartbeat to her scent to the taste of that scent at the edge of his palate. He resolved to do as every Hesperine was inclined to when confronted with a great delight the Goddess had placed in the world— simply be glad.

"Lady Cassia. It is good to see you again." He offered her a bow.

If she noticed it was deeper than usual, she gave no indication. "Good evening."

By moonlight she looked like the woman she was instead of a battered doll set up as a decoration in her father's court. She carried herself with resolve, rather than wariness. That alone reassured Lio a great deal.

"I was concerned for you these past three nights," he confessed.

"We both had reason to be concerned."

"I'm grateful for the opportunity to tell you how sorry I am about what happened last time. You needn't worry, I assure you. Amachos left thinking only that a young Hesperine was too thirsty to last through the dancing."

"His presence here was proof enough for me that it was necessary to withdraw."

"Withdraw?" Lio gave her a rueful smile. "You make it sound like a battlefield."

"Is it not, my champion?"

"I feel the need to remind you I am a champion who regards weapons as a last resort."

"I would advise you to keep your sword close at hand, just in case."

"Do you, my lady, pass a single hour that is not one long series of risk assessments?"

"If I were a farmer, I would weigh my risks according to weevils, storms, and blight. Being what I am, I weigh them according to how close the royal mage comes to seeing me talk to you." She eyed him. "And, despite his charmed existence, I suspect a Hesperine weighs his risks just as carefully."

But oh, what different scales he had than she. "Then what inspired you to risk this again? To what do I owe the pleasure?"

Lio caught a whiff of fear. Much too fresh and powerful to be the remains of what Cassia had felt at the prince's celebration.

Her gaze deserted him, seeking refuge in Knight's direction. "I spoke with the king today. He has not found out."

Did the king always have this effect on her? Always *the king*, Lio noticed. Never *my father*.

Lio put as much certainty and reassurance as he could into his words. "Of course he didn't find out. We've been very careful."

She didn't answer, and the fear heated into something even more powerful, while her hand moved smoothly over Knight's back. Did she even realize how angry she was?

What had her father done to her to fill her with such fury?

Lio hated to imagine what cause Cassia had to harbor rage so powerful against her father. Stories he'd heard and tried to forget now came to mind, tales of what Tenebrans did to one another...what some fathers did to their daughters.

The mere thought that anyone, that *Cassia,* would be forced to endure such a thing was sickening.

"Do you spend much time with the king?" Lio asked carefully.

"No."

Lio dreaded following his thoughts where they led, but he had to know. "You don't see him often?"

"Not particularly." Cassia fiddled with Knight's ear, which the dog endured with a broad grin. "The court and I are only occasionally at the same palace. For example, this year the king had me winter at Namenti and then visited there briefly. Since he brought me with him to Solorum, I have seen more of him than usual."

A surprisingly detailed answer, but delivered in a tone so neutral, an inquisitor would be hard pressed to make anything of it. A great deal of information that told Lio very little. What diplomatic skills Cassia had developed in her young mortal life. It filled him with admiration, but equal grief, because it had not been a pleasure for her, as it had for him—for her, it was a necessary means of survival.

Lio found some reassurance in the knowledge that the king seldom forced her to be near him. If Lucis had perverse intentions toward his daughter, he most likely would not keep her at a distance.

"Do you enjoy being at court for a change?" Lio asked, as if inquiring how she liked the weather.

"Solorum is where I wished to be at this time."

Again, an answer that was not an answer. But one that told him perhaps a great deal more.

She dreaded being near her father, and yet she wanted to be here at Solorum. What could be so important to her that it was worth putting herself through this?

Were her encounters with Lio a collateral convenience or an integral reason for her actions?

PEACE OFFERING

"**F**OR MY PART, LADY Cassia, I'm delighted you are here at Solorum, and I'm sure our own discussions will prove much more fruitful than the debacle at the negotiation table tonight." Lio waited for her to ask, but she said nothing about what had happened at the Summit.

Surely Cassia had heard that right in the middle of Uncle Argyros's most pivotal address, Lord Severinus had called forward a witness against the embassy. The mage from Severitas had filled the embassy's entire speaking time with overwrought tales of Hesperine atrocities, and the Council had lapped up his gory lies. The display had been so excruciating, Lio was sure gossip about it had escaped the secrecy of the ward around the pavilion to take the court by storm. But Cassia showed no signs of awareness or interest regarding the event.

So Lio proceeded to reach into one of the deep pockets of his robe and draw out what he had brought for her each night, just in case. Not such a foolish notion after all. "Every beneficial and promising agreement warrants an exchange of gifts, don't you think? Here is a token of good faith."

She stared at the round, paper-wrapped package on his palm as if she'd never seen a bar of soap before.

"I've noticed you prefer soap to scent oils," he felt the need to explain. Still she looked at his gift with furrowed brows. "It's...very fine."

"The finest from Orthros. The embassy brought a crate and presented them at the Summit, among other gifts that promote good health. I took the liberty of reserving one for you." He shifted on his feet. He was not making a romantic gesture, he reminded himself. There was no reason to feel so unsure standing here before her with his offering in his hand. "The soap does have a fragrance, but I believe you'll like it."

"I thank you." She held out her open hand to Lio while she cast her gaze toward the ground, dipping her lashes with every appearance of humility. The gesture did not befit her any more than her affected laugh. She was clearly accustomed to receiving gifts on her best behavior, probably from men who thought they could buy and own her.

Lio glanced at her hound. "Do you suppose Sir Knight will allow me to hand this to you?"

Now a smile tugged at the corners of her mouth. "Perhaps if you allow him to sniff it first."

"And present him with an opportunity to take off my hand?"

Cassia clucked at Knight and said a word to him. He looked up at her, eyes wide. Woman and dog gazed at each other, communicating through what must be their own sort of Union.

"*Ckuundat*, all is well." How could her voice sound tender and commanding at the same time? "*Hama.*"

Knight backed into a position right at her side. The hound no longer stood between them, but if Lio came much nearer Cassia, he would be within easy reach of the beast's jaws.

With his eyes on the dog, Lio took one step closer. Knight peeled his lip back. Lio waited. The hound stood still, glaring at him.

Slowly, carefully, Lio reached out and placed the soap in Cassia's hand.

They both watched Knight. He watched them.

"I think he has given you leave to proceed, so long as you do not push your luck."

Lio angled a slight bow in Knight's direction. "I will not forget I am on his sufferance."

He let the soap rest in Cassia's hand for a moment, his hand still on the soap. A connection between them, one he allowed the Blood Union to embellish for his senses. Her deep sense of hesitation told him she had no intention whatsoever of using such an intimate gift.

She took the soap and withdrew her hand all too soon. But she did lift the bar to her nose. Lio listened to her take a breath and watched the groove at the base of her throat deepen. She hesitated. Then she took a deeper breath.

"It is very fine," she said again.

"The oldest soap known to civilization and still one of the best. You will never guess what it is made of."

"No, I shall not, for I have not smelled anything like it before."

He smiled at her. "Cassia oil."

She took the soap away from her nose. "Cassia is an *oil?*"

"Not at all. It is a tree."

Slightly, but visibly, she relaxed. "I have never heard of a cassia tree."

"What is your namesake, then?"

"Cassius," she supplied, "a past king's bastard son. All I know about him is that he was notoriously vain, and his name became tradition."

Lio tried not to grimace. "Cassia is an ancient and exquisite tree, whose fragrant bark supplies the world with soaps, delicacies, and medicine."

Cassia drew back, gazing down at her new soap. She cradled the bar in both hands as if the design of yellow flowers on the wrapper were as fragile as real blossoms. "I am sorry. I have brought you nothing."

"Isn't it more appropriate for a guest to offer his hostess a gift to thank her for her generosity?"

Somewhere behind him, the underbrush rustled, preempting whatever comment she might have made. Her gaze shot toward the sound.

"A badger," Lio reassured her without looking that way. "She's dragging fresh nesting materials into her den to keep her two cubs clean and warm."

Now Cassia was looking at him. "How can you tell?"

"It seems we've finally returned to your questions about Hesperine life, and I'll have a chance to answer them properly. Shall we walk and talk?"

She gave him one of her level gazes that meant she was thinking. Debating, probably, what was safer: to sit by the familiar, neutral fountain, near where the mage had appeared the other night, or to wander the wild unknown of the grounds and present a moving target.

Lio would do whatever he must to reassure her it was safe to stay here awhile, with him. "You need not fear someone will find us. My senses would give us plenty of warning. As you have seen, I have the power to conceal us both, if you will be so kind as to stay near me."

She stood there for one awkward moment, turning slightly toward the center of the clearing. "Very well."

Lio extended an arm and started walking, so she might fall into step beside him. Knight imposed his bulk between them, and Lio found it necessary to put more distance between himself and Cassia than he had anticipated. They wandered past the fountain and into the trees on the other side.

"You grow cassia trees in Orthros?" she asked.

"Alas, it is too cold. We import the oils and spices made from the tree." Lio resisted the urge to tell her cassia tasted even better than it smelled.

"Import?" She blinked at him. "No one trades with Orthros."

"Tenebra and Cordium do not. In any case, cassia does not grow here. The tree must have a kinder clime in which to thrive." He studied her chapped hands that held the soap so gingerly. "The Empire is such a place. The Empress herself cultivates prize groves of cassia. Her gardeners have tended the same trees for thousands of years."

"You mean the Empire across the sea, which the Orders claim they once reached in bespelled ships? I thought all that was a tale they spun to impress foolish folk. They expect us to believe the cities are made of sunlight and the people's skin is burnt dark."

"The Empire is as real as the soap in your hands. It is a complex area of the world that comprises countless lands and peoples, each with their own language and traditions. Together, they have built cities out of the light of educated minds, effective governance, and a prosperous economy. There are people in the Empire of every color, for the same reason that here, some people have blue eyes and others have freckles."

She fingered the soap. "You must have actually met people from there."

"So have you. Master Healer Javed and Master Envoys Basir and Kumeta."

Her face lit up. "Now I understand."

"Many Hesperines begin their lives as mortals in the Empire," Lio explained. "'Orthros has two hearts,' in the words of Prometheus, one of Orthros's greatest heroes, who was of Imperial origin. Our kind came to be in Tenebra, but the Empire is no less our motherland. The Empress and my Queens keep our alliance strong."

"Favorable relations between humans and Hesperines," Cassia marveled with an expression of mock surprise. "The mages here would get their robes in a mighty twist if they knew."

"Guests from the Empire are a permanent community in Orthros. They visit for trade, education, or leisure and stay for months or years at a time."

"Humans living among Hesperines? Imagine that." Astonishment escaped Cassia's reserve, but no aversion.

"Our human guests may choose to provide for us with their blood. We honor their generosity with our hospitality, goods, knowledge, and all that Orthros has to offer. Often, our guests decide to stay."

"Forever?"

"It's the pie. We have the most delicious meatless mincemeat in the known world. Oh, and immortality is rather nice, too."

Her half grin seemed far more genuine than her laughter. "With so many people from the Empire happy to give you their blood or become Hesperines, you've no need to kidnap folk from Tenebra to feed on and force convert, do you?"

"Ah, the powerful magic of common sense."

"That's certainly not the kind of magic the Orders teach."

Lio guided them onto a deer trail he was wont to follow. Cassia accompanied him deeper into the woods without a glance backward.

She scuffed her slipper in the hoof print of a deer. "Speaking of magic… something occurs to me."

Lio caught himself looking at the dainty, threadbare toe of her shoe and removed his gaze before she caught him at it, too. "What's that?"

"Unlike badgers, deer don't come out at night."

"They will for me." Lio gave her his most innocent smile.

"Hm. Can you tell where they are and what they're doing, like the badger? Even when they're asleep?"

"Yes. I hear their hearts beating."

She was quiet for an instant. "I suppose you knew I was on my way here."

"And I was very glad for the warning. I would have hated for you to catch me before I'd had a chance to wash after dinner."

Amusement hummed in her veins. "So is it Hesperine magery that allows you to hear so well?"

"Not anymore than your eyes and ears and thoughts are magery. It is the Blood Union."

"The same Union that causes you to share the experiences of those from whom you drink?"

"Yes, and it also binds us to every living creature around us. It is through the Union that the Goddess teaches us. We live attuned to the lifeblood of others, so we may understand the world as they understand it. It is a way of knowing, which comes with the Gift."

She shot him a curious glance. "The Gift?"

She knew the Mercy, but not the Gift? "Hespera's Gift is what makes us what we are. That is our name for her blessing of immortality and the ability to survive on living blood, rather than dead flesh."

A small smile appeared on Cassia's face, and he did not miss the irony in her eyes. "Ah. So your Gift is what humans call your curse. Insatiable bloodlust, banishment from the sun, and eternal exile from the afterlife."

"Yes, that's right. It's quite terrible. I lament my pale complexion more and more with each passing night."

Her snort was definitely a chuckle in disguise. "But worst of all, you shan't be allowed to die gloriously in battle, so you may throw spears with Anthros for all eternity and be waited upon by willing maidens."

"That sounds rather unfair. Aren't there any willing knights serving in the afterlife?"

"Oh no, no knights to wait on me once I get there. I am expected to be a maiden, and willing. But perhaps I shall escape such an exalted destiny, compliments of my mother, for she was not a wife."

Lio refrained from making another jest. If he asked about her mother, would he push their Oath too far? Would Cassia begin to watch her words with him again?

Perhaps a careful, undemanding comment was worth the risk. "I haven't had the pleasure of meeting your mother."

"Me neither. She died."

Regret stung him. "I am so sorry."

Cassia shrugged.

That shrug was so foreign to Lio he knew not what to say. They walked several steps in silence. He could not imagine speaking so dismissively if he had lost his mother, even if he were not as close to her as he was. But then, he had never had to protect himself every waking moment, as Cassia did. Where he came from, an open display of grief was not a sign of vulnerability that could be exploited by an enemy.

Perhaps offering up more details about himself was the most tactful way to invite her to say more—and the only way to make her feel safe in doing so. Lio waited for her to pose another question.

"Did you have kin?" she asked. "Before you…received the Gift?"

"'Received the Gift?'" he said with appreciation. "Not, 'turned from the gods,' or 'transformed into the monstrous spawn of Hespera?'"

She peered up at him, leaning one way, then the other so she could see all sides of him. "No horns, wings, or other bestial features. You don't appear monstrous to me."

"My parents will be reassured to know that, thank you."

He was gratified—immensely so—to see curiosity on her face. Her mask was slipping.

"Your…human parents, or do you have…?" She trailed off.

"For those of us who become Hesperines as children, the ones who rescue us and give us the Gift are our parents. Take my cousin Telemakhos, for example. His is a classic story. Mak was born with a club foot and abandoned on a cliff as an infant. My aunt and uncle found him and brought him home to Orthros."

"Ah yes, the time-honored Tenebran practice of exposure, in which loving parents leave their children to freeze to death or be eaten by bears. If a child is born sickly, lame, out of wedlock, or to parents too poor to feed it, it is a sure sign from the gods they want the babe right back as a sacrifice."

Spoken like someone born out of wedlock herself. "I see I needn't mince words with you. At the Summit we struggle to address the issue without implying Tenebran traditions are barbaric or making our own appear so."

"So you really do transform abandoned children into Hesperines?"

"We cannot create life on our own, you understand…we do not conceive children, as mortals do. But we have the power to restore and preserve life as no mortal healers can. To do this for children is one of the greatest callings and greatest privileges of our kind. We call this the Solace, for we offer refuge and comfort to suffering children. But my mother once said to me the real reason for the name is that children are the solace of all Hesperines."

"What is it like, when you change them?"

"Hesperine parents nurture the child on blood, as humans nourish their own with milk and food."

Cassia did not follow with another question this time. Lio clasped his hands behind his back. Was he about to discover her limits? It was not an easy thing for most mortals to consider. But he would not present his people as anything other than what they were. Especially not to her.

"Admittedly, these children do not have a choice," he said. "But many are so far gone by the time we rescue them, only Hesperine blood has enough healing power to save them. Although we make such a vital decision for them, and they have no opportunity to consent, I must believe the succor we give them is preferable to starvation, illness from the elements, or violence by wild animals."

"Choice?" Cassia shrugged again. "I never had a choice to be born a king's daughter, nor Knight here to be born a hound. What does it signify, choice?"

It seemed her observation saddened him a great deal more than it did her. "Every person's Will is sacred. It is forbidden for any Hesperine to take the blood of another living creature without their consent."

Another moment of silence. Then, "Yet you transform children. Doesn't that require that you drink from them?"

"What? No!" Before he knew it, he had halted in his tracks. Did she actually believe that? Perhaps he should have been more prepared for the question, but it made his stomach turn. "Parents only *give* blood. To... drink...from a child. That's repulsive."

"I see."

He saw the shading in her cheeks and realized it was she who felt uncertain now. "It's understandable you wouldn't know. But none of us would ever take the Drink from someone so young and helpless. The very idea goes against everything that is Hesperine. It's hard for me to imagine anyone would think that of us."

"Tenebrans don't know what is Hesperine. They only know what they fear."

He remembered he was still standing there and started moving again. There remained such gaps in her knowledge of his people, more than he had assumed there to be after she had called the Mercy by name. And yet here she was, willing to listen. To take a risk. That only made him more determined to find out why. "You often seem to know what is and is not Hesperine."

"That's because I know better than to trust what I hear."

If that were the reason, every mistrustful courtier in the palace would be a potential ally. No, there was certainly more to it than that. Lio resisted his desire to ask her directly. If he appeared too curious, she would feel threatened.

"Since humans from the Empire are not frightened of you," Cassia said, "they must drop their unwanted babes on Orthros's doorstep all the time. But I suppose you have no trouble feeding them all."

"Actually, exposure is not practiced in the Empire, and extended families or Imperial institutions provide for orphans. Most children in Orthros are of Tenebran origin, and most humans who choose the Gift as adults are from the Empire. Of course, we are always happy to offer Sanctuary to adults from Tenebra, too. You might be surprised there are people from this part of the world who are willing to brave Orthros for the hope of a different life."

"Rather than endure the fate their fellow humans have in store for them here? No, I should not wonder."

"Every life the mortal world casts aside is a treasure to us. All can come to Orthros for a second chance. We are Hespera's Sanctuary in the world, and it is a matter of sacred principle that we never deny anyone, just as she never denies us."

"So how did you come to be a Hesperine?" Cassia asked. "How old were you when you received the Gift?"

He had promised her honesty. Now was not the time to dither. But he found himself doing precisely that. "If we are talking about life in Orthros in general, my case would hardly be a good example."

"Oh? In what way are you such an exception?"

She was asking him to push her still farther from what was comfortable for her. He did not want his own family history to be what finally drove her too far…perhaps even away from him. If he was finally to witness her disgust, he would hate for it to be directed at him.

She cleared her throat. "Ah. Perhaps it is painful for you to speak of. I beg your pardon."

"No, far from it. It is the best thing that could have happened to me. My father rescued my mother and me from her husband and gave us both the Gift." He paused, listening again to Cassia's silence, and realized how confusing that must sound to her.

"You do not think of your mother's husband as your father?"

"No. I have only one father, Apollon."

"Her husband…sired you…but your father gave you the Gift."

"Yes."

"Do you remember him? Your mother's husband."

Lio looked ahead into the forest's welcoming dark, but that was cowardly. He met Cassia's gaze. "No. My mother, Komnena, was with child when my father transformed her."

"Ohh." Cassia turned toward him, walking a bit sideways as if the better to observe him. "So the tales are true, and Hesperine males do kidnap pregnant women to increase their numbers." She looked him up and down again, her gaze teasing. "You are one of their unnatural brood."

Lio laughed with relief. She hadn't screamed at him in horror or even insulted his mother with accusations of adultery. She mocked her people's ghastly legends. "We hardly make a habit of it. I'm the first in a long time to be born Hesperine."

"Do your people view that favorably?"

A question that would occur to her to ask, after a lifetime of dealing with the consequences of her birth. "Hesperines love all their children with all their hearts. It makes no difference if we are foundlings like my cousin or bloodborn like me."

"Yet you admit you are not a typical case."

"Well, the seven bloodborn who came before me have the gratitude of all our people, but I think it only right that I hold myself particularly bound to them in gratitude. They are legendary for their deeds, especially Prometheus. I am thankful to have such an inspiring example to guide me."

"You are the eighth bloodborn in Orthros's history? Eight is the number of Hespera, which is considered ill-fated here. I am sure among your people, it is a sacred number."

"Yes, a symbol of eternity." He pulled a face at Cassia. "What's more, I was born on the Winter Solstice, both the moons were full, and some very meaningful constellations were in portentous positions."

"No expectations, then."

"None at all."

Cassia glanced up between the trees at a patch of overcast sky. "It makes sense astrology would be important to your people, as you spend all your lives gazing at the night sky."

"We love Hespera's sky like nothing else." Lio followed Cassia's gaze to the hazy cloud cover. At the moment, he could read none of the weighty messages the Goddess had written him in the stars since the moment he had arrived in her world.

Cassia gazed at him again, as if trying to read portents on his face. "So you were born a Hesperine in Orthros. You really aren't Tenebran at all and never were."

"No, but both my parents spent their human years here before they became Hesperines. For the record, Father didn't kidnap Mother. She was delighted to run away with him."

"Her husband was a cruel man?"

"He committed the cruelty of neglect, an abuse second only to the misery he put her through when he bothered to come home. My mother has often said he broke their vows first. The eternal vows that bind her and my father now are far more powerful than mere marriage. I intend no offense against a cherished human institution," he added.

"It is neither mine nor particularly cherished by me. There is no such thing in Orthros?"

"No, Hesperines do not marry. We avow one another, and a Hesperine's partner is not a spouse, but a Grace." There. That did not qualify as revealing too much. He guided the conversation in a different direction. "I gather you are not fond of the idea of marriage."

"Its lack was a great inconvenience to my mother, yet the threat of it is a great inconvenience to me. With or without it, it seems but a bane to women."

"Not fond of your suitors either, I take it." Suitors. The word felt foul in his mouth. As foul as the covetous lords who thought to take on the role and the way they had noticed her at the banquet.

"I'm about as fond of them as I suspect your mother was of her potential husbands. Did she say why she married him? What made him easier to handle than the other possibilities?"

"That's...quite like what she described to me." Lio winced. "Her other option was a man who became violent when he drank, so she chose the one who merely became lustful in his cups."

Cassia nodded. "Wise woman."

"I asked her why she married any of them."

"How else would she survive?"

"That is what she told me."

Cassia looked straight ahead, a line between her brows. What did she make of all this? Lio tried to guess. She was above all practical. She would regard his mother's decision to leave with his father as a strategic exit from a bad situation to an improved one. A clever move for her own survival and that of her child. But did Cassia, anywhere in her thoughts, ponder the magnitude of his mother's escape? The magnitude of love and freedom?

Was there no such escape for Cassia?

He thought he already knew the answer to that question, and it made everything they said and did here suddenly feel confining and aimless. The tide could turn at the negotiation table. The Oath could be sworn. Peace could be won.

And Cassia would still be here, hemmed in on all sides by these same men, fighting this same war. There would be no peace for her.

"Must you marry?" he asked.

"It remains to be seen."

Perhaps he was wrong, and there was still hope. "It would naturally be a pressing question for you, in your position."

"It is useful to the king to have an unmarried daughter, such as she is. The promise of her hand is a powerful incentive in some eyes. Offering or refusing to give her in marriage is a means of influencing interested lords. But once she is married, she is no longer useful in this way. He will not grant her hand unless the benefits of the marriage outweigh the usefulness of the promise of marriage. Just as he will not banish or execute me until the benefits of ridding himself of me outweigh the usefulness of my continued existence. But I am already one-and-twenty, seven years overdue for marriage and well on my way to becoming an old maid. Perhaps I shall ride out my eligible years yet. There." She gestured with one hand in invitation. "I have explained human marriage negotiations. Now tell me of the Hesperine alternative."

Was it his unsatisfied belly that made her calm words so hard to stomach? No. He could not blame his failure to control his outrage on thirst unabated by deer. Only on reality.

"Come now," she urged him. "I withstood your tales of infants suckled on blood. I'm sure I can handle Hesperine mating rituals."

"I will tell you how different our ways are, but I regret that is a tale for another time." Lio came to a halt and turned to face her. The smell of the forest was changing, and the night sky had turned from one shade of darkness to another. He lifted a finger toward the eastern horizon.

"It still looks quite dark to me," she said.

A sign she wanted him to stay? He tried to recapture their banter. "My monstrous senses say otherwise."

That won back her small, amused smile. "Is the sun really harmful to you?"

He snorted. "No. Sorry to disappoint the mages. Anthros's holy light doesn't burn at all."

"Then why the hurry to return before dawn?"

"First, because my uncle insists on punctuality. Second, because… well, as soon as the sun comes up, I can't stay awake." As if on cue, a jaw-cracking yawn overtook him. He smothered it behind a hand.

"One of the members of the embassy is your uncle?"

"Yes, my father's brother. Uncle Argyros didn't kidnap Aunt Lyta, either, by the way. She told him she wanted the Gift."

"Bloodborn and the nephew of the Queens' Master Ambassador and his lady." Cassia's gaze sharpened. "And you say you're just an initiate?"

She was all too perceptive. And clearly less ignorant of political developments than she might like others to believe.

"I am indeed a mere initiate, and I count myself extraordinarily fortunate Argyros himself is my mentor. I endeavor to be worthy of him. Which is why I really must return to the fortress. I shall tell you more about the members of our embassy," he promised. "Next time."

"Well then. I shall bid you good morning, Lio. Rest well. For I shall exhaust you with more questions on the morrow."

28

days until

SPRING EQUINOX

THREADS

ASSIA DRANK HER WINE slowly, letting the heady, spiced vintage warm her. She judged that she had half of her drink left, to match the half of Lady Hadrian's gathering still to come. More than one goblet would appear excessive for someone in Cassia's position.

A flagon of this in her own room before bed would serve her well. She ought to sleep while she waited to hear Perita take her noisy leave. But during the past eight nights that Cassia had continued to meet with Lio, she never could seem to find rest before she slipped out to the grounds. Nor after they spoke, for that matter, if she got back to her rooms with any time to spare before dawn.

Lio's revelations were well worth the lost sleep. The extraordinary details he shared about his world were beyond Tenebrans' wildest imaginings, because they were the opposite of everything Tenebrans imagined about Hesperines.

Even so, this exhaustion setting in upon Cassia was cause for concern. She could not afford to be less alert. She made a point to pay attention now.

Lady Hadrian's loom clacked and whisked, and her tapestry took shape as she and the young women she had gathered about her wove a conversation with their voices. They decorated here and there with laughter at each other's jests. Cassia watched for loose threads: evaded questions or bitter gazes that came out only when the others weren't looking.

Cassia's function was to sit and be a grateful recipient of generosity and, fortunately, not to assist in the construction of the masterpiece Lady Hadrian had been working on all year. It was the duty of the free lords' untarnished daughters to praise the design, make suggestions as to colors, or hand threads to the lady. Confident in his purpose, Knight sat poised and quiet beside Cassia's chair and shed on Lady Hadrian's rug. There was no one with whom Cassia would rather sit and be ignored. She sipped her wine and listened.

"Oh, how I wish Aurelio would perform here!" Lady Biata moaned.

"Aurelio?" Lady Nivalis shook her head. "He would never come to Tenebra. He only performs for the most sophisticated courts in Cordium."

"Why should only vain, greedy princes get to hear his songs?" Lady Biata pouted. "Surely we fearless Tenebrans are worthier of the great Aurelio. If the *king* invited him…"

Lady Dalia sighed. "Nay, when you are the greatest living minstrel, you may refuse whomever you choose."

"They say his hair is as golden as his voice, and his face as beautiful as his songs." Lady Biata fanned herself with one hand, her third goblet of wine in the other.

"No, no, he is Cordian," Lady Dalia protested with a smile. "I am sure he has raven-black hair, burnished olive skin, and eyes so dark you could lose your way in them."

"He's probably ugly," Lady Nivalis declared, "and all the tales about his divine music a lot of Cordian exaggeration."

Lady Dalia's eyes sparkled. "Well, if he is as homely as a fencepost, no one gives it a thought. Not when his fingers are so nimble." She cleared her throat. "On the lute strings."

There came a titter of laughter and a few anxious glances at Lady Hadrian to see if she noticed or disapproved of the suggestive remarks.

Their hostess wove serenely on. "No one shall ever convince me a musician is more agile than a warrior. Only a man who is skilled with his sword can impress me."

Lady Hadrian's entourage let out a tide of delighted laughter, then gossiped thoroughly about the minstrel's exploits—musical ones, of course—and how they compared to those of beloved Tenebran tournament champions. The young women lauded the competitors loyal to Lord Hadrian's faction, while Lord Titus's supporters became targets for veiled insults regarding their manhood, or lack thereof. Only Lord Flavian was never mentioned, for no one could deny Lord Titus's son was the paragon of young Tenebran manhood, but nor could they exalt him in the Hadrian residence.

The ladies must do their part to carry on the oldest, bitterest feud in the history of Tenebran noble families, now that the lords could no longer perpetuate it by the sword. The king had succeeded in forcing the men off the battlefield, but he had yet to conquer the women's weaving rooms.

Cassia had observed time and again that Lady Hadrian caught the thread of every innuendo in her reach, whether about the size of a minstrel's flute or the size of a rival free lord's army. Why did she spend so much time on these weavers who were still learning to keep up with her? Lady Hadrian's position was secure; she could get what she wanted without coddling the daughters of her husband's supporters. She was not prone to vanity and did not require the flattery of younger women to know her own worth.

A tangle in the conversation made the laughter fade. All the good humor was gone from Lady Dalia's gaze. "Surely not, Bee. Please say it is only a rumor."

Now the focus of everyone's attention, Lady Biata drew herself up like a bird ready to preen. "Well, it is a rumor, but is it not one that should concern us? If frost fever has begun to afflict outlying villages in the east, then how long before it reaches us here?"

"It should indeed concern us. Rumors are often the only warning we get before the fever strikes." Lady Nivalis's hands knotted around the stem of her goblet. "We would have done well to heed them last time."

"We shall be better prepared if it ever happens again." Lady Dalia put a hand on Lady Nivalis's arm. "But I'm sure the illness will stay far away from us. No one need worry but the outlaws and beastmen who run wild in the east."

Lady Biata nodded. "Perhaps it is a blessing to rid us of the unholy."

"Or just a lot of heartless gossip." Lady Nivalis looked away.

How many younger siblings had she had? Three, Cassia recalled, all under the age of ten. Until the last outbreak of the fever.

Lady Hadrian observed this exchange, lips pursed, her fingers never wavering in their guidance of the weft. "Let us either lay this terrible rumor to rest or establish its credence. If we can do neither, let us speak no more of such a painful subject." Her head turned slightly, and Cassia realized their hostess's gaze was upon her. "Lady Cassia, I know you can assist us in this. Perhaps the mages of Kyria have word from their sisters in remote areas. Have they given any indication they fear an epidemic may be encroaching on us?"

"They have said nothing about an outbreak of frost fever, my lady," Cassia lied.

"Perhaps they would not speak of it, to avoid creating panic," Lady Biata said to Lady Hadrian.

"Naturally the mages would seek to protect us," Lady Hadrian soothed. "They would not speak of it hastily, but they would act well ahead of time to be prepared for such a threat. Lady Cassia, have the temple mages harvested a winter crop of rimelace? Or made medicine from any stores they might have from previous years?"

No untruth required this time. "No, my lady."

"There now." Lady Hadrian's smile returned, creasing its customary paths around her lips and eyes. "Lady Cassia devotes her time to the goddess in the mages' gardens nearly every day. She would know if anything was amiss. Thank you, my dear."

"I am happy to reassure you."

"Oh, your wine grows cool," Lady Hadrian surmised, turning her smile on one of her handmaidens. "Minica, such good news warrants a full glass."

Cassia spent the rest of the afternoon draining her goblet and hoping she would be awake enough to go out again that night. She was sure she missed a few implications that would have been as useful to her as her knowledge of the seamstress's son. Cassia really must not become careless.

Lio presented a great inconvenience, robbing her of sleep and distracting her thoughts. But the words he gave her each night were worth even more than those spoken to the rhythm of the loom.

HESPERA'S ROSE

THE WEATHER COULD NOT make up its mind. Waiting by the Font, Cassia kept tugging her cloak about her against a sudden drizzle, then pushing it open again when the rain let up. Would that she could be as unbothered as Knight, who sat calmly beside her and gave no indication he minded the drops that clung to his outer coat.

She would get the information from Lio. He could give her an answer for the mages of Kyria. It would be just like reading lips at dawn rites or listening for useful gossip at Lady Hadrian's gathering.

Except that it had to do with the king's politics.

Cassia's sense of unease grew by the moment. It was unlike Lio to take so long to appear. But that might be no reason for concern. Perhaps he simply hadn't gotten away from his uncle as quickly tonight. He would come, and she would ask him the mages' question, for she could not go into her next conversation with the Prisma unequipped. What was one quick question about the Summit, just a simple yes or no? That hardly signified she took an interest in royal affairs.

Cassia peered past the edge of the clearing, trying to see in the intermittent moonlight. Where was Lio? He *would* come, for he must drink, and when he drank, he would know she was here.

He might even now be breaking his fast somewhere in the woods. Cassia shifted on her feet, pulling her cloak close again. What was it really like when he took his nightly draught? She needn't waste time imagining the deed bore any resemblance to the nasty stories Tenebrans told. Instead the memory came to her of Lio sitting poised and mannerly at table by candlelight, drinking Solorum's finest vintage. She had observed him as he had lifted the goblet in one of his long-fingered hands, had seen the rim of it touch his lips, had watched his throat move as he swallowed… She could envision him doing just that, when the dark red liquid he sipped was not wine.

Was it dangerous to interrupt a Hesperine in the midst of the Drink? She was confident in her assessment of his intentions. That did not change the fact that his kind were powerful. Power, when approached without caution, was always dangerous.

"Good evening!" Lio sounded like a young courtier hailing a lady in good cheer before a dance.

She turned to find him loping toward her through the trees. "What's this? I see you approaching on your own two feet. No sudden and magical appearance this time?"

He came to a halt before her. A courtier might be winded. Lio was not. In fact, he did not appear to be breathing, until he did so to speak. "I walked up to you those times as well. You just didn't see me."

"I thought for certain you whisked yourself about, moving on magic in an eyeblink."

He held out an arm ahead of them. "Walk with me?"

Cassia set out into the trees, and Knight took his customary place between her and Lio. The way the Hesperine prowled beside them made him appear restless. How strange for his usual poise to falter. His graceful body betrayed he wished to be on the move, so Cassia set a brisk pace.

Even so, he had to shorten his stride to match hers. "We can use our power to assist in getting from one place to another, although I wouldn't necessarily describe it as a blink. It's more like…" He held up a finger. With his other hand, he reached into a pocket of his robe and pulled out a sizable white handkerchief.

Whyever would someone who did not sweat, sneeze, or relieve himself need a handkerchief?

Oh. Was it messy when they drank?

She eyed it as he unfolded it. Snowy and clean, with a black geometric design embroidered on it. No red stains.

He came to a halt and turned to her. "Hold out both your hands?"

She stopped before Lio, and Knight sat down on her feet. "Shall I reassure Knight this will be like the soap?"

"Yes, please. I should hate to see the state of my silk handkerchief if he deemed it a threat to you."

"*Hamaa.*" She rubbed the toe of her slipper against Knight's furry flank. Grumbling, he shifted himself to lean against the side of her leg instead. She held out her hands in the open space between her and Lio.

If her dog's proximity made Lio anxious, he gave no sign this time. As he draped the handkerchief across her open palms, the motion of his hands was relaxed, as if they did this all the time.

He smoothed the handkerchief over the contours of her hands, and she almost started. Knight tensed against her.

Lio's skin was warm. She felt his body heat through the cloth, as surely as she would a human's. The tales of Hesperines as cold as the grave were all lies.

She gazed down at his hands where he touched the handkerchief upon her palms. She caught herself staring. But she ought to make note of the embroidery, she told herself. It might be significant. It appeared to be a stylized flower of some kind, with a round center surrounded by five lobed petals and five sharp points like thorns.

Lio tapped one point with his finger, then touched the end of a thorn on the opposite side of the flower. "When we use our power to travel, it is not as if we fly about." Now he traced from the tip of the first thorn, all the way across the flower to the opposite point, following the lines of black thread. His finger left a trail of warmth over her palms. "It is more like we ease our own passage. We simply step."

"I wish I understood," Cassia said.

"You already do. You're just overthinking it."

She felt as if she were not thinking clearly at all. "It is very subtle, your magery."

"That is because we work with the world, not against it as the mages of Anthros do. To perform traversals, mortal mages must be as birds in a storm, heaving their rain-laden wings to stay aloft on turbulent winds. Hesperines, when they step, are like fish in a river, swimming with the water's natural current. We enjoy the world. In Orthros, I run on foot every night when I awaken, without using magic. When you go too directly from one place to another, you miss everything in between."

Cassia could think of some shit-filled courtyards at Solorum she would gladly miss. But she suspected that was not his point. She held the hand-kerchief closer to him to give it back.

He didn't take it. "Do you recognize the emblem on it?"

"No. What kind of flower is it?"

"Have you never seen a rose?"

"Oh!" She looked at it again. "It doesn't deserve what they call it here."

"I'm afraid to ask."

She made a face. "Harlot's kiss."

Lio sighed. "They would give such a name to my Goddess's sacred flower. Is it true mages uproot them whenever they're found in Tenebra?"

"I'm afraid so. No one grows them, for that would be heresy. None of the gardeners I've met in palaces or temples even remember what they look like. I've never seen a depiction of one. Until now."

"This is a beloved symbol in Orthros—Hespera's Rose. It appears everywhere, from handkerchiefs to illuminated texts. I'm partial to seeing the design in windows, but I must admit my bias as a glazier."

"Glazier? But you are a diplomat, not a craftsman."

"Every Hesperine must learn four things: a service, a craft, magic, and Ritual."

"What a demanding education."

"Life is best filled with purpose, rather than left to become aimless. Even with four areas of study, many Hesperines find themselves looking for enough to do. We have quite a bit of time on our hands, you see." His smile was halfway to a grin.

If not for his lengthy canines, Cassia wouldn't have believed the blithe youth before her could be speaking of immortality. Hesperines lived forever. Lio was a Hesperine. That knowledge usually hovered in the shadows of her thoughts along with every other Hesperine mystery, vast as darkness itself and just as impossible to grasp. What they spoke of now brought it into the light. The fact was, the person she passed each night with in conversation would live forever.

She had learned a great deal about him, and yet there was still so much of Lio she could not fathom.

"I know of your service to your people as a diplomat. Your craft is glassmaking?"

He nodded, but did not elaborate.

She could see she would have to prod him, as usual, if she was to discover anything more. His self-effacing tendencies were quite the obstacle. He would gladly tell her about his people from dusk to dawn, but when it came to his own affairs, he was in his own way nearly as reticent as she to keep their Oath.

He did not talk like someone whose people had spoken grand prophecies over his head since birth. She might have believed his modesty a diplomatic affectation, except that it was so much work to make him talk about himself.

"Yours is a very exclusive craft," she said. "Glass is so expensive, and the truly fine pieces are rarities treasured as heirlooms. I imagine it must be a challenge to work with."

"In Orthros you can hardly turn around without seeing a stained glass window. Hesperines love light and color, and glass is the perfect medium for both."

"You make stained glass windows?"

"I earned my initiation in my craft with a rose window in this design." He gestured to his handkerchief. Knight's gaze followed the motion of his hand. "But my Ritual mother embroidered this for me. I'm no good with thread."

"That makes two of us. What is a Ritual mother?"

"Ritual mothers or fathers attend our first Ritual after our Gifting and remain our trusted mentors who watch over us and offer us guidance. They are usually a relative, a close friend of the family or, for those given Sanctuary as adults, their Gifters. Mortals' temple parents are similar, I think. In Tenebra and Cordium, don't a temple mother and father accompany parents when they present their newborn to the gods for the first time, when the child is twice-seven days old?"

"What is Ritual? You said it is the fourth thing you must learn?"

"It is a sacred ceremony but also, in a broader sense, our beliefs. You can learn much of it from Hespera's Rose. Each part of the design has a specific symbolism."

Cassia spread the handkerchief out again, holding it in her open hands. "Show me."

Lio took a step closer.

It was just a step. But she felt all too aware of the space between them and how it was one step smaller. Of Knight's tension and stillness against her leg, which told her he accepted, however reluctantly, that she had issued Lio an invitation.

Lio pressed a finger to her hand again. His touch pricked her where one thorn grew from the rose. "The thorns are our most sacred duties, the five acts to which the Goddess calls us. You already know a great deal about those. We must show Mercy to those who suffer, give Solace to the lost, guard the sanctity of each person's Will, strive to live in Union with all, and offer the Gift to any."

Here it was, yet another perfect opportunity to return their rambling conversations to the subject that had prompted them all. The Mercy.

No, this was not the time, she told herself. She needed to wait a little longer. Know a little more. If he told her enough about Hesperines, the night might come when she found her own answers in his words, without ever having to ask.

If she were to succeed, she must spend her carefully accumulated opportunities wisely. Her own questions must come first, before she could consider the risk of any inquiry about the Summit for the mages of Kyria.

"And the petals?" Cassia asked.

Lio spread five fingers upon her hands, as if to part the folds of the flower captured forever in thread. "These represent what Hespera does for us, her greatest blessings. Ritual, through which she first gave us the Gift. The Gift, through which we overcome death. The Drink, through which we can thrive without the death of others. Sanctuary, the Goddess's realm, where we go if death does find us, and which we strive to realize in the world. And Grace…through which we experience abundance. The center of the flower, here, represents Hespera herself, who binds us together, from whom everything grows."

"I thought you said the Gift was a thorn, not a blessing."

"It is both." Lio's touch lingered on the handkerchief for a moment before he withdrew his fingers.

Only to wrap both his hands around hers. Cassia stood very still.

Lio folded her fingers around the handkerchief. "No one in Tenebra would recognize this symbol, nor even a living rose."

"No."

"In that case, it will be no danger if you keep it." His smile, never absent for long, now reappeared in full force. "The fabric resists moisture. It's perfect to wrap soap in once the paper is torn off."

Cassia withdrew her hands and busied them folding the handkerchief, buying time to think. Was there any polite way to refuse this second gift? No need for him to know she had yet to unwrap the soap. Besides, who would tear paper so fine and expensive? Surely it was not to be discarded.

Lio folded his hands behind his back. "Forgive me. Perhaps I am not sensitive enough to how different that flower's meaning is here. I meant no offense."

She glanced up at him quickly. "None taken. Why should your sacred symbol offend me?"

He relaxed, which seemed to bring him a little nearer to her again. "Why indeed? There is no shame in a kiss."

Just the sort of thing a man would say. Usually when he was trying to get said kiss. It was a good thing Lio was a Hesperine, not a man, and that he had none of the seductive powers the tales claimed his kind possessed. "I would think the reference to harlots would offend you."

"And why should it? Women are far more sacred to Hespera than flowers."

Cassia focused her attention on her gardening satchel, tucking the handkerchief inside next to her spade. "You'd best not let anyone hear you say harlots are sacred to Hespera. That will hardly advance your cause, Initiate Ambassador."

"I will tell anyone who will listen the Goddess cherishes all women. Harlots and queens. Concubines and their daughters."

Now she had heard everything. A goddess who thought well of her and her mother. Cassia opened her mouth. But the retort did not come. She could not bring herself to aim it at the earnest eyes looking down at her.

"Thank you," she said, resting her hand on her satchel. Then she pinned her gaze on her feet. The underbrush might trip her. She started walking again, and Knight heeled.

Lio fell into step with her, and for the first time, she walked beside him.

AFFINITY

CASSIA COULD BARELY SEE the impressions in the underbrush that marked their path. The clouds had drawn near again, and the air felt wet with the rain they had yet to release. She clutched her skirts in both hands, wary of stumbling. In a moment, the muddy hem of her gardening dress became easier to make out against the darker ground. The wavering shape at the edge of her vision resolved into Lio's black silk robe, bordered in thick red-and-white embroidery shot through with real silver. She blinked, but the colors only became clearer. She snapped her gaze up to see where the light was coming from.

She closed her lips on a gasp. A soft white glow spilled from between Lio's fingers.

He gave her no chance to protest. "No one will see it, even if they do happen to wander out of their way, this far into the woods. Just like no one saw me talking to you in the great hall the night of the prince's temple day."

"I dare say you can make folk see or not see whatever you wish." Cassia had witnessed plenty of ostentatious magery in the temple. But nothing like Lio's simple spell. It looked as if he held a bit of the stars in his hand. "You're a light mage."

"That is in fact the magic that comprises one of my areas of study."

"Not just conjuring bright baubles," she said with certainty, "but also sophisticated illusions."

"Very handy when I'm trying to have an uninterrupted conversation with a lady at a dance."

He did not deny he possessed powers that could give a mortal cause to doubt the evidence of her senses. Such a revelation would have put Cassia on the alert if he were anyone but a Hesperine. Even when such power was used under the auspices of the Order of Hypnos, it frightened people. Folk usually gave a wide berth to mages devoted to the god of death and dreams, both the necromancers and the illusionists, but especially the most feared of all: thelemancers. Mind mages had the power to read and manipulate your innermost thoughts, to subdue your will and command you to do their bidding.

But Cassia was not most folk, and the illusionist beside her was anything but an Ordered mage. She continued down the path with Lio. "Amachos's poor apprentice would be jealous of how your spell light puts his to shame."

"Strange, isn't it? He and I can achieve similar results, although our powers are of such different natures. This spell light is blood magic, the very heresy his Order despises."

Cassia caught sight of the blood on the tip of Lio's thumb. He must have pricked himself to work his magic. "Summoning light seems a very Hesperine sort of thing to be able to do."

"Very few humans would arrive at that conclusion." He smiled at her. "But light magic is an essential Hesperine affinity. It was one of the arcane paths taught long ago in the Great Temples of Hespera."

"Affinity? Arcane? I've no idea what you mean. You mustn't let my service in the Temple of Kyria fool you—I am very ignorant."

"Of course. Just as you are not a philosopher." He tossed his hand, and the light drifted up to hover over their heads. "An arcane path is what the Mage Orders refer to as a discipline of magic. They like to draw lines between things, but in truth, all varieties of spellwork are paths into the same whole—magic. Your affinity is simply the kind of magic you're good at. It is the same as with any other skill. Anyone can learn to garden, but it may be an ordeal for them, and many of their plants may die before they see a single bloom. You, on the other hand, have a green thumb."

"Well, Hypnos's season has yet to wither my perennials beyond hope, if that's what you mean. It's nothing like your red thumb, I'm sure."

A smear of light appeared on Lio's thumb, and the blood was gone. "You take to it naturally, and you excel at it intuitively, although study or experience will improve your results."

"Not just anyone can learn any type of magic," she protested. "You're born with it, or you're not."

"Is that so?" he asked.

"Of course. That's why the mages keep those with aptitude in the temples and forbid everyone else from using magic. It would be dangerous otherwise."

"Dangerous for whom?"

"Well. That does fill my head with new and seditious thoughts."

"Be careful, fair lady. I may yet corrupt you with my heretical ideas."

"I fear there is no work left for you to do upon me. I was corrupted from the first moment I drew breath."

"In that case, we are two of a kind."

Hardly. His people had celebrated his birth under auspicious stars. "Not a fair comparison. You don't have to breathe."

He laughed. "But I enjoy breathing. How else would I speak with you?"

Cassia bent double to snatch up a branch at her feet, feeling the blood rush to her cheeks. Straightening, she tapped Knight on the shoulder, then hurled the stick ahead.

As he bounded between them, Lio slid out of his way. "I hope I am never the object of his chase."

Actually, Lio was right. At least while they were both in Tenebra, a concubine's bastard and a bloodborn Hesperine were on equal footing. "As I've said before, Knight will never go after you. He only hunts the enemy."

"I rejoice to hear it." Lio smiled down at her again. "I wouldn't like to find out if I can outrun him."

"You continue your habit of running here?" What must that look like, a Hesperine pushing his body to the limit, racing like the athletes before the war games?

"As time allows, yes."

"I cannot help but wonder why you would require such pursuits. I doubt you even need to train to maintain your..." Cassia almost cast a glance up and down Lio's body, but stopped herself from indulging the odd and inexplicable urge. He didn't need her to remind him how the Gift benefited him. "...your skills."

He gave her an amused glance she found even more inexplicable. "The

Gift keeps a Hesperine's body at his or her personal peak of health, but within that optimal range, our bodies do respond to our habits."

"Are athletics popular among Hesperines, then?"

"There is no art my people do not love, and that includes the art of the body. Running is what I enjoy most. But it is my cousin Telemakhos and my dear friend Lysandros who spend every spare hour in the gymnasium."

"How glad your cousin must be that the Gift has ensured his club foot is no longer an obstacle for him."

"With proper care, such conditions need not be obstacles for anyone. Do you know, that's why those of us who are Gifted as children are so much taller than humans or Hesperines who reached adulthood as mortals."

"I thought that must have something to do with your magic."

"No, only with proper nutrition and a safe, healthy upbringing. Tenebrans would be taller if they did not face such harsh conditions here."

She tilted her head back so she could look into his face. "I find it hard to imagine any Tenebran man achieving your stature."

The mysterious warmth appeared in his gaze again, something between humor and pleasure. It gave her the impression he took her statement as a compliment.

"It's a side effect of being bloodborn. I'm even taller than usual for a Hesperine—the tallest among all our people, in fact. It's a good thing, too, for I need all the advantage I can get against my much more athletic cousins."

Cassia returned to the more manageable topic of Lio's family. "I am curious why Telemakhos did not accompany his parents, as his sister Arkadia did."

"He and Lyros are guarding Orthros's borders."

"They are guards?"

"Initiate Stewards in Hippolyta's Stand. Aunt Lyta and her Stand serve as the Stewards of the Queen's ward, the magic that protects our borders. Kadi is the Master Steward and her second-in-command."

"That explains Master Arkadia's military bearing."

"I see you are not one to let appearances fool you. She and Aunt Lyta train equally hard, although they are naturally different shapes. Kadi is one of the greatest warriors in Orthros's history."

"Orthros is ruled by Queens. I should not wonder that females can also be warriors there."

"Indeed, any Hesperine may choose any life path, based on skill and desire. But few desire to pursue the path of war. Our people strive to avoid violence at all costs. Aunt Lyta and her children are the only ones who devote themselves to the preservation of the Hesperine fighting arts, and Lyros is one of the few who sought her training from outside her bloodline."

"Your aunt is...the leader of Orthros's army?"

"She is the Guardian of Orthros."

Cassia was silent for an instant. "Not the legendary warrioress from those hateful marching songs."

"She rather likes those songs, to tell you the truth."

"Those old ballads must be as exaggerated as everything else about Hesperines."

"No, the songs of her deeds are all true."

"She is...shorter than I imagined."

Lio laughed.

Cassia found herself smiling. "The Guardian of Orthros is breathing down the necks of the most powerful men in Tenebra, and none of them have a clue."

"Aunt Lyta and Kadi accompanied the embassy as our protection. In their absence, Mak and Lyros are solely responsible for the defense of Orthros."

Had Lio just told her inside information about Orthros's defenses? He was very foolish after all. "Just the two of them?"

"It only takes two," Lio said with a sanguine smile.

Perhaps not so foolish. "They say Orthros is impregnable, and all those who have tried to enter have lost their way in the frigid mountains and died an excruciating death, driven mad by blizzard wraiths that pick their bones."

"We only do that to unpleasant people."

"Like mages?"

Lio didn't answer that.

"No one dares lay siege to Orthros," Cassia said. "Wars with Hesperines always occur on Tenebran soil. You are in very dangerous territory."

Lio put the back of his hand to his forehead in a dramatic gesture of distress. "I live in fear of a particularly ferocious liegehound who stalks me every night, for I did not heed my cousins' warnings that I should learn to defend myself."

Cassia pursed her lips, trying not to smile. "I have told you. I shall defend you."

"No, you have not told me that before." Lio's tone changed. Did he let his steps weave him a little closer to her, or did he seem so near simply because he was so tall? "With such a capable protector as you, Cassia, I feel very safe indeed."

Cassia had never heard him speak quite like this. Surprise sent an uncomfortable flush across her skin. To her astonishment, she found herself unable to interpret his tone of voice.

But she knew he was indeed unwise, if he took her banter about protecting him to heart. If he felt safe with her.

FREE WITH WORDS

FOR SOMEONE SO SKILLED at reading every minute cue in a person's movements and tone, Cassia was remarkably unaware Lio had just flirted with her.

He had debated the wisdom of speaking in such a way to her, but the lovely answer in her blood proved well worth the risk. This could become…addictive. Saying something that embarrassed her, making her blush, listening to her blood and the pounding of her heart.

His own blood pumped in his veins, awakened but unsatisfied. It was a good thing he had lingered over the deer so long tonight.

Cassia looked away, calling to Knight. The dog loped toward them again with the stick trapped in his jaws, and Lio reluctantly moved aside. Making over her dog, Cassia took hold of Knight's prize by the end with no drool on it. She threw the stick ahead into the darkness beyond the reach of the spell light.

In the hound's absence, Lio once more eased closer to Cassia on the path. How could she miss it? She knew dalliance when she saw it. But perhaps the courting she received had only taught her to watch for deceit, not to recognize sincere interest. Lio—a Hesperine, an ally, a genuine admirer—was far outside the paradigm in which she strove to survive. It seemed she did not know what to make of him.

She changed the subject. "The way you speak of your cousin Mak, it is clear the two of you are good friends."

"We are more like brothers than cousins."

"Brothers are not always friends."

Prince Caelum must have proved that to her on plenty of occasions.

Lio gentled his tone. "That's true. I feel very grateful that in our case, we are both friends and family. In fact, Mak and Lyros are my sworn Trial brothers. We went through the Trial of Initiation together to mark our passage into adulthood, along with our three other dearest friends."

As he and Cassia neared a ruin that had crumbled partway across the deer path, they slowed their pace. At the base of a stone slab that had long ago fallen on its side, Knight was digging and sniffing amid the rocks and dirt with great enthusiasm. His stick must have landed somewhere in the rubble.

Cassia propped herself against the fallen support. "Was your Trial of Initiation very long ago?"

Lio leaned against a slender tree that grew up through the fallen stones across from her. "I fear whatever air of mystery I still possess in your eyes shall not survive this conversation. My friends and I passed Trial only this Winter Solstice, shortly before I came to Tenebra. I'm quite green."

"That tells me very little, for I still do not know at what age Hesperine initiation takes place."

Lio slid his hands into the pockets of his robes. "We all wanted to be initiated together, so we waited until everyone was old enough."

"You are making me fish for my answers tonight, Initiate Ambassador. Before you ask, no, it shall not disturb me to learn you are old enough to be my ancestor."

Lio gave a laugh and hoped it didn't sound forced. Would it disappoint her that he was not as wondrously ancient as she might have imagined? "Guess again."

"Oh, we are playing a guessing game, are we?" She tapped her cheek with a finger in contemplation. "Very well. You are old enough to be a fallen god!"

"Definitely not. Anthros struck down Demergos and left Chera a widow long before I was born. More's the pity."

Cassia's gaze lit with curiosity. "You are old enough to have been an apprentice in a temple of Hespera before the mages of Anthros and Hypnos drove your cult from human lands."

"No, I am sorry to say. Very sorry indeed. I would love to have seen the Great Temple Epoch."

"Hmmm. You were at the first Equinox Summit and knocked back too many pints with the Mage King."

Lio shook his head, smiling. "Hesperines can't get drunk. And you know this is my first journey to Tenebra."

"But what if your first journey began centuries ago, and you have remained here all this time, hidden by your arcane affinity?" In the glow of his spell light, her eyes glinted with mischief. "You wandered the land during the Feuds of Regnum, when the Council failed to crown a king. While the free lords hacked away at each other for a century and trampled the fields into famine, you secretly helped the folk who suffered."

"That was true of many Hesperines at the time, but I was not among them."

The light in her eyes winked out. "You remember when Lucis Basileus did not rule Tenebra."

Lio's humor fled. "Yes. I do."

"Ah. Older than the king with whom you treat. And you shall outlast him."

"There is a vast world of which that is true, Cassia. Your people have a long and honorable history that dates back to a just king and queen, and I hold out hope the Tenebrae have a future brighter than Lucis's present."

"'Tenebrae?' Take care you do not say such a thing at the Summit."

"I know. No one breathes the word 'Tenebrae' in front of the king. No matter that this part of the world has always been called the Tenebrae, a plural."

"Indeed, our glorious king has unified the Tenebrae into a single mighty kingdom called Tenebra, in the singular. He has reforged the course of history and even the name his people have called their own lands for centuries. For the safety of the realm, be sure to drop the treasonous 'e.'"

Ah ha. There was Cassia's opinion on the king, hiding beneath her mocking recitation of his decrees.

Lio grimaced. "It's hard to believe the king considers one extra letter blatant resistance. He demands that centuries of loyalty to Hadria, Segetia, Otho, or Severitas to become loyalty to Tenebra overnight. But the fact remains, this so-called kingdom is really a collection of independent domains under the nominal rule of a king affirmed by the Council of Free Lords."

"It was," Cassia corrected, "until Lucis secured the affirmation, then took royal authority beyond all its traditional bounds and began calling himself Basileus like the Mage King himself."

"An offense to a great man from whom he does not descend," Lio dared say, hoping Cassia would continue to vent her perspective on her father's reign. "No matter how much Lucis postures, everyone knows he has no hereditary claim on the crown. The Mage King's line died out ages ago, and Lucis cannot claim descent from any of the dynasties that have held the throne since."

Cassia's voice became icier still. "He staked his claim not on the blood he carries in his veins, but on the blood he has spilled."

"As firsthand observers of his reign can surely attest."

Then came her shrug. "He is hardly the first free lord to make himself into a king with nothing but the sword."

Thorns. Lio had pressed her too far. Did she not realize it was safe to discuss treason with a heretic?

"Regardless of how his former equals appear to oblige him," Lio went on, "it would be too generous to say the free lords are convinced of his claim. Especially in the east, where there are only homesteads under the authority of the hold lords. The old name of the Tenebrae remains true there."

"You seem to know a great deal about that area," Cassia observed.

"There lies the bluff called the Hilt, the doorstep of the wilds, and beyond, nothing but treacherous rivers and impenetrable forests."

"Ah, yes, the Hilt. A traditional site for offering sacrifices to the gods. Heretics, for example, or unwanted children."

"Hesperines wouldn't know anything about that."

"Of course not."

He could not possibly explain to her how much more there was to it than that.

She had steered the subject back to Lio's people again. But the knot of wistfulness and anger he felt in her had all to do with the king.

Could Lio help untangle it? He put on a grin for her. "I must admit

I learned all I know of the Hilt secondhand, for I am much too young to venture into the wilds as a Hesperine errant to rescue mortals in distress. I'm only eighty-eight. The customary age for initiation is eighty, but of the six of us, I waited for the others the longest."

"*Only* eighty-eight."

"I told you I was young."

She crossed her arms. "You've barely grown your chin hairs."

Lio's grin turned into a real one. It was good to see her return to their teasing, even if it did come at his chin hairs' expense. "I'll have you know I grow a very fine beard. You just have to wait for it. It's merely a side effect of our bodies' natural pace. On the one hand, we mature slowly and ultimately cease aging. On the other hand..." He rubbed his chin. "It takes forever to grow a sunbound beard. It seems to stay at that itchy stage for an eternity. My father's been working on his since before I had teeth, and it's famous by now. Perhaps I shall eventually find the patience."

"Hesperines must take great pride in their hair once it does grow."

"Yes. I have friends back home who would be ferociously jealous of your mane." He let his gaze travel over her hair.

Her flush was pure music. He readied himself for a retort.

But she said nothing about his compliment. "Now I understand why none of the males in the embassy wear beards."

Cassia, without a clever reply? She was one of the strongest people he had ever met, but the one thing that made her falter was a hint of genuine praise. It took so little to put her so off balance. To touch her so thoroughly.

Lio was in a unique position. He was not a suitor, nor even a man. She was not hostile to any pretty words he spoke. He was one person who could give her compliments that did not feel like threats, manipulation, or attempts to control her. He could show her the pleasure of being noticed and appreciated.

Flirtation was only words, and words were the one thing they could exchange freely. Safely.

FORBIDDEN

CASSIA MIGHT BE WATCHING Knight dig in the ruins, but Lio sensed her attention elsewhere. Focused. Undivided. On him.

"So you Hesperine males have your own rites of passage, as our warriors do."

"Actually, all Hesperines must pass the same Trial to demonstrate our mastery of our Gift. The other three friends I mentioned are all female."

Knight pressed against Cassia's skirts, his tail waving like a battle standard as he held up the stick in his mouth. She rubbed the hound between his ears, smiling down at him despite the dirt he smeared on her skirts. Lio might have believed her semblance of playfulness if not for the keenness of her aura.

And the pointedness of her remark. "You have never mentioned any specific females at home in Orthros who are not your elders."

"Have I not?"

Cassia tossed the stick off into the night, and her hound bounded away again. The air around them suddenly seemed very quiet and fragrant of her.

"Tell me about your lady friends," she invited.

He could give her an idea how different it was for females like her in Orthros, without delving into subjects better left back home. "Eudokia is an initiate mathematician and smarter than any of us. She is already an accomplished scholar and calligrapher. Menodora, an initiate musician, not only sings and plays beautifully, but also crafts her own instruments. Xandra is an initiate sericulturalist who provides Orthros with one of our most prized goods—silk."

Now Cassia subjected him to a thorough scrutiny. Nothing gave him the impression her intent was suggestive, as his had been a moment ago when he had caressed her hair with his gaze. But the way she looked at him now had much the same effect him.

He looked back into her gardener's green-brown eyes and resisted the urge to show his true appreciation with a glance that would touch her up and down, from her freckled nose to her muddy hem.

He was quite hopeless. Was it *because* she was so forbidden? He had not thought himself to be that sort of fool, to run headfirst into what he knew would remain unrequited.

"You have a tell," she informed him.

"I beg your pardon?"

"A tell. A gesture a gambler makes whenever bluffing. Ladies may not frequent Hedon's halls, but we witness plenty of games of chance at court." She took a step away from the stone slab and held up her hands. Then she tucked them behind her back and stood up very straight. "You do this every time you lack confidence. Especially when you are about to say words of which you are unsure."

Now it was Lio who flushed. He realized he gripped his hands behind him even now, and he no longer lounged against the tree.

"You are very good," Cassia assured him. "The candidness of your expressions makes others feel they can trust you, while your body language gives nothing away. Except when you put your hands behind your back and draw yourself up."

Lio cleared his throat and slid his hands into his pockets again. "I shall endeavor to remember that at the negotiation table."

"I need not play another guessing game to discover which lady most regrets your absence. Your tell appeared when you said Xandra's name."

Thorns. Cassia had just given him a lesson in diplomacy, indeed. "She most certainly does not regret my absence."

"Ah. So the distance is not unwelcome to her. The question is, then, do you regret your absence from her?"

Lio wished Knight would choose that moment to return with the stick, but alas, it was a vain hope that a liegehound would come to his rescue. Cassia had effectively maneuvered the conversation from a discussion of his people to an interview about everything he had no desire whatsoever to talk about. He should have been more prepared. Hadn't he done the same thing to her often enough? "If I answer that question, you must tell me if I owe anyone an apology for monopolizing your evenings."

"That is not our agreement," she said primly. "We do not make exchanges. We ask and answer openly."

She had him. He could not expect her to uphold their Oath if he did not. And he had worked so hard to make her feel it was worthwhile and safe to speak with him like this. Was it really worth jeopardizing all the progress he had made with her because he was too embarrassed to discuss his romantic mistakes?

Lio bowed. "On my honor, you are right. Although I do hope you will answer my question openly, once I have answered yours."

His interrogator leaned against the ruin again, and the toes of her slippers peeked out from under her gown. "Do you miss her?"

Lio lifted his gaze from Cassia's small feet. Why did his mind choose this moment to wonder whether she had freckles on her toes as well? "I too find the distance quite welcome, I assure you."

"Well, I can certainly understand that. I frequently long for greater distances between myself and my suitors. But I confess, I find it hard to imagine what could possibly go wrong between a lady and you."

She regarded him likelier to succeed with a female than one of her suitors. What a compliment. "We discovered we were unsuited."

"Then it sounds as if it is for the best that you parted."

Lio breathed in the scent of Cassia's determination. She would have her answers out of him, one way or another. He had seldom been so thoroughly subjected to his own negotiation techniques, and never by a young mortal woman.

He could only conclude she was as voraciously curious about him as he was about her. Was that really cause for discomfort?

Lio strolled over to the stone pillar, bringing himself nearer to Cassia in body and Union. Her curiosity tickled his senses as he casually propped an elbow on the stone support. "It never once occurred to me it was for the best. But I think you are right."

"You must have cared for her very much."

Lio cast a glance out into the night, to the north. He grimaced. "I decided to avow her when I was about your age."

"Oh. Considering your explanations of how Hesperines mature, at age one-and-twenty, you must have been..."

"A child, yes."

"Well, it's not as if childhood betrothals are unheard of." She paused. "But sixty-seven years is a very long time to be betrothed to someone."

Lio snorted. "Yes. It is, isn't it? You would think I would realize, if we could endure such a long engagement, we might not be so eager for what was to come after."

A soft, hiccuping sound filled the silence. Cassia was laughing.

Before Lio knew it, he was laughing with her. He laughed over that single, disastrous night with Xandra when everything he had planned for their entire lives fell apart in a matter of hours. Over his years of youthful efforts to impress her. Most of all over his own blindness.

He should have realized long before. What he felt for her was not what he would feel for his Grace. That had not been hunger powerful enough to sustain them for eternity. It had not been the Craving.

He had made a mistake. But not the one he thought he had made. He should not have stubbornly persisted in such a misguided commitment, which had only burdened both of them.

But the end of that commitment was not the mistake.

He could not fight their natures or the nature of the Gift. No matter how thoroughly he had managed to convince himself he and Xandra were meant for each other, they were not. That was a fact.

Not a failure.

He wasn't what she needed. She...was not what he needed.

Lio rubbed his eyes and listened to Cassia catch her breath. Had he really regretted arriving in Tenebra unavowed? If he were Graced, he would not be standing here laughing with Cassia.

He stared at her. Her laughter quieted as if it had never been, and she pressed her lips tightly together. But not tight enough to hide her smile.

"I have never heard such a charming sound," he told her.

"What sound?"

"Your laughter."

"I see why they sent you as an ambassador. You've a gift for flattery."

"You wound me. I thought you knew by now I only speak with the utmost sincerity. You have a lovely laugh."

"It's not as if you haven't heard it before."

"No, I don't think I have."

Cassia waved a hand. "Do not waste your time regretting Xandra, Sir Diplomat. You are young, successful, and handsome. I am certain you will have plenty of more suitable opportunities."

Lio rubbed his mouth to wipe the grin off his face. Cassia had just evaluated him in the same tone of voice as she might describe the condition of a horse's teeth. But she had called him handsome.

He gave her his best bow. "I thank you for your vote of confidence, my lady. I take your opinion to heart."

Knight would choose *that* moment to impose himself on them again. But not between them. After the hound had received his lady's adoration, he lay down on her other side to gnaw on the stick.

"You never know," said Cassia. "Perhaps Eudokia or Menodora is merely waiting to take her chance when you return."

Smiling, Lio shook his head. "Kia and Nodora are my Trial sisters."

"Well, I'm sure there are plenty of other ladies in Orthros, and the dashing athletes Mak and Lyros will not lay claim to all of them before you return."

Lio burst out laughing again. "That is...not a concern."

"Ah, you're in luck. They're already Graced?"

"Thoroughly. At least one good thing happened after our Trial. We are considered rather young to make such a commitment, by Hesperine standards. But they did not let that deter them. They have known what they wanted since we were old enough to understand such things. We all hope to be like the two of them. They make it look effortless."

"You seem very happy for them."

"I am, with all my heart." Lio cleared his throat. "I could not imagine finer partners for my two dearest friends than each other."

He counted one, two, three beats of her heart before she sailed onward. "Forgive me. I should know better than to make uninformed assumptions."

"We do not forbid the same things in Orthros as are forbidden in Tenebra," he reminded her.

"You do not forbid what people will do anyway. In other words, you are not hypocrites."

"There was a time when we were not the only cult that blesses passion." Lio frowned. "I am familiar with the complex history that led to conflicting views. Our Goddess teaches us to practice compassion toward those who believe differently from us and to have patience with their search for truth. I do try to understand how the followers of Anthros have arrived at their ideas, although they violate my convictions."

"Tenebrans' beliefs are very simple to understand," Cassia said. "If you are a man, you may sheath your sword anywhere you please—as long as you are the one wielding the weapon, of course. But if you surrender to a warrior, it is off to the temples of Hedon with you. Man or woman, doesn't matter. If you lie down for the sword, you are unworthy of Anthros, and you'd best make yourself useful in service to Hedon, the god of pleasure and chance—oh, excuse me. The god of fertility and prosperity, I think the Order of Anthros calls him now."

Lio found it difficult to hear her commentary out. "I have read the mages of Anthros tolerate the temples of Hedon as a means of promoting order."

"Yes, they like everyone to keep their vices under the temple roof, where the mages can oversee them. Hedon has plenty of servants to assist in the endeavor. Once forsaken, if you wish to eat, you must earn your bread on your belly or your back."

And humans thought his people were perverse? "I am no stranger to the concept of sacred union, to be sure. Before the Order of Anthros enforced celibacy among all mages, pleasure was a part of worship in many cults. But to turn that ritual into a punishment…to force it on anyone…" Lio's hand tightened on the fallen pillar. "The mages of Anthros impose their cult on everyone else, their 'order' on everyone's lives, and use all other cults as a means to that end. They march over the many sacred practices and beliefs that once thrived, as if they wish to grind that wondrous variety to sand of a single color beneath their heels. They have no respect for anyone's Will but their god's, and as to what it is, we have only their word."

Spell light cast a sharp gleam in Cassia's gaze. "Oh, but the forsaken did have a choice, of course. They could have chosen to obey Anthros. It is perfectly honorable for a man to throw away his life on the end of a real sword in battle or for a woman to earn her bread on her back as a wife."

Lio found himself pulling away from the Union for the first time that night. If Cassia spoke any more bluntly, she would bruise him. But he should not shy away. He must listen. This was the reality she lived in, one his own Trial brothers might have endured as well, had they not been Hesperines. "Surely there are people here who find happiness and comfort in one another, despite the odds. Not all the people I encountered at the palace feast were unhappy in their partners."

"The Cult of Hedon is more predominant in Cordium than in Tenebra, I'll grant you. You won't find many pleasure temples here. Most often, a Tenebran warrior in need of a man to sharpen his sword keeps a favored retainer close at hand. Others prefer their concubines. Much to their wives' relief. Lady Elana encourages her husband to see his concubine as much as possible, so she and her handmaiden Lady Fidela may enjoy themselves without the man of the house around to interfere. Then there is Lady Caro, who uses her position as a widow to attract the very best liegemen to her service. Lady Caro is very smart and effective."

"It seems as if your rules are designed only to make you all miserable."

"They are not *my* rules. I was born in violation of them. My father's god has no use for a whore's bastard, so why should I have any use for him? When Anthros marches all of us who displease him to the pyre, I rejoice that I shall be among that company with you and your Trial brothers."

Lio stared at her. "I wish you could meet Mak and Lyros. They would appreciate you."

Her cheeks were flushed again. She pushed away from the ruin, and Lio rejoined her on the path. Knight moved with her, his stick left behind and tail still.

"Your turn," Lio said. "Do our midnight walks take you away from someone whose company is infinitely preferable to mine?"

"You did not pay attention during my lesson on what is forbidden in Tenebra. Conversing with a heretic is the extent of my secret life. Anything more would be imprudent in my position."

"As adept as you are with secrets? You are very smart and effective, Lady Cassia."

"I am not Lady Caro. I am Cassia Basilis."

Her name said it all. Why the strictures were different for her and ever more binding. But even as the king's daughter spoke of prudence, he had heard the concubine's daughter speak in anger, out of bitter experience. "Yet you have no use for Anthros's rules."

"I certainly don't. Nor do I have any use for activities that are not worth the risk."

Lio felt suddenly he was treading on dangerous ground indeed, not least because it would be presumptuous of him to question her choices on such a personal matter. But also because he felt furious.

He angered anew at the cult of Anthros, which robbed Cassia of such a vital part of who she was. It was sickening. Unnatural. For Cassia, one of the best parts of being alive was not worth the risk. Her own nature was too dangerous for her to experience. As if she would be punished for using her ears or her eyes or her voice.

She did fear punishment for using her voice. She dared not say the wrong word, look the wrong way, or put her foot down on the wrong flagstone in her father's presence.

Lio's head told him he ought to watch what he was saying, but his heart demanded something else. For once, he didn't think about the consequences of his words. He just said them. "Everywhere you turn, you are told to do away with your desires. That they do not matter—nay, that they are an abomination. It is wrong."

Cassia came to a halt on the path and rounded on him, her blood rushing with anger. Because he had spoken out of turn?

Because he had spoken the truth?

Cassia wore her stone face. "The king's daughter has no desires."

"He is not powerful enough to banish them, Cassia. Nothing he says or does can kill them. Shame upon him for trying to chain them so they wear away at you, a curse rather than a blessing. It is immoral to deny such a vital part of anyone."

She let out an artful laugh, just like the night they met, but he knew her better now. He could hear the strain in her voice. He felt as if he could reach out and touch the cord inside her that she held so taut it might snap at any moment.

"To *quell* desire is immoral?" She arched a brow at him, her chin high. "Now that I have never heard. Trust a heretic to say such a thing."

Lio wanted to move closer to her. He dare not. "We understand that desires are sacred. They make us who and what we are. They prove to us we live, that we are thinking, feeling beings with a consciousness separate from others."

"I am no philosopher, as I must often remind you. But it does seem to me you are speaking of the soul. Desire is a foible of the flesh."

"Both body and soul experience desire. Both are part of the Will. Behind every act of Will, there is a desire."

"Well, since we are on the subject, perhaps you may now give me the promised explanation of Hesperine mating rituals."

Lio could not laugh. Not when she was so flippant about something so sacred.

He wanted to tell her just what Grace was and shake all her bitter notions of marriage. But he must stop and think of how much he could say without violating his people's unequivocal rule: Hesperines did not reveal the meaning of Grace to any Tenebran, unless of course that Tenebran was a Hesperine's Grace.

If only Lio could explain why Grace was such an astonishing blessing. In her generosity, Hespera made her people immortal and freed them from the need to consume slain creatures, providing mortal blood as nourishment instead. But when she Graced two Hesperines, her generosity overflowed. She gave them a way to thrive on each other, without the need for any mortal's blood. To be Graced was to know not only sustenance, but abundance.

The great cost at which such a blessing came was, in truth, a kind of blessing in itself. Once you tasted your Grace, no other blood would ever be enough again. The need, the addiction that set in, was irreversible and irresistible—and always mutual. Time and again, Hesperine experience had proved that once the Craving claimed one of you, it claimed the other as well. Even when a Hesperine developed the Craving for a mortal, that human would experience the same hunger in return upon receiving the Gift.

To be Graced was to be truly free, and yet utterly dependent on another. Graces could not live without each other. Well, it was possible for them to survive. Other blood might be sufficient to keep them alive. But Hesperines who lost their Graces seldom lasted long. Everyone regarded the agony of withdrawal as a death sentence. Who could endure eternal Craving without hope of relief? Who would want to?

That was a truth Orthros's enemies must never discover. If the war mages in the Order of Anthros learned of the Craving, they would target Graced pairs, knowing if they slew one, the other's life would already be forfeit.

How was Lio to walk the fine line between his Oath of honesty with Cassia and the centuries of tradition and law that bound him to secrecy? How to describe his people's greatest strength without revealing it was also their greatest weakness?

"Well," he said, "we often refer to avowal as the Hesperine equivalent of marriage, to help make it understandable to mortals. But in truth, avowal bears little resemblance to your legal institution designed to secure a man's right to get a woman with child and ensure his heirs are his own offspring. Avowal has nothing to do with property."

Cassia lifted her eyebrows. "I have yet to hear a mage define marriage as such in the temple on a wedding day."

"How do you define it?"

"As a way for the king to get what he wants in exchange for me or the promise of me. But I do not deny your definition is also true, from the standpoint of the prospective groom who wishes to ensure his heirs have a trace of royal blood, however ill-gotten. Is your people's preoccupation with blood so very different?"

"As different as the moons are from the sun. We do not regard blood as something we can own or to which we have a right. It is a gift. That is the foundation of all Hesperine bonds, but especially Grace. Avowal is the acknowledgment before our people of that bond, which is of the body and the soul, of desire and love, of oath and magic."

"It sounds like a romantic minstrel ballad."

"The minstrels didn't invent love, you know. It has been known to happen to real people."

"Of course they made it up, so we would have songs to quote for reference, when we pretend we are in love."

"Of course. Poetry and pretense have kept the Queens of Orthros together for over fifteen centuries."

Cassia leaned back on her heels. "People tell all sorts of insulting stories about your Queens."

"If you are referring to the tale that they are lovers, that is neither a lie nor an insult. As for the rumors that amount to slander, I suspect mortals spread them out of jealousy."

"An insightful observation on the human mind, Sir Diplomat. Your Queens are two females who hold their throne without the aid of men or gods. Tenebrans cannot fathom it, and so they must decry it." There was no mistaking the curiosity in Cassia's aura. "How is it to serve them? As one of their diplomats, you have surely been presented to them at some point."

Lio almost chuckled. "There is no Hesperine in Orthros who has not spent time with them. They are happiest surrounded by their people."

"What are they like?"

"Kind." An ache of homesickness overtook Lio. "They are our light and our darkness, and we can always look to them to guide and shelter us. Queen Alea began her service to the Goddess as a Tenebran mage of Hespera. She is the only Prisma of our cult who survived the Ordering. Queen Soteira is one of the greatest healers ever born in the Empire. But she too once lost everything to her enemies—the husband she loved, her students...her entire people. Together she and Queen Alea overcame their suffering to give life to a new land. They will celebrate their sixteen hundredth jubilee five years from now."

"They need neither pretense nor poetry." Cassia's voice held a rare undertone of admiration. "Not when they have power."

She would say that. If he regaled her with tales of eternal love the night long, would she see anything in them but goals and motivations, personal gain and power? Lio had lived his whole life surrounded by examples of how Graces loved one another and their children. He was not sure any of that would get through to Cassia.

Was there nothing and no one in her life that proved to her love was real?

"Our Queens have been in love longer than they have been on the throne. They have raised eight children together and bounced every other Hesperine suckling in our long history on their laps. Power? Yes, so much that they could sit on their terrace in Orthros and shake the Hagion of Anthros in Cordium to its foundation. Ask yourself why they have not."

Cassia's face was utterly devoid of expression, but she spoke with absolute conviction. "Because they cannot bear for even one unknown child to feel afraid."

Before Lio could voice his surprise at her declaration, Cassia turned on her heel and walked back the way they had come.

FROST FEVER

LIO WAS CONVINCED OF Cassia's hidden depths, but he could not fathom whence her heartfelt statement had arisen.

He followed her, throwing open the currents of the Blood Union. They buffeted him headfirst against an array of inner defenses that would give any mind mage pause.

No one had ever felt like this to him inside, as if she had turned herself to stone. That momentary, intimate connection that had awakened between their minds at the feast truly defied explanation.

Lio should not be surprised Cassia guarded herself so thoroughly, despite her lack of training in resistance techniques. Strength of Will was the one recourse the untaught mind had against magical intrusion.

Whatever had prompted her confident assertion about the nature of his Queens just now, she was burying all traces of it within her. Lio knew right then he had come too close to something Cassia never shared with anyone. Something that made her feel vulnerable.

"Hesperines care about children," she stated. "That is what I wished to speak to you about tonight. Specifically, a question of medicine."

The revelation jolted Lio back from the ramparts of Cassia's mind and heart. Dare he think he was about to find out the reason for her interest in his people? Could she have been asking him questions on a child's behalf all along?

He had speculated endlessly as to why she had approached him that first night, but he still had no theory that satisfied him. He could only wonder, for he knew if he attempted to press Cassia for what she kept to herself, he would only risk driving her secrets deeper—or driving her away.

At one point, he had hazarded a guess she had a friend or loved one whose suffering had inspired her to ask whether his people might provide the Mercy. He had finally deemed that unlikely, for it seemed she held no one dear except Knight. Now Lio wondered if he had been wrong to dismiss the idea after all.

"I will provide whatever answers I can," he promised. "I regret I have limited expertise in healing."

"I don't need the assistance of a healer, but rather, a diplomat."

If she was trying to approach a difficult matter, he had best do what he could to put her at ease. He smiled. "Then you are certainly in luck. I am at your service, although I am but an—"

"Initiate ambassador. Even better, for a full ambassador's price would be higher."

"I haven't heard the favor yet," he said lightly. "I may raise my price."

"No…for this I think you will offer me yet another boon, out of the goodness of your heart."

"What is the matter, Cassia?" he asked gently. "For whom are you so concerned?"

"My question regards the concerns of another. The Prisma at the Temple of Kyria has just informed me in the strictest confidence about an outbreak of frost fever."

Not the reason she had first sought him out, then, nor a personal crisis. An impending crisis that might affect them all. "Hespera's Mercy."

"You must understand, Tenebrans live in fear of this illness."

"It's infamous to us, as well. It is dangerous enough to adult humans, but if a child catches it…"

Cassia searched his gaze. "I have seen less concern on the faces of fathers told they've lost a new babe to the fever."

"I saw a father die on the temple steps trying to protect his children from me. I do not claim to know how he felt. But any time frost fever strikes, it is a grievous time for Hesperines. That illness casts suffering children into the world like nothing else, and there are so many we cannot save."

"Take heart, for it is far away yet, in villages to the east."

"The eastern Tenebrae?" Lio asked urgently.

"Word from there does not travel swiftly or reliably. I only give the rumor credence because the mages of Kyria take the threat seriously."

"Then we certainly ought to, as well."

"No one else must know there is genuine cause for fear. The mages are not to breathe a word about it outside the temple. However, the Prisma told me in order to ask a favor." Now Cassia waved a seemingly dismissive hand. "One I am hardly in a position to grant, as she should know."

"There is some way I can help?"

"You can tell me if there are any healing herbs among the gifts your embassy has offered the king and whether he intends to accept them."

"We did offer a great many medicinal plants, including rimelace, the only effective treatment for the fever." Lio swallowed. "The king refused."

"Of course. He will refuse anything that might be imbued with malign magic."

Lio shook his head. "Lucis may not have faith in our good intentions, but he knows we are not so foolish or obvious as to attempt to do harm through a gift we offer him before the entire Council."

"But he cannot afford the terror that would spread among those ignorant enough to believe so. His subjects' fear of Hesperine magic has already caused him enough trouble."

"I am so sorry."

"Why are you apologizing?" She huffed a sigh. "It cannot be helped. I will tell the mages of Kyria they must make what preparations they can with whatever they have."

"Don't they cultivate rimelace in the temple?"

"For all the magic they plied to get it to grow, the last crop failed. The weather here is traitorous." Cassia gazed down the deer path that slowly but surely led them back toward Solorum. "I have heard tell that in the Magelands, the Order of Kyria knows spells that can make well-nigh anything grow inside their wards. And they say the goddess's fourteen children by Anthros, the Twice-Seven Scions, empower their mages to cage the wind and make rain fall upward. But such stories don't make rimelace grow in Tenebra."

"It thrives in the ice and snow in Orthros. I regret that does not make it grow in Tenebra, either."

"Foolish peasants," Cassia spat. "Their own suspicions will be the death of their children."

At the harshness of her tone, Lio took a step aside. "They are hardly more than children themselves. They don't know any better."

"They do not wish to learn." She let out a bark of laughter. "How convenient for the king."

Lio had felt her fear, her mistrust, and her anger. But the bitterness welling out of her tonight was more than he had bargained for, a sour taint inside her. They had both seen the man who had sacrificed himself in the bull's place on the temple steps. She had witnessed—and endured—more than her fair share of the king's abuses. How could she feel no sympathy for Lucis's subjects? How could she be so quick to ridicule them?

"How would you try to change their minds?" Lio asked.

"They do not listen to bastards." She said it without a hint of concern. Just as quickly as it had slipped, her mask of indifference was in place again. But she had already shown him what lay beneath.

"If they did, what would you say?"

"The king's daughter has no opinion on the Summit."

"Cassia, you care a great deal about what suffering may come."

"We would all do well to care, before the fever arrives at our own doors."

Someone worried about her own door, he suspected, did not seek out heretics in the middle of the night to help the Kyrian mages. "Did the king's household lose many during the last epidemic?"

As they passed the ruin again, Cassia held her skirts, picking her way through the rubble on the path. "He takes himself and anyone he requires to survive to one of his distant, self-sufficient estates. The royal healer is a mage of Akesios, the third scion, and highly qualified to be locked in the palace. When the peasants stop dying outside the walls, the king emerges again."

"I dearly hope you would be safe within those walls as well." On her other side, Lio levitated to avoid the debris and keep up with her.

"Apparently I qualify as more useful to him still breathing, so yes, he sequesters me on such occasions."

"So if an epidemic comes, it will not be at *your* door. Whose door, then, is the cause of your worry?"

"I do not pretend the body count beyond the fortress does not affect us all."

"Lady Cassia, it sounds a great deal as if you're concerned for the common good."

She snorted. "There is a difference between acknowledging reality and waxing poetic about the common good."

"Acknowledging that everyone in your kingdom is interdependent sounds to me like an expression of appreciation for each person's value."

"That some of us in Tenebra are less callous than the king is no great distinction. I wish there still to be a temple where I can garden and mages willing to let me in. That is all."

"You are fond of spending time with them."

"Gardening for Kyria is an expedient way to reassure the king I am not engaging in any activities of which he would disapprove."

"If you had been at the Summit, you could have learned for yourself what gifts were accepted, so you could easily tell your friends at the temple."

She gave him a flat look that said his point was moot.

"Have you been able to follow the proceedings at all?" he pressed.

"I said I don't have an opinion, not that I don't pay attention."

"Despite how rumors spread, not a great deal escapes the mage ward, I suspect. Very little news must reach you."

"If I waited for news to reach me, I would be dead by now."

Lio winced. "Do you know anything about what has transpired, then, besides the king's refusal of our medicines?"

"Everyone ought to know the terms of the original Equinox Oath. Hesperines shall have the right to children who have been exposed, abandoned, or orphaned without anyone to take them in. Hesperines shall have the right to the dying whose own kind give them no succor and to the dead whose kin and comrades fail to collect their remains. Hesperines shall be permitted to exercise any power on convicted criminals or miscreants acting in clear violation of the law to the detriment of honest people."

"Yes, those are the protections the Oath once afforded us."

"As for what the truce forbade you to do... Hesperines shall not take to them children who are still under the care of their elders—regardless of those elders' treatment of the children, I might add. Hesperines shall not disturb the dying who await mortal aid or the dead whose kin or comrades are coming to claim them. Hesperines shall not set foot in temples, orphanages, or places of burial. Hesperines shall not, under any circumstances, intervene in conflicts between the Mage Orders, the Council of Free Lords, the King of Tenebra or his enemies, or in any way attempt to influence worship or politics in Tenebra."

"Activities in which we have never intended to engage, I assure you."

"So long as your people hold to these terms, you may traverse all lands under the rule of the King of Tenebra without fear of persecution. Should you in any way violate this Oath, then you forfeit the king's protection from mages, warriors, and any subjects of Tenebra seeking to exact…'justice.' Finally, each king, upon his accession to the throne, is to reconvene the Summit and reaffirm this Oath with the appointed representatives of the Queens of Orthros."

"You are well informed about Orthros and Tenebra's past accord, I see."

"Anyone who is not a fool pays attention to how the past affects the present. King Lucis invites you to the first Equinox Summit in hundreds of years, making grand pronouncements about renewing the age-old Oath the Mage King established. Once you are here, he sits and watches the free lords insult and denounce you. The hate Lord Severinus's mage incited early on set the tone for the entire Summit."

"So you did know about that."

"The Council is doing everything in their power to refuse you your traditional right to children without families. Lord Nonus's remarks made it clear the free lords believe you disregard the distinction between abandoned children and those under the care of parents or guardians. He as much as accused you of kidnapping."

Lio listened, and a smile crept over his face despite the grim truth of her words.

"It is telling," she went on, "you have gained little ground regarding the Mercy, either. The terms the king has presented to you appear simply to reaffirm human burial rites, but in doing so they preclude your ministrations to the fallen. Once again it was the free lords' protests that shut down the discussion, conveniently making the king appear blameless. He might as well drive you from the kingdom, at this rate, but he will not, of course. He will welcome you with open arms and let the free lords tie your hands."

Lio did not interrupt her, eager to hear what further conclusions she would draw.

"At best," she predicted, "the current situation will go on. Your people will continue to conceal your activities here and act in the same gray area that has persisted ever since the Oath's lapse. At worst, Tenebra will use the unsuccessful Summit as an excuse to retaliate and attempt to expel you from the kingdom without appearing to have initiated the conflict. I need not say what we all fear, what your people have surely feared since you came. This may well come to war."

Lio grinned down at her. "Why did you need me to tell you about the medicines?"

"I am seeing you tonight and the Prisma in the morning. It will not be until tomorrow afternoon that Free Lord Varinius's best knight, who was present with his liege to hear the king's decision on the embassy's gifts, will see his saddler to gossip about it. The saddler's younger brother works in the kennels and alternates with another man to deliver Knight's food. I am unsure when the saddler's brother will next arrive, and I would prefer not to take action to ensure the other man doesn't come. A bite from Knight takes a long time to heal. The fellow might feel inclined to give my hound the worst cuts of meat from then on."

"What *don't* you know, Cassia?"

"I ask myself that every morning and ensure I have an answer by sundown. If I did any differently, I would not have survived this long."

"I suspect someone who knows so much also does a great deal with her knowledge."

"My influence extends about as far as my own skin. Aside from that, I garden and exercise Knight. I weave, if I must. That is all."

"Never a desire to extend your influence farther than that?"

"Oh, no. I am too fond of my skin." She paused by the Font of the Changing Queen, glancing at the sky, then turned to leave the clearing. "One who looks too far ahead fails to watch one's back."

"Cassia." Lio halted by the fountain, searching for the right words.

She stood stiffly on the other side of the basin from him, poised to leave.

He could never tell her what an immediate and personal impact her news had on him. Early knowledge of the frost fever epidemic would be a boon to someone who mattered so much to him. But that was not his secret to reveal. "I want you to know how much I appreciate you telling me this. You have my gratitude."

Her face was as still and carved as the fountain itself.

"Allow me to explain." Lio rounded the Font, then sat on the edge of the basin to put himself on her eye level. "I am not merely saying thank you. Hesperines mean something more than that when we say you have our gratitude. Those words are an acknowledgment of a bond of gratitude. We say them to show we appreciate the true value of a generous and self-less gift, which warrants a gift in return."

Her expression now changed ever so slightly. If he watched long enough, would he see the statue ease back to life and turn into a woman?

Lio placed a hand on his heart. "Rest assured, my people will do everything in our power to mitigate what is to come. For my part, I will make the most of any opportunity I have to change the king's decision about the rimelace."

"I know."

Before he could see what expression was taking shape on her face, she turned and led Knight back toward the palace.

Lio opened his mouth to stay her, but he stopped himself. She had read the color of the sky correctly. Time was of the essence. He must deliver her forewarning to his people—without implicating his oracle.

A PLACE AT THE TABLE

LIO HAD NEVER THOUGHT he would be in a position to protect his prince, but by the Goddess, if Cassia's warning gave him that power, he would use it for all he was worth.

Lio would put on a show for the fortress guards later. He had no time to waste right now. He stepped directly to Basir and Kumeta's door.

Only the door was closed. Lio sensed no veil to indicate they did not wish to be disturbed. He let the Union communicate his presence on the threshold, and the door swung open to admit him.

Kumeta stood at a battered map of Tenebra that hung on the otherwise bare walls. She had marked nothing, and Lio could only imagine the complex picture she saw as she studied it. She was so still, not a rustle disturbed her plum-colored veil hours robe. But her power roved the boundaries of the small room.

Basir sat on the bed with his travel desk open before him and his legs crossed beneath what must be his veil hours robe. He wore bright orange silk. Lio had never even imagined him in such a color.

Basir gave him a look. "Good moon, Deukalion."

"You have learned something?" Kumeta turned to Lio.

"As I promised, I came to you immediately." Lio resisted the urge to fold his hands behind his back. "A rumor reached my ears during my wanderings tonight, one that you, Master Envoys, are the most qualified to contradict—or act upon."

Despite his appearance of calm, Basir's attention sharpened. He seemed almost eager. It had never occurred to Lio that two Hesperines who were such advocates of caution would be so restless at the pace of diplomacy. But they were the Queens' Master Envoys. Orthros had eyes everywhere—Basir and Kumeta's eyes. They spent every night coordinating their intricate association of informants or gleaning information firsthand in the field. Inaction was hardly their element.

"I have heard hesitant whispers among the humans of an epidemic of frost fever that has begun far from Solorum." Lio looked at each of them. "In the eastern Tenebrae."

"Cup and thorns." Basir threw down his quill. "What a time to have no contact with the Charge."

Kumeta paced away from the map. "When we last left the area, there was no sign of the fever there."

"It could have started since we joined the embassy," Basir said.

Kumeta caught Basir's hand as she neared. "How could knowledge of an epidemic reach Solorum before the prince learns of it?"

"Perhaps he battles it even now."

"Surely he would have sent word," Kumeta said. "Our envoys know to risk contact if the need is so dire. Deukalion, whom did you overhear spreading these rumors?"

"There is talk amongst the gardeners. Those who have contact with the nearby Temple of Kyria seem to think the mages there are concerned." Lio could only pray his carefully constructed omissions were not a very deep hole into which he was digging himself.

"The healers are on the alert already?" Basir looked at his Grace, but did not make Lio privy to the rest of their consultation.

A moment later, Kumeta nodded. "We are of the same mind. It is possible these mortals speak in ignorance, but we will not stake the well-being of the prince's flock on it. Those under his care are so fragile. One outbreak of fever might be enough to devastate all they have worked so hard to build."

"We must tell him," Basir said. "It might give him time to prepare before the epidemic reaches them from whatever starving village it started in. If he knows of it already, he can be the one to advise us."

"The eastern Tenebrae are vast," Lio said hopefully, "and illness does not move as quickly in sparsely settled areas. Perhaps there is still time to warn him."

Nothing would devastate Rudhira like seeing the people he protected suffer. He had enough grief to bear already.

"Tell your uncle what you have learned," Basir instructed, "and that Kumeta and I will return in time for the Summit tomorrow with the mortals none the wiser."

"Keep Javed informed," said Kumeta. "He would do well to keep his medicines ready in case the Tenebrans change their minds."

Lio bowed. As he straightened, he cleared his throat. There was so much he had not had the opportunity to say after his initiation, even though Rudhira had made a rare visit home to support them all during their Trial. And it would be such a long time before Lio saw him again. "If you would, please tell Rudhira Lio says hello."

Oh, a spectacular and eloquent message indeed. It was probably entirely inappropriate to call the First Prince of Orthros by an affectionate name in front of the Master Envoys.

The suggestion of a smile flickered across Kumeta's face. "We will tell him whom he has to thank for this warning, and with what devotion it was delivered."

They were gone before Lio had a chance to reply. He stared at Basir's abandoned travel desk with a stab of unfamiliar emotion. On any given night, the Master Envoys pushed their Hesperine power to the limit for their people's cause. This was just one of many occasions when Basir used his thelemancy and Kumeta her illusions to deliver life-saving information.

Lio could have chosen that life. Should he have?

He checked himself. Diplomacy was his path. The Summit was the opportunity he had always awaited. This was his chance to serve his people and try to influence the course of their future.

At the mental image of Basir appearing before Rudhira in a bright orange veil hours robe, Lio's mood lightened. He struggled not to chuckle. This was not a laughing matter. He had to tell Uncle Argyros the Master Envoys were risking a departure from the Summit—to contact the prince.

Lio sensed his mentor waiting in the common room, as Uncle Argyros did every night, whether or not Lio took the unspoken invitation to coffee on his way in. This time, Aunt Lyta was there too, her aura closely intertwined with her Grace's. Lio entered the common room to find her sitting with her chair drawn close to Uncle Argyros's and her body tucked against his side. He held her in one arm, and where his hand rested on her thigh, her fingers intertwined with his. He sipped his coffee in silence while they spoke without words.

What must it be like to communicate with each other when you had been Graced that long? How must it feel to share knowledge and ideas through an effortless connection, which only grew stronger with each passing century? It was hard for Lio to fathom a joining of the mind more powerful than what his magic could achieve or a bonding of the soul deeper than the Blood Union that bound all Hesperines together. But Union with your Grace, it was said, was beyond anything you could imagine, until you knew it for yourself.

A sense that all was well with the world came over Lio, just as it did when he came upon his parents dancing or saw the Queens embrace. But this time it was fleeting. The burdens he had carried into the room with him ate away at the feeling that things were as they should be. He hated to add his cares to all those that already weighed upon his aunt and uncle.

Aunt Lyta looked up, smiling at him as if nothing were amiss. But her aura, always so vibrant, was veiled tonight. That alone gave away how much worry she sought to hide. "Forgive us, Lio. We were lost in thought."

"Not at all. I'm sorry to interrupt."

"The boy says he's an interruption," his uncle scoffed. "Need I remind you how much trouble your parents went to so we could have the pleasure of your interruptions?"

Lio took his seat at the table, smiling at a memory. "And the trouble you and Aunt Lyta went to so you could have the pleasure of seeing Mak stuff one of your formal robes and use it as a practice dummy as soon as he started training for the Stand."

Uncle Argyros's chuckle grew into a heartfelt laugh.

"We would sacrifice any number of robes to witness that again." Aunt Lyta grinned.

The affection did not fade from Uncle Argyros's eyes. "What is on your mind, Nephew?"

Lio broke the news.

In an uncharacteristic display of strain, Uncle Argyros lifted a hand to rub his eyes. "I must trust Basir and Kumeta's judgment on this matter."

Lio exchanged a worried glance with Aunt Lyta. Uncle Argyros was truly weary if he didn't have the energy to repeat his lecture on the problematic nature of the prince's mission and why it should not be allowed to interfere with the Summit.

"May the Goddess's Eyes light their path," Aunt Lyta murmured.

"And may her darkness keep them in Sanctuary," Lio finished. He composed his thoughts, ensuring all he did not wish to reveal was safely behind his veil. He must tread with the utmost care, lest his aunt and uncle find his words suspect. "There is another matter that troubles me: Lady Cassia Basilis."

"Yes." Aunt Lyta frowned. "We have yet to see her at the Summit."

"I am concerned." Let them feel just how much. They would easily think Lio worried only for his people.

Uncle Argyros took another swig of coffee. "I have not given her as much consideration as I probably ought to have."

Lio had seldom heard his uncle make such an admission. Perhaps he could do the right thing by both Cassia and his mentor by taking it on himself to change her role in the Summit. "Isn't your initiate supposed to mind such details for you so you may devote your attention to leadership?"

"The night I need another to mind my details for me is the night I shall surrender my position before the Queens."

Lio tried not to wince.

The encouragement in Aunt Lyta's gaze told him she at least appreciated his effort to shoulder some of his uncle's cares. She tightened her hand on Uncle Argyros's. "Nonsense, my love. We all learned long ago none of us carry our people's fate alone."

"I have given a great deal of thought to this particular detail," Lio offered.

"What is your opinion on the matter of Lady Cassia?" his aunt asked.

"I know we must pick our battles." Lio let out a humorless laugh. "The Tenebrans pick most of our battles for us, and we have yet to win any. But this may be an issue worth pressing. It is no small offense on the king's part."

"He denies Lady Cassia a seat at the table that is rightfully hers," Aunt Lyta agreed.

Uncle Argyros took his coffee pot in hand. "It offends our sense of justice deeply, to be sure. But if we sought to address every abuse a Tenebran man committed against his daughter, where would we stop?"

Where indeed? If Lio must stop at Cassia, he would still call it a great victory. But if Uncle Argyros did not feel her plight as Lio did, he must give his uncle other reasons to champion her. "It is an offense against us as well. The king is withholding one of only three people he is honor-bound to bring to the table. He is violating the long-standing terms of the Summit."

"Lio is right," Aunt Lyta said. "We as the Queens' representatives are here to swear the Oath with the ruling monarch of Tenebra and his entire family."

Uncle Argyros poured Lio a cup of coffee and slid it across the table. "Of course Lio is right. My initiate knows we must look ahead. Lucis is a formidable king, and his reign appears to be an iron rule, but such things can change swiftly among mortals."

"I appreciate your confidence, Uncle." But their discussion seemed to be veering from the reasons and justifications Lio had intended to present in favor of Cassia's inclusion in the Summit.

"Lio is obviously thinking of the precedent of the Summit of 973," his uncle said. "We were fortunate the king kept his elder son, favored but illegitimate, involved in the negotiations, along with his younger, legitimate son. Upon the king's death, when the two rivals vied for the throne, Hesperines' greatest anxiety was mitigating the suffering the civil war caused, for the Oath would be secure regardless of the victor. Although the younger son prevailed, it could easily have gone the other way."

Lio did his best not to think of the precedent the king's younger son had set when he had ordered his own elder sibling publicly drawn and quartered.

"We do not know what may come to pass," Uncle Argyros went on. "A feared and hated man rules this volatile country. Those who oppose him may yet get the better of him, and what then? A free lord puts himself on the throne with Queen Cassia for a wife to ensure some degree of continuity?"

Aunt Lyta nodded. "Then where would we be, if we had no agreement with her? Right back where we began, forced to negotiate with a new king whose intentions are unknown. Unless Lady Cassia puts her name to the Oath now."

Lio could not believe that was a likely future for Cassia. She would never allow herself to become the puppet queen of one of the suitors she despised. But Lio could not afford to contradict the possibility, if it made Uncle Argyros more ready to help her now. "I do think it is in our best interests to see her more involved in the negotiations. Perhaps there is a tactful way we could encourage the king to allow her to take part."

"We have given ground on almost every matter." Aunt Lyta's eyes flashed. "He ought to give ground on at least one."

"But is this the ground on which we wish to make our stand, my Grace?"

"What reason has the king to refuse?" Lio asked. "Although we take the long view, Lucis clearly does not regard his concubine's daughter as a political threat."

No. Lio knew well that Lucis believed he had complete control of Cassia. How wrong the king was.

"Showing such generosity to her might enhance his prestige," Aunt Lyta pointed out.

Uncle Argyros shook his head. "Bringing a girl child to the table is more likely to draw mockery."

Aunt Lyta's lip curled. "Or admiration. She is evidence of his conquests, after all."

Lio's jaw tightened. "Although we remain unconvinced Lucis wants the Summit to succeed, we can be certain he wishes to appear as if he supports the restoration of the Oath. On the question of Lady Cassia, would he not consider it in his best interests to oblige us, in order to keep up appearances?"

Uncle Argyros said nothing. After a few long sips of coffee, he nodded. "I think this may be one debate we can win. There are so few of them, I should hate to sacrifice even one."

"Then we are agreed?" Lio tried not to sound too eager.

"Yes," his uncle said. "Tomorrow night we shall see if we can get Lady Cassia to the table."

27

days until

SPRING EQUINOX

SUMMONS

"I'M SORRY." CASSIA BURIED her hands in her apron, though there was no more soil to wipe from them. "The king will not accept any gift from the Hesperines that may have magical properties."

The Prisma still smiled. Gray daylight still filled her vestibule and illuminated her patient, benevolent features. The votive Kyria still looked on with a smile carved in stone.

Cassia was all too adept at discerning what lay behind the expressions people held on their faces. A woman of the Prisma's influence and experience would naturally have many such shields at her disposal. That was one reason she had arrived at a point where she seldom needed them. Straightforward speech and action were her way. Cassia found the Prisma's feigned calm more concerning than any outburst of frustration or disappointment.

Cassia gave her fingers something to do, scratching Knight's ear. This tension in her was different from the familiar wariness and fear she knew how to accommodate in herself. "I am sorry."

The Prisma's smile softened a measure. "Thank you for asking on our behalf, Lady Cassia. I take no more pleasure than the king in a bargain with the godsforsaken, but those herbs would have been..." She braced her hands on the altar at Kyria's feet. "...beneficial."

Vital, Cassia translated silently. Lifesaving.

It was another day in Tenebra. Folk cared more about nursing their prejudices than their children, and the king signed his own people's death warrant.

There was no call for despair when all proceeded as it always did. The

Prisma was a mage. She knew more of prejudice against Hesperines than anyone. She should not be surprised.

Yet the Prisma did despair. Only such a strong emotion would require a shield like the one she wore on her face in this moment.

I'm sorry," Cassia said one more time.

"You've done all you can."

Cassia took that as a dismissal. She and Knight escaped back to the garden. He lay down in his usual place at the edge of the plot, but he did not lay his head to rest on his paws, as if he expected to jump up again.

She *had* done all she could. The mages had misguidedly asked her to intervene, and because it was in her best interests, she had obliged. More than she ought to have. She would return to the palace today at dusk, and no more would be said of the matter.

The king had made his decision. That was the end of it.

Another day would pass, another night, another day. She would continue the rhythm her time at Solorum had taken on, swinging between long afternoons in the dirt at the temple and long predawn hours in the woods with Lio.

That rhythm, just begun, broke two hours after dusk. Cassia was in her rooms, occupying herself with her potted garden and waiting for her handmaiden to leave, when the royal messenger arrived.

Cassia stared at him over her rosemary. Hot pain tightened in her belly, and she gripped the handle of her spade. As if that were a weapon that had any power against the man standing by the fire and the words he would say. Knight uttered a quiet warning growl. But even he could not stand against the king.

What now? What had she done now? What did the king want of her now?

"What?" she managed aloud.

The messenger pried his gaze from Knight and looked at Cassia. His face betrayed his anxiety about her hound, but also puzzlement. He was an opponent who wore all his weaknesses for her to see. That was of little use, when the man he served was invulnerable.

"The king," the messenger declared, "requests your presence at the Summit."

The basket, spade and all, threatened to slip from Cassia's lap. She had to make herself hear the rest of the messenger's words.

"…within a quarter of an hour in appropriate court attire, my lady."

"I understand." A lie.

The messenger bowed and escaped. Perita floundered for an instant with darning needle in hand, staring wide-eyed at Cassia. Then the girl abandoned her chair and Cassia's stockings by the hearth and disappeared into the dressing room. There came a flurry of clinks and thuds. The telltale sounds of Perita gathering her arsenal of combs, jewelry, and scent oils Cassia wouldn't wear.

Cassia went into her bedchamber and shut the door.

By rote, she put away her things and undressed. She went to her wash-basin and began to scrub.

Perita pounded on the door. "There's no time for washing, Lady!"

Cassia scoured her elbows for the third time. "I'm coming."

Here in her room she couldn't tell precisely how much time she had, couldn't feel the moments slipping by that were not an invitation to the woods, but an order to the Summit.

The Summit. It simply made no sense to Cassia. She did not com-prehend. She had grown skilled at understanding the king's motivations, even at their most twisted, but this she could not fathom. She only knew she must sit in his presence until nearly midnight without vomiting on her court gown.

CASSIA'S SEAT

CASSIA NEED ONLY SLIP into the Summit and take a seat among the least important. It should not be difficult, should it? Not as grueling as kneeling before the entire court at Caelum's temple day festival with the king looking directly at her.

Cassia led her little retinue of one liegehound and one chandler's daughter-turned-handmaiden on a circuitous route through the palace. Perita said nothing in the presence of listening ears, but her expression spoke for her. She was subjecting Cassia to a thorough scolding for taking the long way. Cassia wound around to one of the side doors that let out into the main courtyard. They made it out the front gate and headed toward the Summit pavilion.

She wished the present would fade into a blur like the moments after she had received the summons. She couldn't even remember whether she had put on the new bronze dress or her old court gown that was barely blue and almost gray. She glanced down at herself. The torchlight told her it was the blue. Gray. No matter. Panic made all her senses sharper than ever. Her gaze fixed on the tiny braids of thread that decorated her belt. She could see every single one that had pulled loose from the worn embroidery.

The walk across the damp grass felt impossibly long, the cool moisture in the drizzly air very far away from her sweating body. The Summit pavilion loomed closer, and her head began to throb. Through the glimmer of the mage ward, she could make out the attendees. The crowd was not nearly large enough to make a silent bastard daughter sitting at the edge of their exalted company feel concealed.

The king was already there. So were the Hesperines.

Walking through the mage ward felt like taking a bath in a tub full of sewing pins. Cassia emerged on the other side with a shudder, fighting to keep her hands at her sides instead of clawing at the pricking sensation on her skin.

One small mercy was that heralds never announced bastards.

"Lady Cassia Basilis," cried the herald.

Every pair of eyes in the pavilion stared at her. She froze like a senseless rabbit before the hounds. She could not make herself move. Terror robbed her of control over her own limbs.

The sight of the men blurred before her until she confronted an army of colorless, nameless faces. Somewhere in that haze, seven pairs of brilliant eyes reflected the torchlight at her and watched her humiliation. The Hesperines could smell her sweat. Through the Blood Union, they could feel her weakness.

She saw herself turn away, grab her skirts in both hands and flee for the shelter of the trees beyond the green.

She could not flee. The king had commanded her to be here. He was watching. Waiting for her to take her seat. To obey.

It had never taken so much effort to turn her body and bend her knees. As she gave her curtsy toward the throne, her legs threatened to buckle. She straightened too fast and turned toward her seat, and the green rotated around her.

She put one foot ahead of her. The ground did not slip from under her. Yet. Every step took her closer to the chair he had allotted her. Each one was an act of submission.

She trembled inside with something that was not panic. Something more than fear filled her with a heat that was not of her body.

Her chair loomed at the very end of the very back row. She sat down hard on the unpadded wooden seat. It felt dreadfully familiar. To Cassia's horror, she felt the urge to curse, cry out…or sob.

Perita took the chair next to her and eased it back in the grass, positioning herself slightly behind. Cassia's vision cleared enough that she realized her handmaiden now directed that scolding gaze on everyone around them, as if daring them. A strange feeling came over Cassia at the knowledge that someone from her own tiny world within the walls of her chambers was here at her back.

And Knight was by her side. She murmured a command to him, and he seated himself at attention. All his training for ceremonial occasions came to the fore. But his tail flopped over her feet, and for the first time that night she felt sure she would not vomit, if only because she did not want to soil his fur. She made herself lift her chin and look up.

Lord Titus began to speak, and finally, thankfully, the hostile faces and beautiful gazes turned away from Cassia.

Over the throbbing in her ears, she gathered that Lord Titus welcomed everyone to another thrilling night of winning honor and making history through useless and disastrous negotiations. She tried to focus. She had to listen. She was sitting in this foreign battlefield unarmed, and words were all she could reach for.

Lord Titus bowed toward the Hesperine delegation, which sat hemmed in by his own faction on one side and Lord Hadrian's on the other, right across the table from the royal dais. At last, the royal spokesman took his seat.

With the other mortals, Cassia pinned her gaze on the Hesperines. Not Lio. All of them. It meant she did not have to look at the king.

When Lio rose from his chair, Cassia nearly startled. Under the concealing fur of Knight's tail, she dug her toes into the ground. She must not give any sign this particular Hesperine meant anything to her.

Lio turned to face her and offered her a bow. "We the embassy, on behalf of our beloved Queens of Orthros, offer our heartfelt welcome to Lady Cassia."

She glared into his brilliant blue eyes. Curse him, curse him, what was he thinking? Was he begging for disaster?

He faced the free lords with a smile. "So too do we give thanks and respect to our honored host for this opportunity to resolve our regrettable differences. We rejoice to see that tonight, the Summit has taken yet another step toward adherence to the traditions we all cherish."

Such artful words from both sides. Did no one realize to what degree the king tolerated the Hesperines, the free lords, and the world at large by bothering with this verbosity and ceremony? This was not his way.

Cassia could still hear his blunt, ugly words that had once decided a much different negotiation on a long-ago night. She could see, instead of the colorful awnings of the Summit pavilion, the mud-smeared walls of a tent. She could feel a different chair creaking beneath her, but oh, how much the same it had felt. How difficult it was, then and now, to sit still and quiet.

No, no. She could not allow this. She must maintain control.

She must see and hear and feel what was before her, not what had been. She must not permit this…this force inside her, whatever it was… to rise and burst out as her tears had that night.

Lio spoke again, reminding her. This was not that negotiation or that tent, although she was still that girl. The ones who brought terms before the king now were not those who had destroyed her world. These were Hesperines, the only ones who had tried to put it back together.

She was listening not to a traitorous free lord's messenger, but to Lio. The same voice that talked and laughed with her in the secret darkness was now speaking with eloquence and maturity, delivering the words his people had delegated to him, surely a great honor.

"Once again His Majesty shows bold and decisive leadership in his commitment to a true restoration of the Equinox Summit, according to the terms that have withstood the test of time. We appreciate the significance of His Majesty's decision, and we look forward to pledging our own commitment to the traditions of Tenebra and Orthros, when we swear the Equinox Oath with everyone of Lucis Basileus's blood."

Cassia bit down on the inside of her lip to keep from making a sound.

She understood the king. Lucis had no reason to want her at the Summit. Except to oblige his guests.

It was the Hesperines who desired her presence. Suddenly, inexplicably, though they had taken no notice of her absence all this time. Someone had convinced them they should want her here.

It was Lio. He was the one who had broken the fragile rhythm of her days beyond repair.

The emotion within her that was trying to emerge—she recognized it. She never let it in. It was far too dangerous. But it had come. Anger.

ANGER

L IO FELT THE SLAM of the hatch as a vibration in the ground beneath his bare feet. The thud echoed through the woods.

Cassia was a powerful flame, and he felt like nothing more than a moth. If he drifted too close, her anger would consume him.

He altered his course and ran for the hatch. She marched toward him, Knight loping at her heels, her anger lashing out before her.

Anger was better than fear. Wasn't it?

She was only halfway to the fountain when he caught up with her and fell into step beside her. She halted in her tracks and rounded on him. He stilled.

"What were you thinking?" she seethed.

Her anger whipped again, ensnaring him and yanking him closer. There *was* fear underneath. No. Panic.

"Cassia, when you arrived at the Summit tonight, I sensed you were angry. I did not realize—"

"No, you didn't realize at all." Her words came in a breathless rush, her tone a warning on the edge of an outburst.

Purely on instinct, Lio lifted his hands and reached out to her to reassure her.

She backed away.

He froze with his hands in midair. Of course. This was Cassia. His touch was not worth the risk, except through a handkerchief. She had no use for his touch. Especially in this moment.

He turned his mistake into a placating gesture. Far too much like one might make when facing an armed opponent.

"You told the other Hesperines about me," she accused.

"*No.* I promised you I wouldn't. Politics were all I had to speak of to convince my people the king must not deny you your seat at the Summit. Tonight was the first time we broached the subject with Lucis, and we were all surprised when he acted on his decision immediately. I had no chance to tell you—"

"It's your fault he summoned me to the table!"

Your fault. The words lanced Lio, even as her sense of betrayal took hold of him. For an instant all he could think of was her pain, and his own regret rubbed salt in the wound. "I thought you might be…"

What? Pleased? That he had dragged her before the one man in the world she least wished to see?

The man she had willingly placed herself near in order to achieve her own ends.

"…that you might find the opportunity useful," Lio finished.

"Useful?" she spat.

Lio pulled back from her fury, attuning himself to his Gift again, anchoring himself in his own skin. He had misjudged. Catastrophically.

She took a step forward, advancing on him. "One does not attempt anything 'useful' with the king watching. I spend every waking moment laboring not to draw his attention. Every move I make to accomplish anything 'useful' must be considered and reconsidered and considered again so he does not suspect I am interested in—or capable of—achieving anything 'useful.' If he thinks for one moment I know more than he has mandated that I should, or I lift a finger to accomplish anything in his domain, then it will already be too late for me."

The words and the anger and the desperation roared out of her. Lio could have thought of something to say. But he didn't.

Had anyone ever heard her say such things, much less *listened* to her?

He stood still and silent under the onslaught.

"How could you think I want a place at his table? How dare you presume to arrange it?" Her voice broke as the depths of her terror had broken the surface already.

Lio had tapped into her worst fears. An instant of regret overtook him again that he had done this to her. But then came certainty.

If one never lanced a wound, it festered. If one never stared fears in the face, they only grew more powerful.

"You don't know what he's capable of!" Cassia cried. "You don't know what he's done. I do. I am the only one who does, and because of that, I must never give him reason to think I am a danger to him. I know better—far better than you and your foolish, idealistic embassy—how to pick my battles with him."

She shut her eyes, and Lio could feel her fighting to regain composure. She had lost control. That frightened her as much as the king did.

"No," she amended. "I know not to pick fights at all. I go nowhere near the field." She looked Lio in the eye now. "I am the king's pawn. But I will not be yours."

"You are no one's pawn."

Her anger hit him like a slap in the face. If she had been anyone else, she might have cursed him and actually reached out to strike him with a hand. But Cassia did not call upon the gods, and Cassia did not strike out at anyone.

"What would you call me, then?" she demanded. "Your wreath of victory? How proud you must feel to have exerted real influence upon the course of the Summit for the first time. You convinced your people to take your view, and you even moved Lucis Basileus himself on his throne. Congratulations, Initiate Ambassador Deukalion. Your first triumph as a diplomat—you succeeded in putting Lady Cassia where you want her."

"Under the Goddess's Eyes, Cassia, I swear you are not some kind of notch on my spear! Hespera's Mercy. I am not a Tenebran lord who thinks himself entitled to power over others' lives. I am a Hesperine—a heretic. The truth is, I am no more welcome before the king and Council than you are. The Summit is a rare chance for me to influence them, and I thought to use it to aid you in achieving influence as well. I will not deny I felt a sense of triumph. But only because I thought I had truly helped someone. Helped *you*."

"You wanted to help me, and *this* is what you did? What were you thinking?"

"I was thinking it is a shame upon this house that you are forced to make do with scraps of influence, when those who wield the power are unworthy of it. You deserve a seat at that table more than anyone there. If no one in this godsforsaken palace will give you what is rightfully yours, then I shall hold them accountable."

No flicker of surprise or comprehension in her eyes. Just her mask, a new one tonight, wrought of indignation. "That is not how things work in Tenebra."

"I know, and it isn't right."

"Self-righteous Hesperines! Always claiming to know right and wrong! To have a solution for everything! How dare you?"

He swallowed, stifling the urge to rub a hand through his hair. "A good question. One you have every right to ask. I presumed a great deal, didn't I?"

She didn't answer. She didn't have to. He saw it now, and he could not confront it without feeling shame.

He had forced her hand. Just like everyone else who surrounded her. Especially the king.

That was what Lio had done. He had made Cassia feel powerless. How could he do that to her?

How had he managed to descend to that level in his attempt to give her more power? For all his good intentions, he had put her in a place she had no desire to be—and at the king's behest. Lio had influenced his people, they had influenced the king, and like a puppet master, Lucis had pulled his daughter to the table on the end of her strings.

No one had asked Cassia.

"Forgive me." Lio bowed his head. "I had no intention of putting you in this position. I should have consulted you."

"You should never have considered it."

"If I had come to you first and offered to secure you a seat at the Summit—"

"I would have told you I do not want it."

"Don't you?"

"Of course not!" She raised her voice again. "How could you ever think I would?"

"I think if you weren't afraid, you would."

"How dare you," she said again, "presume to know what I want. How dare you come here and upset everything I've worked for!"

"It would indeed be wrong of me to say I know better than you what you want or what's best for you. I speak only of what you have decided you want, your own desires you have expressed to me."

"I've never said anything of the sort to you!"

"You've been telling me, showing me night after night what you want. Not to be in danger. Not to endure suffering. The information you need to protect yourself and stay one step ahead of those who would cause you harm. The opportunity to use that information to your advantage. And beyond that?" A sad laugh escaped him. "To have Knight by your side. To get to work in the garden instead of having to do any weaving. Such modest wants. Far too modest for someone like you."

"Oh, I see! I fall short of Hesperines' lofty standards of desire and Will. My wants are insufficient!"

"There can be nothing wrong with your wants. They are, by definition, yours to decide. Only think how they might grow if you did not have to stunt them. Your *life* is insufficient for *you*. You deserve more."

Her riposte was long in coming this time. But as the silence stretched on, Lio felt the cool air on his skin and a lightness in his chest. Her anger, easing. Giving way to something else too complicated and fraught to name.

"I want to keep breathing, Lio. I'm a girl child and a bastard. Either reason alone would be enough. The king could have left me to the wolves the hour I was born, and even now he could consign me to the headsman at his pleasure. Every day I peer into my own grave, and the only reason I am not buried yet is that I do not try to right wrongs. I do not give a thought to what I deserve. I think about what I need and what I can manage, and that is all I have any call to think about."

"You're wasted on *necessity* and *managing*."

"You do not understand the way of things here."

"No, I do. I understand that you're intelligent and determined and braver than any man who charges out onto a bloody battlefield with a sword. You shouldn't be locked away in some neglected wing of the palace or even the walls of a temple garden. Forgive me for thinking to put some tools in your hand that would help you dig your way out."

She stared at him. Her face was blank. But Lio sensed a war in her spirit. A foolish sense of hope overtook him.

Without a word, she turned on her heel and walked away.

He let her go. He didn't know what would come of it, if she would ever agree with what he had said. But he did know that what he'd said had reached her.

26

days until

SPRING EQUINOX

DIRTY HANDS

THE AFTERNOON WAS WANING, and the Prisma still had not called Cassia away from the garden. Perhaps she would manage to escape back to the palace without the mage asking her to do anything else about the rimelace. Cassia's luck had held. It seemed word had not yet reached the cloistered halls of the temple about the scandal at the palace, that the king's bastard now blemished the noble Summit.

Cassia lifted her hoe from the soil at the end of the row and leaned on it. Another bed turned over. Soon it would be time to move onto the next. She straightened, stifling a yawn. It was always that Hesperine's fault she did not sleep. Now she would only see him at the Summit, but it was his fault that she would have to attend each night, and that she would lie awake in her chambers afterward, battling her own weakness. It would surely win, and the cramps in her stomach would drive away sleep.

As she headed for the nearest well, Knight got to his feet and followed. She drew a bucket up and cleansed first her spade, then her hands. Knight watched her expectantly, knowing clean hands meant petting would resume.

She was about to start scrubbing the dirt from under her fingernails when another pair of hands entered her vision. Elegant ivory fingers took hold of the other bucket on the opposite side of the well. Cassia glanced up to find Irene had joined her. She gave the mage a nod as civil as she gave to anyone.

Irene's beautiful, rosy lips curled into a smile that did not reach her eyes. "You must feel very privileged."

Cassia's instincts warned her that her luck was about to run out. Irene was not to be outdone by her brother, Free Lord Tyran, although their family had raised him to sit upon the Council and bartered her to the temple in her childhood as a badge of their devotion to the gods. Cassia knew she would always be Irene's favorite target, for she lacked what Irene was most proud of—elevated, legitimate birth—and possessed what Irene wanted more than anything. A life at court.

Cassia followed her customary policy of giving Irene as little as possible to use against her and simply raised her eyebrows in an interested expression.

"A seat at the Summit," the mage fawned. "What a truly unusual condescension from His Majesty."

"Yes."

Irene rounded the well, still smiling as if this were a harmless chat over the buckets. Closing in for the thrust, Cassia guessed. Knight maneuvered himself into the space between her and the mage. Irene shifted on her feet with an eye on her sky-blue robe to ensure it was not touching the dog. But she did not back away.

"I confess to being surprised at you, Cassia. You have always shown yourself to be aware of your place, as befits us all to be. Perhaps you have misunderstood the Prisma's generous kindness to you. Has your little garden plot gone to your head and emboldened you to reach out of the dirt for a seat at the table?"

"I sit where the king bids me."

Irene's smile widened, but her eyes narrowed. Just a squint in the sun to anyone looking. But Cassia, under the full impact of her gaze, saw it for the warning it was.

"As a handmaiden of Kyria, I am called to assist my fellow women in remaining on the path of virtue. When I notice a female about to stumble, it is my duty to warn her of the pitfall waiting to trap those who are susceptible to corruption."

Cassia showed Irene the face she wore before the Summit.

"It may by exhilarating to sup on rich fare," said the mage, "but only those born to it can dine with grace. Those who were not will always appear gluttonous. Woman was born to lay the table, not sit at it. And some women were born only to grow the food that shall be laid." Irene's gaze fell to the dark lines under Cassia's fingernails. "An ambitious gardener will only soil the linens."

"I assure you," Cassia replied in her mildest tone, "I scrubbed my fingernails quite clean before answering the king's summons to the table last night."

Irene gave a shrug that said *hew your own crypt.* "Some dirt is too ingrained for the eye to see."

Cassia gazed back at her steadily. "I could not agree with such wisdom more."

Irene's gaze sharpened to blade-point. "*Some* of us see it, no matter how deep it is hidden. Some of us can spot presumption...unseemly pretentions...while others are duped into seeing only virtue."

A dozen different parries occurred to Cassia, and for an instant she indulged an uncharacteristic desire and imagined saying them. If she engaged, she could outduel Irene so effectively she would leave the mage bleeding.

Where had this unfamiliar thirst for battle come from?

There was no call to strike back against Irene. There was no reason for these same accusations to rankle Cassia. Bastard. Tarnished. Unwomanly. Presumptuous. No wedding vows had constrained her mother. Therefore the daughter too must be uncontrolled, uncontrollable. Always violating the proper bounds the gods had placed on her, lusting for men, riches, or power. Cassia had heard it all before. She spent every day laboring to be acceptable, and they still believed her capable of every transgression.

Irene was just more of the same. A woman who regarded other women as a threat to her. A daughter trying to make what she could of the life her father had ordained for her.

In fact, Irene was a great deal like Cassia herself. The only difference was that Cassia only worried about real dangers. Irene's jealousy drove her to see threats where there were none.

"Certainly," Cassia said, "we should all strive for a greater level of insight. With the goddess's help, we ought to all pray to become better judges of character."

Irene's lips pressed together. "Oh, yes, Cassia. Pray. And hope that when you fall, the gods hear and are merciful enough to catch you." She took her bucket in hand and turned her back on Cassia to walk away.

Cassia gazed down at her hands, which were clean of everything except those little smudges under her nails. Knight nudged her, reminding her she should be petting him. She gave his ears a thorough rub. Satisfied the threat was gone and they were on schedule, he wagged his tail.

If only her own course seemed so simple as the one that governed his life.

She glanced at the sinking sun. If she did not dawdle, she had just enough time before dusk rites to talk to the Prisma.

When she stepped into the antechamber, her heart pounded, warning her what her body would do to her if she went through with the plan she was about to propose. The knot in her belly agreed with Irene that Cassia had no place even attempting this. All her life, Cassia had agreed with that, too. Everyone had. Except Lio.

Curse him. She was not doing this because of what he had said. She was doing it because she wanted her hours at that table to produce more than another night of sweating and nausea. Because she was just corrupt enough to want a place at that table and just virtuous enough to want to use it to erase the look of despair she had seen on the Prisma's face at the news there would be no medicine.

The vestibule door opened, and thankfully it was sympathetic Deutera who invited Cassia inside. Cassia entered with one hand on Knight's ruff to steady herself, and Deutera departed, shutting the door behind them.

The Prisma stood before Kyria, half turned away from the door. She had draped her apron over a nearby chair in anticipation of dusk rites. "Lady Cassia. Can I do something for you?"

Cassia cleared her throat. Her stomach seemed to have leapt into it and lodged there to stop her words from coming out. She swallowed. "Actually I came to ask if I might do something for you."

The mage turned, wearing a smile that must have cost her a great deal of effort. "Do not feel you have anything to make up for, child. The rimelace is out of our reach."

"Perhaps it isn't."

The Prisma's brows lifted over her tired eyes. "You think there may yet be a chance?"

Cassia swallowed again. "It would require broad permission from you, but if it is acceptable to you, I will do my part."

"Please, go on."

"If you will allow me…" Cassia's belly flopped. Her sweat-soaked gardening dress would need washing when she returned to the palace. When she escaped…and fled toward her fate. "…I could convey to the Summit your concerns about the frost fever and plead on your behalf that they reconsider their decision regarding the Hesperines' gift of healing herbs."

The Prisma came to her and took her hands. Her grip, firm but gentle, stilled Cassia's shaking.

Cassia dropped her gaze to their joined hands. The Prisma's were strong and callused from hard work, brown from time spent in the sun. The little marks and discolorations on them were not unlike Cassia's freckles, although she had been born with hers, and the Prisma had earned hers through a life of harsh endeavor and exposure to the elements. Cassia could imagine the hands that held hers had saved many lives, while Cassia's had been busy clinging to her own.

"You have overcome a great deal to suggest this," the Prisma said. "I appreciate what more you must overcome to act on it. Kyria bless you for acting."

Cassia resisted the urge to tighten her hold on those hands. For steadiness. For…comfort? "Then you will permit me?"

"Lady Cassia, I would not be ashamed before the goddess to beg you."

Cassia swallowed again. "What message shall I deliver to the Summit for you?"

"Tell the truth about the outbreak. Inform the king and Council they must take immediate action to provide the medicine if they expect my mages to protect anyone. We are out of time. We must have the rimelace now, or there will be no hope." The Prisma gave Cassia's hands a squeeze.

Cassia flexed stiff fingers and returned the gesture. "I will wait no longer to speak."

CASSIA SPEAKS

ASSIA SPENT THE HOUR before the Summit in her bedchamber, emptying her stomach until nothing came but dry heaves. When Perita finally dared enter despite the absence of a summons, Cassia knew dusk had fallen. She was out of time.

Perita hovered a pace away for a moment. Cassia, her head still over her basin, imagined the girl wringing her hands.

"You are too ill to go," Perita said.

"I must go."

Knight stood still and strong while Cassia used him as leverage and got herself to her feet. She paused to swallow repeatedly. Perita waited a moment, then closed in, a damp cloth in each hand. She pressed a cool rag to Cassia's forehead. The other, which Perita must have warmed at the fire, she used to wipe Cassia's mouth. Cassia made herself stand still and not jerk away. Embarrassment trembled in her already tortured belly. Then tears pricked at the back of her eyes. The final humiliation.

With her usual diligence, Perita undressed Cassia and slid her finest linen tunica and bronze court gown over her head. They would be soaked with sweat in moments.

Cassia could tell herself how many lives she might save. How glad and grateful the Prisma would be. That at least one person at the table would not judge her. He wouldn't even gloat that he had told her so. He would congratulate her afterward. None of it was enough to get her out of this room, knowing she would speak before the king. Without his permission.

Cassia clutched at Knight's ruff, leaning some of her weight on him. Even he was not enough.

Perita knelt and wrestled Cassia's slippers onto her feet. She was dressed. No more excuses to delay.

"We must go." Perita twisted the knife.

Cassia realized she could no longer see the room before her, just dark blotches on her vision. She lost her sense of where the floor was.

Anger surged inside her. Her own body was going to betray her and prevent her from going anywhere. All this effort, wasted. She was going to tumble right to the floor in a dead faint, powerless to stop it.

She flung out a hand, reaching for anything to steady her. Wood met her flesh. Bedstead? She gripped it with all her strength and dragged in a breath.

She would not succumb. She refused. She would not be powerless.

Her vision cleared, the roar in her ears eased. She could hear Knight whining and Perita asking her if she was all right.

Cassia straightened. "I am ready to go."

Every step from her room to the pavilion was an act of will. She did not look at anything but the way in front of her own feet. Not at the free lords taking their seats. Not at the Hesperines across the table. Not at the Mage King's throne and...him.

She pushed herself through the final obstacle of the mage ward and walked straight to the herald with her skin stinging. She kept her head down at a modest angle, but looked in his eyes.

He stared at her, his lip curling in an uncertain expression. She must not give him a chance to speak.

She held out her hand, showing him her dirty fingernails and the Kyrian mages' seal. The bluestone medallion engraved with the goddess's glyph felt smooth and weighty on Cassia's palm. She focused on it. "On behalf of the Prisma of the Temple of Kyria at Solorum, I submit myself as a speaker before His Majesty, the honorable Council of Free Lords, and His Majesty's esteemed guests from Orthros."

Silence was a little bubble around her and the herald. It grew, swelling out and out. The herald looked her up and down. The whole Summit did so, she knew. But she only had to look at the herald. He bowed and retreated. Cassia did not watch, but she heard him murmuring, and the voice that answered in low tones was Lord Titus's.

Sooner than she expected, the herald returned. "On behalf of His Majesty, Lord Titus conveys his welcome and invites you to speak once His Majesty's business is concluded."

At the very end of the night. She would have to endure through all the debates. "Convey my thanks to Lord Titus."

She was doing well. She had managed to get the words out of her mouth. Now she was finding her chair. Sitting down. Correcting her posture.

One moment at a time. She would defeat each as it came.

She did not hear the discussion. She tried to comfort herself with the knowledge that the speeches were more important to the free lords than her little scene before the herald, and no one had time to speculate as to her intentions. The free lords' voices blurred together, and then the musical tones of the Hesperines—not Lio, everyone but Lio. Her battle with herself allowed her to spare just enough thought to realize he was not speaking tonight.

The king never spoke at the Summit. That was the one certainty she could rely on.

To keep staring at Lord Nonus's left heel was an excellent strategy. She would appear as if she were paying attention, but the king remained outside her peripheral vision.

An eternity passed, one moment at a time.

Then Lord Titus announced for the king what His Majesty did not want. "On behalf of His Majesty, I ask the honorable Council of Free Lords and our esteemed guests from Orthros to hear Lady Cassia Basilis."

Would the king lift a hand and put a stop to Cassia's plan then and there?

She stood. The green's dampness seeped around the leather soles of her slippers and through the upper fabric.

No one spoke. No one called out to halt her.

The king was not going to prevent her. That meant she would face his judgment later. Most likely behind the closed doors of his solar.

She felt as if she were swimming against a strong tide as she walked past the rows of chairs. Knight must be at her side, but she was aware only of herself and how she carried herself forward.

When she approached the table, a space to stand actually awaited her there. Some of Lord Hadrian's councilors had shifted their chairs farther apart. How had he convinced them to do that for her?

Cassia came to stand at the table.

The sheer number of eyes staring at her did nothing to diminish the power of those two pale, icy blue ones she knew were among them.

If she had to kneel before him in this moment, she would never get up. But the Summit was the one occasion she could remember in her entire life when kneeling before the king was not required.

On this occasion, Cassia was not even a member of the court. She was a representative of the temple.

She reached out and laid the mages' seal on the table with a thump. All eyes turned to the glyph on the medallion: a circle within a circle. A child within a womb. The world within the goddess.

Cassia must look back at them. A timid plea was not enough. She must speak with knowledge...with authority.

She curtsied deeply to the table at large in recognition of the entire Summit's authority, then lifted her chin. Swept her gaze about the entire gathering. Those sky-blue eyes to her left almost caught her. She fled them.

A different pair, deeper, darker, gleamed at her. She must not hesitate upon them either. Must not look for approval in them. She was not here to prove Lio right.

She became aware of the night insects chirping. It was time to speak.

"The Prisma thanks you for hearing her agent." The words came. "Within the secrecy of these wards, she wishes to divulge a grave truth to you, my lords."

The words were her map, her safe path. Focus on the words.

"The Solorum mages' sisters in eastern Tenebra have borne witness to cases of frost fever."

Gasps, murmurs, grunts of surprise. She had dealt the most powerful blow she could tonight, and it had struck.

"Even those of us without the Prisma's expertise understand it is only a matter of time before the fever reaches every corner of the kingdom, as it has in years past. She need not remind you only rimelace is an effective remedy for children who fall ill. The gods' will is mysterious, and they saw fit not to bless the temple with a healthy crop, despite the mages' finest spellwork and most earnest prayers."

The gathering had fallen silent. She wished they were still muttering. It seemed like it might have made the most difficult part easier. Cassia licked her parched lips. She looked at Lio's uncle's forehead, then each Hesperine's in turn. Finally at a lock of black hair across Lio's own brow. "With respect, the mages implore you, our esteemed guests, to show Orthros's benevolence and generosity yet again. They ask that you once more extend the offer of your gift of medicinal herbs."

Now she cast a glance around the Council again. "Lords and fathers of Tenebra, the temple asks that you consider their dire need and the danger to our children. They request that the honorable men who speak for Tenebra…and His Gracious Majesty…reconsider their decision, now armed with knowledge of this threat."

Cassia turned. She fixed her eyes on the hem of the king's robe, and she gave him the mere curtsy owed to he who presided over the Summit.

She had gainsaid the king.

As if she had not just come as near treason as she might ever in her life, she turned back to the lords and curtsied again. "Thank you for granting the mages of Kyria your ear."

Victory. Escape.

But she did not flee. She took the Kyrian seal in hand and walked back to her seat. This time she could no longer attempt to make herself an extension of the chair. She heard the debate going on before her. She had started it.

Gazes sought and found her. Heads bent and whispered. She saw Lio exchange a long, meaningful look with his Grace-cousin Javed, the healer. Lio's uncle murmured to them in the Divine Tongue, and Javed gave an answer Cassia did not need to understand. She already knew what the Hesperines' reply would be.

Javed stood and bowed to the Summit, turning to include everyone. Especially Cassia.

"As the representative of Queen Soteira and all healers in her service, I would like to thank the mages of Kyria for their honesty." He looked right at Cassia and gave her a nod. "I hope Lady Cassia will convey to them our deepest respect for their courage and the delicate way they have handled this difficult truth, which must certainly be contained to avoid public panic."

Cassia nodded in return. Her stomach thumped, but did not pain her.

Javed continued his address, a lesson on the dangers of frost fever that revealed the depth of his knowledge and reminded the Tenebrans of the stakes. Was Cassia the only mortal there who recognized how sincere his concern was? With a healer's sympathy, he made it known the Hesperines were more than happy to provide the rimelace and other medicines. Cassia had issued the threat. There could be no more effective follow-through than Javed's heartfelt plea.

After he concluded and took his seat, the free lords' murmurs resumed and grew in volume, promising an intense debate. Lord Titus excused himself from the table and ascended the dais. Amachos lifted his hands, and an inner ward encircled the king and the other two men. It came down again almost as soon as it had gone up.

Lord Titus's eyes looked hollow as he returned to the table. A moment of silence dragged on before he spoke. And Cassia knew what the reply would be.

"His Majesty's answer is the same."

Cassia did not listen to the rest. There would be no debate. There would be no appeal. Only Lord Titus's meaningless attempt to garnish the king's refusal. But no one could make a death sentence palatable.

Cassia did not feel like she would vomit again. She was not afraid. Her anger had deserted her.

She sat, silent, and did not feel anything at all.

VICTORY

LIO FOUND CASSIA SITTING on the rim of the Font, her arms around Knight. He drew a deep breath to smell her scent and let out a sigh of relief.

When he drew near, she looked up at him. "I do not rescind my protest of your effort to bring me to the table. You should have asked me first. But if you had, I hope I would have had the courage to say yes."

"You changed your mind. Cassia, I am so glad."

"What a momentous night, when a Hesperine heretic helped a bastard girl, his fellow godsforsaken, to the table."

"As for not asking you first, I am sincerely sorry."

"I accept your apology. I was glad for my place at the Summit. As the free lords' children die in their arms, they will remember my words and know the king is to blame."

Lio sat down beside her, the closest he could come to offering her solace. "Don't quit the field yet."

"That's the difference between us, Lio. I know when it's time for a strategic retreat, and I'm not too proud to make it."

"Retreat, after what you did tonight? After such a victory?"

She gave her head a single shake. "I lost. Naturally."

"Far from it. You laid waste to every man there who did not wish to hear you speak…and to your own fear."

The Light Moon was a mere slip overhead, but the Blood Moon's gleam caught in Cassia's gaze, revealing for once the hidden depths of her emotions to his sight as well as his Gift. "Then why doesn't it feel like a victory?"

"Doesn't it?"

Her arms tightened around Knight, but her eyes shone brighter.

"The war isn't over yet, and your ally from Orthros has arrived." Lio gestured to himself. "With an offer of reinforcements. Let it be noted I am consulting with you before charging in this time."

"What more could we possibly do, Lio?"

"We can give the herbs to the mages."

She sat up straighter, her feet hitting the ground. "Madness."

"Necessity," he countered. "Strategy."

She was already shaking her head.

He spoke quickly to make as much of his case as he could before she went back to being angry with him. "The king refused the herbs. That's the end of it, as far as he's concerned. It does not matter to him what becomes of gifts for which he has no use. He assumes the rimelace will sit with our other goods in the fortress until we return to Orthros. If those herbs disappear from our possession, he will never know."

"No."

"Cassia, think on it. What other choice do we have?"

"Not to attempt the impossible."

"You already have. And you do not regret it."

She surged to her feet, and Knight moved with her. "Don't—"

"Don't what, Cassia? Test your limits?"

Her gaze flashed, and this time, her temper did not make Lio feel guilty or alarmed. Actually, he found it satisfying. Intoxicating.

"Don't instruct me on how to deal with the king."

He held up his hands. "Not at all. You're the expert, and I need your help."

"I will not help you conspire." Her voice was cold as ice, her spirit afire. "I have a previous commitment to my continued survival."

"I would never suggest this if I thought we could not do it safely."

"You should make a greater commitment to your own survival." She jabbed a finger at him. "Have you no appreciation for how dangerous I am to you? You risk yourself and your entire embassy every time you dare gaze too long upon one of the king's possessions."

"I am not afraid, for I know better than to believe he owns you."

Cassia's anger took hold of Lio, but he did not pull away. The fierce pulse of her blood exhilarated him. Her fury was a primal, beautiful power trembling on the surface, ready to break free.

"Think of the lives we could save, Cassia."

"What use is it if one temple in all of Tenebra has enough medicine for one outbreak? What does it matter if we save folk from frost fever, when a bad tooth or bandits or their own king may be the death of them next year?"

"It matters that those people will not die because of something we could have prevented."

Her arm came up like a weapon, pointing back toward the palace. "Lay the blame at his door. Where it has always been."

"Where will the mages lay the blame?" he asked. "If they're anything like the healers I know in Orthros, they'll take it to heart when so many die under their care. They'll blame themselves."

"How dare you try to make me feel guilty enough to help? *You* won't endanger your own life by trying to save them."

A few herbs, a danger to her life. What a broken world she lived in. But Lio had spent too many hours in the king's presence to question her fears. Tenebra and its king were twisted enough to brand an act of kindness an act of treason.

Lio could see it now. A young woman trying to save children's lives and bring aid to the devout mages who had placed their trust in her. It would be trivially easy for Lucis to call her instead an ungrateful, undisciplined bastard daughter who flouted his authority and consorted secretly with heretics.

And Lucis would, simply because she dared go against his decision. He dealt swiftly and emphatically with anyone who did not show him absolute obedience. It was the reason why the Tenebrae had become Tenebra and why Cassia's life had been one long war.

For her to be caught violating any decision of the king's was enough to bring his punishment down upon her. For her to be involved with a Hesperine would truly be the death of her.

Lio had known this journey would be dangerous, that it would take him from the refuge of Orthros and plunge him into a harsh reality. But even here in Tenebra, he felt confident in his elders' determination to protect him and in his own power.

He expected to live forever. He had never known what it felt like to fear for his own life until he had felt it with the woman before him.

He had known before he came looking for her tonight there was only one way they could do this.

"Cassia, I would never put you in greater danger than I am willing to face myself. I wouldn't even suggest this, unless I intended to shoulder my fair share of the risk. I will come with you to the temple."

She was silent for an instant, but her astonishment was palpable. "Nonsense. That is the least circumspect, most unwise way we could possibly approach this. It would make much more sense if you simply brought me the herbs here and I delivered them to the temple on my next visit."

"And then you would shoulder all the risk. Where would you hide the herbs in the hours between our meeting and your arrival at the temple? Who might discover them in your possession? How would you explain where you had come up with a shipment of the very rimelace you implored the embassy to provide? I can see that and many other possibilities for failure running through your mind, and I will not stand by while you face them alone."

Her surprise blossomed into something more powerful that made her look away. He was learning to reach her within her armor. His words had touched her, even though she gave no indication.

"You are right," she replied. "There are many ways in which we might fail. Too many."

"We shouldn't underestimate ourselves. We can accomplish this without the king ever knowing."

"Arrogance is the surest path to failure."

"I'm not being arrogant. I'm being realistic." What would her retaliation be, if he kept using her own words against her like this? He'd best tread carefully. "Make an appraisal of our capabilities and tell me if you think we cannot succeed."

"The mages will never let you near the temple. What makes you think the Prisma will even agree to deal directly with heretics?"

"Did you not speak for her at the Summit, when you asked us for them outright?"

"The request was hers, yes, but that was when the king would receive the gift on her behalf."

"Would she not be all the more amenable to Lady Cassia accepting it for her?"

Cassia's pulse began to pound anew. "They'll know. The whole temple will know I've had contact with you."

"Certainly not. We will act with perfect discretion. We will go to any lengths necessary to ensure only those whose interests align with yours know you are involved." Lio leaned forward. "I've set out my terms, now you decide yours. Think on it. Take as much time as you need. The herbs aren't going anywhere."

The rest remained unspoken between them. The frost fever would not wait. It drew nearer.

Cassia swallowed, and the motion of her throat drew Lio's gaze to her neck. How sweetly he could drive away her fears, if they had met anywhere else but Tenebra. If they were anyone else but Initiate Ambassador Deukalion and Lady Cassia Basilis. But if that were the case, she would not live with such fears. And he would have tasted that sweetness long since.

"It would be best if no one but the Prisma knew," Cassia said slowly. "If she would grant us a private audience by night... But how in the world could you accompany me to the temple without raising the alarm? Doesn't Amachos keep a close eye on the whereabouts of every member of the embassy?"

Lio waved a dismissive hand. "The only methods of detection he will have learned here in Tenebra are unsophisticated and vague. This isn't the Magelands, where specially trained masters keep watch for Hesperine intrusion every hour of the night."

"You seemed worried enough when Amachos happened upon us before."

"That's because you did not stay put inside my concealment. But you see, I managed to veil you all the way back to the palace without him noticing."

She went quiet. "You did?"

Lio smiled.

"Oh." She cleared her throat. "You were worried before I left, though."

"I was concerned about controlling myself in Amachos's presence without anyone to help me listen to my conscience."

Her curiosity was easy to sense. "I did not know you felt such personal antagonism toward him."

"I try not to. The point is that taking us both to the temple without alerting Amachos is within my abilities. Are you familiar with the basic principles of magical perception?"

"I wasn't paying attention during that part of my training for entry into the Order of Anthros. Enlighten me."

"Anyone capable of magery can sense magical power, including an act of power by another mage." Lio stopped himself before launching into examples of the various forms of magical power that could be sensed in other beings and the natural world. He really was getting better at being concise. "How easily one mage detects another's spells depends on a number of factors, including their respective levels of skill, experience, training, and familiarity with that particular arcane path. There are as many techniques for detecting magic as there are for concealing one's magic from detection."

"Well, I have seen you have a knack for concealment."

"Hesperines admittedly devote a great deal of time and study to that in particular."

"Yes, I suppose being hunted for centuries by the Mage Orders might inspire you to do so."

"One of the easiest but also most effective ways of hiding your own magic is to allow greater power to hide it for you. A great deal of magic going on at once in close proximity will befuddle the senses of anyone trying to sense you. The more powerful magic will bombard the mage who tries to perceive your working, and if yours is more subtle, it will be lost in the clamor."

"So it's as if all the minstrels are playing at once, but different songs. You can only make out the melody of whoever is playing the loudest."

"Perfect analogy."

"Is your way of traveling, as you demonstrated with your handkerchief, a very loud song?"

"Not for a Hesperine alone. To step from one place to another is innate magic—very hard for a mage to detect. However, bringing a mortal with me requires an active working."

"I remember what you said about working with the world rather than against it." She frowned at him. "I suppose that makes you a fish swimming in the current of a river, and I am a bird you are trying to bring with you."

Lio laughed. "You will not be in danger of drowning, I assure you, although it may be as uncomfortable as wet feathers."

"I never imagined magic could make so much sense," she remarked. "The Orders make it sound like obtuse nonsense."

"Of course. They guard their knowledge jealously, for their power is built on the ignorance of others."

"So how would a knowledgeable heretic suggest we obscure the magical working required to get us both to the Temple of Kyria?" Cassia asked.

"Keep in mind the king has lodged the embassy in Solorum Fortress, a site more military than magical. There are no spells on the barracks. It is easy for Amachos to keep watch on us when we're in our quarters."

"So that's why he feels safe letting nothing but human guards patrol the fortress. He's able to sense any mischief you might get up to from afar."

"Which is why all our mischief must be committed elsewhere. For example, small spells are quite easy in the palace, because it's covered in centuries of all sorts of magic Amachos has no hope of scrubbing away. He has also added his own wards and such, but those are painfully obvious and thus easy to avoid."

Cassia watched Lio keenly, absorbing and gathering all he said to her, as was her way with information that might prove useful to her. Even without delving into her mind, he could feel it at work.

He went on, "Naturally the Temple of Anthros is drenched in magic, although I wouldn't dare set foot in there, even if I brought nothing more than my innate aura with me. I would be a blatant note of discord in Anthros's battle music. The Sun Temple is Amachos's domain, and by now he has surely intertwined his own magic with the spells in the very walls, to the point that my mere presence would alert him."

The way Cassia pursed her lips when she was concentrating had a charming effect on her mouth. "So if you were to perform some act of magic at the Temple of Kyria, which is the Prisma's domain, Amachos couldn't sense it under the Kyrian mages' own spells. Although the women in the temple would certainty know."

"Precisely."

"I think I see. You could step to the temple, and Amachos wouldn't sense your arrival."

Lio nodded.

"If the Prisma knew to expect you, do you think she could...I can't believe I'm volunteering her for this. In theory, could she conceal your arrival from her fellow mages in the temple?"

"That depends on her strength as a mage."

"I suspect she is powerful," Cassia ventured. "Not that I am any judge of such things. But I've seen her mend skin and bone without a needle and thread."

"Then her power is considerable," Lio said with admiration, "and after her many years as Prisma, her temple's magic will be as close to her as her own. She could certainly cover my step into her domain under one of her workings. Her fellow mages would feel only Kyria's own magic at work."

"You are not worried she will expose you?"

Lio leaned his arms on his knees, folding his hands. "When you and I made our pact to speak freely with each other, you pointed out it is in both our best interests to keep each other's confidences. Doesn't the same principle apply here? If the Prisma exposed us, she would expose herself."

"I wasn't sure that was enough to satisfy you. You seem to value the notion of trust more than I do."

He knew better than to ask Cassia whether she trusted the Prisma. Trust was always the wrong word to use with Cassia. "What is your opinion of her?"

Cassia hesitated. But Lio knew that had more to do with her hesitation to speak well of anyone than any lack of admiration for the Prisma. Cassia wouldn't be considering this, if she didn't trust the mage.

"Since I've been here," Cassia said, "her actions have shown her only goals to be the good of her temple and the welfare of her patients. She cultivates her prestige as a means to promote the well-being of those in her care, rather than for her own benefit. Her idea of pleasing the goddess is helping people, not holding them to precise standards. She has always dealt fairly with me."

"I have complete confidence in your assessment. For that reason, I trust the Prisma." Lio hated to go on, but if he withheld anything from Cassia at this point, it would only bring disaster. Above all, she had a right to know everything and weigh her own risks accordingly. "I believe the Prisma's intentions are pure, and that she has a justifiable motivation for misrepresenting the frost fever to others."

Cassia took a step back. "What do you mean? What do you know about the fever?"

"I have it on good authority there is no outbreak of frost fever in eastern Tenebra." Lio wished he could tell her he had it on the authority of the Master Envoys. Rudhira's people were safe. Lio's warning had not been necessary. Although it had been appreciated. He wished he could tell Cassia that, too.

"How would you know something like that?" she asked.

"Let's just say someone like a free lord's knight's saddler's brother told me and leave it at that, shall we?" His humor deserted him as quickly as it had come. "Will you take my word on it?"

"Your people care about children," she said, as she had before.

The only *yes* he would hear from her, but a yes nonetheless. "We do, Cassia. And I believe the Prisma does as well. If she has invented this rumor about frost fever in the east, surely she has a good reason."

Cassia began to pace before the fountain. Knight stood on guard, watching her progress back and forth. "There is simply no harmful reason for her to try to convince the Summit she needs children's medicine. Rimelace has no dark purposes. What dishonest dealings could the Prisma possibly have in mind? Selling rare medicine to smugglers so she can buy shoes for the orphans?" Cassia snorted.

"What do you think her motivation could be?"

"I can think of only one reason. The same reason she had for telling no one of the fever in the first place."

"To avoid frightening the people."

Cassia halted. "Yes. Perhaps people would panic if they knew the truth. For example, if the truth were that the fever is closer than eastern Tenebra."

She fell silent. Lio waited for her next protest of their plan. But none came. Her expression of concentration turned grave.

She had decided. He had convinced her.

"It won't work," she said. "The king won't miss the herbs, but the other members of your embassy will."

Lio tried not to let his hopes sink. Just last night she had railed against him at the mere suggestion he might have revealed their encounters to the others. He would lose all the ground he'd gained with her, if he pointed out his fellow Hesperines would gladly consent to this plan and were perhaps the only people this side of Orthros who would be no danger to her.

He must hide still more from everyone in the embassy. First these meetings with her. Now a plot.

He was going to trust the goodwill of a human mage he had never met without even telling his own people.

Where would the deception stop?

It could stop when no lives were at stake. If his family and the Master Envoys knew what he was considering, they would agree. They would support his decision for the sake of the children who must be protected.

They would understand it was safer for them if they did not know. If Lio misstepped…if he fell…he would take the fall alone.

"I can make sure they don't notice the herbs are gone," Lio promised.

Cassia's eyes narrowed. "They're all older than you. Even you are sometimes in awe of their power. How can you hide such a thing from them?"

"They don't expect me to hide anything. It's easy to keep a secret from others when they believe you have no secrets."

"You didn't really answer my question."

Lio considered his next words. Her pulse sped up, and for once it did not lure his fangs from his gums. It only reminded him he was losing her.

"Your elders must not find out, Lio. No one must find out." Her heartbeat fluttered into panic again.

He could almost see the terrors that haunted her mind's eye. A political catastrophe for all Hesperines—but for her, a death sentence.

Involving fewer of Lio's people might mitigate the damage to their cause. It wouldn't protect her.

But Lio could protect her.

"No one will find out," he promised. "My magic will see to that."

"Forgive me if I do not stake my life on illusions."

Lio bit his tongue, and not for the first time. This was his one failure to keep their Oath of openness, for it was the one truth that might shatter their promise. Once she knew he was a thelemancer, would she think he had been manipulating her all this time? She did not bat an eye at fangs and blood, but if she believed he had deceived or, worse, controlled her, she would turn against him in a heartbeat.

But if she believed the truth, that he was using his magic on her behalf, she would realize he had the power to keep her safe.

Lives now depended on Cassia's willingness to stake hers on Lio's power. He had to take the risk and confess the true extent of his power. He must have faith in her courage and the strength of the Oath they had forged together, if he wanted her to have faith in him.

"Cassia, I'm powerful enough to make sure six elder Hesperines don't know the herbs are gone."

She drew a breath, her mouth curling in one of her sarcastic expressions. He expected a dismissive remark, but it never came. She considered him.

"Do Tenebrans truly doubt the existence of the Mage King and the Changing Queen?" he asked.

"Such heroic figures make for good stories around the hearth fire, but don't seem very real when your belly is empty. They do seem very convenient for living kings who need a precedent to justify royal authority."

"I can assure you the Mage King and the Changing Queen were real, and they would be ashamed of Lucis. As you know, I'm too young to have known them, but I grew up listening to my father's stories of when he met them during the Last War."

Her lips parted.

He rubbed a hand over the back of his head. "Uncle Argyros negotiated at the very first Equinox Summit. Hence the Queens have sent him to reaffirm the Oath ever since."

She blinked, then shook her head. "Well, your aunt is the Guardian of Orthros. Why shouldn't your uncle be Silvertongue? Just don't tell the minstrels two of their favorite villains are a pair. The resulting compositions would not help the diplomatic situation."

"I'll be sure to keep it to myself. Unlike Aunt Lyta, Uncle Argyros isn't terribly fond of being a ballad sung to give folk a scare on a winter night."

"You need not defend him to me. I would never believe your uncle used thelemancy on the Mage King to trick him into letting your people escape."

Lio smiled. "Indeed, there was no bewitchment involved, only some of the most brilliant negotiations in history, from both sides."

"So tell me, who is your father?"

Lio laughed. "Not a diplomat. He has a reputation for being quite… passionate…in all that he does."

Cassia crossed her arms. "You take after him."

Lio sat back. "Do you really think so?"

"You're much too passionate to be a diplomat."

Perhaps she was right, but he smiled at her. "Everyone tells me I am conscientious and well-behaved."

Now Cassia snorted.

He grinned. If such an expert judge of character said he was more like his father than he thought, he felt inclined to believe her.

"Your father is a great deal older than your mother," Cassia observed.

"A winter romance, to be sure."

Cassia's brows lifted, but if she was filling in the blanks about his passionate father's long years unattached, she did not say. "Your uncle is much older than you."

"But it is not my uncle who is steward of the medicines we brought. That cargo is Javed's responsibility."

"You said Arkadia gave him the Gift," Cassia reminded him. "She's only three hundred and eighty-six, but she is Argyros's daughter. Doesn't the power run in the entire bloodline?"

"Kadi and Javed are indeed heirs to Uncle Argyros's power. But my uncle is my father's younger brother. That was true even before they were Hesperines, but most significantly, my father received the Gift first. Uncle Argyros is vastly older than me, but not older than the blood that made me what I am. My father has nurtured my mother and me on his blood for almost ninety years. I'm still learning what to do with it all, but I have a great deal of power."

Cassia looked at him as if she weren't sure what to make of him.

As if he fascinated her.

Just like the first time she'd seen him, she was not afraid.

Lio took a deep breath. "Besides, I have a dual affinity."

She put a hand to her chin. "Let me think. That must mean you are adept at two arcane paths."

"You are a quick study."

"Bloodborn on the Winter Solstice under two full moons *and* possessed of a dual affinity? How unfortunate for you."

"I'm afraid so. In any case, my uncle is not only my mentor in my service, but also in one of my arcane paths. He has devoted decades to bringing me to the level of his skill. He tells me he has never taught anyone with quite this much magic, except his own daughter Nike, my eldest cousin." Lio glanced down at his hands. No, he should watch Cassia's reaction. He looked up at her, hoping this would not be the moment he finally saw fear in her eyes for the first time. He cleared his throat. "I'm one of the three most powerful mind mages in Hesperine history."

Lio listened to Cassia's heart thump in her chest, and then he heard her laugh.

That sounded nothing like the first time she had pretended to laugh, nor even like the winsome chuckle that had emerged from her when they had first laughed together. This sound was bright. Defiant. Free.

She was standing in the dark with a mage of the night who could rob her of her Will, and she knew it, and she felt safe.

"I'm glad you're on my side," said Cassia.

Lio had thought he put her off balance. But those words coming from her made his world shift. This was more than a success. It was a gift. Cassia had not simply deemed his magic to her advantage.

She had decided Lio was on her side.

"I am at your service," Lio pledged.

"I will speak with the Prisma tomorrow, and we shall see what she makes of our plan."

25

days until

SPRING EQUINOX

INTERMEDIARY

"**S**URELY THERE ARE ALTERNATIVES we might pursue." As Cassia said the words, she wondered when she and the mages of Kyria had become *we.*

"I appreciate your determination." The Prisma's sigh betrayed how tired she was. She sank into her chair beside the altar. "But when you are my age, you will understand there comes a moment when you must acknowledge all the alternatives are exhausted and it is time to admit defeat."

How strange for anyone to tell Cassia she was the one who did not know when to give up.

The Prisma's hand tightened on the altar, as if what she really wanted to do was lift that hand and slam it down. "I fail to see how the Hesperines can grow anything in that wasteland of theirs. Did you know Orthros is covered in constant night for most of every winter? The sun doesn't even make it above the horizon. How do plants thrive when they are trapped in darkness?"

A strange and powerful image came to Cassia's mind. A mere fantasy of Lio's world, surely. But it struck her powerfully.

An endless wood in an endless night. No glimpse of the sun, just moonlight that never faded. Living, growing things thriving in the shelter of that darkness, nurtured by a white glow like Lio's spell light.

"It is their magic," Cassia said. "They can help things grow."

"I ask my goddess of life and harvest every day how such an irony is possible, that heretics can coax healing out of ice better than Kyria's hand-maidens can out of her own soil, and I still don't have an answer. Frigid as Tenebra is, it isn't cold enough for rimelace to thrive without the aid of magic. And our magic was not enough." The Prisma rubbed her face in both hands.

Cassia shifted on her feet. They wanted to carry her to the door. But she stood riveted by the image of despair before her: this powerful woman slumped in a chair with her head in her hands.

Even as Cassia prepared her thoughts, she prepared a defense in case her own words turned on her. She supposed the Prisma's vestibule, all things considered, was not the worst place to utter heresy. In her compassion, the mage might dismiss Cassia's suggestion as the misguided notion of a young person desperate to help.

"There may still be a way."

The Prisma lowered her hands and lifted her head, her eyelids drooping in exhaustion. "I wish there were, child."

"I must beg your clemency before I speak further. If what I am about to say offends you or the goddess whose domain this is, let my words be forgotten…and forgiven…as if never uttered. I only wish to help."

The mage's brows lifted. "What could you have in mind?"

"The king will not accept the herbs. But you and your temple could."

The Prisma blinked, then her gaze sharpened. Her keen mind was clearly working, racing through the possibilities. The consequences.

Cassia pressed on. Tightening the rope about her neck. When had she volunteered for that? "The king wishes to hear no more about rimelace. He assumes it will return to Orthros with the Hesperines. What matter if it happens to be left here at the temple instead?"

"He refused them," the Prisma said. "Therefore they belong only to the Hesperines."

"Yes."

"But would they agree?"

"Yes."

"How can you be sure?"

"The Summit has given me the opportunity to observe the embassy firsthand."

"How much can anyone really observe about such creatures?"

"As much as she can observe about the king or the free lords after a lifetime of watching her back."

At that the Prisma grimaced. "You do well to remind me. You are young only in years."

The comment added fuel to Cassia's words, and they became easier to say. "I am confident the embassy's chief desire as far as the herbs are concerned is to extend the offer as a display of goodwill. Naturally, you and the mages would be able to tell if there were any insidious spells on them. Here in this sacred place, unholy magic would be revealed." Silently Cassia apologized to Lio. But he was a diplomat. He knew one must often say words one found distasteful, for the greater good.

The greater good. Now those were words Cassia would have thought sounded more like Lio than her.

But the Prisma was shaking her head. "This is madness."

See there. Cassia was not the only one who thought so.

"There are too many obstacles," the Prisma lamented. "Too much risk. I can't believe we're even having this conversation."

Was Cassia losing ground? "Surely the goddess would want us to prevent suffering above all. Surely that makes this...not wrong."

"It's not our consciences we need to convince, child. It's the king and the heretics I'm worried about."

"We have satisfied ourselves the king has no cause for ire, and he will not under any circumstances learn of what goes on in Kyria's domain. We also know the Hesperines will agree. What other obstacles could there be?"

The Prisma let out a breath that might have been a bitter laugh. "Aside from those small uncertainties? The little matter of how the daughters of Kyria are to have a conversation with an embassy of heretics staying in the capital, without offending the gods, the Orders, or the king."

"That is the least of our problems. I will act as intermediary."

The Prisma stared at Cassia for a long moment. At last she rose from her chair and rested her hands on Cassia's shoulders. "If you are willing to take on such a thing, who am I to refuse?"

Cassia lost an instant to her own surprise, too startled to speak.

The Prisma *had* known what she asked, when she requested Cassia first bring information to her about the rimelace. She, who brought people out of danger for a living rather than thrusting them into it, had asked anyway.

And was accepting now.

"I can see how necessary this is," Cassia said. "I know you would not have asked in the first place, unless the need was dire."

"I will not deny it. But I will thank you, and I will pray for you and commend you to the goddess. This won't be easy." She patted Cassia's shoulder. "Saving lives seldom is."

24

days until

SPRING EQUINOX

SACRED RUINS

L IO OBSERVED CASSIA AS she lowered her nose to the bundle of rimelace he held for her. She drew a deep breath, then exhaled, bringing her scent to him mingled with the fragrance of the plants. The combination took him aback and uncoiled a new longing inside him, a blend of frustration and homesickness.

"What do they smell like to you?" he asked.

She glanced up from the herbs, her brow furrowed. "Like a winter snow and a spring morning at the same time. Impossible."

"They smell like Orthros," he said in agreement.

"I've never seen rimelace of this quality! How do you preserve them in such a perfect state?" She studied the herbs in the glow of his spell light. With a gentle touch, she fingered the array of tiny, fragile white petals on one flower. "They're bursting with blooms. See what a pale green the stems are and how the leaves are edged in white? Those are sure signs your people harvested these at their peak. Even the roots are intact. With all the parts of the plant, we can do great things. And you've brought so much." She stared again at the basket by Lio's knee. "You could carry Knight in that."

"I'm sincerely glad no one's life depends on me doing that."

"If you weren't an illusionist and a mind mage, I would wonder how you ever managed to sneak something that large out of your quarters after tonight's Summit, right under six elder Hesperines' noses."

"Light and mind magic used together do produce the most convincing results. When I returned to the fortress last night, after you told me the Prisma agreed and we finalized our plan, I seized an opportunity when Javed and Kadi were in the common room with my aunt and uncle. I relocated the basket of rimelace to my room and left an illusory decoy in its place. A very believable one, rest assured. When I departed for a drink tonight, no one knew I took the real basket with me."

"I see now why you were not in favor of my plan to take the herbs to the Prisma myself." Cassia hesitated. "There are many reasons why it would have been a challenge for me to manage this alone."

Lio knew what an admission that was, coming from her. Now was not the time to point out that in addition to crafting illusions, carrying the heavy load was no trouble for him as a Hesperine, even if he was far from being an athlete of Mak and Lyros's prowess. "I think it proper for me to carry the basket, as it is my people's gift to the temple." Lio returned the bundle of rimelace to the pile in the basket, then took the small canvas healer's satchel from his shoulder and handed it to Cassia. "However, I would like you to present this to the Prisma, if you would."

When she opened the flap, she sucked in a breath. "Seeds."

"So the mages of Kyria can begin cultivating their own from our stock. If they're willing. I can't promise it will grow as it does in Orthros, but it should have a much better chance of survival than any rimelace from Tenebran seeds."

"I didn't realize…this is…it will make a real difference."

"I'm grateful you think it is enough."

"It is, Lio. It is enough." She closed the satchel with careful hands and gazed at the invaluable cargo, not meeting his eyes. "Thank you."

The notion overtook Lio to lift his hands and wrap them around hers where she held the satchel. His wiser self mounted resistance, and she put the bag on her shoulder with her gardening satchel before he had time to resolve the argument.

He heard her take another breath, as if to brace herself. "I suppose we're ready to go."

"Now all we need is a starting point that has its own magical aura to disguise our departure." He nodded toward the fountain. "This does hold considerable power, but I know of an even better place."

Cassia frowned at the Font of the Changing Queen. "It feels no different from the palace to me."

"Naturally. You can feel the magical history of the Tenebrae everywhere, especially the ancient history from the time before the Orders established their laws to restrict magic use."

At his use of the kingdom's traitorous name, she gave him a sly glance. "The artifacts from the Mage King's time are powerful, then, as legends say?"

"If the fountain feels to you as the palace does, you do not need to ask me that question."

Cassia shrugged. "They don't raise the hair on my arms like Amachos's finger twiddling. They feel…full. Like rain clouds."

Now that was a revealing observation indeed. Lio refrained from comment only because he sensed Cassia's tension mounting. She turned her face away and glanced into the trees.

Was she worried about what they dared to do tonight? How far they dared go?

"I can assure you, nothing in the deeper woods will trouble us," Lio said.

"Of course. Knight is more than a match for a few wolves."

Lio exchanged a look with Knight, his forlorn, the dog's satisfied.

"Besides," Cassia added, "if they're anything like the deer, Knight won't have to bestir himself. You will have the predators eating out of your hand."

Lio smiled at her. She looked away quickly, but he did not miss the change in her pulse, the new flavor in her scent. Just like the night of the festival, when she could not seem to stop looking at him across the crowded great hall.

He took a step closer. "I promise I'll keep you safe, Cassia. Tonight it is my turn to protect you."

"Well then, champion," she said lightly, "let's see this place you've chosen for our magical concealment." She strode away from him and past the fountain.

Lio paused to secure the cover over the basket and hoist the load onto his back. He and his spell light caught up with Cassia and entered the woods at her side. "It is an astonishing find. I could scarcely believe my senses when I first happened on it."

"Now I am curious."

"It would be wise to stay close to me. With the Light Moon veiled tonight, we must rely on my magic to light the path." With his free hand, he gestured upward, where the Goddess's white eye was an imprint of light on the sky. The circle glowed softly as if hidden behind her eyelid, but too bright to be truly concealed. The Blood Moon, nearing fullness, cast a reddish aura over the trees.

"Is a veiled moon considered a bad omen among Hesperines, as it is among Tenebrans?" Cassia asked.

"We celebrate all phases of the moons, although each holds a different significance for us. Don't you think that tonight, it looks as if Hespera is winking at us?"

"Imagine that. I've never had a goddess as a coconspirator."

The branches soon became too thick for them to see either of the moons, and darkness wrapped still closer beyond the reach of Lio's spell. Cassia slowed her pace, following his lead. But she would not meet his gaze. The tension in her was not all worry. He wondered how much effort it cost her not to look at him.

Did she not realize she could look? That looking cost them nothing?

Lio guided them along one of their usual ways, and before long they passed the fallen rubble across the path, beyond which they seldom went far. But tonight he would lead her much farther. He took a fork in the trail, and the deer track plunged them into ferns and the shelter of even older trees.

The thick underbrush and narrow gaps between the tree trunks pressed Lio and Cassia closer together. He listened to her heart flutter and tried not to smile at the frustration he sensed in her. His senses attuned to the flush of her skin and the tension low in her belly. She was so aware of him, here within reach. It had never been so hard for him not to reach.

As they approached a weeping willow whose fall of branches blocked their way, he steadied the basket on his back with one arm and extended the other to push the tree's bare limbs aside for Cassia. She slipped right past him, her body within a finger's breadth of his, and ducked under the shelter of his arm.

"Is it very far?" she asked.

"I'm afraid so. We should head a little to the left, past that holly bush." He sent his spell light ahead of her to mark the way.

She set off in that direction, putting still more distance between them.

Knight stalked forward, on the alert, shouldering through leaves and fronds and making way for her. Every now and then, he fidgeted and cast a glance at Lio's spell light.

Following behind Cassia, Lio could look at her without consequences. As she waded through the underbrush and low shrubs, holding her skirts in both hands, a glimpse of her ankle appeared and arrested Lio's attention. What a pity her stocking prevented him from confirming his theory about the full extent of her freckles.

It was a cold Tenebran night, but Cassia was rosy-cheeked and trying to catch her breath by the time the ruin emerged ahead of them. Lio watched her approach the white marble structure where it stood in its sanctuary of thorns with an honor guard of ancient ash trees. She halted before his sacred place, and he marveled. At that moment, the most powerful aura in his senses was Cassia. Her determination and worry, certainty and doubt were their own kind of magical beacon.

"Do you know why something so strong and beautiful lies in ruins?" he breathed.

She gave her head a shake. "People build things, they die, then all they labored so hard for is forgotten."

"This will never be forgotten."

She cast a startled glance over her shoulder at him, then at Knight, whose hackles were on end. "You can't mean..."

Lio joined her before the ruin and put his free hand on the capstone of the arch over the doorway. He rubbed his thumb across the faint impressions of the glyph there. Although the lines were eroded, his own Gift responded in recognition to the magic in the glyph stone. "Many shrines were abandoned during the Ordering. The cults that once lovingly tended them died out. Not this one. This cult was driven out, but they survive. In fact, we do not die."

He heard her feet move, felt her body heat draw nearer. "This was built to honor Hespera."

Lio nodded, letting his hand rest on the glyph stone as if the joy and welcome in that magic could seep through his skin.

"I can scarcely believe it." Cassia lowered her voice. "I thought all your people's sacred sites were completely destroyed this side of Orthros."

"This one nearly was." Lio ran his hand along one of the remaining pillars. "A blast of war magic did this damage. But that mage, whoever he was, must have been in a hurry. Or under duress. He didn't do a thorough job. Then, much later, some other mages did some sort of cleansing ritual." He sighed. "Kyrian, I think, for the evidence of their spells feels like your gardening dress after you've been at the temple."

"But some of your people's power is still here?"

"Oh, yes. It cannot be purged that easily."

Cassia stepped back and heeled Knight close to her, folding her hands in front of her. As if to give Lio space and time.

He hadn't known she had any respect for anyone's gods. But she had called the Mercy by its name, and now she stood patiently and waited for him as he paid his respects to a lost Sanctuary of his Goddess.

He focused on the grooves in the worn capstone that had once been the cup and thorn of the Goddess' glyph. He brought his thumb to his mouth and pricked it on one tooth, then smeared his blood on the symbol. The ruin's power rushed to life and breathed into him.

After a moment, Cassia cleared her throat. "Is it acceptable for me to come inside?"

"Of course. Everyone is welcome in Hespera's safe places. Although the Order of Anthros now maligns her as chaos and violence incarnate, she was once known to all as the goddess of Sanctuary and Mercy. People saw darkness as her gift of protection and blood rituals as a reminder that we must all make sacrifices for the good of others. In the Great Temple Epoch, wanted criminals and honorable warriors sought her blessings side by side, and her mages turned none away."

"I begin to understand why her worshipers became a target."

"Yes, Cassia. You understand well that such things rarely have to do with genuine devotion to the gods or a true commitment to the common good, and all too often with more pragmatic motivations. The Orders of Anthros and Hypnos and the lords and princes who colluded with them had many reasons for vilifying the Cult of Hespera, but most were political."

"Sheltering folk they wanted to hang wasn't popular, I take it."

"I would not want to oversimplify a complex history. But I often think to myself they cast my Goddess from the pantheon for the crime of loving everyone."

"Do not regret that fate, Lio. You are fortunate not to belong to the world Anthros rules." She looked into the ruin's shadowed interior. "You should rejoice in your freedom."

"Join me," Lio said.

Her gaze swiveled to meet his.

"I made sure the structure is safe. No chance of a cave in." He ducked under the archway and into the antechamber of the shrine.

Before Cassia could follow, Knight whipped around her and halted in her path, his back and his hackles to Lio. The hound let out an altogether different kind of warning growl. At her.

Lio stood very still. "Cassia, he never bares his teeth at you!"

"See how different his body language is? He isn't threatening me. He's putting himself between me and the threat." She gave Lio a rueful smile over the beast's back. "He's trying to protect me from myself."

Lio hesitated to answer, wary of trespassing on her bond with the animal. "Protect you from me, you mean."

"Hmm, on closer consideration, it does seem possible that entering a profane shrine with a notorious heretic of the male variety might endanger my reputation."

Lio couldn't find it in himself to laugh. He had thought he'd earned her guardian's tolerance. If Knight revoked it tonight, the hound might prove the greatest threat of all to their plan.

Cassia spoke to Knight in their training tongue, her voice adamant. She pointed to the ground at her side, snapping her fingers. Petite Cassia and enormous Knight faced each other, both standing tall, neither breaking the stare.

Cassia's tension transformed, and her new unease was an erratic current in the Blood Union. Although she stood resolutely on one side of an invisible line in the soil, her hound on the other, Lio could feel how off balance she was.

"If I can get him to enter the shrine, will your spell effect him?" she asked. "Can you take him with us to the temple?"

"It will be a challenge." What an understatement. Attempting to use his magic on Knight was the part of their plan Lio had been dreading most. But he kept his tone gentle. "He is bred, born, and raised to resist Hesperine magic. That is his nature and one of his greatest strengths. But it does mean it will require an immense effort on my part to bring him with us."

Cassia didn't answer right away. Her unease trembled, ready to overflow. Finally she asked, "Is the strength of the spell you would need to take Knight with us more likely to draw unwanted attention?"

This was difficult for her, and Lio owed her answers as honest as her questions. "The great expense of power would definitely be a greater risk, although I believe the shrine would still be enough to cover us. However… enduring my magic is likely to be extremely distressing for Knight. I suspect it will feel as uncomfortable to him as Anthros's magic does to me, and it is likely to antagonize him. Like any good dog following his instincts, he may lash out at the perceived threat."

Cassia squared her shoulders, and her shaky emotions stilled as if she gripped them in an iron hand. "He will stand watch for us here. He understands staying at the end of the row and guarding for me, even when I have to walk to the other side of the garden."

She held Knight's gaze and began to speak to him, alternating between Vulgus and their private tongue, from loving praises to firm commands.

At last Knight ducked his head, lowered his tail, and went to Cassia's side.

She knelt down and wrapped her arms around her dog. The spell light cast a sheen in her eyes that hadn't been there a moment ago. "*Doon.* Yes, dearest. Right here. I know it's hard for you, but you cannot go with me this time. You must be a good dog and stay. *Doon.* It's all right. I'll be just through that door. You must do me a great favor and guard outside, so no one comes in after me. *Hekna glaan.*"

Centuries of breeding, ancient magic, and a lifetime of training bound Knight to Cassia's service to the death, but Lio had no doubt her debt to her beloved hound was just as powerful. Had the two of them ever been out of each other's sight since the day Knight had bonded to her?

Lio left the basket of herbs inside the shrine and went outside, approaching Cassia and Knight slowly. The hound looked up at him. Lio looked down at the hound.

No sign of teeth. Promising.

Lio knelt on the dog's eye level and eased himself near Union with Knight. Instead of a mind filled with placid welcome, what greeted Lio was a solid wall of wariness. The dog tensed all over and flared his nostrils. He was indeed far more intelligent and aware than an average animal.

Lio halted where he was, holding the path to Union open, but going no farther along it. "Good evening, Knight. You know me. Lio. Your lady's willing champion, remember?"

The dog stood still, his ears cocked.

"You can understand me just fine without any help, I can tell. But to reassure you, I'll put everything I have on the table. See?" Lio spread his hands. He attuned himself to a powerful heartbeat and deep breaths that brought thousands of smells. Then he let Knight hear his heart and smell what he smelled.

"Do you feel that, Knight? You're a liegehound. I know that you and I can't ever achieve real Union. I don't want to make either of us uncomfortable by trying. But if we could, and you allowed me a few moments to experience the world inside that hard head of yours, I know I'd find all my senses focused on only one person. I would feel like nothing mattered except keeping her safe. If you spent a moment in my equally hard head, you'd see exactly the same thing."

Lio heard, in the absence of the sound of Cassia's breathing, that she was holding her breath.

"So you see, Knight," he concluded, "we are of one mind in any case. If you stay here by this door and guard it all night to make sure your lady can feel at ease, then I will stay at her side and protect her with all the power I possess, until I return her to you. Together, you and I will see to it no harm comes to her. Can you trust me to do that?"

Knight got up off his powerful haunches. Lio made himself as still as only a Hesperine could, not even breathing. The dog's massive head drew closer, closer, filling his vision. Two wet nostrils flared, then blew a breath in his face. Raw meat. Muddy paws. Savory treats and Cassia's fingers.

Knight proceeded with his examination, sniffing Lio all over. Lio lifted his arms slowly, the better to let the dog nose at his sides. Finally Knight drew off.

The dog turned his back to Lio and the ruin, faced the dark forest, and planted his rump in the foliage with an air of finality.

Cassia got slowly to her feet. She took one step backward toward the shrine. Knight looked over his shoulder at her, tensing as if to get to his feet, but he stayed where he was.

"The greatest diplomatic feat I have ever witnessed, Initiate Ambassador."

"If I do say so myself, I believe we are the only people in history who have ever persuaded a Tenebran liegehound to guard a shrine of Hespera. The Goddess must be smiling to have such an unusual and capable protector tonight."

Cassia cast one long look at Knight, then turned away.

Her safety was now entirely in Lio's hands.

A HERETIC IN THE TEMPLE

LIO FOLLOWED CLOSE BEHIND Cassia with his spell light and his hands out to offer assistance in case she stumbled. "Be careful. Last night I did my best to clear a path in here, but there's still a great deal of rubble."

She picked her way through the shrine's antechamber. "You mean you can't move ancient stones as big as me with your eyes closed using a single wiggle of your little finger?"

Lio chuckled. "My magic is more akin to that of my mother, who is a master theramancer, a mind healer. It's my father who's the architect. Even before he was a Hesperine, he was a lithomagus, a mage with an affinity for stone. As I've said, I don't take after him in many ways."

"Of course. Just as I am ignorant and unphilosophical."

Lio grinned at Cassia's back. "Wait here, if you will. I'll go ahead into the Ritual Sanctuary to ensure the way remains safe."

"Very good. I'm sure Knight will question you upon our return to be sure you adhered to his rigorous safety standards."

"I hope I can count on you to be my character witness." Lio retrieved the prized basket of rimelace and swung it over his shoulder again before he took a Hesperine step into the ruin's inner room. "Everything is as I left it. Come ahead. I think someone of your height can make it through the doorway without difficulty."

Cassia ducked under the broken column that leaned across the doorway and joined Lio in the Ritual Sanctuary. Her gaze traveled over the slivers of tile on the floor, a mosaic night sky now shattered into fragments, and the two intact pillars at the back of the shrine that, strong and undamaged, still flanked the alcove that would once have held the votive statue of Hespera. "I'm sorry your goddess's shrine is in such a sad state. What a wretched welcome to Tenebra."

It was so unlike her to express concern. Her words touched Lio more than he could say. If he dared say, he suspected she would withdraw again. Best not to call attention to her sympathy. "It gives me as much solace as grief to discover a place where Hespera's magic still dwells on this side of the border. It is so good to find a piece of home."

"Her sacred thorns outside are growing strong." Cassia stepped into shadow and went to stand by the wall. She examined the dry, blackened vines that clung there. "So why aren't these?"

"I wish I knew."

Carefully avoiding the thorns, Cassia touched a hand to one of the few shriveled leaves that still dangled from the stalks, but it crumbled in her hand. "They're too damaged for me to identify them. Do you suppose they were roses?"

"That would be my first guess."

"What a shame. I suspect it would take a garden mage to rescue plants this far gone." How wistful she sounded.

"I mourn the roses. But the magic here lives on. I could ask for no better cover for my spell than a site already infused with Hespera's power. I can only thank the Goddess that Amachos has not recognized this place for what it is."

"I suppose the Anthrian and Kyrian magic used here stand out to the Royal Incompetent's senses, and his Honored Masterfulness doesn't notice the heresy lurking."

Lio laughed. "That is my theory. What poetic justice, that the very spells that destroyed this place and sought to purge Hespera from her own Sanctuary now disguise its true nature."

Cassia turned away from the dead vines, folding her hands. "Tell me what to expect. I am no stranger to discomfort. I only wish to be prepared."

"Do not concern yourself with tales of mages suffering from traversal. With a Hesperine's power to assist, magical travel is not as taxing for a human. The more power the Hesperine employs, the more comfortable the mortal's experience."

"Well, I am in luck, then. You've power to spare, by the sound of it."

"And so do you. You are a strong woman. Children and elders require extra care, and if a human is ill or injured, it can be unsafe to step at all, however…"

She grimaced. "No wonder heart hunters and their hounds are such a threat to Hesperines. You cannot simply step away to escape if you are trying to rescue fragile mortals."

"I'm afraid so. Heart hunters stoop to using children or injured humans to lure us out. But not to worry, as your liegehound is quite chivalrous. And you are not fragile, Cassia."

She lifted her chin. "I am ready, then."

"The return trip will be even easier," he added, "as you acclimate to my magic."

"Very well. What do I need to do?"

Nothing, he almost said. He could step with her while they stood apart. But that was not the most secure, comfortable, or elegant way to involve her in his magic.

And this was too precious an opportunity to waste.

"Come a little nearer," he invited.

Her steps brought her once more into the moonlight that spilled down into the Ritual Sanctuary.

"In blood magic," he said, "the divine and the natural are inseparable. Magic and the senses empower one another."

"So your magic will work on me better if…"

Lio held out his hand to her.

Her gaze fell on his fingers, but she hesitated only an instant. Once she had made up her mind, Cassia would not be stopped. In the name of achieving her ends, she would do anything. Even touch him.

The first sensation of her skin on his, the mere brush of a bird's wing, swept through Lio's entire body. She perched her fingers on the tips of his, barely touching.

"Touch strengthens the spell." He wrapped his hand around hers.

Her hand was so small in his, but he could feel the calluses on her palm and the strength of her grip. He could smell the sap and soil under her fingernails. For a moment they stood like that, both their hearts growing loud in the silence. Perhaps loud enough even for her to hear them.

He let his magic drift out around them, into the darkness and the light. Then he pulled his power close. Her lips parted, and she took a breath. He wrapped her up in his magic, layer upon layer, but ever so gently. Her eyelids drooped, even as her heart pounded louder.

The herbs over his shoulder and the temple of a different goddess waited. He had made a promise.

Lio called to mind the imprint of Kyrian spells he always sensed on Cassia whenever she had been at the temple. That power and the directions she had given him formed a map in his mind both magical and mundane. He went forward first with his Gift, then with his feet.

Stepping through the Prisma's ward was neither unpleasant nor difficult, only a little strange. Lio slipped between tendrils of magic that felt like the vines of some plant species he almost recognized. They clung to him as if they were unwilling to let him go.

But they never touched Cassia. He cradled her in his power and carried her through.

For an instant, they slipped through the world together, free of everyone, wrapped up in his magic.

Then they were standing in a small room awash in candlelight. She dropped his hand as if it were a hot iron. He resigned himself. When she took a deep breath and teetered stiffly away from him, he resisted the urge to steady her.

The magic that surrounded them inundated his senses. A great deal of that power, potent but not malevolent, emanated from the person who stood before them in a white hood and robes of office. Of about Cassia's height, she was a small woman, but her magical stature was greater than that of any mortal Lio had encountered in Tenebra. He rested the herb basket on the ground at his feet and bowed deeply to the Prisma.

Cassia hastened to place herself between him and the mage. "Prisma, allow me to present Deukalion Komnenos, Initiate Ambassador to Tenebra in service to the Queens of Orthros. Initiate Ambassador, this is the Prisma of the Temple of Kyria at Solorum, Daughter of the Harvest Goddess and Mother to her Handmaidens."

The Prisma inclined her head. Lio would not have expected or wanted any further greeting. She was a woman who should bow to no one.

She said nothing, and he was quite aware the burden of speech was on him. It was he who entered her temple on her benevolence.

"Prisma, please accept my heartfelt thanks for your forbearance in allowing one such as I to set foot here. It is a great honor to be a guest in Kyria's domain."

Silence fell and stretched on, and Lio could feel the Prisma scrutinizing him with her magic. He stood still under her examination, doing his best to emanate goodwill. He did not need to investigate to sense the power that guarded her. The ward she cultivated around her person declared loud and clear she had no intention of his unholy Blood Union sinking thorns into her. Lio had no intention of dishonoring her wishes.

The Prisma's ward was a tangle of magic within countless others that protected Kyria's house, just like the temple's stone walls that Cassia had described. Within those defenses, spells grew blithely everywhere, untrained to the trellis of intensive study. Generations of workings as fleeting as annual blooms and as enduring as oaks had come and gone, and countless thrived now. Lio could also feel the gardeners who tended the spells. The temple housed dozens of mages with auras both shallow and deep, but all were bright, living mortal women who drank and breathed magic.

Lio hardly knew how to express his awe. When was the last time a worshiper of Hespera had set foot in a temple of Kyria? When had any Hesperine been privy to such a glimpse down this path into magic?

Lio snatched careful glances at the votive statue of Kyria that stood, life size for a Tenebran woman, on the altar behind the Prisma. He sensed no disgruntlement from the mage and hoped it was permissible to look at her goddess. Lio did not find Kyria anywhere near as beautiful as Hespera. There were some of his own prejudices he did not try to overcome. The harvest goddess stood with perfect posture, wearing a distant smile. The sheaf of wheat she held in one hand made Lio think of a switch, and she brandished a shuttle in the other. There was little doubt as to the destiny this austere mother ordained for the unborn child she carried in her heavily pregnant belly.

But there was nothing austere about the auras of her mages, whose spells were almost enough to drown out the suffering that lurked somewhere in the temple. Almost. Pain was a beacon to any Hesperine, and the temple's infirmary was filled with it. Lio tried to ignore the ache and waited for the Prisma to choose to reveal her thoughts.

Cassia bridged the silence. "I find the gift the initiate ambassador has brought to be great indeed, Prisma, although you will be a much better judge of that than I."

"Let me see," the Prisma replied.

Lio stayed where he was and let Cassia open the basket. What a time for him to be so aware of how near she came to him as she took the next step in their joint endeavor. How close her hands were to his knee as she withdrew one bundle of rimelace from the basket.

Cassia carried the herbs to the Prisma. From the voluminous sleeves of the mage's robes, two wizened hands emerged and hovered over the bushel of rimelace. The Prisma's power spilled out, steady and cool, and again it struck Lio how strange and familiar Kyrian magic felt at the same time. Like some lost cousin of the power he felt Javed and other Hesperines work in Queen Soteira's Healing Sanctuary.

When the Prisma stumbled, Lio startled. It was hard for him to stand on the other side of the room and watch her distress without lifting a finger. But Cassia already had an arm under the Prisma's. Leaning on Cassia, the mage lifted her head and looked right at Lio. For the first time he caught a glimpse under her hood.

Her lined, weathered face far surpassed Kyria's beauty. "I suppose you know what you've brought me."

He bowed again. "Forgive me. I should have predicted how forcefully the rimelace's natural magic might respond to power as great as yours."

Cassia glanced between them with the expression she wore when she was studying, trying to draw out meanings.

"Like calls to like," Lio explained to her. "The Prisma's power, directed at a plant, is a mother calling her own child."

"And these particular children answered as if Mother promised them sweets," the Prisma said.

The remark surprised Lio, and he felt he might have gotten another real glimpse of the Prisma.

She let out a breath, and her strongest emotions escaped the shelter of her magic. Her relief and bitterness were ice and fire in the Blood Union. "So many lives in this single basket, Hesperine."

"I rejoice it is within our power to help. The suffering and death the frost fever brings are specters we all dread."

"Why seek to stop it? Is it not harvest time for you?"

"No. It is the season when the crops wither in the fields faster than we can gather them, and we can do nothing but weep for the waste."

"What do you know of wasted lives?"

"I? Nothing. I've enjoyed an idyllic life in Orthros and never suffered a moment in my life. But the seven babes my mother lost before me were not so fortunate. I've seen the look in her eye when she remembers. Those miscarriages and stillbirths happened because all she had to eat was the meager crop she scraped out of the dirt on her knees, while her husband and kin wouldn't lift a finger to help her. But it has taken her a Hesperine lifetime to realize it was not her fault I was the only child she could save."

The lines in the Prisma's face deepened. Lio needed no Blood Union to sense her compassion. It was woven into the very fabric of the ward that hid her from him.

"She ought to be proud of you."

Lio was so taken aback, he found himself at a complete loss for a reply. Unable to find the right words, he bowed to the Prisma still more deeply.

"Look at what else he has brought you, Prisma." Cassia pressed the satchel into the mage's hands.

When the Prisma saw what was inside, she gasped aloud, just as Cassia had.

An unmistakable breath of excitement wafted from Cassia. "Seeds from the hardy Hesperine crop. Just imagine how they will thrive with the aid of your magic."

The two women bent their heads over the seeds, discussing their plans in rapid murmurs. Lio listened in appreciation and relief to their talk of row arrangements and soil composition, dilution ratios and solvents. It appeared his offering had been accepted.

As they conferred, he tried to make the most of the extraordinary privilege of visiting the temple. He opened his senses to the Kyrian magic, which washed over him and pushed back against him. He was an interloper, a heretic, and a male. He was not about to squander such a chance to educate himself about the magic the women worked here.

Without disrupting Kyria's power with his own Gift, he let her odd and alluring magic imprint its shapes and layers, flavors and scents on his awareness. Only the impressions of distress from the infirmary disturbed his observations. Once again the patients drew his Hesperine heart to them, and the Union honed in on them in spite of him. Well, his study would be incomplete if he did not get a sense of what illnesses and injuries the mages treated and their healing methods. Careful to maintain his control, Lio examined the auras of the ill.

A shiver moved over his skin. So cold. Always shivering. Couldn't ever get warm. If only the cold didn't hurt so. It had started in his fingers and toes, but it was moving upward now. When it reached his chest…

Lio flared his nostrils, and he could smell their fear and loneliness. He felt as if he could reach out and gather each sweating, shaking little body into his arms.

Hespera's Solace, how he wanted to.

"What is it?"

Cassia's voice drew him back. She and the Prisma were staring at him, the older woman wary once more.

Lio blinked hard and cleared his throat. He gave Cassia a long look. Did she know?

He met the mage's gaze. "Twenty-four, Prisma. That is no small number."

Her face paled within her hood. She gripped Cassia's shoulder. "What one does not know is no danger."

"Understood." Lio drew a finger over his cheek, tracing a line from his ear to his chin to indicate the boy who had a cut on his face. "First," he said firmly.

The Prisma nodded. She too must sense how far gone that boy was and that he must be treated before the others. She put a finger to her lips, and Lio bent his head in acquiescence.

Cassia looked between them, her gaze keen. All she said was, "How will you explain the rimelace to the others? What should I say if I am asked?"

"A miracle from the goddess that appeared in the temple in answer to our devoted prayers, a reward for Tenebra's piety." The mage studied Lio. "No one should question the mysterious ways she delivers such blessings."

Cassia turned to rejoin him, but the Prisma caught her hand. "Kyria bless you, Cassia Basilis. Take care."

"We all want the same thing, Prisma. That makes tonight safe."

"I can see that." She gripped Cassia's hand for an instant, then let her go.

Cassia came to Lio's side. Although the Prisma watched, he offered her his hand.

She did not hesitate to take it.

Most likely all it meant was that she was in haste to escape the scene of their indiscretion. But it warmed him nonetheless.

In a moment they were back in the shrine, and the echoes of his own Goddess's power welcomed them.

Joyous barks erupted outside. Lio had never actually heard well-behaved Knight bark, despite the hound's highly developed vocabulary of growls, whines, and menacing stares. Perhaps this was the real secret weapon of liegehounds: deep, roaring bays loud enough to split a Hesperine's ears. Lio tried not to grimace as Cassia withdrew her hand. She hurried under the pillar and out of the Sanctuary.

Lio hung back and gave her and Knight time to reunite before he followed her outside. As he departed the Goddess's shrine, he ran his fingers over her glyph one more time. Then he approached Cassia where she sat in the underbrush with Knight's head on her lap.

"How do you feel?" Lio asked her.

She ran her hand over her hound. "No ill effects. The first step was disorienting, I admit, but not difficult. You must have used a great deal of magic indeed."

"I gave you my word I would do my part."

Cassia looked up at him. "Lio, I must thank you for all you've done tonight."

He knelt among the ferns across from her. He wished he could tell her what those words meant to him. Perhaps it was time he did, regardless of how she reacted. "Your thanks are precious to me."

She did not look away this time. "As is your honesty to me."

Hespera's Grace. He would risk trespassing in any foreign temple to hear her say such a thing. "I will always protect the Oath of honesty between us, Cassia."

"Will you tell me what you and the Prisma know?"

"I'm not sure I ought to thwart her considerable effort to protect you. She would not wish to repay your kindness with danger. Yet I think it should be your choice whether you wish to take on the risk."

"Would it be so dangerous for me?"

"The Prisma certainly thinks so, which makes me wonder. I do not know everything, so I am uncertain as to the true degree of risk involved."

"It has to do with the rimelace?" Cassia guessed.

"Yes."

"Then if the secret became known, I might fall under suspicion in any case, for I spend so much time there and have advocated for the king and Council to accept the medicine." She paused, silent in consideration. "If I did not know, I might not be prepared if something were to happen. I might not see it coming. What you don't know is often a greater danger than what you do know."

Lio waited, unwilling to sway her decision.

"Tell me," she finally said. "I would rather know the secret and decide what to do about it than let it catch me unawares later."

"Very well. Have you been to the infirmary lately?"

"Yes, I help the healers prepare medicinal plants from time to time."

"Are they treating any children?"

"A couple. One of the orphans twisted an ankle in the fields, and a farmer's child is recovering from an affliction of the skin."

Lio shook his head. "The temple is treating twenty-four children who are seriously ill."

Cassia frowned. "Not in the infirmary."

"The Prisma must have them in quarantine, then. Good. Are any of the mages absent?"

"The Prisma sent out a party to aid the villages sickened with frost fever, but…"

"Most likely, they never left, and they're caring for the children in hiding. I'm not sure who else knows."

"Deutera is stewardess of nearly all the Prisma's confidences. But why keep this a secret?"

"Because the children have frost fever. The epidemic is here, and it's contained within the walls of the temple."

Cassia sat frozen for a long moment. Then she slid out from under Knight and surged to her feet. "What would possess the Prisma to do such a thing? If the illness were to spread from within, we would lose our healers first."

"She seems a woman who would take all the lives in Tenebra upon herself."

"Yes. That is just the sort of foolish thing she would try to do." But it was not ridicule or disapproval that drove Cassia to pace back and forth between the thorn thickets. Lio could feel the worry she disguised with harsh words. "They must have diagnosed the children and taken them into hiding before the nature of their illness became widely known. That would prevent people from panicking and even casting out the children. But their families must know."

Lio got to his feet. "Could they be temple orphans?"

"No, none of them are unaccounted for. These are someone's children whom the mages smuggled into the temple."

"Now we understand the motivation for the Prisma's pretense about illness in the east. She needed an excuse for her desperation to procure the medicine. So the question is, where did the illness really begin? Where are the children from and whose are they?"

Cassia pressed her lips together. "If there is a secret within a secret, it is probably wise to stop at one."

Lio wasn't sure he could. Not when he had experienced those fragile young humans' misery and terror. They felt so alone in their hiding place, torn from everything familiar with no one to help them feel safe. Did families wait in fear of losing them? Or were the little ones truly alone, with no one to worry if they ever made it out of the temple alive?

But it wasn't his secret, although tonight's events had made it known to him. Those children were by rights under the Prisma's care, thus by the Oath, he as a Hesperine had no claim on them except his compassion.

"I suppose you are right," Lio said. "We should pursue our questions no further. Will you tell the Prisma I did not heed her request to keep silent with you?"

"Only if I must for her safety or mine. Until then, we shall all go on as we were."

Would they really? Would fully armored Cassia return to her silent battle and give him a passing glance across the Summit pavilion tomorrow night as if nothing had changed? After a night of such confidences and risks on each other's behalf, Lio felt that nothing could be the same. Least of all between him and Cassia.

23

days until

SPRING EQUINOX

THE DRINK

THE MOONS HAD BARELY risen when Cassia arrived at the fountain. Although the Light Moon was still veiled, the Blood Moon shed enough light to reveal she was alone.

It had surprised all the Summit's attendees when the recess had turned into the end of negotiations for the night. With the free lords bickering so amongst themselves, there was nothing else to be done. The king must let them have their squabbles so they could continue to believe they had a say and he could continue to appear faultless in the lack of progress toward the Oath.

Cassia should be troubled by the stalemate, but she welcomed the early escape to the grounds and the knowledge that the Summit would drag on for who knew how long.

She had yet to ask Lio the real question that had brought her to Solorum to seek out the Hesperines.

Cassia gazed into the dark trees and confronted the knowledge that the day, *that* day, was almost upon her. Her fingers closed reflexively upon her gardening satchel, at the thought of what she carried there.

Suddenly she felt alone. She had spent the day at the temple, swept up in the mages' rejoicing over the wondrous appearance of the rimelace. Knight stood patiently beside her, and she knew Lio was here somewhere. But the sense crept over her that she was adrift without anchor. The storm would never end, and there was no one to guide her into harbor.

Cassia set out into the trees on the far side of the clearing. Lio must know she was on her way. It would not surprise her if he preferred meeting at the shrine from now on, in a haven where he could use his power more freely. He was probably waiting for her there.

The forest cut off the red moonlight, and darkness closed around her. She unhooded the small lantern she had brought with her, but the candlelight barely touched the shadows. Without Lio's guidance, she had to pay very careful attention to find her way through the tall undergrowth and between the broad tree trunks. More than once, the deer path seemed to disappear from beneath her feet as if the ferns and darkness had swallowed it. The woods looked *bigger* than they had years ago when two girls, uninterested in ruins, had made forbidden excursions to a pond that seemed a much more appealing destination on a summer day.

The forest felt so much more vast when she was alone.

A glimmer of light off to her right caught her eye. A hint of red moonglow amid the trees. Another clearing, one she and Lio had passed the night before. She was going the right way.

A flicker of motion in the clearing arrested her gaze.

Cassia hooded her lantern. Careful where she put her feet, trying not to make a sound, she eased closer to Knight.

Another flash of motion. She fumbled in her cloak to douse the lantern entirely.

From the clearing up ahead spoke a voice she knew. "Come to me."

Cassia caught her breath. Then she heard hooves in the grass. She let out her breath again, as quietly as she could.

She motioned a stay command to Knight, patting his chest with the flat of her hand. It was a testimony to his loyalty that, knowing what lay ahead, he obeyed.

She crept forward, although she knew what she would see. *Because* she knew what she would see. That call had not been for her. Yet she chose to answer it. She halted in a deep shadow at the edge of the moonlit clearing and watched.

Lio knelt at the center of the glade, awash in blood-red light, and before him stood a young doe. As he gazed at her in silence, she lowered herself to the ground, folding her hocks beneath her.

At the touch of his hand, she stretched out her neck and rested her head on his lap. He ran his slender fingers over her coat, and her sides rose and fell with a sigh. He lowered his head, as if to whisper in her ear.

The doe did not flinch, but Cassia did, the moment his mouth opened on the animal's neck. The Blood Moon outlined the taut tendons in his jaw and the undulations of his throat. And yet his hands remained still and steady. He, the monster of the night, touched a beast with greater gentleness than humans touched their own kin.

Cassia stared, unmoving, until his throat stilled and his jaw relaxed. He paused a moment, then lifted his head. There was no blood on his lips. She did not even catch a glimpse of red moonlight on gleaming fangs.

The deer got to her feet, letting his hands slide off of her. With a shake of her head and a twitch of her ears, she strolled away into the trees.

His gaze did not follow the doe, but rested instead on his own hands. After a moment, he cleared his throat and looked at Cassia.

He had known she was there all along, of course. He had chosen to let her watch.

Cassia took a step forward into the reach of the moonlight. "She wasn't even afraid."

"She had no reason to be." He held out a hand. "If you care to join me, I won't bite."

Cassia drifted farther into the clearing. "I know you don't bite. Except the willing. She was, I take it?"

"Animals make their cooperation or disapproval clear, and we strive to respect that. There is never any excuse for causing them distress. The doe was friendly and curious."

"You weren't even using your mind magery on her?"

Lio shook his head. "Animals already know what so many humans don't realize about Hesperines. We are harmless."

"I wouldn't call you that."

His hands tensed in his lap. She was coming to recognize the almost imperceptible body language of Hesperines, which had seemed opaque to her at first. Or at least, she was learning how Lio's body spoke. He was worried about what she thought of the scene she had just witnessed and its implications.

"Not harmless," Cassia said. "Safe."

Now his fingers relaxed. "Is that what you'd call us?"

She nodded. "You could enthrall any creature, couldn't you? But you wouldn't."

"Indeed, that would be a grave violation. Hesperine law forbids us to abuse the insight the Blood Union affords us. Mind mages have a particular responsibility to understand and uphold these laws. The power and precision of thelemancy goes beyond even the Union. Because we can manipulate the Will, it is our duty to be its foremost defenders. Only in very rare, specific circumstances may we use magic to influence a human's mind."

"So there are occasions when it is permissible?"

"Only when there is no other way to save someone from harm."

"Does that include saving yourself? Might you put an unwilling human into a trance and drink if you were starving?"

"Any Hesperine would seek sustenance from animals first. I hesitate to imagine a situation so desperate that option would not be available."

"I fear my thoughts are trained to consider the worst eventualities," she said by way of apology.

"We do everything possible to prevent such eventualities. Our laws do provide for situations in which we must use our power to neutralize an aggressor...or make someone answer for a crime. But I think you would find Hesperine justice quite different from what passes for justice in Tenebra."

"That's why you resort to the king's negotiation table. It is, of course, a mockery to describe anything that goes on there as a negotiation. But I think the king is the butt of the joke. He plays with his soldiers and his mages, but you could take anything you wanted."

"As you said, we wouldn't."

"No. You would petition the monster on the throne to give it to you." She let out a laugh that tasted bitter in her mouth.

Lio was not laughing. "Can you imagine the consequences, if we resorted to force? The only reason the Last War can be called that is because we keep ourselves a kingdom away from Cordium and only enter Tenebra peacefully and discreetly in small numbers. Think what would become of your people if we were less careful—or if the time comes when they once more force us to defend ourselves."

"I guarantee I will ponder how different our fate would be at your hands than the king's, the next time he sentences another one of his dependents to death."

"You and I both know that the moment conflict erupts between mortals and Hesperines in Tenebra, Cordium will rush to your kingdom's 'assistance.' I am not sure even Lucis would have the power to keep those hounds from their natural prey, and I know it is not only Tenebra's sovereignty that would be a casualty. The Cordians would burn their way across Tenebra on a new crusade to destroy all Hesperines."

"And your people would grieve because you would be the reason for our suffering at Cordium's hands."

"You must wonder why we do not simply give up on the Oath and withdraw from Tenebra so that there is no chance of conflict."

"I have never wondered why you are so dedicated to your goddess's mercies. If you never left Orthros, who would rescue infants from the wolves? Who would ease the pain of the dying?" Cassia would not let her voice waver. She would not. "Who would give the desecrated the dignity of their final sacred rites?"

Lio rose to his feet so fluidly she did not really see him move. "I am glad my uncouth display has not tarnished your opinion of us. As always, you see things as they are."

She came nearer still. "I never trust what I see. I trust the evidence of bloodshed, however. That never lies and is seldom open to interpretation."

"I'm sorry your truth requires such grisly proof."

She halted in front of him. "If you were anyone but a Hesperine, I would tell you I do not want your pity."

He appeared taken aback. "Cassia, it is not pity."

"I know." She turned away from Lio. What a coward she was. The gloom between the trees welcomed her gaze, much easier to face than him. The trees could not see the fear in her eyes.

The tension and sweat and pain that always waited to drown her now rose over her like a tide. Her belly quivered, threatening to sicken if she subjected herself to memory. If she looked at what she always carried inside her.

Cassia willed the words out, as she had willed herself to the Summit table. "The most generous deed ever done on my behalf was the work of your people, and it was not an act of pity."

TRUST

LIO KNEW HE HAD passed the final test. He had proved himself
trustworthy.

If he had not, Cassia would never make a confession that cost her
this much. In the face of suffering so powerful, there was no such thing
as controlling the Blood Union. Her nausea rose in his own belly, and
her panic heated and chilled his skin by turns. Every muscle in his body
strained with hers against the urge to flee or strike out blindly against any
target at hand.

Her own words made her sick with horror. This went beyond their
Oath of openness. But she had spoken, and even now she stood just out
of reach, trying to go on. Lio listened to her take a breath to speak, then to
the silence in which her words would not come. Still, she gasped another
breath for a new attempt.

From the first night she had approached him, she had said things to
him she told no one else. With him, she broke the silence that was often
all that stood between her and her own mortality. Perhaps he was finally
about to understand why.

He must not push her. He tried instead to encourage her, to offer her
a path into what she was trying so desperately to say. "You have met a
Hesperine before?"

It worked. Her breath hitched, her voice came out ragged, but she
spoke. "Three of them. A flock of swans come to carry away the slain."

"Goddess bless. Cassia. I am so sorry." Lio struggled to respect the
distance between them and not go to her side. "Now I understand. When
you talk of the Mercy, you are speaking of someone you lost."

She cast a quick glance over her shoulder, not quite meeting his eyes. "Not a remarkable story, of course. Humans died, your folk came to clean up my folk's mess." She shrugged, once more trying to wield the sharp edge of indifference. But she barely had hold of her weapon, and she brandished it in shaking hands.

Lio took just one step closer. She tensed, but did not move away from him. So he dared try to comfort her. "My people have eternal memories. We never forget the fallen. I don't know what happened, but I can say with certainty that the Hesperines who were there still remember the face and name of each person to whom they gave the Mercy."

Her hands rested at her sides, but they curled into fists in the folds of her skirt. He smelled salty moisture in the air.

She was crying.

Knight appeared at the edge of the clearing and strode to her side. Lio had never seen the hound disobey a stay order. But now Cassia's beast pressed himself against her skirts, nudging her fist until she uncurled it and buried her fingers in his fur.

Watching Cassia's shoulders quiver, Lio had never felt so frustrated and powerless. He prayed she would understand his words for what they were. Not a demand to know more of her secret pain, but an offer of sympathy. "Would you tell me your loved one's name, so that I may remember as well?"

He listened to her soft, quick breaths. Not sobs to anyone's ears but his. "It is still a mystery to me, your concern for the dead. The ones beyond your reach. But I learned long ago you are their kindest keepers."

"To honor them is a sacred trust."

"Nothing is sacred here." Her heart thundered as she confessed her private heresy to him. "For that reason, I am glad your people persuaded me to leave her in their hands. Much better that she be borne away in a Hesperine's arms than subjected to the mockery of a funeral rite in that pile of stone my father calls a temple. The only god who dwells there is his own ambition."

"You're speaking of your sister."

"Solia. My kind, gentle sister, who belonged on the throne. She was the answer to all our prayers. The light that awaited at the end of the king's cruelty. I was living evidence of his betrayal of her mother, and yet Solia cared for me as if I were her own child. She never laid others' transgressions at my door. I loved her."

Everything in Lio demanded that he reach out and offer Cassia the solace of touch. It was the right thing to do, to give her a simple, physical assurance that another shared her pain. He could not. The bounds of his role as a diplomat, the standards of modesty her people imposed on her, and Cassia's own pride stood in his way. In all his struggle to understand human strictures, he had never hated them as he did in this moment.

As always, all Lio was permitted to offer Cassia were words. He gave her the best ones he had, speaking them in Vulgus, so they would mean something to her. "I carry your grief in my veins."

She swiveled to face him. The tears quivering in her eyes made those windows on her soul seem enormous. "The Hesperines I met that night said those very words to me."

"Those are our sacred ritual words, an invocation of empathy." Indeed, words were the best gift he had to offer. Not just his words, but the opportunity for her to speak her own. "Would you like to tell me about her?"

"You know our history."

He knew the date in the scrolls. But now he understood it. "The day after tomorrow is the anniversary of the Siege of Sovereigns. It will mark fourteen years since Solia fell at the hands of free lords who rebelled against royal authority. The king gave in to every ransom demand, but the traitors were not satisfied. In their lust for power, they resolved to remove Lucis from the throne and destroy his line, beginning with their captive, the seventeen-year-old princess. The king avenged her and brought her remains back to Solorum…but they were damaged, and her body was kept covered during the funerary rites in the Sun Temple. So says history. Would you like to tell me the truth, Cassia?"

The Blood Moon's light glinted in the fullness of her gaze. "Yes."

What would the night of the siege look like, feel like, taste like if Lio could use his thelemancy to relive the memory with her and truly share in her past? He could not know. He could only experience the flashes her mind and heart cast into the Blood Union. He must rely on her words to understand what she had endured.

Cassia began to walk. This seemed her only concession to how desperately she wished to run away from the past into which she was about to lead Lio. He stayed by her side and prowled with her around the boundaries of her cage.

Once the trees were thick around them, she began. "In those days, Solia was the king's only legitimate child, his rightful heir. For that reason, he needed her. I thought she was the only person in the world who was safe from him."

ANOINTING

CASSIA PEERED OUT FROM under the dressing table. "Is this it, Soli? Does this mean you're really getting married?"

"Of course not, Pup." Solia smiled down from her perch on the dressing stool. Her golden hair shone like the auras around goddesses in temple stories.

Cassia scooted closer to her sister's shins. "But you're doing the fall dance with Lord Bellator today. Everyone says that means you're supposed to marry him."

"When a lady dances the Autumn Greeting with a suitor, that does usually mean their fathers will begin talks to arrange a betrothal. But it's different for me."

"Why?"

"Because I am the king's daughter."

At that moment, Lady Iris returned to the dressing table. "There now, My Princess. I have sent all your other attendants away, so it will be just the three of us." The handmaiden smiled at Cassia, then looked at Solia in the mirror, resting a hand on her shoulder.

Solia reached up and gave Lady Iris's hand a squeeze. "Thank you."

"Regardless of what comes to pass after today, Your Highness, this is the only time you've ever had a partner for the Autumn Greeting. Every woman deserves to enjoy her promise dance."

Solia didn't answer.

Lady Iris reached for something on the dressing table. Glass clinked on wood. There came the pop of a cork. Suddenly the whole room smelled like flowers. "This is the only time you get to use the ceremonial fragrances, which the myths say Kyria herself wore when Anthros took her as his bride. Mark my words. The sacred scents of autumn will make you feel like the goddess you represent in the dance tonight." The pop of another cork, and a new cloud of sweet smells. "Allow me the honor of anointing you, My Princess."

Solia held out her hands.

Cassia watched Lady Iris roll up Solia's embroidered velvet sleeves. The handmaiden began to spread one of the scent oils over Solia's hands. The fragrance smelled so good. Why wasn't Solia smiling?

Lady Iris used each oil on Solia's hands, face, and hair. When the handmaiden corked the bottles at last, Solia's lovely fair skin gleamed, and her wavy blond locks were smooth and shiny. Lady Iris proceeded to dress Solia's hair with fancy blue velvet ribbons. At last Lady Iris nestled a circlet of solid gold atop Solia's hair, the delicate filigreed one they saved for very special occasions.

Cassia didn't like the fragrances anymore. She had a headache, and Solia looked like she felt sick, too.

Her work done, Lady Iris gazed at Solia in the mirror once more. "Isn't our princess the most beautiful woman in the world, Lady Cassia?"

Everyone knew that was true. Cassia burrowed nearer against her sister's skirts. "Oh, yes."

"Come up here, my brave little Pup." Solia patted her lap.

Cassia crawled out from under the dressing table and climbed into her sister's lap.

Solia wrapped her arms around Cassia and cradled her close, looking at her in the mirror. "Do you know who is the most beautiful girl in the world? You."

Cassia blushed with pleasure. She didn't have golden hair and fair skin like Solia and Lady Iris. But if Solia told Cassia she was beautiful, it must be true, no matter what anyone else said.

Solia planted a kiss on Cassia's cheek. "Don't worry about the fall dance. Father and I are playing a game with Lord Bellator. We will win, and I won't have to marry anyone. I'll get to stay here at Solorum with you. Just think of all the pretty flowers we can add to the garden when spring comes. You know I'll need your help, for the flowers always grow best when you plant them."

"Can I help you with the game?" Cassia asked.

"You're such a good girl. But you don't have to help with Lord Bellator. I will take care of everything. What I want you to do is keep learning how to be a lady. Do you remember what I taught you?"

Cassia nodded proudly. Soli taught her how to be a lady every day, and Cassia was getting very good at it. Much better than she was at reading.

Solia smiled at her in the mirror. "All right. What's first?"

"A lady always listens carefully."

"Exactly. What's next?"

"A lady always tries to understand what's going on."

"Very good. Third?"

"A lady always keeps secrets."

"Yes, that one is important indeed. Keep going, my little lady."

"A lady always keeps ivy. A lady always dresses correctly. A lady always honors the queen. A lady can walk through fire!"

"Perfect, from start to finish, my clever Pup. You learn so quickly!"

"Your Highness," Lady Iris interrupted. "You are expected at the temple. It is time for Lady Cassia's nurse to take her back to her own rooms."

Cassia should try harder to be good. But Solia wouldn't scold her for telling the truth. Cassia confessed softly, "I don't want to go with Nurse."

"I don't want you to go with Nurse, either. But it will only be for a little while. I'll be back from the dance before you have to go to sleep." Solia hugged her even tighter, hiding her face against Cassia's neck. "No matter what happens, you will always be with me, understand?"

"Even if you have to get married someday?"

"Yes, Cassia. I will never let anyone, neither Father nor a husband, part me from you."

SILENCE

I WILL NEVER LET ANYONE *part me from you.*

    Cassia silently recited Solia's promise to herself again. Hugging her knees, she tucked her cold feet deeper under her skirt and watched their father. From her place at the back of his tent, she could look between all the tall men and see their father's arm, his shoulder, and his blond hair. Not his face.

But he wouldn't be worried. She was sure of it. He never lost.

She hugged her knees closer. Somebody would get hurt again, but Father would win, and Solia would get to leave Lord Bellator's castle. Then they would all go home to Solorum. When spring came in a fortnight and a half, she and Solia would plant new flowers in the garden.

Nurse's sharp fingers tapped Cassia between her shoulders. She startled in her chair and dropped her feet to the ground. She must be on her best behavior so she would get to stay here and see Solia as soon as she came out of the castle. Cassia didn't want to lose her special privilege of remaining with Father in his camp instead of having to travel onward with his court.

Cold seeped up through the pelt on the floor from the icy dirt beneath, chilling her feet even through her leather shoes and soft wool stockings. She eyed her new puppy. Knight sat next to her chair, his back paws sprawled to one side and part of his belly peeking out of his fur. He didn't look like he was cold. Would he mind sitting a little closer to her? With a nervous glance at Nurse, Cassia leaned down and gently picked up her dog the way the kennel master had shown her, then set Knight on her feet. His body was warm, his fur soft. He wiggled a little, then stretched out over her shoes and laid down his head.

The tent flap flew open. Cassia leaned to one side to peer through the crowd at the man who entered. He was wearing Father's blue and gold livery, like many of the men who had come in and out today. Cassia straightened her back and listened.

The messenger bowed low. "My King."

He sounded anxious. Cassia gripped her hands together in her lap.

Her father's silence was an order for the messenger to speak. The only thing worse than telling Father something he didn't want to hear was not talking when he wanted you to.

The man finally went on. "It appears Lord Bellator was informed of Her Highness's whereabouts at Your Majesty's pleasure palace at Desidia. He knows Your Majesty authorized Lord Altius to pay court to Her Highness there."

Lord Hadrian's gruff voice erupted in a string of words Cassia wasn't allowed to say. He always sounded like he wanted to hurt someone. "Whose tongue shall I cut out for betraying our future queen?"

"The rat's identity remains unknown, Your Lordship. We know Her Highness's party left Desidia safely, but before they could join the court on the road to Solorum, Lord Bellator waylaid them. He brought her here to Castra Roborra with the aid of Lord Evandrus. The princess's guard could not withstand the combined forces of two free lords." The messenger cleared his throat. "Now we stand against four. Lords Reman and Mareus have joined Her Highness's captors inside the fortress with their own warriors."

"I see," said Father.

Cassia struggled not to cry. She must not shut her eyes and stop listening. *A lady always tries to understand what's going on.*

"So Reman and Mareus have thrown in their swords as well," Lord Hadrian snarled. "The cowards who call themselves 'sovereign' free lords. If they have aligned with Bellator and Evandrus, this may prove far more dire than a simple demand for ransom."

"The traitors will not manage to put aside their petty squabbles for long," Father replied. "This union against Us will be short-lived."

Horns sounded in the camp. Cassia jumped in her chair again. The tent flap snapped back once more, and strangers crowded inside to present themselves to her father.

"Is Lord Bellator prepared to receive Us in the castle?" Father asked.

"Lord Bellator will grant nothing in exchange for nothing," one of the strangers answered.

"Admit Us into Castra Roborra, and his wedding to my daughter will take place. We made Our terms clear."

"Lord Bellator has no further interest in your daughter for that purpose."

"Then he is a fool."

"My lord instructs me to say you are the fool to think you could deceive him."

Cassia widened her eyes. They had dared to insult her father. Now she knew who would get hurt today.

But the stranger, Lord Bellator's messenger, continued. "My lord is now wise to your intentions. Your support for his courtship of your daughter amounted to nothing more than empty promises to win the concessions you desired from him. As soon as you got what you wanted, you planned to withdraw the offer of marriage. Even now you are in talks with Lord Altius about a betrothal between him and the girl, as if you think my lord would stand by while you barter a place in the line of succession to his rival."

"Lord Bellator is mistaken," Father said calmly. "Lord Altius has no claim on my daughter's hand, and no man in this kingdom has a claim on my throne."

Cassia had known the secret. Father was playing the game with Lord Altius, too. Solia had explained why she had to go to Desidia so Lord Altius could spend some time with her. But she had reassured Cassia she wouldn't marry him, either. Father always won.

Lord Bellator's messenger must know he was losing, for he sounded angry. "You do my lord the insult of lying to his face. Your deceit has come to light, and you can no longer deny you are forsworn. The Autumn Greeting is a promise of betrothal, one on which you never intended to deliver. My lord will not tolerate your faithless disregard for your oaths, nor will the Sovereign Free Lords of the Tenebrae endure your violations of their ancient rights, promised them in the Free Charter laid down by our ancestors."

All the men in the tent started talking at once, some of them quietly and others, like Lord Hadrian, loud and angry.

"Lord Bellator offers new terms." The messenger spoke over everyone. "You will return all the gifts he bestowed upon you, thinking he paid a bride price. Along with them, you will cede Regnum Ceposum to its rightful sovereign, Lord Reman. You will reaffirm Lord Mareus's exclusive right to collect tolls for passage across the Palla River. You will…"

The names went on and on, and although Cassia tried to make sense of them all, there were too many she hadn't learned about yet. At last, the list ended in the only name that mattered.

"You have elevated yourself above the lords who were once your peers," the messenger concluded, "and presumed to make yourself the first of a new royal dynasty. If you do not agree to the terms as dictated, my lord shall see to it you are also the last of your line. You have until nightfall, at which time, if you have not delivered, Sovereign Lord Bellator shall order the execution of your only scion and heir, Solia."

Cassia stared at her father. Now it was certain. Father would kill Bellator and the other lords so Solia could come home.

Their father did not move in his chair. "I refuse his terms."

The tent was silent.

The messenger's face twisted into disbelief. "This is not a bluff. If you refuse, her life is forfeit. Your only heir."

"I have the sword to get me another."

Cassia clutched her middle. The wail came out of her anyway.

"Silence that noise," the king ordered.

Nurse tried to pull Cassia to her feet. But Cassia's whole body shook, and she could not stand. The sobs would not stop. It took one of the soldiers to pry her off the chair. He took Knight by the ruff and carried them both, whimpering, out of the king's presence.

In the confines of her own tent, Cassia wailed while they waited for nightfall. She tried to hide her crying in her blankets, but it was not enough. Nothing could stop the whole camp from hearing her shame.

CATAPULTS

THE LIGHT IN THE tent had faded by the time Cassia managed to
be silent. If she was not quiet, Nurse would make her drink an
infusion. If Cassia had to take it, she would fall asleep.

She could not sleep, not while this was happening to Solia. She held
Knight's soft, floppy body close to her and swallowed her tears.

She was still awake when she heard the catapults.

A shiver moved down her back. It was night. She had heard the guards
say the siege would not begin until dawn, when the rest of her father's
army arrived.

Had they come early to rescue Solia? She heard the crunch of heavy
boots on the icy ground outside and the clank of swords. Voices mixed
together, and she couldn't understand.

She eased out of her bedroll and scooted toward the tent flap. A furry
form wriggled close. With one arm around Knight, she raised the tent flap
an inch. A chill crept inside.

Nurse's arms wrapped around both of them and hauled them back.
Her crooning words drowned out the voices outside. She pulled a thick
woolen cap onto Cassia's head and down over her ears, and all chance
to hear clearly was lost. Wrinkled hands pressed her face against a bony
chest, as if expecting her to start crying again. But that wouldn't help now.
If someone was attacking the castle to help Solia, Cassia had to know.

In a display of obedience, Cassia crawled back into her bedroll and
hid her face against Knight instead. Nurse let out a sigh. Her hand came
to rest on Cassia's back and stayed there for a long time. Cassia lay very
still and slowed her breathing.

It seemed she waited forever. If Nurse tried to stay up the whole night, Cassia didn't know what she would do. But eventually Nurse withdrew her hand, and a blanket rustled as she settled into her own bedroll. At long last, she began to snore.

Cassia put her mouth close to Knight's keen ear and whispered one of the new words she had learned from the kennel master. "*Baat.*"

Her puppy laid his head on his paws and waited in the bedroll while Cassia found her cloak by feel. With it tucked under her arm, she crept to the back of the tent and squeezed between the floor pelts and the wall. Cold bit at her skin as she slithered out onto the ground. The slush of ice and mud made it hard to keep quiet, so she moved very slowly.

The huge moons loomed overhead. She unfolded her cloak and wrapped it close around her. She could see no one else from where she stood. The noise from a moment ago had all gone quiet. It didn't sound like anyone from their camp was attacking the castle. Surely someone, somewhere, was still talking about what had happened.

Cassia was actually very good at being quiet, except for when she had cried today. She got a lot of practice making herself unseen and unheard, and everything in the camp was much bigger than her, which meant there were lots of good hiding places. She darted from one to another, listening.

Finally faint voices caught her attention, and she followed the sounds. She crouched at the back of one of the long tents where the soldiers slept.

"They sent her retinue over the walls first," a man said. "What was left of them. Then her."

Cassia slid to her knees. She couldn't think. Maybe they didn't mean what she thought they did.

"I can't bear to think of it," came another man's voice.

"Then don't," a third said, "and whatever you do, don't say it."

"I don't care if it is treason. I'll say it. It's immoral, what he's done."

"Hypnos take you. I won't be caught listening to such things."

"It's you I hope Hypnos takes," the first man cried, "and the king with you. Someone ought to speak the truth aloud. How could he do such a thing to our Solia? He abandoned her. *Her.* Left her to suffer and die.

There's no telling what they did to her before the end. We don't even know if she had her rites. This is unholy, leaving her and the guards and servants who died for her on the field without a proper burial. You heard the royal mage. Honored Master Orumos said the—"

His voice faltered. "The Hesperines are abroad tonight. They will desecrate her before dawn."

MERCY

CASSIA SWALLOWED AGAIN AND again. She mustn't be sick. They would hear her.

Heavy footfalls sounded inside the tent, and all speech ceased. Lord Hadrian broke the silence. "I thought I heard a disturbance."

No one answered.

"What I thought I heard troubled me. Words that sounded like treason, which gets soldiers killed. But I've had orders shouted in my ears since I was a scrap. I must have misheard. Speak up, men! Tell me what I really heard."

The man who had started all the talk answered. "Yes, my lord. I would give my oath in the temple that no words were spoken which were treasonous against the *rightful* monarch."

"Good. The king decides whether he can spare any men to retrieve the fallen. The king decides if he can trust the enemy to honor a white flag and not rain arrows from the walls, and if he can afford to lose the men who might not make it back. He also decides the severity of the message he needs to send the enemy in order to make it clear he is not concerned about the security of his position on the throne."

"Of course, my lord."

There came the sound, almost inaudible, of a heavy hand falling to rest on a broad shoulder.

Lord Hadrian's voice was quieter than ever before. "What I'm certain I heard were the words of a man willing to sacrifice anything for the sake of our rightful queen. Our Solia. Such a man puts to shame he who would not do the same."

"My lord," said his soldier, "I won't let this go unsaid, if the king has my tongue for it. You've been in council with him for hours. You shouted yourself hoarse. If starting the siege could have saved her, you'd drive the battering ram yourself. If the kingdom was yours, you'd hand over ever acre for her sake. Every man here knows you did all you could."

Lord Hadrian stalked out of the tent and out of earshot.

Cassia managed to sneak out of camp and into the woods without being seen. She had to climb a tree a couple of times so her father's patrols wouldn't see her, but they weren't on the lookout for a girl. Once she got past them, there was no one in the forest to stop her.

She started running. Icy wind tore at her face as she raced between the towers of the trees, and tears came to her eyes again. She should be afraid. But she wasn't. She didn't care what happened to her, as long as she made it to Soli.

No one would go back for Solia unless Cassia did. She had to find her sister before the Hesperines came.

When she reached the edge of the woods, she crouched down in the darkness where the moonlight didn't reach between the trees and bushes. She peered out of her hiding place.

An enormous field of grass, blue and bare under the moons, lay between her and Castra Roborra. The fortress's walls rose up, up into the night. She couldn't see any movement on the ramparts. The field was equally still, smudged with a few patches of white snow and dark blue shadows.

Her whole body broke out in a sweat in the icy air. Those dark shapes weren't shadows.

They were bodies.

Cassia knew where she was headed, now. The only way to get there was to cross the field. There were no hiding places between her and…Soli.

Cassia looked at the castle one more time. She didn't see anyone moving on the walls. Maybe the lords in the fortress would let someone come get Solia after all. Father could have sent his warriors. But he hadn't.

Cassia had to go. She had to be brave for Solia.

She crept out of the trees.

Her only warning was the barest touch of warmth on her skin. Then strong arms held her fast, and the ground was far away below her feet. She started to fight, kicking and striking out with all her might. But the grip on her was impossible to break. Over her captor's shoulder, she watched the field and Solia slip away.

A single arrow quivered in the grass. At first Cassia didn't understand. Then it became clear to her. The arrow had come from the direction of the castle and landed right where she had been standing.

She stopped trying to struggle. All her determination drained out of her, and all she could do was lay limp. Her captor's hold gentled. Cassia found herself cradled close to a body both soft and strong, and a hand stroked her hair.

"Easy, little one. You're safe." The voice was female, deep, with a strange, lovely accent. "I'll keep you safe now. Nothing in the world can harm you while I protect you."

The forest surrounded them. The person who held Cassia eased her onto her feet and let her stand, holding her shoulders to steady her. At last Cassia saw her rescuer.

Kneeling on Cassia's eye level was a beautiful lady. She wore a black cowl and long black robes. Her skin was the fairest Cassia had ever seen. There was shadow all around them, the kind of deep, dark shadow that was safe to hide in.

They were not alone. The lady's two companions towered over Cassia. They too wore hoods pulled close around their star-pale faces and sky-dark eyes. Cassia could see them because of a gentle glow in the air, like mist, only made of light.

Cassia stared, too frightened to utter a sound. Fear kept her frozen. Helpless. She stared at the ground, at her numb feet and the layers of embroidery on the woman's black robe.

No, she wasn't a woman. Cassia knew what she was.

A warm, smooth hand cupped Cassia's cheek and urged her to lift her gaze. She looked at the lady's beautiful face again. Everyone said they were beautiful until you saw their fangs.

The Hesperine smiled.

Cassia gasped. Her smile was…kind. Her eyes looked sad. Sad for Cassia.

An ache threatened in Cassia's throat. She couldn't cry. Not again.

"Don't be afraid, little one," the Hesperine said. "We would never hurt you."

Cassia swallowed, trying to find her voice. No words came out.

Cassia's rescuer glanced at the other two Hesperines. She spoke to them in a language Cassia recognized, the same one the mages used in the temple. One of the other Hesperines drew near and knelt down. Without disturbing her hood, she reached up and pulled a mantle off her shoulders, then made to wrap it around Cassia.

Cassia jumped and backed away.

Her rescuer laughed softly and let her go. "What a fighter you are."

"But you don't want to go out there, sweetling," said the second Hesperine. "It's not a safe place for a child."

"I have to go. To find—" Cassia shut her mouth. The Hesperines were already here. There was no hope of getting to Solia first. What would they do to her? When would they stop pretending to be kind and show what they were really like? Cassia's lips trembled.

Her rescuer reached for her again and rubbed her arms. Cassia wanted to flinch and move away, but those hands were so gentle. They warmed her through her cloak and made it easier to control her shivers.

"How brave you are," her rescuer said. "Tell us who you are looking for, and we will help you in your honorable purpose."

"No," Cassia cried. "You're not here to help. You're here—to take her away, not to let me—take her back—home. She should—at least get to come home—and be next to her mother. I should at least be able to visit her under the temple."

Cassia had not thought that far ahead until now. Imagining Soli like that made her feel sick again.

She found herself cradled between two warm bodies that smelled good. This time her tears fell on a soft black robe, and the hands that stroked and rocked her were not thin and cold like Nurse's. The way the two Hesperines held her made her feel safe and important.

"Who are you looking for?" Her rescuer's voice was steady and sure. She sounded like the kind of lady who could make sure everything was taken care of. "If you tell us, we will find her for you."

"I have to protect her," Cassia protested.

From the Hesperines?

Or from Father?

"I know you want to do the right thing for her, but how will you find her without getting hurt?" asked her rescuer. "I am sure she would not wish you to be in danger for even a moment. And even if you could get to her safely, how would you carry her all the way back home by yourself?"

Cassia clenched her hands. She had to try, because no one else would.

Except the Hesperines.

Cassia's rescuer wrapped firm, gentle hands around her fists and looked at her again. "I promise we will not do anything for her until you tell us you will permit it. Is that all right with you?"

"You s-swear?"

The Hesperine put one hand on her chest. "By your gods and mine, I give you my word."

"She has blond hair and blue eyes and a—a secret around her neck. M-my *sister*," Cassia wailed. "Soli."

She wanted to explain, to scream at someone what their father had done. But as soon as she said Soli's name, she couldn't speak. She could only cry and keep on crying. She didn't care anymore how useless and weak it was. She wept in the Hesperines' arms.

Soli was dead.

Cassia sobbed until her whole body was exhausted and her belly ached. Her rescuer held her on her lap while the second Hesperine cleaned Cassia's face with a soft cloth. The two ladies talked to each other in the Divine Tongue. They kept their voices quiet, but Cassia could tell they were very angry. Only not at her.

The third Hesperine must have left while Cassia was crying, because now that one returned. From the direction of the field.

The third Hesperine got down on her eye level as well. This one was a lord, but he looked just as kind as the ladies. He held out one large hand and opened it. "Is this your sister's secret?"

Cassia stared at the carved wooden pendant that rested on his palm and the ribbon that dangled from it. She had never seen them anywhere except around Solia's neck. In the Hesperine's big hand, the familiar symbol of ivy vines twisting in and out of each other looked smaller than before. It felt wrong to see a strange male with Solia's secret. But he held it very gently, and it was clear he knew how important it was.

Cassia nodded.

He took both her hands in one of his big ones and gave Solia's pendant to her. "It's your secret now."

Cassia stared down at the necklace. In her hands, it felt very big. He was right. She should take care of this for Solia now.

Cassia's rescuer asked her, "Why have you come to find Soli all alone, without anyone to help you?"

"Because he wouldn't."

"Who wouldn't, little one?"

She didn't want to talk about him, or even say his name. But the Hesperines were going to help her with Solia, so she answered the question. "F-father."

Her rescuer exchanged glances with the other two Hesperines again. "Where is your father?"

"The camp on the other side of the woods. But I won't go back without Soli."

She resettled Cassia on her lap. "Do you know why we are here?"

Cassia had thought she understood, but now she realized she had been very wrong. She shook her head.

Her rescuer explained, "Our Goddess, Hespera, has given us a very important duty called the Mercy. When people harm one another, Hespera wants us to help."

"You," Cassia whispered, "can help Solia?"

"It is difficult for a child," said the second Hesperine.

"Yes it is." Cassia's rescuer hugged her close. "But this one has been forced to grow up quickly tonight. How old are you?"

"I will be eight next month."

"The Mercy is distressing to think about, but I can see how brave you are. Because you are here to help your sister, I think you should be allowed to know how we will help her. I think you are big enough for me to tell you what the Mercy is. But if it sounds too frightening, you can tell me to stop, and I will not say any more. Very well?"

Cassia nodded.

"There is nothing wrong with being afraid," her rescuer added. "Your sister would be so proud of how strong you've been tonight. If you don't want me to go on, you don't have to feel ashamed, do you understand?"

Cassia held Solia's necklace tightly. She didn't feel brave. But the Hesperine said she was, even though Cassia had cried in front of her. "I understand."

"After a battle, sometimes the fallen on the field are still alive, but they are too gravely wounded for any healer to help them. We ask them if they want us to save them and turn them into Hesperines. If that's not what they want, we make sure they don't feel any more pain, and we wait with them until they go to be with their own gods. If they don't want to wait, they can ask us to send them swiftly on."

Cassia gasped. "Is Soli a Hesperine now?"

"I'm afraid your sister had already departed when we arrived. Only one of her guards needed us to ease his journey into the next life."

Cassia's throat closed. It was really true. Soli was gone.

"Do not be sad that it is so," her rescuer said. "It means she didn't lie there in pain or fear, not even for a moment, for she went quickly to your gods. They must be so happy to see her, if she is anything like you."

"No, she isn't like me," Cassia cried. "She is beautiful and good and everyone loves her. She is so much better than me."

"Is that what she told you?" the Hesperine asked.

Cassia shook her head.

"What did she say to you?"

Cassia thought about all the things other people had said, and then about what Solia said instead. "She told me I am b-beautiful and good and that she loves me."

"Then that is what you must say to yourself. That is what she wants for you."

Cassia felt more hot tears at the back of her eyes. "How can you help her, if she's already gone?"

"Sometimes it is not possible for families to give their loved ones proper rites," said the Hesperine. "Even when they want to very much. So we take it upon ourselves to care for the fallen on behalf of those who loved them. We give them our Goddess's sacred rites and honor them as we would our own people."

Cassia hung her head. "I love Soli and want to give her rites. But I can't. I'm not enough."

She had failed.

The Hesperine put a hand under Cassia's chin again and lifted her face once more. "Do not ever be ashamed. You have done a courageous deed tonight, and your sister is proud of you. She knows you love her, even now."

"How will she know it if I have no grave where I can visit her?"

"It doesn't matter where she is or where you are. She will feel your love."

"How do you know?"

"Because you showed her you love her while she was with you."

Cassia looked into the Hesperine's eyes, and she could see tears there. "Someone you love is gone too?"

"My brother. He was taken prisoner. I couldn't help him that night. Will you let me give his Mercy to your sister?"

Cassia reached out and touched the tears that slid down the strong, beautiful lady's cheeks. Tears just like Cassia's own.

When she wrapped her arms around her rescuer, the Hesperine froze, as if taken by surprise. But then she pulled Cassia closer than ever.

They held each other for a long time, and Cassia cried again. But this time she didn't feel ashamed.

At last Cassia's rescuer drew back and set her on her feet.

"Please take care of Solia," Cassia requested.

"It will be my honor. For your trust in me, you have my gratitude."

"Thank you." Cassia tried to give a lady's curtsy like Solia had taught her, but her knees wobbled, and she almost stumbled. Three pairs of Hesperine hands steadied her on her feet.

"Can I—" Cassia hesitated.

"Yes?" Her rescuer waited.

Cassia whispered, "Can I see her before you take her away?"

The Hesperine who had found Solia's secret answered. "She would rather you think about all the times when you were together. Remember what she looked like when she said she loves you, and imagine what she looks like now, feeling your love in the safe, happy place where people like your sister go."

Cassia nodded in silence.

Cassia's rescuer touched a hand to her cheek. "Will you tell me your name, so I can remember it, along with Solia?"

"Cassia."

"Cassia. I am so sorry about your sister. I carry your grief in my veins."

The Hesperines carried Cassia all the way back through the forest. They strode right past the king's guards, who did not look their way. That was the last thing Cassia remembered before she rested her head on her rescuer's shoulder and fell asleep with Solia's secret clutched in her hand.

LIGHT

"MY NURSE WOKE ME at daybreak, when it was time for the women and children to leave. The rest of the king's forces had arrived to begin the Siege of Sovereigns."

Cassia came to a standstill. Their journey had brought them back to the clearing where they had begun. Lio halted beside her, unwilling to breathe a word that would interrupt the conclusion of her tale. Unready to break his memorial silence for Solia.

"Not a soul within Castra Roborra was spared," Cassia finished. "Free lords and warriors, servants and pages, horses and dogs. For every hostage fired over the walls, a dozen traitors' heads decorated the ramparts. It was the shortest rebellion in the history of Tenebra—and the last.

"For his winning strategy, Lord Hadrian's reward was to watch his king put his best men at the front of the attack. Time and age took care of my nurse. Of all those who witnessed the king's decision that night, only Lord Hadrian and I survive."

With shaking hands, Cassia reached inside her gardening satchel and pulled something out. She held it up for Lio to see.

On the end of a faded, tattered length of ribbon swung Solia's wooden pendant, an elaborate triquetra of ivy vines without beginning or end.

"I will never forget. Nor should you, Lio. Now you know the true nature of the monster you face each time you sit down at his table."

Lio listened to Cassia's blood ache with emotion and heard the spasms thumping in her belly. She had just relived the worst night of her life, and she was still on her feet.

He wanted to do more than hold her. He wanted to take her blood and her pain into his mouth, into himself, and bear it with her until her burden eased because they carried it together. Until she felt more than grief and knew comfort.

He stood where he was, at arm's length, and echoed Cassia's rage and despair. "How could he do such a thing to her?"

"She was dangerous to him. She won the people's love in her own right. There wasn't a soul in Tenebra who didn't look forward to the day when they bowed to her instead of the king."

"There were past kings among her mother's ancestors," Lio recalled. "Solia's claim to the throne must have inspired many people to imagine."

"I believe it was more than mere imaginings."

"Cassia, do you mean...?"

"As a girl, I didn't recognize the signs, but looking back in the years since, I have come to understand. She knew things. Things the princess should not have known, which no one else in Tenebra except the king himself knew. I still wonder if he ever realized the full extent of her reach. But he realized enough, and he acted on his knowledge before she had a chance to endanger him with hers."

"Are you saying Solia was preparing to challenge him for the crown?"

"We will never know. But I ask myself: why would she make a point to gather so much information, unless she planned to use it against him?" Cassia lowered the ivy pendant into her satchel once more. "She will always be my queen."

"Now I understand just how much you lost."

"Everything. Except my life. It was a gift from your people, and the king shall not take it from me."

Lio took a step closer. "I cannot express how grateful I am to my people who found you that night."

"Your people have done more for me than I could ever ask. And yet here I am to ask for one more boon. It's why I made sure to be at Solorum during the Summit, contrary to the king's wishes. Why I first approached you. You see, there is just one thing the Hesperines did not explain to me that night: where your people take the bodies of the fallen to give them Hespera's sacred rites. So please, if it isn't too much to ask. Would you tell me, Lio? Where is my sister's final resting place?"

Now Lio understood. For fourteen years, Cassia had waited for her opportunity to meet a Hesperine again. The Summit might be her only chance, and she had seized it. She had faced her worst memories and most primal fears and risked taking action to make sure she was at court. She had chosen to suffer through countless confrontations with her father. Again and again, she had endured the dread of her own death at his hands, a terror all too justified by what he had done to her sister.

All this, so she could ask a Hesperine this single question.

Lio had never been called upon to deliver words so important to anyone as what he told her now. He would try to give her an explanation both gentle and unflinching, as his people had that night. He could only pray she would not be disappointed.

"We do not inter our fallen, as mortals now do," he explained. "Nor do we honor them with the ancient tradition of the funeral pyre, which mages have now claimed as their exclusive rite. When we perform the Mercy for humans, we treat their remains as we treat those of our own people."

When he took her hands in his, she jumped. She was raw with emotion, but she let him gather her hands together, palms up.

"First, we offer a libation." Lio lifted his wrist to his mouth and drew blood.

He flexed his hand over Cassia's. Neither of them breathed as the crimson droplets splashed into her cupped palms. She held her hands together so tightly he could see them shaking.

He cupped her hands in both of his to still them. "Everything you can touch is, in its most fundamental nature, light. You. Knight. The ground beneath our feet. It is also true that all the light you can see has the potential to become a person or a hound or fertile soil."

Her brow furrowed, and her lips pursed. She was trying so hard to understand.

"To change light into something you can touch," he continued, "it takes a monumental act of power. Far more power than any Hesperine or mage will ever possess. We can only wonder if that mysterious transformation, which we know is possible but cannot achieve, is the essence of creation itself. The act of power by which we ourselves, as living beings, are made."

Cassia listened to him with all of herself, from her pounding veins to her searching gaze.

"The most we can do," said Lio, "is turn that which we can touch into light."

He nurtured a spell light to life from his blood, bathing her hands in a white glow.

"When Hesperines are slain, our bodies do this of their own accord. So that is what we do, through a wholehearted and devoted effort of magic, for all fallen mortals who are entrusted to us. In that moment of transformation, a release of spiritual power occurs, which carries on it their final thoughts, feelings, and memories. Hesperines partake of these through the Blood Union so they can know and remember. For all time, they carry with them a part of those to whom they have given the Mercy."

Cassia did not look at him, only his spell light. Emotion wavered inside her like more tears ready to spill over.

"I am so sorry, Cassia. There is no grave, crypt, or mausoleum where you can go to pay your respects to Solia. But what I want you to know is this. Every light mage learns that although we can banish light, summon or change it, we can never destroy it. All the light that ever was in this world remains and always will. You see Solia every time you look at the sun, moons and stars, or even the flame of your own hearth fire."

"I am holding her in my hands."

"Yes."

Now at last Cassia met his gaze. "You have my gratitude."

Lio did not move or breathe. He stood holding light with Cassia and prayed in silence. Asking his Goddess to comfort her. Saying thanks that he had been able to. He had not spoken the wrong words. He had given Cassia something to hold on to.

"Don't apologize, Lio. What you've told me does not grieve me. I think it would have been too hard for me to understand as a child, when all I could think about was making sure my sister received the burial rite I had been taught was correct. When magic was something only mages did, which frightened me. Your people were right not to explain everything then. But I am grateful…so deeply grateful…that you have told me now. I'm glad I found out from you."

"It is a privilege to be the one to tell you."

"Solia was too great to be put to rest trapped in the ground. A crypt, or even an entire temple, would be too small to hold her. What better memorial for my radiant sister than light itself? What better resting place than this living one, which she shares with all your people who have gone before? Although I could not share in her final moments, I could not ask for finer bearers of her last thoughts than three of Hespera's immortal Gifted. If you cross paths with your fellow Hesperines who performed the Mercy for her, please thank them for me. This is the second thing I have wanted to ask of you. If you ever have a chance, tell them they have my gratitude as well."

To think, somewhere in the world there were three Hesperines who had known Cassia's name before Lio had. "I cannot fathom who they could be. There *is* no Hesperine account of the Siege of Sovereigns, nor of you, I am sorry indeed to say. If you had not told me, I would never have imagined any of my people were there that night, nor that your name was known to us. I promise you, I will not rest until I find out who they are and give them your message." Lio caressed Cassia's hands. "I think Solia would want me to thank them for her as well, not only on her own behalf, but for snatching her beloved sister from the path of an arrow."

"They shepherded her into death and me back into life. I cannot... there are no words for my debt to them. I can count on one hand every person in the world to whom I owe anything. One of them is Solia, and four of them are Hesperines."

"Cassia... I am humbled. It is an honor beyond measure that you count me among them."

"After all you have done? I owe you beyond measure."

"Hesperines do not practice debts. Only gifts. I will find the other three with whom you share a bond of gratitude, and I will give them mine as well. I cannot bear to imagine a history in which you did not survive that night to stand here with me."

When he reached for her, her eyes widened. As he closed the distance between them, his light spell dissolved into a glowing haze and enveloped them. He wrapped his arms around her and pulled her close.

She was a bundle of bone and soft hair and tension. She stood in his hold, her arms tucked against her, unmoving. He ran one hand down her back, slowly, feeling the ridges of that proud spine she always carried so straight. With his other hand, he touched the back of her head.

She let him slowly, gently lower her face to his chest.

He had never felt anything like the sensation of holding her. Exhilaration raced through him at the knowledge. He had reached for her. She had not pushed him away.

Her arms unwound. Her hands unclenched. One came to rest right over his heart.

She breathed a sigh. "I feel like I'm under a spell."

"I would *never*—"

"I know. And yet I feel as if you have."

He dared to slide a hand under her hair and touch the soft skin at the nape of her neck. "I could do that, Cassia. Touch your mind and sweep away all your fear and anger and pain so you did not know they had ever been. But I wouldn't do that, because you have a right to every single one of them."

When her arms came around his waist, he felt like he had won. They had won, together, their battle against her fears. She clung to him, and he finally learned what her touch felt like, what it felt like to touch her. Her temple, her cheek, her slender, stubborn shoulders. The curve of her waist.

He held her and touched her until she slid out of his arms and back into the trees. He watched her retreat through the darkness. She walked not with the march of a lady, but with a fluid step that made her hips sway.

22
days until

SPRING EQUINOX

DAY TERRORS

THE SICKLE WAS IN *his hand. The bull's roar spurred the frenzy inside him. Fear put unnatural strength in his swing as he brought the weapon down.*

The bull's wide eyes met his. Torch flames lit the blade as bright as the sun.

But the pain erupted in his own back. So fast. Fire-hot. His own blade flew from his hand, out of reach, while the one in his back impaled him.

He fell forward onto the animal, felt its sides heaving under his body. Together they exhaled.

Lio let out a yell on that breath and opened his eyes. He jolted up off the bed, but two hands held his shoulders and eased him back down. Currents of power shot through his mind and blood. Magic, frigid and potent. That was what had shaken him awake.

"Easy, Cousin." A familiar, steady voice. Neither a frightened bull nor an angry soldier gazed down at him.

Lio heaved a sigh. "Javed."

His Grace-cousin straightened, releasing his shoulders. "A real day terror, that one. Grace-Father sensed your distress even through your veil. He had to Call you three times to make you come around."

"Uncle Argyros performed the Night Call on me? *Three times?*" Lio shuddered. No wonder he felt as if thousands of years of glacial movement had just occurred inside his veins in the course of a few heartbeats.

"I suggested I ought to be the one to come in and check on you. I think answering his Call is enough without also waking to find him looming over you."

"Sunbound dreams." Lio sat up slowly, glancing around him to get his bearings. After a day terror like that, even his cell in the fortress felt like a haven. "That wasn't the least bit embarrassing."

"Just be glad I'm the only one who crossed your veil. Grace-Mother and Kadi would be beside themselves if they heard the way you were screaming."

"Does *everyone* know the intimate details of my troubling dream?"

"Basir was going to wake you if your uncle didn't. Talk about a chilling experience."

"Pray he and Kumeta don't include that in their next report to Rudhira." Lio rubbed both hands over his face and muttered another curse. "I feel the need to point out I'm not an uninitiated newblood, and you don't all need to fret over me so. For the record. I know my protest will go unheard."

"I'm afraid so. Your parents told us to take care of you."

Lio sighed. Despite the embarrassment that rankled him, he felt a wave of the homesickness that became more familiar to him each night. "I can see my feeble assertions that I can take care of myself are fruitless. No one can resist a decree from Apollon and Komnena, not even their son."

"Their only child," Javed reminded him, "and the future of Blood Komnena."

Lio slid out of bed on the side opposite Javed and pulled on his veil hours robe. The garment still smelled of Orthros. He went to the basin and washed his face, persisting in the same nightly ritual he would have observed at home. The cold water braced him like a physical Night Call. "You know I don't take it for granted, Javed."

"Of course not. Neither do we. You can't expect any of us to take it lightly that you're here in Tenebra where you're vulnerable. Even if you come to no harm, this place may take a toll on you."

Javed had an adroit way of turning the subject back to what ailed his patient. Lio stalled, drying his face with one of the rough-spun barracks cloths. Cleaning spells might be more convenient, but the mundane ablutions his people practiced now gave his tense hands something to do. "I will always be grateful for the Queens' dispensation to travel Abroad." He joked, "I suppose some prying from my elders is a small price to pay for such an honor."

But Javed did not laugh. "A day terror has struck every one of us at some point, Lio. We all fear what misery we may endure when we are trapped in the Dawn Slumber, unable to escape our dreams."

Lio turned to face Javed again and abandoned any attempts at lightness. "I appreciate your concern, Javed. I'm very grateful Uncle woke me."

Javed nodded once and gave one of his slight, disarming smiles. "I won't stir the veil. But you know where to find me if you wish to invite me behind it."

Javed's own veil felt like that smile. Had he let it fall for one moment since they'd left home? With Kadi, perhaps. But not in front of his patients. And everyone was his patient.

"You know where to find me," Lio reminded him. "This place takes a toll on all of us."

"Oh, don't worry about me. I was a human physician errant with mortal patients. That has a way of preparing you for anything."

Lio sighed. "I won't stir the veil, either, then."

"No veil to stir." Javed lifted a hand in farewell and headed for the door. "I prescribe you a run and a decent drink. Don't wait. Negotiations are on hold tonight."

"As well they should be. Tomorrow is the fourteenth anniversary of Solia Basilinna's death. The whole kingdom ought to mark the occasion."

"Yes, we're told the Tenebrans are preparing to begin a day of mourning at dawn."

"The pain is still fresh for those who loved her."

"Try not to dwell on mortality. Your physician advises you to exercise, drink up, and get a solid day's Slumber tomorrow. His Grace advises him not to begin their night seeing to his patients."

Lio grinned. "Apologize to Kadi on my behalf. I see you already have plans for your free night."

With a wolfish smile, Javed stepped out the closed door.

Uncle Argyros and everyone else were certain to be waiting on the other side for a full report. Best to go out a different way.

Lio donned a simple, knee-length tunic of breathable cotton and stepped to one of the fortress's upper corridors. Let the guards see him without his formal attire. The sight of Hesperine knees wouldn't make their eyes fall out, nor would his bare feet render the ground he walked on barren. He would return and change into something more suitable before he met Cassia.

He wanted to be at his best to offer her support. That meant he must arrive free of his own dark dreams and his thirst.

As soon as Lio got out of the fortress, he loped for the nearest tree line. Under the cover of the woods, he surged into a run. He wanted not to think, only to run.

Bare feet on the ground. Finding purchase between the roots and undergrowth. Angling around trunks and between tree boles. If he gave into instinct, he could win a few moments of pure relief, when his mind quit and his reflexes, his body, his senses took over.

They honed in on the scent of freshly soaped skin and the throb of her heart. Cassia was already here.

Cup and thorns. Exertion and her scent made him feel he was in a desert with his oasis in sight. For an instant, it struck him that not a deer, but Cassia awaited him tonight.

Hespera help him. He should not be in her presence in this condition. The drink he had let her witness last night had been his third. Tonight he hadn't even begun to tame his thirst, and here she was.

Because she didn't want to be alone. She wanted his company. Even his comfort.

She trusted him. That gift beyond value should be all the motivation he needed to maintain his self-control with her.

Union drew Lio toward the clearing where she had taken him into her confidence the night before. He slowed as he approached, letting her hear the sound of his feet in the brush so as not to startle her. He entered the glade to find her waiting on the opposite side with Knight lounging at her feet. She leaned against an aspen tree, her hands pressed behind her back, her buttocks propped against the trunk.

Hands he had felt on his chest the night before. Buttocks he had watched as she retreated, hips that had given her away. As the warmth in her blood now did.

Let her see him in his tunic as well. She would never admit it, but the sound of her pulse and the change in her scent told him just how much she liked his present attire. A Hesperine's bare knees and feet seemed to affect her like a charm, not a curse.

Her gaze fixed on his face a little too deliberately. "Good evening."

"Well met." He drew closer. Just close enough.

Did she wish to speak of what would begin at dawn? Or did she seek to escape from it with him? He would not probe her open wound. He must let her indicate what conversation would be the greatest solace for her.

"Forgive me for interrupting your habitual exercise," she said.

"Your company is an infinitely better remedy than running, I assure you."

"Remedy? What could possibly ail you, Sir Hesperine?"

He sighed. "An immaterial, but eternal, malady. We are vivid dreamers, and yet no dream, no matter how troubling, is sufficient to awaken us from the Slumber. I confess, day terrors have given me no peace of late."

"Nightmares from which you cannot wake? That sounds like one aspect of your Gift that is a curse."

He cleared his throat. There were other times he didn't want to leave his dreams and wake to the reality that Cassia was not in his bed, but on the other side of a clearing.

"I happen to have something that may be of use to you." Cassia dug in her gardening satchel. She pulled something out and tossed it to Lio.

Hesperine instinct sent his hand out, and he caught her offering. A charm smaller than his palm. The square of undyed homespun was stitched on all four sides with thick green tapestry thread and stuffed with something fragrant. He held it to his nose. He couldn't name the plant, but the scent of its leaves and flowers wrapped him in an inexplicable sense of reassurance.

"The Prisma mentioned some of the children at the temple were having nightmares," Cassia explained. "I think she wasn't talking about the orphans. I made a few dozen of these charms to ward off fever dreams."

"That was very kind of you."

"I fear the true horror of my sewing skills is painfully apparent, but the betony inside is the best remedy there is for nightmares. I grow it in my window boxes and dry an ample stock so I always have some on hand."

On hand in her satchel, next to Solia's secret, it seemed. "You are quite the alchemist."

"The power is all in the plants. Betony has potent benefits, and not just for children. It works best when kept close during sleep, perhaps under the pillow or in a pocket. You must tell me if it works on Hesperines."

"I look forward to finding out." He fingered her gift, lifting it to his nose again. Almost to his lips. "Thank you, Cassia."

"You'll be glad to hear we finished preparing the first batch of rimelace at the temple today. The mages haven't even stopped to sleep. Officially the Prisma is having the medicine delivered to the east, but the children already received it, I suspect. We were right that few mages in the temple know about their hidden patients." Now she gave him her arch smile. "You've been trusted with quite a confidence, for a heretic."

He smiled at that as well. "The rarity of my experience is not lost on me. If there ever comes a time when it is safe to tell others what we did, I may become the first Hesperine in history to write a firsthand account of the inside of a Kyrian temple."

"You would write it down? Centuries from now, I suppose, when all the troubles of this age have been laid to rest, except between debating scholars." She said it with the carelessness that defined her carefully fashioned court banter.

Lio's thoughts shied away from her vision of the future. He could not bring himself to consider a time when he could no longer be near her except in the words of a history text. "I am writing an account of all my experiences here. *A Chronicle of the Equinox Summit of 1595*. It will be a continuation of the study I began in my initiation treatise."

"Is that like your stained glass window of Hespera's Rose?"

"Yes, just as the rose window secured my initiation in my craft, my treatise met the requirements for my advancement to initiate ambassador."

"What was the subject of your work?"

Lio folded his hands behind his back before he could stop himself, then realized he must look foolish making such a formal gesture in his athletic attire. "*The Reign of Lucis Basileus, King of Tenebra, and its Implications for Hesperine Diplomacy*. You must understand, the situation in

Tenebra is one of the most critical problems facing my people. I wanted to do something meaningful with my work by addressing an area where there is real need."

She did not appear to take offense at his interest in the tyrant she hated. Far from it. She smiled softly. "I am not surprised, Idealist Ambassador Deukalion."

He returned a rueful smile. "My chronicle of the Summit will be far superior to my treatise, for it will not rely on theory, but on firsthand research. I've always hoped to add original material to the diplomatic canon that provided my education. I never imagined I would have the opportunity so soon and such an incredible embassy to document."

"Even after all that has happened, you are still excited to be here. Is Tenebra not enough to wear you down?"

"I would not trade this experience for anything." He found himself looking at her a little too long and rather too honestly. Her pulse answered. Lio returned to the subject at hand. "You are welcome to read my chronicle, Lady Circumspect, if you wish to satisfy yourself I have left out all the details that may not be safely committed to paper."

She gasped and covered her mouth. "You would teach a bastard girl the Divine Tongue so she might read heretical texts!"

"I would. Or you could simply read my parallel text in the vulgar. In fact, I would be glad to have a native speaker's evaluation. My mother will read it later, of course, but her Vulgus is ninety years out of date."

"I am hardly the one to ask for help on a scholarly matter."

She hadn't said it didn't interest her, only that she didn't consider herself qualified. That gave him hope she was not merely seeking a polite way to excuse herself. "You have more insight into these events than any scholar. I would value your opinion."

"I am flattered. But I doubt I would get through it before current events become ancient history. I can read words on lips at a hundred paces, but words on a page?" She shuddered. "Takes an eternity."

"I see." Her intellect was yet another aspect of her that was going to waste. Lio tried not to let his disappointment show. "Reading was not deemed relevant to your education."

"Not since I was seven."

"I'm sorry. I had no intention of imposing such a task on you." Nor of bringing up painful memories. Lio winced inwardly.

"No need to apologize. I certainly don't regard your invitation as an imposition. I wish I could be of more help."

"I value your interest alone."

She pushed away from the tree, narrowing the distance between them ever so slightly. "Perhaps I can be of assistance in a different way. It's the least I can do."

"No exchanges between us," he reminded her. "Only openness."

"That Oath governs our speech, yes, but all you have done for me goes far beyond words. Words are not enough to thank you. I would do something for you in return."

She *did* feel closer to him. She had not reequipped her armor after what she had shared with him last night. After their one, unforgettable embrace. Dare he hope that was not to be their only one?

Lio took a step forward, toward her offer of warmth. "There should be no debts or obligations between us. But a gift for a gift? Far be it from me to refuse your generosity."

Cassia matched him, a step for a step, her small foot rustling in the grass. "You are thirsty."

Her words thrust him into a fantasy world where she was coming to him with a single intent. To slide into his arms again, but with a different purpose this time. To lift her head and look into his eyes without any fear in hers. To bare her throat.

If only.

But of course that wasn't what she meant. "I'm all right for now."

"You must always be thirsty." Another step toward him. She had to tilt her head to keep her gaze on his. More of her throat came into view. "Here you are, far away from home, forced to make do with deer."

"No Hesperine shies away from a test of self-discipline. It's good training." And he was failing the test miserably right now. His control seemed unable to recover from that stray thought, that imagining of what he wished her words meant. Not even Knight's gaze on him was threatening enough to banish his wishful thinking.

Cassia stepped closer still. Goddess help him.

"Human blood would satisfy you much better, wouldn't it?"

Did she *want* to torture him? He stood speechless. He had no reply that would not betray him.

"But only if the human is willing," she went on. "That is acceptable, according to your laws."

"Of course," he blurted.

She looked into his eyes. The liquid rhythm inside her undulated faster, harder. "I am willing, Lio."

OFFERING OF BLOOD

L IO'S THOUGHTS GROUND TO a halt. Then eased into motion again
on the realization he had not been dreaming.

He dare not go a step nearer to her. Not till he was certain.
"Cassia. You are offering..." *Your blood. Yourself. To me.* "...to share your
blood with me?"

"Yes."

She was. She really was. Willing.

Lio's reality shifted. Cassia had just redrawn the rules of it.

Every rule he had agreed to abide by as an ambassador still stood. The
rules that defined her life could still punish her. He was still a Hesperine,
and she was still a mortal from whom the king, the gods, and Lio's duty
to the Queens' embassy forbade him to drink.

But Cassia no longer forbade him. That changed everything.

She searched his gaze. "Are there other impediments? Or does my
permission satisfy the requirements?"

They had taken the law into their own hands already for the simple
rewards of companionship and the high stakes of frost fever. Would he
draw the line here, at her blood?

Lio felt none of the caution with which he so often struggled. He did
not need to deliberate. His decision was crystal clear to him.

"Yes, Cassia. Your consent is all that matters."

"Then we are agreed?"

These were not the words he had imagined her saying to him on such
an occasion as this, and that was not the expression he had envisioned on
her face. But ardent words and declarations of passion were not Cassia's

way. It had cost her a great deal to even consider issuing him such an invitation, of that he was certain. Far more telling than the mask she wore was what lay beneath.

He let the Blood Union take him, and before he knew it, he had closed the distance between their bodies and all that lay within. He heard her gasp.

She lifted her face. Close enough to kiss. Her lips parted. "I am not suggesting anything indiscreet, of course. As you've so tactfully explained before, desires of the flesh do not accompany the Thirst. That is something else, which you call the Hunger."

"You would not wish me to do more than drink from you," he said softly.

"You know I do not find such activities prudent." Her eyes widened slightly. "I assumed your perspective was the same."

Her pulse beat a swift flourish to his slower, thundering heart. A flush glazed her cheeks, a mirror of the heat under his own skin. Yet she spoke of discretion. Of prudence.

Anger burned through Lio, but it was not his own. A dread for dawn overtook him. He longed to sleep and sleep and awaken when the coming day was over, as if it had never been. Then another day, another room loomed in his thoughts, awash in candlelight. A powerful presence hovered over him. He dare not lift his gaze from the fur-trimmed hem of the royal robe that filled his vision.

The voice above him spoke evenly, but seemed to boom around him. *...it is necessary to remind all concerned your blood is mine to use as I see fit, and mine alone.*

Lio backed away, and Cassia jumped. The vision broke, and he stood once again in the clearing under the Light Moon's slim crescent and the burgeoning Blood Moon with Cassia awaiting his decision. To accept what he had wanted since the moment he had met her. Or to push that gift away.

This time the frustration that overtook him was entirely his own. So close. So far. Nothing would be truly shared between them, if she offered thus.

"Perhaps I have assumed too much." Confusion flickered in her eyes. "I thought you thrive on human blood in general, but I did not consider the possibility your tastes are more particular. If you do not find my suggestion appealing, please, speak openly as we've agreed."

Not appealing? Her blood, which tormented him in his dreams every Dawn Slumber, his deliverance from his nightmares? "You speak of agreements and what is acceptable, but to share your blood with someone is nothing so mercenary."

"Mercenary!"

"If there was ever a time when there should be no negotiation between us, it is now. I don't want you to share with me as a means to an end."

She took a step back. "To what end would I make you a means? I have nothing to gain from this. I'm trying to do you a…"

Had she been about to say the word *favor*?

"I thought to do this for you," she amended.

"I don't want you to do it for me." His teeth punished him for protesting such a plea from her. "If you share with me at all, it must be for both of us. But certainly not for the reasons you have in mind tonight. I want to be more to you than a means of revenge. More than a tool to spite your father."

He had trespassed. All the anger he had felt within her surged to the surface. Her eyes flashed, and her blood raged.

Her words were longest in coming, but at last they too lashed out. "I try to do you a kindness, and you…accuse me of such a thing. You, Lio. Accuse me of trying to use you!"

He felt no triumph, although he had struck the mark. "I do not intend it as an accusation. It is simply the truth."

"I'll thank you not to claim you know the truth of my motivations better than I do."

"I can feel it in you. Do you not feel it in yourself?"

"I'll have none of your heartwarming magical truths on this occasion. The transcendent glory of your Blood Union has led you astray. *He* is not the reason. He has nothing to do with this. I am too wise to consider any act of revenge against him and too occupied trying to stay alive to engage in petty acts of spite. And even if that were not the case…"

Hurt welled out of her. Lio had endured a broad spectrum of her emotions, from her temper to her grief.

He'd never felt this hurt with the knowledge he had caused it.

"I do not want him here, Lio. He has no place here, tonight, with us."

"That's precisely what I'm trying to say. I don't want this to be about him."

"Will you not accept my assurance that it isn't?"

"How can I, when you hear his voice in your head when I draw near?"

The flush drained from her cheeks. "How *dare* you? After all your claims you would never trespass on my mind."

"I didn't have to. You were shouting your thoughts as if they were a battle cry. You want me to drink your blood so you can have the satisfaction of handing a piece of the king's property to the enemy. Merciful Goddess. That is not what I want for us. I will have no part in it."

"Such high standards." Cassia's voice was cold as ice. "I see what I have to offer you is not to your taste."

Lio fought to sever their Union. Her anger burned, even as she intoxicated him. If he went any closer to her now, he would not listen to his better judgment, but his aching mouth, hollow belly, and everything southward.

Her aura sank under a lifetime of disappointment. "Of course. Who would want to drink the king's blood? Now that I think of it, it makes me sick, too."

"By the Goddess, that couldn't be farther from the truth. Your blood is not his. Body and soul, you are not his. I will not help you act as if you are."

"You deny I would taste like him?"

"*You* taste like…cassia and pure Will and your garden."

She fell silent for a moment. "How can you be sure?"

"Because I have spent every night in Union with you and I know what's in your blood. My taste *is* particular. I have never in my life thirsted for anyone as I thirst for you. It has been so since my first night here, when all my senses picked you out of the crowd on the greensward, and I longed to know who you were. I would have you share with me for the same reason. Because you want it. Because you, Cassia, want it for yourself."

She held her chin high, and her pride was a thread inside her she clung to like a lifeline. "Well. I see I have overestimated my insight into Hesperine ways. Since I have so thoroughly misjudged, I shall leave you to your customary drink."

She turned her back on him and marched off. At the edge of the clearing, she tossed back over her shoulder, "My offer stands, however misguided."

Knight insulted Lio and his ancestors with an eloquent string of growls and escorted his lady away.

When Lio knew Cassia was out of earshot, he rammed his fist into the tree.

The bark gave a satisfying crack, the trunk a creak. His blood made a red stain on the pale aspen. The pain of his split knuckles distracted him from the rest of his body for an instant, before his hand healed.

It was a good thing she had left when she did. He couldn't have said another word around his unsheathed fangs. And he wore no formal robes that would conceal just how "indiscreet" he longed to be with her.

He could have said yes and backed her up against this tree. He could have his teeth in her right now. The taste of her, Cassia, on his tongue. Her blood pouring down his throat and heating him within. He could be showing her what it felt like. Finding out if she would ask for more than his fangs inside her.

And she would have been thinking about the king and her sister and revenge.

Instead of dealing the aspen another meaningless injury, Lio took off running.

21

days until

SPRING EQUINOX

DAY OF MOURNING

CASSIA WOKE TO THE thought of what his arms had felt like around her. The feeling had been powerful in its newness, astonishing in its potential to comfort rather than unnerve her.

She felt as if he had only just let her go. Perhaps she had dreamed of him. Or perhaps the memory of his embrace was just that strong, that it outlasted their angry, wounding words and held through the night, into the dawn.

Dawn. The realization fell upon her. Her moment of reprieve in the memory of Lio holding her was over.

The day had come. The day of her year that was, just as it had been twice-seven years ago, a trial by fire until tomorrow came and it was finally over. And here she was at Solorum for the first time since she had last been here with Solia.

Cassia did not want to open her eyes.

But she couldn't close her ears, and they told her Perita moved about in the room beyond. There came the inescapable sound of the girl stoking the fire with an iron poker to keep breakfast warm.

Cassia wanted no food. She wanted no dawn. She would accept the gloomy dimness of her room, such as it was, over what awaited beyond.

Moments from now, the Sun Temple would be brimming with mourners. The black door to the tombs would be the focus of dawn rites. The highborn would descend into the crypt to offer gifts to the sarcophagus engraved with Solia's face. They would pray over the vacant stone and believe they prayed over their lost queen's bones.

As every year, Cassia would not be there. The king thought her presence would be an act of remembrance. Of defiance. A reminder of what she knew.

But he was wrong. That dark hole meant nothing to her. That he forbade her to mourn there only freed her from pretense. Freed her to memorialize the truth of that night when the catapults had delivered their verdict and all she could do was try not to scream...

She was free to remember that her sister now dwelt in light, not the grave.

Cassia's mind fled back to the memory of how Lio had reached for her after she had told him the truth. The brush of his sleeves. Then the sureness of his arms around her. Finally, the sensation of his hands. His fingertips on the nape of her neck. His palm sliding down her back.

How could her heart ease so, while her cheeks began to flush at the thought? It seemed she had some proper degree of maidenly modesty after all. That must be the reason his touch made her skin heat.

She had overcome all her modesty and caution to offer him her blood. And he had said no.

If she dwelt on that, it would have the power to hurt her again. She couldn't afford any more pain. Not today. She had no comfort to waste. She could not bear for her anger to push him away.

His embrace was a solace he had given her only once, but once was all it took to make a good memory. She imagined herself back in that moment and hung on tight. For once, she gave her thoughts free rein. For once, she relived a moment she did not want to escape.

Perhaps if she allowed herself to think of him, she would get through the day.

So far she did not feel the tears threatening. She pushed away the hot tide of her emotions and put herself back in the cold night air and into his warm arms. His hands stroked her hair. Drifted down her back...down...

Lio's gesture of comfort proved a potent antidote. It got her out of bed and into her clothes. Kept her under control through breakfast. Helped her stay silent and composed in front of Perita.

Was the memory of Lio holding her enough to last her through the entire day?

Oh yes.

She returned to the sheltering darkness of her room and thought of Lio.

Until Perita pushed open the door and let in the firelight. "Lady. There's a messenger here."

"What?" Cassia's mind was so far away, she had not heard him arrive.

"You'll have to come out to the hearth room. He's here with a message from the king."

The words invaded and dragged Cassia back to where and when she was. Her fragile hold shattered, and emotion filled her, too fierce to withstand, until she had to stand up and move. She wanted to turn right around and pace back into the depths of her bedchamber, but Knight let out a growl and marched into the next room.

She followed him. Ochre light fading at the window told her it was dusk. Knight stood on guard across the hearth rug from the messenger. Cassia could see the white of the man's eyes. A young man who was not the enemy, but another of his pawns.

"*Het,*" Cassia said. "*Dockk.*"

Knight let out one last snarl, then came to her, circling her with the same unbearable agitation she felt. She looked at the messenger to indicate he should speak. She had no words for him.

The young man delivered the same message as always. Cassia tried not to hear it but could not escape the words. "…king…summons…"

He expected her to appear before him on this day. At sunset.

She should never have come to Solorum. This audience with the king would teach her what a mistake she had made. This would be her point of failure, when she must admit being near him on this day at this hour was too much for her. Not worth any gain.

Not even finally knowing the truth?

Not even meeting Lio?

The walk to the king's solar was harder than anything she had ever done. Even speaking at the negotiation table had not been this difficult. Only one thing kept her feet moving: the memory of comfort that took her away from where she was going.

Some part of her remembered it was utterly foolish to rely on anyone for help, even just the memory of someone. But she could spare no thought for such concerns. Lio's hold on her got her to the king's door.

She commanded Knight to be silent. She would not have him growl at the king with her fury and earn a punishment for protecting her. He could not protect her in this room. But her own thoughts…yes, they could.

She just had to think about Lio's face above her. Not the king's. The carpet pressed into her knees as she knelt. No, she wouldn't think about that feeling, only Lio holding her. Not the king's voice. Lio's voice and her own, speaking openly in the night.

I have told you. I shall defend you.

With such a capable protector as you, Cassia, I feel very safe indeed.

Flashes of awareness about her surroundings came to her. The king wasn't wearing black. The chamberlain was leaving the room. Business as usual. Of course.

I promise I'll keep you safe, Cassia. Tonight it is my turn to protect you.

She focused on those words until she was almost chanting them in her mind.

She realized she was not going to retch at the king's feet. She was able to listen to his words enough to know if they required a response.

"Your humble work in the temple gardens reveals itself to be untoward, when it transforms into such a brazen display. I thought you knew better than to draw such attention to yourself. Do not mistake your attendance, which is merely symbolic, for a place at the table."

He was talking about the Summit? Now? He had chosen this moment to chastise her for speaking out. He had waited till she was on the ground to land his next blow.

…you're intelligent and determined and braver than any man who charges out onto a bloody battlefield with a sword. You shouldn't be locked away in some neglected wing of the palace or even the walls of a temple garden.

Cassia opened her clenched teeth enough to say, "Yes, Your Majesty."

"What were you thinking?"

Cassia swallowed. Why must he expect more from her than silence today, of all days?

Because he knew that made it harder for her.

"I was thinking…" *That you've committed enough murders.* "…only of the lives the mages might save."

He did not raise his voice, just let his words do the beating for him. "You should have come directly to me with their request."

You would have refused even more quickly. "Yes, Your Majesty."

"Such a public defiance of my decision is not acceptable."

But now they know you would let their children die, just like your own. "I understand, Your Majesty."

He sat up in his chair and leaned forward, and Cassia nearly jumped out of her skin.

"You do *not* understand," he corrected her. "If you understood, you would never have placed the Kyrian mages' pleas, however pitiful, above my command. This is precisely the sort of behavior I warned you I would not tolerate from you, when I generously agreed to permit your presence at court."

She felt him looming over her.

"Look at me."

When her head remained bowed a moment longer, he repeated the command.

"Look at me."

Cassia struggled to breathe and fought to compose her face. No, coming into this room today was not the hardest thing she'd done. Keeping the fury from showing in her eyes must surely be the greatest challenge she had ever faced.

She would never forgive him for what he had done. Every breath she took would keep her anger burning. Her anger was even more powerful than her fear.

Cassia lifted her head.

His blue eyes bored into her. "You will no longer visit the Temple of Kyria. The palace, the Temple of Anthros, and the greensward are the boundaries of the kingdom in which you now reside. The next time you make it necessary for me to call you before me, I shall redraw the borders at the walls of your own chambers and fortify them with guards at your door."

"Yes, Your Majesty."

"You will continue to attend the Summit. But you will never again rise from your chair. If you stray in the slightest, if you dare for even one moment to be anywhere other than where I have ordered you, I will put you in your place, just as I have done to every other woman who thought she could defy me."

Cassia must make sure he saw no response in her eyes. No grief. No fear. No defiance. Nothing.

"You are nothing," the king said.

She told me I am beautiful and good and that she loves me.

Then that is what you must say to yourself. That is what she wants for you.

"You are what I command you to be and nothing more. Do not forget again."

Do not ever be ashamed. You have done a courageous deed tonight, and your sister is proud of you.

"Yes, Your Majesty."

"I am your king."

He dared to say such a thing on her day of mourning for a world in which he would not have been her king, and she would have knelt instead before her queen.

But the day would yet come when he no longer was her king. All she had to do was survive him.

I do not want to imagine a history in which you did not survive that night to stand here with me.

"Yes, My King."

"Get out of my sight."

When she got to her feet and backed away, she did not flee. With Knight as her honor guard and memory as her talisman, she walked out of the room.

FLINT AND STEEL

SOLIA'S DARK ROOMS ENFOLDED Cassia. She could not risk filling them with candlelight, not so close to the king's wing. But if she got no clear look at them ever again, they could always look as they had when she and Soli had been here together.

Folk were keeping vigil long into the night, and the votive lights and open chamber doors had made it hard for Cassia and Knight to move through the halls unnoticed. But having withstood her encounter with the king, she would not let a palace full of well-meaning mourners prevent her.

She carried her unlit candle out into the garden, where the walls had no eyes and overgrowth shielded her. Knight stayed close by her as she knelt amid the broken tiles at the rim of the dry pool. The blue and gold pattern on the tiles looked blue and silver in the moonlight and was as beautiful as ever. Cassia found one tile that was still whole and set her candle on it. She bade Knight sit behind her, where his fur would be well out of danger, before she retrieved flint, steel, and a scrap of tinder from her satchel.

A breeze slid down through the trees, snatching sparks as soon as she managed to produce them, casting them away into the damp undergrowth to fizzle out. By the time her hands slipped and her flint gouged her palm, she was crying. She kept on, ignoring her blood dripping onto the tiles.

When a tall shadow cast by moonlight fell across her hands, she did not startle. She breathed a sigh. A sense of relief stole over her.

Lio knelt down across from her. "May I join you? I do not wish to intrude."

On any other night she would have kept her head down to hide her tears. But there was no shame in proper mourning. She lifted her face. "I'm glad you've come."

More of a welcome than she had intended to give him. Not as much as he deserved. Judging by the look on his face, more than he had dared hope for.

Why did he want welcome from her and take it so to heart? Of what value was her favor, which he worked so hard to win?

She owed him more words, thanks for what he had done for her today. She tried to think of how to tell him. She had not shamed herself before the king, and she could not have won that battle without Lio's help. His embrace had given her courage. He and her Hesperine rescuers and her sister had all been part of her...strength.

The only words that came to her were, "How did you find me here?"

His gaze fell to the red droplets on the tiles. "I followed the scent."

Of course. Her blood. Which she had tried to give him, and he had not wanted.

"Cassia, I..." He ran both his hands through his hair. "When you didn't come out to the grounds, and I smelled your blood, I... All I could sense was your distress. So many atrocities can befall a woman in this place."

She had witnessed many displays of fear, and she'd spent her life grappling with her own. She hadn't seen such fear for *her* on another's face.

There was no call for him to look at her so. He was someone from another world. He did not have to risk her secrets and confront her pain. Why did it matter to him if she was safe?

He would not accept anything from her. Why would he give her so much in return for nothing?

For the same reason three of his people had rescued her on this night all those years ago.

Kindness.

The tears simply would not stop, even now, when she willed them to. Cassia held out her injured palm. "It's all right. See? It's nothing."

Lio held out his hands. "May I?"

The shiver that moved through her had nothing to do with her weeping. He was asking her to place her blood in his hands. Surely he did not intend to collect on her offer after all. Not now.

If he did, did that disturb her?

Slowly she extended her palm closer to Lio. Behind her, Knight made no move, only watched in silence.

Lio gathered her injured hand in both of his. The smoothness of his skin made her all the more aware of the calluses on her own from wielding a spade. His long fingers dwarfed hers, but were so gentle.

As he gazed down at the cut on her hand, she looked up into his face and caught her breath. The blue of his eyes had receded to the barest rim around the fathomless black of his pupils. She was not looking at a benevolent Hesperine stranger. This was Lio. She knew there was no spell in his touch or his gaze, but she could not look away.

VIGIL

THE FRAGRANCE OF HER blood promised him he held everything he had ever desired in his hands.

Lio might never forgive this accursed country that his first whiff of what lay in Cassia's veins had been mingled with grief and fear. He had known instantly whose blood he scented on the wind. In a single moment he had felt as if he had just made a profound discovery, and he was about to lose her.

The feeling hadn't retreated, even now, although he knew a wayward flint had been the only threat to her. This time.

He held the gift of Cassia's hand in his, which she had not refused to bestow. The pace of her pulse told him this one touch was enough to stir her response to him, which she fought so hard to stifle within herself. He could taste the scent of her blood, a divine tease of what it would be like to drink her. It would take nothing more than to lift her hand to his mouth, and the blessed scent would become flavor, and Cassia would no longer be sitting across from him, but flowing in his veins.

He could heal that cut with his mouth. Then open another. Somewhere that would bring her even closer and give her even greater pleasure.

And she would call it payment instead.

The heat in Lio's veins turned from yearning into frustration. How could Cassia deny this meant more?

Perhaps she did not deny it—she simply didn't feel it as he did.

What she did feel tonight was fourteen years' worth of grief, and he was sitting before her overwhelmed with temptation, thinking only of desire.

Shame cooled his blood. He reached into a pocket of his robe and pulled out one of his remaining handkerchiefs. He spat onto it. How romantic. She had no idea how much he wished to employ the alternative instead.

Cassia sat still and patient as he cleaned the blood from her hand. He waited for her to realize.

"It's gone!" She flexed her hand. The motion of her fingers in his tantalized him. And she was only touching his hand. "Thank you."

It was my pleasure, he almost said. "You're welcome."

"Do others try to take it from you? Steal your spittle or your blood or your hair?"

Trust Cassia's mind to go to the direst consequences. "It doesn't work that way. Just like only living blood straight from the vein can nourish us, our bodily substances only have healing properties when they come straight from the source. Removed from a living Hesperine, their power fades."

She withdrew her hand, but not quickly, and only to hold it in her lap and study where the cut had been. "It's like a bit of your immortality..."

The musing drew Lio to lean closer to her. He wondered what words she had left unsaid. A bit of his immortality...given to her. On her. In her. Erasing a mark, but leaving one too.

As he brought his body physically closer, the Union brought him near her grief again, and he wondered if she was only thinking of what tonight meant and how different his immortal life was from her human existence. Her blood drying on the tile still scented the wind, a promise to him, a warning to her.

"Cassia, may I be of assistance?"

She looked up at him, her hollow gaze filling with emotion. "You already made Solia a memorial light without compare."

"Would it be acceptable for me to help you light your candle?"

"It would be a grave thing, if I didn't manage to light a vigil candle for my own sister. But lighting it together with a fellow mourner...that's an honored tradition as well."

Lio dared take her hand again.

She wrapped her fingers around his. "I didn't think Hesperines could start fires with magic."

"Actually that's not really my area. I was thinking I might place myself between you and the wind."

The corners of her mouth relaxed. "That would be a great help."

He had almost made her smile, on this night. He must count his blessings and be patient.

He arranged himself on her other side, whence the wind came. "This must be the garden where you and Solia planted flowers together."

"Yes. Her rooms are through that door." Cassia gestured, then put her flint, steel, and tinder into position again. "We were always together here."

She grew quiet, and he recognized the silence of reverence. It was the mother tongue of his people. She had learned that on this night twice-seven years ago.

He was so very glad he was here to speak it with her now.

On the fourth strike, a spark caught her tinder, and she pressed the budding flame quickly to the candle wick. She bent near and breathed, and the candle flared, casting a golden aura on the broken stones. Putting away her flint and steel, she brought out Solia's pendant, which she laid at the base of the candle on the unbroken tile.

Cassia sat very still before her small shrine, gazing into the candle flame. At her sister and everyone Lio's people had lost, brought to life by her own hands and breath. The light filled her eyes and spilled down her cheeks in a new flow of tears.

A strange and wistful thought came to Lio's mind of a past that had never been. What if the Hesperines who had found Cassia that night had not returned her to her father, but offered her Solace instead? What if they had found Solia alive, and her Mercy had been to receive the Gift?

Here in their garden, the Blood Union echoed with Cassia's wishes for a different fate. Lio doubted she shared his imaginings. But this was a night to grieve for lost loved ones and lost futures.

"My mother's name was Thalia," Cassia said. "She was murdered a few hours after I was born."

The sudden revelation made Lio start where he sat. "Hespera's Mercy. I cannot imagine…"

"The king came to see her after the birth. He was in her room when a mercenary, an apostate war mage, infiltrated the palace to assassinate him.

But even mages can die on swords. Lucis managed to slay the intruder and save himself."

"But not your mother?"

"During the struggle, she was caught in one of the assassin's spells. She really did die from Anthros's magefire, just as everyone says fallen women deserve." Cassia's lip curled. "Lucis laid the blame on one of the lords he wished to be rid of. I don't know if that's really who hired the assassin or not...it could have been any of the king's enemies. It doesn't matter. It was the king's fault. He didn't kill my mother with his own hands, but he might as well have. She died because of him, just like Solia."

For a moment Lio was speechless, trying to grasp it. How did Cassia live with the knowledge the king was responsible not only for her beloved sister's death, but also for the years she had never had with her mother?

"Solia never allowed anyone to speak ill of my mother around me," Cassia went on. "She told me I was the best thing that ever happened to Thalia in Tenebra. Can you imagine? My mother actually wanted me. Despite my father. Soli said I was the hope that kept my mother from despair."

"I can certainly imagine that."

"At least she spent the final months of her life expecting her child. At least she got to have me. Only for one day. But it was the day that mattered."

"Yes, it was."

"After Solia was no longer there to protect me from the gossips, I came to understand my mother's situation. Lucis found her in a temple in Cordium on his first visit there as king. Everyone says she was *fortunate* to escape service to Hedon to become a powerful man's concubine. Just as they say his first wife was fortunate to become queen, and his second to give him a son. Their good fortune was to die for him."

"I am so sorry."

"He would have gotten rid of me, too, if not for Solia. My sister persuaded him not to expose me and to put me in her care instead, although she was still a child herself. I'm alive because of her and you. Hesperines. I am the only woman who has survived him." Her gaze was still lowered to the candle, but her chin lifted. "I am not nothing."

Lio's throat ached. His whole being ached for the three mothers that man had destroyed, for the loving sister this kingdom had lost, and most of all for the tired, battered, but unbroken woman beside him. Thank the Goddess he could at least do this one thing for Cassia. Sit with her and feel.

Or perhaps a little more.

"Cassia," he said softly. He lifted his arm in invitation.

She slid nearer.

He wrapped his arm around her and drew her close to him. She settled against his side, nestling in, holding on. A sense of succor enveloped him. His, hers. Theirs.

20

days until

SPRING EQUINOX

MORE

NOTHER EMBRACE TO GET her through another day.

If Lio had not kept vigil for Solia with her, Cassia could never have endured preparing to celebrate the monster who had murdered her sister.

The king had allowed his subjects their night of tears. Now he demanded days of effort to ready a victory festival like no other. All must rejoice over his triumph at the Siege of Sovereigns. None must know they celebrated his defeat of all goodness and reason. He expected Cassia to do her part to raise the banners and bury the truth.

The king's feast was important enough to bring the Queen of the Kitchens down off her throne to demand an extra pair of hands. If Cassia had known the cook would choose now to accept her previous offer of help, she would never have set foot in the woman's domain. That moment of shortsightedness now sentenced Cassia to an afternoon in the din of the sweltering kitchens, where she must weave table decorations that required a gardener's skill while Knight was subjected to dirty looks. At least they gave him and Cassia as wide a berth as they could manage in the bustle.

She worked the prickly sunsword and fragile everblossom into center-pieces until her fingers were in shreds. Gloves would make it impossible to achieve the complex ceremonial weavings, and she cursed Tenebran superstition. But spending the day staring at the work in her hands meant her gaze was never far from that smooth patch of skin on her left palm that had last night been torn. She could still see in her mind's eye Lio's handkerchief, damp from his mouth and stained with her blood.

"The other Hesperines will smell my blood on it," she had fretted before they parted.

"No they won't." Lio gave her a smile that was half mischief, half mystery.

"Perhaps I should take it with me, just in case."

"I can't risk Amachos sensing Hesperine spittle about your person." Lio winked. "Besides, I'll run out of handkerchiefs if I keep giving them to you, and then what will I do next time you need your champion to provide one?"

Cassia almost laughed, before a new thought struck her. "Lio, will Amachos sense what you did to my hand?"

"If you touch His Honored Masterfulness with that hand within the next half hour, it *might* make his senses sneeze. You aren't planning to play any tricks on the Royal Incompetent in his sleep tonight, are you?"

In the middle of the godsforsaken kitchens in the godsforsaken palace, Cassia nearly smiled at the memory. She envisioned asking Lio to do something for the welts on her fingers when she saw him tonight.

For she would see him tonight. The king's exercise in hubris would not deny her that, no matter what this so-called festival demanded of her.

She never expected something much more mundane would keep her trapped in the palace.

When she returned to her rooms with Perita after a hasty dinner in the kitchens, Cassia expected it would be only a matter of time before the handmaiden disappeared to relieve the frustrations of the day with her guard.

But Perita wasted no time busying herself about the chambers. Even after the arduous day, she sought out every possible task that might be necessary and set to it. She worked fast and with utter concentration.

By the time Cassia retired to her bed, the scent oils sat on the dressing table in perfectly arranged rows, her slippers were clean of a fortnight's worth of garden stains, and the handmaiden was eying a carpet they hadn't disturbed since their arrival as if it warranted a beating.

Cassia lay in her bed, pretending to sleep as usual while Knight slept in truth, and listened to the girl whacking the carpet at the window. Cassia had never seen Perita in this state.

It must be a lovers' quarrel. If Cassia were wont to groan aloud, she would have. Of all nights for Perita to discover her guard had been shining the sun rod on other fields or for him simply to decide he was tired of watering the same plot.

It should not matter so. Cassia should not, must not learn to rely on these nightly excursions. But it had mattered that sundown would bring more than the end of another day of her father's reign. Night would bring a conversation with Lio.

He had found her in Solia's garden. He had dared to enter the palace walls without permission. Was there a chance he might venture further if he became worried about her?

No. Of course not. It had been risky enough for him to come to the garden. She should not entertain the thought of welcoming him here in her own rooms. That stretched the bounds of prudence too far, to say nothing of propriety.

Perita's activities did not quiet until well after midnight, and even after that, Cassia could hear the rustle of the sewing basket. It sounded as if Perita had settled down to a long session of stabbing frail stockings with needles. Even if there had been silence, Cassia's own frustration would have kept her awake.

Now there was nothing ahead of her but another day of centerpieces and sore hands.

She had nothing to aid her tomorrow except the memory of the cool caress of his magic on her skin. The warm moisture from his mouth. And the handkerchief, where that moisture mingled with her blood.

She must have more than that to carry with her and to anticipate. After everything she had withstood the past two days and everything she must still endure without losing her composure, she felt she…ought to have more.

She wanted more.

19

days until

SPRING EQUINOX

SNOWFALL

CLOUDS HAD ROLLED IN during the second afternoon of festival preparations while Cassia had been trapped in the kitchens yet again. Rain was sure to fall tonight.

She listened for the sound from her bedchamber between the splash and drip of her wash water. Leaving her tallow soap to drain on the lip of the basin, she rubbed herself dry with a rag, careful to pat her stinging hands.

In the quiet, she realized. She could no longer hear Perita.

Cassia scarcely stopped to wonder at the cause of her luck, whether an attempt by the girl to reconcile with Lord Hadrian's guard or to court a new lover to spite him. Cassia donned her clothes and paused only for a moment to toss what she would need into her satchel. She did not allow herself to worry whether her keeper would return at the usual hour or not.

A gamble. She would take it.

When she arrived at the garden door, she pulled her hood close around her face before heading outdoors. But as she dashed across Solia's garden, it was not rain that fell upon her.

Cassia paused in the middle of the garden and lifted her face and hands to the sky. Fluffs of white spun about her and alighted on her brow, her mouth, her fingers. A sudden, late snow.

By the time she and Knight reached the end of the tunnel under the walls, she could feel a powerful cold creeping in from the grounds. She braced her shoulder against the half-frozen wood and gave it a mighty heave. Winter breathed in through the hatch.

Knight sat a few paces back in the tunnel, out of the snow's reach. He looked at her with large eyes.

"I'm sorry, darling. *Dockk.*"

Without a whine, he obeyed her command. She gave him an extra pat before he loped past her to lead the way into the night.

Perhaps she ought to have been circumspect, but she couldn't find it in herself to be concerned. She dashed through the woods without thought for being seen or heard.

She was soon under the shelter of the thickest and oldest trees. Their expansive canopies welcomed the snow, shivering in the wind and passing the caress of winter down to her. Before long she too was frosted in snow.

The path turned white before her eyes. She let her hood fall back and her cloak fly open. She grasped her skirts and her satchel close so she could run faster. The dark streak beside her reassured her she and Knight still ran together.

The flurry became a gale, telling her she was in a clearing. She paused to catch her breath, bracing herself on the Font of the Changing Queen. Snow mantled the stone falcon and drifted down into the basin, filling the Font to overflowing. She left her handprints on the basin's rim, revealing the carved ivy leaves that twined around it.

She ran on. Trees were dark pillars that held up the vaulted ceiling of the snowstorm. Cassia wove between them, rushing along the narrow aisle in the underbrush that was the deer trail. She swerved around the frosted rubble in her path just in time.

She almost didn't see the shrine when she was right upon it. It emerged out of the night like some conjuring made of living snow and not stone. The doorway was a beckoning darkness that promised shelter. For a moment, Cassia thought she could imagine Orthros.

She plunged inside. The singing wind eased to a steady embrace of sound. The snow on her clothes began to melt and drip onto the stones at her feet.

On the other side of the threshold, Knight sat in the snow with his ears plastered against him and stared at her.

She had seen betrayal in the eyes of liegehounds whose masters did not return their devotion. Cassia now searched her companion's gaze for a sign she had gone too far.

She saw a miserable, confused, wet dog. But no hurt.

"You are such a good dog, my darling. Why don't you come in out of the cold? It's nice in here. There's nothing dangerous, I promise."

She showered him with reassurances as she slid her satchel off and opened it. She pulled out the blanket she had brought, Knight's favorite to lounge on at the end of her bed. She laid it down in a spot that was free of debris, crooning for Knight to join her inside. He eyed the blanket with unmistakable longing.

Cassia pulled out her most effective means of persuasion. At the sight of his favorite chewing bone, Knight's ears lifted ever so slightly.

"That's right, love. We're safe here. There's no need to stand out in the snow. You're such a good dog. You've been so patient all day with the nasty folk in the kitchens. You've earned a bone and a warm blanket."

Knight took one step forward and gave the threshold a sniff, then a thorough investigation.

"We're so alike, aren't we? We're both very cautious by nature. Yes, that's right. Give it a good sniff to make sure it's safe."

Cassia persisted, tempting and luring, praising and commanding. When Knight made up his mind at last and stalked over the threshold, her heart lifted. As he gave himself a ferocious shake, flinging slush all around, she let out a laugh.

He investigated the entire perimeter of the room, sniffing and occasionally digging amid the rubble. Cassia silently apologized to Hespera and Lio's people for desecration by muddy paws. At least Knight didn't take a notion to mark his territory. He concluded his rounds at the door to the inner Sanctuary, where he let out a sneeze, then backed away. As he returned to Cassia's side, his tail gave a sopping wag.

She treated him to a thorough rubdown with a large cloth from her pack. When she was done, he laid down to his blanket and his bone without further protest.

"So easy to please, my dearest. I used to think my wants were simple, too."

Cassia moved further into the ruin, and Knight watched her go, content to stay where she had bid him. She ducked and slipped under the half-fallen pillar and through the door to the inner room. The soft darkness and scents of snow and stone closed around her. How strange that she could not see snow blowing in through the skylight. She peered up at the opening. Snow collected there as if on glass.

Hespera's magic endured indeed. What mage centuries ago had cast such a powerful spell on this place that it lived on even now? Had he or she imagined that power might, in the distant future, give refuge to someone like Cassia? Now, as then, the magic protected the hopeful who came here to attempt an offering of blood.

Cassia took a seat on a heap of rubble. Lio would know where to find her. He would sense the change of heart these past three days had wrought in her. And if he didn't...she would tell him. She would somehow find words for what she had never known and dare to speak them aloud, and he would understand what she was trying to say.

He would not tell her no a second time.

WANTING

For a moment, Lio simply let himself take in the sight of her. Cassia sat on a throne of ancient, broken stones, wringing out the long rope of her hair with both hands. Her gown clung to her skin as snow melted upon her body and pooled in the tangled cloak that had fallen at her feet. In the shelter of the shrine and its magic, steam rose from her damp clothes. Her breaths soughed around him, echoing within the stone walls of the Sanctuary.

Had the shrine and its magic not sheltered her from the elements, Lio would have feared she would catch her death. He worked a spell light from Will alone and started toward her. Before he reached her, she was on her feet. Something in her eyes made him halt and drove everything he had thought to say from his mind.

She stood, shaking, her shoulders squared and her chin held high. "I've been thinking about what you said the night you would not drink from me."

Their breaths mingled. Lio inhaled the warmth pouring off of her, out of her, and started to answer.

She held up a hand. "Please. I must explain."

"I shall listen."

"I am not eloquent. I do not know how to speak of such things, but by our Oath, I shall find a way."

"You have spent your life gathering words. Do not doubt your ability to speak your own."

"Thank you." Cassia swallowed. "Actually *thank you* is where I must begin. I have not had occasion to say it to anyone in so long that I hardly know how anymore. There have been no gifts in my life for fourteen years.

I have lived instead by thefts and bargains and forgotten what a gift really is. It seems fitting the last one I ever received was from three Hesperines, and now one of their own has shown me true generosity again. You reminded me that a gift is something given without thought for your own benefit or any expectation of receiving something in return. To try to pay for such a thing dishonors it. To try to buy more gifts with favors is worse still."

"When all you know is bartering, it is hard to believe someone would keep giving to you at no cost."

"But I do believe. I may not put much stock in the gods, but there are things I hold sacred. I would never use you. Not you, Lio."

Of all the things he might have expected her to say, he would never have imagined those words. He was so unprepared, he had no reply. He could only stand and feel he would rather be on his knees here in the shrine it seemed Cassia had just reconsecrated.

"Nor do I wish to use myself, least of all because of *him*." She looked away, but only for a moment. "However, I cannot deny that is what I have done. He regards me as a tool. I resigned myself to that and even shaped myself to it. To use myself, even against him, is to become…" Her lip twisted. "…nothing more than what he commands me to be. That is not who and what I am. I am better than that." She held Lio's gaze. "Tell me what my thoughts are shouting now. You will not hear spite or a thirst for revenge. Only rebellion. What, pray, is wrong with that? Why shouldn't I rebel? Why shouldn't I, for just a few moments, get to feel free?" Her voice rose. "The blood in my veins is *mine*. No one shall decide what becomes of it but me. And I want to share it with you."

Lio's fangs unsheathed on reflex, and warmth gripped his groin. "Cassia."

"I've brought a gift. It's for you. And for myself."

Twin desires flared to life inside Lio. His raged through his blood. Hers unfurled, fragile and strong, new and hungry. He listened to her give voice to it for the first time.

"I thought such feelings weren't a part of me. But they are, Lio. I want to, with you. I *want*."

His heart began to pound, summoned by those two long-awaited words. He should think, but no, he didn't need to. Those two words were all he needed to hear.

He reached for her. She came into his arms.

He drew her close, and the dampness in her clothes soaked into his robes. He could feel her pulse in her whole body, living and throbbing under her skin. Tonight he would taste her pulse. His heart would beat to it.

He took a few steps back, drawing them deeper into the room. "It will be just as you said. Nothing indiscreet. No imprudent activities."

"I don't doubt you."

That was the closest she had ever come to saying aloud that she trusted him.

He kept going until his back came up against a pillar. The intact support of the rearmost wall, which had stood for centuries. That wouldn't fall down around them, no matter how eager they became.

Lio let her go.

She stood there, poised against him from shoulder to knee, her hands balled into fists on his chest. She gazed up at him with wide eyes.

He held up his hands for her to see. "One to support your head. One to support your waist. Aside from that, I will only touch your neck."

Her throat moved as she swallowed. She nodded.

At her agreement, Lio caressed her head, then slid his hand under the damp tangle of her hair. At his touch, she shivered again. Her head eased into his palm. Yes, just a little more. There. She rested her head completely in his hand. He placed his other at her waist, a light touch above her hip.

"I'm not holding you," he said. "If at any point you want to stop, or what I'm doing makes you uncomfortable, you're free to step away, you see?"

"Yes."

"And Cassia." He waited for her to meet his gaze again. "You can tell me what you don't want. Or what you do want. I will heed you."

She licked her lips as if her mouth had gone dry, surely unaware how powerfully sensual the little gesture was. "Very well."

He smiled at her. She would become well acquainted with his teeth presently, so he showed her all of them.

Her gaze riveted on his mouth. Her lips parted.

How he wanted to begin with her neglected lips. He had never imagined she would allow him an intimate Drink before they had even kissed. But she had set down her terms. He would abide by them. And they would mean her blood in his mouth tonight.

His gums throbbed, and his fangs unsheathed further with each passing moment, readying for her. But she did not look away. Brave Cassia. A fresh rush of saliva filled his mouth, and he swallowed hard.

He lowered his head slowly, so as not to startle her. Even so, he felt her tense against him.

"Relax," he whispered.

"Very well." Her fingers curled into tighter fists.

He let out a soft breath upon her skin where her neck and shoulder met. A little of the rigidity in her body gave way to another shiver. "Relax," he soothed. "You need not doubt me, Cassia."

And he refused to doubt himself. She had come to him at last. She wanted this. He would show her how good the Drink could be.

Bracing himself, he let his lips brush her skin. Oh, how satisfying to touch his mouth to her freckles for the first time. He ran his lips lightly over that spot again, savoring the texture of her skin.

"Lio—"

He froze.

"You said there would be nothing like a kiss."

He swallowed a chuckle. "I'm afraid the deed does require my mouth to be involved. There's nothing for it. You'll have to put up with my lips on your neck. That doesn't count as a kiss, does it?"

She was silent for a moment, but she did not draw away. "How much more of that are you going to do before you drink?"

He lifted his mouth to her ear and whispered there. "As much as I need to, to help you grow accustomed to the feeling of my mouth on you."

Another measure of tension drained out of her. Her hands seemed to melt upon his chest and his upon her waist. He could feel her heart pounding against his breast. He could only hope it would not alarm her when his response to her became more and more obvious where they pressed their bodies together.

But he must let her feel it. She would come to understand.

He wavered between hope and doubt. Surely she would recognize her response to him for what it was. She would come to realize what she felt was desire for him, just as he desired her. How could they—the two of *them*—share the Drink, and she remain unmoved?

"Very well," she whispered.

He lowered his head and kissed her neck again.

Patience, patience, he instructed himself. For a few moments, he allowed himself nothing more than gentle teases of his lips in that one little place between her neck and shoulder. He waited, and he was soon satisfied she would not tense up again. He let his tongue dart out.

At that mere taste of her skin, he sucked in a gasp. She did not utter a sound, nor even draw breath, but a little jolt moved through her body. He reassured her with a touch of his hand under her hair, and his other hand caressed her waist compulsively. At the next touch of his tongue, she held steady.

Proud Cassia. She was no docile doe. She came to no one's hand. Lio would consider nothing a greater gift than if he could win her to him not with magic, but with his words and mouth and hands. Not with manipulation, but with openness and honesty.

Her skin tasted even better than she smelled. The storm had washed away the odor of tallow soap and bathed her in the scents and flavors of the forest. There was the warm sweetness of clean skin, flushed from a recent scrub. He tasted the salty tang of sweat and the savory musk of excitement. There was no mistaking the flavor of a female's body responding to something that pleased her. He *did* please her.

With a sense of relief, Lio parted his lips wider and laved her skin with his tongue. He let himself explore a little, mouthing up to just below her ear, then down again, all the way to the shoulder of her gown. Blessed Goddess, she was so good. And he hadn't even yet tasted what awaited *under* her skin.

He let his tongue taste her, warm her, preparing the way for what would come next. Her skin heated, and the flavor of her excitement grew stronger. He steadied his hand on her waist, forcing his fingers not to tighten. When he tangled his hand deeper in her hair, she brought her face closer to him. Her mouth came to rest near his ear, and he listened to her breaths. He opened his lips wider and sucked gently on her neck. Her breathing quickened. He eased her head farther back, baring her neck to him.

His teeth strained in his gums, and another ache answered below his waist. So close. Patience, patience.

He opened his mouth wider still and did nothing more than rest the tips of his fangs on her skin.

She stilled. Lio stopped breathing, forcing himself not to move. The temptation of her skin on the tips of teeth…everything in him wanted to bite down, close over her, bury him in her at last.

But he would not do that with her frozen in his arms, panting, as if she were prey.

He nipped gently at her, and sensation fired from his teeth, into his mouth, and through the rest of his body. Her gasp pressed her closer. He held back a groan.

He alternated little nips and licks with long, suckling strokes of his tongue. And as he persevered, his reward was that she lifted her chin, pressing her head into his hand. She stretched her back, lengthening her torso against him. Did she realize what that did to him? She clutched at the front of his robe, tangling her fingers in the silk.

Without breaking the rhythm of his kisses, without giving her time to brace herself, he bit down.

She jerked in his hold, and they took a harsh breath together. Her skin gave and broke, and his teeth sank into soft, moist flesh. Oh, *yes*. Nothing had ever felt like this, having his mouth full of her, feeling her pulse against his teeth.

He flared his nostrils. He wanted to taste everything. They were past the hard part now, and he could show her what it really felt like. At last, he gave into his instinct to suck.

Now it was he who jerked against her. A rumble in his throat…had he cried out? He didn't know, couldn't think.

Cassia flooded his mouth and every part of him. A feast in a single swallow. He flexed his throat, downing the banquet only for another to fill his mouth and veins, to consume his senses. She was all he had smelled and felt and seen and wanted. But so much more.

Nothing…no one…tasted like this. This was what it should taste like. Feel like. Her.

He was working his mouth on her, puncturing and suckling, pulling more of her into him. He recalled he had begun this with a plan, some notion to be patient. But all that mattered now was getting her into him, and him deeper inside of her. Yes, that was right, for she was throwing her head back even now, pushing herself up onto his teeth until another layer of her flesh gave, and his fangs penetrated deeper.

PLEASURE

THERE WAS SOMETHING WRONG with her. This was not supposed
to happen. It didn't hurt. No, it had at first, but even that pain
had felt…so good…it felt so good even now, and not just on her
neck. All over her body.

Cassia squeezed her legs together, tucking her arms against herself.
She realized she was pulling him closer. She tried to stand still, but it was
so difficult. Her whole body felt so tense that she wanted to move. But
this tension was not like anything she had felt before. It made her anxious,
but it was not anxiety. No, it was a powerful heat, an anticipation, like
holding her breath and waiting for something to happen…something
to change…

She had to contain herself. These wild feelings threatened her mastery
of her own body. But the sharp digging of his teeth, their pressure at her
throat urged her to move.

She could feel him drawing warmth and liquid out of her, suckling it
into his mouth, and it felt as if he sucked it from somewhere much deeper
within her than her throat. That same liquid heat seemed to gather low
in her belly.

Her pulse throbbed, pumping her lifeblood into Lio's mouth, and
she felt that throbbing pulse everywhere. In her head, in her chest.
Between her legs.

He had said it wasn't always so. Drinking didn't always mean lusting.
But she felt the firm ridge pressing into her belly, growing harder with
every moment. *This* drink, her blood, made Lio lust.

How could the touch of his mouth cause her to take leave of her senses like this? How could her body ache deep within, as if his teeth in her neck meant the same thing as having the rest of him between her legs?

She flattened her hands on his chest, ready to push away. But just then he released his grip on her neck, only to bite down anew. A rush of sensation flooded her to the tips of her breasts and the bottoms of her feet, hot and rousing. She felt more awake, more alive than she ever had.

She panted for breath, and her breasts felt heavy. Her nipples had hardened as if she were freezing, although she felt hot from top to toe. The firm tips pressed into his chest painfully, making her want to shift her hips. Oh, she had to hold still.

But that tightness inside her coiled, unbearable, from below her navel…down deep…right into the emptiness inside her that marked her as a woman. Nothing and no one had ever touched her there. She had never felt sensation there. How could nothing but his two careful hands and his mouth at her neck do this? How could it feel…so good…

Her body thwarted her. Sensation thwarted her. She could no longer control the effect it had on her, this strange and powerful feeling. It had a name. Pleasure.

Her knees buckled, and his arm came around her just in time. He held her tight against him, and she squirmed in his hold, moving the parts of her the sensations would not leave alone. But shifting her hips back and forth this way did not relieve the pleasure. It only increased it. And it rubbed her over and over against the evidence of Lio's lust. Nothing but thin layers of cloth separated his body from hers, which seemed so primed to receive him.

He would not…he had promised he would not…he would do nothing more than drink from her. She could withstand nothing else, for this alone was making her come undone. And yet it went on. The pleasure could not possibly get any stronger, but it did.

His teeth slipped out of her, sending rivulets of sensation through her and trickles of warm moisture down her neck. "Cassia." His voice had never sounded like this, a low purr in his throat. "I swear, I will give you as much pleasure from this as you are giving me." He shifted his hold on her, lifting her higher in his embrace. An inch lower, and his hand would wrap around her buttock. "Let me touch you."

She could only shake her head. The motion woke an ache in her throat, just like the one inside her. She moaned.

In one long stroke from her collarbone to her throat, he licked up a hot trail of her blood. "Please let me touch you. I promise you'll enjoy it. It will feel even better than this."

More than this? She couldn't take any more. She shook her head again, and the room spun.

"I'll just have to do my best as we are, then," he breathed.

Before she realized what he was doing, he shifted her head to bring the other side of her neck to his mouth and drove his teeth into her again.

Pleasure-pain speared her throat and her womanhood. Her body bowed in his hold, and her hips moved again and again. She could not stop. In an instant the motion was no longer something she did, but her body did of its own accord. Her back arched, serving her up to him, and her hips began to writhe. Then the writhing moved within.

She tossed her head back, mouth open to gasp for breath. She could only breathe and feel.

To the deepest core of her body, all was feeling. Motion and sensation, grasp and release, burst after burst of something beyond pleasure. In the sensate haze, she felt his teeth and lips clamp onto her as if they were a part of her own body.

The tide over her senses gave way to gentle ripples and a wave of warm lethargy. She went limp in his hold, gulping at the air. He wrapped both arms around her and held her close.

Slowly he eased his teeth out of her, and every part of her shivered with an echo of pleasure. He lapped at her neck, first one side, then the other, where she felt the lingering trickle of her blood. The ache in her neck eased. But the sensations between her legs quivered to life again. Her body was not done with her. It might begin again any moment, given its way.

The realization sent a pall of shock and excitement through her, and her heart began to pound again. His lust was still unsatisfied compared to his thirst. And here she was, her thighs parted and her hips tilted against him, trembling inside. Although the wetness of her blood on her neck was gone, she could feel the moisture between her legs. Oh, he would have an easy entry indeed.

The image came to her unbidden of him turning her and pushing her back against the stone. His hands hiking her skirts around her waist. Her legs…parting for him…wrapping around him…while he took her body the way he had taken her blood.

She found the floor with her feet and stumbled backward. He steadied her, but did not hold her. Dizziness assailed her, but she stepped out of his reach and leaned against the wall, narrowly missing a vine of thorns. She had to leave. As soon as she could walk.

The spell light had gone out and left them both in shadow. Lio's eyes shone at her through the darkness, catching all the moonlight that reached them through the storm. "Cassia. You are magnificent."

It took a moment for his words to sink into her muddled thoughts. She wasn't sure what she had imagined would be the first words out of his mouth afterward. But she certainly hadn't expected praise. In his voice, the most genuine one she knew.

Her face heated even more. "Thank you."

His glowing eyes narrowed, a sign he was smiling. "I hope you don't feel it was a one-sided exchange."

After a lifetime of surviving on her wits and words, Cassia had nothing. No ready response for such an occasion as this. Her mother might have. Other women whose bodies were their tools surely had an arsenal of things to say after such an encounter to produce just the desired result.

Cassia found she did not want to think of her mother or anyone else in this moment, and she did not want to say any of the sort of words she was used to speaking.

She swallowed. "I…ah…I felt our agreement…broke down at some point."

She heard him shift in the dark. His gaze wavered.

"That is," she said, "it did not feel like what we planned."

"No?" he asked softly. "What did it feel like?"

She would never, no matter how she tried, find words to answer *that* question. "I could not possibly describe it. I was too occupied feeling."

Those blue eyes came swiftly toward her, and the next thing she knew, both his hands cupped her face. "I am more delighted to hear that, from you, than I can possibly say."

He was touching her again. Standing so close. Her nose filled with his scent, a mixture of plants whose names she did not know. Layers fresh and floral, crisp and woodsy, rich and aromatic.

His hands slid downward. So gentle. Now he touched her neck, and she realized she felt no pain as she would if he had touched torn flesh. The punctures had closed, and all that remained were pinpoints on her skin that were strangely sensitive. Even her hands no longer stung. He had done all that with a single bite.

Only a bite. It was obvious he wanted more. She must leave.

"Before you go," Lio said, "may I ask you one thing?"

"Yes," she said in surprise. He wasn't trying to keep her here?

"Since we seem to have left our agreement behind, may I kiss you? We have yet to know that pleasure, although your blood runs in my veins even now."

Her pulse throbbed in her cheeks, and she shifted on her feet, tucking her legs together again. They had already gone far beyond a kiss. "I take it Hespera does not object to such activities in her sacred places."

Lio's laughter was soft and throaty. "Why would she, when such activities *are* sacred?"

Cassia reached out into the darkness. Her hands met his chest. She did not think about what lay below. She splayed her hands on his breast and slid them a little. It turned into a caress. She could feel his heart beating. His heart. Full of her blood. Pumping her blood throughout his body. A part of her was inside him.

She tilted her face upward and stepped closer. She couldn't see his mouth, but she lifted hers for him.

His eyes descended. Down, down. *He* had no trouble finding her in the dark. The lips that had spent tonight on her throat now touched her own.

His mouth was warm. He began as he had on her neck, with light, gentle touches. She knew what came next. Hesitantly, she parted her lips for him.

He pressed his mouth more firmly against hers. A little rough, so very gentle. He had been telling the truth. It felt even better.

His tongue delved between her lips. Her mouth filled with heat and moisture. She tasted a metallic hint, as if she'd bitten her tongue. Her blood lingered in his mouth. But beneath that, Lio. Now she could taste him.

She tried moving her tongue inside his mouth. He began to move his lips and tongue as well and somehow turned it into a rhythm, inviting her hapless probing into his deliberate motions.

Was this what men's mouths tasted like? Surely not. Nothing and no one could taste like Lio. He was a wine she could not name, whose flavor transformed the longer she tried it, first sweet, then heady, then so rich she wanted to moan.

His kiss was slow and leisurely and tender. A strange and unexpected warmth came over her. She could not place it. A fine feeling, a safe one... That's what it was. Contentment.

He pulled his mouth away, and she realized they were both panting again, and she was pressed against him.

"Good night, Cassia."

He backed away. His eyes dipped, and she realized he had bowed. Then he was gone.

The room felt so empty. He had left so abruptly.

If he hadn't, they would still be touching. No, it was good he had left.

Cassia crossed the room and sat on the stones again, pressing her hands to her face. She would collect herself, then find her way back. The sound of the snowstorm she had long since forgotten still continued outside, soft and steady. Another good soak must surely clear her head.

CASSIA'S BLOOD

LIO WAS SURE HE would never, as long as he lived, taste anything better than Cassia's blood while she climaxed.

It took every bit of will he had to abandon her there in the ruins. He didn't bother trying to walk back. He was far past that. He took himself straight to his rooms with one step and dropped his robes on the way to his bed.

He rolled onto the pallet, bracing himself on his arms. His body begged him for relief, but mad as it was, he still fought for control, unwilling to end such a night as this with a solitary release here in this empty bed.

He had tasted her first climax. What a privilege. What a *drug*.

He could become addicted to that taste. To the thrill of her reaching her completion in his arms, with his teeth in her neck. But Goddess help him, he might not survive it again.

Lio groaned. She had been so wet. He could still smell her arousal. He could still taste her blood.

He could feel her in his blood.

With each pump of his heart, his Gift surged through him anew. Power had become viscous joy in his veins. This was the Feast. This was Cassia.

Cassia, always so controlled, so imprisoned within herself. She had come undone. She had been wild in his arms. How easily he could imagine her here, spread out on his bed, wild beneath him.

Lio gave in and put his own hand to his body where he hungered for her touch. He bared his teeth. Self-discipline be forsaken. He could not lament any pleasure brought on by what she had given him tonight—and the promise of what they would share when next they met.

18

days until

SPRING EQUINOX

TOUCH

"ANOTHER DAY IN THE kitchens," said Cassia. "Garlands of king's wort, no less."

Knight replied with a sympathetic gaze through the doorway from the shrine's antechamber. He stretched out more comfortably on his blanket.

"What would I have done if Perita hadn't gone out tonight and I couldn't get away?" Cassia gave her small fire a gentle blow, stoking the little blaze with a spare branch. A handful of sparks and flame leapt up, and shadows played on the broken stones scattered about the Ritual Sanctuary. "There now. I can only hope Hespera does not object to me bringing this mortal element into her house."

"We too once kept sacred flames burning in her temples, before fire turned on us. But sympathetic hands have lit this one tonight."

Cassia heard him, felt him even before she glanced up to see Lio kneeling beside her. Very close beside her.

"I didn't get the impression you were cold last night," he said.

She smiled, blushing. "No. I just thought I might like to see you better this time."

"My spell light was not enough?"

"It went out. It seems you were somewhat distracted."

His gaze warmed with amusement and a great deal more she was not so used to seeing there. "Afraid there might be monsters in the dark?"

"Ha!"

He grinned, and it struck her again how much of an effort he had once made not to give her a real smile.

"I am not afraid of those fangs," she informed him.

"I'm very, very glad to hear that." He leaned forward, and his lips were on hers for the second time.

The kiss was swift and gentle and unstudied. An impulse. Cassia put out a hand to steady herself. It came to rest on his shoulder. His lips were firm, their motions soft, his tongue slick and warm sliding over hers. Four sizable canines pressed against her mouth. One scraped her tongue, then her lip.

Tilting her head, she adjusted her mouth on his, the better to feel his teeth. Two long, thick canines on top, two smaller ones on the bottom that were no less sharp. She ran her tongue over his top left fang, studying its shape.

Lio made a startled sound in his throat. Almost a moan. Did that feel good to him? Cassia probed his top right canine with her tongue. He parted his lips wider, leaning into their kiss. Yes, he definitely liked that.

Carefully she licked his fangs, exploring each one up and down, under and behind. She felt them lengthen. The base of his fangs emerged from his gums, and it seemed his teeth grew thicker. She dared to draw her tongue over the tip of one. She felt a sharp, teasing pain and tasted blood.

Lio drew back, flushed and smiling even more.

Cassia stared. Had she done *that* to his fangs?

Did that mean the same thing as what happened to a male's other parts?

His tongue darted over the fang tipped with her blood, and he swallowed. "Not afraid at all, I see."

She looked down at her fire and applied herself to its tending again.

He cupped her face in his hand, inviting her to keep looking at him. "I take it no kiss is forbidden this time?"

She let him turn her head. "As we discussed, our agreement has rather…"

"What agreement?"

"Yes, just so."

He kissed her again, and she sat very still, all her focus on the sensation of his lips on hers. A moment later he pulled back and eyed her fingers as if dessert had just arrived on the table ahead of dinner. She realized she had let her free hand wander down his chest.

"I take it touch is not forbidden this time, either?"

Cassia dropped her gaze, and it landed on one of his hands, which he braced on the stone beside her thigh. "It is as if you have already touched me."

"I have." With two fingers, he traced the curve of her neck and shoulder.

"No, I don't mean there." She struggled to explain. Did this even make sense to him, what she was trying to describe? She sighed and prodded the fire again.

"Cassia, you can speak freely with me. That is what we do." He wrapped his hand around hers where she held the stick.

At his coaxing touch, she loosened her grip and let her makeshift poker fall. "I felt as if…"

He drew her hand to him. "You felt. Tell me. I would love nothing better than to hear. For what I felt was…unlike anything else I have ever experienced."

She frowned. She would usually dismiss such words as flowery flattery. But she could tell when Lio was teasing her and when his words were heartfelt. "It was…unexpected…for you as well?"

"I knew it would be good. I had no idea how good. Was it so for you?"

"I suspect you already know the answer to that question."

"I still treasure your words."

She studied his face in the firelight. Treasure indeed. Secret treasure. "I felt as if you touched me in places where you didn't." She whispered, "I felt pleasure there."

His eyelids dipped, and his smile changed. "Did it disturb you?"

She scowled at him. "Yes. I had no intention of feeling pleasure there."

"But once you did, did you enjoy it?"

"Pleasure is, by definition, enjoyable, is it not?"

His laughter was warm and rich…and kind. "I found it enjoyable too. Goddess bless, how I enjoyed it." He brushed Cassia's hair back from her neck. "I tasted every instant of your first pleasure."

A tremble went through her, as if she were soaked to the skin like she had been last night. Treacherous body.

She wiped a hand on her skirt. Wasn't there a trace of soot there? "It is as if you have already touched me. So I have no objection to you actually doing so."

He caught both her hands. "Not objecting is not the same thing as wanting."

She sat with her hands in his. Again, he would not do anything unless she invited him. Unless she spoke. He would make her say it.

No. He made her do nothing. He always waited for her to ask. To want.

"Lio." She did not recognize her own voice. "I want you to touch me."

Despite the fire, the blue of his eyes had shrunk to a rim around the shining black of his pupils. She recalled the way he had looked at her in the garden when her hand had been bleeding. She could no longer deny she had longed for him to put not his handkerchief, but his mouth to the cut.

Lio bent his head and opened his mouth on her palm, just like she had imagined. He kissed her there, tasting her skin with his tongue, and in a moment gave her other hand the same treatment. She felt it everywhere she had felt his bite.

"I want you to touch me." She swallowed. "Where I felt as if you had."

He lifted his head. "Only tell me where that was."

Heat flushed her face. She listened to people praise and curse their own bodies and each other's, and occasionally denigrate hers. She avoided a healer's probing at all costs. She did not speak of such things. She, always listening, never speaking. What fascination could it possibly hold for Lio to hear her talk about her body aloud? What purpose could it serve for her to draw attention to her form, which was surely not what allured him?

"I suspect you would be more entertained by talk of my blood than the rest of me."

He drew back. "I thought you knew better than that by now."

Silence fell between them. The spell that had enfolded her receded and left her cold.

"I am not lily-livered about it, Lio. I know your thirst is what draws you to me. I have no objection to that."

"Is that what you think?"

"Men have many reasons to be interested in me. Never has it been any particular feature of my body. It's usually my royal blood. But that's not what you want. You want just…my blood. There is a great difference."

Confusion warred with comprehension on his face. "Cassia, if you're trying to say I care nothing about your parentage or politics, only about you, then you are right."

Had she? She had been thinking he was a Hesperine in an unwelcoming kingdom and thirsty for more than deer, and she was perhaps the only woman in Tenebra mad enough to regard his bite as a pleasure. But perhaps she had been feeling and trying to say something else entirely.

Now he had said it. And he meant it.

He drew close again. "I want you. If you think that means your blood is somehow more important to me than the rest of you, then you are very mistaken."

"You're saying what happened last night was not just the Thirst. That was the Hunger."

"There is a difference, a very clear difference for us." He ran his thumb down her cheek. "For us, I wish for more than the Drink. I want us to enjoy the Feast together."

"So...you want both. To drink my blood, and to lie with me."

"To share your blood while we make love."

The way he said it in his magic voice, with his hand doing magic things at her temple, made it sound like some secret, marvelous ritual she had never heard of. But she knew all it amounted to, blood or no blood. "If that's what you wanted, why did you leave last night after only drinking from me?"

"Because you have not said that's what you want."

But he was a male, far from home and recently unattached, and she was the only female within reach. She frowned. "When you left so quickly, I thought there must be some reason why we shouldn't. Or can't."

"I think it's a little late to worry about violating the terms of the Summit, don't you?" He nibbled the inside of her wrist, where her pulse beat.

Her pulse quickened. Far too late, indeed. "I don't mean political reasons."

Lio sat back, the image of patience, holding her hands in his. "What's worrying you?"

"I confess to having some questions about...Hesperine-human relations...we have yet to discuss."

"I left something out when we talked about Hesperine mating rituals? Do allow me to clarify."

"When you healed my cut, you said your power wouldn't draw Amachos's attention unless I touched him with my hand. Does the same hold true if we…"

"Make love? Yes." Lio appeared to be trying not to smile. "Even more than the Drink, the Feast invites a Hesperine's essence into a mortal. The infusion remains for several hours, until the human's body fully synthesizes the rejuvenating magic. But that magic is a trace of innate Hesperine power, rather than an active working. Only extraordinary physical proximity would give a mage on Amachos's level any inkling there is something amiss."

"Well, he doesn't want to tarnish himself standing too close to me, so we needn't worry on that score. But there is something else…"

"Allow me to reassure you."

"Well, of course I dismiss the notion that such activities with a Hesperine are fatal to a mortal—"

Lio made a choking sound.

"—but in other cases, it is more difficult to separate rumor from fact." Cassia cleared her throat. "Surely it is also untrue the deed turns a human into one of you."

Lio rubbed the bridge of his nose. "First of all, no, what's in my underlinens is not an instrument of certain death. You'll also be glad to know the Gift isn't something you can catch like a disease. The transformation will only occur if a mortal drinks a Hesperine's blood, and in considerable quantity."

"I see."

"As a matter of fact, we carry no diseases at all and cannot conceive children. We're rather popular with Imperials, you know."

No doubt. She watched the light and shadows vie on his exquisite face. "Why do you want more than my blood, Lio?"

As soon as she asked, she thought how useless the question was. She had already told herself the answer. He was male, his bed was empty, and she was here.

But she wasn't satisfied with that answer.

Again, the new feeling took hold of her. She wanted more than she was accustomed to expect.

If anyone would give her answers that defied her expectations, it was Lio.

He pressed a kiss to the back of her hand. "Because I admire you."

"That's a very strange reason to lust after someone."

His laugh sounded neither surprised nor daunted. "You think it strange I am drawn to your bravery and intelligence? That I am foolish with desire for someone as passionate as you? Think how I would feel if you turned that gaze of boldness and resolve upon me while I held you. Who would not count himself fortunate to be your choice, when all your choices are so carefully made?" His gaze swept over her with all the power of a physical touch. "To say nothing of your lovely form that holds all this within."

She would have scoffed at such words applied to her. She did not consider herself brave, only fond of living to see another day. She made a point not to seem clever and prided herself on her dispassion. She had never attempted nor wanted to be lovely.

But she could not scoff, because this was Lio. Every feature of his face and every line of his body bespoke he was in earnest.

How would she feel if he turned that look upon her while she held him?

"You see something entirely different in me than others do."

He propped his hands to either side of her and leaned in close, until every part of him was just a finger's breadth away. "That is because I have seen through your eyes."

The spell had returned. They had not broken it beyond repair. She gave herself leave to touch him. She had looked at him for so long without touching. Now she placed her hands on his shoulders and felt them. Just as strong and broad as she had imagined. She ran her hands down his arms, and his silk sleeves caressed her in return. At last she let her hands come to rest upon his and traced one of his long fingers with her own.

Such a strange and wonderful sensation, touching this body so different from hers. Not just because he was Hesperine and she human, he male and she female, but because he was another person, and she was touching him. In a way she had never thought she would touch anyone.

He lowered his lips to hers and kissed her slowly. With each motion of his mouth, he deepened the kiss. It was like his bite, a touch so intimate, but only one touch. His lips on hers, and no more. His tongue pushing deep into her mouth, placing him inside her, like his teeth, like the promise of more than that, while he kept his hands unmoving under hers.

She thought he would draw away and stop to breathe, but he didn't. He didn't have to. He kissed her, careful and unrelenting. Finally she pulled away to gasp. She heard him draw one breath.

"Where do you want me to touch you?" he asked.

The sensations were everywhere, just as they had been last night. "My breasts."

"Oh, yes."

He cupped her face as he had the night before and again slid both hands down her neck. But now he continued. His hands came to rest on the front of her gown. There was so little there, she wondered how he had found them. She didn't even have enough to put in a breast band. But she wore one, because it made them even flatter, and that made her feel safer.

Lio ran his thumbs down the front slit of her dress and the laces that held it closed. "So tight. We must free you from this."

"Yes," she said foolishly, "that would be necessary."

He smiled. "Allow me."

His hands did not move. Cassia felt her laces stir against her chest. Before her eyes, the knot at the top simply untied. One hole at a time, her laces came undone until, with a flourish, they fell in her lap.

Without her gown laced tightly to keep it in place, her tunica's slit front flopped open. Then the length of linen she so assiduously secured about her breasts each day gave way and slid right out of her clothes. She watched her breast band land on the stone beside her.

She tried not to gape. "What affinity is that?"

"Just an essential Hesperine skill."

Lio's large hands filled the front of her dress, enveloping her breasts. Awareness burned down through her body. She thought it might be shame, but no. It was too sweet to be shame. He was cupping her breasts in his palms, and she liked it.

He applied gentle pressure as he moved his hands. She fought not to gasp aloud. This was enough to undo her, and it was only the first of many touches that would grow ever more forbidden.

He was watching her face. He smiled softly.

With his palms, he grazed her nipples. They had pressed hard and aching into nothing but clothes last night, but now, into Lio's hands.

He caught her mouth in a kiss and was soon moving his lips and tongue in coordination with his hands. She tightened her fingers around his arms, trying to brace herself in the wake of the sensations. They threatened to overwhelm her, but just when they became too much, he altered his touch again into something new, and too much became not enough.

He took her nipples between his thumbs and forefingers, gently squeezing and tugging, sometimes pausing to thumb the very tips. When had she become so painfully sensitive there? How had her breasts become something that could feel so much?

He broke the kiss, although his hands gave her no reprieve. "Where else, Cassia?"

"This…we can continue with this."

"But there's more."

Yes, she knew there was more. It awaited even now, impossible to ignore. The emptiness between her legs responded to his touches as if waiting to be filled by the very hands that wrought such pleasure elsewhere.

"My belly," she began.

"Mm. Yes."

He pulled his hands out of her gown, leaving her chest half-exposed and thoroughly flushed. With slow caresses, he made his way down her ribcage to her stomach. The sensations taunted her even through the fabric. Oh, but she was hopeless.

Lio gave her quick, probing kisses as he traced his thumbs in a line below her navel. He applied pressure, massaging her belly, her womb. That pressure moved downward, inward, and she shifted under his touch.

"More?" he asked.

It could not possibly be more intense than what she had felt last time. It would not break her to feel the rest.

"Yes," she said.

His smile was wicked now. "Where?"

She swallowed, then cleared her throat. "Lower."

His fangs flashed in the firelight. "How much lower?"

Her heart was in her throat, but she said it. "Between my legs."

"Yes, Cassia." He stroked the tops of her thighs, then reached down for the hem of her gown.

He hardly even lifted her skirts, did not even bare her legs to him. Just slid those graceful hands under and slipped them between her ankles. With his palms and fingers flat against her skin, he took his time moving upward.

By the time he reached her knees, Cassia had arrived at the conclusion that the inside of her legs was an unfairly sensitive place. When his hands slid up her inner thighs, she struggled to breathe.

He caressed her there, resting his forehead against hers. "Here?"

"Yes."

"Where else?"

"My…that is…" The heat on her cheeks grew uncomfortable, and her body tensed again. Oh, she couldn't say it aloud. She simply could not speak the word *sheath* in front of Lio while he was touching her like this, much less the other, blunter names for that part of her body.

His thumbs traced little circles on the insides of her thighs, and he traded breaths with her. "Do you not like the word your people use? Are all those warlike metaphors distasteful to you? If so, perhaps you would prefer Hespera's word instead."

"I don't know it."

"*Krana,*" Lio murmured against her mouth.

"Krana," Cassia repeated, naming her body with a new word. One in the Divine Tongue, but one she had never heard in the temple. "Yes."

At the gentle rubbing of his hands in invitation, she shifted, easing her legs farther apart to let him in. The linen around her loins surrendered its hold on her just as her breast band had and made way for Lio's hands.

At the touch of his fingers on the hair that guarded her, she tensed. He traced her boundaries. So gently. The teasing touch did not feel strange. No, far from it. He firmed his touch then, rubbing her, and the abrasion felt very right indeed.

"How high shall I go?"

She gripped his shoulders. "Inside."

"Let me hold you."

"Very well," she whispered.

He moved one hand behind her to rest, warm and supportive, on her buttock. His other hand covered her curls, giving her one last caress there. Then his fingers dipped inside.

Her heartbeat leapt and pounded. His fingers were inside her. *There.* It should have felt foreign to have another's hand there in her most secret place. A male's hand. *Lio's* hand. But her body responded as if it were the most natural thing in the world. His fingers slid easily into the wetness.

Smoothly and gently, he explored her. He pressed equally gentle kisses to her lips, and slowly, she slid her hands up his shoulders and wrapped her arms around his neck.

He drew one of his fingers upward, toward the top of her cleft, where her flesh was so swollen. He touched one fingertip there.

She gasped into his mouth, tightening her arms around him. He made a sound low in his throat, like one might over a delicious meal. And touched her again.

She scooted her hips backward, and his hand was there to hold her steady. He braced her behind with one hand and with his other, teased that pinpoint of sensation. She felt the compulsion to squeeze her legs together, to escape the onslaught of feeling. But that was a coward's way out.

And that would make it stop.

She held onto him and eased her legs farther apart.

He broke his mouth from hers, even as he took her invitation to caress her further. "Oh yes, Cassia."

He kissed his way down her jaw and began to suckle her neck with his lips and tongue. His attentions at her throat and between her legs blurred into one deluge of sensation. When his teeth opened over her skin, she knew what he would do. She felt no hesitation this time.

His teeth sank into her just as he gave her the most exquisite caress upon her most sensitive place. Her toes curled in her slippers, and little shudders made her move her hips. That pushed her closer to the pleasure. Her body clearly knew what to do. She obeyed her instincts and, as she had the night before only against their clothes, began to tilt her hips, forward and back, forward and back.

Oh. *Oh.* It was wondrously different to do this with him touching her.

His teeth tightened on her throat. His hand tormented her, sometimes rubbing, sometimes flicking the barest touches over that minute spot that now seemed the center of her entire body. She clung to him, legs splayed, and moved with his touches.

The ferocious pleasure seemed to last only a moment before her insides tightened, then convulsed. Deep, deep down. Far, far without. Everywhere he had touched her. Everywhere she had not known she could feel. Her whole body shuddered in his hands, anchored on his fangs.

As the spell of ecstasy drained away and her awareness of the shrine returned, his teeth withdrew, and she felt adrift. But he wrapped his arms around her and held her. She rested her forehead on his shoulder. Harbor. She tucked her face against his neck, her cheeks burning with awareness of what they had just done, of how close she wished to hold him afterward.

She realized she still sat there with her legs spread, her skirts puckered at her knees where his body pressed near. He must be lusting as hard tonight…perhaps harder…than last time, although she could not tell from this position.

She had never wanted to think about another's body between her legs. The idea of hard flesh thrusting into her had never given her pleasure. But Lio was unlike anyone she had imagined before.

Was he going to ask? Was *she* going to ask?

He untangled himself from her and retreated to the other side of her fire. His eyes were wide, his pupils still dilated. The color ran high in his cheeks, thanks to her. But there was no trace of blood on his teeth. All she saw on his beautiful mouth was the redness and swelling brought on by her kisses.

Her own voice emerged husky and thick, the unrecognizable, sultry tones of a temptress. "You have not satisfied your desire."

"I want you to be satisfied as to yours, before you must think of mine."

He disappeared, leaving her hands empty and reaching after him.

17

days until

SPRING EQUINOX

LIO'S MISSION

IO WOULD NEVER HAVE gotten through the king's victory dinner if not for Cassia. The whole boar who had been the victim of the prince's temple day had been enough to try the limits of any Hesperine's endurance. Tonight the main dish was venison. To avoid wondering if he'd known the deer, Lio focused all his senses on Cassia.

She watched him from her seat in the back corner of the hall, and her fragrance told him where her thoughts drifted. He need only dwell on the fare that awaited him when at last they could escape to the shrine.

The doors of the great hall opened again, and in came a draft from the corridor, along with more guests. Cassia's scent sharpened with wariness, and Lio frowned. The enemy she dreaded most, tonight's celebrant, sat at the head of the hall for all to see. Which of the court's numerous lesser threats had just put her on guard? Lio sorted through the newcomers' scents. Four bored, oily ladies ambled in, and with them swaggered five unwashed males bearing freshly cleaned steel. The odd man out must be one of Cassia's self-styled suitors.

Well, Lio would not allow anyone to make this event worse for Cassia than it already was.

At last the humans' orgy of death over their dinner plates came to an end, and an army of servants arrived to clean up the battlefield. Lio and the other members of the embassy retreated to their post at the periphery of the milling crowd of humans, while the king's household hefted the tables and removed them to allow for dancing.

Lio's uncle leaned close. "Don't feel obligated to stay any longer."

Standing on Uncle Argyros's other side, Aunt Lyta wore a fixed, benevolent smile that would only fool the mortals. "By all means, Lio. Take your opportunity."

"I find my appetite has deserted me," Lio answered. "I'm not in the mood for deer."

Through the Blood Union, they shared a covert wince.

"Just don't wait too long," Uncle Argyros cautioned.

"I'll be all right for a while yet." It was no dissimulation. Two nights on Cassia's blood, and Lio felt he could take a run all the way to the Empire and back, and not even the ocean could stand in his way. He couldn't ever remember feeling so exhilarated, so at home in his own body. His Gift had never felt so potent in his veins. Was this how it felt when real desire and thirst aligned and were satisfied? Lio glanced through the crowd, trying to spot her. "I stand by my earlier intention. I still want to go through with my plan to mingle."

"'Mingle'?" Basir joined the conversation.

"Lio…" Uncle Argyros still sounded dubious, despite the time they had spent in the fortress debating this subject.

Lio reiterated his case. "They invited us to the banquet and dance. They offered us dinner, although we refused it. Is not the dancing an open offer as well?"

Uncle Argyros's brows had descended over his eyes. Basir and Kumeta subjected Lio to their direst glares.

"I know you still have your doubts, Uncle, but consider. We are here to promote understanding between our two peoples. What does it accomplish if we remain distant and aloof throughout our stay? The humans think we'll taint them if we so much as occupy the same air. Should we not venture out of quarantine and—gently, tactfully—challenge those assumptions, in the hope of disproving their fears?"

"Who better to represent us," Arkadia put in, "than a handsome, nonthreatening young fellow who is unattached?"

"My dearest," Javed said, "did you just refer to Apollon's son as nonthreatening?"

"He should take it as a compliment." Kadi's eyes twinkled with mischief.

Lio gave everyone his most nonthreatening grin. "I am determined to rectify our image as maniacal seducers of innocent maidens. How am I doing?"

"Keep your lips shut over those teeth," Aunt Lyta advised.

Lio rubbed a hand over his mouth, then pulled it away to reveal tightly closed lips and his most solemn expression. He managed to coax a chuckle out of his aunt.

Their jesting belied the seriousness of their situation. With the specter of failure looming over them, they needed all the humor they could muster, gallows humor though it might be.

"This has been a thoroughly depressing journey," Kadi declared. "Shall we not enjoy watching the shrinking violets dance with Lio?"

Aunt Lyta exchanged a bemused glance with her daughter. "I see no harm in it. The free lords could not possibly become more hostile to the Oath than they already are, even if Lio crumpled every one of their ladies' petals."

"I will strive to be gentle." Lio smiled to himself. If only they knew it was not the flowers, but the gardener he had in mind. She never wilted.

"There is more at stake than the sensibilities of a few blushing maidens," Kumeta protested.

Uncle Argyros spread his hands. "We are outvoted."

"There are only three of them," Basir intoned without a trace of humor.

"Four," Javed said. "I think it would do Lio good."

Javed had no idea what an effective prescription he had just issued. Lio shot him a grateful glance. "Physician's orders. I must dance."

His uncle met his gaze. "Do not interpret this as a lack of confidence in your good manners, however…"

Lio nodded. "Don't overestimate their tolerance. And be careful."

"Never forget the precise amount of space human dances maintain between male and female partners. An invitation to a young, unmarried woman would be considered a favor to her under normal circumstances, but not in your case. Best to avoid eligible ladies until you prove yourself to their mothers. A dance with an older lady is a favor to *you*, so take it as the great compliment it is."

"They're *all* younger than Lio," Kadi pointed out.

Her father pressed on. "If she is married, request her husband's permission before applying to her. If she is not, approach her father first. You may not ask the same lady to dance more than once, and certain dances are only open to those of a precise status—"

Lio held up a hand. "I will be mindful of all the fine points of human decorum, which I studied before we departed Orthros."

His uncle nodded in surrender.

Lio bowed to them all with a flourish and turned toward the crowd of guests preparing to dance.

For the first time it occurred to him what a daunting task he had shouldered. He must dance with as many ladies as possible, so as not to draw undue attention when he finally achieved his true goal. That meant he would have to run a gauntlet of frightened women and angry stares from their men before he gained the reward of dancing with Cassia.

He entered the fray and made his way toward Lord and Lady Hadrian. First, he would approach two of the king's allies who, willingly or not, supported the royal attitude of welcome toward the embassy. Lady Hadrian was above reproach, and it was easy for Lio to sense her strength of Will. She was unlikely to shy away, no matter how he unnerved her.

The energy humming in his veins made his senses keen and his tongue keener. He felt certain he would find just the right words to say and never miss a step in the dance. He could do this, and he would accomplish it with grace.

What a difference it made to be fully nourished. More than that, to be nourished by her. Cassia had given him this power, turned him into this extraordinary version of himself.

His efforts tonight would be worth it. He would have her hand in his, her beside him amid the music. He would learn how she moved when she danced. Just once, without having to hide, they would get to do something all lovers enjoyed. And he would occupy her company for at least a little while as a shield against whichever suitor she was trying so hard to avoid.

CASSIA'S CHOICE

ASSIA STARED. SHE GAVE herself leave to continue doing so. Everyone was.

Lio bowed before Lady Hadrian and extended his hand.

Cassia had read his courteous invitation on his lips and Lord Hadrian's permission on his. The warrior's hand an inch away from his sword hilt said more. Lady Hadrian's posture declared pride, her pallor aversion. With iron grace, she took Lio's hand, her back stiff as a bastion as she let him lead her into the circle of dancers.

Two things made it difficult for Cassia to continue observing objectively: the vicious grasp of jealousy and the knowledge that, because Lio danced at all, there might exist the possibility he would dance with her.

She felt like a stranger to herself. She had never considered herself a jealous person. That made one foolish and created more problems than it solved. She simply could not afford such petty feelings. Nor had she ever longed to dance before tonight.

With all the other women in the room, she watched the one she desired take the floor with someone else and burned with the wish that it was her.

None of the dancers laughed. No one smiled. The minstrels played, the liegehounds bristled, and the court gawked. A Hesperine had dared to behave like a normal guest.

Not that anyone could mistake Lio for a normal guest. His fluid movements put the most acclaimed dancers in the court to shame. Cassia could not begin to guess where he had learned the steps of the ancient Tenebran circle dance, but he went round without missing a single clap, leap, or hand clasp.

She watched the faces of those whom the dance brought into his grasp. More than once someone almost ruined the pattern of the steps because they hesitated to take his hand. But take it they did. For the king was watching.

So was Amachos, like a bird of prey at the king's hand. A step behind him cowered his apprentice, the only person in the room whose face revealed the full extent of his dismay.

A large figure intruded between Cassia and the spectacle.

Knight let out a growl, pushing her backward. Her gaze was level with the emblem on the man's tunic, a fisted gauntlet on a brown shield. The arms of Free Lord Ferus.

She did not meet his eyes. Let Knight do that on her behalf, for her would-be suitor could not imagine the hound's expression to be encouragement. Cassia let her gaze and her hand rest on Knight's shoulder. Lord Ferus could not mistake the meaning in that: she need only say a word, and her hound would protect her.

"Still hiding behind your pet, I see." Was Lord Ferus in a state of constant scorn, or was that rumble from his barrel chest the natural sound of his voice?

"If you know your dogs, my lord, you will not mistake mine for a pet."

With his back to the dais, Lord Ferus reached for Cassia's wrist. Knight's teeth snapped, and the man snatched his hand back just in time to keep it.

He sneered at her hound. "Just a dance, girl."

"You have not asked my father."

"Hiding behind your hound *and* your father." Lord Ferus drew himself up, using his full height to loom over her. "He'll regret making me freeze my bollocks riding east, only to find no bride to warm my bed when I arrived."

How sorely mistaken Lord Ferus was. It was not to the king, but to Cassia whom he owed the damage to his manhood.

His breath fanned her face with the odors of gamey venison and too much wine. "Mark my words, chit. Next time we meet without the king peering over my shoulder, I'll lock the door and settle things the traditional way. Marriage by claim is still law in this kingdom, and he'd best not forget it. The first sword in wins the sheath."

She tightened her hand on Knight's ruff. That little reminder to Lord

Ferus should be enough. Dropping careful words in the right ears to keep the man at bay should be enough. But it wasn't. Not anymore. She *needed* to speak out. To deal her own blow.

Cassia looked Lord Ferus in the eye. "You shouldn't be so eager to expose your weapons, after their recent close call with the frigid weather."

His lip curled. "One dog isn't enough to protect you from the weapons I have."

The threat should have sent a chill down her spine. The sight of him towering over her should have frightened her. For the first time, that was not the case.

She had banished him to eastern Tenebra using a cloak and a few well-placed words. She need only choose how she would like to teach him another lesson.

She outmatched him.

Cassia gave Lord Ferus a smile so cold he could never mistake it for flirtation. "It is a mistake to believe my dog is all that stands in your way, or that he is the greatest threat to you."

"I'm equal to the challenge," he declared. But that bold retort was not enough to hide the flash of surprise in his gaze.

Lord Ferus turned on his heel and stalked away.

The coward had decided to keep the king's tolerance of his presence for one more night. The bully thought he left the field the victor. But he left with the knowledge Cassia could take him by surprise.

Would he take it to heart? Oh, certainly not. Lord Ferus was so unequal to the challenge of Cassia that he would keep waving his war hammer at a straw target while she toppled him from behind with a puff of air.

Her anger did not feel like a wild force threatening her control. Her fury was a part of her, focused and strong, honing her courage. When the rematch came, Lord Ferus would not walk away.

The circle of dancers moved again, and her enemy was gone from view. The first dance came to a halt and presented her with the vision of Lio bowing over Lady Hadrian's hand. The lady was not precisely smiling, but her posture was more relaxed than before, her gray brows arched in surprise.

From the corner of her eye, Cassia noticed a figure approaching the throne. Her gaze darted to the dais, even though she wanted to look away. Lord Adrogan bowed before the velvet robes in the chair, then looked at her over his shoulder. The strapping blond lord gave her a suggestive smile as if bestowing a rare treat. His smoldering gaze promised he would completely understand if Cassia lost her head in gratitude and delight.

But when he retreated from the foot of the throne, he made his way toward a young lady on the opposite side of the room. He had been refused. What a shame. Cassia had been ready to teach another suitor it was not the king's refusal that ought to worry him.

Cassia watched Lio approach Lord and Lady Galanthian next. This time no one interrupted her observation of the initiate ambassador's performance.

Lio's formal black robes showed off his height to the finest advantage. The high collar drew the eye to his graceful neck, and the cut of the silk suited his broad shoulders and lithe torso. His bell sleeves and floor-length hem whipped around him as he danced, tantalizing Cassia with all she could not see. All she had seen the night she had first offered him her blood, when he had worn naught but a tunic for his nightly run. The image lingered in her mind now. Long, lean legs. Big, bare feet.

He spent the third dance with Lady Caro, the admired widow who was in possession of her own estate. Their faces and conversation came in and out of view. They spoke of the flax her fields produced and the linen for which her looms were renowned. She betrayed her fascination when she began to ask Lio questions about silk.

Xandra must have taught Lio all about silk. Cassia suffered another alarming stab of envy.

At the end, she watched his mouth hover over the lady's hand. His lips moved again. Lips Cassia had felt on her. *The pleasure was all mine, my lady.*

Cassia lost count of how many times Lio danced and how many other women's lips she read speaking to him. She gathered the conversations to her for warmth, although they burned. Her legs ached from standing and her throat ached from all the words she could not say. She stayed out of the way in her faded gray-blue gown with its fraying belt. For the first time, she found no comfort in the knowledge she blended into the wall.

The man who eventually approached her to claim a dance was not one who had asked the king for permission. In fact, he was not a man who asked for anything. She looked up at Lord Hadrian in surprise.

"You're wasting here by the wall." He held out his hand.

One did not tell Lord Hadrian no. An offer she could not refuse had never been so welcome to her. He might well be the only safe partner in the room. Her only opportunity to join the dance and be brought into a pair of slender, pale hands for just an instant.

Cassia took Lord Hadrian's weathered hand with a smile. It was only polite, after all. "I would fancy a chance to stretch my legs."

He nodded. This was another fine thing about Lord Hadrian. He was a man of few words, although he never had trouble making his meaning clear.

She bade Knight stay at the edge of the crowd and joined Lord Hadrian a couple of paces away in the long line of dancers. Neither of them spoke as a new song commenced, and they began to weave in and out of the others, swapping places, then coming to face one another again. The silence in Lord Hadrian's company was a boon. It gave her time to brace herself.

She caught glimpses of gleaming dark hair and robes at the far end of the line. She used the moments in which he drew nearer to prepare. To ensure she showed no reaction when, at last, the pattern caused them to meet.

Her vision filled with black and red, white and silver. Two hands took hers, smooth as silk, strong as magic. He steadied her and set her mind to spinning at the same time. She felt she was floating. She dared a look into his face.

She knew right then his concealing illusions were in full force, and she needn't have struggled so to compose her own face. Lio was showing his fangs.

"Who was that creature, Cassia?"

"Who?" She wanted only to think of the divine creature in front of her.

"The man who threatened you. What is his name?"

"Free Lord Ferus? He is of no concern."

"You faced him with courage and dignity. He is no match for you, to be sure. But he does not deserve a rematch with you."

The dance tore her away. It brought her back to Lord Hadrian, and she felt bereft.

When the music delivered her into Lio's hands once more, his eyes flashed with an emotion she had never beheld in him. Fury. "Shall I teach him a lesson on your behalf? Would you like me to give him a taste of Hesperine justice?"

"Lio, you can't—"

"Oh, but I can. The Oath denies criminals protection from Hesperines. There is nothing to stop me, and as a mind mage, I have just the skills to assist Ferus in understanding the true meaning of his threats. I promise you, the coward would swallow his boasts until he choked if he endured even a moment of real empathy with those who have suffered the violation he just described."

As Lord Nonus took Cassia's hands, it was good he did not deign to talk to her, for she was speechless.

Lio could not seriously be considering using thelemancy on Lord Ferus. Could he?

She changed partners three more excruciating times before she had her chance to warn Lio. "You can't brand Lord Ferus a criminal for his threats, even if he acted on them. Marriage by claim isn't against the law in Tenebra."

"This barbaric kingdom may not have convicted him, but it would be easy for me to discover what crimes he has already committed."

"Lio, you are here on a mission of peace. You've devoted your life to it. One breach of the agreement—one unauthorized use of your magic on a lord of Tenebra—"

"I never agreed to uphold peace at the cost of justice."

When Lord Hadrian reached for her again, she was not certain Lio would let her go. But he did, only to watch her retreat down the line of dancers with an expression she had never seen in anyone's eyes for her sake.

She waited until the moment when she could take his hands again. She held them fast. "You *must* leave Lord Ferus to me."

Lio gave her a glimpse of his sharp canines again. "I cannot stand by while he says such things to you. While he thinks of you in that way. I want to reach into his thoughts and purge—"

"Contain yourself, my champion. I excel at dealing with such boors." Reluctantly, Cassia let go of Lio's hands to turn in place.

As they spun, Lio shot a glance across the room at Lord Ferus. "I know you can protect yourself. But there shouldn't be a need for you to."

"As long as there is, I deserve my rematch with Lord Ferus."

"You are right. You have shown him you do not fear him. You will teach him to fear you. When that moment comes, let your reinforcements stand at your side. When you bring your words against him, let my magic magnify your voice."

"Thank you, Lio. I am truly fortunate in my ally. But I will bide my time, and when the opportunity is right, I will take care of this myself."

He held her tightly. "Cassia, promise me you are truly safe from him."

"It is I who have driven him on three wild goose chases already. He is finally beginning to see I am not the goose, and he is not the hound. I promise you I shall end the hunt once and for all. You must promise me you will not do anything to jeopardize your position as a diplomat."

Lio pulled her as close as the dance allowed. "Very well. I give you my word I will not act—as long as you are not in immediate danger. But Lord Ferus had best pray to mighty Anthros the Summit never ends. For the next time he and I meet without the king peering over my shoulder, I'll lock the door and settle things the Hesperine way."

The dance brought Cassia to Lord Hadrian and the crowd to a standstill. The commander bowed, and she gave him a deep curtsy. Now that she was out of the reach of Lio's veil, she could only hope Lord Hadrian blamed the dance for her flushed face and shortness of breath.

It was not the crush of guests that made her feel hot from head to toe. It was not wariness that made her unbearably tense, beside herself with energy she could not contain. It was her own boldness. And it was that other person in the crowd, upon whom she may not look, upon whom she could not stop looking.

She retreated to her place by the wall. How could she be so precisely aware of Lio at every moment, as if he were some magical beacon and her senses under a spell that made her home to him?

He wove his way slowly through the crowd, exchanging polite remarks. Neither Lady Dalia nor Lady Biata shied away as he neared, but he passed them by. Lady Nivalis watched him come within range, but he did not take the invitation in her gaze.

He was walking toward the throne.

He was so tall the king did not tower above him. Lio gave not the abject bow of a vassal, but an elegant gesture of respect befitting a foreign ambassador. Cassia didn't look at the king, only at Lio. She could not read his lips from this position. What was he saying? It didn't matter. She knew what the king would say. Lio would receive the same answer as the unworthy contenders before him.

Cassia had the power of refusal. She could see to it neither Lord Ferus nor Lord Adrogan touched her. But she still did not have the power to choose Lio as her partner tonight.

At least, not for a dance. But afterward?

As soon as midnight neared, bringing the king's fraud to an end, she could make her own choice. Under the cover of darkness, with Hespera's Eyes as her only witness, Cassia's Will was her own.

She watched her choice bow to the king again. Lio took a step back from the dais, then turned to the dance floor again. She waited to see which woman would next receive the gift of his invitation and fail to appreciate it.

His gaze found and held hers. He strode through the crowd, and now they did retreat to make way. Everyone in the room was watching him… and Cassia. Her heart pounded, but not with panic.

She savored the perfection of Lio's strategy. The king was refusing all her suitors tonight. The initiate ambassador was not a suitor. A Hesperine was entirely ineligible. According to that criterion, he was as appropriate a partner as Lord Hadrian, whose marriage vows already bound him. Except for the little detail that Lio was a blood-drinking heretic. But just as the king had allowed Cassia to attend the Summit at his guests' insistence, so too would he allow her to dance with one of them.

Lio presented himself before her at the appropriate distance, but his gaze seemed to do away with the space between them. He was no less stunning by firelight than under the moons. He looked utterly out of place, a jewel among stones. "Do you, Lady Cassia, wish for a dance?"

A brilliant scheme. A flawless invitation. The crowd might dismiss the unusual phrasing of his question as a foreigner's odd choice of words, but she cherished his private message to her. *Do you, Lady Cassia, wish?*

Do you, Cassia, want it for yourself?

She wished. She wanted. Nothing and no one would stop her from saying yes.

"With pleasure, Initiate Ambassador Deukalion." Cassia slid her hand into Lio's in front of the entire embassy, the court, and the king.

Strains of lute and the patters of drums set a rousing pace. He had chosen the perfect dance. A spirited one, but one that kept two partners close to one another more than any of the other pattern dances.

"This is our dance." His voice wove around her, well and truly a spell. "No one will interrupt or hear a word we say."

Before she could find the right words to thank him for such a gift, they began to move, and he took her breath away.

His supple power had lured her from across the room. Now, so near, his body seemed to summon something out of hers. This was dancing as she had never known it. Her body was not a tool for keeping her partner at a distance. Her body was part of her, which gave her the power to turn feeling into action and bring him closer. She threw off her limbs' rigid discipline, let the music banish her tension, and moved with him.

The steps brought them shoulder to shoulder, his words near her ear. "I waited all night for this."

He was not fighting for breath. She didn't know where she would find the air to speak. But she would not waste this rare moment. "I hoped."

He smiled. "Wanted."

"More than I can say."

"I would gladly dance with every woman in this room again, just to hear you say so."

At arm's length, then near, then far away. They clapped, and his sleeves slid back, exposing wrists and forearms still concealed in tight undersleeves. His sensual grace teased her from under a veil of silk. He was as light on his feet as light itself, and yet every time he grasped her hands she felt the sureness in him.

Every touch of his hands brought them close, but not close enough. She loved the distance between them that let her look at him and hated it for keeping his body too far away. His movements were exquisite, but not near enough to her. Not against her.

She wanted to *feel* him dance. To hold him while he moved. To find this rhythm skin to skin, their bodies rubbing, his hands roaming, nothing more between them. That dance, too, would defy all she had known and expected. He would join himself to her, and it would be like his bite, his kiss, his touches. She would enjoy it.

This was desire. Lust. She was capable of it.

The dance dragged her away again and wasted valuable moments while other hands gripped hers. Then Lio was waiting to take her to him again. To this brief treasure of a dance, and this chance to speak freely.

"I want more, Lio."

She saw surprise in his gaze. Eagerness. Longing.

She pressed on before words deserted her. She let her own new, strange, powerful longing drive her forward and found words she had never had before. "Don't leave so soon tonight. Stay with me."

His eyes shone. "Are you sure? You don't have to rush yourself."

She could hear the music around them, hear the dance nearing its end. But she looked only at his face and felt only his hands. "I want to see you bare and touch your skin. To know what all of you feels and tastes like. Just as you take my blood inside you, I want to take part of you inside me."

She would never forget the stunned expression on his face. He almost lost his place in the dance. Now it was he who struggled for words. She watched every shade of emotion his face revealed to her, aware too of his body, leaning toward her as if the space between them were a string pulled taut and ready to snap.

"Cassia." His resonant voice had descended into new depths. "I swear I won't part myself from you till dawn."

The full implication of his words took root in her thoughts, so ready for them. She could have him with her, against her, inside her till the sun rose. "I hope dawn doesn't come."

"Where I am from, the sun never rises."

The dance came to an end. She must drop his hands. They could not linger here.

"I'll be waiting," he promised. He swept away into the crowd. A moment later, she could no longer spot him in the hall. He had departed for his nightly drink.

Nay, his feast.

FALLING

ALL THAT REMAINED OF the night must be hers. Cassia could not afford to gamble on Perita's plans. This occasion required precise arrangements.

When Cassia made it back to her rooms in the hour before midnight, Perita looked up from a lap full of mending and narrowed her eyes.

Cassia felt all too aware of the heat that lingered in her cheeks. She stood straight and still as always, but the thrumming in her body felt like an audible chorus she had carried into the room with her for all to hear. "Are you not making merry with your family tonight?"

"That's all right, Lady."

"You know you are more than welcome to take the night off, Perita."

"Thank you, m'lady, but I'd just as soon not wake to mending that still needs doing."

Cassia resisted the urge to take the mending in hand and hurl it out the window. "In that case, have you brought me that new batch of soap yet?"

Perita ducked her head. "I'm sorry, no, Lady."

"You were trying to finish the mending first," Cassia conceded. Why did she feel the need to concede anything? "But that can wait until after I've had my bath. Surely your father is still awake on a festival night like this and can spare me some more of his tallow soap."

Cassia readied herself to face her handmaiden's usual protests that the soap the tallow chandler made from his leftovers was destined for laundry and not fit for humans. But tonight the girl kept her vocal opinions on her father's craft to herself.

Perita stood and deposited her work, needle and all, in the chair in her stead. "Yes, Lady."

Cassia went into her bedchamber as if that were all. As soon as she heard the door to the corridor open and shut, she hastened back into the hearth room. She picked up the mending, carefully fishing Perita's needle out of the folds. A freshly laundered tunica. Not for long. "Knight, *dockk.*"

He pressed closer to her, sniffing and curious at this unusual activity. When she began to give him a rubdown with the tunica, he swished his tail.

She returned the garment to the chair, dropped the needle in its midst, and carefully collected any obvious tufts of dog fur. It would not do for Perita to notice before her eyes started burning.

By the time Perita returned, Cassia lay stretched out on her bed with her eyes shut to create the appearance of exhaustion. But all she could see behind her eyelids was Lio's face when she had said those words to him. All she could think of, lying here on her back, was what it would feel like to lie beneath him.

She went into the hearth room to collect the soap from a pouting Perita. Without a glance at the mending, Cassia returned to her bedchamber in customary silence and went through the motions of preparing for bed.

When she heard the coughing, she went to stand in her doorway. No sign of Perita by the fire. Cassia walked past the abandoned mending and into the dressing room. There the handmaiden stood over the washbasin, rubbing a wet cloth over her face.

"Perita? Is aught amiss?"

The handmaiden startled and looked up. At the sight of her, Cassia felt an unfamiliar discomfort. The girl's eyes were swollen and streaming with moisture that was not from the rag, and her hands were red with the first signs of a rash. In the silence between them, Cassia could hear Perita wheezing.

"I'm so sorry," Cassia said.

"Can't be helped." Perita turned her face into the cloth and coughed again. When the hacking spell ended, she stood there with her chest heaving and labored to get her breath. "I thought it was clean before I started mending it."

"I'm so sorry," Cassia said again.

She stood, her hands at her sides, as Perita washed her hands. No amount of water would ease the welts rising on her skin.

"Perita, you must take the medicine the mages gave me for you. Don't do any more work tonight. Just drink the tonic and get some rest."

"Thank you, Lady." Perita turned away toward the cabinet where they kept medicines.

If Cassia were Hesperine, would she hear the rattle in Perita's chest as the girl struggled for air? Would she feel her fear?

Cassia turned on her heel and deserted the room. She returned to Perita's chair by the fire and sat down to finish the mending. In the dressing room, glass clinked on wood. A stopper came out of a bottle with a pop. Cassia's thread knotted, and she tore out her work and started over.

Presently she heard Perita throw back her blankets and crawl onto her pallet. Within a quarter of an hour, Perita's wheezing gave way to the easy, steady breaths of sleep.

Cassia put down the mending and went into the dressing room. Kneeling beside her handmaiden, she touched Perita's shoulder. The girl did not stir. Cassia patted her flushed cheek. With a groan, Perita turned her face away and burrowed deeper into her blankets. An instant later, her breathing resumed its restful rhythm. Cassia breathed a sigh of relief and a hushed thanks to the mages for medicine that worked. With unintended side effects like heavy sleep.

Cassia dumped the unfinished mending into a covered basket by the hearth and made for her bedchamber. She knelt before the chest at the foot of her bed. As she opened the lid, her palms broke out in a sweat. She rubbed them dry on the blue-gray gown she still wore before she began rummaging through the rest of her meager wardrobe.

Two plain, practical gowns, as far from beautiful as possible, as she had intended. Two fine, elegant gowns, as unattractive as she could make them and still meet the requirements for appearances before the king. That was all.

It probably meant little, what she wore tonight. Lio had never seemed to care about such things…and in any case, she would not be wearing it for long.

But it did seem to mean something to her. What did she wish to be wearing when he disrobed her?

She crouched there on the floor of her room, aware of her colorless, ratty hair and skin chapped from daily washing. She could not stop it: a flash of an image in her mind's eye. Solia, resplendent in a velvet gown, her hair a veil the color of the sun, with the sheen of fragrant oils upon her skin. Anointed for her promise dance. Embalmed for her death.

Cassia shut out the memory and stared into the darkness of her own room, breathing in the fragrance of the floral charms she kept in her clothing chest.

This was not the same. She was not the same. And Lio...he was from a completely different world.

How did she wish to anoint herself not to make, but to break the most binding mortal vows? What did she wish to don not as a betrothal gown, but as a vestment for her presentation to Hespera?

No husband would ever take her maidenhead as a marital right. She would gift her virginity to a Hesperine as a reverent treachery, a forbidden pleasure, an unashamed offering to his profane goddess. Tonight Cassia would fall as far as she could under the Eyes that saw all women as sacred, no matter how forsaken.

FIRST TRYST

TONIGHT HIS DESIRE WAS even more ravenous than his thirst. This was true hunger. Lio rejoiced in it.

Even if it did mean one more drink from the deer. Lio peeled his tongue off the roof of his mouth and grimaced at the aftertaste. He paused in his effort to ready the shrine for Cassia's arrival and cast a cleaning spell on his own tongue so she would actually want to kiss him.

He had thought he could never force another swallow of deer blood down his throat, now that he had tasted her. But for her sake, he could and had. Coming to her tonight on a full stomach would result in the best experience for her. He must ensure he had the patience and self-control she would need from him.

He ran both hands through his hair again. He'd been training in self-discipline longer than she'd been alive, and tonight he had taken all the appropriate steps to manage his thirst. That was the best he could do, and indeed the correct way to prepare for such an occasion as this. It must surely be enough.

No, there was one more thing to do. He must simply trust himself.

"And trust you, Goddess. You've brought me to her, of that I have no doubt." He smiled to himself at the realization. "Therefore she must be in good hands."

He flexed those hands, coaxing a bit more moonlight into the ruin he had come to think of as their own. Thanks to the ruins of spells, the chill of winter did not reach here. But the Goddess's Eyes peered in at every crack, both waxing with promise. Only a little more bending from him, and the light in the Sanctuary would be at the perfect level for Cassia's sight... There.

I want to see you bare…

Those words, on *her* lips. Unforgettable. Erotic. Divine.

Just as you take my blood inside you, I want to take part of you inside me.

Tonight they would live out her wants. And his. There was no difference anymore.

Her presence at the edge of the woods awoke his senses as surely as a kiss. He let his awareness of where he stood fall away and gave himself up to the Blood Union. He walked the path to the ruins under her skin, drifting with her between lingering patches of snow. He breathed with her, feeling her heartbeat as a caress that throbbed in his gums and groin, reminding him he still wore his own body.

Moonlight bathed her, and she thought she could feel it, as one felt the sun. Yes, as a Hesperine felt the moons, one cool and silken, one warm and pulsing, more than just light. A fresh night wind ushered Cassia forward, her only attendant other than the four-legged one who guarded her. Anxiety coiled and uncoiled within her as she fretted, then talked herself out of fretting, then fretted again. But her worries faded beneath the rush of something much more powerful. Desire was a spice in her scent, a fierce heat coursing through her veins, priming her body deep within, where he would touch her.

With a groan, Lio pulled himself back into his own skin. If he had any intention of proceeding slowly, he must rein himself in. Now. He focused instead on his Gift, the source of his power but also the foundation of every self-discipline exercise. He sought to attune himself to the Goddess's blood within him, which always seemed boundless and perfectly measured, wild and in rhythm with the course of the universe.

But tonight he felt the Gift singing in his veins, rousing his blood. Even his power was overtaken with this hunger. It was beyond control. But Goddess knew it was wonderful.

He heard Cassia's slippered feet on the broken floor of the antechamber, followed by Knight's lumbering footfalls. Then came the rustle of a blanket and the swish of a wagging tail.

Lio stepped out into the antechamber. Cassia was kneeling, silhouetted in the moonlight that poured in through the doorway. For a fraction of an instant, she was a shadow even to his eyes. Then his pupils adapted and revealed her to him anew.

Cassia turned her head. Their gazes locked. He smiled at her, and her eyes filled with things he intended to drink down the whole night through. She untied her cloak, and her fingers dawdled at her throat before she let the garment fall away. Her gaze dipped to his mouth. If the silence stretched between them an instant longer, he was going to begin their feast then and there.

Cassia stood and gave him a smile he had never seen, a shy one. "I think we have permission from Knight to go off by ourselves."

Lio offered the hound a bow, then Cassia his arm. She slid her hand into the crook of his elbow, turning it into a caress. Merciful thorns. It was definitely time to get her alone.

"Hold on tight." He took a step forward and into the next room.

Cassia blinked and glanced at him, then at the solid wall between them and where they had been standing. "That is never at all like your handkerchief analogy."

"Really? I thought the comparison rather inspired, myself."

"No, it's much more like…going through a door…" She shook her head.

"Does it disturb you?" he teased.

She gave him a pert smile. "No. I'm quite fond of your magery, which spares me having to stoop under the rubble…and unwraps breast bands."

He grinned. "Why, I think you're rather acclimated to my magic by now."

But her smile faded, and her anxiety fluttered to life again. Her voice grew soft, self-conscious. "You look very fine. Like the moonlight followed you in here."

"Thank you. I did invite it, so you would be able to see well." He moved back so he was no longer blocking her view of the room. "And every lover has a right to expect roses, especially upon a first tryst."

Her eyes widened. She drifted to the nearest wall and reached out to cradle a single bloom in her hand with the utmost care. It looked as if she cupped blood in her palm. She lowered her face to the rose and drew in a deep breath. Her eyes fell shut, and her lips parted.

"How?" she breathed. "They were dead last night."

"I don't know," Lio confessed. "They were like this when I entered. But I can tell you it happened since I began drinking from you. Since I offered *our* blood on the glyph stone."

"It is you who carries healing in your veins. It must have taken all these nights of your blood to resurrect them."

"Or three nights of your green thumb."

Cassia rubbed a petal between two fingers, testing its texture, as gentle as if she expected it to disappear. "As long as I live, I shall never behold a flower more beautiful."

Watching her stand against a curtain of thorns in her gardening dress with a blood red rose in her hand, Lio could not agree more.

Her gaze fell to the pile of blankets he had arranged for them in the middle of the room, which he had cleared of stones and debris. All that littered the floor now were rose petals, apparently shed in the vines' eagerness to bloom.

"You thought ahead much better than I. I confess I envisioned us…" She trailed off.

"The visions you described earlier were…life altering. Please don't stop sharing them with me now."

Her heart was thundering, and her cheeks flushed as if he had kissed her. No matter how many times they spoke of this, it seemed, that blush would always overtake her.

But the same defiance she had shown at the Summit table was a note in her scent, a chord in her voice, a chorus in her blood. "I assumed we might proceed against the pillar, the way we first began, only this time with *my* back against it and my legs wrapped around you. Or with me sitting on one of the stones there, and you kneeling in front of me, as before, only this time with my skirts around my waist. Or perhaps…"

"Please. Go on. Please."

"…with you sitting and me on your lap, riding astride you. You know, the act is deceptively simple. It occurs to me there are many more ways to achieve it than I have yet imagined."

Lio fought not to take hold of her and show her what he thought of her imaginings. If he touched her this instant, he would not stop for anything, and their first night together wouldn't proceed slowly at all. He focused on keeping the arm's length of space between them as he gazed at her rosy face, which was still turned upon the room at large.

He had hungered for her in these past nights more than he had ever hungered in his entire life. But he had waited so long to feel that way. He had looked forward to this moment in his life for so long it would seem strange to her. As much as he ached for her, he did not want to rush. He wanted to live every instant of this to the fullest, even when his wanting bordered on pain. He refused to risk missing something she might say or do if he only *waited* and allowed this night to proceed on its own, without him pushing it to its inevitable conclusion. For that conclusion…that climax…*would* come, and it *would* fulfill all their expectations.

He hoped.

"May I recommend a horizontal arrangement on soft blankets to begin with?" He gripped his hands behind his back, this time for no other reason than to keep himself from touching her. His voice seemed to have plummeted downward along with his blood flow. "Before we broaden our horizons to encompass your…excellent suggestions."

"Thank you, Lio," she said quietly.

"Of course. The first time should be as comfortable as possible."

Moonlight, roses, and a bed amid the ruins were all he had to offer her. That and a spare bar of soap as a gift. And yet she seemed more than satisfied.

Soap…cassia soap. That was the new snap in her scent now mingling with the fragrances of roses.

"You bathed before you came." He grinned. "With my gift."

Her gaze slid to his, and she wore a secret smile. "Yes. My ritual ablutions."

"I hope you liked it."

"Very much, actually. It made my skin feel so much softer than usual."

He shrank the distance between them and let his nose roam the air above her scalp. She had even washed her hair in it. A sure sign of approval. "It suits you. But you always smell divine to me."

He struck gold, and she treated him to her genuine laugh. "Now I understand the secret of my allure. I knew all that bathing would serve me well one day. Is the tallow soap not as off-putting as I imagined?"

"It is the person under the tallow soap who smells better than any flower."

Lio glanced down to see not her nose, but her gaze roaming over him. She touched the breast of his robe, and he felt the impact of her small, tentative hand to the depths of his body. He watched her trace one swirl of embroidery. Her finger followed the curve of cerulean thread, then dipped into the circle of sapphire blue fabric directly above his left nipple.

"I've never seen you wear this before. It's different from your court robes."

Looser. Fortunately. "My veil hours robe. Every Hesperine has one."

"Veil hours?"

"The time of night devoted to our families, friends…and lovers." If he kept reciting the culture lesson, perhaps he would not lose his mind over the way her fingers played across his breast. "The veil hours robe is what we wear among those to whom we are closest. Those we trust."

Cassia ran both palms down the front closure of his robe, her voice steady and unapologetic. "I have no veil hours robe. You will have to accept me coming to you in my gardening dress."

He took one of her hands and lifted it to give himself a reprieve, but also to turn her all around. She spun, and her skirt twirled about her as if the practical, dark green wool were the finest festival attire. The lingering smells of soil and water, growth and life wafted into the air, along with a breath of contentment. Hers. A rare whiff of the consolation she found only in the garden. How seldom he sensed that.

"This is my favorite gown you have," he told her.

She let out a sigh. "Good. For it is the only scrap I have that I do not hate."

As the spin brought her round to face him, he kept hold of her hand. "I'm delighted to hear that. I would be sorry to learn you hate something I have so often imagined you wearing while I make love to you."

A breath made her breasts rise and fall, and her fingers curled closer around his.

"Tonight, however," he said, "I would like to take it off of you. And let you take mine off of me, as you wanted."

"Yes. It must be so."

His teeth, already long unsheathed, surged further out of his gums. Cassia reached up and touched his top left canine. From root to tip, she ran one finger down his fang. His body responded as if she had bestowed the same caress much lower.

"Cassia." He had best say this now, before the remnants of coherent thought deserted him. "Before we proceed, if there is anything you wish to talk about…or ask me…any other concerns you have…"

"Ah." She had mercy on him, returning her hand to his chest. "You have indeed lived with fewer strictures than I. But we humans live close to matters of the flesh, even forbidden ones. I am far from ignorant."

"I understand that. Even so, knowledge isn't the same as personal experience." He let go of her hand, only to put both of his at her waist. "I don't want anything to worry you."

She looked down, but her lashes hid only her gaze from him. He could feel the tension creeping into her body. Her anxiety was a tide in the Blood Union that threatened to rise.

"I wish to offer you every possible reassurance," he said. "With your permission, I can make tonight much easier for you."

"What do you mean?"

"Every mind mage completes some training with Orthros's physicians, even those of us who do not specialize in healing. We learn that any pain of the body begins in the mind. I know how to affect that part of your thoughts so that nothing you experience tonight will hurt at all. This is not like hypnosis or anything of that sort. It would not influence your Will, only ensure your comfort."

Cassia frowned. "Wouldn't it be rather…uncomfortable…for you to try to maintain a spell like that while we are…otherwise occupied?"

Lio tried not to smile. "Thelemancy is a great deal more intuitive than a light spell. It is certainly within my abilities to use my power to improve your experience, if you will allow me."

She leaned closer to him. "I am uncertain I wish to sacrifice any of the experience. I want to know what all of it feels like. With you."

Lio slid both his arms around her waist. "You will feel everything. I will not rob you of an instant of pleasure. Only enhance it by making sure no pain interferes."

She was silent for a moment before she answered. "You have protected me with your mind magery on more than one occasion."

"I will gladly do so again, but only if you are comfortable with my presence in your mind. That is all it would be—my presence. A connection. I would never read your private thoughts."

"Will it feel anything like the Blood Union?"

"Yes. A great deal like that, I believe."

"A way for a mortal to have a taste of that? I would like to know what such Union feels like with you."

He cupped her face in his hand, as she had the rose moments before. "Thank you for your confidence in me."

"If you did examine my secret thoughts, you would find little there I have not already said to you aloud. Is this not a natural result of our Oath? And is it not also natural that…since I want you in my body…I would feel the same way about your mind?"

Hespera's Grace. Cassia had just disarmed the last of her defenses and thrown open the gates. She would let him into her beautiful, guarded mind. He lowered his forehead to hers. "I promise you will enjoy every moment of it. There is a reason we call lovemaking the Natural Union."

"I like that much better than what men here call it."

"This will be nothing like what you've heard them say, Cassia. Self-control is the greatest strength of every Hesperine. I am not an experienced lover, but you can rely on me to be a considerate one."

"I suspect you're too modest. I know you will have had no shortage of lovers."

"Oh? And how do you know that?"

She pulled her face back from his. "It is not forbidden among your people, and you are obviously greatly desirable by Hesperine standards."

"Such a complimentary analysis," he teased. "But I confess to being more interested in your assessment according to human standards."

She let out a little huff, almost a laugh, as if it should be obvious. "To our eyes, you are…"

Words seemed to desert her. Perhaps playfulness was not the best way to help her maintain her already fragile comfort with the situation. He searched for what he might say to soothe her unease.

But she spoke first, her voice a hushed murmur he had never heard from her before. "You are beautiful beyond imagining."

He held her gaze, drawing her hand slowly nearer his mouth.

"But you've been told that by more sophisticated females than me." She looked away.

That was a source of anxiety for her? The thought of how she might compare to some hypothetical past lover of his?

He placed a languid kiss on her open palm. "The regard I treasure most is that of she who is careful in giving it. What you want to share with me tonight is higher praise than any I have ever received."

She was indeed speechless. Her struggle with what to make of his words was written all over her body, in her scent and the sound of her heart. But by the same signs, he could sense her heart opening. Thirsting.

How well he understood thirst.

"I've never had a lover," he told her.

She looked at him as if he had just spoken in a foreign tongue.

He raised his eyebrows. "You find that so hard to believe? This from someone who has labored to avoid it herself?"

"You have none of my reasons to avoid anything! I fail to understand how you have escaped having any number of lovers in your bed and why you would wish to."

"It is a choice, not something that overtakes one like a wave, before which one must flee for one's life."

Again the huff. "If Xandra expected to avow you, I cannot imagine her refraining."

Lio couldn't resist rubbing a finger over Cassia's bottom lip, which protruded stubbornly. "As intimate as we were, we never made love."

That raised the color in Cassia's cheeks, although her expression became quite composed. "Ah. I see. I knew you could not have achieved your dexterity without some degree of personal experience."

"Desirable, mobbed by potential lovers, and dexterous. High praise indeed." He chuckled, letting his gaze slide up and down her. "No, I am no stranger to the female form. But I have yet to know anyone's as intimately as I intend to know yours tonight. I've never wanted anyone as I want you."

"But you've no lack of feelings and wantings, and…"

Oh, he should not continue to tease her, but those words were priceless. "I'm very happy to know you haven't found my feelings and wantings to be lacking."

"There must be some stricture then, which you haven't told me about, regarding…"

He waited to see what word she might use, but she made no boldly sensual declarations this time. When it became clear she was waiting for him to answer, he obliged her. "Xandra and I explored only as far as our thirst allowed. It is forbidden to drink from anyone who is not yet of age—even when both of you are underage. As you can imagine, it is rather challenging to make love to someone without giving into the temptation to drink. Thus we are encouraged to wait until after initiation for our first Natural Union."

"Do young Hesperines usually do as they're encouraged?"

Now it was Lio's turn to blush. "Well, some of us do."

"For the first time I have an inkling how you earned a reputation as conscientious and well-behaved. You waited for her. For *eight extra years*. And then she rejected you."

No, it was not wishful thinking on Lio's part. Cassia really was indignant. On his behalf.

He smiled down at her. "It was more a mutual admission of defeat than a rejection, and it was the third best thing that could have happened to me."

"But after her... I have seen how beautiful Hesperine ladies are. And I know how popular you are with guests from the Empire. Orthros must be full of...willing possibilities."

"After Xandra, I fled to Tenebra at my earliest opportunity, and it was the second best thing that could have happened to me. Guess what the very best thing of all is." He lowered his mouth to place a kiss on Cassia's neck.

Her breath tickled his ear. "You must have tasted someone as... good...as me...before."

"No one," he said to her shoulder. "You are the best."

He nipped her, drawing a little jump from her and a tiny fleck of blood. He licked it away slowly, enjoying her skin as much as her blood, until his kiss healed the nick as quickly as his teeth had made it.

Her hands fumbled for his robe, then drifted southward to rest on his belly. He stood very still, except for the kisses he feathered on her neck. He didn't want to interrupt her impulsive caress. She slid her hands up ever so slightly, then down. He allowed himself to imagine for a moment they would descend further. But she let them rest at his waist, gripping and clutching as he moved his lips on her skin.

"I..." she murmured.

"Yes?" Goddess help him. It was the longest wait of his life. But he would stay himself until Cassia gave him another signal that he might proceed.

How well worth the wait, each time she deemed it safe to welcome passion.

"I can hardly believe I am to be the one, Lio. Your first choice."

He met her gaze again, so she would see in his he spoke only truth. "Then we are on equal footing tonight, for I feel the same when I realize you have chosen me."

She eased nearer to him. Then lifted herself on tiptoe. Her arms slid around his neck, and he realized. For the first time, she was not going to allow him or invite him to kiss her. She was going to kiss him.

THE FEAST

LIO'S BLOOD POUNDED, URGING him to commence the Feast. But he was not about to disrupt these first overtures that were all Cassia's own.

Her fingers ventured into his hair, and she guided his face down toward her. When she pressed her lips against his, he felt that first contact from fangs to feet. She hesitated, as if waiting for some signal. He nudged her with his nose, placing his hands loosely at her waist again, to encourage her without taking the lead.

She took them onward, further into that kiss. First just lips on lips, a delightful exploration of the surface. But her mouth became determined, eager, sooner than he could have hoped. She opened her mouth a little, and he offered his lower lip for her consumption. She gave it one, two experimental tugs. But no, that was not all she wanted. Her tongue darted between his lips, seeking an opening.

He let her lick and kiss apart his lips, then lick and suck her way into his mouth. Oh, no, he wouldn't stop her for anything. Not now, when she was dining on his lips and tongue and fangs with greater alacrity than he'd ever witnessed her devote to a plate of food.

She paused only to gasp a breath. With that breath, she said one word. "Lio."

The sound of his name on her lips, a seduction, a declaration, did something to him. He felt more himself than he ever had. Sure of who he was. Glad to be Lio and alive, to be the one she wanted and to want her.

She joined their mouths again, and now they were devouring each other. Her heartbeat vibrated in his chest, as if their blood already flowed as one. He embraced her fully, holding their bodies together, and she flexed her hips into his in affirmation.

He parted their mouths to muster some space between them, just enough to begin disrobing her. He swept his hands up her body, and he must have let more power touch her than he knew. She shivered as if she felt his magic on her skin. Her swollen lips rounded in surprise, but not displeasure. Her clothing answered to his touch as willingly as light. The front laces of her gown slipped free and drifted to the floor to land with a whisper amid the rose petals. Her dress fell open, and he eased it down off her shoulders.

She looked up at him, panting, her gaze daring. He kept going. The gown pooled around her waist and caught there just below her navel, gathering about the slight curve of her lower belly. She had not even worn her tunica or the tight band that always confined her chest. Her small breasts were free and bare before him, two brown freckled moons, crowned in twin dark peaks that swelled before his eyes in the cold air.

Self-consciousness crept out of the night and gripped him, crippling in its force. He stood before her clothed from neck to ankle, and yet he felt more naked than he ever had in his life. This was Blood Union. This was how she felt standing before him in nothing but her skin. Utterly exposed. Utterly vulnerable. She was fighting the urge to put her arms over her chest to hide herself.

She put her hands to her waist and pushed her gown to the floor.

He could not take his eyes from her. This was Cassia, unbound. Her chin high, her gaze on his face, her whole body shivering. Her fists clutched at her sides, only drawing his gaze downward to the triangle of dark curls at the apex of her thighs. His gaze halted there a moment, but soon plunged downward still to her locked knees and slender ankles and, at last, her bare feet.

"You *do* have freckles everywhere," he said.

Her breath hitched. She didn't understand.

"Cassia," he tried to explain. "I lay awake at night thinking about kissing each and every one. I'm going to be busy for a *very* long time."

Her response struck him, a bolt of light to the chest that radiated to fill him. She had no name for it. He suspected she had forgotten what it was called long ago. But he knew it well—happiness. He could not help but beam at her. He realized how that must make his teeth look, but only smiled more.

Her fists uncurled. She reached for him. She started at his high collar and made her way down his robe, unfastening the clasps with one compulsive caress after another. Self-control would be marginally easier with one last layer of fabric between them, but he would have to manage. She wanted to see him, as he had seen her. It was only fair. It was entirely wonderful.

He wondered if she would subject him to the brush of fabric and her touch all the way to his ankles. But when she had him bared to the waist, she took fistfuls of silk and embroidery and pushed his robe over his shoulders, banishing it to the floor.

Air and moonlight and her gaze struck his bare skin, and his straining arousal surged to pain. He blinked to clear his vision, to see the look on her face.

Thank the Goddess, no fear in her eyes. Not even a hint of alarm at the evidence of his desire. She had learned to fear men's lust. Apparently his lust was in a different category. In fact, she hadn't yet taken her eyes off of it.

"You must tell me Hespera's word for this. What Tenebrans say is entirely insufficient."

"*Rhabdos*," he blurted, giving her the metaphor they favored without a detailed translation. He was out of lessons. In fact, running low on intelligible words altogether.

Not so with Cassia. Her tongue emerged to wet her lips. "You are beautiful beyond imagining," she said again. "But I have dared to imagine. Now I shall dare to do more than imagine."

Such a gaze. Such a flow of words from her. Lio tried to appreciate it, but his entire world seemed to shrink to her hands reaching out to touch his stomach. His skin and muscles tightened at the contact, and his breath halted in his throat at the sensation needling through him. And Cassia hadn't even touched his rhabdos yet.

He had never felt like this. This was how it was supposed to feel. This was right.

She traced upward with her fingers and fondled the modest growth of hair on his chest with great concentration. He didn't sport the pelt of which her countrymen could boast, but she gave no sign she was disappointed.

She stroked the line of hair that ran down the length of his stomach. Past his navel. And kept going along the path he had been absurdly proud of ever since it had grown in.

He caught her hands in both of his. "Cassia. Your pleasure first."

Her gaze lifted. Her eyes were wide. Trusting.

"Cassia," he said again, without other words now. His entire language, just her name.

He stepped onto their blankets and knelt before her, still holding her hands. She followed him down, and their mouths found each other again. He eased them back onto their bed amid the rose petals.

Then he was touching her everywhere, and she was welcoming him. He put his hands where his gaze had been moments before, everywhere her freckles marked the way. Sight and fantasy realized into touch.

He came to know the shape of her breasts he had barely met the night before. Where all the little buds and ridges were in her dark areolae. Precisely which way she liked best for him to drag his tongue across her small, hard nipples, and how often she liked for him to pause and tease them with nothing but the tip of his tongue, right at the center where they were so sensitive.

He discovered her small feet fit perfectly in his long hands, and that she had never imagined the pressure of his thumbs in her arches could make her squirm with pleasure. He discovered it pleased her well indeed to have her knee tucked up close to him, her foot in his hand while he licked her breast.

She made no sound other than her swift, uneven breaths. He found himself panting with her, as if he too must breathe to survive. Scent brought him the fragrance of her arousal, and their Union brought him her arousal itself.

He wanted to thrust into the wetness he could smell, let the grip of her body push back against the pain of his need. But that look of trust in Cassia's eyes sustained him. He mastered himself and bade his body wait for hers.

He dare not attempt to touch her mind, not yet. Thelemancy was like the Drink. It didn't always inspire desire. Between them it would. She was not ready yet.

She was panting hard now, her hips rocking as if begging for him. He caressed his way from her foot to her thigh and slid his hand between her legs.

For the first time, she found her words again. "Yes. Lio. Touch me there again."

Wonderful. They had established a precedent for her voicing her desires, and she didn't intend to stop.

He slid a finger inside her krana as she had liked the night before, only to find her much tighter. The heat of her body sank into his skin, and he wondered when his finger had developed ambitions to be as sensitive as his fangs.

"More than your hand," Cassia clarified.

Oh yes. If only it were more than his hand. "We don't have to do it quite this way, Cassia. You could have me under you instead."

She blinked glazed eyes. "Will it not please you this way?"

He spared a breath for a laugh that almost came out as a groan. "Every way will please me. But is this what you want?"

"Yes. Just like this."

He heard and felt her certainty. She had decided. She would be under him tonight.

"Your pleasure first," he said again, through gritted teeth.

"Lio," she protested, but the motion of his hand seemed to preempt whatever else she would have said. With his other, he kept playing with her foot. She moved her hips eagerly, with all the passion he had been so delighted and astonished to discover in her. He had not been wrong. She was so tightly chained within herself, but once she threw off her shackles...

She arched off the blankets with a gasp, pushing herself against his hand. One sigh after another passed her lips as the contractions inside her clutched at his finger. He supported her where she braced her foot against his palm. Her blood rejoiced in her veins, and saliva pooled in his mouth. He wanted to drink her climax. But that would mean not getting to watch her.

She relaxed back on their bed, wet and hot and pliant upon his hand. He tucked her foot into a warm fold of the blanket. Now was the time.

He eased his body down, bracing his forearms on either side of her, and opened his mind to hers. At the first rush of her thoughts, he gasped. He could taste her satiation and her longing, her eagerness and her reticence. The sight of her face, the sound of her buttocks shifting on the blanket, the warmth of her skin under him inundated his senses with every facet of her.

He gave her mind a probing caress. No instinctual barriers rose against him; she was not aware of his presence yet. He put one hand on her head, another at her waist, his teeth at her neck. She tilted her head back, baring her throat, laying her feast out before him. A nudge from his leg on the inside of hers, and she slowly, hesitantly, parted her legs too.

He stilled himself above her, breathing with her, and eased not his body, but his inner self against hers. No object or direction, simply mind upon mind. Pure Cassia touched him for an instant, and a groan caught in his throat. Her thoughts soughed and shifted in welcome.

Lio focused on the precise, intuitive techniques of thelemancy, reaching for another measure of self-control. He must go deeper. No doubt she would feel this intrusion. This would be when her mind mounted resistance.

He must enter gently. As he had with his teeth in her neck, he must prove to her this too would feel good to her. If he succeeded, he would finally get to feel what it was like within the ramparts of her mind.

Lio braced himself and slid his thoughts into her own.

Cassia gasped and breathed him into her. Her mind swept open, dragging him deep, and he plummeted. No control. No precision. Just him in her, her in him.

Lio fisted his hands in the blankets and braced the muscles in his back to keep from thrusting into her body as well. He felt the chill air on his back and the hot, damp fabric under hers. His arousal throbbed, while her satisfaction weighed heavy and relaxing on his loins. Thirst scoured his veins as wonder infused hers. She could feel him inside her, and she was not afraid. The sight of his own face flashed in his vision before he felt the touch of her fingers on his cheek, which brought him back to himself.

Blood of the Goddess, what was this? Not thelemancy. Not magic. More.

Cassia took Lio's face in her hands and guided his mouth to her neck.

He buried his face against her shoulder and ground his teeth. He had promised her no pain. He dared to move his mind within hers. Her thoughts parted for him, then closed around him as she clutched at his shoulders. With a gasp, he delved into her mind. The way was sure and ready for him, all the way to the tender place he sought. Lio found the tipping point between pain and pleasure and carried her over the sweeter edge.

Cassia arched beneath him and threw her head back. With his mind buried deep in hers, Lio sank his teeth into her throat and his rhabdos into her krana.

Her body wrapped tight and wet around him. Her blood welled hot where his teeth pierced her. At last. Exhilaration jolted him, gripped him, and tightened in his back until he instinctively thrust deeper inside her.

They both went utterly still.

He knew what she felt. He knew what she needed. Lio reassured her with a shaking caress upon her hair. He began to suckle her vein, giving her the one pleasure she never feared.

NATURAL UNION

S O THIS WAS WHAT it felt like to have a male's flesh inside her. The last barrier was torn, the most secret part of her body exposed and penetrated. She was open to him, her body and mind and blood. Trapped on her back beneath him, at his mercy.

That flesh was hard and filling. That male lay still and patient upon her, his back rising and falling under her hands as he gasped in air, not out of survival, but because he wanted it. Only his mouth and tongue moved, drawing at her neck with hunger he could not hide.

This was what it felt like to have Lio inside her.

He was a warm fragrance under her skin, a bright caress within her. She felt him in her heart and heard him in her thoughts, a presence in the dark she could not see, a voice in the night to which she answered. There was no name for the sense that told her Lio himself was inside Cassia herself, as surely as his body was inside of hers and her blood was in his veins.

She lay shaking beneath him and held him close. What was this sweet, raw thing? She felt it on her skin where he lay upon her, inside her where his flesh was lodged. In her chest where her heart thudded against his. In her mind, where he touched her in a place more sensitive than anywhere on her body.

It was intimacy.

A warm ache began in her throat and threatened to spill out in tears. Was this the Blood Union? She didn't know. But it was *their* Union. It was trust made into ritual. Their Oath made into pleasure.

She felt so much. She wanted so much.

The pressure of his teeth at her throat filled her with familiar, uncontrollable excitement, an undertone to the throbbing between her legs. His hand caressed her head again, and his tongue stroked a trail of blood from her skin. She knew what he was saying. *Relax, Cassia.*

She uncurled her hands and lay back, letting her legs slide apart. But in one place, the tension refused to drain from her. Her flesh deep within was so tight around his.

When he pulled back and slipped out of her, she could not restrain a gasp. As her chest lifted, his arm slid beneath her. He held her, cradling her against his mouth, and pressed his rhabdos into her again. Solid warmth glided through the need within her.

The grip of his bite tightened, as if by reflex, then eased. His jaw was rigid with tension against hers. She caressed his face, tangling her fingers in his hair.

As if he had been waiting for that sign from her, he began to move between her thighs. He withdrew, then slid within her again, suckling her throat in time to his retreat and advance. Each time he drove a little deeper than before.

His presence in her thoughts heated and grew in intensity. Pleasure scathed her, and she gasped aloud. His power pulsed to the rhythm of his feast, and Cassia moved her hips with each rhythmic, hypnotic stroke.

The tears slid down her cheeks at last. He steadied her in his embrace. She held onto his shoulders, shifting beneath him to seek relief from the torturous pleasure. If she just angled her hips a different way…and perhaps pulled her knees a bit higher like this…

It could get better. It did get better. Just like the first time he had pierced her with his teeth. Now she found herself parting her thighs wider to make way, to allow him deeper. Her blood rushed in her veins and swelled into his mouth.

His gentle invasions became thrusts. His power took her breath away. His smooth, limber body moved on her. Inside her. For her. She had not known. She had thought his hands alone had woken all the raw, forbidden places she had, but this was more.

There was no place within her he did not touch. There was no part of him she did not hold.

Cold air struck her damp throat as he lifted his head. For the first time, she saw blood on his lips. Dark liquid trailed down his jaw and dripped onto her breasts. His eyes locked on hers, gazing into her as his lower body bore down and he penetrated her again.

No, it didn't frighten her.

His swift, forceful thrusts built up the unbearable pleasure inside her. She curled her hips closer against him, dragging her feet down his back. It was going to happen again.

His head descended, and his mouth closed around her vein to suckle her into her peak. Her back arched, and she held on tight to him as her hips began to jerk, thrusting her onto his rhabdos. The deepest places within her gripped, not empty this time, but finding him to hold and suck.

Her mind, her heart, her Will held fast to him. His presence waxed outward to fill the darkness all around her and inward to the deepest reaches of her. An ephemeral wave of pleasure overtook her. Not hers. His. But her body responded, and the end of her climax became the beginning of another.

His fangs sank deep into her throat and clenched hard as his rhabdos drove into her one last time. His whole, powerful frame went rigid, trapping her shivering, bucking body under his. Sudden, unexpected warmth streamed into her. She was drinking him.

When at last he went still, his lips felt soft on her throat, still covering her where his teeth rested in her flesh. He did not withdraw from between her thighs. She kept her arms and legs close around him.

She was lying in the night goddess's shrine in the forbidden reaches of the woods, utterly naked and entwined with a well-fed Hesperine. The feeling clawing its way out of her was fierce and wonderful. It drowned out all the names men called a woman like her.

As long as she lived, when she thought of lying on her back with a male body upon her, this was what she would feel and remember. No man could ever touch her the way Lio did. It was not in their power.

The truth was, she still had no idea what it felt like to endure a night in a man's bed. She had no desire to find out. It was a Hesperine who had taken her maidenhood, along with her blood. And given her his virginity and this…this moment…this feeling in return.

HOURS BEFORE DAWN

WHEN HE PARTED THEIR bodies, Cassia discovered she had to make herself let him go. But the deed was done.

He collected himself, untangling from her. Then he stretched out his long, lean frame beside her and wrapped one arm around her middle.

He seemed to want to pull her closer. She obliged, and he pulled her very close indeed. It seemed his plan was to hold her now. She found she approved this plan wholeheartedly.

His embrace felt like the comfort he had offered her at her worst moments. Except he was naked, and she had just bedded him. She didn't know what to do with that concoction of safety and excitement. She only knew his body was the warmest thing in the room. After a moment's hesitation, she slid her feet against his legs. He didn't pull away. In fact, he reached down and retrieved the blankets, covering them both.

She became aware she was sore. She ached in all kinds of places she never considered relevant to the act, not to mention the more obvious ones. She squeezed her thighs together. They slid damply against each other.

Under the privacy of the blankets, Cassia touched her fingers to the wetness on the inside of her thigh. She brought her hand close to her face and gazed with heating cheeks at the milky mixture. His and hers.

Lio propped himself on one elbow and looked at her hand, then at her. He was the picture of satisfaction, his eyes hooded, his body languid and relaxed, his smile holding the secrets they had just committed together.

"I thought you didn't—" she tried to explain. "That is, I didn't know you have—"

"My dearest Cassia, are you trying to ask me to explain the mysteries of corrupt Hesperine seed?"

That surprised a laugh out of her, although she blushed. They had just made love. How could she blush over this? Why was this the first thing she had said to him after what they'd just done?

He fondled her hand. "Yes, I do and I have, although what my body spills in you cannot get you with child."

Her face burned hotter, but as always with Lio, she found herself saying the things that were so hard to put into words. "I like the thought that I'm carrying part of you inside me, mysterious as it is."

He brought her hand slowly to his mouth. His lips closed around her fingers, then he slid them slowly back out, sucking gently. His nostrils flared, and his eyes slid shut. "Your maidenhead bled."

She swallowed, watching his face in the moonlight, and her imagination progressed from having him for the first time to having him again. There was a name for a woman like her.

A name that didn't exist in Lio's vocabulary.

She touched his cheek. "There are still hours before dawn."

His expression gentled. "That was difficult for you. Tomorrow night will be better."

"Tomorrow night is a long time from now."

"Do you feel any soreness? My bodily fluids should diminish your residual discomfort, but tonight was...demanding."

She moved gingerly. "Surely it's like when you bite me, and the pain goes away quickly."

"It can be."

He waited, holding her hand on which he had tasted a smear of blood, and she realized what he was saying.

"Shall I do that for you, Cassia?"

She tucked her thighs together, even as she said, "Yes."

"Then I shall give you a kiss," he whispered. As he moved his graceful frame down her body, the blanket caught about his waist and slid away.

Now he positioned his head and shoulders between her legs, where his lower body had been. She caught fistfuls of the blankets in her hands, tilting her head back, and stared up at the skylight. She could feel the moonlight and the night air and his breath upon her loins. That feeling of being exposed, weak, on the verge of humiliation overtook her again.

But Lio was taking hold of her hips, cradling them in his careful hands. "Goddess bless. You did bleed."

She felt the flick of his tongue in the dampness there, then a long, steady stroke. Pain she had not expected flared to life, and she fisted her hands tighter, trying not to flinch. His tongue laved her again, probing the wound. The pain eased, and she let out a grateful sigh of relief. His mouth pressed closer, and his tongue stroked deeper. The discomfort faded, giving way to the feel of his kiss.

He bathed her with his tongue, as thorough and eager as he was at her neck. She shivered, her skin breaking out in goosebumps. His mouth was on her womanhood. He was feasting on her there.

His mouth parted from her, and an instant later she felt his tongue on the inside of her thigh. Rose petals peeled away from her skin and gave way to his mouth. He kissed and licked his way up to the crease of her leg, drawing his tongue through the groove.

"I missed some," he informed her, before his mouth returned to her center.

She gasped when his tongue dipped lower, licking the skin between her krana and the opening of her buttocks. Her skin burned. She felt pleasure even there. He must have known, in the way he always knew. His tongue grazed her there again. Playfully. The muscles between her buttocks tightened.

But then he drew his tongue up. Higher. Yes, he was going to. He would lick her *there*.

He did not lick her. He took her most sensitive place in his mouth and began to suck.

She bit down on her lip to keep from crying out. She had thought herself at his mercy…but this… He clutched the most vulnerable part of her in his mouth, amid those fangs, and he drank her pleasure as if it were blood. Her body bowed of its own accord, tilting her hips, offering her pleasure up to him. They were so far beyond forbidden territory there was no such thing anymore.

Gripping the blankets, bracing herself, she lifted herself to look. His dark head nestled in the vee of her legs, moving gently with the motions of his mouth. Her knees spread, her feet pressing against his lower body, toes curling. It was a dark and beautiful vision, and she could not look away.

She watched her own body undulate, watched his hands clench and unclench on her hips. Her lower belly clutched tight, and she could no longer see, only feel, as her head fell back, and her body writhed on the blankets again. He did not stop. He kept sucking, drinking, and her body kept answering, every stroke a new kind of ecstatic pain.

At last he gave her mercy and lifted his head with a gasp. She did not see him move, but suddenly he was there above her, his face close to hers. His mouth gleamed wet in the moonlight.

"Again." His hard flesh nudged where his mouth had been.

"Yes."

He filled her in one rough, silken thrust. No pain now. Only her body stretching to welcome him, to hold him.

"*Yes,*" she cried.

She felt the imperceptible return of his mind to the door of hers. He made no demand. He waited for her with hopeful eagerness. She stretched the new sense she hadn't known she possessed and invited him in. With a gasp, he plunged into her thoughts again, stirring the currents of intimacy between them once more.

His body rose and fell upon her, in motion from head to toe, every motion concentrated on that locus of their joining. He spoke to her now in nothing but deep, rough groans as muscles bunched in his hips, driving him into her. He was gorgeous. And he was inside of her.

As his rhabdos pulsed and emptied inside her once more, she watched his face and beheld the pleasure he took. In her. His thoughts called out like a shout. To her.

She was the one still holding him when the night beyond the skylight changed in a way she had learned to interpret all too well.

He moaned and lifted his head. "Accursed sun. It always rises eventually."

"The wonderful thing is, it always sets again afterward." Her voice had become that rough, husky one she didn't recognize—no, the one she was coming to know.

His gaze darted across as much of her as was visible amid their tangled blankets and intertwined bodies. His expressive face said more than words. He looked at her as if she were a night falling at dawn, or a moon rising in the sun's stead.

"You enjoyed it, then," she said.

"Cassia, I—" He broke off, as if searching for words.

Had her question surprised him? Didn't it make sense for a woman to ask her lover if she had pleased him?

"I fear this time, I cannot be free with words," he said. "For I know none fine enough for you."

With that, he pulled her close again and tucked her head under his chin. She shut her eyes, resting her face on his chest. She must face the day, but after it, there would be tonight. And then, the night after that...

Cassia lay there and thought about what to say. She opened her mouth once, shut it. Opened it again a moment later, only to press her lips closed again.

Finally, she opened her mouth and kissed his chest. Why was that easier than speaking?

"I'm so glad it was you," she whispered against his skin. "You are so good to me."

16

days until

SPRING EQUINOX

A STRANGER TO TRUST

CASSIA WOKE TO THE indistinct gloom of her bedchamber, unsure how many hours she had slept and how many remained before the day would release her, and the night would be here again. Night and Lio.

She stretched beneath her blankets. Even the aches felt good. She had not felt so rested, so relaxed since she'd come to Solorum...nor since long before that.

She didn't care what time it was. Even if the king summoned her to demand why she had not attended dawn rites like a pious little bastard, she would appear before him without remorse and lie to his face. She would think about last night and feel brave enough to get through the audience.

Eagerness was what got her out of bed, and cassia soap was what she took in hand at her basin. When she had sneaked back into her empty rooms early that morning, she hadn't needed to worry about cleaning up the evidence of their tryst before her handmaiden's return. Before she and Lio had parted, he had worked a cleaning spell, which had felt lovely and left both of them tidy and fragrant.

There was still a trace of his mysterious scent on her skin. She added cassia soap to it, not to wash away what they had done, but to remind herself.

She did not lament the necessity of secrecy. This secret was a delight to keep. When she was with Lio, she felt they were in another world, far removed from everything else in her life. She wanted it always to remain so.

Always? That meant, she must remind herself, for the length of the Summit.

A spurt of anger drowned out the pragmatic voice in her head. As she often had lately, she found she preferred the anger. She let it drive away all thought for the future. Best to focus on what lay directly ahead. Wasn't that always what she did?

No, it was not. What she had always focused on was surviving one more dawn. That paled in comparison to what she now resolved to do: live for today.

She walked out into the hearth room in her unremarkable brown dress, prepared to face her handmaiden and questions. Are you ill, Lady? Why else would you sleep so late, Lady? Should I call the king's healer, Lady? No, no, and certainly not.

But Perita was not at her post by the hearth. Cassia told Knight to stay on the rug by the fire and headed for the dressing room.

Perita stood at the window with her back to the door, hunched over a basin on the dressing table. The girl could hide her face, but not the sound of her vomiting.

With a sinking feeling, Cassia considered the likely reason for a young woman in her handmaiden's situation to be ill like this in the middle of the day. The slant of the sunlight suggested it was no longer morning, but every woman was different. The recent turbulence in Perita's relationship with the guard began to make sense.

How to broach the subject? Perhaps Cassia should simply begin by asking if the girl was all right. A meaningless question, but a show of concern. "Perita—"

At the sound of her name, she jumped. But by the time she turned to face Cassia, her mouth was clean and her face composed. "Good morning—nay, afternoon, Lady."

Perita busied herself with the window latch. Damp, cool air crept into the room, relieving the odor of sickness.

Cassia tried her question. "Are you all right?"

"Of course, Lady. I'll go get you something to eat." Perita devoted great effort to refolding a cloth.

Cassia stalled, trying to think of some way to approach the issue. When an eighth son had gotten Lady Hadrian's youngest handmaiden with child, one conversation with Her Ladyship had been sufficient to get the man to the altar. For any woman in Perita's predicament, her lady's advocacy was the best hope she had.

Ha. Poor girl, to be cursed with such an impotent advocate as a bastard daughter. Cassia was utterly dependent on the king's whims. Thus so was Perita.

Impotent? Cassia's anger protested. Was she impotent, who had spoken before the Summit and smuggled medicine to the temple in the company of a Hesperine?

And taken that Hesperine as her lover.

"Perita, do you love him?"

The girl went still. She ducked her head, as if studying the towel. "I'm sure you needn't concern yourself with such things, Lady."

"Are you with child?"

Perita's face disappeared into the cloth. A moment later she said clearly, "Of course not, Lady."

"You've helped me, Perita. A great deal. I wish to help you in return."

"I'm glad you find my service satisfactory."

Cassia stood and waited. Perita dropped the towel into a basket of soiled linens.

"Confide in someone you trust," Cassia urged her. "He can be made to treat you honorably."

Perita gazed out the window as if something of great significance lay there for which she was responsible. Cassia gave her another moment. But Perita said nothing.

Cassia retreated to the hearth room, closing the door behind her. She went to stand at the other window and looked out on the same trees that had just now held Perita's undivided attention. Cassia's knuckles turned white gripping the windowsill.

A damp, snuffling nose pressed under one of her wrists. After a moment of that, Cassia had to detach one hand from the windowsill and transfer it to Knight's ears. She pulled his head against her, giving him a good rub, and soon the sound of his tail thumping the floor broke the silence of the room.

"Why is it so hard, Knight?"

Thump. Thump.

"How fortunate you are that your loyalties are so straightforward. That trust is so easy and complete. If everyone were like you and me, things would be much easier, wouldn't they?"

Thump.

"My handmaidens are never with me long enough for us to matter to one another."

Snuffle.

"But then, I never try."

Cassia frowned down at her hands. They wanted to take hold of the old shutters that fortified her window here in the king's palace and break them off their hinges.

"It's so hard. I am a stranger to this idea of trust."

She wrapped her free arm about herself, thinking of how she welcomed Lio's arms around her. How she had lain down beneath him without hesitation.

"No," she amended. "I once was. But even now, no one has any reason to trust *me*." She heard the shutters in the other room close with a bang. "Everything here seems built to thwart us."

ACROSS THE PAVILION

YOU ARE SO GOOD *to me.*

Lio couldn't stop thinking about what Cassia had said. He straightened in his chair, casting another glance around the Summit table. How much longer before negotiations commenced? Waiting gave Lio's mind too much freedom to drift. To roam everywhere on Cassia's body where he had been last night.

What a night.

Lio rubbed a hand over his mouth. Sunbind him, his fangs weren't behaving. He kept his mouth shut, a challenge in itself with his canines in this state. He had to stop thinking about how many times she had climaxed. He definitely mustn't think about what he had to look forward to again later tonight.

Lio studied the banners that hung around the Summit pavilion and made himself review which coat of arms belonged to which free lord. His thoughts refused to focus. It seemed last night had expended all his capacity for self-discipline, considerable though it was. Now he was hopeless.

He knew his veil shielded him, and he had time to collect himself behind the broader veil that Uncle Argyros maintained over the embassy to allow for private conference. But Lio still felt as if he waved a great banner over his own head announcing to all his fellow Hesperines just where he had been last night and what he had been doing.

Javed leaned closer. "Don't pretend your fangs aren't bothering you."

Lio choked on a protest.

His Grace-cousin frowned. "I can see you trying to swallow your own teeth to keep them from scaring the humans. Will you not reconsider the thirst suppressant I offered you?"

Thirst. Well, at least Javed hadn't said *hunger*. Lio's secret was safe. For the moment. "Are we really going to continue this conversation in front of the entire Summit?"

"Grace-Father's veil isn't enough to make you feel at ease having such a discussion with your physician?"

"Sometimes you are too comfortable with bodily matters, Javed."

"Lio, now is not the time to be stubborn."

"I can see Kadi's influence on you." Lio smiled. With his lips closed. "I assure you a thirst suppressant is not the sort of assistance I need."

"This is the very same treatment I give Graces to soothe the Craving when they must spend time apart. Mak and Lyros could vouch for how effective it is. They devastated my supply during their Ritual separation."

"Only until they couldn't stand the side effects anymore. Don't remind me about those eight nights."

If it were not the Queens themselves who decreed two Hesperines must spend eight nights apart to demonstrate they were truly Graced, Lio would question the wisdom of the custom. The Craving was hard proof. He hadn't been sure Mak and Lyros would live to see their avowal, at least not with their sanity intact.

Javed waved a hand. "The side effects aren't nearly as bad as everyone says."

"I did my service in the Healing Sanctuary," Lio reminded him. He didn't have to go on. Nothing Javed said could convince him the suppression of one's thirst *and* hunger, not to mention the resulting…depletion… weren't horrible side effects.

"It would offer you some relief," Javed said in his most patient, tactful tone.

"I'd rather be miserable."

"Some *comprehensive* relief," Javed added.

"No."

The healer sighed. "In that case, the only comfort I can offer you is a reminder. It will not always be like this. The Goddess knows and loves your Grace, although you have yet to."

Lio found he didn't wish to contemplate that time-honored Hesperine adage. He didn't want to think about the Grace in his future or, in fact, anything to do with the future at all. The pleasure of the moment was too sweet.

Lio had already wasted so much time and effort carefully constructing a plan for eternity, which had all come to naught. It was a fine, rare feeling to want nothing more than the present.

He was his father's son, after all. Apollon knew how to enjoy the moment and live fully, and he did everything with his whole heart. It was high time Lio followed his example.

He need not think of anyone except she who claimed his devotion in this season. Indeed, nothing short of his total attention was worthy of Cassia. But if he dwelt on precisely what attentions he would show her tonight, he wouldn't get through the negotiations.

Lio watched figures approach from the palace, hoping for distraction. Another free lord arrived with a following of lesser nobles who had weaseled their way behind the mage ward as his retinue. Among the sycophants was Lord Adrogan. One of the men who thought he could wheedle Cassia into a temple wedding.

Lio lounged back in his chair and rubbed a hand over his mouth again. He wasn't prone to such savage feelings, but gloating had never felt so good.

I'm so glad it was you.

His hand tightened on the arm of his chair. He could not simply gloat. Lord Adrogan was the least of the offenders.

Cassia's words would never cease to haunt Lio. They told him too much about what she had expected from her first encounter. Or rather, what she had not expected.

You are so good to me.

Should he have said what he had wanted to say? It went against his grain not to shower her with reassurance.

I'll always be good to you, Cassia.

Perhaps silence had been the right decision. He would be good to her every moment they were together. But he had no right to promise her anything to do with always.

It was definitely time for Lio to stop thinking too far ahead.

A more ostentatious party neared from the direction of Solorum Palace. The king and his retainers.

When Lucis entered the pavilion, Lio stood with the rest of the embassy. The man's stench cast a pall over the entire greensward, not an odor of the body, but of his dessicated heart. The memories Lio now carried in his veins burned within him. Cassia's memories of the king's crimes.

Lucis took his place upon the dais, and his playing pieces arranged themselves in their ordained formation, heir and dogs, mage and apprentice. The king surveyed the Summit as if his gaze could rearrange them too. Lio stood straight, his hands at his sides. When the man's gaze reached him, he returned it steadily.

Cassia, master of the impassive face, would have been proud of Lio's expression in that moment. The king did not even realize the initiate ambassador's bow mocked him.

A small figure glided into the pavilion, her hound and handmaiden in tow, and Lio's court face almost faltered. Without a glance his way, Cassia walked along the farthest row of chairs. Lio realized he had perhaps another heartbeat before he was guilty of resting his gaze on her longer than was appropriate. He turned his attention to taking his seat beside Javed.

Lio heard her footsteps halt. The chair creaked as she sat down, then creaked again as she shifted on her seat, as if seeking a more comfortable position. He rubbed a hand over his mouth.

The wind stirred the air under the pavilion, and her scent reached him. Too faint for anyone but a Hesperine to smell. And the only Hesperine who understood what it meant was him.

The fragrance of cassia soap on her skin invited him to their next feast.

NOTHING TO DO WITH WISDOM

L IO SMOOTHED HIS VEIL and made coffee. He must not allow anyone
in the common room to discern how eager he was to be gone.

How much longer before Aunt Lyta and Kadi finished tonight's
ward? The sooner they joined everyone, the sooner Uncle Argyros could
make his announcement, and the sooner Lio could go to Cassia.

Lio debated pleading thirst so he could escape right away. But his
uncle had not asked if he could wait until after his nightly drink for this
conference. It must be important.

Lio busied himself serving the coffee. He set steaming cups in front
of his uncle and Kumeta, careful not to spill anything on the documents
spread between them on the table. As Kumeta smiled her thanks, her gaze
scarcely rose from her dispatches.

"Thank you, Nephew," Uncle Argyros said kindly, but he did not smile.
His attention drifted away from his diplomatic correspondence to the
packets in front of Kumeta. "As risky as it was for you and Basir to make
your surreptitious visit to the Charge last week, it was certainly a fortuitous opportunity to retrieve our correspondence. The envoy dispatches,
however, have placed a greater burden of reading on you two than the
diplomatic correspondence has on Lio and me. Might I be of assistance?"

"That's generous of you, Argyros." Kumeta sorted through the pile
and separated a stack, which she slid across the table to him. "These are
the reports I am at liberty to share with you."

Uncle Argyros gave her a rueful look. "Some secrets are too dark even
for a founder of Orthros?"

"What you know can hurt you," Kumeta answered.

Uncle Argyros nodded. He began working his way through the envoys' dispatches with greater efficiency than Lio had lately seen him devote to any diplomatic missive.

"Argyros," Kumeta added, "if any of the secret reports mentioned Nike, you know we would tell you."

Uncle Argyros's expression eased. "Thank you, Kumeta."

Lio delivered two more cups of coffee to the other end of the table, where Basir and Javed sat in utter silence over a game of Prince and Diplomat.

Lio tried to sound nonchalant. "Javed, I didn't know you brought a Prince and Diplomat set."

"It's Basir's," Javed replied. "It compromises neither portability nor craftsmanship, wouldn't you agree?"

Lio glanced at the folding board and the pieces, which appeared to be carved of reed. "Indeed, it is a beautiful work. Light as a feather, I'm sure."

"A gift from my Grace," Basir said with relish.

"You are truly devoted to the game, I see." Lio had never known Basir to divert his attention from a pile of dispatches.

Javed pursed his lips and picked up the scroll piece nearest him, moving it a few spaces.

Basir gave him a concerned look, then moved a knight and knocked the scroll from the board.

With a hiss of displeasure, Javed sat back in his chair, rubbing his eyes.

"Don't be so hard on yourself," Basir said.

"I should just go back to reading my medical text. It's the latest research from the Imperial university. Fascinating."

"You sound like the soul of enthusiasm." Basir tapped the board in front of Javed. "Come now. You and I haven't enjoyed a game in far too long."

"You're right. No telling when you and Kumeta will get to spend this much time with us. We should enjoy it as much as we can." Javed returned his attention to his pieces.

Lio fetched himself a cup of coffee and sat down to watch their game. His gaze fixed on the shrine piece. Cassia was waiting. The sun sat untouched at its place on the board, never in play, but always threatening.

Suddenly Javed broke his meditative silence. "How many Hesperines errant have we lost this year, Basir? What is the actual count?"

Basir sighed. "Javed…"

"I know names mean more than numbers," Javed insisted, "but how many?"

Lio sensed a veil enfold their end of the table.

"It's our worst year this century," Basir answered quietly.

"Why are you playing this game with me when you could be helping Kumeta with the dispatches?"

"Because you do not need to subject yourself to the latest research on fever treatments for children."

"Cup and thorns." Javed rubbed his eyes again.

"How many patients have you lost this year?" Basir asked.

Javed offered no reply.

"None," Basir answered for him. "You do not lose patients. You would do well to remember that."

"Every child in Tenebra became my patient the moment I joined the Summit, and I cannot count how many of them I'm going to lose to frost fever while the medicine they need is sitting in my luggage."

Javed's veil slipped. Lio gritted his teeth at the pain in the Union. He pushed his coffee away.

"There is no frost fever in the east," Basir reminded them.

"There's frost fever somewhere," Javed said, "because the Kyrian healers asked for the rimelace. It's only a matter of time, and when it comes, no one will be able to do a thing about it. Least of all me."

Lio opened his mouth to speak.

And shut it again, and bit his tongue.

Goddess, forgive him.

"Basir is right," Lio said. "The game is just what we all need. Shall I be your second, Javed?"

"Thank you, Lio. But it is too late in the game for you to join as my second."

Lio halted in the act of pulling his chair closer. All he could do was lift a hand in acquiescence.

"After the Summit." Kadi strode through the door in conversation with Aunt Lyta. "It could not possibly influence the diplomatic outcome."

Aunt Lyta shook her head. "It would not be wise."

"Wise?" Kadi halted in her tracks. "No, it wouldn't be. It has nothing to do with wisdom. It is a matter of honor. Of love."

Kumeta buried her nose in the dispatches. Basir fixed his gaze on the board. Javed and Argyros did not interrupt their Graces, so Lio followed their example.

"The honorable thing is to respect her decision," Aunt Lyta said.

"What if she needs us?" Kadi demanded.

"She has my warding and your father's thelemancy. She is well armed."

"She might need us even if she isn't in danger. We are right here in Tenebra, and we are not to even try to look for her? How can you bear it?"

"We did try. I must learn to bear it, because she does not want to be found."

"I haven't tried. I'm her sister. If I—"

"If your father and I couldn't find her, no one can."

"Kadi," Uncle Argyros said.

She looked to him, her gaze afire.

He gestured to the seat beside Javed. "If you would, hear me out for just a moment before you deliberate further. What I have to say must inform everyone's course of action."

At length, she gave one nod and joined Javed. They shared a speaking look. Aunt Lyta sank into the chair next to Uncle Argyros and shut her eyes.

He set his coffee aside to wrap an arm around her. "We must acknowledge the Summit is failing."

"Uncle—" Lio began.

Uncle Argyros shook his head. "We knew it might. We see now that it is. Our relationship with Tenebra is only deteriorating further. Every night poses a greater danger to all Hesperines who are Abroad—including us."

"We are equal to it," Kadi said. "Swords and a few backwater mages are no match for us."

"This is a diplomatic endeavor," said Uncle Argyros, "not a war campaign. The negotiations must not, under any circumstances, escalate into conflict. An open contest between Hesperines and Tenebrans, especially in this setting, could turn a stalemate into a war."

In the silence that fell, Uncle Argyros and Aunt Lyta's memories of the Last War loomed in the Union.

"Our embassy has broad authority to act on Orthros's behalf," Uncle Argyros went on, "and to make difficult decisions in response to any unforeseen situations we encounter here. However, the Queens' mandate has a very specific limit. We are to put safety ahead of success. If there is any serious danger, I am to bring us home. Immediately."

"No," Lio said.

"Lio," Uncle Argyros interrupted, "I have gathered everyone for an announcement, not a discussion."

"We can't leave yet." Kadi spoke the horrified protest running through Lio's mind.

Uncle Argyros held up a hand. "We are not leaving tonight."

Thank you, Goddess.

"However," Uncle Argyros said, "everyone must be prepared to depart at a moment's notice, in case the worst should come to pass. If there is no immediate threat, we will leave at the Equinox as planned. If, however, my fears turn out to be justified, the moment will come when we must quit Solorum in haste."

"What immediate danger could there be?" Lio protested.

"We do not know," Uncle Argyros answered, "and that is the problem. It is clear the king never wanted the Summit to succeed. His dissimulation has gone on far too long to be anything but deliberate. He is using the free lords' divisions to avoid a resolution. He would see to it they obeyed him if he really wanted a truce with us. Would you say that is an accurate assessment?"

"It is," was all Lio could say.

"Which begs the question, why did he bring us here if he never had any intention of renewing the Oath?"

"As a stunt to manipulate others," Lio argued. "To send a message to the free lords, the Mage Orders, and the people."

"That remains a possibility, and if we are merely a tool for making a statement, that is a lesser misfortune. If, however, that is not the reason…"

"You think he has some other purpose."

"A motive we have yet to understand, which has made him willing to go to great lengths. Such a careful plot could only be a threat to us. We must be ready to preserve ourselves."

"Be ready," Kumeta echoed.

"When the king makes his move," said Basir, "the Charge needs the embassy to be out of the way."

The Union throbbed with Javed and Kadi's unspoken exchange.

"We'll be ready," he said.

She took his hand.

Lio let his gaze fall. "I understand."

He sensed his elders' relief. Good. Uncle Argyros believed that Lio accepted the state of affairs and that he would cooperate without further protest.

No one suspected Lio would never surrender that easily.

A NECESSARY MONSTER

L IO HAD BEEN SURE of the message Cassia had sent him with her soap.
She wanted him again tonight.

Yet here he was, waiting alone at the shrine nearly an hour after
negotiations had ended.

She couldn't be having second thoughts. Could she?

Lio paused his pacing and focused one more time, reaching beyond
their Sanctuary with all his senses. He could feel the shaft of moonlight
on his head, the cool magic in the stones around him, the heartbeats of
the forest's wildlife. Cassia still wasn't anywhere on the grounds.

Something had prevented her. The only question was whether it was
a danger to her.

Lio slipped to the edge of the grounds with one measured act of power
and descended into the hatch without opening the door. But once there,
he relied on his feet to carry him forward.

He wanted to step to Cassia's side now and let nothing stand in his
way. The mage certainly wouldn't be an obstacle. When Lio had left the
fortress, he had assured himself Amachos's aura was in the Sun Temple.

Even so, Lio must use his power with the utmost caution when entering the palace walls. Now was not the time to test the limits of what he
could achieve under the cover of the palace's magical aura.

The eyes the Goddess had given him revealed the confines of the dark
tunnel to his sight, even in the near absence of light. His speed and long
stride ate the distance to the garden's entrance. This time he used the door.
He eased out into the shelter of the ivy, careful to shut the postern behind
him and let the leaves fall into place.

Cassia was not here either, in what had once been her refuge under her sister's care. Lio must search within.

For the first time he hesitated, forcing himself to consider what he was about to do. He was going to trespass under the palace roof. He could not afford a single misstep.

For once, Lio wanted nothing more than to shrug off the responsibility that rested on his shoulders. He didn't want to think about his obligations to the embassy. Cassia might need him, curse it. He wasn't a diplomat tonight. He was her lover.

He wouldn't make a mistake. That was all.

He climbed the steps to the door Cassia had pointed out to him before. The portal to her sister's realm was crowned by the first stained glass window Lio had seen in Tenebra.

On another occasion, he would have paused to appreciate the work's fading beauty, still visible under the effects of weather, neglect, and time. He might also have smiled to himself, realizing why the door let him in without making a sound. The hinges reeked of the scent oils everyone but Cassia wore. More feminine scents and the aroma of contentment welcomed him inside. Solia and Cassia had both been happy here. But a jarring note of wariness lurked beneath.

Lio's senses heightened in warning. He could smell the king's malodorous presence from here. He wasn't far from Lucis's chambers.

Even a mortal could have walked silently across the rugs where Cassia and Knight had played, past the curtains and tapestries that absorbed as much sound as dust. Through another door with scented hinges, and Lio was in a hall lit by moonlight.

If Knight's odor hadn't been enough, the smells of tallow soap and garden soil, faint beneath the fresher scent of cassia soap and roses, would have made her trail easy to follow. Lio would have no trouble finding her rooms.

His senses clamored as he stalked closer and closer to the intersection of two halls, nearer and nearer the smell of the king. Lio halted at the crossroads. His gaze fell on the large door at the far end of the adjoining hall. He listened.

Lucis slept within. Lio could hear the king's even breaths and steady heartbeat. Astonishing. The man actually had a heart in his chest. And a small army of bodyguards to ensure it kept beating through the night. They were quite awake.

How easy this was.

Lio could walk right past them, ignorant minds that they were, and they would never sense him.

More than men guarded the king, of course. But after learning Knight's ways, Lio felt brazen in dealing with liegehounds, and the plethora of herbal charms and hedge magery about the king's chambers would not halt a Hesperine. It was the hum of Amachos's wards that announced it would take a show of power to enter. But a sorcerer of Lio's caliber could get through those spells and be gone before the royal mage had time to lift a finger.

And, with one stroke, Lio would set off a chain of events like one spell igniting another. The king's death would create a void of power. A free lord would raise himself to prominence as Caelum's regent, probably Lord Hadrian. His rivals under Lord Titus would declare war on the usurper, and the feuds would resume. In one night, Tenebra would regress hundreds of years into its devastating past. The maimed kingdom would be a ripe target for Cordian intervention.

The king was a monster, but a necessary one.

Lio would be mad to remove him. So why did the cost of such a crime seem just as high as the cost he and his people would pay when they left this place without having committed a single error? When they returned home without an Oath. Soon.

Lio had to see Cassia. He had to break the news to her.

He turned his back on the king's door. Lucis ought to be grateful Hespera had ordained a path of peace for her Gifted. The man would never give thanks where it was due. He would never imagine the Goddess his people had forsaken had, in this moment, been all that stood between him and his own destruction.

In contrast to the sleeping king, the wakeful denizens of Solorum palace were easy to evade and did not delay Lio. He found himself in an out-of-the-way residential wing and halted before a door that bore the scents of Cassia and Knight's frequent passage.

He felt Cassia within—wakeful, frustrated, anxious. But not afraid or in pain. Thank the Goddess. She was not in danger, at least not tonight.

She had no wards to guard her, only Knight. There was a mild spell fragrant of the Temple of Kyria and a pungent but feeble charm whose purpose Lio could not divine. Inherent traces of magic had accumulated here over the centuries, like everywhere in the palace, but the strongest auras within were natural. Cassia had not exaggerated when she had said she grew potent plants. Even in winter dormancy, her garden filled her chambers with natural power. Plenty to hide a Hesperine from a mage on the far side of the complex, if said Hesperine was responsible in his use of power.

If this were Orthros, where there was no need for secrecy, he would have indicated his presence and waited for her to invite him in. Or she might have beat him to it and been waiting at the door with a kiss that made her plans for the night quite clear.

Despite their circumstances here in Tenebra, he couldn't just throw respect to the winds. He couldn't commit such a grave offense against his own lover as crossing the veil. Although Cassia did not in fact have a magical veil over her chambers, the Hesperine expression fit the notion of Lio entering her chambers in the middle of the night unsure of whether she wished it.

He had been confident the soap was her way of signaling she wanted a tryst, but had she really meant for him to come to her rooms? She had not explicitly asked him, and he saw now there was no immediate danger from which he must protect her. He had neither her express permission nor just cause for his intrusion.

Cassia would have a hearth room, though, the middle ground between a Tenebran woman's domestic sphere and the outside world, where males might enter to petition for her time. Perhaps it would be acceptable for Lio to venture that far and check on her.

The best he could do in these circumstances was risk trespassing upon her to give her the opportunity to tell him herself what she wanted. If she was offended, he would take his leave and any well-deserved censure she leveled at him.

She had been glad when he had found her in the garden the night of Solia's memorial. If all he did tonight was take a moment to assure her of his concern for her, that would be most welcome to them both, he thought.

He stepped through the closed door and into where Cassia lived.

Four bare walls. A low ceiling. A hearth too small to push back the Tenebran cold. The embers in the fireplace cast a dying glow on a ragged rug and two wooden chairs.

A half-darned stocking stained with grass and soil sought to escape the sewing basket. Lio grinned at a hole worn by Cassia's big toe. Her loom gathered dust in one corner, while moonlight shone through a lone window upon a motley assortment of pots, buckets, and troughs bursting with thriving plants.

On his left, a door stood slightly ajar. Beyond it beat Cassia's heart.

Lio went closer. The scent of her soap and frustration drifted out to him. He opened himself to the Union still more. Her misery saturated his senses. He heard a bed creak, then the muffled thump of a pillow suffering violence. He couldn't help smiling to himself. She did not seem happy with the prospect of missing their tryst.

His smile faded. He had to speak with her. She had a right to know what he was here to tell her.

He knocked on her bedchamber door. "Cassia? It's me. May I come in?"

HAPPINESS

LIO HEARD CASSIA GASP.

"What are you doing here?" she demanded.

He winced. "When you didn't come to meet me, I got worried about you."

By the time he finished speaking, the door had swung open. The way she clutched his arms and pulled him inside her bedchamber did not feel like she was about to throw him out. In fact, she was shutting the door behind him.

"It's too dangerous," she whispered. "What if Amachos senses you? And Perita might be back at any moment."

"She won't hear a word we say, anymore than the court could hear us as we danced." An irrepressible smile overtook him. It was fear for him, not rejection he heard in her voice. "Amachos is very, very far away in his temple doing magely things, or perhaps sleeping off the sun god's fire spirits. It was foolishly easy for me to come in here undetected. I might have tried it before, if I'd thought you wished it."

Cassia breathed a sigh of relief and gave him the fine surprise of sliding her arms around him. For a moment he just savored the sensation of her holding him, and him getting to hold her back. No hesitation. No fear she would pull away.

"If I'd known that," she said, "I would have told you how much I wished it."

All the words he had planned to say deserted him. He should tell her now, but he didn't want to. He wanted nothing more than this, the sensation of her nose pressed against his chest, the feel of her skin through the wool of her tunica as he slid his hands down her back. The fabric was a negligible barrier, compared with a castle, its king, and the dictates of Anthros.

Cassia sighed into Lio's veil hours robe. "I've been lying here waiting for my chance to go out to the shrine. I'd just about given up. Yet here you are."

"Why couldn't you leave? Is everything all right?"

"Perita is only paying her mother a quick visit for a women's tonic. She would come back to find me gone. What she knows, the king knows as well."

Lio held Cassia closer still. "The person who mends your stockings is one of the king's spies."

"Of course."

"I can scarcely imagine the toll it must take on you to know she is watching you all the time."

Cassia frowned. "It's not a comfortable situation for Perita, either. I always know the king has demanded a report when she comes back looking frightened."

"It is a shame the king has put the two of you in this position."

"No one is sorrier than I." The Union twinged with Cassia's guilt. "Something has gone wrong between her and her lover, so she's not spending the night with him. I can't risk leaving my rooms."

"You must evade the king's informants just for a breath of fresh air. I am aghast you must fight a war for every little enjoyment."

"Enjoyment is not the word I would choose to describe our time on the grounds. Nor would I say little."

He drew her to him again and nuzzled her nose. "What word would you choose?"

"Happiness. Great happiness." As soon as she said it, she drew a breath. Almost a gasp.

He realized what those words meant to her. She aired them as if they had long lain in disuse. She had not thought of them in a long time, perhaps never thought of them consciously.

Lio lifted a hand from her only long enough to prick a finger on one fang and cast a spell light so she could see his expression. He buried his hands in her hair and tilted her face up toward him. "Yes. Those are exactly the words I would choose."

He sensed he had indeed chosen the right words, and that even without Blood Union, she had seen what she needed in his eyes. She wanted to know she gave him the same happiness he gave her.

The words he still left unsaid pained him. His awareness of time pressed in on him. Time had never given him grief. It had simply never mattered. In Orthros, it barely seemed to pass at all, and it brought only the growth of his own power. Not the waning of precious things. Not loss.

But here in Tenebra, it was Hypnos's Dream. The last month of winter spun onward to its inevitable end at the Spring Equinox.

Why now, when he and Cassia had only just begun, must their time grow short? If only he had more time with her, he might turn this budding happiness into something even greater. Joy.

He kissed her to silence himself and push away the words he dreaded saying. He who had begged for the chance to come to Tenebra and face reality now longed only to shut out the harsh truth. When he let Cassia come up for air, he strove for a light tone. "No convenient pillars here. Shall we try a bed instead?"

She gave her chuckling laughter. "I am not difficult to please. Anywhere will suit me, as long as I'm trying it with you."

"Goddess help me, Cassia. The things you say drive me mad."

He had beheld her by moonlight, firelight, and now almost no light, clothed and naked, standing and lying beneath him. But the sight of her now aroused him anew. Her hair was a tousled mess, her eyes heavy-lidded from lack of sleep, and her tunica hanging askance off her shoulder.

Behind her, the bed awaited. Her pillow and blankets were twisted as if she had battled with them. The thought of him had kept her frustrated and awake. She had longed for him to warm her through the night. Now he would.

It would have been a wholly erotic situation, if not for the dog who took up most of the bed.

Knight crouched atop the blankets, ready to spring. It appeared their truce did not cover the lady's bedchamber.

"Easy there, my friend," Lio said. "We talked about this. Please accept my apologies for the blood magic. I'm sure the scent doesn't make this easy for you."

Cassia faced her hound, shielding Lio behind her. She said a few crooning words to Knight, then reached forward and pulled the dog's favorite blanket off the end of the bed. She used it to make a place for him on the floor by the door instead and offered him his chewing bone.

When Knight jumped down, Lio felt the impact of the liegehound's weight through the stones under their feet. In record time, the dog posted himself on his blanket at the door and mouthed his beloved bone.

"My thanks," Lio said to Knight, careful not to smile and bare his teeth.

Cassia turned to Lio, knotting her hands. "My bed smells of dog. It's worse than the tallow soap."

"No comparison between good, honest dog smell and dead animal smell." Lio urged her closer to the bed.

She halted in her tracks. "You'll get liegehound fur all over you."

Small price to pay to have Cassia all over him. But he cast a hasty cleaning spell on her bed. "Does that reassure you?"

"It's barely big enough for two. Your feet will hang off the end. And look how low it is. It doesn't even raise one above the chill of the floor."

He eased her against the edge of the mattress, and her knees buckled. "I'll keep you warm."

"I promise there are no fleas. My Kyrian wreath keeps them away." She waved toward the flora hanging above the bedstead while she buried her other hand in his robe.

He paused to kiss her, reaching down to push her tunica up over her knees so he could slide between her legs.

Her arms wrapped around his waist, and her body rubbed his arousal. "The other charm isn't…diminishing you…in the least."

"Charm?" he repeated, his thoughts already far ahead of their state of dress.

"Chastity charm. That garland with the chillvine and prickle buds. Every woman is expected to sleep under one to ward off males with impure intentions and guard against lustful thoughts."

"That explains why it doesn't affect me. My intentions are entirely pure." He wrapped his hands around her buttocks.

"I'm still convinced it doesn't work. I suffer from very lustful thoughts when you're not here. And especially when you are here."

"Incompetent Tenebran mages." He kissed her again.

She opened her lips to him. He moaned encouragement, penetrating her mouth with his tongue in anticipation of all tonight would bring. Again. And again.

He lifted his mouth long enough to ask, "Would you like to tell me these lustful thoughts of yours? Perhaps I can allay them."

She shook her head, one wayward strand of hair in her eyes. "Tonight you must tell me your thoughts. Say where you wish for me to touch you."

His hands tightened on her of their own accord. "You never cease to astonish me."

She brought her hands around to his belly. "Perhaps tonight, you would like for me to feast on you."

His imagination took her words and ran away with them. The vision came to him of Cassia rising up on her knees and lifting her lovely mouth to his neck. She would part her lips, and there would be her fangs, sharp and unsheathed with arousal. She would press her mouth to his throat, he would feel her tongue there and the razor tips of her canines. Then would come the fierce pleasure-pain when she fastened onto him and began to suck...

Her hands drifted still lower, pulling him out of his wild thoughts. Although she brushed his rhabdos lightly through his robe, he gritted his teeth.

"I am no Hesperine, but a human woman can still feast on her lover."

Reality replaced his fantasy with something almost as wild. All he could say was, "Yes."

She unfastened his robe from collar to thigh and let it fall open. And then she stopped. Waiting, he realized, for him to speak.

He lowered his mouth closer to hers. "Kiss me, Cassia, and don't stop."

She did as he asked and covered his mouth with hers. Her hands caressed his bare chest, as if unconsciously, while she probed his mouth with her tongue. He felt her searching, delving to find what pleased him. She raked her tongue over his top left fang with confidence borne of her previous experiments. He gave a short groan of confirmation.

She licked his fang so that her tongue bled, giving him a foretaste of tonight's feast. The delicate sensation of her tongue sliding on his gum, then his fang, then teasing its tip made him press closer to her and drag his hands farther up her thighs. She continued, this time on his top right fang. Then the bottom right. Then the bottom left.

He was not sure he would last if she did this everywhere he had in mind. But between her ministrations, he found himself mumbling, "Don't stop."

"Where shall I go next?" She pulled back, smiling with mischief. Turnabout was fair play, and she was enjoying it.

"Downward."

"And don't stop."

"Please."

She sucked his bottom lip in her mouth, then kissed her way along his jaw. She was proving herself to be a bold lover, now that she was unbound. No telling what pleasures she might be willing to explore with him, if they only had more time.

No. He must not think of the future and how short it was. Only of this moment.

She mouthed her way down his chest. Over his heart, she paused, then detoured to his nipples. Oh, she was wreaking revenge indeed for how he had pleasured her. Lio clenched his jaw, tilting his head back. Did she know what that did to him? She did, for she was doing the same to his other nipple now.

"Cassia," he pleaded. "Downward still."

She obeyed, and as she ventured farther, he took hold of her shoulders. When he felt her tongue sliding down the trail of hair on his belly, he wondered how he would withstand it when her mouth finally reached his rhabdos.

Her breath washed over his agonizing erection. "Downward still?"

"Cassia," he said, not sure if he was begging for more or for a reprieve. "Please."

Slowly, almost gingerly, she took him in her mouth. Pleasure blazed through him, tightening every muscle in his body. His hands clenched on her shoulders, and he gasped a breath.

"Suck," he breathed. "As I do at your neck."

She closed her lips around him and tightened her mouth and tongue.

He let out a groan, almost a shout. She understood it for what it was, a cry of pleasure, not pain. Or perhaps both. Holding him tightly inside her mouth, she slid her head back. Speech deserted him, and he braced his legs against her bed.

Having discovered what pleased him—what undid him—she applied the strategy relentlessly. He buried his hands in her hair, holding her to him, then letting her pull away. He flexed his hips in time to her rhythm as she took him deep, then suckled him and withdrew. He was not sure who was moving whom now, who led their advance and retreat.

Just as she had watched him love her with his mouth, now he could not take his eyes off of her. He watched her head bobbing in his hands, her lips around his rhabdos, until he lost control. He threw his head back as pleasure gathered in his loins and erupted out of him. He felt her mouth and tongue working and her throat closing. She was swallowing him, gulping him down as eagerly as he spilled inside her.

Lio leaned heavily on the bed, amazed he was still on his feet. Cassia retreated carefully, releasing him from her mouth and tongue. He watched her swallow again and lick her lips.

"You never cease to astonish me," he repeated, as soon as he was capable of speech.

Almost shyly, she wrapped her arms around his waist again, holding his legs between her thighs.

"I'm glad you're holding me up," he said. "Otherwise I don't know how I'd stand up after that."

That wasn't just a smile. That was a grin. "I was hoping to work up your appetite, rather than exhaust you."

"You succeeded at both. I'm ravenous."

In one move he stepped back, swept an arm under her knees, and planted her on her back on the bed. Her genuine laughter filled the room. There were great benefits to Hesperine speed and agility.

He surprised her yet again with how quickly he set his mouth to her vein. She gasped and held him closer to her. He drank with more abandon than ever before, giving them both the gratification they wanted. By the time she was panting and twisting under him, the taste of her had set his veins alight again, and her blood had glutted his rhabdos.

So too did her blood glut his Gift. His magic flooded his veins, and a shudder wracked him. His mind reached for hers, ready to join their thoughts without preamble. He barely checked himself in time. What was he, a newblood drunk on his first taste of power?

He thought to slow down now, to ready her still more with caresses. He slid her tunica up past her waist. But when he made to touch her krana, she took his hand in hers. Parting her thighs, she tilted her hips up to demonstrate what she wanted.

No pain to worry about this time. Only immediate pleasure. With a groan of satisfaction, he slid his rhabdos inside her, giving her neck a long, firm suck.

Goddess bless, she felt good inside. So tight. The heat inside her sent shivers of pleasure through him. And the way she moved… She rocked beneath him in swift, impulsive motions. He thrust as fast in return, his fingers tangled in hers.

His magic pulsed in time to their lovemaking. With each surge of power, he felt her shudder. He had to regain control.

"Lio," she breathed in his ear. "Your mind magery…"

He tensed, but he could not still their rhythm, not with her rocking like this under him, not with her blood filling his mouth and his magic striving toward her. He must find a way to slow down, to…

She nuzzled his ear. "Lio. Will I not…feel you…in my mind this time?"

Lio pulled back his head, licking her blood from his mouth. He gazed upon her swollen, parted lips and her skin flushed with far-gone pleasure. Somehow he managed to speak. He had to know. "Is that what you want? Every time?"

"Can we?"

"Yes."

"Please—!"

Relief and delight seemed to drive his Gift right out of his skin and under hers, and her mind enfolded him. Just as she clasped his shoulders and arched nearly off the bed, he thrust hard between her legs. So right. So effortless. Their thoughts, befuddled with desire, entangled and held tight.

"Tell me," she said between pants, "what you want."

This was the stuff of fantasies. Long, tantalizing fantasies he had entertained in that solitary room in the fortress. Now he was here in her bed, inside her. "Wrap your legs around me."

Her slim legs came around him, her thighs gripped, and he felt her feet tuck against the small of his back.

"Ohh. Yes. Cassia. Tighter."

Her legs closed more firmly about him as she clenched her krana within to hold him tight inside her. His groan turned into a growl. She clenched, released. Again. He spilled hard into her. His power surged out of him and flooded her mind. She clutched him to her with her legs as her own climax clutched him inside, drawing him into her.

When pleasure no longer hazed his vision, he became aware of the blood still spilling from her throat in a sluggish trail. He lowered his head again and began to close the wound with gentle licks. She sighed under him and caressed his head. She still hadn't released him from the embrace of her legs, although her limbs had relaxed.

Her sighing continued at the pleasure his mouth and tongue wrought on her wound. He smiled against her neck. Once merely woke the hunger inside her. It would take at least twice to satisfy it.

Her thoughts fluttered amidst his own, and images, ideas brushed his mind. He paused to withdraw from inside her, then slid his hand between her legs. He plunged his fingers into her wet krana as she had been imagining. A beautiful, fleeting smile appeared on her face.

He stroked and probed her, reawakening all the places he had just pleasured. Her eyes slid shut. He slipped one finger deeper inside her. Curling it, he pressed gently up into the roof of her channel and slowly withdrew his hand. Her eyes flew open, and her jaw dropped. He smiled and continued to acquaint her with that particular place inside her. In moments, she was tremoring under him again, this time in slight, soft motions that sent powerful echoes through the Union.

They lay tangled together, and he rested his face between her breasts. He was sure his power must be levitating him a bit, for she did not complain of his weight. He could give up hope of taming his Gift at a moment like this, when they were both so satisfied.

So happy.

He didn't have the heart to rob her of that. He wouldn't tell her what his aunt and uncle had said. There was still a chance they might be wrong. And if they were right…Cassia would soon read the signs around the table, and she would not need Lio to be the bearer of the news they dreaded.

No, there was still hope. Perhaps there were yet strategies Lio and Cassia might attempt together to sway the course of events. They had defeated frost fever. Could they not set themselves against the Summit again?

Lio breathed in the scent of Cassia's skin and listened to her heart where it beat beneath his ear. With her, he felt they might take on anyone.

15

days until

SPRING EQUINOX

THE LAWS OF MEN

NEVER BEFORE HAD CASSIA invited an invitation to one of Lady Hadrian's gatherings, but today it might well prove worth the sacrifice. It hadn't been easy to drag her achy, unrepentant body to dawn rites. But her reward had been catching Lady Hadrian as everyone left the temple. It had only taken a few words about a disastrous weaving project and a desperate need for expert assistance. Cassia had secured herself and Knight a place in Lady Hadrian's weaving room for the afternoon, surrounded by the usual devotees.

"Oh, that is a troublesome snarl." Lady Hadrian brought the knots in Cassia's length of tapestry to a swift resolution. "Let us do it again. Once you see how this thread is woven in, you'll understand quickly, and it will be easy for you."

"Thank you, my lady." Cassia watched Lady Hadrian's demonstration. The other ladies' hand looms soughed on as they paid more attention to their own work than to the bastard who received their hostess's generous condescension. Glad the young women's focus was on their gossip and not her, Cassia listened.

"Lord Tyran's guards?" Lady Nivalis scoffed. "His brigands, you mean."

Lady Dalia sniffed. "The disreputables he employs would not last a day in Lord Hadrian's service."

"Lord Hadrian would never tolerate such conduct," Lady Nivalis agreed.

"Have you heard Lord Tyran at every feast?" Lady Dalia asked. "He goes on and on, bragging about his friendship with Lord Titus's son. Just another of Lord Flavian's bootlickers without a scrap of honor."

"Of course Lord Hadrian's man has the right of it," Lady Biata declared.

Talk of guards already. It might prove even easier than Cassia had expected to gather the gossip she had come seeking. Everyone here would be interested in a scandal in the barracks. Although the highborn were these ladies' obsession, no one escaped their notice. In that way, they and Cassia were all alike. They knew how important it was to know. Cassia had once thought what separated them was her use of such knowledge for survival, and theirs for advancement. From her seat at the table, this division did not appear so distinct anymore.

"How many of Lord Tyran's guards?" Lady Dalia asked.

"Three cowards," Lady Nivalis answered, "against one of Lord Hadrian's men."

"He dispatched every one of them to Hypnos!" Lady Biata exclaimed. "He left two of them to sleep in their own blood near the practice yard and delivered the third to Lord Hadrian's solar at the crack of dawn."

Everyone cast a glance at Lady Hadrian, who continued her silent lesson for Cassia.

"That must have been shocking." Lady Biata sounded exhilarated.

"Imagine that," Lady Nivalis mused. "Lord Hadrian's guard marching through the halls of Solorum with the remains of his enemy."

"Lord Hadrian's man was the victor," Lady Dalia concluded. "In trial by the sword, the survivor is in the right, with the gods as his witness."

"Apparently the palace guards think they know better than the gods," said Lady Nivalis. "They're calling it murder."

"Our men have been at war with Lord Titus's faction for generations," Lady Dalia protested, "and it has never been murder."

"Do you know how the fight started *this* time?" Lady Biata asked with relish.

"I need not ask," Lady Dalia returned. "One man is Lord Hadrian's. The others serve the Segetians."

"But this was not merely your usual feuding," Lady Biata gushed. "According to the gossip coming from Lord Tyran's direction—"

Lady Hadrian lifted a hand from Cassia's weaving project, and the room fell silent.

"Dear Bee," Lady Hadrian said, "how unfortunate that anyone has bothered your ears with the words of such unpleasant men. I can only imagine how distasteful that was to hear, my poor dear. You need not think on it any further."

"Oh, yes, it was most distressing," Lady Biata simpered. She took the hint and refrained from repeating any testimony of the opposing faction within Lady Hadrian's hearing.

Lady Hadrian's expression had grown pinched and grim, although she continued to demonstrate the technique of seamlessly adding a brilliant but fragile color of thread to the weaving. Cassia nodded to show she was paying attention.

"He languishes in prison awaiting his untimely execution," Lady Biata informed everyone.

"How can they believe him responsible, when Lord Tyran's guards outnumbered him?" Lady Dalia lamented.

"Lord Tyran claims Lord Hadrian's guard slaughtered the men without cause," Lady Biata replied. "Insidious lies, of course."

"It's military discipline. The laws of men." Nivalis's tone held a bitter note Cassia recognized. "There's no thwarting them."

"In that you are right," Lady Hadrian cut in. "That is the sad truth of the matter. Let us speak of it no more."

THE WAY OF THINGS

WAS THERE STILL TIME? Cassia left the weaving party as soon as she could without arousing suspicion, for she did not know if she had fortnights, days, or mere hours before the guard's execution.

Regardless, it was not much time to convince Perita to go against months of silence and a lifetime of knowing her place.

Cassia found her handmaiden in her hearth room. Perita sat by the fire with her head bent over the tiny stitches that were coming undone from the blue-gray belt. There was plenty of thread on her needle, and most of the damage still lay ahead of her. One might suspect she had just picked it up.

"Hello, Perita."

"Afternoon, Lady."

After a moment of difficult silence, Cassia took Knight into the bedroom and bade him stay on his blanket. The last thing she should bring to this negotiation was dog fur. After she washed her hands and changed into a clean gown, she returned to the hearth room and took her chair across the rug from Perita.

Moments dragged on. Perita did not speak.

Cassia cleared her throat. "How much time do we have to find a way to get your guard out of prison?"

The girl jumped out of her skin, and her finger narrowly escaped a vicious stab from the needle. At last, she met Cassia's gaze.

"The more you tell me," Cassia said, "the better chance we have of seeing that his life is spared. How long?"

Perita searched Cassia's eyes. The handmaiden's gaze was as sharp as that needle. Cassia did not look away.

Let her look. Let her see all Cassia was and was not. Let her decide for herself why Cassia was doing this.

Although, it might not hurt for Cassia to make her case in words as well.

She drew a deep breath and tried, with great difficulty, what always came so easily with Lio. Speaking. If she learned to do it with other people as well, might it do more good than harm?

In this case, in this one case, perhaps.

"I haven't anything to gain by helping you," Cassia said. "Winning you to my side, you may be thinking, so you don't report to the king. That would be a useless attempt on my part. We both answer to the king, and we always will."

Deliberately, Perita secured her needle in the fabric of the belt. "What is it you want in return then, Lady? I'll be straight with you. I'm desperate enough. Name your price, and I'm likely to pay it."

"I don't want anything."

Brow furrowed, Perita studied Cassia. "If there's a favor you've a mind to call in later, I'd as soon know now."

"No. No favors." Cassia swallowed. "I just want to help."

She looked and saw no trust in Perita's eyes. And suddenly, Cassia thought she could see through Perita's eyes.

The tyrant king's mercenary daughter was coming to her in her hour of despair, dangling hope in front of her, cruel hope, and she didn't know what new trap might be waiting if she took the bait. What new trial she must find the strength to endure, in order to make something of the lady's offer.

"Of course you need to know why," Cassia said, "when I have never been of any help to you before."

"Neither of us can be of any help to the other," Perita said softly. "It's the way of things."

"No. It is no longer the way of things."

Those words, Cassia knew not why, broke the dam. She watched the expressions on Perita's face. Perita was smart—she never wore a stone face, but she only showed about three of her faces to Cassia, all acceptable ones. Now Cassia saw how much lay beneath. Perita's confusion gave way to a grimace of anguish and wetness in her large eyes that threatened to overflow.

"When you say it like that, my lady, I believe you."

Cassia had not realized how she'd sounded. So sure. Like someone with authority. Even power. "I will do everything in my power to help the two of you," she promised.

Perita clapped a hand over her mouth. Tears traced over her cheeks and the backs of her knuckles.

Cassia sat with her hands in her lap, feeling unarmed against the girl's pain. "I'm so sorry," she tried. Yes, sympathy must surely be what Perita wanted and what would keep her talking. "What is his name?"

Perita scrubbed her eyes with the back of her hand. "Callen."

"He is good to you? You care for him?"

"We'd do anything for each other." Perita's chest shook from her effort to contain her sobs.

Cassia sought more words. "How did you two meet?"

"When the court was at Namenti. We girls started going to watch the fellows in the practice yard. We all picked favorites to cheer for. It gave us something to cheer about, and the fellows something to fight for. It all seemed like such a merry game until we came to Solorum." Her face crumpled again.

"What changed?"

Perita sucked in a breath. Then her despair resolved into an iron calm.

Cassia really hadn't seen Perita before. She had been looking with the wrong eyes. Otherwise, she would have learned to respect Perita long before this moment.

"Nothing is a game here at Solorum," Perita said. "You'd think the guards bring the ghosts of all Lord Titus's and Lord Hadrian's ancestors with them into the practice yard. Lord Tyran's men are the worst. He's in Lord Titus's faction, you know, and his guards never let anyone hear the end of it. Especially Verruc. He's one of Lord Tyran's 'favorites.' He and his two cronies are always bullying Lord Hadrian's men."

"Did Verruc's band pick a fight with Callen?"

"You can't pick a fight with Callen. He's a steady man, not prone to petty squabbles. He respects Lord Hadrian's orders not to make the feud worse. He would never do something like this without just cause. He killed Verruc and the other two in honorable combat, then took himself to Lord Hadrian to confess."

"Yes, the way Callen turned himself in has made quite an impression on Solorum."

"That's Callen. He doesn't deserve this. But Verruc's liege is calling it murder. It's Callen's word against a free lord's."

"It is unusual for the palace guard to interfere in trial by the sword. Surely Callen's comrades vouched that he challenged Verruc and the other two in accordance with honor and won by the will of the gods."

Perita's gaze fell. "There were no witnesses." Then she lifted her chin. "If you want evidence Callen is in the right, know that Lord Hadrian takes Callen at his word."

"I will take you at your word, Perita."

Perita straightened in her chair. "Thank you, my lady. You'll find I'm as good as my word."

"Tell me, has not Lord Hadrian intervened on Callen's behalf?"

"He personally offered Lord Tyran double life price for all three soldiers. Lord Tyran accepted a small fortune for the other two, but he wouldn't take money for Verruc. Said he wanted 'justice.'" Perita's mouth twisted.

"No doubt the palace guard insisted they had 'no choice' but to enact the letter of the law."

The king would not intervene. Not when he was secure of Lord Hadrian's loyalty and struggling to keep Lord Tyran's. Lucis was the law's most faithful defender, as long as it was convenient for him.

"Even Lord Hadrian couldn't stop the arrest," Perita said. "Callen went without a fight, of course."

"What about Lord Titus?" Cassia asked. "He is usually a reasonable man. He could talk Lord Tyran into a more moderate response."

"Lord Titus said he'd have Lord Flavian look into the matter."

"Lord Flavian is away on an errand for the king and not due to return for a month. Does Callen have that much time?"

Perita closed her eyes, then shook her head. "It's not the headsman we've to fear. Callen won't last till the next execution. It was a dreadful fight. His victory cost him." Perita swallowed hard. "Yesterday you came upon me when I'd just got back from visiting Callen in prison. I've a strong stomach, my lady. But the shape he's in…"

"His wounds have gone bad?"

Perita nodded, her gaze haunted. "But I had to see him. Father officially agreed to our betrothal just so I'd have the right to visit Callen."

"You and Callen intend to marry?"

"Oh, yes. We made a promise to each other on tournament day. My father had the butcher in mind, but when Callen spoke to him, Pa took one look at Lord Hadrian's colors and forgot to be stubborn. Even so, Callen insisted we wait till he rose a bit higher in the ranks, so he'd have more to offer. He's got his mother and sisters to support, so taking on a wife, too…" Perita's voice wavered. "They can't…I can't…do without him, my lady."

"You will not have to do without him. First of all, we must see to his wounds. You know the mages the Kyrian temple sends to Solorum every few days?"

"Well, yes. They assist the household with garden magic and healing. But I've never seen them set foot in the western wing of the king's prison, my lady."

"This afternoon will be a first, then. I'm forbidden to meet with them, but it is hardly my fault if we happen to be visiting the prison at the same time, hmm?"

"Callen's youngest sister could get word to them. The king wouldn't pay any mind to her comings and goings." Perita's composure had returned. "But I won't see him survive prison just to face his sentence. If there's aught we can do to spare him from the headsman, my lady, I'll do all I can to serve you in seeing it through."

"Information is where all such efforts must begin. The more we know, the better."

"I'm afraid I've told you all I know."

"If we understand the reason for the incident, it could help us prove Callen's deed was justified."

"There's no reason in it, my lady. At least, if any man remembers a reason for the feud, I've never heard him explain it."

"As you say, Lord Hadrian and his men do not pick fights. No one has sacrificed more to keep the feud at a standstill."

"If only the other side saw it that way, my lady."

"Was Verruc a particular rival of Callen's?"

"Yes. He envied Callen's victories."

"I see. So the rivalry had become personal. How did Verruc and his men manage to ambush Callen alone, though? Callen is clearly too honorable to accept a challenge under dubious circumstances and too sensible to fall for a trap."

"It's dangerous at night, my lady, even for off-duty soldiers."

"The fight happened at night?"

"Verruc had the character of a thief, not a warrior."

"Lord Tyran and his men are notorious. His own misconduct sets the example for theirs. Their camp is circulating a great deal of gossip about the incident."

Cassia observed the hint of expression around Perita's mouth, the blankness in her gaze, the odd stillness of her hands where they rested upon the abandoned mending.

"Callen went straight to his liege to tell the truth," Perita said. "That won't stop Lord Tyran's guards from making up lies."

"In that case, I would like you to be the one who educates me about their gossip, so when I hear it from others, I will know better than to believe it."

"It's not fit for your ears, my lady."

"I'm only barely a lady. You need never hesitate to speak frankly with me."

"Oh, I couldn't, my lady."

Cassia considered Perita. *We'd do anything for each other,* she had pledged just a moment ago.

"I can understand you'd be hesitant to repeat nasty rumors about Callen. Think of it as spying on the enemy's weapons, so we may properly arm ourselves against them."

"Please, my lady. Don't ask me to speak of that."

Perita was indeed clever at showing the right face at the right moment. But Cassia was very good at watching faces and reading lips. And there were some lips that begged to be read.

Cassia knew all about words unspoken that you longed for someone to hear, although you could not say them.

"I can understand your anger," Cassia said. "Hold on to that. It will serve you well. But...do not fear. You don't have to be afraid."

Perita's mouth was still.

"I know the wounds lies leave behind," Cassia went on. "Wounds that seem like they will never heal. I know the fears that come even when you're alone, when threats seem to grow into something larger than words. I have only recently found the courage to fight them myself, but if I am certain of anything, it's that they are easier to conquer when you are not alone."

Perita's lips trembled.

Cassia clenched her hands in her lap. "I have no right to ask you to make me your ally. But if you choose to give me that chance, I will be discreet and reliable." Cassia took a deep breath and braved Perita's gaze again. "You can trust me."

Perita spoke. "I'm the only one who saw what happened. Me, a woman, who can't stand witness in matters of law. Even if I could testify...no one would listen to me once they found out I was there that night."

Perita, unflinching, did not look away. As if daring Cassia to judge her, as everyone else would do if they knew what Cassia did about where Perita went at night.

A woman's word was worth little, a whore's worth nothing. And that's what everyone would call Perita, if the truth got out.

"I know they would not listen," Cassia said. "I know what they would say. My mother knew, too. But you will hear no wounding words from me. *I* will listen."

Perita drew a breath. "Verruc didn't ambush Callen." Another breath. "Verruc ambushed me."

Cassia reached out. She found her hand moving slowly, as if she expected someone to strike her. As if she expected the person she reached toward to shy away for fear of being struck. But Cassia closed the distance between them, and no one stopped her. Cassia put her hand over Perita's.

Perita didn't shy away.

Cassia searched for words and found them all insufficient. This was not the time to speak.

She listened.

"Ever since we got to Solorum," Perita began, "Verruc wouldn't leave me be. He saw me with Callen when the girls and I came by the practice yard. I don't know if Verruc really wanted me, or just to spite Callen, but he made up his mind he'd have me. I kept telling him no, but he accused me of just being coy. When he finally realized I wanted nothing to do with him, he started threatening me. Boasting of what he'd done to other women. It got to the point where I had to watch my back everywhere I went, for if Verruc ever caught me alone…"

Fury boiled up in Cassia, powerful and without warning.

Cassia knew the primal fear all women shared of what could happen to them when their protectors weren't watching. But she had always faced that threat with Knight at her side. And her lineage, however much she hated it, made the king's retribution a threat.

Perita had no royal name to make a man think of consequences. She didn't even have an animal to protect her.

Was there no one you could turn to? Cassia wanted to ask. But she knew the answer. What could a tallow chandler do to protect his daughter from Verruc, a favorite of Free Lord Tyran's? Perita's father knew better than to expect advocacy from the king's household.

Perita knew better than to expect advocacy from Cassia.

"I couldn't tell Callen. I didn't want to start trouble in the barracks. This sort of thing happens all the time, and the girls and I know to look out for each other. I just didn't go anywhere alone…except to be with Callen. Nowhere's safer than with him. But Verruc set a trap for me."

Cassia scarcely breathed. She feared to hear the rest.

"Somehow Verruc knew where Callen and I meet at night. As careful as we've been, after no one's ever found us out. He got his two cronies to delay Callen. When I went to the place…*our* place…there was Verruc."

No. No, Cassia didn't want it to be true.

Sweat beaded on Perita's face. "Callen saw through it. He killed the other two on the spot and came straight to me." She gulped a breath. "He got there in time."

Relief made Cassia weak all over. "Are you all right?"

"Callen didn't give Verruc a chance to lay a hand on me."

"Is there anything you need? If you have even a scratch, I will see to it you receive the best care from the Kyrian healers."

Perita shook her head, her face ashen. "Thanks to Callen, Verruc never carried out any of his disgusting threats. All he got away with was talk. Just a lot of words."

"Wounds," Cassia said again.

Perita shrugged, but she was shaking. "We're used to that, aren't we?"

Cassia's anger flashed again like a clear light. "We shouldn't be."

Perita gulped again, her sweat trickling down her face, her whole body shivering.

"I know what it's like to live in fear," Cassia said.

Perita's breath came in frantic gasps. "I was so afraid."

There was no rattle of illness in her chest, which medicine might ease. Just as there was no elixir that could untie the knots in Cassia's belly after she had seen the king.

"I still have—nightmares." Perita swayed in her seat. "About—about—what he tried—to do."

Cassia had no betony charm at hand. She put her own hand in Perita's. "You're safe now. I swear to you. No one will threaten you ever again."

Perita held on tight, resting her forehead on Cassia's hand. For long moments, she heaved breath after breath, while she never shed a tear. Cassia steadied her with a hand on her shoulder until her rapid, ragged breaths eased into sighs of relief.

While Cassia had wallowed in her own affairs, Perita had struggled through each day bearing all this. She had lived with the fear of what Verruc would do to her if he got the chance. She had lived through the ordeal of a close call. She had gone to a safe place to see the one she loved, only for her enemy to desecrate her sanctuary and try to violate her.

Cassia had thought only of herself. She had used Perita to further her own ends. She had risked Perita's health for a night of pleasure.

"I am so sorry, Perita. I should have realized. How I regret every time I sent you on a meaningless errand…put you in real danger just for a bar of soap in the middle of the night…"

"My sister walked back with me." Perita hiccuped.

"Like your friends and family, I should have come to your aid. Please… could you find it in your heart to…forgive me?"

"You've so many problems of your own to contend with."

"That is no excuse."

Perita sat up slowly. "Can you forgive me for betraying you to the king?"

"There is nothing to forgive. That was not your choice."

Perita's eyes flashed. "None of this was my choice."

"I know. Little of it has been my choice, either, but I cannot deny I had more choice than you, and I squandered it. No more. I will help you see justice done."

"Callen won't even tell Lord Hadrian he killed Verruc and the others for my sake. He'll choose death before he lets this ruin me. And yet I can do nothing for him. But you can, my lady."

"We can. Together. My voice is yours."

THE WESTERN WING

AROUGH, PUCKERED SCAR RAN from the prison warden's left brow to his cheekbone. An eye peered out from beneath his mangled lid, and his other narrowed to match.

Cassia endured his glare with her chin high and let him study the small army she led: her handmaiden, two Kyrian mages, and a liegehound. Callen's youngest sister was perhaps their fiercest fighter of all, but they had left her in the sunshine outside. The dungeons beneath Solorum were no place for a girl of six.

No sound emerged through the closed door behind the warden. Were its massive oaken panel and iron reinforcements enough to trap the groans of the dying, or was it magicked?

He planted his feet and crossed his arms. "This is the western wing."

"That is why we are here," Cassia replied.

"The men beyond this door have been sentenced to execution. Consider them already dead. There is no work of the gods to be done here, except by Hypnos."

Deutera's veil concealed her expression, but not her resolute tone. "Kyria's work does not cease while they still draw breath."

"The sooner they stop, the better for them." The warden's left eye lagged in its socket as his gaze swiveled to the mage. "I won't have you prolong their misery nor the king's duty to feed them. Save your magic for the deserving."

"The headsman's axe is a hard enough fate," Deutera said. "Kyria would not have them suffer while they await it. Would you begrudge them the comfort of our ministrations in their final days?"

Cassia knew a retreat when she saw it. The warden abandoned the lost argument and pinned his gaze on Perita instead. "You've already had your final visit. Returning in the company of mages doesn't change the rules."

Cassia hooked her arm in Perita's and held her close. "Perita is my companion. She goes where I go."

"And who are you?" he finally asked.

She smiled. "Cassia Basilis."

The warden's scowl deepened. He bowed, barely. "My lady."

"You have not heard of my works on behalf of the Temple of Kyria?"

"As I said. Hypnos is my god."

"You are not aware one of your prisoners is promised to a member of my household?"

"Dead men don't keep promises."

"I keep mine. Let me pass. Relief from pain is the least I owe my hand-maiden's betrothed."

The warden subjected them all to the sort of sneer men gave women they regarded as meddling nags.

Cassia drew herself up into the posture she had learned from the kennel master many years ago and spoke in the tone best suited for training dogs. "Warden!"

His gaze snapped back to her.

"Perita will be permitted to see Callen, and the mages will be permitted to tend his wounds."

His sneer remained, but he relented, "As you wish…my *lady.*"

He waved a hand at the guards who stood at attention behind Cassia's retinue. The two men came forward to the prison door. Their strength made the massive barrier swing as easily as a lady's dressing screen.

As Cassia and her company filed past, the warden gave her a parting glare. Knight answered him with a growl.

"You'll leave before dusk rites," the warden ordered. "If the goddess takes a notion to send you back for more good works another day, I'll want to see a seal from the king."

Cassia smiled at him with the coldness that had sent Lord Ferus running. She imagined what she might do if she had the sword the warden carried at his hip. Next time, she vowed, she would have something better than a sword or the king's seal. She would have a letter of release for Callen.

The stench of the western wing assailed them. The mages didn't flinch, and Cassia wondered if magic on their veils shut out odors. If she had not helped in the infirmary before, she might not have been able to stomach it. She and Perita pressed their scented handkerchiefs tightly to their noses.

Perita was brave to come here and confront Callen's suffering a second time. Did she want comfort? Cassia wouldn't find out by not offering. She offered Perita her arm again, and Perita leaned on her.

The two guards' heads nearly brushed the low ceiling as they escorted Cassia and her companions down a wide hallway. Sputtering torches lit the passage at intervals. Between the lights gaped holes of shadow filled with iron gates, groans, and most of the rank odors. They came to an intersection where two more hallways led off at angles. More lights in the dark, more barred doors, more men who would die at the king's command. Cassia had lived in her own version of his dungeon all her life, although she had never set foot here.

How many of the prisoners deserved this fate? How many were like the men who would have died for the chance to carry Solia's body off the field, who had died against the ramparts of Castra Roborra to punish her murderers?

The guards herded them down the right-hand hallway, and the passage narrowed around them. Now that Cassia's anger had taken on a life of its own, it was hard for her to shove it down. Impossible, in fact. She could only channel it and make it into a fuel for her more lucid thoughts.

Their escort took them past more turnoffs and into a crooked off-shoot of the hall that felt like a forgotten corner of the world. No sun had touched these stones since these walls had been built here in the bowels of the Mage King's palace. The legends were true, and he had been a just king, Lio said. How golden had that age been? Had the western wing been a bastion of justice instead of a cruel jest of Hypnos's?

Cassia could hear Perita sniffing softly as the guards unlocked the cell, but the door's screech soon drowned out her quiet weeping. The still, prone form at the back of the cell, discarded on the squalid floor, was a man. The one Perita cared for. The broken body before them was the one Perita held at night, the one that loved her.

Cassia let the mages go first and slid her arm fully around Perita to hold her up. Wouldn't Cassia need an arm to lean on, if anything befell Lio? Yes, she would. For just a moment, before she wielded every secret she knew, every tool at hand, every bit of influence she could muster against those who had done such a thing to him and made sure they never harmed him again.

Staring at Callen, Cassia experienced a moment of astonishing clarity. It was stronger than anything she had felt in many years. No, it could not compare with anything she had ever felt before.

The mages knelt beside Callen, subjecting their clean, fragrant robes to the filthy ground without any hesitation. Deutera kept her lantern hooded and set it down near enough to give them light without blinding him. Before Cassia could ask if she would rather wait outside, Perita drew herself up and stepped forward. Cassia went with her, and together they knelt beside the mages to offer their help.

Cassia was indeed grateful for her training, such as it was, in the compassionate but hard school of the mages' infirmary. Callen lay in his own offal, his skin slimed with the sweat of a high fever, his hair matted with dirt and rotten rushes from the floor. It was hard to tell how many of the dried bloodstains on his clothes were his own, but the wet mess of pus at his left knee made it clear which wound was the cause of his troubles.

Cassia looked through the grime, gore, and suffering. She saw a man with a strong jaw and well-proportioned face, a long-boned frame and broad shoulders strong from a lifetime of training. A wilted luck charm of spring blossoms peeked out from one cuff of his tunic. They could tell his youngest sister he still wore the wrist chain she had made for him.

Deutera looked at Perita, and the light in her eyes made it clear she smiled beneath her veil. "Don't fear. Between the four of us and Kyria's magic, we'll have him clean and treated before we leave today."

A sigh of relief, almost a sob, burst out of Perita. She reached out a hand to Callen and caressed his forehead, pushing back a tangle of sandy brown hair. "Do you hear that, love? We'll set you to rights."

His eyes opened. "Perita."

"See there?" The smile around Deutera's eyes deepened. "He knows you. That's a good sign."

"Perita," he said again, the way one might utter the name of a goddess.

"I'm right here, love. Everything's going to be all right."

KINDNESS

WITHOUT KNOWING THE MEANING of the closing words of dusk rites, Cassia might decide the final prayer meant anything. She uttered it thinking of the cost of war to those who tried to fight with honor. She doubted Anthros actually gave much thought to such things, for he loved the results of war too much. He must love King Lucis above all.

Cassia descended from the gallery without waiting to file out behind the crowd. As she had that morning, she caught up to Lady Hadrian with as much propriety as she could manage while striding so fast onto the greensward with a liegehound trotting alongside her.

Lady Hadrian turned so neither of them must squint into the sunset. "Lady Cassia. Has another question about your weaving project come to mind?"

"Not at all. Your help earlier made everything clear. Thank you again."

"You know it was a pleasure for me."

"I wish I could speak of pleasures now, but I must beg your attention to a grave matter. You recall the guard everyone spoke of this afternoon?"

"I can hardly forget." Lady Hadrian shook her head. "As I said to the other young ladies, I would sooner not speak of it. My husband feels the situation deeply, as do I."

"I believe I can help."

Lady Hadrian's gaze sharpened. Cassia recognized the keen expression of a woman who was more accustomed to taking action than resigning herself to a situation she could not influence. "Please, go on."

"Did you know Callen is betrothed to my handmaiden, Perita? He was only waiting for his next recognition from Lord Hadrian before he sought your husband's approval of the marriage."

"I had no idea. What a tragedy this is for her. Rest assured, if there is anything my lord and I can do for her, we will. We will not abandon any of our dependents' loved ones."

"Nor will I. Perita and two Kyrian healers are with Callen now."

Lady Hadrian sucked in a breath. "Lady Cassia, allow me to thank you on my lord's behalf. You have done what we could not. Fealty dies at the door of the western wing, although the men to whom we owe it still breathe. Once the feud delivers a man into the prison warden's household, neither side has any more power to aid him."

Cassia clasped her hands, suddenly tense, but not in the fearful way to which she was accustomed. What a strange hour this was, when all the politics that made Lord and Lady Hadrian powerful stood in their way.

And the powerless bastard and her silenced handmaiden delivered the solution.

"I will not allow Perita to come to grief over this," Cassia declared, "nor will I stand by and see death be Callen's reward for honorable combat. I know Lord Tyran has proved resistant to your efforts on behalf of justice. Perhaps he would be more open-minded toward an intervention from me."

Cassia held her breath and waited. Perita ostensibly served Cassia. Perita really served the king. If Lady Hadrian felt the need to adhere to the fact of the matter, rather than the appearance of it, Cassia's efforts would perforce become more complicated.

"Your willingness to intercede does you credit," the lady approved.

"I wish to return your kindness to me, and your lord's."

It was a rare moment when Cassia spoke words to produce a desired effect and realized only afterward they were in fact true. She had learned not to look for kindness. So she had not seen it in repeated invitations to leave her isolated rooms. In a cup of that delicious spiced wine she would never ask for, but which never ran dry as long as she visited. In dances without consequences. There had been kindness there all along.

She should have seen it. Her seven-year-old self had on that night long ago, when Lord Hadrian also could do nothing.

Here today, Cassia could.

LIFE PRICE

NEARBY ON THE GREENSWARD, Lord Hadrian stood with a few other lords in low-voiced discussion that was surely a preamble to tonight's negotiations. His lady took him aside, and Cassia made her case again.

"Good," Lord Hadrian said. "I will see Tyran give you his answer now."

With that, he sent his retainer to find Lord Tyran, who even now approached the Summit pavilion. Men as important as Free Lord Hadrian did not trot across greenswards, but had others do it for them. Men like Free Lord Tyran who were trying to be important frowned and delayed a moment to soothe their dignity, then came to see what their liege lord's rival wanted of them.

As soon as Lord Tyran drew near, Knight tensed, and Cassia's own tension mounted. The man moved like a wolf eager to spring. Cassia felt sorry for both his concubine and his betrothed. The arrogance in his eyes made his bow to Lord and Lady Hadrian into mockery. He was half Lord Hadrian's age and half as broad, although the young lord flaunted his slight advantage of height. His black hair was well-groomed, his chin cleanly shaven. He attired himself in the short tunic and tight breeches fashionable among Lord Flavian's hangers-on, unlike the long tunics and looser braccae Lord Hadrian's generation still wore. But Lord Tyran had something else in common with Lord Titus's son: a real sword arm hiding under his velvet sleeve.

Lord Tyran was the man who had not only allowed, but enabled Verruc to commit his crimes. Cassia was glad Perita had decided to remain at Callen's side. That she had entrusted this confrontation to Cassia.

Perita shouldn't have to endure it. Cassia owed it to her to see this through for her.

Lord Hadrian said not a word, but held out a hand toward Cassia.

Lord Tyran gave her a belated, halfhearted bow. "My lady. That's a fine dog you have there. Shame the royal kennels don't breed them except upon the king's orders. I'd fancy a pack of hounds like yours at my heels. His Majesty's bitches make the best in the kingdom."

Cassia laid a hand on Knight's shoulder. "It is a shame Knight and I were not present when a guard under your command ambushed an innocent person in the middle of the night. If we had been, your soldier would not have received the honor of a warrior's death. Verruc would have met the end he deserved. On the ground with my dog's teeth at his neck."

Lord Tyran was actually too startled to speak. Cassia was off to a good start.

She didn't give him a chance to gather his thoughts. "Alas, it fell to a man to put a stop to Verruc. A good man who is now in prison awaiting execution."

Lord Tyran set his jaw. "One of Hadrian's men murdered three of mine in cold blood under cover of darkness. Hadrian, shall we educate Lady Cassia on the law?"

Lord Hadrian's silence made an effective refusal.

Lord Tyran spoke in a painfully patient tone. "If the man was of exceptional value to his lord, which Verruc was, that gives me the right to reject the fine and demand instead a life for a life."

"I am aware of the law and that you accepted only two life prices from Lord Hadrian. I am making you my own offer. I have ample weight in gold and jewels right here." With a sense of satisfaction, Cassia untied the heavy purse from her belt. Her suitors' gifts would not buy her hand in marriage, but the freedom of a common man who was worth more than all of those courtiers put together.

Lord Tyran's eyes narrowed. "What value does a murderer's life have to you?"

"Callen is an honorable warrior and my handmaiden's betrothed."

"Well, well. Callen's gotten himself betrothed. That's a recent event. I wonder what reason a girl might have to yoke herself to him in such haste."

"Callen's imminent execution is a powerful motivation for making such a commitment, I should think. I want him to survive to see his wedding."

"What a vehement defense. Is your companion so desperately in need of a husband she must scrounge for one in the dungeons?"

"We would all do well to seek husbands there, when the finest men in the kingdom are consigned to prison cells for protecting us from derelicts."

Lord Tyran smirked and took a step nearer. "That is the great mystery of the matter. No one knows what drove Callen to butcher my men. It was a baser urge than protectiveness, I dare say. You wouldn't be able to enlighten us, would you?"

"I know Callen gave his word he had just cause for his actions. I also know your guards have wagging tongues. Which do you think I regard as more reliable?"

"If wagging tongues concern you, you ought to ask your handmaiden if she spends her nights where a girl in her position ought to."

Lord Tyran's retainers snickered, while Lord Hadrian's expression darkened, and Lady Hadrian tightened her hand on her husband's arm.

"How dare you?" Cassia advanced on Lord Tyran. "You question the honor of my companion? You question the honor of my household?"

He gave a laugh. "If you are going to suggest someone else's dependents are guilty of improper conduct, you should first ensure your own are blameless."

"You discredit no one but yourself with your insinuations. My handmaiden is a woman of great character. She is worthy of only the highest praise, and I am fortunate to have her as a companion."

"How well do you know your dependents, Lady Cassia?"

"Lord Tyran, are you questioning *my* diligence? *My* judgment? *My* honor?"

Lord Tyran put on a confident, handsome smile that did not reach his eyes. "I assure you, my lady, those remarks are not directed at you."

Cassia took yet another step nearer. "Any remarks about my handmaiden are remarks about me. Her troubles are my troubles. Her enemies are my enemies."

His eyes narrowed. He gave a shallow, but significant bow. "Well. I will see to it they do not forget that...should I meet any who qualify."

"I think we understand one another, Lord Tyran." Cassia held up her purse. "Therefore, my offer stands. Will you accept Verruc's life price from me?"

Lord Tyran cast a glance at the prize in Cassia's hands, then at Lord Hadrian. "Too old to go to war and dancing with young women instead? You'd be better off quitting the field and the floor."

"The lady invited me to dance, and I said yes. One does not refuse His Majesty's daughter."

Lord Tyran turned a more considering eye upon Cassia. "I've never known the king not to charge into battle himself."

"He leads the charge that shapes the kingdom," she replied. "Meanwhile I am left to my dancing."

"Hm." Lord Tyran almost smiled. "Promise me a liegehound from the royal kennels with that purse, and we have a bargain."

"A dog of Knight's breeding costs more than Verruc's life price, and I am already paying you more than your due, for I have not deducted the fine for assault."

Lord Tyran's smile was gone. "You have no proof Verruc attacked anyone."

"You will refuse the king's daughter a dance?"

"The king has not given me permission to dance with you."

"Our little turn about the floor is beneath his notice," she reminded Lord Tyran. But her sway on him was weakening. Her threats were enough to shock him out of his complacency and make him realize he could not disregard her. But she did not truly frighten him.

Yet. That day would come. That was her silent promise to Perita and every other woman who had suffered under this man's ill-deserved leadership.

In the meantime, Lord Tyran had made it all too obvious he was vulnerable to bribes. Cassia coaxed, "Are you sure you do not wish to promise me a dance? It would be a shame to miss such an opportunity. We might speak of so many things while we danced…things even more valuable than liegehounds."

Now he smiled. "A lady so adamant as yourself is sure to be a leader among the court's dancers. I can imagine how fruitful any conversation with you must be."

He recognized her words for what they were: the offer of a favor. She had convinced him she was influential enough to deliver.

Cassia wanted to send him running with his tail between his legs. But she had already known such victories for justice were few and far between. She could curb her disappointment, if not her anger, and do whatever she must to free Callen this very day.

One never knew what might befall Lord Tyran later.

"What do you say?" Cassia prompted. "Shall we dance?"

He bowed deeply. "Lady Cassia. I will gladly accept your purse…and a future dance. Just the two of us."

She gave him a curtsy in return and placed the bag of coin in his palm. But she did not release it.

"Ah yes, of course." He lifted his free hand at his retainer. "Retrieve one of the heralds from the pavilion."

Assured she would soon have Callen's pardon in writing, Cassia let go of the purse. Presently one of the men who recorded the proceedings for Lord Titus joined them with a travel desk propped on his arm. It was the herald she had shown the seal of Kyria the night she'd spoken at the Summit.

"Do you have a scale?" Cassia demanded of the herald.

"That won't be necessary." Lord Tyran sifted through the contents of Cassia's purse, letting gold rings and jeweled ear baubles slide through his fingers. He smiled at her over the treasure and lifted one delicate neck chain to his lips. "I will accept my lady Cassia's word."

A statement from Lord Tyran, the scratching of the herald's quill, and Cassia held in her hand a slip of paper worth Callen's life.

Lord Tyran gave her one more bow and a smile that threatened of their future dance. Bouncing the purse in his hand, he departed to rejoin the growing crowd in the pavilion.

As soon as he was out of earshot, Cassia turned to Lord and Lady Hadrian.

He smiled at her. "Well done."

She had seldom heard him praise anyone. She gave him a deep curtsy. "I thank you, my lord."

In front of everyone on the green, he gave her a bow, one much deeper than a bastard had any right to expect.

Her cheeks flushed. "The Hesperines haven't arrived yet. We have just enough time before the negotiations begin."

Now Lord Hadrian leapt into action, his element, and headed for the palace and the king's prison. As Cassia fell into step with him and Lady Hadrian, she saw he still wore the rare smile. Was he looking forward to the expression on the warden's face as much as Cassia was?

The best sight of all would be the look on Perita's face as she helped her beloved Callen out of that cell.

BEAUTY

ONIGHT LIO TOOK CASSIA'S absence from the ruin as an invitation and wasted no time making his way to her rooms. He didn't even pause at the king's door. He didn't want to think about the king or anyone else in this sunbound palace, only to go to her.

His awareness of her at the Summit had made the excruciating negotiations bearable. While the free lords' fears had crippled yet another attempt to resolve tensions about the Mercy and Lio's hunger had threatened to defeat him, Cassia's scent had been heady with boldness and triumph. What had she been up to today?

When he entered her rooms, he found Cassia seated by the hearth in the light of a gentle fire. Knight lay dutifully in the open door of the bedroom, surveying his domain.

Cassia smiled at Lio. "Sir, manifesting through a closed door is even more remarkable than appearing suddenly before me in the woods. I dare say I am the only lady in the palace whose champion can accomplish such a feat."

He grinned at her. He felt he had left all the hopeless events of the night on the other side of her door.

The Blood Union echoed with her sense of victory. "I have given Perita the night to herself."

Lio stalked closer to Cassia. "Which means we have your chambers to ourselves?"

"Mm. Until dawn."

As he drew near, Cassia stood and went to the chair across from her, pushing it a little closer to her own seat. She gave Lio a shy smile of welcome.

He took the chair she offered, and she did not return to her own. He leaned back, enjoying his awareness of her standing behind him. She slid her hands over his shoulders, giving him a gentle rub.

The naturalness and intimacy of the moment took his breath away. As if they need not hide. As if they might share without fear of consequences.

Her hands slid upward, easing under his hair to caress his neck. He stretched his legs out before him and tilted his head farther back to rest against her.

She smiled down at him. "I would offer you a glass of wine, but I have something else you like even better."

He reached up and brought her hand to his mouth. He placed a kiss on the soft skin on the inside of her wrist, where her pulse beat. "I come for an evening toast, and you offer me a nightlong feast."

The thrill that went through her at his words teased his senses. She stepped around to face him. The chair on the other side of the fire seemed too far away. He drew her to him with her hand, to see if she would take the invitation. She did, and he gathered her in his lap.

Her body fit against his as if they were made to sit just this way. He wrapped his arms around her, savoring the feel of her bundled on his lap, her head tucked against his shoulder, her hip pressing in just the right place to tantalize him.

"What did you do today?" he asked her. "You are as pleased as the bear that got the honeycomb. Did you hatch a plot while I was sleeping, and does it have anything to do with this change from drugging your handmaiden to dismissing her for the night?"

"You are still too passionate to be a diplomat, but your perceptiveness may make up for it."

He ran his fingers along the outside of her thigh. "I only regret I was not here to assist you." He had been locked in the fortress. In those sunlit hours while he slept, she lived a whole, dangerous life. It had never irked him this much before.

But he was the one whose lap she curled up in at the end of the day to confess her secret plans. He was content with that. More than content. Only he wanted all the rest too.

How had gaining so much made him want so much more?

He listened with rapt attention as she told him of Perita and Callen. His heart went out to them in the way a Hesperine's always did, which made such things difficult to hear. What engrossed his heart was how Cassia's vision of herself progressed in the telling. She related nothing but facts, but what those facts meant to her was that she had set out to right an injustice for no other reason than a desire to help. She had broken her silence and tried to earn a friend. And she had succeeded.

Lio was the one who heard her speak of it and the one who understood how important it was in a world defined by the irrevocable sound of catapults in the night. One woman had listened, and another had been heard. One Cassia had managed to ensure one Perita's safety and happiness and give one Callen back his life.

"She's with him now," Cassia finished. "Lord and Lady Hadrian have provided him with a safe place to recover in their servants' quarters. Perita will have plenty of help while she cares for Callen through the night according to the healers' instructions."

"Congratulations, Cassia. That was well done indeed."

She tensed in his embrace, looking away. "It was the least I could do."

"No, it was not."

The firelight set her hair and lashes agleam, but her gaze was shadowed, cast toward the hearth instead of him. "I," she began. "When I saw Callen there in his cell, I thought…"

What was it she struggled to explain? "That must have been difficult."

Cassia curled closer to Lio. All the most pleasing parts of her moved against him, and he tightened his arms around her.

"It just about killed Perita," Cassia said, "to see the man she loved in that state. I thought how I would feel if I were her, and how I would do anything to keep him safe and by me."

Lio didn't breathe. He didn't move. He just held Cassia, not daring to respond or remark on those words, for fear she would retreat if he called them what they were.

For fear his own wanting for those words would become too strong, and the knowledge he could not, must not want them would become far too painful to bear.

This was the nearest she might ever come to telling him she…

"Cassia." He nuzzled her neck. He could only drink from her, make love to her. Pleasure was all he could give her in return for those almost-words.

She reached up and caressed his face, turning him to her as she turned in his lap to bring her throat closer. He kissed her there, a rough, thorough kiss that quickened her pulse under his lips.

"This chair…" he murmured against her throat.

"…is not nearly so sturdy as a pillar that has stood for centuries."

"Precisely."

She slid off his lap and stood before him. "There's a reason I brought half my bedclothes to the fireside."

That inviting pile under her feet was indeed a heap of blankets. Her bare feet. Moisture filled his mouth at the sight of her toes and their freckles peeping at him from under the hem of her gardening dress.

Her fingers went to the little hollow under her throat, luring his gaze upward. She watched his face as she unlaced her gown. She pulled the dress open slowly, inviting Lio to feast with his eyes. Her shoulders emerged. Then the top contours of her breasts.

Her hands were not clenched into fists. She did not shove her dress off in an anxious rush. She slid her arms out of the sleeves and let the fabric fall away to reveal her breasts to his gaze. Slowly, so slowly, she let her gown slide down over her body to fall at her feet. She stood before him wrapped in nothing but the long mantle of her hair. The powerful fragrance that reached out to lure him to her was not that of a woman who felt exposed.

She felt bold. Strong.

She saw herself.

He said her name. It was the only word he could find that was sufficient praise.

He knelt before her. Her hands came to his head, trailing sensations over his scalp as her fingers played through his hair. With his hands on her hips, he placed a slow kiss on her belly and felt her muscles twitch with anticipation under his tongue. He let himself devour her, feasting only on the taste of her skin from one hipbone to the other, from the crown of hair at the vee of her thighs, to her navel and upward to the crescents under her breasts.

Her hands descended to his shoulders, and she began to work his veil hours robe off of him at the same seductive pace as she had disrobed. Halfway down his chest, she knelt in front of him to let her fingers wander further still. When she reached his waist, he caught her hands, pulling her arms around him. She held him tightly as he swept her hair back away from her neck.

When his teeth pierced her, she gave a sigh and melted into him. Her welcome made him moan. The taste of her, again, struck him as powerfully as the first time. He wrapped his hand around her bare buttock and held her close against him as he feasted, his other hand tangled in the length of her hair.

He drank his fill in long, fast draughts. He reveled in her. If her words had not hinted at it, if the way she held him did not make it clear, he would have known from this new taste in her blood. He could actually taste it, this powerful thing flowing in both their veins, which they dare not name.

After he was sated, he kept drinking for the sheer joy of her. She kept holding him, now spreading her knees and clutching him between her legs, nearly climbing on his lap where they knelt with his robe tangled between them. He traced one finger between her buttocks and felt her flinch with pleasure at his caress. He slid his hand farther and dipped his fingertips in the moisture between her legs. She arched her back, tilting her backside to let his hand reach deeper into her krana.

The arousal in her blood became a more powerful drug than blood itself. He lifted his head with a gasp. He licked and kissed the wound just enough to close it, drawing new shudders from her.

There was no deciding who would state their wishes tonight. Without speaking, he leaned back, and she pressed forward, and he let her push him down onto his back on their blankets. A thrill went through him at her straddling him, as much his excitement as hers.

She pulled his robe away, laying him bare to her. Firelight played across her umbrous skin, casting her freckles in light, then darkness as she lowered herself over him.

He took her hips in both his hands, steadying her as she found her way. She was beautiful, her small breasts swinging slightly as she fitted herself over him for the first time. Then hot moisture touched the head of his rhabdos, and she was pressing down, covering him in her.

Lio snapped his teeth shut. His feast had made him painfully thick and ready, her fiercely tight with need. She made it halfway down his shaft before she had to retreat and advance again. She caught her lower lip between her teeth, thrusting her hips down as he thrust up, and this time she took him completely.

He could not hold back a groan. She let out a rough sigh. Almost a moan, but not quite. For all her bold words, she was otherwise so quiet through their pleasures.

But her body spoke. She began to move on him, slowly at first. A pleasure to watch and to endure. As she found the way she moved under him worked well in reverse, her gentle exploration intensified to a reckless rhythm. With his hands and his thrusts, he told her *yes. Don't stop. You are beautiful when you lose control.*

She rocked harder, swifter on him. She bit down harder on her lip. He reached up and pulled her closer until he could take that lip between his. The kiss turned into a mime of their lovemaking. He thrust his tongue in her mouth.

She feasted on him. He tasted her blood where his teeth nicked her, felt her teeth on his tongue. The flavor of her full pleasure bloomed in his mouth an instant before she came apart utterly. She bucked and shuddered on his rhabdos, her body rubbing over his. He held her to him, wanting to hold every instant of this, of her.

She was incredible. She was everything he wanted.

He wanted this feast on each other never to end.

A cry wrenched out of him as he spilled inside her. His whole body arched, lifting them both off the blankets. For a handful of moments, all he felt was their perfect, simultaneous pleasure pumping together in a single beat.

He fell back under her, taking great gulps of air that filled him with her scent. He listened to her panting, felt the wild flutter of her heartbeat against him. Happiness broke out of her like a second climax, and he shivered.

But that rush of emotion faded as quickly as it had come, and he knew they were thinking the same thing.

The Equinox was barely a fortnight away. A mere fortnight. The blink of an eye.

She did not speak for a long time, just allowed them this. Cassia, who allowed herself nothing, let them lay in silent, blissful denial.

That lured Lio to allow himself something. For a moment, just one moment, he imagined waking to this. To Cassia. Her blood, her body, her passion that had been trapped inside her for so long and was only just beginning to emerge.

Cassia. Night after night. No end in sight.

That was a future they could never have.

ONE FORTNIGHT

L IO HAD NEVER FELT such sickening certainty. He had spent his life
looking forward to his future. He had seldom dreaded anything. Now
he held Cassia and knew he must let her go.

He had never felt anything so crushing as the knowledge that he could
not look forward to her.

Why was he thinking like this? He was not looking for his Grace. He
had learned his lesson with Xandra. There was no comparison between
her and Cassia, but he knew better than to see his Grace in every person
with whom he shared. He no longer expected to discover his partner for
eternity so early in life.

He wasn't thinking of Grace. He wasn't asking for eternity. Just time.

He wanted what he and Cassia had, that was all. Something this good
deserved time. It might last a very long time indeed.

They would never have a chance to find out.

The idea of Cassia running away with him to Orthros was sheer fantasy. Such a thing was not possible in the world where she lived.

She was throwing off the king's shackles as never before, declaring
her freedom night after night. But when dawn came, she must be where
Lucis expected to find her, just as Lio must return to the fortress so the
guards could lock him in.

Lio had the power to free Cassia from Tenebra. He could do it, as
surely as he could walk into the sleeping king's bedchamber and put an
end to Lucis's tyranny once and for all. But the initiate ambassador knew
all too well that taking the king's daughter home with him would create
a disaster no less catastrophic than would assassinating Lucis himself.

Seducer. Violator. Kidnapper. In one stroke, Lio could do the right thing by Cassia and make himself a monster in the eyes of her people. He would give the humans here every reason to believe he was exactly what he labored so hard to convince them he was not.

He had come here to prevent a war upon his people, not give Tenebra a reason to start it.

Cassia had said a great deal about how she only served herself. That had been before frost fever. Before Perita and Callen. Lio knew Cassia was no more willing than he to pay for happiness with the blood of their people.

He would be a fool to think she would accept his offer of freedom, even if he made it. She was the greatest living expert on how Lucis made many pay for one subject's disobedience.

Cassia slid off of Lio, as if in echo of his thoughts. Even the Blood Union did not feel like enough to keep her close to him. She lay right next to him on the blankets, skin to skin, but she already felt so far away.

"The negotiations tonight…" Her tone was conversational, as if no great doom loomed ahead. "…what an utter waste. Imagine Lord Otho blaming Hesperines for his grave-robbing problem to cover up his inability to control the bandits in his domain. Just when I think I have seen all the free lords' idiocy, they descend to new depths."

"A disaster," Lio agreed.

"At this rate, it will be forever before they agree on anything. Fortnights. Months, perhaps."

Lio shut his eyes. His most immediate dread, he found, was this conversation. He had escaped it upon their last tryst. Not so tonight.

"That's the thing about diplomacy," she said. "It often proves to be a surprisingly slow and lengthy process."

Lio rolled onto his side and lay face-to-face with her. He took her cheek in his hand. "Cassia."

She met his gaze. Brave Cassia.

"The Queens will recall us at Equinox, Oath or no Oath."

Her face betrayed nothing, but her real reaction was a blow.

"You must understand," he said, "the embassy cannot remain in Tenebra when the rest of our people leave Orthros Boreou. The night after Spring Equinox is Migration Night. When the hours of darkness shorten in the north, all Hesperines journey to our home in the south, Orthros Notou. There the darkness grows longer, and the Empire is near. When summer arrives here, it will be winter there."

"Winter out of season? It sounds like a different world."

Lio struggled to find words that would make that distant place seem closer to her. But he found none. It felt impossibly far away from her to him, too.

"But you'll return?" she asked.

"Yes. At the Autumn Equinox, we come north to Orthros Boreou again."

They gazed at each other in silence. He would come back to Orthros Boreou, but not to Tenebra. They both knew the first Summit in centuries would also be the last, perhaps for centuries more.

"Goddess knows I'm sorry," he said.

"Don't apologize. I am used to such things. Good things don't last long in Tenebra."

"Goddess," he said again. A prayer. A protest. *Goddess,* he asked her in silence. *Why?*

"I expected nothing, Lio. And yet we will have one more fortnight. A whole fortnight of…what I never imagined for myself. That's more than I ever asked for."

All her life she had survived on crumbs. A fortnight was not enough of a feast to make up for that.

A fortnight out of the countless years that lay ahead of him was not. Enough.

"It may be…not quite that long." At last he twisted the knife. But she deserved to know.

For the first time, he saw it in her eyes. As if she wanted to shake her fist at someone. But she had no gods she trusted enough to ask why.

"What?" Her voice sounded thick.

"The negotiations are…a catastrophe. The king seems pleased to watch the free lords destroy peace before his very eyes. My uncle fears that all along, the king has had a malicious purpose for convening the Summit."

"Of course he has." She sounded hollow now.

Lio fitted his hand to the dip above Cassia's hipbone. As if he could hold her. "If Uncle Argyros is right, we will not stay. When the Queens sent us, they commanded us to put our safety first and return immediately if we suspected danger. My elders will not disobey."

Cassia's expression steeled. "If the king is planning something, we must discover what it is."

Lio slid his arm around her waist. "That's what I wanted to ask you tonight. Would you be willing to undertake another plot with me? The stakes will be even higher than the lives threatened by frost fever. As hard as that is to imagine. A war between the Mage Orders and Hesperines errant on Tenebran soil…"

"You are the stakes, Lio. War or no war, I will help you."

He pulled her close and buried his nose in her hair. "Thank you."

"We will do whatever we must."

"If we uncover the king's plot and I warn the others in time, we may be able to protect ourselves and mitigate the diplomatic damage. Or, if we can determine he has no ulterior motive…"

"Then it will be safe for you to stay until the Equinox."

His throat tightened. "I want my fortnight, Cassia."

Without saying another word, she pulled him down to her, and he tucked her beneath him in silent agreement. They would make the most of every night they had.

14

days until

SPRING EQUINOX

WHAT DEAD MEN SEE

I N THE SERVANTS' QUARTERS of Lord and Lady Hadrian's residence within the palace, everyone went about according to their wont, as if the world were not coming to an end. For their world wasn't. It was only her own Cassia fought to rescue. It was only she who felt so keenly aware that every day, every moment counted.

Even if she could discover Lucis's plan in time, it would win her no more than a fortnight with Lio.

There must be something she had yet to discover that would be the leverage she and Lio needed. There had to be an opening somewhere, however slight, evidence of a strategy they could undertake. She would go everywhere she could today, listen to everything within reach of her ears. She had begun at dawn rites and would begin again after dusk rites, when the maneuvers on the greensward would continue.

The peace of Callen's room stemmed the furious tide of her day. His quiet, even breathing. The sun streaming in the window over his bed. The sleepy calm on Perita's face. Cassia had not a moment to spare, but spare it she would for Perita. This endeavor of growing trust was unfamiliar. Cassia didn't know how often one must tend the seedling for it to thrive. When a gardener was unsure of such things, she kept a close eye on her plant, didn't she?

Cassia bade Knight guard the door and stepped further inside Callen's room. Perita appeared genuinely glad to see her. The plant was not in danger of wilting today.

Cassia nodded in greeting and took the extra chair. She studied their sleeping patient. "How is he?"

Perita kissed his hand. "Out of danger. The mages said he's likely to wake from the sleeping draught anytime now. They left plenty of pain tonic in case he's hurting when he rouses, and Lady Hadrian's household has scarcely let us alone for a moment. They've been so kind." A grim expression crossed Perita's face. "Callen can't go back to the barracks, at least not for a while yet. I fear…never mind. No sense worrying about what will come next. That's like throwing the gods' blessings back in their faces."

Rivalries died far less easily than men. Perita had reason to worry about what might happen once Callen returned to his service in Lord Hadrian's guard.

If Callen rejoined them at all. Cassia eyed the wounded soldier's knee, but the blankets hid it from view. Kyrian magic had saved his life and his leg, but would Callen ever march again?

If Cassia had lent her aid sooner, would his fate have been different?

"Come what may, Perita, my promise to you was not merely for a day."

"My lady…I know." Perita shook her head, her face alight. "This morning, all the gossip has changed. It's all over Solorum. Not the terrible things Lord Tyran's guards were saying about me. The words you said to him, for my sake."

"Our words. If not for you, I would not have found the words to say, or known it was time to speak."

"If not for you, I'd never have been able to tell anyone the truth."

"Would that I could have done more. Lord Tyran should have paid you the fine for Verruc's crimes against you. Where is your justice?"

"The maggots, not the magistrates, can be trusted to carry out justice on Verruc, for me and all the women he wronged."

"Well, I cannot argue with that. But Lord Tyran is still due for sentencing. I am not done with him, I assure you."

"I'm afraid you aren't. You promised him a favor. For Callen and me."

"Yes, and I would do it again."

"My lady, he's dangerous."

"So are we."

Perita smiled. "Aye. That's why I want you to know I'll be watching your back. You'll need my ear to the ground from now on, I expect."

Cassia returned her smile. "Let's make that favor backfire on him most terribly."

They fell into their first comfortable silence.

Not long after, Lady Hadrian came by. She spoke with her usual perfect decorum, asking Perita a slew of interested and informed questions on Callen's condition. She always had the right words to say to everyone, of any station.

"If I might pull you away for a moment, Lady Cassia. It won't take long." Lady Hadrian smiled. "If Perita can bear for us to leave her alone with Callen for a moment. We'll be just within reach in the corridor."

Perita smiled. "Thank you, Your Ladyship."

"By all means, my lady." Cassia accompanied their hostess out of the room.

Lady Hadrian led her and Knight into the corridor and just out of earshot of Perita. Seeing the expression on her face, Cassia feared she was about to receive more praise and gratitude for which she had no reply.

But Lady Hadrian refrained. "I hope you will join me for another weaving party the day after tomorrow."

"Gladly. It is generous of you to include me. I'm sure my project would be hopeless otherwise."

Lady Hadrian chuckled. "It is you and the other young ladies who show your generosity to me by consenting to be a captive audience." Cassia opened her mouth to protest, but Lady Hadrian held up a hand. "I do not require unconditional enthusiasm, nor do I expect the pretense of it. In fact, you will find all I ask for is good company."

"The company around you is always the best."

"A benefit—a consolation—of my position. It delights me to have young ladies like my daughters around me. My husband must always be at the king's side, and I at my husband's, while our daughters are seldom at court, as you know. We could not do without Sabina to look after her younger sisters. We are so proud of how capably she assists us in the management of our households and estates. It is one of His Majesty's generosities to my lord, that she may stay in Hadria."

"What a boon to your younger daughters and your people, that your eldest is always there to see to their needs."

What a boon to Sabina, that she was far from royal machinations. How Lucis must slaver to serve up for his own ends the female heir of the most powerful free lord in Tenebra. What piece of his soul had Lord Hadrian bargained away to protect his beloved daughter? How much of Lord Hadrian's soul remained to him, after he had paid so much of it in service to Lucis? Did he, who made the king strong enough to stop the slaughter of the feuds, find it worth the price?

"Sabina is a blessing to us and our people. She has her father's strength of will." Lady Hadrian laughed. "And his temper."

Cassia smiled with the lady and said nothing. Perhaps the most generous reply was silence that allowed Lady Hadrian to speak of her daughter.

Her tone was wistful. "I hope you will meet her one day. Before Sabina left court, she and your sister were great friends."

Cassia shifted her feet to make sure the floor was still there.

Lady Hadrian had broken the silence.

Cassia had always suspected Lady Hadrian knew what the king had done to Solia, for it seemed she was privy to all her husband's secrets. Now, after what she'd said about keeping her daughter away from the king, Cassia was certain.

For the first time in fourteen years, one of the few survivors who knew the truth had spoken to Cassia of her sister.

"I would treasure any friend of Solia's." There. Cassia, too, had invoked her aloud.

"We do the best we can for Sabina…and for you, Cassia, although you are not often at court with us, either. Our princess bade us take care of you in her absence. We took that to heart when Her Highness did not return. I hope we have not failed to fulfill Solia's wish."

Cassia's throat closed.

Lady Hadrian gazed back at her in silence. Waiting, Cassia realized. For thanks? Or for…forgiveness?

"You have my gratitude," Cassia said, although Lady Hadrian would not understand the full significance of those words. "No one in Tenebra has been kind to me as you and His Lordship have. Not since we lost her."

The lady's perfect, tense posture changed to the relaxed poise of relief. She did Cassia yet another kindness and guided them into a different subject. "My lord and I look after our own, down to the last man. The mages provided us with further details of Callen's condition, which I thought to share with you."

"Please."

"By the time the mages were able to attend to his wound, it was too late for even magic to restore his leg to full strength. He has not lost his life or health, but he will no longer be able to serve in the field."

"That is...not the news we hoped for. I cannot say how much I regret it."

"My lord and I share your regrets. Callen came into my lord's service as a youth and has proved himself honorable and capable. His character and ability earned him a place in my lord's capital guard. He had a promising career ahead of him."

"Surely he might still serve you in a different capacity."

"The gods have seen fit to bless my lord and me with seven healthy daughters. Yet we feel we are wealthy in sons as well. My lord's soldiers are also his heirs, who shall inherit all he has labored to achieve for Tenebra. We will not leave Callen stranded without a future, especially not now, when his and Perita's hopes rest on his livelihood."

"House duty, perhaps?"

"Given my lord's position, even our house guards must be battle ready at all times. However, service in a less demanding household would be an excellent situation for Callen. Which brings me to the favor my lord and I wish to ask of you, if you would assist us yet again."

"If there is anything more I can do for Callen, consider it done."

"What do you think of taking him into your employ as your body-guard? Ensuring a lady's day-to-day safety would be well within his capabilities."

Cassia's heart sank. "I would, certainly, but I fear such a decision is farther out of my hands than paying Verruc's life price. Only the king can approve an addition to his household."

"My lord can easily settle it with your father, if you are amenable." Lady Hadrian gave Knight the sort of look one turned upon an ancestral tapestry that could not be taken down, no matter how ragged it became. "You need a capable man at your disposal."

Cassia resisted the urge to protest that Knight was more than enough protection. It was the truth, but now was not the time for protest of any kind, not when she was so close to having both Callen and Perita assigned to her. It would be an ideal situation for the couple.

And a fine situation for Cassia as well. A real soldier in her service? She had never imagined such an asset. If anyone could convince the king to let Cassia have a soldier, it was Lord Hadrian.

"I cannot express how delighted I am at your suggestion, Lady Hadrian. Nothing would please me more than to have Callen and Perita by me. They would be assured of my support for their marriage." Cassia could already predict the king's decision on that score. It pleased him when people married. Spouses and children were means of control. He would think having Perita's husband under his thumb would make it easier for him to extract anything he wished out of his spy within his daughter's rooms.

He would be wrong. Cassia and Perita had each other's backs, and Callen's, too. None of them would be victims of the king. Never again.

"It's settled then." Lady Hadrian smiled.

Cassia envisioned a day when she might smile so and be assured of such things being settled by her own hand.

One hound, one handmaiden, and one soldier were not a vast household by any means. But Cassia found she felt a great deal wealthier now than she had before she had surrendered all the gold and jewels she possessed to Lord Tyran.

When she returned to Callen's room, Cassia found Perita out of her chair and sitting on the bedside. His eyes were open, his hand clasped in hers. Cassia took a step back, unwilling to interrupt a private moment. But it was hard to be surreptitious with Knight at her side.

Perita looked up and beamed. "My lady. He's awake!"

Cassia took that as an invitation and ventured inside. "So he is. A pleasure to meet you at last, Callen."

"My lady." Callen nodded his head on the pillow. A wry smile, or perhaps a grimace, crossed his lips. "I'd bow if I could."

"Don't give that a thought." Cassia took her seat again.

"I owe you a great deal more than a bow, my lady." He was quiet for a moment, and he struck Cassia as a man who spoke only well-considered words. "If there is any way I can thank you, you have but to say. My lord Hadrian permitting, I will do as you ask."

"You owe me nothing. It is I who wish to thank you for keeping Perita safe."

He pulled Perita's hand closer to him. "If I'd known what was going on, I'd have put a stop to it sooner."

"And gotten yourself arrested sooner." Perita stroked the back of his hand.

"With no regrets," he replied.

"Callen," Cassia said, "I hope you will allow me to show my gratitude by promoting you into royal service. Would you consider accepting a position as my bodyguard? Lord and Lady Hadrian have given me the happy news they are willing to spare you for my sake, for I am in great need of someone of your skill."

Perita and Callen exchanged a surprised glance, hers hopeful, his conflicted.

"Service to the king is not easy work," Cassia warned him. "Perita has told you, I am sure. But she can also tell you it has its advantages. For my part, I can assure you I will treat you fairly and lend all the assistance I can to make it possible for you to marry as soon as you wish."

Callen's gaze fell and lingered on the blankets over his knee.

"Of course," Cassia said, "you'll need time to think on my offer and discuss it with Perita."

His gaze lifted to Perita and finally came to rest on her hand that held his. "Thank you, my lady, but I'm fit enough to answer now. I would be honored to serve you."

A smart man, to hold fast to that hand, instead of a lost cause.

"Thank you, my lady." Perita was...glowing.

Cassia cleared her throat. "You can remain here until you're on your feet again. You are to take your time healing, Callen. I'll want you completely fit before you report for duty."

"Yes, my lady," he said obediently. He knew the promise of time off when he heard it, judging by that smile.

But the look Perita exchanged with Callen now was not a lovestruck one. "You should tell her what you told me. See if it isn't something she'd want to know."

"It's nothing to concern you, my lady," Callen hastened to say.

"It's just the sort of thing to concern her," said Perita. "My lady likes information."

Cassia was more fortunate in her companion than she had known. "Perita is right. Any insight you have to offer would be invaluable, Callen."

The inside of the barracks was the world of men. Cassia had few eyes and ears there...and none at all in the prison wing where men were sent to die.

Callen shifted in his bed, wincing when he let his lower half move too much. Perita busied herself arranging his blankets more comfortably. His gaze followed her, as if he sought an anchor to save him from slipping back into what he saw in his mind's eye.

"Not every man in that place is given the privilege of waiting for the headsman. Some of them are..." Callen hesitated. "This discussion isn't fit for your ears, my lady."

"I have not had a soft upbringing in a lady's tower. And you know already how strong Perita is."

"Aye, that I do."

"What did you see in the western wing? What are they doing to the men?"

"Torturing certain of them for information. That's no surprise, but what's strange is who, and how. As mad as I got with fever, I'm certain it was him I saw coming down every night. At first, when I was still lucid, I...I may have acted a great deal worse off than I was, so they'd leave me be. They thought me too ill to be of any use, even before I really was that far gone. I was still clearheaded enough at the beginning to be sure it was him. Otherwise I wouldn't say this."

"Who?" Cassia tried not to sound too eager.

"His Majesty's mage." Callen's tone was almost apologetic. "Honored Master Amachos."

What could the royal mage want with doomed prisoners? How could she use it against him? "What was he doing there, Callen?"

"I have to warn you, my lady, it hardly seems possible. I wouldn't normally utter such nonsense. I'm not a fanciful man."

"Go on."

"He…*burned* them…till they talked. Shot fire right out of his hands. Just like in the legends." Callen gestured with his own hands. "I saw him twitch his fingers at a man in the cell across from me and…never mind. Normally a man would need a hot iron for that. The length of the cell was between them, and all the royal mage needed were his bare hands. But that's impossible, of course." He met Cassia's gaze. "No mages from Tenebra can do that."

"You're exactly right, Callen." There was only one place where such skills were taught, and even there, only the elite learned them.

"What do you make of that, my lady?" Perita asked, nodding. She already knew.

There was only one thing they could make of it. Amachos was not from any temple in Tenebra.

He was a war mage from the Order of Anthros in Cordium with power to rival a Hesperine's.

"His Majesty appointed Honored Master Amachos out of Namenti," Callen said staunchly. "Everyone knows that. Isn't that right, my lady?"

Perita patted his hand. "Of course. I'd stand before the king and answer to that."

"That's the fact of the matter," Cassia agreed. "Which is why, after you have told me everything you saw and heard, Callen, no matter how strange and wild, there is no reason for any of us ever to speak of such impossibilities outside this room."

SOLIA'S SECRET

ASSIA HAD KNOWN AMACHOS was dangerous. As soon as she noticed his passionless demeanor, she should have tried to discover what lay behind it. If she had dared venture into politics before—if she had only *acted*—it might never have come to this.

Now it might already be too late.

And yet she could not make a move until she had a strategy. Even with every scrap of information Callen had given her, she did not yet know enough.

She sat at his bedside awhile longer, sat useless and still in her chair and tried to keep her fear from showing, when all she wanted to do was leap into action. Callen slipped back into sleep. Perita watched him in silence. Cassia thought hard.

The king must be aware of Amachos's activities in the prison, as surely as he already knew Cassia had been down there. She had yet to discover if there would be retribution for how she had taken matters into her own hands and whether or not Lord and Lady Hadrian's involvement would cushion the blow. Cassia could not afford to think on it now.

The mage's interrogations in the western wing could never have taken place without the king's sanction. That meant Lucis knew exactly who and what Amachos was.

The king himself was hiding a war mage in their midst. The deception had been going on all along. Lio's uncle had been right to fear. The Cordian Order of Anthros had not sent a war mage to smile and watch the king make amends with the heretics.

It was unlikely the conspiracy reached far. The king would never risk word getting out that he had welcomed Cordium into Tenebra with open arms and lied about it. The Tenebran mages, the free lords, the people, everyone would be up in arms.

The prison guards of the western wing would dispose of the burnt corpses of the mage's victims. They didn't ask questions when the king ordered them to clean up a mess. The only ones who bore witness to Amachos's real power were men deemed already dead. Callen alone had lived to tell the tale.

The plot Cassia and Lio must thwart surely began and ended with the mage and the king. Amachos had been conspiring with Lucis each day during their private audiences.

The answers Cassia now sought could be in only one place. The one unbreachable fortress in the kingdom. The king's solar.

The only way to know what he was planning was to get an ear behind that door.

Cassia had never been in that room except on her knees. The king had never said anything she could use against him, only words he used against her.

What could she possibly do?

The secrets she knew were not enough. Real answers…real weapons…lay out of her reach.

Cassia realized she had closed her hands around the edges of her chair. She felt immobile. As if she must make herself a part of that chair. She was the one who must sit. Who must try to be still. Who must not cry out or wail or weep.

She who moved too much was pushed to her knees. She who spoke too loud was silenced.

She was pushed and silenced until she sat and watched and choked her own grief back down inside herself.

Cassia uncurled her hands.

She would not stay on her knees. She would not be silent. By all the uncaring gods of Tenebra, by the goddess no one in Tenebra listened to anymore, she would not sit in this chair and watch the king be the death of another person she loved.

Cassia got to her feet.

Perita's gaze met hers. Cassia held a finger to her lips. Her companion nodded once. Then Cassia escaped the quiet, ordered residence.

A single afternoon. That was how much time Cassia had for her first attempt to get behind the solar door.

Her only attempt.

Now was not the time to shy away from the truth. The last woman who had learned the secrets the king kept in that room had paid for them with her life.

How had Solia known so much? She had certainly never explained such a dangerous secret to her seven-year-old Pup. But Cassia had heard the conversations between her sister and Lady Iris. The details had made little sense to her as a child, but now she recalled them with the understanding of a woman. She could appreciate the breadth of the information her sister had possessed and, she hoped, draw some conclusions about how Solia might have obtained it.

Solia had known things the king would only discuss with the highest ranking and most obedient. She had surely relied upon a most sophisticated web of informants, but even that could not sufficiently explain how she had always known what the king's next move would be.

But in a secret conversation between the king and one of his loyalists, there was no one to report their words to the princess. Could it be she had relied on the same tactics Cassia employed—her own eyes and ears?

Could Solia herself have been the spy in the solar?

If the answer could be found, it would be here at Solorum. Cassia had access to Solia's old rooms and any clues that might remain there. This was perhaps the best, the only chance Cassia had ever had. She would not squander it.

The king was in his solar even now. Amachos might be joining him for their afternoon conference any moment. Cassia knew what she had to do. There was little time for preparation and no room for caution or self-defense. She must discover for herself what the king was planning, in the way only one of his daughters could.

When she got back to her rooms, she began to collect everything that might assist her. Knight paced back and forth across her chambers with her. She wasn't certain what she would need, but more scent oils might prove necessary casualties if a door threatened to squeal. She would need a tool if she were called upon to coax a loose stone out of the masonry to reveal a hidden compartment or passageway. She put several vials and her spade into her gardening satchel.

Cassia hesitated, fingering Solia's pendant. She drew the talisman out and lifted it over her head.

For the first time, the ribbon hung about Cassia's neck, and she saw the ivy symbol upon her own breast. It was not as heavy as she had expected. As she tucked the secret out of sight under her tunica, the wood felt strangely warm on her skin. A shiver went through her.

She pushed herself out the door of her chambers and set her course for Solia's rooms. Her hands shook. The sweating had started. She tangled one hand in Knight's ruff and tried to distance herself from the nausea rising in her.

This was the route she traversed to get to Lio each night. Today it was the route that would take her to the information she needed to keep him safe.

He seemed invincible. But he wasn't. Amachos had the power to harm Lio. He was the kind of mage who hated everything Lio was. He must only be waiting for an excuse—or a cue from the king.

In broad daylight, it took thrice as long to make her way to Solia's rooms without being seen. The pace of her progress made Cassia begin to sweat with frustration instead of fear. Her nausea receded and left in its wake the pure tension of urgency. She shook with something more powerful even than the anger that had become her strength in recent days. More compelling than the fear that had always governed her life.

She refused to be afraid. She refused to lose. Amachos would not harm one hair on Lio's head, nor put a single one of his people in danger. Cassia would not allow it.

She would give her own life instead, if that's what it took.

She hovered at the edges of the royal wings for a quarter of an hour, waiting for a break in the traffic of soldiers and officials to and from the king's solar. The break never came, and her sense of urgency became too great. She spent another quarter of an hour backtracking and leaving the palace by a side gate. To exercise Knight between the palace and the temple, she told the guards.

The hatch on the grounds was harder to get open from the outside. Pain shot down her back as she hurled it open, and the same spot twinged again when she pulled it shut over her and Knight.

She raced down the tunnel. In the garden, a careful glance reassured her this was still an empty, forgotten place. She slipped into Solia's rooms, thankful she had been trespassing here and leaving the lock undone. Quickly and quietly, she shut the garden door behind her.

It was dark as night until her eyes adjusted from the sunlit outdoors. Even then, the heavy drapes left the room too dim to see. Cassia could not search for answers like this.

She took a deep breath, then went from one window to the other, throwing back the curtains. Swarms of motes hovered in the bands of sunlight that flooded in, and she blinked away the sting of the dust.

She turned to face the room. For the first time in fourteen years, she saw Solia's sanctuary.

The vacant crypt in the temple received attention every day, but this memorial to Soli's kindness went untended. Everything here did look smaller, except for the big fireplace. The curtains that had been so elegant were now dull. Carpets and side tables, padded chairs and an embroidery frame slept under a gray shroud. Beneath the dust, Cassia glimpsed a threaded needle and a note in her sister's writing, which lay just where Soli had left them upon her departure for Desidia.

The little dressing table near the fireplace still held the princess's collection of delicate glass vials. The oil within them gleamed at Cassia.

In three steps she crossed the room. In one motion, she brought her hand down.

She stopped herself just in time, before the back of her hand swept them off to shatter on the hearthstones.

That smell. That faint acrid note under the fragrances. What was it?

Cassia bent nearer, waving her hand above the vials to bring their fumes to her nose. A chaos assailed her. Sickly sweet florals and cloying fruits, even more pungent after fourteen years of aging. But the bitter smell was there. She had not imagined it.

The odor was familiar. One that teased her memory...old memories? Recent ones? If only she could place it.

She braced herself and inhaled deeply again. Behind her, Knight sneezed. Cassia had to pause and bury her nose in her sleeve to ward off a sneeze of her own before she sniffed again. One of the many memories she had buried rose to life.

She was seven again. She hugged Knight in one arm and a doll in the other, tucking her knobby knees closer so none of her stuck out from under the dressing table. The hem of Solia's tunica brushed against her as her elder sister sat down on the stool before the table. Cassia and Knight both sneezed. What an awful smell. Solia did not seem bothered by it, though. She was sliding on the gloves her handmaidens told her she must wear to bed to preserve her delicate complexion. Next she would wrap her long, beautiful hair under her sleeping net to protect it, too.

What was that smell?

Cassia was fourteen. Flattery won her an hour in the royal apothecary's storeroom. He bragged her ear off about the rare concoctions he kept for the king, stroking his own pride while he unwittingly gave her an education. At the very last, the bony man adjusted his skullcap and leaned close. From a bronze lockbox, he withdrew his greatest treasure: a magically potent botanical oil His Majesty had purchased from the Cordian Order of Anthros for an undisclosed sum, which the royal armorers would soon use to treat a new suit of mail for the king.

The apothecary had visited the Order's gardens in Cordium personally and seen the herb, which had seven-fingered leaves that looked like tongues of flame. A temple's entire annual crop produced enough oil to cover only one suit of armor, but the warrior who wore it could walk under a rain of fire arrows without fear. It would do nothing to stop magefire, but against mundane flames, there was no more powerful protection. No wonder the Order of Anthros maintained their mages' exclusive right to grow the herb and guarded the magical secret of how to prepare its oil.

Although the apothecary did not allow Cassia to touch the elegant cut glass bottle, he let her smell its viscous golden contents. A bitter odor burned her nose and made her chest feel tight. It reminded her of something. But no, that could not be. The likes of her had never come so near the rare, prized oil before.

Flametongue.

Cassia opened her eyes and rifled through the dusty bottles on Solia's dressing table, bringing each one to her nose in turn. When tears came to her eyes, she knew she had found it. It was a slender vial of pink glass with a tassel about its neck and a little fabric label bearing an embroidered lily. But the cork had shrunk in the intervening years, and the seal was no longer enough to hide the odor.

How had Solia gained possession of such a thing? More importantly, why would a princess need to protect herself from fire?

A lady can walk through fire.

Solia *had* told Pup her dangerous secret. She had taught it to her little sister until Cassia could recite it in her sleep.

Solia had hidden her best secrets in plain sight. She had not taken the vial of flametongue with her for safekeeping on that final journey. She had left it behind for a reason.

For Cassia.

Cassia's gaze went to the fireplace. The enormous fireplace that was large enough for a grown man to stand in without hunching over.

The hearth had been cold a long time now, but all those years ago, it had never been without a merry fire…just like the hearth in the solar, which even now the servants kept hot at all hours of the day and night to accommodate the king's ceaseless schedule.

Only inner walls separated Solia's fireplace from the king's. A person could literally walk to the solar from here, assuming she could walk through fire…*and* stone.

Cradling the vial of flametongue oil in one hand, Cassia stepped near the hearth and peered inside. Just dust, ashes, and cobwebs. She leaned in and gazed upward. Not even she could fit up there, and she was smaller than Solia had been. Cassia studied the blackened back wall of the fireplace, scanning the uneven rows of stones and the seams between them. She could see no gaps or loose mortar, although it was hard to tell under the coat of soot. Perhaps it was time to begin tapping stones.

Best to solve one problem at a time. Cassia glanced at the vial, then at her clothes. Even if she stripped, it would take forever to rub it over every inch of her, and then the irreplaceable oil would be spent.

A lady always dresses correctly.

Cassia whispered the words to herself now as she glanced around the deserted chambers. No solution would have been practical for Solia except keeping a treated garment on hand to slip into whenever she went spying. She would naturally keep the remainder of the oil in reserve in case she had to mend a tear and treat that bit of the fabric again. Just like a knight with his suit of armor, who must get it repaired and re-oiled whenever a mace dented it.

Might the garment still be here? Solia would have hidden it well. Even so, it must have been something that would not look out of the ordinary in her possession, if its hiding place was discovered or she was caught wearing it. No handmaiden who got a whiff of it would know enough about flametongue to identify the scent. Unless that handmaiden was Lady Iris, whom Solia had trusted with her secrets. Cassia could only hope no one else had found the priceless garment and, mistaking it for odorous laundry that could not be rescued, disposed of it.

Cassia got to her feet and went into the next room, Solia's dressing room, to commence a search. She went through the ranks of wardrobes and dug through the heirloom chests, only to discover many of them empty. A princess's finery cost a king's ransom, and unlike drapery and furniture, it was not an ancestral fixture of these chambers. Caelum's mother had sported a wardrobe in the latest fashion, but Cassia had recognized the colors and patterns of the costly fabrics. She had hated Lucis a little more each time she saw his poor young bride wear a gown made of scraps of Solia's. The late queen really had been laid to rest in the royal crypt. They were all gone now, Solia and both queens and Cassia's mother, too.

She would be the next to join them. But she would not go to her grave in submission. She would take the king's plans with her.

Cassia found no false bottoms in the clothing chests or hidden compartments in the backs of the wardrobes. She sniffed every scrap the magpies had left in the dressing room, from Solia's simpler work gowns to her tunicae to her sleeping gloves. Even a handful of feathers that had shed from one of her elegant hats, which was long gone. None bore the telltale scent of flametongue.

Cassia searched her way back to the bedroom. She studied the items that sat on the little tables and opened drawers to go through their contents. A wooden hairbrush. One of her own dolls. A few books that had been favorites of Solia's, which Cassia had as a child aspired to read, once she got better at it.

Cassia focused on her quest, on analyzing each thing she found for its usefulness. Everywhere she disturbed the dust, she ran the feathers in her wake to scatter the grime and hide any prints that matched the size of her hands. If she thought beyond usefulness, if she contemplated what these objects meant beyond expediency, emotion would cripple her, and she would not succeed. When the lump in her throat became too painful, she thought of Lio instead.

Cassia knelt beside the bed's carved oak platform and held her breath to search the musty mattress for a tear. That was where Solia had always hidden the books she didn't want anyone to know she was reading. She had never permitted her little sister to read them, either.

Cassia flipped through them now, looking for more secrets, and she had to cover her mouth to stifle a surprised laugh. She couldn't follow the text very well, but the images were lavish. One volume on warfare, one on statecraft, and another on matters every woman wished to understand before she went to her marriage bed. Or the arms of her lover.

Cassia must not let her train of thought go in that direction, not to what marriage prospects had brought on her sister. Nor to the new question that now burdened her. Had Solia ever in her short life had the opportunity to know tenderness or pleasure with a partner she did not fear? Cassia was sure her sister would be glad for her now.

But that wasn't enough. She wanted to know her sister would be proud of her. Not only because of what she had done the night of the siege, but because of what she would do today.

There must be somewhere else she could look. Something she had missed. In her mind she ran through the hazy images of her childhood, everything she had seen Solia wear, searching for that smell. All she came up with was that same memory of her own favorite hiding place under the dressing table, of the clink of bottles, of the whisper of Solia's tunic against her shins…

Cassia returned to the dressing table and sat on the floor. She wrestled her full-grown self into the tight space underneath the table.

The smell seemed stronger under here. Was it just the vial she still carried? She tucked it away with her other oils and closed her satchel tightly. No, the smell was just as strong. She sniffed the air, following her nose.

It brought her to the dressing stool and a latch in the wood under the seat. It was stiff with disuse, but Cassia managed to pull it, and the upholstered top of the stool popped up. She opened it and found a heap of delicate golden fabric. The very tunica Solia had been wearing in Cassia's memory. It was all here. A pair of sleeping gloves, matching slippers, and the hair net with a veil. Not a bit of soot stained them, and not an inch showed signs of having been charred.

No time to waste. Cassia tore out of her plain, modest, oh-so-acceptable brown dress and all the trappings she wore underneath.

She donned Solia's armor.

Letting the veil down over her face, she discovered it was sheer enough to see and breathe through, but the odor of flametongue was suffocating. No wonder Solia had used scent oils rather heavily. This smell must have lingered on her skin.

Solia's pendant had swung out of hiding as Cassia had changed and now swayed at her neck as she knelt before the fireplace. She clutched it in one hand, and ivy leaves pressed into her palm. A whisper of awareness teased her skin. Another memory rose in her mind unbidden.

A lady always keeps ivy.

As Solia tucked the last strands of her hair under the net, Cassia caught sight of the talisman on her sister's chest. Ivy leaves peeked at her through the fabric of Solia's tunica. Her sister saw her peering at it and knelt at her eye level, pulling out the symbol. She set it in Cassia's hand. Cassia shivered as if she'd jumped in a warm bath. The wood felt nice, like a handful of good dirt that had been sitting in the sun. She peered at the scratchings around the ivy symbol. "Are those letters too? Can I learn to read them?"

"They are a very, very old kind of letters. Even I don't know what all of them mean."

"Mage King letters?" Cassia had asked, wide-eyed.

"No, his queen's letters," Solia had whispered. "It's a women's secret. Just between us."

Cassia had grinned in delight. She loved all the secrets her sister shared with her. She loved being trusted.

A lady always keeps secrets.

Now Cassia looked at her sister's secret pendant in the afternoon light, and although she still could not read the words, she had a new appreciation for what they might mean. The Mage King's wife had been a powerful sorceress in her own right. A Silvicultrix, wise in Lustra magic, an ancient power that could not be Ordered. The old magic of plants and beasts was a lost art like the letters on the ivy pendant, unless you believed the tales wizened village alchemists told in the back corners of the kingdom to give their great-grandchildren a scare.

The Changing Queen might have needed her own garden once she left the wilds and consented to live in her husband's halls of stone. Cassia could only wonder if these chambers had not always been given to the king's eldest daughter. Rooms and their purposes had a way of changing in that much time. There was no way to know. But she knew what the aspiring queen of her time had taught her.

A lady always honors the queen.

"*Baat*, Knight. I need you to stay here and watch my back." She heard him flop onto the carpet behind her, as if even after all these years it were the most natural thing in the world. Not that anyone would sneak up on her in here. But it felt good to know Knight would be waiting for her when she came back out.

She stepped into the fireplace, and ash shifted under the slippers that were too big for her. She put her hands out before her and braced them on the hearth's back wall. She ran her fingers over row after row of stone, feeling for an opening, tracing paths in the soot.

"A lady always keeps secrets," she breathed. "A lady always keeps ivy. A lady always dresses correctly. A lady always honors the queen…"

What did Cassia know about the Changing Queen, besides the lost words that now hung about her own neck? All she had to go on were a lot of overwrought ballads.

"The Changing Queen. Also sung of as the Life of Tenebra. The Hawk of the Lustra. The Mage King's Mage. The Sun's Wife. The Warrior's Heart." Cassia dug her nails into the mortar between two blocks that would not budge. She plowed the depths of her memory for any other name, title or honor that might apply to the ancient queen.

"There's one thing none of her epithets mention. It's associated with her, isn't it? It's in the garden, on the fountain and the pendant, even on the throne...ivy. *Hedera.*" Cassia smacked her palms against the stones. "But the Changing Queen's people would have called it something else, wouldn't they? That old word rural Tenebrans still use, which so confused me when I was learning their ways of gardening. *Ebah?*"

Cassia's hands sank through solid stone into empty space.

CASSIA'S TREASON

ASSIA WALKED THROUGH THE stone at the back of the hearth as if it were one of Lio's illusions. The moment her entire body was on the other side, all daylight disappeared.

She turned around. In the gloom, she could just make out the solid wall that cut off her view of Solia's bedchamber and Knight and the sun. Her hand darted out as if of its own accord. She watched it disappear into the stone. It felt nothing like moving through the ward around the Summit pavilion. In fact, she couldn't feel the wall at all.

When a familiar nose snuffled the tips of her fingers through her glove, she grinned in relief. She could get back through, and Knight would be waiting for her. She reached far enough to give him one last pat on the head, then pulled her hand back and faced the tunnel.

What little light there was came, she realized, from her. She glanced down. Solia's odorous tunica gave off a faint, soft glow like a gentle fire. Flametongue indeed.

Cassia moved forward as hastily as she dared in unfamiliar territory. But she found no soot, no rats, and no side passages down which she might become lost, only an inaudible whisper everywhere. Magic. In the pendant at her neck, she felt…an answer. As if it were a plant turning toward the sun.

A sensation of heat made her slow her steps. She put a hand near the wall beside her, careful not to push through. Warmth radiated from the stone. The wall behind a hearth should feel hotter than this, but through Solia's glove, it was merely pleasantly warm.

Cassia pressed her ear nearer the wall and listened. The rumble of male voices, at least half a dozen. She picked out the timbres she recognized. The king's soldiers. This must be one of the antechambers that served as a guardroom. She was getting closer.

Soon the tunnel did bring her to a side passage, which led to the left. She made a mental note of where it was and stayed in the main tunnel. Before long, she came to a right-hand passageway. She must take care not to become lost.

She tried to keep the layout of the royal wings in her mind as she proceeded, but she was familiar only with Solia's rooms and the king's solar, which left gaps in her mental map where Caelum's and the late queen's chambers were. The truth was, in this strange, magical non-hallway, inside the palace but apart from it, Cassia was not entirely certain the usual logic applied. This was the old magic. Was up still up and down still down? Were left and right where they had been a moment ago?

A lady always tries to understand what's going on.

Cassia paused to consider how best to navigate and how she might mark the passages she had already explored. In the silence devoid even of her footsteps, the sound of a familiar voice drew her attention. It was moderate in volume, as always, but she would know those measured, nasal tones anywhere.

She followed Amachos's voice around a corner and to a place against the wall where she could best hear it. She could not make out his words through the stone, only the timber and modulation that characterized his way of speaking. When abrupt words joined his, Cassia did not jump. She felt only satisfaction. That was the king's voice. She had found him.

His secrets were hers for the taking.

A lady always listens carefully.

Cassia leaned near the wall, and heat flushed her skin from without and within at the knowledge of her own brazenness. Shutting her eyes, she eased her body sideways through the thick layer of stone.

Amachos's muffled words became distinct sounds she could hear over the crack and snap of a fire. Her ear was through. The mage spoke in the Divine Tongue, not with the formal cadence of a prayer, but the naturalness of conversation. With whom?

She held still, uncertain whether she should pass any further through the barrier. The knowledge that she stood with most of her body inside a wall disoriented her, and she kept her eyes shut. She had no desire to open them and find her vision filled with stone, even though she knew it could not bury her.

She felt half deaf without facial expressions and body language to reveal to her the other meanings of the conversation in the solar. She couldn't even see to whom Amachos was speaking. But if she went any further through the wall, wouldn't they see her? How much protection did the magic offer?

A lady can walk through fire.

Cassia could not afford caution. She had made that decision already. She had come here today to risk everything.

Her heart pounding, she tucked her elbows against herself, turned toward the room, and leaned. Forward…just a little more…

When she opened her eyes, she found herself face-to-face with a member of the royal guard.

He looked right at her, but his eyes did not meet hers. His gaze slid over her and away. He crouched and turned to the side, reaching for something next to the hearth. A stick of firewood, which he tossed into the flames. Cassia jumped as a shower of sparks leapt up at her.

The guard stood, dusted off his hands, and returned to his place at the wall.

Could it be this easy? She took a deep breath and stepped out of the wall.

A fire roared at her feet. Flames bathed her body in warmth, and the soft linen of Solia's tunica swayed against her skin like the rippling air. It was ticklish. Cassia felt the wild urge to laugh.

The king sat a mere pace away in his great oaken chair, holding real court on his true throne, and he could not see her. As Cassia watched him, he leaned back against the padded leather and gazed into his fire.

He was gazing at his own worst enemy.

Cassia had seldom felt so certain of anything in her life. Here and now, she promised herself. This was the first step, but only the first. She would not stop. She would not be stopped.

She, Cassia, would defeat the king.

He glanced across his desk, and she followed his gaze to the royal mage. Amachos stood with his head bent, in conversation with his apprentice. The young man listened, nodding. Then he swallowed.

On Amachos's other side, a soldier waited. He turned to give the mages a steely glare, and Cassia saw his maimed eye. The prison warden.

"He's beneath your concern, Your Majesty," the jailer said.

"Not a living creature or a single corpse in my domain is beneath my concern."

"His leg went bad, Your Majesty. He was mad with pain and fever from the moment he came in. Too ill to notice anything or give it credence if he did."

Cassia's gut clenched. Callen.

Amachos lifted his head. "You are certain?"

"Yes, Honored Master. No room in my line of work for being uncertain. I make sure dead men die. I make sure they don't talk, either, except to us. As you know, I make them talk a great deal to us."

"I have instructed my apprentice to take care of the guard, if necessary." Amachos leveled his gaze at the young mage. "This would be a valuable opportunity for him to test his skills—and prove them."

"Not necessary." Lucis delivered his verdict. "The guard was Hadrian's before he came under my direct command. The girl he wants for a wife is also in my service. Regardless of what he saw, he knows better than to speak out of turn."

Cassia exhaled, and her veil rippled before her face.

Amachos pursed his lips. "Very well. Even if this Callen were lucid enough to see anything and fool enough to repeat it, what would others make of such wild tales? A half-dead guard ranting about a respected mage from Namenti? Who would take his word over mine?"

Cassia smiled.

"His only visitors since he got out have been the future wife and his new lady." The warden snorted. "Doubt he'd make himself a laughingstock to the two females about to start giving him orders."

Snickers came from another part of the room. Cassia peered in that direction. The guards at the door.

Her smile widened. Of course, she and Perita were just a couple of foolish women, the new bane of Callen's existence. Not a threat in the least.

"That is all," said the king.

Amachos muttered something else to his apprentice.

The guards tramped out of the room, and the young mage slunk after them. The soldiers and the apprentice had left the master and the king alone.

"So, Honored Master Dalos," Lucis prompted.

Cassia reasoned the mage's ruse would not be complete without a false name. Amachos from Namenti was really Dalos from Cordium.

"I have sufficient evidence to proceed," the mage stated. "The confessions of the prisoners I interrogated and especially the inside information from my trusted source are more than enough. It is time I apprehended the remaining Eriphites and took action against those who have harbored them."

The Eriphites? *Those* were the heretics he was after?

Dared Cassia believe Cordium had sent him for that reason? It seemed too much to hope he would go after human prey when he had the greater prize of the Hesperines before him.

Could it be that the Cordian Order of Anthros was not ready for war? Perhaps their lackey Dalos, when faced with seven of Hespera's Gifted, was simply too afraid to challenge them. Too weak in magic to stand against their power.

Perhaps everything would be all right after all.

The king picked up the jeweled goblet in front of him and took a swig. "A trivial matter."

"Beneath me, in fact. To think, from the entire Cult of Eriphon, there are only two dozen survivors, and all of them children."

Cassia's mouth went dry. It couldn't be.

"The concerned parties in my Order would say that left untended, they will prove ample seed to grow the corrupted vine anew. If even a single sprout of a virulent weed is not put to the pyre, the infestation will return, and so forth. Your own magistrates will tell you they are thieving brats who will grow into violent bandits. In some of the free lords' domains here in Tenebra, isn't it still legal to hang thieves, regardless of their age?"

"No need to sentence them in my courts. It is a matter of temple law, which I leave in your hands."

"Excellent, Basileus. I will deliver them to the Temple at Namenti as I promised the Prismos there, as my payment for his cooperation with my appointment. It's astonishing the Eriphite cult has resisted the Tenebran mages of Anthros for generations, yet I have succeeded in tracking down every last one of them in a matter of fortnights."

"Once I fully open my borders to the Cordian Orders, I am certain the competency of Tenebran mages will improve under your guidance."

"Their competency and their obedience. Beginning with the nearby Temple of Kyria. It is an outrage they have been harboring the brood of heretics all along. Such a thing would never occur in Cordium. This is what comes of too much self-determination, especially among females."

"Who is your source inside the temple?"

"A mage called Irene. At least one of the women there knows her duty. She took it upon herself to investigate suspicious activity in the temple and discovered the Prisma's crimes. Irene is clever to take advantage of the opportunities I have the power to promise her, rather than tie her future to the insubordinate. She will be useful when I enact my reforms."

"You have succeeded in cultivating supporters already, I see."

Cassia clenched her hands into fists. Irene. How could she do such a thing to the women with whom she'd spent her life? They were her temple family, who had cared for her and tried to help her be happy in the life she had not chosen.

How could she sentence children to death?

Cassia didn't know. She was so glad to realize that. She couldn't imagine doing such a thing.

She could imagine destroying the few prospects available to the seamstress's bastard. Bringing Lord Adrogan's fury down on his concubine. Treating Perita with cruelty. She could also imagine what more might one day have seemed necessary, even acceptable.

But what seemed necessary to her now was to protect the children, to stand with the women of the temple, to not squander Perita's trust. The only course that seemed acceptable was to burn Dalos's plans to the ground before his very eyes. The Prisma had her own useful informants, and one of them was standing here, discovering Dalos's crimes.

"I will remove the children and make an example out of the Prisma and her supporters first thing tomorrow. I trust I can rely on you to ensure your subjects mount no resistance on the temple's behalf. I gather this temple is nearly as beloved as Namenti, and most of the mages there come from the ranks of the nobility."

The king's hand came to rest on the hilt of his sword. "After tonight, the free lords will not be in a position to wring their hands over the activities of the daughters they have stashed away inside the temple walls."

For the first time, Cassia heard Dalos laugh. There was more expression in that one cackle of laughter than in any of his recitations at dawn rites. The sound sent a shiver down her spine.

"Your thoroughness never ceases to amaze me, Basileus. We shall work well together indeed. I have yet to meet a lord, prince, or king who rejoices more in destruction."

"I am not a man who rejoices. Merely one who is not hesitant to act. You can guarantee the spell will be as effective as you promised?"

"Effective? It will be devastating." Dalos sounded self-satisfied, not unlike the king's chief architect when he pronounced a round of renovations complete. "As I explained, I have seated the magic in the throne, which is still potent with latent power from the time of the Mage King. The Hesperines will not recognize the threat until it is much too late."

Oh, it had been too much to hope the Eriphites were Dalos's real target. Far, far too much to hope.

"I did not plan this for so many years to proceed in haste now," the king said. "If the time since the Summit began has not been sufficient to build your spell to the necessary strength, you still have a fortnight to perfect the working. Are you certain we should act tonight?"

"I have had plenty of time to make ready," Dalos purred, "and it will take only an instant to release. This will be the last night of the Summit."

"I require you to be certain before you enact your spell. Are you absolutely confident in your assessment of the Hesperines' power?"

"My circle has had sixteen centuries to become confident. The healer, Javed, is not a threat. Our information on the two quiet ones, Basir and Kumeta, is admittedly scant, but we know envoys are nothing more than glorified couriers attached to the diplomatic service. They are certain to be less powerful than their leaders, whom I am well-prepared to confront."

"You have said Argyros and Hippolyta are two of the most ancient Hesperines in the world. They are valued targets, are they not, whose deaths are likely to enrage their kind?"

"After a feud that has spanned two millennia, my circle will make an elder firstblood and his mate our offering to the god of war, and I shall be the one to sacrifice them." Dalos smiled. "I shall put an end to that abomination Hippolyta, the Guardian of Orthros, and one of her monstrous daughters. I rejoice too that so much of Silvertongue's arcane knowledge will die with him, as I shall be able to dispatch his upstart nephew at the same time. I shall release the spell when the initiate ambassador is speaking, so I can watch Argyros's face as he beholds his legacy begin to burn."

Then and there, Cassia made one more promise, this time to Dalos's god. She would not rest until she served Anthros's own mage up to him on a funeral pyre.

"Not even the Hesperines with all their unnatural instincts will be able to react quickly enough to prevent the destruction." Dalos snapped his fingers, and a flame appeared at his fingertips. "Of course the free lords will die instantly."

Cassia's mouth fell open behind her veil.

The king fixed the mage with a gaze she recognized. "Not a single witness can survive."

"I leave no loose ends, Basileus. The Hesperines, finally showing their true nature, will be the villains who massacre the Tenebran nobility. The king and his kin will be the only survivors of the heinous sorcery. I will be the hero responsible for the royal family's survival and the destruction of the blood goddess's servants." The mage waved a hand, and his fire spell went out. "No one will live to contradict the story. No one in Tenebra will feel safe. They will know they need a strong king and the powerful mages of the Cordian Orders to protect them from the encroaching darkness of Orthros."

"I am pleased the Order has sent such a skilled emissary."

"Those who refuse the Order refuse the god," Dalos intoned. "The free lords who protest our influence here in Tenebra obstruct Anthros's will, and a king such as yourself is pleasing to the god of war. So say my superiors who concern themselves with justifications. They are all too happy to see the free lords no longer an obstacle to us and you empowered to carry out your will upon a cowed nobility."

Cowed? The nobility would be maimed beyond recovery. Cassia's mind ran through the list of influential titles that would fall to young heirs vulnerable to the king's influence, how many bloodlines would end, how many holdings would revert to the crown. Her mind totaled the benefit to the king and accounted for all his considered motivations.

Her heart wanted to scream.

Lio. Lio and Argyros and Hippolyta, Arkadia and Javed, Basir and Kumeta. Dalos thought to kill them all in one blow.

Along with Lord Hadrian, who danced with Cassia without expectations. Lord Titus, who announced her at the Summit table with a civil tongue. And dozens of other men, some of whom never gave her a second glance, others who looked at her with lust or derision. But they too were men, and those who loved them would grieve. There were lords who would not be mourned, but even the corrupt and malicious played their role in the siege, each of them one more row of stakes in the field between the king and what he wanted.

The king must not get what he wanted.

"The kingdom will be rid of all dissenters," Dalos said. "My Order shall have your welcome in Tenebra—within the reasonable bounds of authority we have negotiated, of course. You shall have the full power of our Order behind your throne and the sanction of our god. A satisfying outcome for all concerned."

"And yet your superiors are not satisfied. They ask for the authority to appoint still more positions in addition to the royal mage, the highest in the land. They request even more land grants than I have promised them out of the holdings that will come under my control."

"To withstand the coming conflict, it would not be unwise to allow them to fill other key positions with my colleagues and to establish more temples here under the auspices of truly skilled Cordian mages. But that is your decision, of course. You know my feelings on the matter." Dalos waved a dismissive hand. "The administrators will busy themselves with questions of offices and appointments and land grants. But we, the war mages, the battle ready…" His tone heated with fervor. "We will focus on the true target. You have promised us the greatest prize we could ask for. The one for which we have fought these many centuries. We of the Aithourian Circle will not forget what you, Lucis Basileus, have placed within our grasp."

"Don't forget what it costs me to offer up my kingdom as the stage for your renewed persecution of the Hesperines, in exchange for your Order's blessing upon my reign."

"You turn your kingdom into a stage for glory." Dalos paced forward and braced his hands on the desk, nodding at the king's sword. "You are a warrior, as am I. But you live by the sword, I in aging halls filled with scrolls. It has been too long since those born with my gifts were permitted to exercise them. We no longer go to war alongside kings and set battle-fields alight with our magefire. We pledge our lives to Anthros as we always have, giving up worldly titles, property, marriage—everything for the promise of magic. Only through utter devotion can a man achieve true power. It was a worthy sacrifice once. But what destiny does our Order lay before us now? We put down bandits! We lower ourselves to protecting ignorant peasants from wild animals! Or worse yet, we stay in the temples in Cordium, occupying ourselves with theory until we render our magic impotent. It disgusts me."

Dalos drew himself up. The flames in the hearth leapt higher, as if to go to him, but Cassia could not feel them burn.

"What is a warrior without a war? What is a war mage without the Hesperines? At last, I shall duel worthy opponents, power against power."

"Such a battle could prove cataclysmic."

"Fear not. When you asked the Order of Anthros for an expert, you received him. It was no boast when I told you that as a member of the Aithourian Circle, I am one of the only living experts on the destruction of Hesperines. Aithouros himself, who led the Order's attacks on the Great Temples of Hespera during the Last War, founded our circle and served as its first Synthikos. We alone are the guardians of his arcane mysteries."

"I look forward to seeing a practical demonstration of your illustrious qualifications."

"I promise the tournament will not disappoint you. Having begun my career as the current Synthikos's apprentice, I remain his right hand to this day. I am privy to secrets other masters in the Order and even my own circle will never be permitted to study. There is a reason the Akron himself wielded his supreme authority over the entire Order of Anthros and hand-selected me for this venture, with the support of my Synthikos."

"So long as your ancient arcane secrets function as expected. You will recall that here in Tenebra, we have more recent firsthand experience dealing with Hesperines."

"Rest assured my circle knows the creatures' ways as no one else can. The Hesperines are masters of stealth and manipulation. It is their way to hide themselves behind their magic here within your own borders. When threatened, they retreat to their unholy domain in Orthros, a land covered in the shadow of their Queens' magic, deadly to any mortal who would set foot there. But when you harm any of their kind, they go mad like mother beasts that will stop at nothing until they rend you apart."

"It is especially fortuitous, then, that they have sent one of their initiates into our reach."

"Yes, for they guard their young most fiercely. Once we destroy Deukalion, the Hesperines hidden in Tenebra will come out in force. Any cowards who do not rise to the challenge, we will hunt down. Our confrontation with them will be enough to make the Queens themselves stir from their throne and answer our battle cry at last." Dalos laughed the way one might in a lover's bed. "Your leave to make war is the finest gift indeed. Oh, how we will make war."

Cassia had heard enough. She had only a few hours to warn everyone who mattered. She took a step back, ready to withdraw and bolt back through the secret passageway.

"One question, as an old friend." The mage's voice deepened.

Cassia halted.

Without an invitation from the king, the mage took the chair on his side of the desk and sat in the royal presence.

From his decanter of wine, the king filled the empty goblet beside his own and slid it across the desk. "What would you like to discuss?"

Dalos took a sip of the wine and savored it in his mouth for a moment. When he spoke again, all trace of his nasal tone was gone. His voice was rich and smooth, his words articulate. "Have you reached a decision on what you wish me to do regarding Cassia?"

The king shook his head. "Not yet."

Cassia's racing heart seemed to slow. Everything seemed to grind to a halt.

What would the king need to decide, but whether she was to survive the mage's spell?

"I need to know so that I have sufficient time to prepare before my working." The mage's tone had never been so clear and cold before.

She listened to Dalos's voice, the voice of the man who might be the one who killed her. A realization thawed her frozen thoughts.

She had heard that voice before.

The mage had spoken to her that way when the king had ordered her to his solar to humiliate her. It had not been her imagination.

The king went on, as if nothing had changed. "I will inform you before the hour comes. I must speak with her once more before I make my decision. I will have her brought to me as soon as you leave."

If Cassia were prone to cursing, she would have now. The king would send his messenger to her rooms, and she would not be there.

"She has demonstrated uncharacteristic behavior of late," the king said. "Speaking out on behalf of the temple. Pressing the issue of the guard. She has forgotten she must ask my leave before she breathes, eats, or shits. I must make sure her restless aspirations will not be an inconvenience."

"The hour draws near," the mage warned. "Do not wait too long."

"Indeed. I have waited too long already for the day when I have expended her usefulness and can finally be rid of her."

"I look forward to taking care of her for you." The mage caressed his goblet, then took a long, slow swallow.

"One more conversation with her, and I will be sure."

Yes, Cassia had heard all she needed to.

She would not appear for the audience that would decide her fate. It didn't matter now. She knew what she must do.

She had spent her whole life trying to survive the king. Today she had a greater goal. To protect Lio and the Hesperine embassy, the Prisma and her mages, the only surviving children of a lost people, and the entire nobility. To see to it the Last War was indeed the last.

Lives all over Orthros, Tenebra, and Cordium were in Cassia's hands.

The weight of those lives felt enormous. Larger than the man in the solar, the magic in Dalos, the castle pressing around her, or the kingdom it symbolized. But the weight did not push her to her knees. It kept her on her feet and drove her once more into the depths of the palace walls, this time at a run.

SAPLINGS

CASSIA MANAGED TO BEAT the royal messenger to her rooms and toss her court attire into her satchel. When sundown came, she would have to appear at the Summit as if nothing out of the ordinary had transpired, or everything she had worked for today would be for nothing.

Before the king's runner darkened her door, she slipped out of the palace again and made it back onto the grounds. She couldn't smell the woods for the odor of flametongue that lingered in her nose. As she ran, she sniffed her sleeve to confirm her brown dress smelled only of cassia soap. It would cover the flametongue that clung to her skin, if not clear her head.

If only Solia's treated garments could protect Cassia from Dalos. But flametongue could only lead her to the mage's secrets, not safeguard her against his magic. Solia's treasures were best left in their hiding place in her abandoned rooms. Cassia might need them again.

If she survived to need them.

Cassia wrapped her fine clothing in her cloak and hid the bundle under the foliage at the base of the Changing Queen's fountain. For an instant, she met the hawk's gaze.

"Look out for me?" she asked the fountainhead.

She bade Knight follow and wove her way across the grounds under the cover of the woods. When they came out on the road she always took to the Temple of Kyria, she halted just off the shoulder, where the trees and a bend in the path kept her and Knight out of sight of the palace gate.

She was not too late. She could see the two Kyrian mages up the road making their way toward Solorum. Cassia waited for them to draw nearer and spot her.

Deutera and the young mage who accompanied her waved and detoured off the road, picking their way through drying mud to join Cassia under the trees.

Cassia offered them as much of a smile as they were accustomed to seeing from her, much more than she felt equal to at the moment. "How fortunate that I encountered you! I was just thinking how I regret I won't be able to accompany you when you visit Callen. I looked in on him earlier, for my presence is required elsewhere this afternoon."

"How has he fared today?" Deutera asked from behind her veil.

"Well, thanks to you. Perita has observed him every moment and can inform you of his condition. I fear I must hasten to my next obligation, but first I wanted to ask if you would be so good as to carry a message to the Prisma for me."

"Of course. She will be glad to hear from you."

"I thank you. Here is what you can say to her from me. Please relate my message in precise detail, as the specifics may influence her decision on the matter."

"We will convey your words faithfully," Deutera assured her.

"Irene has told Honored Master Amachos about the Temple of Kyria's exceptional crop of saplings," Cassia said with great care, "the ones I have been helping the Prisma tend. He would love nothing better than to have her young trees to burn as offerings in the Sun Temple. The number he requires is two dozen."

The younger mage nodded, her eyes bright with interest. Deutera's brow had gone pale and clammy above her veil.

Cassia held Deutera's gaze. "Once Amachos sees the Prisma's gardening methods for himself, I am certain he will take an unprecedented interest in Kyria's affairs."

Deutera caught Cassia's hand in hers. "I understand. Thank you for letting us know in advance about the honored master's plans. I would never have imagined Irene would take so much upon herself."

"I would remind the Prisma of the other mage upon whose expertise she and I have relied, the one whose work on sapling blight proved so beneficial, especially to the tree with the scarred bark. That Gifted gardener would certainly be willing to take the trees off her hands as well, but to see them harmlessly transplanted in a different temple so they might grow and thrive under other mages' loving care. You must tell her right away, and she must reach her decision quickly. Honored Master Amachos will pay her a visit first thing tomorrow to request that she make a gift of the trees to him."

Deutera uttered what sounded like a prayer, then turned to her companion and instructed her in the Divine Tongue. The girl took her leave and headed toward the palace.

"She will see to Callen while I return to the temple." Deutera spoke fast and low.

"I must know the Prisma's decision by nightfall, or it will be too late to get word to our fellow gardener in time for it to matter."

Deutera did not ask who this gardener was or how an anonymous mage could help. "Wait here. I will return with her answer in a moment. Thank Kyria I'm the other mage in the temple besides the Prisma who can accomplish a traversal."

"That takes a tremendous amount of power. Isn't it dangerous?"

"A small price to pay. With the votive Kyria as a focus, I will manage."

A current of magic nearly knocked Cassia off her feet. When she regained her balance, Deutera was gone.

If Cassia had possessed the energy to pace, she would have. Instead, she stood with an arm around Knight and waited. Anthros drove his accursed sun still further down the sky, and she knew the king's messenger arrived in her rooms to find them empty.

When Deutera reappeared, Cassia had to take hold of the mage's arm to keep her on her feet. Sweat soaked through Deutera's robes. More costly moments escaped before she was able to catch her breath, much less speak. But Cassia held her up and waited without pressing her.

"The Prisma's answer is yes," Deutera heaved. "Give the message to your mutual friend. At midnight tonight, she will meet the other gardener in Kyria's sacred grove and deliver the entire crop of saplings so they can be transplanted in the other temple."

Cassia wrapped an arm around Deutera. "Tell her thank you."

"Lady Cassia, the expression on the Prisma's face as she struggled to decide— Who could this other gardener be? What sort of mage would put that look in her eye?"

"She will need your help, Deutera. She will need you to support her tonight and to tell her afterward that she did the right thing. You will find you must set aside what you have assumed to be true. For the children's sake, and the Prisma's."

"I don't understand."

"You will." Cassia pulled away, watching to see if Deutera could stand without aid. "Will you be all right on your own?"

The mage nodded, wiping sweat from her brow with the back of her hand. "I will not stop until my work is done."

"Take care. I must go and deliver the Prisma's message. You have my gratitude. Please tell the Prisma that for me as well. Those exact words."

The mage nodded and signed a glyph of Kyria over Cassia with a shaking hand. "Goddess preserve us all."

Lio would surely be saying the same prayer before the night was through.

SIEGE

IT WAS SHOCKINGLY EASY to approach Solorum Fortress in daylight. Cassia spotted only a handful of men strolling the walls and standing about in the shadows of the towers. It seemed the earnest watch did not begin till nightfall, when an army of guards would patrol the walls with keen eyes and sweating brows. Even then, they sought to keep the monsters in, rather than keep humans out. No one expected a mortal to want inside with the Hesperines.

It had been simple to make her way around the entire Solorum complex under the cover of the forest, a reversal of Lio's nightly route to her. This approach from the north was well-shielded. The woods hid Cassia from the guards' sight, and a tall tree gave her a decent view of what she was up against. The only challenge now was the line of cleared ground between the trees and the walls. She could not afford to wait for the cover of darkness.

For the second time in her life, Cassia gazed out across a vast, open field at the walls of a fortress and knew she was the only one who would go.

She clambered back down the tree and slid to the ground, landing a little too hard. Knight wove about her jarred legs, sniffing her as if to check for injuries.

She knelt down in front of him and held him. "I have to be stealthy, my dearest. You have to stay here."

It took her four trips to the edge of the woods before Knight did not follow her. His sense of danger was so strong. But his obedience still remained stronger, and it was no lie she needed him to watch her back. If she ran into trouble on the way and had to make a hasty retreat, she wanted an ally to retreat to. Even if all he could offer her was the reassurance she was not alone.

The truth was, if they found her out, retreat was unlikely. Even if she did escape, what then?

Escape. The mere thought filled her with longing she could scarcely bear, and more anger than she could hold. There would be no escape for her.

From the cover of the trees, she studied the walls that separated her from Lio. Only narrow slits for archers interrupted the otherwise unbroken expanse. The sun that struck those openings was swallowed by blackness within. She eyed the towers. Windowless. This was not a fortress ready for a siege, which it had not seen in ages, but it was built for one.

Moments slipped by as she observed the pattern of the guards' patrol on the ramparts. She tallied their steps. The time it took them to make their rounds changed subtly with each circuit, for they were not being diligent. But that was all right. It meant they were moving slower than they should. In the time they were not on this side of the wall, she could make it from the trees to the fortress.

But there remained the problem of the locked gate. The portcullis she couldn't see from here, which faced the greensward to the south, was the more formidable of the fortress's two entrances. The north gate on this side was set deep into the wall and barely large enough to admit a single horse and rider. If would-be invaders managed to enter the recess, the fortress's defenders might pour any manner of painful things down onto the enemies' heads before they reached the door. Assuming they got near at all.

The gate stood elevated above ground level at the top of a narrow flight of steps. During a siege, the path between Cassia and the stairs would be covered in sharp pickets or other such menaces. But those sorts of stakes were of no use at all against Hesperines.

Cassia waited. The instant the patrol rounded the corner of the walls and traipsed out of sight, she took off running.

For a few dreadful moments she raced across open ground with the sun beating down on her. Every instinct in her keened with wariness. She kept her gaze fixed on those empty walls until she came too near the side of the fortress to see what lay above her anymore.

She dashed up the stairs, into the recess, and stopped just in time to avoid hurtling right under a large grate open to a chamber above. She held her breath and listened.

There came the muted but unmistakable tread of boots on stone somewhere far over her head. The guards had already rounded the corner. Cassia waited, frozen.

No shouts. Not even a curious voice drifting down from the ramparts. She let out a silent, shaking breath. So close. But they had not seen her.

She waited awhile longer, listening for any movement on the other side of the grate in the roof of the recess. She heard nothing. Whatever chamber lay above seemed to be deserted at the moment.

Now she faced the obstacle of a locked and barred door designed to withstand sieges. She had never felt so reckless and unprepared. She had thrown herself headlong into this desperate attempt, and now she must discover the hard way whether she was as useful in such a crisis as she was at gradual maneuvers.

She ran her hands over the door's surface, digging her nails into the barest seams between its planks and at the edges of the iron reinforcements that crisscrossed them. No handle. No keyhole. There weren't even any hinges visible for her to douse in the fetid oil she'd brought. She paused, flattening her hands on the door, and leaned her face near. The hairs on her cheek did not rise, and she felt no telltale tingle on her palms. No spells, at least not that she could detect with her senses, such as they were. She eased back and studied the door frame for any weakness, looking it over, down and up.

Up to the grate that served as an outlet for boiling oil, arrows, sewage, or any other unsavory substance that might impede an invader. But in this case, the grate was by no means an impediment.

A soldier could never fit between those bars, but an underfed girl could.

Cassia's momentary relief gave way to trepidation. It was far above her head, and even for an underfed girl, it would not be a comfortable passage.

She did not even have Knight to give her a leg up. She would have to find what handholds she could on the door itself and scramble up the wall, then catch the bars with her fingers and pull herself up.

Cassia waged her wars in the hearth room, the weaving room, and the garden. She was hardly equipped for such a physical feat. But she hoped these past two fortnights of hard work at the temple might grant her just enough strength that her body didn't fail her.

The first thing she did was tie her hair out of her way and strip until she wore nothing but her slippers. Cold assailed her skin, but she faced her foe without a tremble. Standing naked in broad daylight before the door of Solorum fortress, she took a bottle of scent and a rag in hand and began to oil herself.

The rag kept her hands clean, while it took three different oils to get her breasts, ribcage, and hips properly greased. She didn't stop until she was slippery as a fish from wrists to ankles. At last she bundled the empty bottles in her satchel with her clothing and tools and slung her bag onto her back.

She was ready. She lifted her knee and braced her foot on the door. For once, her stupid slippers were an asset. Too cold in winter, sweaty in summer, always letting dampness from the ground soak through to her feet. But now they were more flexible than any protective shoes might have been, and yet they offered her toes a modicum of protection from the rough iron of the door. She squeezed her toes into the slim hold where the flat iron bar met the wood and reached up to find a handhold on the stone door frame, which protruded from the sheer wall with a lip about the width of her thumb.

It took three tries and many awkward rearrangements before she managed to crawl up the face of the door, then turn its frame into a foothold while her hands found purchase in a few moss-eaten, crumbly grooves in the wall above. By the time she brought herself within manageable reach of the grate, she felt emboldened.

But her victory so far would mean little if she could not make it the rest of the way.

She double checked her toeholds and left handhold, then carefully pried her right hand from the wall and lifted it. Slowly she reached up, cautious not to upset her balance. Closer. There. She wrapped her right hand firmly around one bar of the grate.

A breath to steady herself. She tugged, testing the grate's strength. When it held, she yanked harder. It didn't so much as rattle. Old and nasty as this place was, it was built to last. The bars should hold her weight.

Her steady grip on the grate made her motions surer as she lifted her left hand and took hold of another bar. Braced between the grate and the lintel of the door, she let her arms and legs rest for a moment. But only for a moment. No time to waste.

Holding fast to the grate, she walked her feet up the wall. A reasonably comfortable approach, but when she had her body parallel to the grate, hanging by her hands with her feet flat against the adjoining wall, she realized the logistical problems of sending her feet between the bars first. To Hypnos with it. She would have to go headfirst and pull her entire body weight up.

But first, to make sure her tools made it through with her. With one hand, she worked her bundle carefully off her back, squeezed it through the bars, and gave it a shove so it landed beside the grate.

For her own entry, she chose the gap between the two bars nearest the door, for that would allow her to brace herself on the wall for as long as possible. The one small mercy of the situation was that the bars were parallel to the doorway, and she would not have to twist to fit herself in sideways.

But by the time she got herself into position, her limbs and belly were trembling, and her throat was tight and prickly with unshed tears of frustration. Hair hung in her eyes, and she tried without success to blow it out of her way. Sweat trickled down her back. Her palms would be next, and then where would she be? She felt awkward, foolish, and helpless, nude and clinging to the side of a fortress large enough to crush her.

No, she was *not* going to fail, not at such a ridiculous task. She would not lose her chance to warn Lio because she fell from a godsforsaken murder hole.

Cassia had to turn her head entirely sideways, but it did fit through the gap. Once she was able to face forward again and get her shoulders through, she felt a little encouraged, but that was also when her arms began to burn in earnest. She slid one up through the grate, then the other. Now she was braced on top of the bars, the iron digging into her arms painfully, her toes still grappling for purchase on the wall. She gritted her teeth, let her legs swing free, and heaved.

In the end there was little analysis and cleverness to it, just a lot of wrenching, bruising, and sucking her breath in so hard her stomach hurt. Her breasts, small as they were, were squeezed painfully on the way through, and she thought her hips would be her undoing. With bruises on her pelvic bones, knees, shins, and other places she could not think to tally, she collapsed on top of the grate, all her limbs now within the fortress.

She'd done it.

She gulped in breaths. Daylight coming through the grate showed her a long chamber that was empty except for the abandoned refuse of siege equipment. There was no door, just an open archway leading into a hallway. Cringing, Cassia crawled off of the grate, onto solid stone floor, and into a shadowed corner behind an empty cauldron.

She used her gown to wipe as much oil off herself as she could. It wouldn't do for the guards to smell her coming. She donned only her tunica and satchel, discarding the rest in the cauldron.

Then she scrambled into a crouch and peeked around the doorway. The corridor appeared deserted. It was a low, narrow passage devoid even of weapon racks and martial banners, lit only by a single torch.

She darted out and snatched the brand off the wall. It took scarcely a moment to carry it back to the cauldron and set afire the only evidence she had been here. Fragrance gave way to smoke as she watched her brown dress, kerchief, and underlinens burn to ash.

Solorum Fortress had fallen to an army of one.

THROUGH THE VEIL

I T HAD NEVER OCCURRED to Cassia she would be so good at committing treason. Her body, which she so often berated for showing fear and weakness, had been her strength today as she had climbed through that murder hole. Now the skills she had learned because of the king were precisely what she needed to see his plan brought to nothing.

She had no magic powers that let her walk past guards unseen in plain sight, but she did have a lifetime of experience to rely on. If there was anything she excelled at, it was subtlety. She crept around corners, crawled behind furniture, and sheltered in empty rooms. As guards passed by, she bided her time before following silently in their wake. Heady, how easy it was; nerve-wrenching, when she considered the stakes.

The guards were worse gossips than the women in the kitchens, and she quickly learned by eavesdropping that the embassy had quarters on the ground level. As she made her way downward, the growing absence of guards confirmed what they had said. They clearly avoided this part of the fortress.

By the time she reached the door to the ground level barracks, she was utterly alone. The only people here with her were asleep in the rooms beyond.

Her heart pounded even harder than it had each time she'd risked discovery above. She pressed an ear to the door. When she had passed the last window on the floor above, she had seen it was not yet dusk. She had a little time. She must hide herself in Lio's room and stay there until he woke.

And hope the others who woke first did not sense her. It was a good thing she knew he had a room to himself. It was a very, very good thing the Hesperines were kind. To find herself their captive would be a relief, if she did not know they would be the ones who came to harm, if they were found to harbor her.

Cassia lifted her head from the door and took hold of the handle. This one wasn't locked.

The door swept open with a groan. Again she had to remind herself how much stone lay between her and the guards and that it took far more than creaky hinges to wake a Hesperine. She closed the door firmly behind her. The meager light that came from the corridor winked out.

She felt she could reach out and touch the darkness around her. She recognized that darkness, knew it as she knew her own past. It was the same power that had wrapped her up in safety the night the Hesperines had saved her life.

She breathed in the darkness and shivered. It was a hint of music she could almost hear. An embrace that told her all would yet be well.

Was this the ward Lio had spoken of, which protected them in their sleep? Would it let her pass?

Cassia took one step forward. The hair on the back of her arms stirred as if a gentle wind soughed around her. She took another step. The magic enfolded her and held her close against its silken breast.

A sense of direction made her walk forward and to her right. Her mind knew it made no sense, but it felt so natural, she did not stop to question. The part of her that simply walked that way knew exactly what she was doing.

Her hand came to rest on a door handle. The shadows promised untold mysteries slept within. She pushed open the door, and the familiar, intimate caress of Lio's magic drew her in.

Soft spell light illumined a small, ascetic room for soldiers. The single occupant of the bed looked much too beautiful to even exist here. Lio slept on his back in a graceful sprawl with his feet hanging off the end of the bunk. All that covered him from waist to ankle was one blanket. One she knew well. Did it still have bloodstains from the night they'd lost their virginity on it? She let her gaze drift up his long torso to his bare chest. Around his neck, on a length of twine, hung the betony charm she had given him.

Here in this room, the magic that had led her to his side seemed stronger than her pain. She felt certain no one could intrude over this threshold. She felt safe and hidden, as she always did with him.

Cassia went to him and slid her bruised body into his bed. There was just enough room for her to tuck herself against his side under their blanket. She took a deep breath. Roses and Lio. His body was so warm next to hers.

Let him wake to her just this once.

AN IMPOSSIBLE DREAM

T HE FINEST DREAM HE had that day was his last one, right before
waking. He dreamed he did, in fact, awaken. In that awful little
room in Solorum fortress. But Cassia was there in the bed with
him, waiting for them to greet the night together.

Lio stretched. She melted closer to him, twining her leg around his,
her arm around his waist. He luxuriated in the feeling of his own body and
hers against him. His appetite uncurled with the same languid pleasure,
and he felt his fangs swell.

All he had to do was roll over, and they could begin the night with the
Feast. This was how it should be.

"Lio."

The first thing he heard as he awakened: her saying his name. So right.
He rolled over. So easy. Now he was face-to-face with her, belly to belly.

He swallowed the moisture that had come to his mouth. "You have
soot on your nose."

She reached up to rub at it, then at her eyes.

He blinked at her. He should ask her why she had soot on her charming little nose. But the only question he could think was, where would he
drink? The inside of her thigh would be so good. But her neck was much
closer. He kissed her while he was trying to decide.

She hung onto him and opened her mouth to him. She was eager. She'd
been waiting for him to wake up.

"Sorry I kept you waiting," he mumbled as he found his way to
her throat.

"How long does it take for you to wake up? I mean, be really awake?"

"Mmm wide awake."

That was the inside of her thigh against his rhabdos. She could feel how awake he was. And there was her throat against his lips. His tongue found her pulse unerringly.

"Lio, you're not thinking straight."

"Thinking's not really mmm...mmportant." But when he took his first breath of the evening to smell her, fragrance assailed his nose, and a thought did occur to him. "Did you grease another door?"

"I greased myself." She made a noise of disgust. "I'm surprised you even want to touch me."

He wrapped his hand around her buttock and pulled her closer. "I always want to touch you." Talking was so much effort when he could be kissing her throat, but this was important. "If you think..." He kissed her. "...we need mm...more lubricant...we can find sommthing you like better than those oils."

Her laughter didn't sound right. Like she was sad about something. Well, before she knew it, she would be feeling nothing but pleasure.

He decided on her neck and took a bite out of her. An appreciative groan poured out of him. She was so good. She wriggled closer to him, and as he sipped her, they worked her under him and got her tunica up to her waist. The bed was too narrow. Didn't matter. She was wrapping her legs around him.

"We don't need more lubricant." She sounded breathless already.

How right she was. She was wet, and he slid right into her, and her krana held him fast. Oh, she was so good. He began to thrust instinctively, just enjoying her. She gripped her legs tighter around him, just the way he liked. Like she couldn't stand to let him go. He thrust harder, deeper. Her blood grew warmer and surged into his mouth. Goddess bless, he needed this. She was so good.

It was that good for her too. No sad words now, just her sighs of passion. He thrust harder. Her fingers dug into his shoulders. He dug his teeth into her and thrust harder still.

Her climax came fast, too fast. But that was all right. They could do it again.

He sucked every last drop of her pleasure from her throat, then drove himself as deep into her as he could and stopped thinking altogether. Just felt his body releasing in long, hard pulses, felt everything inside him surging into her until he was spent and replete.

Nothing felt like this. He wanted to wake to this, to her, and no one else.

No, he wasn't awake. He was dreaming. Cassia couldn't possibly be in his bed in Solorum Fortress.

Her blood in his veins sent energy coursing through his body. He felt her flesh wet and soft around his, too vivid to be an erotic dream.

"I'm so glad you didn't stop," she was saying. "There's no time, but I had to have you again. Just one more time—" She broke off. Her voice was neither sleepy nor satisfied. She was in pain.

Her heartache shredded through the last heavy remnants of his Dawn Slumber.

This wasn't a dream.

"*Cassia.* What are you *doing* here?"

"Rescuing you."

He pulled out of her with her blood running down his chin and the wetness from inside her on his body. It was one of the most erotic moments of his life and they could *not* be doing this. "You shouldn't be here."

She sat up in what little room the bunk afforded. "I had to be here the moment you woke, to warn you. There was no time for me to wait for a safe meeting."

"How did you get in?" Too many questions assailing him, and he was asking the least important ones.

"I climbed through a murder hole."

The sight of the bruises that mottled her hips finally got him fully awake and painfully alert. In his thoughtless lust, how badly had he caused her injuries to pain her?

In moments he had the wound on her neck properly healed, her tunica all the way off of her, and clean cloths doused in water from his washbasin. He worked in silence, reciting to himself every curse he knew. He draped the icy cloths over the worst bruises he found, like the mess on her right pelvic bone, to give her some relief while their tryst finished healing her. He wasn't about to put a cold rag on her most sensitive places. He finished with a cleaning spell upon both of them. As the smell of the oils dissipated, she breathed a sigh of relief.

"I had no idea," he finally said. "I would have been gentle."

"I wanted it just like that, Lio. Like nothing was wrong. Bruises heal."

He couldn't bear the sadness in her smile. "I'd go over every inch of you and speed them along still more, but I suspect there's no time."

"How long before your uncle expects you to appear?"

Lio spat on an extra towel and set to work on the bruises on her other hip bone. "Judging by how long I've actually been coherent, about half an hour from now."

She covered her face in both her hands and rubbed it. Apparently she hadn't counted on how long it took before the Dawn Slumber wore off.

That one moment of apparent strain, and then she was off, speaking swiftly and factually, as if delivering a diplomatic address instead of sitting on his bed injured and naked with him rubbing spittle over her bruises. "Amachos is a fully trained war mage from Cordium. His real name is Dalos."

The rag slipped from Lio's hand.

"Whatever time he spent at Namenti was a ruse to ensure no one would object to his appointment. He promised the temple there a favor in exchange for their cooperation. In secret, the king granted the Cordian Order of Anthros the right to appoint the royal mage of Tenebra, and they sent Dalos as their official representative."

There was no time for him to interrupt her with shocked questions. He was too stunned to articulate useful ones if there had been.

"While the king has been stalling negotiations with you, he has been negotiating the terms of his new alliance with the Cordian Order of Anthros. In exchange for the Order's endorsement of his rule, he's granting them unprecedented authority in Tenebra. He's bought the war mages for his cause, and his payment to them is a war with your people. Dalos is mad, Lio. Slaughter is pleasure to him. You should have heard him talking about reviving the glory days of his order."

"You didn't go near him," Lio said in denial.

"I heard every word he said to the king." She finally rubbed the soot off her nose. "Don't ask me how."

"Hespera's Mercy, Cassia. You could have been—"

"I wasn't. And I made it here in time for one last feast…" Her voice quavered. "…before I tell you that you must leave now and never set foot here again."

"Slow down. We may yet have our fortnight. I'll tell the others, and my uncle will decide—"

"They're going to seal their new pact this very night," she interrupted. "I warned you the king is beyond reason. Dalos plans to assassinate the entire Summit."

Lio stared at her, then shook his head, trying to clear it. "He doesn't have the power! We would have sensed it."

"He's been building a spell into the throne all this time. They've been stringing you along with the promise of an Oath while Dalos prepared his working. Now he's ready to unleash it."

"Impossible."

"He'll say your embassy murdered the Council of Free Lords for their unwillingness to renew the Oath, that when diplomacy failed, you resorted to violence. Dalos will claim credit for eliminating you as a threat and saving the royal family. Tenebra will clamor for war with the Hesperines, and Dalos believes your Queens will be angry enough to give it to them. They are trying to draw you out, goad you into meeting them in battle."

"He has no idea how he oversteps himself."

"They will begin with the persecution of Hesperines who act in secret here in Tenebra." Cassia's aura and her pulse throbbed with emotion. "The very Hesperines who saved my life and gave the Mercy to Solia might well be among them. I will not allow this to happen."

"Don't fear, Cassia. Dalos is no match for us."

"When Callen was in prison, he witnessed Dalos burning prisoners to death with his bare hands. If Perita hadn't realized what Callen saw was important and persuaded him to tell me, I never would have known the truth about Dalos. Thanks to them, we've discovered what he really is and have some idea of his abilities. But I cannot judge how his power will measure against yours. I heard him boast to the king he's from an important circle within the Order of Anthros."

A chill spread through Lio's veins. "He couldn't be *that* Dalos. His aura isn't strong enough. He's just a mediocre warder. He didn't mention the Synthikos of the Aithourian Circle, did he?"

"That's exactly what he said. He was the Synthikos's apprentice."

To think, Lio had once faced him alone in a deserted forest. "I can scarcely believe it. He's one of the highest-ranking, most powerful war mages in the entire Order of Anthros. All of us know him by reputation. His kind go out of their way to make sure of that."

"Then he is a real threat to you, as he claims."

"As a fire mage, his strength lies in our greatest weakness. He'll also have an arsenal of the Aithourian Circle's specialized revelatory spells for unveiling Hesperines and battle wards to counter us."

"Dalos said he learned how to fight Hesperines from the secret teachings passed down by a war mage named Aithouros."

"Aithouros killed more of us in the Last War than any other mage in history or legend. He led the assaults on our villages and temples. He started the fires with his own spells. He had so much blood on his hands by the end that death was too good for him. Hesperines curse the day he went to Anthros's Hall, where the god of war must have seated the mage at his right hand as a reward for destroying so many Hesperines who forsook the sun."

Cassia's eyes were empty of all feeling, but her aura blazed with anger. "If all of you leave now, Dalos will never have the chance to live out his fantasies of being the next Aithouros."

"Of course I'm not leaving."

"Your family are Dalos's targets! He knows who your aunt and uncle really are."

"An Aithourian would. He would also be arrogant enough to challenge them and foolish enough to end up like Aithouros."

"What happened to him?"

"He tried to stop our people from escaping over the mountains into Orthros. Aunt Lyta killed him with her bare hands."

"A grudge like that will drive a man to do unimaginable things. Dalos will go to any lengths to destroy her and Kadi."

"He did not seem particularly worried about Basir and Kumeta?"

"He disregards them and Javed. He does not fear any of you."

"A dangerous error. It will be his last."

She took hold of his arms. "Lio, he—he's going to release the spell during *your* speech. He wants to strike at your people through their future—you. You have to escape. Now. The Summit is starting in…"

"Little more than an hour."

"There's no more time."

He gathered her into his arms and helped her tunica back over her head. "You said yourself he plans to assassinate everyone who attends the Summit, not only the embassy."

"Without anyone to blame, he won't dare go through with it. The only safe course of action is for you to return to Orthros. The embassy's desertion will be an insult, but it won't have the entire nobility rallying for war."

He eased her arms into her sleeves. He hadn't had time to kiss the bumps on her elbows. "I am not. Leaving *you.*"

She was silent for a moment, letting him gently straighten her tunica around her hips. "The royal family is Dalos's badge of heroism, remember? Even if he tries something, the king's family will survive."

"Cassia." Lio gentled his tone. "Did you hear him say for certain that includes you?"

"They didn't specify what they were planning to do with me," she admitted. "But I haven't been *that* much trouble over the herbs and Perita's man. Besides, Lord and Lady Hadrian vouched for me about Callen. I'm in no danger."

For all her strategizing, it seemed she still would not lie to him, even to convince him she would be safe if he went through with her plan. Thank the Goddess their Oath still held. But the Blood Union didn't lie either, and it told him there was an ocean of omitted words beneath the true ones Cassia spoke on the surface.

Lio donned his formal robes by rote, trying to get at what Cassia wasn't telling him. "Don't go to the Summit."

"I must be there. If I don't appear, it might give the king reason to believe I'm involved, that I know something." She was on her feet now and stepping into her slippers, which must have come off while they made love.

He was so glad he hadn't stopped.

A strange and bitter emotion filled him, one he'd never felt before.

Worse than disappointment. It was betrayal. He didn't know who had betrayed him, but he felt he'd been cheated. He was angry, and he didn't know who to blame.

He and Cassia had just made love for the last time, and he hadn't even known they wouldn't have another chance.

"Cassia, promise me you'll be safe."

She drew near and straightened his collar, her gaze fixed on his robe in utter concentration. Her hands didn't even shake. She was only shaking inside. "Of course I'll be safe. The king and his mage have much greater concerns than a bastard girl. You have to leave, because you have to take the children from the temple away with you. Tonight. Otherwise they will be Dalos's next victims."

"The children? What could that monster want with the Prisma's little ones?"

"It's his favor to Namenti. They're the last surviving Eriphites. The Tenebran mages of Anthros have been—"

"—trying to stamp out their cult for hundreds of years, but they've been too resilient. Goddess bless. I'm not the only heretic the Prisma let in her temple."

"Dalos knows she's protecting them, and as soon as he's done with you, he's going after her temple. The children can't be there when he arrives, for their sake and the Prisma's."

"As broad-minded as the Prisma is, what makes you think she'll let us Solace them?"

"I already offered her your help and secured her agreement. I wasn't certain it was a risk your uncle would be as willing as you to take, but for the children's sakes—"

"He won't hesitate." Lio pulled Cassia closer, unwilling to let her hands out of his. How could he leave a woman like this behind?

"The Prisma has agreed to meet with you and the rest of the embassy," Cassia said. "You know where Kyria's Grove is?"

"Not far from the southeastern boundary of the king's grounds, in the direction of the temple."

"The Prisma will bring the children there at midnight."

"You never cease to amaze me," he said softly, reminding her. He studied her every feature as time pressed in on them, as if he could take some final drink of her with his eyes. "We need to decide how much we'll tell my uncle and the others. About us."

She looked into his eyes as if there were something inside of him she needed to drink as well. "Tell them what you will, for I have nothing to hide from your people. I am not ashamed of anything you and I have done."

He pulled her to him and held her. That was not enough to convey how much her words meant to him. How much *she* meant to him.

He had never known emotion could ache in his veins like physical pain. He couldn't tell anymore how much was his pain and how much hers.

"You're rescuing us," he said. "Who will rescue you?"

"I don't need rescuing. The king hasn't decided I'm a traitor yet."

"Goddess knows I'm sorry for the danger I've put you in."

"Don't you dare apologize for anything." She let him go. Why was she letting him go? "It's almost time. Go and save your people, Initiate Ambassador Deukalion. And if you ever meet your fellow Hesperines who gave the Mercy to my sister, say to them that I too carry their grief in my veins."

The ache had moved into his throat. "I will. One night, they shall know all you have done for our people."

"You know I would have done this just for you, Lio. I will never let him hurt you."

He wrapped his arms around her one more time and gave her one more kiss. The kiss he would have given her in bed, if he'd known.

You're saving my life, but leaving you will kill me.

Come with me.

He could not ask her. He would not ask her. But the words would burn inside him over and over again after he left, if he didn't say them. *Come with me.*

He parted his mouth from hers and gasped a breath. "Come with me, Cassia."

He had said it. Her answer would hurt, but it hurt worse not to ask.

She didn't weep. There wasn't even an expression of anguish on her face. She stepped back from him, her body utterly rigid, her face made of stone. "If I disappear on the same night as the embassy, we give the king a blank writ to fill in with any story he wishes. How you seduced me and put me under your thrall, or how you kidnapped me against my will. He would have justification for a mage war against all Hesperines without lifting a finger."

Facts. Awful facts. Lio had known the answer would hurt, but not like this.

"It will come to war anyway. Perhaps not tonight, but it's only a matter of time." Lio had never heard this in his own voice. Everything he'd ever asked for, he had been given. The most important things, he'd never had to ask for at all. Now he was begging. "Don't give this up when war will come anyway."

"War won't come."

"Lucis wants a war to give to his allies. You said yourself he gets what he wants." *Don't ask me to leave you to that*, he wanted to plead. *Don't expect me to leave you at his mercy.*

Her eyes blazed. "No. He does not get what he wants. But if I go with you, no one will be here to make sure of that."

"You—" Lio started to say. *You can't fight him on your own.*

The words stuck in his throat. He had been about to say *that* to her? He wanted her so much he would say something that wrong?

She had spent her whole life cowed. She had lived in fear of the king, caring for nothing but her next breath, since she had lost her sister. Even before then, since she had been born.

Lio had encouraged her to see all she was capable of, celebrated her every rebellion.

And now, when she declared what she wanted, he dared question her? He dared tell her she could not fight?

"I don't want to do what's best for Tenebra or Orthros," he protested to himself, to Cassia, to his Goddess. "I want what's best for us."

"I know."

But one thing mattered more. "I want to do what's best for you."

"You always have."

"Tell me what is best for you now, and I will do it."

He heard her breath hitch. Her jaw trembled. A crack in the stone. No. A glimpse of the real granite beneath.

"Go," she told him. "Be safe and happy in Orthros while I stay here and fight."

"I will do as you say. But do not ever imagine I will be happy."

"But we *were* happy. Lio." That catch in her breath again. Her eyes gleamed. "There are so many things I need to say. But I only have time for one. *Thank you.*"

He had made a promise to go. He didn't know how he would keep it. How was he going to do this?

He made a move toward her, to touch her, hold her.

"Lio?"

They both jumped at the sound of the voice on the other side of the door. Javed. They were out of time.

"Coming," Lio called.

A pause. "Is everything all right?"

No. And he didn't see how it would be ever again. "Fine. Just a dream. No, I don't want you to come in. Yes, I'll be a moment late."

"Easy, Cousin. Take your time."

Cassia was shaking her head. "No time," she whispered.

"You're not going back the way you came, not after those bruises. At least let me help you out of here."

"Won't someone sense you use your magic?"

"It won't take much. My magic flows in you now."

She held out her hand. He took it and pulled her into his arms before she could protest. Just one more time.

He was astonished his power even obeyed him and took them out of the fortress, when everything within him rejected the knowledge he was helping her leave him.

The moment they were amid the trees, she slid out of his arms and fled.

Their last chance to touch, to speak, slipped out of his grasp.

He was Hesperine. He could catch up to her on a thought. It took every scrap of Will he had to watch her go.

He would watch her go. He would keep his promise to leave.

But not while she was throwing herself into a war mage's trap.

DEUKALION'S ADDRESS

L IO HAD NEVER IMAGINED the most crucial negotiation of his life
would be with his own people. With the Queens' hand-chosen
embassy, no less.

When he entered the common room, their concern enveloped him.
He halted by his seat but did not take it. Their worry intensified. He could
see it in their eyes and feel it in the Union, and it stung like salt on an
open wound.

Cassia had no one to worry for her, except him.

Lio wanted nothing more than to tell these loving people, his people,
about her. She deserved their love. She should be here beside him, receiving their gratitude. He wanted them to know she was the hero of this hour.

But there was no time to make them realize that. Lio knew precisely
what he must and must not say to this audience to win them to his point
of view. He could spend what little time they had attempting to persuade
his war-weary elders that Lucis Basileus's daughter was trustworthy, and
the youngest member of the embassy was not blinded by his infatuation
with her. Or he could build his argument on their trust in their own Lio.

He would say or withhold whatever he must in order to succeed. Cassia had risked everything to make sure the embassy could escape, and she
was determined to go to the Summit to cover their departure, even if it
cost her life. He would not allow his plan to fail and make her sacrifices
mean nothing.

"Lio." His uncle studied him. "What could it be that you wish to say?"

I am not ashamed of anything you and I have done.

Lio would treasure her in secret. He would inform the embassy of every risk *he* had taken and every injunction he had violated. He would accept whatever judgment his Queens passed upon him, for he was not ashamed.

To think, his diplomatic ambitions had been what mattered most to him when he had arrived in Tenebra. His future as an ambassador meant so little in comparison with all that might be lost tonight.

"I have a course of action to propose," Lio announced.

Uncle Argyros set down the scroll he held and let it roll shut. "What is wrong?"

"Twenty-four fugitive children, the last surviving members of the Cult of Eriphon, are hiding in the Temple of Kyria. The Prisma has agreed to let us bring them home to Orthros, but we must do it tonight, for Amachos is out for their blood—and ours."

Utter silence met his pronouncement. The Blood Union clamored with their reaction.

Lio pressed onward. No time. "Amachos has concealed his true identity. He is really Dalos of the Aithourian Circle. He's planning to assassinate us and the entire Council of Free Lords at the Summit. Tonight."

The Union roared. Uncle Argyros was on his feet. Aunt Lyta and Kadi had beaten him to it by a heartbeat.

Aunt Lyta braced her hands on the table as if the map of the battlefield in her mind were spread out before her. "How have you learned this? How certain are you?"

"Certain enough to stake all our lives on it, or I would never have spoken."

"Explain," Uncle Argyros commanded.

"I've been trespassing inside the palace."

The storm in Argyros's aura faltered. All he said was, "Lio."

The shock and worry and love that emanated from his uncle in turn was more difficult to bear than any anger. Lio searched the Blood Union for what he dreaded most: disappointment. But his uncle's response was too complex, and there was so little time to read him. Before Lio could be certain, Basir's anger consumed his focus.

"How long has this been going on?" the Master Envoy demanded.

"Since we arrived."

"Your Queens have not authorized you to engage in subterfuge, youngblood. That is the duty of the envoys. You are a diplomat, an initiate, I might add, in whom they have placed extraordinary trust. This is what you have done with it?"

Kumeta joined in her Grace's outrage. "You simply decided one night you would become the Queens' spy? With no training and no one at your back? You could have gotten yourself killed."

Or he could have killed the king.

Lio did not confess this temptation. Nor did he engage in a petty defense of his abilities. He stood tall under their scrutiny.

Aunt Lyta's gaze was keenest of all. "We might all have gotten ourselves killed tonight, I take it, if Lio had not appointed himself to eavesdrop on our enemies."

"The king's daughter," Uncle Argyros cut in.

Lio met his gaze without hesitation, prepared for him to make the connection. His uncle would not arrive at the truth.

"That is how you were aware of her presence here," Uncle Argyros said. "Also the rumors about the epidemic of frost fever in the east. All this you have learned not from conversations you overheard during your nightly drink, but from deliberate trespassing?"

"Yes," Lio confirmed.

"Here I've been," Kadi burst out, "sitting on my hands and struggling to behave! All the while I was longing to see action, Lio was taking the lead. You could have asked me to come with you."

Javed covered his face in one hand.

Kadi's eyes flashed, and Lio was no longer looking at his cheerful cousin, but a Master Steward of Hippolyta's Stand. "Why didn't you ask me for help? You know I am not so fastidious about the rules as you yourself are. You know what it has cost me to wait in Orthros with my hands tied for nearly a century, uncertain whether Nike needs my aid. While I walk her patrol night after night, I wonder if I fail her again each time by not going errant to find her. See now what good it has done our elders for me to hold myself back to soothe their hearts." Kadi brought her fist down on the table, and her parents jumped. "What wouldn't I give for a chance to act, just once?"

Javed rested his hand over her fist. "Are you holding yourself back when you save lives at the border? How many would have died before I had a chance to heal them, if you had not acted?"

She uncurled her fingers and held fast to his hand.

"Kadi," Lio said, "don't doubt for a moment I hold two sisters' love for one another in reverence. I wasn't trying to exclude you—only protect you and everyone else."

"You, little cousin, trying to protect me? And all of Orthros too? When did it become our youngest diplomat's duty to take up the calling of the Stand and the Charge?"

Power and emotion quivered in the air around Aunt Lyta. "I want to know why my youngblood nephew discovered a war mage in our midst, when we who have faced Dalos's kind in battles to the death have not sensed a trace of his magic. To hide that much power takes a ward of equal power, which gives away the caster's strength and defeats the purpose. The ward he carries about is *not* that strong."

Kumeta shook her head. Lio had never seen her look so haunted. "It seems we must consider the possibility the enemy has developed new workings unknown to us. If anyone could achieve such an innovation, it would be the Aithourian Circle. There is a great deal of their secret research into which we have no insight, even those of us who are active in Cordium."

Basir exchanged a glance with her, clearly holding two conversations at once. "Regarding Dalos's power, we can no longer make conjectures with any degree of confidence. Argyros, we advise you to proceed under the assumption the war mage possesses any number of abilities of which we have no knowledge. Expect him to take us by surprise."

"Understood. Nephew, there is more you can tell us."

"A great deal more."

Lio delivered the finest address of his career. He informed the embassy of everything Cassia had overheard and made sure not a single lie passed his lips. It was true he had infiltrated the royal wings; the conversation between the king and the royal mage had really taken place. It grated on his conscience to take sole credit for everything, but for her sake, he would say anything he must.

Uncle Argyros put him to the test. "What you have said still does not explain how you came to have personal dealings with the Prisma of the Temple of Kyria."

"After the king refused to accept our gift of medicines, one of the temple's representatives approached me when I was alone on the grounds. I was astonished at her daring…" He had been, that first night when Cassia, so proud and fearless, had come to find him. "…and even more so that she set aside her prejudices for the chance to help others." Lio had seen it when no one else had, her desire to act that she hid so well. "She negotiated a direct exchange of the rimelace."

"I'm not missing any herbs," Javed protested. Even as the words came out of his mouth, a startled expression crossed his face. "I'll be sunbound. Those are an *illusion,* Lio?"

"I'm sorry my deception has burdened you with grief." One apology Lio had no qualms in offering his friend. "But do not despair of the children, Javed. The Prisma knows as well as we do there is no epidemic of frost fever in the eastern Tenebrae."

Javed grimaced. "The children. Of course. The malnourishment and exposure to the elements they must have suffered as fugitives and orphans would make them prime targets for frost fever. It's a wonder any of them survived long enough for the Prisma to take them in."

"I don't know how the mages of Kyria managed to locate the Eriphites ahead of the mages of Anthros and get the children to safety, but I am certain the Prisma has her own sources of information. She learned just in time that the royal mage is planning an imminent raid on her temple. The Kyrians' representative approached me again to inform me we may Solace the children." *She came to my room. I made love to her. I will never taste her again.*

And she was about to sit down at the Summit across from a war mage who looked forward to committing murder.

Lio laid out the details of the Prisma's plan to meet at the Grove. "She would rather surrender the children to Hesperines than see them suffer the punishment for heresy."

"Deukalion, your passionate determination to help does you great credit." It was the kindest thing Kumeta had said. "That is what we all believe in. But you are young. Your upbringing in Orthros predisposes you to trust. Here in Tenebra, you must consider less benevolent motivations. It's possible the Prisma's seemingly compassionate proposal is a trap."

"I spoke in detail with the Prisma herself when I delivered the rimelace to her vestibule. I found her to be a great mage and a woman worthy of respect."

"You went inside?" Basir hissed.

There was no mistaking the wonder in Javed's voice. "You've been inside a temple of Kyria."

"And I came to no harm."

"She could have planned the encounter to build trust with you," Basir said, "to make you believe it would be safe to bring the rest of us to her later. The children could be a tale she offers up as bait—"

"I felt each one of them dying. They are no tale, and our herbs are the only reason they still live."

"They may still be bait," Basir returned. "It would be a master stroke for the Prisma if she delivered the Eriphite heretics and the Hesperine embassy to Dalos in one move. The Order of Anthros's favor would secure her future and that of her temple."

"He doesn't need her to deliver us to him. He thinks we will be at his mercy tonight."

"She doesn't know that," Basir said. "To escape Dalos's trap—provided we succeed—only to go willingly into an encounter with another powerful mage would be a shameful risk of precious lives."

Lio looked the Master Envoy in the eye. "Do not imagine for a moment that I would ask all of you to take such a risk if I did not cherish those lives."

"Deukalion." The gentleness in Kumeta's tone made Lio look at her in surprise.

She rounded the table and came to stand beside him. He stood still, feeling as if too fast a movement might banish a gift.

Her hand came to rest on his arm. "Basir and I are not the gentlest protectors. That is because we have borne too many losses already. The Blood Errant was acting on our information when the war mages captured Prometheus."

"You cannot hold yourselves responsible for what befell him! Everyone knows your information is the only reason any of the Blood Errant survived that night."

"Yes. Basir and I provided the very best information possible, and still we lost Methu. We did not make a single error, and still we live with the knowledge that we could not prevent his capture. In our dreams, we watch him suffer the fate we know awaits all Hesperines the Aithourian Circle takes to Cordium as prisoners. A heretic's public torture and execution on the Akron's Altar. How do you think we feel at the thought of you wandering alone in the palace with Dalos looking over your shoulder?"

Lio bowed his head. "Devotion like yours is exactly what makes me regret nothing I have done."

She let him go. "I know. You are so much like him, bloodborn."

Lio had listened to the tales about Prometheus all his life and heard that title of bloodborn laid upon them both. He always heard he reminded them of beloved Methu, and he always answered that he would strive to be worthy of that praise.

No one had ever said he was *like* Prometheus.

Tonight Lio answered, "Thank you."

"There is time later to debate the wisdom of Lio's actions." Uncle Argyros's gaze lingered on the closed scroll in front of him. "For now, we must reach a decision."

Lio knew the reckoning would catch up to him later, but it seemed so distant as to be unreal, separated from him by the Summit pavilion where Cassia would soon take her seat with the intention of paying with her life for his people's safety.

Aunt Lyta stood in silent council with Uncle Argyros, then looked to Basir and Kumeta. "Your recommendation, then, is not to trust the Prisma?"

Lio felt Basir study him through the Union.

"We advise you to consider both possibilities," Basir said. "We are ourselves uncertain."

Kumeta's bitterness returned to the fore. "We must choose to stake either our own lives or those of twenty-four children on our uncertainty."

The Blood Union shivered with Aunt Lyta's anger. "Already Dalos puts us right back in the Last War."

"Rudhira would want a say in this," Kadi broke in. "He should take part in any conflict with the circle that took Methu. The Blood Errant may have disbanded after they lost Prometheus, but you know our prince still craves justice. He will hold any Aithourian accountable, though he and Nike and Uncle Apollon tracked down the war mages personally responsible for Methu's defeat."

At the mention of the infamous crusade, Lio tensed. He and Kadi watched Argyros flinch.

"No." The Union rang with the finality of Uncle Argyros's refusal. "We cannot afford for the prince to escalate the situation."

"Methu was Rudhira's Trial brother, and Nike their Trial sister," Kadi protested.

"Listen to your father," Aunt Lyta said. "Even if we could risk communication with the prince, we cannot risk exposing him. Think how he would react. He would give no thought to protecting the ruse under which he lives here in Tenebra."

"And he would regret it later," Kadi conceded, but her expression hardened. "We shall have to deliver justice on his behalf."

"I'm afraid I agree we should not attempt contact with the prince," Basir said. "Orthros Abroad is his domain, and we should by rights seek his sanction. But with an Aithourian just outside the fortress walls, we must not risk magic we once assumed was safe."

"We must act without our prince's counsel," Kumeta agreed.

Uncle Argyros spread his hands to indicate the seven of them. "Our Queens have empowered us as their ambassadors to use our judgment. It lies with us to determine if we should meet with the Prisma and how we will respond to Dalos's threats."

Lio must work harder to convince them of the truth. Goddess, let him not lose the ground he had gained. He had told them all he knew, and still they feared a trap awaited them in Kyria's Grove. What else could Lio say, short of exposing Cassia as the mediator who had negotiated his truce with the Prisma? Cassia, ever wary, had judged this worth the risk.

I tasted the truth in her blood. We can rely on her plan.

That, Lio's most powerful proof, was the one his people would not accept. Cassia was his revelation. They would dismiss her as his youthful folly.

What an irony. The Hesperines would see a human as a deceiver who had seduced one of their innocents for her own ends. Mortals were not the only ones blinded by their mistrust.

"We have a quarter of an hour before the Summit." Uncle Argyros exchanged another long look with his Grace.

Aunt Lyta nodded once.

He took her hand. "We have reached our decision. Lyta and I will not return to Orthros with the weight of even one child's uncertain fate upon our hearts."

Aunt Lyta's posture had shifted, perhaps instinctively. She stood poised in a battle stance. "We have faced far greater dangers than a Kyrian mage. Argyros and I shall retrieve the children, whether the Prisma has laid a trap or not."

"The children are orphans and fugitives." Basir sighed. "We are doubly within our rights to take them."

"A point to bear in mind, my friend," Uncle Argyros answered. "Though the Oath still lies broken, our tenets endure."

Kadi stepped forward. "What is your plan of action, Mother?"

"The embassy will take shelter at Rota Overlook, the Sanctuary I showed everyone on our way here. I had hoped we would not need to resort to one of our safe havens, but Rota is among the oldest, and its Sanctuary ward has never failed us. This will not be the first time it has harbored Hesperines on the run from an Aithourian. There we'll divide into two parties. I will lead one to the Grove, while the other waits hidden at Rota."

"What of Dalos's assassination plot?" Lio asked. "How will we respond?"

"We will weave a veil to hide our departure," Uncle Argyros said. "Even if Dalos searches for us when we fail to appear at the Summit, we can trust the Sanctuary to conceal us until midnight, when we meet with the Prisma."

Lio had achieved one victory of persuasion. Now he must win one more. "What if we leave, and Dalos assassinates the Summit anyway?"

Again he found himself the object of all their gazes. The force of their Union, concentrated on him, made the hair at his nape stand on end.

"If we are not there," Kumeta said, "Dalos will have no one to blame for his crime and thus be unable to go through with it. Removing ourselves from the situation is the solution."

It was a shame Lio could not tell Kumeta about Cassia. The two of them might actually see eye-to-eye. "What if he claims we appeared and murdered everyone? No one will survive to bear witness that we never arrived. He can say anything he wishes about what transpired under the cover of his mage ward. We will not be here to gainsay him, and a great many will be dead."

And one of the mage's victims—Goddess, please no—might be Cassia.

Lio prayed the others would agree with him. The truth was, when he went to the Summit, he did not want to go alone.

"Only our power can shield everyone from Dalos's assault," Lio said. "A single Aithourian is no match for one of us, much less the entire embassy."

"Temper your overconfidence, youngblood," Kumeta told him.

"Dalos underestimates us," Lio replied. "He dismisses you and Basir as messengers! A testament that you will always have the better of the Aithourian Circle. Seven hundred years and counting, and your identities remain a mystery to the war mages. They still have no idea the envoy service is our people's web of observers and saboteurs. He is not prepared to face the Queens' Master Envoys, the spymasters of Orthros."

"We do not have an accurate assessment of his power," Basir argued, "and he has spent the entire Summit preparing his spell. His working may well have become something greater than himself."

"Something greater than the Guardian of Orthros?" Lio asked. "Greater than Elder Firstblood Argyros? Greater than Master Steward Arkadia and her Grace? I think not."

"I would send Dalos the way of Aithouros," said Aunt Lyta, "if our Hesperines errant would not pay the cost when his circle comes for revenge. There is a time to stand and a time to stand down."

"What of the cost the Tenebrans will pay within the hour?" Lio asked. "Their king and their temples have betrayed them. Their heretics are their only protectors tonight. When Dalos releases his spell, we must be there to counter his attack."

Lio's elders did not answer. They were listening.

"Regardless of how it affects our relationship with Tenebra," Lio declared, "we must do everything we can to protect the people at the Summit, because it is the right thing to do." He should stop now, but he didn't. "And because Kadi has suffered in silence long enough, waiting to act on her sister's behalf. Javed knows making wounds, rather than mending them, is sometimes what saves lives. Basir and Kumeta have fought on with their thirst for justice unquenched for too long. You, Uncle, and you, Aunt Lyta, know that if Methu had lived, Nike would never have left us, and you still wonder if an Aithourian mage is the reason she has never come home. And as for myself…I want my chance at that war mage, and I want to see the king's plan crumble underneath him."

Lio wanted to behold Cassia in that moment of triumph.

The light in Uncle Argyros's eyes had become something Lio recognized. That was…yes, it was. Pride. "If your father were here, that's exactly what he would say to me."

For the first time that wretched night, Lio felt he had more than just his own strength of Will to carry him through. He felt hope. He began to feel he was not alone. "Uncle, I know you and Father are not always of one mind. But there was a time when you were. If the two of you had not stood together against the Orders during the Last War, none of us would be standing here tonight. It was you and Father who kept Hespera's surviving worshipers alive long enough for the Queens to gather the scattered flock and shepherd them to safety in Orthros."

"We did that so our children could live in an age when Hesperines do not make war. I taught you to be what our people need in this time—a diplomat."

"Do not imagine for a moment I love your teachings any less tonight than I ever have. Do not doubt my commitment to words over war. But think what else I have learned as your initiate. There is a time when we do everything right, and words still aren't enough."

Uncle Argyros went still, his face and aura at their most stoic. "I have considered it my responsibility as your mentor to confront you with challenging truths. Tonight you have subjected me to the same discomfort."

"Uncle," Lio began. But he had promised himself he would not back down, and he would not apologize, no matter what the cost. "If the Queens could be here tonight, how would they respond, if Apollon proposed he and his brother stay and fight an Aithourian war mage?"

"They would tell him he must not consider such a thing under any circumstances. Then they would send Apollon and me home to guard the children, and they would attend the Summit and see to the matter themselves."

Despite everything, Lio could not suppress a grin.

"We are charged with acting in their stead," Aunt Lyta declared.

Kadi faced her mother. "I want this chance to defend our people alongside you. I *need* this chance to act. Nike would want us to. For Methu."

Javed stood close at her side. "I would not stand by while Dalos brings suffering upon so many."

Uncle Argyros looked to the Master Envoys.

"We have worked from the shadows long enough." Kumeta held out her hand to Basir, her gaze daring him.

Slowly, Basir placed his hand upon hers. "Some risks are worth taking."

Aunt Lyta entwined her fingers with Uncle Argyros's. Whatever discussion ensued, whatever past battles they recalled to each other, it occurred only in the private Union they shared. There was so much of their history younger souls would never know.

At last Aunt Lyta spoke to Uncle Argyros aloud. "My heart would have died long ago, if you did not strive to calm the war to which it calls me."

"You know I love you, not in spite of your warrior's heart, but because of it." Uncle Argyros smiled.

Lio had never seen such an expression on his uncle's face. That smile was as fierce as a predator's.

"Do not look so eager, my Grace," Aunt Lyta said, but the same light blazed in her eyes. "We must set a good example for the young ones."

Uncle Argyros's smile broadened. "And so we shall. It has been too long since one of the Aithourian Circle accounted for his crimes."

TO THE GALLOWS

CASSIA COULD NOT HAVE let Lio touch her one more time. If she had, she would not have said no. She would be with him right now, instead of racing back across the grounds. Toward the Summit.

She could, at this very moment, be leaving for Orthros with Lio. She could be free.

She must get to the Summit on time. That was what mattered now. She had retrieved her blue-gray gown from its hiding place by the Changing Queen's fountain and now looked as she always did, as if nothing were amiss. She smelled not of flametongue or scent oils, but of Lio's cleaning spell.

Lio.

Everything was going according to plan. So far. Everything was going to proceed just as she had imagined.

Nothing would stop what was about to happen.

She focused on the logic she had laid out before Lio. She must give the king no opportunity to accuse the Hesperines of suborning his daughter. She must stay here, so she did not become the next justification for war. The best way to prove she had not been the one to forewarn the embassy of danger was to walk headfirst into that danger as if she had no idea what Dalos was about to do.

She must walk headfirst into whatever fate the king had chosen for her when she had not answered his summons. Her failure to appear had surely been the only sign he needed to be sure of his decision.

Cassia tried to comprehend the knowledge. She was going to die.

Vela Roth

Knight wove back and forth beside her, almost tangling with her legs. He whined with the agitation that overtook him when something was wrong that he didn't understand. She buried one hand in his ruff to steady them both. To keep herself on her feet and moving toward the Summit.

She didn't want to die.

Be safe in Orthros, while I stay here and fight.

She couldn't die now. Not when she'd just discovered the words she'd said to Lio were true.

She didn't want to die for anyone. She wanted to live. To her very roots, she wanted to live so she could *fight*.

Cassia kept walking out of the trees, onto the greensward. She fell into step with the crowd of people bound for the pavilion.

The Mage King's broken throne towered ahead of them.

She didn't want to survive to avoid the grave she feared, which had swallowed two queens, her mother, and Solia. Nor to keep breathing within the walls of her silent rooms for one more day, nor to rattle about the halls of another deserted royal keep, nor to weave one more tapestry so she was unobjectionable.

She wanted to fight. For them. For herself. For the day when she would look her father in the eye and she would not be afraid, because she knew she had won. She would see the fear in his eyes, because he knew he had lost.

Knight balked in Cassia's path, his hackles rising, and forced her to come to a stop. The lords walking in front of them turned wary eyes on him. Their gazes lingered on Cassia's tousled hair and wrinkled gown and became derisive.

Cassia resettled her grip on her hound's ruff. "*Dockk,* Knight."

He spun around and faced her, baring his teeth. Giving her warning. He would not let her walk into certain danger.

Watchful lords passed by all around them. She could not cry, not here and now.

She would not weep, whatever happened today. She only wept with Lio.

She buried her other hand in Knight's fur as well and knelt down to speak for him alone. "I know."

He let out a fierce growl.

"You deserve a better fate. I do not want to ask this of you. But...I need you with me. We have to go forward."

Cassia willed him to understand and obey, for this was in his nature. To lay down one's own life for those one loved.

She got to her feet and looked him in the eye and put all her Will into the command. "*Dockk,* Knight."

Knight marched to the pavilion at her side, his tail out behind him like a banner of triumph.

There was no chance to save herself. No cloak to bargain to Hypnos, no purse of baubles that would turn his gaze, no words of persuasion that would move him. The bargaining power was her life, and she had put it on the table.

She had done the right thing.

But she wished she could have done more.

If so much as a slip of rope would swing her way, she would grab onto it to keep herself from hanging and claw her way out of the king's noose. If there were any way she could live through this, she would realize the vision she had spoken of to Lio. She would fight, beginning now.

Cassia took one last look at the moons in the night sky before she stepped under the pavilion. Torches and bright martial banners swallowed her. As she took her seat, the king's gaze came to rest on her.

She did not turn away. She looked into his eyes. She didn't sweat, and her heart didn't pound.

Until seven graceful figures approached from the fortress, their robes gleaming in moonlight that outshone the torches.

FIRE AND LIGHT

THE MOONLIGHT LIO GATHERED under the pavilion cast Dalos's face in sharp relief. Even now there was nothing out of the ordinary in the mage's demeanor or magical aura. There was no sign at all the mage was preparing what would most likely be the greatest spell he ever cast.

The man was truly skilled. Frighteningly skilled, if Lio was honest with himself. He had confronted the Aithourian mage alone one night, not knowing what a threat stood before him, and he had lived. He knew he might not be so fortunate tonight.

Although he dared not look at her, Lio picked out Cassia's scent among the odors of the lords to remind himself why he had made this decision. Why he was willing to risk never making it home to Orthros.

In time, perhaps, his parents would come to understand.

"You know what I'm going to say," Uncle Argyros had told Lio just before they left the fortress.

"Of course," Lio answered. "And I know you'll also say it's no reflection on my abilities."

Uncle Argyros gripped Lio's shoulder. "I will rot in Cordium before I place one of our youngest on the front lines. I will never allow my failure of diplomacy to cost my initiate his life, nor will I return to Orthros to give my brother and Grace-sister the news I failed to protect my nephew. I insist you go to the Sanctuary immediately while the rest of us attend the Summit. When we, Goddess willing, rejoin you, you will remain there with those who are not going to meet the Prisma. Do this, if not for your own sake, then for your parents."

"I understand, Uncle. *When* we all make it back to Orthros together, I'll make sure Father and Mother know you tried to keep me out of danger. But you would have to rob me of my Will and have Aunt Lyta and Kadi chain me at the Sanctuary with one of their wards to keep me from your side."

"In that case, you are to remain within arm's reach of me at all times, and I relieve you from speaking before the Summit. I will stand in your stead."

"We mustn't change the program at this hour. Dalos might suspect we know something about what is to come."

Uncle Argyros's emotions disappeared behind an impenetrable veil. He gave Lio's shoulder a squeeze, then let him go.

Aunt Lyta took both of Lio's hands in hers. "You must do exactly as we have agreed, nothing less, nothing more."

"I have not come this far to make a misstep now." Lio would not fail his people, nor the humans whose lives depended on them.

He would never fail Cassia.

To Lio it seemed her anger filled the pavilion along with the attendees now taking their seats. No one sensed that fury but him, just as no one noticed the slow buildup of light under the canopy. But Lio let her anger at him sink into his veins. If he could have spared even a trace of his magic from his working, he would have found some way to communicate with her that he had not just destroyed everything she was trying to achieve. That she need not doubt him.

He didn't have to tell her, did he? By now, she knew.

He breathed their Union in, letting her fill him, brace him. His Gift welled within him, potent and ready, thanks to her blood and her fury. Amid all Cassia's anger and fear—for him, for herself—the one thing he did not sense was doubt. He felt what he had seen in her eyes the first night they'd made love.

Cassia, who trusted no one, trusted him.

He knew in that moment, whatever was about to happen, he would never regret it.

Lio was careful to keep the growth of the light subtle and steady. While the moons' power came to him, the Tenebrans saw what they expected to see. The moons were bright tonight, but their torches brighter, of course. The waxing Blood Moon tinged the Light Moon's silver with copper, and the mortals paid little mind to the celestial glow that was now stronger than their fires. Dalos appeared to pay the youngest Hesperine no mind at all.

The last free lord settled in his chair, and the Hesperines took their seats as if this were not the night the Summit would come to an abrupt and violent end. Lord Titus began his opening remarks without an inkling the mage on the dais behind him intended to silence him forever.

Lucis watched the proceedings like the spider he was, squatting on the throne at the center of his web, waiting for his prey to be delivered.

Dalos subjected them all to his bland smile.

Lio's mouth was dry. Running through him with his fear, there was also a new and strange exhilaration. Any moment now, he would face death. But he had the Gift to save him, and he would tap the Goddess's blood within him as he never had before. He would truly wield his own power.

The speeches had never been so excruciating or so meaningless. Lio kept his face blank as a veil and his power steady as the moons themselves while one, two, then three free lords raised their objections and issued demands.

Lord Tyran sat back down. To give the embassy the floor. Lio's heart hammered against his ribs. He shifted in his chair, preparing to rise.

Uncle Argyros's signal rippled through the Blood Union. One last check, one last encouragement. The way Lio braced himself made his own Gift shake inside him.

Lio stood.

Nothing came.

He eased into his remarks and began addressing Lord Tyran's points one by one. The waiting became worse.

The only mistake Dalos made was to watch Uncle Argyros. For Lio saw when a hint of satisfaction appeared in the mage's eyes.

Dalos swayed on his feet. Power erupted out of thin air where he stood. The mage's real aura. As soon as it manifested, his spell eclipsed it.

Was this what the sun looked like?

The golden, blinding flash slammed into Lio's light. But his people were already there, their magic bound up with his. They were on their feet, infusing all their protective power into the moonlight Lio had provided as material for their warding magic.

He felt them all. Basir and Kumeta's zeal. Javed's strength and Arkadia's valor. Argyros and Hippolyta's breathtaking, ancient power, anchored in him, made ferocious by her. Aunt Lyta was the ward's architect, Kadi its artist. They built it on the foundation of Uncle Argyros's magic, and Javed, Basir, and Kumeta lifted it high.

Lio was blind as an unborn child under the onslaught of fire, but he felt powerful as a firstblood. He could no longer feel his body. He had become his power, pure magic in the night, flowing with the others but distinct from them. One with all, but standing on his own.

How could they have doubted they were equal to the task?

Pain burned into Lio and reduced that thought to a cinder.

Was this what it felt like to gaze into the sun until it destroyed your eyes?

THE HERETIC AND THE BASTARD

THE SCREAM CASSIA HAD kept inside her for fourteen years tore out of her throat.

Flame roared down from the Mage King's throne. Every shred of light under the pavilion rose to meet the fire, and a translucent white barrier throbbed into being. The cascade of flame broke against the pale, ephemeral shield.

The free lords screamed with Cassia, letting out battle cries and shouts of alarm. There was no escape. Dalos's ward penned them like animals. Chairs crashed against one another, boots pounded in the grass, and the swish of steel echoed as swords leapt from their scabbards. But there was no enemy to fight. Heralds and retainers scrambled for refuge beneath the council table while the warriors staggered about with useless blades in hand and squinted into the clash of magics. Light was all that stood between them and the flame.

Cassia watched the anguish on Lio's face. Everything within her demanded she run to him. Part of her remembered she must do no more than look, but she could scarcely hear that voice. What held her in place was the certainty she must not distract him from his people's spell.

The Hesperines stood as still as always, their hands at their sides. Only their faces betrayed the magnitude of the power they channeled. They bared their fangs.

Was there nothing Cassia could do?

Even as she cursed that she must stand and watch, she felt it. Felt *him*.

Lio was all around her. She sensed him as surely as she might feel his arms around her body. She looked down at herself. Moonlight clung to her, a soft and glowing film over her skin, her clothes, her hair. The same light that marked the boundaries of the Hesperines' ward.

Did the lords not see it? The moonlight was a veil upon their heads and a mantle around their shoulders. The light was everywhere, even clinging to Knight's fur, which stood on end. But he bared his teeth at the throne, not the Hesperines.

They were so powerful. She had known, but now she saw.

Despite that impossible, horrific flame towering over them all, Cassia felt safe.

Until a second wave of fire erupted behind the first.

Tongues of blue shredded through orange as if cannibalizing the lesser fire. Sapphire flame licked at the Hesperines' shield and began to gnaw.

Cassia held onto her chair for support as she watched the wall of light creep toward the crowd.

She tore her gaze away and stared at the Hesperines. Two globes of light pulsed in Lio's hands, one liquid red, one blinding white. She could see his body trembling. Argyros stood at Hippolyta's back, his arms wrapped around her, holding her up. Her head had fallen back, and she held her hands out as if begging the moons themselves to come down to her aid.

Their shield retreated another measure.

But the light that cloaked every human in the pavilion only drew closer. That power...it was Lio, wasn't it? Part of him and all of his people who made the spell. Might Cassia find a way to reach them through that power, to help them?

It was a wild notion. She barely knew how magic worked. But she had seen Lio smear his blood—their blood—on an ancient stone, and she had touched the roses their offering had brought to life.

While the free lords fell helplessly into a fighting formation behind the ward, Cassia dropped to her knees between Knight and her chair. From her satchel, she drew her spade. She put her tool's sharp edge to her palm and laid open her own flesh where Lio had healed her.

The tremor threw her onto her hands and knees. A flash of white light blinded her, and tendrils of red coursed across her black vision. Her head filled with the smell of blood.

Through the burn of light and her own tears, a pair of jewel-blue eyes met hers. She could see in Lio's gaze that he was smiling.

Darkness fell.

His gaze broke from hers. Cassia heaved at the air and wrapped an arm around Knight by feel. She became aware of the blood trickling down her hand and the handle of her spade she still gripped in the other. Let the free lords think a wayward weapon had caught her palm in the confusion. Let them scoff at her for brandishing a gardening tool in the face of danger.

As the dark shapes around her manifested, she realized the blood on her spade didn't matter, for the free lords weren't looking at her. They surveyed the scene upon the dais.

Cassia stumbled to her feet and went closer, blinking at the backs of the crowd. Now that the mage ward around the pavilion was gone, gasps and outcries echoed across the greensward. Together she and Knight pushed their way through the onlookers. The lords moved away from her sharp shoulder and Knight's snapping jaws until the two of them found a spot where they could see.

Lucis had stepped down from his throne. He stood over a prone body in red-gold robes.

Dalos lay spreadeagled at the foot of the Mage King's chair, face down in the ivy that carpeted the dais.

Caelum sat frozen in his seat, his skin pale and sweaty as if he were about to vomit or faint. Dalos's apprentice was already on the ground. Only the uneven rise and fall of his back revealed he was alive.

Lord Hadrian mounted the dais. He paused to murmur to Caelum and grip the boy's shoulder. Then he knelt and reached for Dalos's neck as if to search for a pulse. But Lord Hadrian jerked his hand back.

Lucis lodged the toe of his bejeweled velvet shoe under Dalos and flipped the mage over.

Fear drained from Cassia as bile rose in her throat. Dalos was dead.

His body was untouched from the waist down. But where his heart had been…it could not be called a wound. Flame had hollowed him from his belly to his mouth and left a chasm of charred flesh and seeping fluid. As if he'd swallowed all the fire he'd conjured.

Cassia turned away, swallowing hard, and got out of the press of bodies for some air. She could look at Lio for a few more moments.

But he was no longer in sight. The free lords, dumbfounded, surrounded the empty seats at the table where the Hesperines had stood.

Lio was gone.

"Cassia."

She froze at the sound of his voice. Her imagination? Another whisper of magic?

She felt his hands frame her face. Not his moonlight, his real hands. She could see nothing, but he was there.

"You never cease to amaze me." Lio was definitely there. "I thought I wouldn't get one more taste of you, but then you shed your blood into our spell."

She stood still, not daring to move or speak, and shut her eyes. She breathed in his scent, feeling his body inches away from her, his palms on her cheeks, skin to skin. She willed him to feel in the Blood Union how she treasured this moment.

"Dalos didn't ward you like he warded the king and the prince," Lio said. "His spell might or might not have reached your chair."

She might have died. There was no way to know.

"But you're safe now." Lio's soft words reassured her. "Dalos's own spell rebounded on him. He'll never threaten you again."

She had lived. She had begged for a scrap of rope, and she had received Lio, who had severed the noose and carried her from the gallows.

No one had saved Cassia in such a long time. Deliverance was the most astonishing feeling. The only thing as good was knowing she had saved him, too.

Lio's breath was warm on her mouth. "The heretic and the bastard won."

His kiss was so light, so gentle. She would weep later when she remembered it. But not now, not when he was touching her. His hands caressed her, not gentle at all, but ardent.

Then he let her go.

She opened her eyes to see a crowd of mortals in the dark Tenebran night lit by smoking torches and the distant, but brighter light of the moons.

FOR ALL OF TIME

THE MOMENT LIO LANDED at the Sanctuary, six pairs of hands reached out to steady him.

"Those were the most frantic moments I've endured this century," Aunt Lyta snapped. "What would we have told your parents if you survived a battle with an Aithourian war mage, only for us to misplace you between one step and another?"

"You never lag behind when we travel." Kadi supported Lio's back with her arm.

Javed held Lio's shoulder. "He's also never used that much power at once before."

Let them ask their questions. He would endure any interrogation in exchange for that last stolen moment with Cassia.

Lio's elders hovered around him under the shelter of Rota Overlook. The bluff rose dark and sheer over their heads, cutting off the moonlight. But the light within his veins was still cold and forceful and sweet. His ears brought him a chaos of sounds, his nose inundated him with scent. He struggled to regain his self-control.

The Union invited Lio to share in their relief, to celebrate the realization that they had lived. The giddy power in his blood beckoned him toward euphoria. But his heart was too heavy to answer.

He had left all his rejoicing behind at Solorum. He felt no triumph. He would call nothing victory that he did not celebrate at Cassia's side.

"What a gift the Goddess delivered to us in our hour of need," Aunt Lyta declared. "I can't believe one of the mortals got a cut in the scuffle and provided fresh blood for our spell when we needed it most."

"The scent was female," Javed remarked. "There was only one woman in attendance tonight. The blood must have been Lady Cassia's."

Lio's whole body tensed. It hurt to hear her name.

"I wonder what the king's daughter would think if she knew she helped the heretics," Kadi mused. "She never seemed too happy to be at the Summit with us."

"Whatever her own thoughts on the matter," Uncle Argyros remarked, "it's a good thing for her neither she nor anyone else knows she aided us, however unwittingly."

Basir held Kumeta in the shelter of his arm. "Our success should never have hinged on an accident."

She leaned into him for support, or perhaps to support him. "Everything about Dalos and his working was unprecedented. I fail to see how we could not sense an aura as powerful as his and why it suddenly became perceptible to us only an instant before he cast his spell. And the spell itself…"

Basir tightened his arm around her. "We knew he had stored a great deal of power in the throne and the monument's own magic would feed his spell, but that second blast of fire was beyond belief. From what reserves could he have drawn *that?*"

"I have never felt a single mage layer a spell in that way." Aunt Lyta's mouth tightened. "If I hadn't known Dalos fought alone, I might have imagined ranks of mages behind that wall of fire."

"We need to report what we witnessed tonight to our scholars in Orthros," Kumeta said. "There are strange developments in the Aithourian Circle, and it will only become more dangerous for us not to understand them."

The Goddess did deliver gifts in the hour of need, sometimes through the words of another. What Basir and Kumeta said reminded Lio that Dalos was no longer a threat. They had not failed to counter the Aithourian's spell. They would take some of his arcane secrets home to strengthen their people, while the infamous mage's mission to Tenebra had ended with his life. The embassy had averted war.

For tonight. Just as Lio had said to Cassia, war would yet come. And what then?

They would all go back to Orthros, borne on the Gift. Before the night was through, Lio would be at home in the beloved halls of House Komnena. But not safe. None of them were truly safe anymore.

Although he had helped spare them tonight, he could not truly protect his people. That was beyond his power. All he could do was fight for them.

That was more than he could do for Cassia. She would fight alone.

All he could do for her was be a steward of her secrets. Her grief. Her memories. Their memories together... *Goddess.* That was one thing no one could ever take from him. Her blood ran in his body and pumped through his heart. He would carry her inside him for all of time.

Goddess, I don't want to think about all of time.

That great expanse ahead of him seemed vast and dark. Eternity no longer felt like the safe darkness he had known, but a strange void with no beacons in the sky.

THE TRUTH

THE KING TOOK THE course of action he always did, when matters spiraled out of hand. He tightened his fist.

He barked one order after another from the dais. Messengers set off in all directions. Retainers carried Dalos's body and the unconscious apprentice away toward the Sun Temple. Caelum's bodyguards escorted the prince back to the palace. Everyone else obeyed Lucis's command to remain under the pavilion, except those who strayed to its edge to vomit. It was not just the heralds who spilled their dinners, but hardened soldiers as well. Even Tenebra's fighting men seldom witnessed mutilation of the magical kind.

Cassia stood where she was and waited to see what the king's first move against her would be.

The problem with an iron fist, she observed, was that it could not hold words. By their very nature, words slipped through even the strongest grasp.

The words traveled in furious murmurs and stifled exclamations.

War mage. War mage. War mage.

"…bastard was a war mage from Cordium…"

"…so keen to smite the heretics he cared nothing for our lives!"

"Nay, he must have sensed the monsters brewing some spell. What else would prompt such an attack?"

"What prompts the foxhound to hunt fox?"

Cassia listened and watched. The king was watching as well. But everyone's lips kept moving.

"…Namenti betrayed us…or were they betrayed?"

At last came the hushed whisper she had awaited. She could not pinpoint who spoke the words, only that they first took to the air here on the edge of the pavilion, farthest from the throne.

"Did the king know?"

Did the king know? Did the king know?

Quelling looks grounded the whisper. But it fluttered inside Cassia's thoughts still, and she knew it would in others' as well.

A fist could hold no one's thoughts.

Could Lio still feel their Union? Wherever he was in this moment, could he feel through their pain what she felt now? Together they had not just won the battle. They had begun a war.

Hers to fight alone, now.

One of the king's guards appeared before Cassia. A footfall behind her told her another soldier stood at her back.

She turned a serene expression on each one in turn, her hand resting on Knight's head. Her hound stood at attention and angled his body so he could watch both threats.

Whatever came, they were ready.

"Lady Cassia," the guard before her said, "we will escort you to your chambers."

With her chin high, her back straight, she sailed out of the pavilion. The guards hastened to fall into step with her.

Her remote little rooms were waiting for her, and within them, Perita. "My lady!" She left off pacing before the fire and raced to Cassia's side to fuss with her tousled hair, muddy hem, and everything in between. She spared one scowl for the two guards who posted themselves inside the door. "Leave me to my work. You've got no orders to keep watch over my lady's bath."

One of them gave a snort, but they removed themselves to stand guard outside the door instead.

Perita shut it firmly behind them, then guided Cassia to the fireside and pulled off the rumpled gown. "Oh, my lady. All afternoon, the king's messengers demanding if you'd returned, and me putting them off..."

"*Thank you*, Perita. You are a wonder."

Perita fixed her gaze on the chair she was pulling up for Cassia. "Thank you, my lady."

"I'm sorry you had to suffer their harassment."

"That was hardly the worst of it, for when we saw—" Perita's voice trembled. "What was it, my lady? Like the Sun Temple fires laid siege to the pavilion. I didn't know if you—" She broke off.

Cassia took Perita's hands. "You will hear many stories in the days to come."

"Give *me* the truth, my lady. Those of us with any sense ought to know what really happened and tell the fools not to believe wild tales."

"You and Callen and I knew the truth first. Amachos was a war mage from Cordium."

"Was that *his* fire, my lady?"

"It was. The Summit was peaceful tonight when, out of nowhere, Amachos cast a terrible spell. He would have killed the embassy from Orthros—and every Tenebran who stood in his way. The Hesperines could have fled or defended only themselves, but they didn't. They stayed and risked their lives to confront Amachos and protect us from him. You should have seen their magic, Perita. I will never forget. Everyone who stood under the pavilion tonight owes the Hesperines their lives."

Keeping only the most dangerous secrets as her sole trust, Cassia started the spread of the truth, beginning with Perita.

LIO'S SOLACE

"BASIR, KUMETA, I ENTRUST our waiting party to you." At Aunt Lyta's words, the heady triumph hushed, and weary auras rose to alertness once more. "If we do not return by moonset, depart without us."

The Master Envoys released one another. They took positions on opposite sides of the Overlook, their backs to the ridge and their eyes on the forest.

"Mother—" Kadi began.

Aunt Lyta interrupted with a smile, though her grief threatened to drown the Union. "I can no longer reason with the thirst in you. I could not reason with Nike when it took hold of her. I would not listen to reason when I journeyed from one end of the Empire to the other to quench myself learning the arts of war."

Not a ripple of emotion escaped Uncle Argyros's veil. "I did not reason with her. I went with her. War can only quench thirst."

Javed took Kadi's hand in his, tracing the shape of her fist. "Are you sure?"

"If you are."

"We're sure." Javed wrapped an arm around her shoulders and pressed a kiss to her temple, where his braid hung.

Kadi turned to Aunt Lyta again. "For the first time since Nike left, I feel certain of what path I should take. Battling an Aithourian, I have seen our enemy's face. I see my rightful place between the fire and our people. In the Stand, at the border. I have always been where I belong."

Her father's veil slipped. Her mother's eyes widened.

"You're not going errant?" Aunt Lyta asked.

Kadi smiled. "Javed and I have changed our plans."

Javed nodded. "I had no intention of abandoning the children of Tenebra during an epidemic of frost fever, but I believe we will be taking my patients home with us tonight."

"I wish we could say the same for Nike." Kadi swallowed. "But she, too, knows where she belongs."

"Come with me to the Grove tonight. I need you in my party." Aunt Lyta touched a hand to her daughter's hair. "Every mother wishes her children remained sucklings forever. But if that were the case, you and I would never have the fun of fighting together."

Kadi grinned. "I think we made Nike proud."

"Yes." Aunt Lyta's voice thickened. "I can no longer deny I miss having one of my daughters at my side in the face of the enemy."

"Keep me at your right hand, Mother. And don't worry for me. No place is safer."

Uncle Argyros drew near and dropped a silent kiss on Kadi's hair.

Javed released Kadi. "I will come to the Grove to provide any immediate care the children need. Besides, I want a firsthand impression of the Kyrian healers."

He turned to his travel trunk and retrieved his healer's satchel. Lio realized the embassy's belongings were neatly stacked under the Overlook, his own trunk among them. He would not have to leave behind any of his mementos of Cassia.

Kumeta looked at Javed with a bemused smile. "In the instant we fled the scene of a war mage's demise, you thought of our belongings back in the fortress and stepped them along with us? That reminds me of someone I know."

Basir inventoried the trunks with a glance. "How resourceful of you, Javed. It is wise never to waste supplies, even under duress."

"I wasn't about to leave my medicines behind when taking a journey with two dozen children recently recovered from Frost Fever. Besides, it would be a crime to allow Grace-Father's coffee service to fall into the hands of Tenebran barbarians."

Uncle Argyros chuckled and patted Javed on the back.

Lio did not join Basir or Kumeta at their posts. "You already know my decision, Aunt Lyta."

Uncle Argyros sighed. "I cannot enforce my wishes upon any of you."

Basir turned slightly, looking back over his shoulder. "If Lio's trust is not misplaced…"

"He will be an asset," came Kumeta's voice from the other direction. "The exchange will go better with Lio as our mediator, since he has already established a truce with the Prisma."

Lio bowed to each of them and let the Union convey how deeply he valued their newfound confidence in him.

"Lio, directions, please," Aunt Lyta said.

It was easy for Lio to envision the location of Kyria's Grove. The challenge was keeping the rest of his thoughts from bleeding into the Union, which flowed strong and open between all seven of them after their collaboration on such a great working. Lio secured his veil about his memories of Cassia, and his Gift leapt to his aid more readily than ever. Her blood still empowered him. With the strength she had lent him guarding their secrets, he turned the Blood Union into a map for the others.

With their minds intertwined, Aunt Lyta issued the command. "We go."

They stepped into an empty and silent Grove. Oaks towered overhead, older than any trees Lio had seen in Tenebra, testament to the strength of the harvest goddess. His own Goddess's moonlight shone through the bare branches and filled the clearing the massive trunks guarded.

Lio and his fellow Hesperines positioned themselves in a strategic formation as Aunt Lyta instructed. When her power, along with Kadi's, began to saturate the moonlight all around them, Lio once more amplified the light.

"Don't overtire yourself," Aunt Lyta cautioned. "We may yet need you in reserve if all goes ill."

"I'll pace myself," Lio promised. The truth was, his power was nowhere near exhausted.

Uncle Argyros's magic was a watchful gaze that hung over all of them. Javed's power rose, reassuring as a healer's emblem, a sign of peace the Prisma could not mistake. Their show of power would tell her they were well-defended but meant no harm.

There came a hint of other magic in the night. In a moment, Lio recognized the power he had felt when he had visited the temple. A Kyrian warding spell, drawing nearer.

Javed was the first to cock his head, listening. A moment later, Lio heard it as well. Footsteps. Scent and Union revealed twenty-four little lights in the darkness that smelled of medicine and warm milk, herded along by six stronger lights fragrant with incense, all wrapped in a tight weaving of the Prisma's protective magic.

Lio felt his fellow Hesperines relax slightly, although they held their magical preparations steady. As the Kyrians' auras drew nearer, his people's admiration increased, reaffirming Lio's own. They felt the strength and honesty of the Prisma's magic.

Just after midnight, by the position of the stars, the Prisma appeared at the edge of the Grove. The younger mage at her side matched Cassia's description of Deutera. Although Lio couldn't see her face, he could sense her faithful, happy nature—and the deep wariness she felt in this moment. Behind her, four more veiled women waited with their young charges.

The children were delicate shadows under the trees, cast by the occasional wink of green light that revealed the presence of the Prisma's ward. Lio looked at their faces one by one and saw that some were trusting, some frightened, others just sleepy.

Deep and green as the Grove itself, the Prisma's magic trod ahead of her out of the trees, both welcoming and resistant to the Hesperines' power. She followed her spells and came forward into the clearing.

Halfway between the Hesperines and the trees, she halted, her face in shadow under her hood. It struck Lio as strange to stand here before the Prisma with his aunt and uncle, his cousin and her Grace. One of the secrets he had longed to tell them and fought so hard to keep had now come to light. The boundaries of his whole world had shifted since he'd come to Tenebra, and tonight he was no longer sure where those boundaries were.

"Prisma." Uncle Argyros bowed. "We cannot possibly express our gratitude for this unprecedented invitation."

The Prisma's hood turned to take in each of them. When she looked in Lio's direction, the motion of her head paused. Would the look he gave her be enough to convey reassurance…and the need for secrecy? If she mentioned Cassia's name, his efforts would be for nothing.

"Unprecedented indeed," the Prisma said. "Never in all my years of service to Kyria have I treated with Hespera's kind. But now it is Anthros who demands a blood sacrifice of me."

"Hespera does not ask for blood," Uncle Argyros said. "She seeks only to give it for others."

"Receiving her blood is a high price to pay for survival, even for those trading one heresy for another."

"I remember when neither the children's path nor my own was heresy," Uncle Argyros replied. "Eriphon was a pastoral god, the Herder of Demergos, as he was known. In those days, my brother was a mage of Demergos and I of Hespera. The Eriphites sometimes carried letters between us on their wanderings, as they traveled with their herds from one sacred grazing ground to another."

"I am not as old as dead gods," the Prisma returned, "but I am old enough to remember when I thought better of my brothers at Namenti. I believed they would take these children into the fold with a kind and guiding hand, not make them suffer for their parents' transgressions. It is they who have betrayed our gods tonight, not me."

"We are ready to aid all those who stand up in defense of the falsely accused. I do not believe for a moment Eriphon's cheerful goatherds ever descended into banditry and bloodlust. Surely their only crime was their refusal to give up their traditions. Everything else, they must have done in defense of their own lives and families."

"They would not obey the Anthrian command to give up their pilgrimages and settle in one place to worship in a temple. There's no hope for their cult now, but I held out hope for their children. Until it also became heresy to fulfill my goddess's command to give a home to orphans."

"I cannot imagine how you achieved the feat of their rescue, nor what would have become of them without your compassion."

"I won't betray the trust of those who brought word of them to me. Suffice it to say, their plight reached my ears. We found them living like animals in a cave with the corpse of their late caretaker. Age and the elements claimed her life while the other adults were away on a desperate search for provisions. Before it turned into a tomb, the cave was a refuge the Eriphites maintained for their young and elderly. I am convinced they would have come back to their children, if they still lived."

"Their sacrifice will not be in vain. Hespera has homes for these little ones."

"Tell me what you have in mind for my children, and I will tell you if Hespera may have them."

Lio felt the others' surprise and growing respect for the Prisma. She was bold indeed to not mince words with Hesperines who, her gods taught her, would not hesitate to destroy her.

Uncle Argyros gave a nod, almost another bow. "We have complete respect for your position and the hesitations you must have."

The Prisma's magic flared, and Lio knew she was testing them with more than her words. Aunt Lyta and Kadi's magic held steady. The three mages prowled about each other like mother bears.

Aunt Lyta offered the Prisma a close-lipped, reassuring smile. "We are not blessed with our own offspring as humans are. Every young life is sacred to us, to be nurtured and cherished above all else. Among our people, these children will never again know danger, deprivation, or loneliness. We will keep them out of harm's reach, no matter what may come between our kind and yours."

The Prisma's hood turned to Lio again. "Let the boy speak, for he has already proved himself to me."

Lio bowed deeply to her and, at Uncle Argyros's nod of agreement, came forward. "I am honored by your confidence in me, Prisma."

"My gardener is very suspicious by nature, but she vouched for you."

It was clear he and the Prisma were of one mind. They must leave Cassia's name out of this. "I appreciate the value of her good opinion of me and the risks she took to form it firsthand."

"You might have used her very ill when I sent her to you, but you treated her with greater care than her own kind have."

It was an unexpected balm to him, this one last chance to speak to another of Cassia. "She deserves her people's respect, and she has my people's gratitude."

"I have questions about your people. You grew up in Orthros, you said."

"I was born and raised there."

The mage's eyes narrowed, and she looked him up and down. Her magic probed his aura. He loosened his veil as a demonstration of goodwill.

Finally she gave a nod. "If what I see here is the future that awaits my children, I may rest easy. Answer me, boy, and do not think your nocturnal powers will conceal a lie from me. Has any Hesperine ever demanded blood from you?"

"No, Prisma. They have only given it to me."

He sensed her disgust, but she continued her questions. "Have they ever committed slaughter or sacrifices before your eyes?"

"Certainly not. I have only seen them save lives, and they taught me to do the same."

The venerable mage watched Lio's face, while her magic watched his heart. "Have they ever demanded you participate in orgiastic rituals?"

"No, Prisma, unless you consider a lady's consent to a private tryst with me to be such a ritual."

"Hmmph," was her only reply. "What of your living arrangements? Impervious to cold you may be, but children need a home."

"Orthros is a land of strong, beautiful houses built of stone. Our geo-magi bring warmth out of the ground to make our homes hospitable. We clothe our children in comfortable robes that are practical for play. Children perform no labor," he said firmly. "They devote their time to learning, so they may grow strong in both mind and body and discover their aptitudes."

She did not say whether these answers satisfied her. "What further sign of good faith do you have to offer me?"

Four elder auras waited behind Lio, listening, and before him, six powerful women. Twenty-two pairs of wide, confused eyes gazed at him from between the oaks. Two pairs stared into the middle distance, unfocused. Unseeing.

Lio swallowed and let his power take stock of the other children's condition. There was the boy with the scar on his cheek. He was younger even than Cassia's brother. He held a girl who appeared barely old enough to walk, a younger sister perhaps, for she had a mop of dusty-brown curls just like his. Her eyes were closed, and her head lolled on the boy's shoulder.

"I am no healer," Lio said, "but even I can sense how much stronger the children are now. You did not lose a single one."

"Yes, they all lived."

It was bitterness, not pride, that Lio heard in the Prisma's voice. The mage's grief rose to join his own.

"No one can stop the fever from leaving its mark," he said.

"We did all we could."

"May we show you how we will carry on your work? If you would permit us and my elders deem it wise, we could demonstrate how our healing can benefit the children. Perhaps this would assure you of our intentions."

"We would be more than happy, should the Prisma accept this proposal." Uncle Argyros turned to Javed.

The healer came forward and bowed. "Prisma. If you will allow me."

"You may examine them from where you stand."

"Thank you." Javed's magic reached for the children like a gentle, affectionate hand. They huddled closer together, but their alarm quieted. "Prisma, I stand amazed at your skill and dedication. The healing you and your mages have performed on these children astonishes me. I will personally see to it your labors were not in vain. The two boys who lost their sight to the fever will see again, and the girl who has not awoken will wake."

"They are not too far gone for your art?" the Prisma asked.

"No. Our ministrations will make their bodies whole again. We have another kind of healers as well who can tend the wounds in their minds."

"Do not spin fantastic tales to influence my decision," the Prisma warned. "The truth will serve you better. Food in hungry bellies does more to impress me than miracles."

"Allow me to show you. I will bring the girl out of her sleep here and now."

The Prisma hesitated while the stars moved inevitably across the sky. Whatever her lingering doubts, she must know she was running out of time and solutions. Dalos was no longer a threat, but the king knew the Prisma's secret. A word from him to Namenti, and the Tenebran mages of Anthros would descend upon the Temple of Kyria. When they came, there must be no children for them to find, only a model temple that proved Dalos wrong. At last the Prisma gestured to Deutera.

The other mage knelt by the boy with the scar and spoke softly to him. "This man is a healer, and he has offered to help your sister get well. Take her and go stand next to the Prisma."

Holding his sister close, the boy came forward with a scowl worthy of a mighty knight. A scrawny girl made to follow him, tugging two toddlers along with her. At the edge of the Grove, Deutera stopped her and held her back.

The boy stood tall, but didn't stray far from the Prisma's skirts. She rested a hand on his shoulder. "This young man and the young lady you see there with Deutera are the oldest among the children, ages ten and seven. The younger ones have been in their care since they lost their elders."

Javed knelt before the boy. As if by unspoken agreement, Kadi also drew near. The look the boy gave her was marginally less wary than the one he turned on Javed.

"My name is Javed, and this is my lady, Arkadia. We haven't any children of our own yet, but I get to spend time with many people your age because I'm a healer. The Prisma has told me I may help her treat your sister."

The boy glared at him in silence.

"I can see you take very good care of your sister." Javed smiled softly. "Would you please keep holding her while I work a healing spell?"

"What's wrong with her?" the boy demanded. "No one will tell me."

Javed looked at the Prisma. She hesitated, and then she nodded.

Javed lifted a hand, not fast enough to be startling, and caressed the girl's curly head. "Fever is very dangerous for anyone, but especially for someone as young as your sister. The fever grew so hot that it harmed her brain. Because of the damage, she can't wake up, and even if she did, she wouldn't be in her right mind."

The boy's tears spilled into the Blood Union, although his eyes were dry. "You can't really heal her," he accused.

"Certainly I can. I will awaken her this very night, and in time, I can help her be herself again."

By the time Javed finished speaking, the girl stirred in her brother's arms.

The boy gasped and looked at his sister. She lifted her head, blinking sleepy eyes, and wrapped her arms around his neck.

"It's going to be all right now," the boy told her.

The little girl blinked again in confusion, but she smiled at her brother.

"She recognizes you," Javed said. "All shall be well."

"I have seen enough." The Prisma's voice quavered.

As she and her mages brought the children into the clearing, Lio's resolve and the flow of his Gift and everything within him that had carried him this far drained out of him in a rush. He watched as the women took their leave of each child with encouraging words and gentle touches. The prayer to Kyria the Prisma said over the small band rose up into the trees and echoed in her magic.

As she turned to go, she halted before Lio. "Take good care of my children for me."

"You have my word." His breath hitched. "Take good care of your gardener. For me."

She looked at him from within her hood with knowing eyes. "You have done right by her. Unlike these children, she has a future here in Tenebra, and she is not alone."

Lio's last connection with Cassia retreated through the woods.

A silent call had gone out, and Basir and Kumeta had joined them. Even they were smiling. Lio watched Basir kneel before a little girl and compliment her on her rag doll, while Kumeta wiped a smudge of dried milk from the child's lip. Lio had never once heard the war-weary Master Envoys laugh until this moment, when they helped the other elders keep twenty-four small, exhausted humans on their feet a little longer.

Kadi and Javed lingered with the scarred boy and his sister. The two Graces shared a long look over the children's heads. Kadi's aura was aglow, Javed's full of longing. Lio suspected he saw before him his two newest cousins and the continuation of one of Orthros's founding bloodlines. Uncle Argyros and Aunt Lyta would finally have their grandchildren.

Dalos was dead, and the Hesperine embassy would escape with no fewer than twenty-four orphans for Orthros to welcome into Hespera's embrace. Even Basir and Kumeta's burden of grief lifted in the face of such a victory.

Lio stood waiting for a sense of triumph to visit him at last, but it did not come. He had felt it with Cassia after the battle. Now it was over.

Before he had left Orthros, following the rules had always been the right thing to do, and doing the right thing had always felt good.

Here in Tenebra, in order to do the right thing, he had broken every rule that mattered. He knew he had acted rightly. But he felt worse than he ever had in his life.

"You did well." Uncle Argyros's aura shone with approval.

Lio turned to his uncle. When he had envisioned the end of the embassy, he had longed to hear those words of praise. Tonight he certainly hadn't been sure his mentor would deem him worthy of them. Now he struggled to take comfort in them. "Thank you."

"Lio, do not be so downcast. It may still lie before you to account for your decisions before our Queens, but do not doubt they will rejoice at the outcome."

"I do not fear that reckoning."

"Then what could possibly trouble you?"

Lio had kept his own counsel so much that night, against his habit, that the truth came out of him. "I feel like I failed."

"Failed?" His uncle clasped his shoulders. "We came for a dead Oath, but we return home with these young lives instead. That is a finer success than I could have imagined."

"I cannot help thinking of who we can't save."

"Ah. In that case, there is nothing wrong with you."

Lio raised his brows.

"That is our way," Uncle Argyros said. "Deep down no Hesperine can escape the feeling that we must not rest until every soul in Tenebra lives under the Goddess's Eyes. There are no lost causes, but there are some causes only the Goddess herself can rescue. You must not dwell on the people beyond your reach. It took me centuries to learn this. Heed it now and spare yourself many years of burdens that are too heavy to bear. Blessings like these children are what keep us going. Think of them, not those we cannot save."

But Lio would think of her. He could not keep from it, and he refused to. He would never stop thinking of her.

Aunt Lyta asked a question, and Lio's uncle released him to walk over and rejoin her. Uncle Argyros's concern lingered where he had stood. Lio drifted after him, reaching within himself for the strength to help with the children. It would take patience and attention to put them at ease during the journey home. The embassy must travel all the way to Orthros in steps small enough for the children to tolerate. But as their combined power carried the little ones from Sanctuary to Sanctuary, there would be no war mage on their trail.

A night breeze slipped through the Grove and touched Lio's face. A scent broke through his numbness.

Tallow soap and betony.

He startled and looked around him, searching first the trees, then the clearing with all his senses.

He followed his nose through his people and the children, past Aunt Lyta and two toddlers.

Lio found himself before the seven-year-old girl. The child who had become her fellow orphans' only mother.

When Lio's shadow fell over her, she went very still. She looked up, up at him, her eyes wide. Her dress bore old stains, and her hair was full of snarls, but her skin was pink and clean. She smelled of fear and courage, tallow soap and dried flowers. A bundle over her shoulder smelled of bread and cheese the mages must have entrusted to her. Her little hands, now relieved of her younger charges, held fast to one of Cassia's betony charms.

Lio knelt down on the girl's eye level. "I know who you are. You have been very strong and taken good care of the other children. May I ask what your name is?"

She stared at him in silence.

"My name is Lio." He gestured to the fragrant token she held. "You have quite a treasure there. There's nothing better than a betony charm to keep you safe from bad dreams."

A look of determination came over the girl's face. "This is for the others. I don't have bad dreams."

"Really?"

She shook her head vehemently.

"Not a single bad dream, ever?" Lio moved his hand slowly and reached into his collar. He drew out Cassia's talisman. "I keep a charm just like yours, see? I have bad dreams all the time."

The child glanced from her charm to Lio's. "Do they frighten you?"

"Yes. Sometimes I feel very scared."

The girl's lip trembled. "Where are we going?"

"To my home in Orthros."

"Is it far?"

"It won't feel far. We will get there before dawn."

"Will the others have enough to eat?"

"Oh, yes. All of you will have everything you need."

She squared her shoulders. They shook. "Then I will let you take them there."

Lio tried not to smile. His teeth might yet frighten her. Instead, he extended a hand. She watched him reach toward her.

He closed his hand over her small, cold ones where she held the betony charm.

"It's all right," he said. "Hold on tight to me, and I will keep us safe all the way to Orthros."

"I'm not afraid."

"Of course not. I can see how brave you are. That's why I hope you'll hold my hand on the way. I'll feel braver with you next to me."

THE KING'S NOOSE

W HEN CASSIA OPENED HER door again, the guards stood
to attention. Their gazes traveled over her flawless hair, her
bronze court gown and clean slippers. She reminded herself
again to be freer with praise around Perita.

The guard who had scoffed at Cassia's companion spoke up, his tone
patronizing. "You'll be remaining in your rooms for the time being, my
lady. For your safety. Your entertainments in the garden and sport with
your hound must wait until His Majesty tells us the danger is past."

"I am going to see the king. I trust his solar is not on the list of dangerous, forbidden destinations?"

The guard frowned. "His Majesty has not sent for you, my lady."

"He sent for me this afternoon, and I was unable to attend him. I will
do so now."

The soldiers exchanged glances with each other.

The sarcastic guard muttered to his comrade, "Go hail the nearest of
the king's messengers and send him to ask if His Majesty wishes to see
Her Ladyship. Then get back here to your post."

Cassia subjected the subordinate guard to a glare and was satisfied to
see him halt in his tracks. "The king doesn't want superfluous messengers
going back and forth at a time like this. Do you have any appreciation for the
disastrous matters he attends to even now? He wants his orders obeyed, and
he issued the order for me to appear hours ago. You will take me to him."

It clearly took an effort, but the guard in command wiped the scowl
off his face and bowed. His subordinate jumped to follow suit.

It was they who had to struggle to keep up with Cassia on the way to the king's solar. Her steps didn't falter. Her heart pounded only with the force of her conviction.

The king's wing was in chaos. Everyone from free lords to messengers raced in and out. Lord Hadrian stood at the door of the solar, a bulwark against those swarming the main corridor and the guard room. He sent a great many interlopers back the way they had come and barked for those who'd been summoned to get inside.

A chill crept over Cassia, and the hair on her arms stood on end. An instant later, a black robe swept past her. A mage of Hypnos had come to perform the final rites for his fellow mage. Even Anthros's own must feel the touch of his brother, the god of death. Dalos's apprentice watched the black-robed mage pass by. The young man huddled in a niche against the opposite wall, observing the proceedings with his expressionless gaze.

Cassia found a bench in one of the niches and sat.

It was three hours before Lord Hadrian had the opportunity to tell her she might go back to her rooms, and she politely declined. It took still more hours after that before the furor died down into a manageable bustle. Night was receding from the windows high in the wall above when Lord Hadrian finally approached her again.

"Go ahead, Lady Cassia." His expression gave no indication of what awaited her.

The solar was still crowded. There was no room for Cassia to kneel, with so many people going back and forth, she reasoned.

She gave the king a curtsy and remained on her feet.

One by one, he dismissed the others in the room with a glance or a flick of his hand. But it was too late. She still would not kneel.

He got to his feet on the other side of the desk. Braced his hands on it. Leaned forward. "What is the meaning of this interruption?"

"You summoned me, Your Majesty."

"I summoned you this afternoon, and you failed to appear."

"Yes, Your Majesty."

"What do you have to say for yourself?"

"My handmaiden has conveyed my excuses to you. Knight and I were on the move all day to fulfill his exercise regimen. It would have been a challenge for any messenger to keep up with us."

He leaned closer. He stared into her eyes. The monster that had loomed over her all her life crept nearer.

He was so predictable.

Here he was, reusing the same strategies, falling back on the same tactics. Next he would turn her into target practice and spout insults to vent his frustration over all he had lost today.

She did not look away. And something in the familiar vision before her changed. In his dead blue eyes, she saw a flicker of surprise.

"How dare you," he spat.

"I beg your pardon, Your Majesty?"

What would he do now? Command her to lower her gaze? Bring his guards in and push her to her knees?

He would not keep her down.

She was ready with a retort for any accusation of treason he launched at her. She had Perita and Callen and even Lord and Lady Hadrian to vouch for her.

She would find a way out of this, and she would live to walk through fire again to take up her vigil in Solia's armor.

Do what you will, she told him silently.

He began to chastise her. Not even in his icy, controlled tone of anger. He shouted in her face.

The words blustered around her. Disobedient. Bastard. Mine. More powerful words had already taken root inside her, and the king's insults found no ground.

Finally his tirade abated, and he leaned on the desk. She could hear him panting. "Get out."

"You have yet to tell me why you summoned me, Your Majesty." He had yet to say whether he had wanted her to live or die this day. What he still intended.

"I am your king. Do not question me. See to it that girl of yours keeps your court gowns in good repair. The seamstress will measure you for another tomorrow. When Lord Titus's son arrives at Solorum next month, you will dance with him."

"I shall look forward to a new gown." A small smile came to Cassia's mouth. "I think I should like a red one this time."

She did not give the king the opportunity to repeat his dismissal. She backed away, observing his figure hunched over the desk. When she emerged into the corridor and turned around, she found early morning light flooding down from the windows.

Lio's day had just ended. He might lay sleeping in his own bed. She must not think of how far, far away Orthros was from Tenebra. She must begin her day.

Cassia could accomplish great things with nothing more than a damaged cloak, and she could draw very informative conclusions from a new dress. A traitor slated for execution did not need another court gown. What Lucis had intended her fate to be at the Summit, she did not know. But his plan for her now was clear. She would be staying with the court for some time. He thought the game would continue as it always had, with suitors to be strung along and her to be bartered about, or brought down on her knees before him when he needed to remind himself he was king.

How wrong he was. Nothing would ever be the same.

SPRING EQUINOX

LAST CALL

LIO CLENCHED HIS HANDS. The sample of crimson glass before him fractured.

His stomach was the source of the fire. From his hollow belly, the heat raged through his limbs and seared upward out of his throat, parching his mouth. He felt as if he had swallowed Dalos's spell.

The curse eating Lio from the inside out would not be so swift.

He raked his gaze over the half-finished sketches of roses that covered his worktable. Through the broken shards of red, not red enough for their roses, he saw distorted images of his insufficient drawings. Somehow he had thought he could cut out his pain in glass, heal their parting as he pieced together a tribute to her. He had imagined that somewhere in this chaos, he could craft himself some peace. But his symptoms gave him none.

On his first night without Cassia, his misery had been easy enough to explain. Their parting was a fresh wound, and suddenly returning to a diet of deer blood after he had been feasting with her would naturally leave him miserable.

By the fourth night here at home, his emotional and physical distress had appalled him. Frustration unlike anything he had ever known took hold of him, and he directed it at himself. How could he let his pining and hunger reduce him to this? He admonished himself he must be stronger for his people, his family—for Cassia. Leaving her behind was what she needed him to do.

But by the eighth night, the agony was more than anyone could be expected to bear.

Denial had become his most powerful ally, his only protection against the truth. Tonight it threatened to desert him.

He could scarcely believe this was the Spring Equinox. The fortnight he and Cassia had once hoped to spend in each other's arms had dragged by at the pace of years, each hour more excruciating than the last. He had learned to long for the Dawn Slumber as much as he dreaded it. Sleep brought relief and dreams of her. But then he must awaken from them. When the sun set, he must return to reality—his hunger.

He stared down at his hands. The shadows they cast across papers and glass trembled. He braced his palms flat on the worktable, trying to hold himself upright.

His bastion of reason was crumbling. Over a millennium of Hesperine philosophy and research offered only one answer. The very one he had done everything within his power to ignore, deny, and explain away. But the verdict was clear. There was no other possible cause for what he was experiencing.

This was the Craving.

In the silent moonlit sanctuary of his chambers, Lio went still and heaved a breath.

Cassia was his Grace.

Fear engulfed him, a second gnawing agony. Sudden, astonishing joy beat it back down. Frozen and wordless, he sat with the truth for a while.

He had found his Grace. Of all the people he had known and ever would know, this was the person to whom the Goddess had matched him.

Cassia. She was the one. The only one.

This mortal he had known for barely a season. This person he knew better than anyone, wanted more than anyone. It seemed beyond belief, a wondrous surprise, a fresh, strange reality. It seemed right, as if it had always been so, like the paths of the moons in the sky.

It had all been real. Everything he and Cassia had felt. How much they had wanted.

The floor tilted beneath Lio, and his stomach rose in his throat. A splitting pain in his head answered. As he scrambled to find a grip on the edge of the worktable, scraps of paper scattered, and panes of glass hummed.

He knew now there was no way to heal this. Except one.

How much time did he have to find a way to Cassia before it was too late?

The answer lay within him. The collective experience of his people could only tell him each Grace was different. Lio's own hunger was his calendar, his strength of Will his only recourse.

Until he had Cassia's blood again. Cassia. Lio's Grace—and the only obstacle between King Lucis and the Next War.

How could the Goddess have chosen this for them?

Cassia didn't know. He had left her in Tenebra without a hope or a promise, without any real declaration of his feelings for her. He had bedded her for four nights and then left her. That was all. How could he?

It was too late. There was no way to make it right now.

Two of the most ancient mages in the world, the most powerful Hesperines in existence, had closed the border between Orthros and Tenebra. Lio and his Grace were on opposite sides.

He was too near vomiting to cry out and shivering too hard to slam a fist onto the table. His frustration erupted out of him in a blast of magic.

Every pane of glass in his workshop shattered. An aurora of slivers hovered in the air around him, whining, then fluttered to the stone floor with a chorus of tiny chimes. His outburst of power echoed back at him within the confines of the veil that covered his empty residence.

In the following silence, he sensed the first whisper of the Queens' spell. The appointed hour had arrived. It was midnight, and they were making the Last Call.

The most powerful magic in Lio's world rose like a tide. Ancient and fresh, brilliant and dark, the Queens' power sang into the night, and no Hesperine could listen unmoved.

From here to Cordium, all of Orthros Abroad would know. It was time to come home. The Queens never resorted to the Last Call unless cataclysm threatened. After tonight, wherever they were and however long they had been away, all Hesperines errant would understand the consequences of the Summit.

The Queens had closed the borders. No one could enter Orthros except in answer to their summons. And once you came back, you could not leave again.

Lio was trapped here, and the Last Call would not bring Cassia home to him. Even if the summons were for her…would it matter? He had tried to sway her with an invitation of his own, and she had refused.

Where was she at this moment? Goddess, was she safe? She who set herself against the most dangerous man of her time.

Did she feel Lio's absence? As a human, she could not experience the Craving. But surely she felt their parting in her own way. She must. She was his Grace. *He* was *her* Grace.

What would she say to him tonight, if he could ask her again to leave Tenebra forever to remain at his side? Would her answer be different?

No panes rattled, no stone groaned, but the force of the Queens' spell built pressure against Lio's ears and made his heart pound anew. His own Gift leapt within him in answer to theirs.

Under any other circumstances, it would have fascinated him to experience the only Last Call the Queens had made in his lifetime. In the face of danger, he would have relied on his family for strength. He would have found solace in assisting with preparations for their imminent migration and looked forward to what the coming season in Orthros Notou would bring. Instead, he was locked away in his chambers under the cover of the most powerful veil he had yet woven.

He was out of time.

Within the hour, Orthros Boreou would be deserted. With the rest of his people, he would be on the other side of the world. Cassia would be out of his reach.

He had to do something. Anything. And he must do it now.

He scoffed aloud at himself. A heroic notion, but a useless one. What could he possibly do to communicate to her what she meant to him, much less repair his mistake of leaving her? There was no way he could go to her with the ward standing between them. All the power he possessed was not enough when set against a working of the Queens'.

Any spell of his would pale in comparison to theirs. In fact, his would go unnoticed altogether.

He truly wasn't thinking clearly, or it would have occurred to him before. The same laws of magic that had helped him and Cassia accomplish so much together in Tenebra were on their side now. Under the cover of the Queens' spell, Lio could attempt a working with no danger of implicating Cassia. Even mortal mages would feel the Last Call and tremble in their shoes at the power that came down from the north. Solorum's temples would be astir over the great wave of blood magic and never notice if another Hesperine's power reached into the palace and touched one particular lady.

Here in the final hour was Lio's opportunity. His only one. He must make it matter.

Lio swallowed again, fighting down nausea and the fear that he would fail. With each passing night, it became more difficult to accomplish routine tasks in his condition. He had no idea if he could manage an ambitious working. Even at his peak, causing his spell to manifest at a location on the other side of the Queens' closed ward would be a monumental undertaking. He had never attempted anything like this, especially without time to research and prepare.

It didn't matter how difficult it was. He had to try. No, he had to succeed. For Cassia.

They were Graced. They were each other's future. He must give her a sign of how important she was to him, a promise to hang onto.

He must make sure she knew. Their last night together had not been the end. It had to be true that this was only the beginning.

EQUINOX OATH

CASSIA WOKE WITH A gasp. The magic was an unseen flare of light, beckoning her to harbor. A siren call that filled her with such longing, she could not breathe for its beauty and her own pain. But it was also the tide of darkness, and it welled around her until she thought she would drown beneath it and never need air again, only the embrace of this spell.

Cassia stumbled out of bed and nearly tripped over Knight. He whined, then growled, then whined again, twining about her legs.

"*Hama.*" Cassia went to the window of the room that was now her bedchamber and threw open the shutters.

There was no light to be seen except the round moons above her. Blood and light, they were both full tonight, the Spring Equinox. Such an alignment had not occurred in many years, it was said. An ill omen, Tenebrans called it. But Cassia knew the Hesperines must be celebrating beneath the Goddess's open Eyes.

Could anyone else besides Cassia feel this swell of magic? Her gaze darted along the wall, two windows over. The shutters of Perita and Callen's new quarters stood closed. The newlyweds were apparently unconcerned.

The magic's embrace pulsed all around Cassia. The working wrapped closer, wondrous in its power.

Across the greensward, the windows of the Sun Temple lit with fire-light, although the spring observances had ended at dusk. The new royal mage must feel the disturbance. Every woman in the Temple of Kyria had sprung out of bed, Cassia was sure. Why was she the only one here in the palace who felt that clarion call?

"Cassia."

She clapped a hand over her mouth to keep from crying out and spun to face the direction of his voice. But there was no one in her bedchamber.

"Cassia," Lio said again. "Cassia."

Nothing could feel this beautiful but Hesperine magic. Only magic could carry his voice to her here in Tenebra.

She stumbled farther into her room. As she moved out of the way of the window, the light of the full moons spilled in behind her.

In their glow, she saw him. Lio, with his jewel-blue eyes and beautiful face, stood before her in his veil hours robe, which she had pulled off of him the night they first made love. An instant before she threw her arms around him, she realized she could see the other side of her room through the swirls of embroidery on his robe.

Disappointment halted her in her tracks. An illusion.

But *his* illusion.

Knight sat down at her feet and cocked his ears at the apparition. She put a hand in his fur.

"Cassia," Lio said a fourth time, his tone urgent. This time she saw his mouth move and his gaze on her. He looked stricken and joyful at the same time.

"Lio, can you see me? Hear me?"

"Listen," he said. "Please."

"Speak to me," she pleaded.

"Can you feel the Queens' summons? It is the Last Call, our warning bell in times of danger. Their spell will cover mine. I don't have much time."

The light in the room dimmed. A cloud passing over the moons. His image wavered.

"No," she cried. She stopped herself before she reached out a hand to what remained of the mirage. What if her touch banished him?

"The Queens closed the border the moment the embassy returned. Those who answer the Call can enter, but no one can leave. I am bound here in Orthros."

Cassia mouthed his name, listening.

"I should never have left you." The clouds must have moved again, for the Blood Moon's light hazed the room. Lio's apparition stood stark and ast in crimson. "By the Goddess's blood, I swear I will come back ɔr you. Trust me. I will find a way. I just need you to wait for me. Please."

She held her breath. If only he would give her more words.

"Cassia. I *need* you." The magic around her ebbed, and Lio's image began to fade. "Wait for me."

Silver moonlight flooded the room once more, twining with the tendrils of his unraveling illusion like veins of light.

"No!" Cassia burst out. "I will not wait for you. You think I would idle here in the palace walls in Tenebra and wait for you?" She took another step toward him, her fists at her sides. "Mark my words. I will not rest until I bring you to me. This I swear. I will make a way."

She stared at the illusion until he became nothing more than a ghostly impression with blue eyes, then merely a brighter gathering of moonlight. A moment later she was alone again with Knight and the moons themselves. The powerful working was over. Lio was gone.

She could not hold him. Not tonight. But the night would come when she fulfilled the vow she had made to herself each night since he had left, which she had now spoken aloud to him.

She *would* hold him again.

Cassia and Lio's story continues in
Blood Grace Book 2, *Blood Solace*.
Learn more at
vroth.co/solace

GLOSSARY

Abroad: Hesperine term for lands outside of Orthros where Hesperines errant roam, meaning Tenebra and Cordium. See also **Orthros Abroad**

Adrogan: Tenebran lord, one of Cassia's unwanted suitors. Attempting to court her, he gives her an expensive shearling cloak. She uses his gift in a scheme to secure a place for herself at court during the Hesperines' diplomatic visit.

affinity: the type of magic for which a person has an aptitude, such as light magic, warding, or healing.

Aithourian Circle: the war mages of the Order of Anthros, sworn enemies of the Hesperines, who have specialized spells for finding and destroying Hespera worshipers. Founded by Aithouros in ancient times, this circle was responsible for most of the destruction of Hespera's temples during the Last War.

Aithouros: fire mage of the Order of Anthros who personally led the persecution of Hespera worshipers during the Last War. Founder and namesake of the Aithourian Circle, who continue his teachings. Killed by Hippolyta.

Akesios: god of healing in the Tenebran and Cordian pantheon. The third scion, or third son, of Kyria and Anthros. A lesser deity alongside his brothers and sisters, the Twice-Seven Scions. Men with the affinity for healing magic become mages of Akesios.

Akron: the highest-ranking mage in the Order of Anthros, who holds the ultimate authority in the Order that dominates all other mages.

Akron's Altar: the altar in Corona upon which the Order of Anthros executes heretics by immolation, where many Hesperines have met their deaths.

Alea: one of the two Queens of Orthros, who has ruled the Hesperines for nearly sixteen hundred years with her Grace, Queen Soteira. A mage of Hespera in her mortal life, she is the only Prisma of a temple of Hespera who survived the Ordering.

Amachos: royal mage of Tenebra, recently selected by King Lucis to fill the vacant office after the death of the previous royal mage. A mage of Anthros with the rank of honored master who previously served at the influential Temple of Anthros at Namenti. Has a weak affinity for warding.

Anaklastia: the fourteenth scion, youngest daughter of Kyria and Anthros. A lesser deity alongside her brothers and sisters, the Twice-Seven Scions. In the Tenebran and Cordian pantheon, Anaklastia is considered the goddess of the moons, who fights to keep them from Hespera's unholy grasp.

Anaklastia's Mirrors: Tenebran and Cordian name for the two moons. Mortals believe them to be made of steel and that the white moon reflects Anthros's light, while the red moon shows the blood he spills. Their myths hold that the moons wane because Hespera seeks to wrestle the Mirrors from the grasp of the goddess Anaklastia.

Anthros: god of war, order, and fire. Supreme deity of the Tenebran and Cordian pantheon and ruler of summer. The sun is said to be Anthros riding his chariot across the sky. According to myth, he is the husband of Kyria and brother of Hypnos and Hespera.

Anthros's fire: a flower commonly grown in Tenebra, used by humans in combination with the herb sunsword to ward off Hesperines.

Anthros's Hall: Anthros's great hall beyond the mortal world. Tenebrans and Cordians believe that men who please the god of war in life are rewarded with an afterlife in his Hall with his company of eternal warriors.

Anthros's pyre: Anthros's eternal, holy flames, where he punishes those who displease him.

Apollon: Lio's father, an elder firstblood and founder of Orthros. An ancient Hesperine renowned for his powerful stone magic and prowess in battle, he once roamed Abroad as one of the Blood Errant. Now retired to live peacefully in Orthros with his Grace, Komnena. In his mortal life, before the Ordering, he was a mage of Demergos.

apostate: rogue mage who illegally practices magic outside of the Orders.

arcane path: Hesperine term for a magical field of study, such as war magic or blood magic. Known as a discipline of magic in the parlance of the Mage Orders.

Argyros: Lio's uncle and mentor in diplomacy and mind magic. Graced to Lyta, father of Nike, Kadi and Mak. An elder firstblood and founder of Orthros like Apollon, his brother by mortal birth. The Queens' Master Ambassador, who attended the first Equinox Summit and every one since. One of the most powerful thelemancers in history, known as Silvertongue for his legendary abilities as a negotiator. In his human life, he was a scholar in a Great Temple of Hespera.

Arkadia: Lio's cousin, daughter of Argyros and Lyta. With her mother's affinity for warding and aptitude for the battle arts, she serves as a Master Steward in Hippolyta's Stand. Joins the Hesperine embassy to Tenebra to ensure their safety during the Equinox Summit.

Aurelio: most famous minstrel in Tenebra and Cordium, whose songs are universally beloved.

Autumn Greeting: ancient courtship festival of Tenebra. When a woman shares this dance with a man, it is considered a promise of betrothal, after which their fathers will arrange their marriage.

avowal: Hesperine ceremony in which Graces profess their bond before their people; legally binding and an occasion of great celebration.

Basilarion: title of a prince of Tenebra.

Basileus: title of the King of Tenebra, appended to the name of every monarch who takes the throne.

Basilinna: title of a princess of Tenebra.

Basilis: title of a non-royal female relative of the king, outside of the line of succession.

Basir: Hesperine thelemancer and one of the two spymasters of Orthros, alongside his Grace, Kumeta. His official title is "Queens' Master Envoy" to conceal the nature of their work. They accompany the Hesperine embassy to the Equinox Summit to provide information that could assist with the negotiations.

Bellator: Tenebran free lord who was promised Solia's hand. When he realized the king did not intend to deliver, he kidnapped her and held her for ransom inside Castra Roborra before murdering her. Led the short-lived rebellion that ended there with the Siege of Sovereigns.

Biata: young Tenebran lady who is one of Lady Hadrian's followers and frequents her weaving room. Prone to gossiping.

Blood Errant: group of four ancient and powerful Hesperine warriors who went errant together for eight centuries: Apollon, Nike, Rudhira, and Methu. They performed legendary but controversial deeds in Hespera's name.

Blood Moon: Hesperine name for one of the two moons, which appears red with a liquid texture to the naked eye. Believed to be an eye of the Goddess Hespera, potent with her blood magic.

Blood Union: magical empathic connection that allows Hesperines to sense the emotions of any living thing that has blood.

bloodborn: Hesperine born with the Gift because their mother was transformed during pregnancy.

Caelum: Solia and Cassia's thirteen-year-old half-brother, only son of King Lucis, crown prince of Tenebra.

Callen: guard in Lord Hadrian's service, of common birth but exceptional honor and skill. Perita's lover.

Cassia: Tenebran lady, illegitimate daughter of King Lucis and his concubine, Thalia. Hates and fears her father, who regards her as a tool to be used in his schemes. Relies on her own cleverness to survive his ire and trusts no one but her liegehound, Knight. Remarkably, she does not share her countrymen's aversion for Hesperines.

Castra Roborra: fortress in Tenebra belonging to Lord Bellator, where he held Solia captive and ultimately murdered her. Site of the Siege of Sovereigns.

Changing Queen: ancient Queen of Tenebra who reigned during the Last War, the Mage King's wife and co-ruler. As a Silvicultrix, she was a powerful mage in her own right. Her name in Vulgus was Hedera, while her own people knew her as Ebah in an older language. Also known as the Hawk of the Lustra.

the Charge: the force of Hesperines errant that serve under the First Prince's command. See **Rudhira**

charm: physical object imbued with a mage's spell, usually crafted of botanicals or other materials with their own magical properties. Offers a mild beneficial effect to an area or the holder of the charm, even if that person is not a mage.

Chera: goddess of rain and spinning in the Tenebran and Cordian pantheon, known as the Mourning Goddess and the Widow. According to myth, she was the Bride of Spring before Anthros destroyed her god-husband, Demergos, for disobedience.

Cordium: land to the south of Tenebra where the Mage Orders hold sway. Its once-mighty principalities and city-states have now lost power to the magical and religious authorities. Wealthy and cultured, but prone to deadly politics. Also known as the Magelands.

Corona: capital city of Cordium and holy seat of the Mage Orders, where the main temples of each god are located, including the Hagion of Anthros.

Council of Free Lords: a body of Tenebran lords who have the hereditary authority to convey or revoke the nobility's mandate upon a reigning monarch. Their rights and privileges were established in the Free Charter.

the Craving: a Hesperine's addiction to their Grace's blood. When deprived of each other, Graces suffer agonizing withdrawal symptoms and fatal illness.

Dalia: young Tenebran lady who is one of Lady Hadrian's followers and frequents her weaving room.

Dalos: war mage from Cordium with an affinity for fire, one of the highest-ranking, most powerful in the Order of Anthros. Began his career as an apprentice to the Synthikos of the Aithourian Circle. Zealous about his circle's cause of destroying Hesperines.

Dawn Slumber: deep sleep Hesperines fall into when the sun rises. Although the sunlight causes them no harm, they're unable to awaken until nightfall, leaving them vulnerable during daylight hours.

Demergos: formerly the god of agriculture, now stricken from the Tenebran and Cordian pantheon. His worshipers were disbanded in ancient times when the mages of Anthros seized power. According to myth, he was the husband of Chera, but disobeyed Anthros and brought on his own death and her grief.

Desidia: the King of Tenebra's pleasure palace. Solia was traveling there when Lord Bellator and his fellow rebels waylaid and kidnapped her.

Deukalion Komnenos: Hesperine diplomat who journeys to Tenebra with the embassy during the Equinox Summit. An initiate Ambassador, he is young and inexperienced, but he is dedicated to the cause of peace and has a powerful dual affinity for thelemancy and light magic. Surprised by Cassia's tolerance, he risks violating the terms of the Summit to discover more about her.

Deutera: respected mage at the Temple of Kyria at Solorum, the Prisma's right hand and trusted confidant.

Divine City: see **Corona**

Divine Tongue: language spoken by Hesperines and mages, used for spells, rituals, and magical texts. The common tongue of Orthros, spoken freely by all Hesperines. In Tenebra and Cordium, the mages keep it a secret and disallow non-mages from learning it.

the Drink: when a Hesperine drinks blood from a human or animal; a non-sexual act, considered sacred, which should be carried out with respect for the donor. It's forbidden to take the Drink from an unwilling person. *Or Hesperine sacred tenet, the commitment to thriving without the death of other living things*

eastern Tenebrae: wilderness east of the settled regions of Tenebra, sparsely populated by homesteads under the leadership of hold lords. Officially under the king's rule, but prone to lawlessness. Hesperines roam freely here.

Ebah: see **Changing Queen**

elder firstbloods: the ancient Hesperine founders of Orthros. See **Argyros**

the Empire: vast and prosperous human lands located far to the west, across an ocean from Tenebra. Comprises many different languages and cultures united under the Empress. Allied with Orthros and welcoming to Hesperines, many of whom began their mortal lives as Imperial citizens. Maintains a strict policy of isolation toward Tenebra an Cordium to guard against the Mage Orders.

the Empress: the ruler of the Empire, admired by her citizens. The Imperial throne has passed down through the female line for many generations.

envoy: according to common knowledge, a messenger attached to the Hesperine diplomatic service. In fact, envoys are the Queens' spies who gather information from the mortal world to protect Orthros and Hesperines errant. See **Basir** and **Kumeta**

Equinox Oath: ancient treaty between Orthros and Tenebra, which prescribes the conduct of Hesperines errant and grants them protection from humans.

Equinox Summit: peace talks in which the Hesperines send ambassadors from Orthros to meet with the King of Tenebra and renew the Equinox Oath. Each mortal king is expected to convene it once upon his accession to the throne.

Eriphites: worshipers of Eriphon, branded heretics by the Order of Anthros and seen as wild bandits by Tenebrans. The temples have struggled for hundreds of years to suppress their cult.

Eriphon: lesser deity, pastoral god known as the Herder of Demergos, whose worship was also banned during the Ordering.

errant: a Hesperine who has left Orthros to travel through Tenebra doing good deeds for mortals.

Eudokia: Hesperine youngblood, one of Lio's Trial sisters in Orthros. An initiate mathematician, calligrapher, and accomplished scholar.

Evandrus: Tenebran free lord who assisted Lord Bellator in Solia's kidnapping and joined forces with him inside Castra Roborra during their rebellion.

the Feast: Hesperine term for drinking blood while making love.

Ferus: a Tenebran free lord, the most threatening of Cassia's unwanted suitors.

Feuds of Regnum: period of Tenebran history when the Council of Free Lords failed to agree on who should be king. The ensuing civil war between feuding nobles caused widespread destruction and suffering.

First Prince: see **Rudhira**

flametongue: rare herb whose oil can be used to fireproof armor or clothing against mundane flame. Offers no protection against magefire, but still prized by the few royals and nobles who can afford it. The Order of Anthros forbids anyone but their mages to grow and prepare it.

Flavian: young Tenebran lord, son of Free Lord Titus and heir to Segetia's seat on the Council. Despite his family's feud with Hadria, he is admired by women on both sides of the conflict as a paragon of manhood.

Font of the Changing Queen: stone fountain on the grounds of Solorum Palace that dates from the time of the Changing Queen. This historical monument is a subject of legends, which say it ran with blood the day the Mage King died.

Free Charter: founding document of the kingdom of Tenebra, an agreement between the Mage King and the lords regarding the rights and privileges of the nobility. Grants the free lords influence over the royal succession.

free lord: the highest noble rank in Tenebra. Has a seat on the Council of Free Lords and the heredity authority to vote on whether a king should receive the nobility's mandate.

frost fever: contagious illness that is dangerous for adults but especially deadly to children. Tenebra suffers periodic epidemics of frost fever due to poor sanitation and nutrition.

geomagical warming plate: a magical device created by a Hesperine with an affinity for geological forces; emanates heat and can be used for brewing coffee.

the Gift: see **Hespera's Gift**

Gifter: the Hesperine who transforms another, conveying Hespera's Gift to the new immortal. For Hesperines transformed as children, their Gifters are their parents. For adults, their Gifter remains a lifelong mentor and usually becomes their Ritual parent.

glyph: sacred symbol of a deity. Each god or goddess in the pantheon has a unique glyph. Often used as a pattern in spell casting or carved on shrines and temples.

the Goddess's Eyes: the two moons, the red Blood Moon and the white Light Moon; associated with Hespera and regarded as her gaze by Hesperines.

Grace: Hesperine sacred tenet, a magical bond between two Hesperine lovers. Frees them from the need for human blood and enables them to sustain each other, but comes at the cost of the Craving. A fated bond that happens when their love is true. It is believed every Hesperine has a Grace just waiting to be found. See **Craving**

Grace-family (Grace-son, Grace-father, Grace-sister, etc.): the family members of a Hesperine's Grace; compare with human in-laws.

Grace Union: the particularly powerful and intimate Blood Union between two Hesperines who are Graced; enables them to communicate telepathically and empathically.

Great Temple Epoch: the historical period when the Great Temples of every cult flourished across Tenebra and Cordium, and all mages cooperated. Came to a cataclysmic end due to the Ordering and the Last War.

Great Temples of Hespera: powerful, thriving temples where mages of Hespera worshiped and worked their magic in peace, before they were branded heretics. Razed during the Last War.

Guardian of Orthros: see **Hippolyta**

Hadria: domain of Free Lord Hadrian

Lady Hadrian: Lord Hadrian's wife, a mature lady above reproach in the court of Tenebra, admired for her graces and respected for her political acumen.

Lord Hadrian: one of the two most powerful free lords in Tenebra, who commands the fealty of many other free lords and lesser nobles. His family has been feuding with Segetia for generations. Known for his loyalty to the throne, but also for honor superior to the king's.

Hagion of Anthros: the most powerful and sacred temple of Anthros in Corona, where the Akron presides over the Order of Anthros.

Healing Sanctuary: infirmary in Orthros founded and run by Queen Soteira, where humans are given care and Hesperines are trained in the healing arts.

heart hunters: warbands of Tenebrans who hunt down Hesperines, regarded by their countrymen as protectors of humanity. They patrol the northern borders of Tenebra with packs of liegehounds, waiting to attack Hesperines who leave Orthros.

Hedera: see **Changing Queen**

Hedon: god of pleasure and chance in the Tenebran and Cordian pantheon, patron of sexual acts and gambling. Styled as the god of fertility and prosperity by the Order of Anthros in their attempts to promote morality. The Orders allow prostitution and gambling within the temples of Hedon, where they can control these activities.

Hespera: goddess of night cast from the Tenebran and Cordian pantheon. The Mage Orders have declared her worship heresy punishable by death. Hesperines keep her cult alive and continue to revere her as the goddess of the moons, Sanctuary and Mercy. Associated with roses, thorns, and fanged creatures. According to myth, she is the sister of Anthros and Hypnos.

Hespera's Gift: Hesperines' immortality and magical abilities, which they regard as a blessing from the goddess Hespera. The practice of offering the Gift to all is a Hesperine sacred tenet.

Hespera's Rose: the most sacred symbol of the Hesperines, a rose with five petals and five thorns representing Hespera's sacred tenets. Frequently embroidered on clothing or represented on stained glass windows. Based on real roses, which are the Goddess's sacred flower and beloved by Hesperines. The mages uproot them wherever they're found in Tenebra or Cordium and punish those who grow them for heresy.

Hesperine: a nocturnal immortal being with fangs who gains nourishment from drinking blood. Tenebrans and Cordians believe them to be monsters bent on humanity's destruction. In truth, they follow a strict moral code in the name of their goddess, Hespera, and wish only to ease humankind's suffering.

the Hilt: cliff in the eastern Tenebrae where mortals often expose unwanted infants as sacrifices to the gods. Hesperines stay secretly active in the area to rescue and Solace the children.

Hippolyta: Lio's aunt, Graced to Argyros, mother of Nike, Kadi and Mak. Greatest and most ancient Hesperine warrior, a founder of Orthros. Known as the Guardian of Orthros for her deeds during the Last War and for establishing the Stand. Always accompanies Argyros to the Equinox Summit.

Hippolyta's Stand: Orthros's standing army, founded by Hippolyta. Under her leadership, they patrol the border with Tenebra as Stewards of the Queens' ward. So few of the peaceful Hesperines take up the battle arts that Nike, Kadi, Mak and Lyros are the only Stewards.

hold lord: Tenebran lord who holds a homestead in the eastern Tenebrae.

House Komnena: Lio's family home in Orthros, seat of his bloodline, named for his mother. See also **Komnena**

the Hunger: a combination of sexual desire and the need for blood, which Hesperines experience with their lovers.

Hypnos: god of death and dreams in the Tenebran and Cordian pantheon. Winter is considered his season. Humans unworthy of going to Anthros's Hall are believed to spend the afterlife in Hypnos's realm of the dead. According to myth, he is the brother of Anthros and Hespera.

initiate: Hesperine who has achieved initiate rank in their craft or service, more advanced than a student but not yet of full rank. Attained after the young Hesperine completes a significant crafting project or research treatise that meets with their mentor's approval.

Irene: mage in the Temple of Kyria at Solorum, sister of Lord Tyran. Looks down on anyone of lesser birth. Longs to be at court and feels bitter about her life in the temple.

Lady Iris: Solia's handmaiden and closest companion, who died with her at the Siege of Sovereigns.

Javed: Lio's Grace-cousin, avowed to Kadi. Has an affinity for healing and accompanies the Hesperine embassy to Tenebra to offer his expertise as a physician to the mortals.

Kadi: see **Arkadia**

Kia: see **Eudokia**

the King: see **Lucis**

Knight: Cassia's beloved liegehound. Solia gave him to Cassia as a puppy so she would have protection and companionship.

Komnena: Lio's mother, still rather young by Hesperines standards. Fled a life of squalor as a Tenebran farmwife and ran away to Orthros with Apollon, who Gifted her while she was pregnant and raised her son as his own. Now a respected mind healer.

krana: Hesperine term in the Divine Tongue for vagina.

Kumeta: Hesperine light mage and one of the two spymasters of Orthros, alongside her Grace, Basir. Her official title is "Queens' Master Envoy" to conceal the nature of their work. They accompany the Hesperine embassy to the Equinox Summit to provide information that could assist with the negotiations.

Kyria: goddess of weaving and the harvest in the Tenebran and Cordian pantheon, known as the Mother Goddess or the Wife. Her season is autumn. According to myth, she is married to Anthros.

Kyria's Grove: orchard of sacred oak trees under the care of the Temple of Kyria at Solorum, close to their boundary with the king's grounds.

Last Call: a powerful magical summons that the Queens of Orthros issue only in times of imminent danger. Calls all Hesperines errant home from Abroad to seek safety in Orthros behind the ward.

the Last War: the cataclysmic violence sparked by the Ordering sixteen hundred years ago. When the Order of Anthros sought to suppress all resistance to their authority, magical and armed conflict ravaged Tenebra and Cordium, destroying the civilization of the Great Temple Epoch. Peace came at the cost of the Hesperines' exile and the Order of Anthros's victory, while the Mage King secured his rule in Tenebra.

liegehound: war dogs bred and trained by Tenebrans to track, hunt, and slay Hesperines. Veil spells do not throw them off the scent, and they can leap high enough to pull a levitating Hesperine from the air. The only animals that do not trust Hesperines. They live longer than other canines and can withstand poison and disease.

life price: under the law of Tenebra, the fine a murderer is required to pay to their victim's kin or liege, in cases where they do not demand a life for a life. Scales based on the victim's rank. If the murderer cannot or will not pay, their kin or liege is responsible for the fine.

Light Moon: Hesperine name for one of the two moons, which appears white with a smooth texture. Believed to be an eye of the Goddess Hespera, shining with her light.

Lio: see **Deukalion Komnenos**

lithomagus: a mage with an affinity for stone. Can manipulate stone with magic for architectural, agricultural, or battle purposes.

Lucis: current King of Tenebra, who reigns with ruthlessness and brutality. Born a lord, he secured the crown by might and political schemes, and he upholds his authority by any means necessary. Cassia often bears the brunt of his cruelty.

Lustra magic: Tenebran name referring to old nature magic. Practiced in ancient times by the Changing Queen. The Orders have never been able to understand or control it, and most knowledge of it is now lost.

Lysandros *or* Lyros: Lio's Trial brother and Grace-cousin, avowed to Mak. Also a warder and warrior serving in the Stand.

Lyta: see **Hippolyta**

Mage King: Tenebra's most famous monarch who ruled sixteen hundred years ago, widely considered by Hesperines and mortals alike to have been a just ruler. He and his wife made the original Equinox Oath with the Queens of Orthros. A fire mage and warrior, he ruled before the Mage Orders mandated that men must choose between wielding spells or weapons.

Mage Orders: the magical and religious authorities in Cordium, which also dictate sacred law to Tenebran temples. Responsible for training and governing mages and punishing heretics.

Magelands: see **Cordium**

Mak: see **Telemakhos**

Mareus: one of the Tenebran free lords who participated in Lord Bellator's rebellion against King Lucis, present at Castra Roborra for Solia's murder.

Menodora: Hesperine youngblood, one of Lio's Trial sisters in Orthros. An initiate musician, admired vocalist, and crafter of musical instruments.

Mercy: Hesperine sacred tenet, the practice of caring for dead or dying humans

Methu: see **Prometheus**

Migration Night: event twice a year when Hesperines travel between hemispheres to avoid longer hours of daylight. The night after Spring Equinox, they vacate Orthros Boreou in the northern hemisphere and migrate to Orthros Notou in the southern hemisphere. The night before Autumn Equinox, they change residence again, leaving Orthros Notou and returning to Orthros Boreou.

mind healer: see **theramancer**

mind mage: see **thelemancer**

Mount Frigora: peak in the Umbral Mountains on Tenebra's northern border, location of the fortress holding their Summit Beacon

Mourning Goddess: see **Chera**

Namenti: Tenebran coastal city on the southern border, near Cordium

Natural Union: Hesperine term for sexual intercourse

newblood: Hesperine youth, no longer a suckling child but not yet an initiated youngblood

Night Call: magical summons a Hesperine elder can perform on a less powerful Hesperine to prematurely break them out of the Dawn Slumber.

Nike: Lio's cousin, a warder and warrior second only to her mother Lyta in strength, a thelemancer second only to her father Argyros in power. One of the Blood Errant alongside her uncle, Apollon, and her Trial brothers Rudhira and Methu. After the surviving Blood Errant's campaign to avenge Methu, she remained Abroad alone and has now been missing in action for over ninety years.

Nivalis: young Tenebran lady, one of Lady Hadrian's followers who frequents her weaving room. Daughter of Lord and Lady Galanthian. Her three younger siblings died in a past epidemic of frost fever.

Nodora: see **Menodora**

the Oath: see **Equinox Oath**

Order of Anthros: Mage Order dedicated to the god Anthros, which holds the ultimate religious and magical authority over all other Orders and temples. Bent on destroying Hesperines. War mages, light mages, and warders serve in this Order, as do agricultural and stone mages.

Order of Hypnos: Mage Order devoted to Hypnos, which holds authority over necromancers, mind mages, and illusionists. Oversees rites for the dead designed to prevent Hesperine grave robbing and illicit raising of the dead by rogue necromancers. The Order of Anthros's closest ally in their effort to destroy Hesperines.

the Ordering: historical event over sixteen hundred years ago, when the Order of Anthros came to prominence and enforced its doctrines upon all other cults, who had previously worshiped and practiced magic freely. New mandates forbade warriors from practicing magic and required all mages to enter temples and remain celibate. The war mages also branded all Hespera worshipers heretics and destroyed their temples. The Ordering caused the Last War and the end of the Great Temple Epoch.

the Orders: see **Mage Orders**

Orthros: homeland of the Hesperines, ruled by the Queens. The Mage Orders describe it as a horrific place where no human can survive, but in reality, it is a land of peace, prosperity, and culture. Located north of Tenebra.

Orthros Abroad: the population of Hesperines who are errant in Tenebra at any given time. Under the jurisdiction of the First Prince, who is the Queens' regent outside their ward.

Orthros Boreou: Hesperine homeland in the northern hemisphere, located north of and sharing a border with Tenebra.

Orthros Notou: Hesperine homeland in the southern hemisphere, near the Empire.

Perita: Cassia's handmaiden, tasked by the king to spy on her. Secretly having an affair with Callen.

Prince and Diplomat: board game and beloved Hesperine pastime; requires strategy and practice to master.

Prisma: highest ranking female mage in a temple

the Prisma of the Temple of Kyria at Solorum: powerful mage who leads the women of her temple with pragmatism and kindness.

Prismos: highest ranking male mage in a temple.

Prometheus: legendary Hesperine warrior and martyr. As a member of the Blood Errant, he was the close comrade of Nike, Rudhira, and Apollon during their travels Abroad. Captured by the Aithourian Circle before Lio's birth. Orthros still mourns his death.

the Queens: the Hesperine monarchs of Orthros. See **Alea** and **Soteira**

Queens' ward: the powerful Sanctuary ward cast by the Queens, which spans the borders of Orthros, protecting Hesperines from human threats.

Reman: one of the Tenebran free lords who participated in Lord Bellator's rebellion against King Lucis, present at Castra Roborra for Solia's murder.

rhabdos: Hesperine term in the Divine Tongue meaning penis.

rimelace: flowering herb that requires extremely cold conditions. Difficult to grow in Tenebra, even with the aid of magic, but thrives in Orthros. The only known treatment for frost fever.

Ritual: Hesperine sacred tenet. A ceremony in which Hesperines share blood, but in a broader sense, the whole of their religious beliefs.

Ritual Circle: area where Hesperines gather to perform Ritual, usually marked with sacred symbols on the floor.

Ritual parents: Hesperines who attend a new suckling's first Ritual or who give the Gift to a mortal who becomes a Hesperine as an adult. They remain mentors and trusted guides for eternity. Comparable to Tenebran temple parents.

Ritual Sanctuary: innermost chamber of a shrine or temple of Hespera, where sacred rituals were performed by mages.

Ritual separation: eight nights that Hesperine Graces must spend apart to demonstrate their Craving symptoms and prove their bond to their people; required before avowal.

Rota Overlook: a hidden Hesperine Sanctuary near Solorum, where an old, enduring Sanctuary ward offers protection to Hesperines traveling Abroad in hostile situations.

Rudhira: First Prince of the Hesperines, eldest son of the Queens of Orthros. Once a warrior in the Blood Errant, he now leads a force of Hesperines errant known as the Charge.

Sabina: Tenebran lady, eldest daughter of Lord and Lady Hadrian. With no brothers, she is the heir of Hadria and runs the estate while her parents are at court.

Sanctuary: Hesperine sacred tenet, the practice of offering refuge to anyone in need. *Or* Hesperine refuge in hostile territory, concealed and protected from humans by Sanctuary magic.

Scions: lesser deities in the Tenebran and Cordian pantheon, the fourteen children of Anthros and Kyria, comprising seven sons and seven daughters. Each has their own cult and mages.

Segetia: domain of Free Lord Titus

Severinus: Tenebran free lord with deeply held prejudices against Hesperines, who attends the Equinox Summit to undermine the embassy's efforts at peace.

Severitas: domain of Free Lord Severinus

share: human or immortal with whom a Hesperine is romantically involved, sharing blood and intimacy.

Siege of Sovereigns: King Lucis's assault on Castra Roborra after the murder of Solia. Ended the rebellion of the nobles who styled themselves the sovereign free lords and resulted in the death of every living thing in the fortress.

Silvertongue: see **Argyros**

Silvicultrix: in ancient times, a nature sorceress with command of Lustra magic. The Changing Queen was known to be a powerful Silvicultrix.

Slumber: see **Dawn Slumber**

Solace: Hesperine sacred tenet, the practice of rescuing and Gifting abandoned children.

Solia: late Princess of Tenebra, King Lucis's legitimate daughter and heir before the birth of his son. When she was seventeen, rebel lords kidnapped and murdered her. Beloved by nobles and commoners alike, who still mourn her.

Solorum: ancestral capital of Tenebra, royal seat of the king.

Solorum Fortress: castle built for the defense of the capital by seven successive kings over the course of two hundred years. The Hesperine embassy is lodged here during the Equinox Summit due to the humans' fears.

Solorum Palace: oldest palace in Tenebra, built by the Mage King, still the most important royal residence for the King of Tenebra.

Soteira: one of the two Queens of Orthros, who has ruled the Hesperines for nearly sixteen hundred years with her Grace, Alea. Originally from the Empire, she was a powerful mortal mage with an affinity for healing before leaving to found Orthros alongside Alea.

the Stand: see **Hippolyta's Stand**

stepping: innate Hesperine ability to teleport instantly from one place to another with little magical effort.

Steward: see **Hippolyta's Stand**

stinglily: plant that produces a severe skin rash on contact.

suckling: Hesperine child

Summit Beacon: bonfire on the border between Tenebra and Orthros, which the King of Tenebra lights to announce to the Hesperines he wishes to convene the Equinox Summit.

Sun Temple: see **Temple of Anthros at Solorum**

sunbound: mild Hesperine curse word.

sunsword: herb commonly grown in Tenebra, used by humans in combination with the flower Anthros's fire to ward off Hesperines.

Synthikos: the leader of a mage circle.

Synthikos of the Aithourian Circle: head of the elite war mages of the Order of Anthros, a position their founder Aithouros once held.

Telemakhos: Lio's cousin and best friend, son of Argyros and Lyta. A warrior by profession and warder by affinity, he serves in the Stand. He and his Grace, Lyros, are newly avowed.

temple day: the day a Tenebran or Cordian child is presented to the gods in a temple for the first time at fourteen days old. Celebrated every year for the rest of their lives.

Temple of Anthros at Namenti: one of the most powerful and influential temples in Tenebra, which uses its wealth and position in the city of Namenti to resist Cordian influence on Tenebran worship.

Temple of Anthros at Solorum: temple in Tenebra's capital, once an ancient site of outdoor Anthros worship that was later walled and roofed by kings. The temple of the royal mage, where the king and his court attend rites.

Temple of Kyria at Solorum: most influential and respected temple of Kyria in Tenebra, located near the royal palace. Houses orphans and provides healing services to the surrounding area. Due to their reputation and magical power, the women here enjoy a great degree of autonomy.

temple parents: friends or relatives who accompany a child's parents when the newborn is presented to the gods in the temple for the first time at fourteen days old. They remain advisors and surrogate parents for the rest of the child's life.

Tenebra: human kingdom south of Orthros and north of Cordium. Agrarian, feudal society ruled by a king, prone to instability due to rivalries between lords. Land of the Hesperines' origin, where they are now persecuted.

the Tenebrae: former name of Tenebra, a plural indicating the free lords' independent domains under the nominal rule of a king affirmed by the Council. King Lucis has since changed the name to Tenebra, singular, to symbolize how he has united the kingdom under his absolute power.

Thalia: Cassia's mother, King Lucis's concubine. Murdered the day Cassia was born by an apostate fire mage attempting to assassinate Lucis.

thelemancer: a mage with an affinity for thelemancy, or mind magic, which gives them the power to manipulate others' thoughts and control their Wills.

theramancer: a person with an affinity for theramancy, or mind healing, who can use magic to treat mental illness.

the Thirst: a Hesperine's need to drink blood, a non-sexual urge like a human's need to drink water or eat food.

Titus, Free Lord of Segetia: one of the two most powerful free lords in Tenebra, who commands the fealty of many other free lords and lesser nobles. Segetia has been feuding with Hadria for generations.

traversal: teleportation ability of human mages; requires a great expense of magic and usually leaves the mortal mage seriously ill.

Trial circle: age set of Hesperines who go through the Trial of Initiation together. They consider each other Trial sisters and brothers for the rest of their immortal lives. Although not related by birth or blood, they maintain strong bonds of loyalty and friendship for eternity.

Trial of Initiation *or* **Trial**: Hesperine rite of passage marking an immortal's transition into adulthood.

Twice-Seven Scions: see **Scions**

Tyran: young, ambitious free lord of Tenebra, loyal to Flavian and eager to stoke Segetia's feud with Hadria. Known for allowing and even enjoying his soldiers' misconduct toward commoners, especially women.

Umbral Mountains: mountain range spanning the border between Tenebra and Orthros.

Union: Hesperine sacred tenet, the principle of living with empathy and compassion for all. See also **Blood Union**

veil hours: Hesperine term for the time of night devoted to private hours with friends, family, or lovers.

veil hours robe: Hesperine garment worn during veil hours, only in the presence of those with whom a Hesperine has a close relationship.

veil spell: innate Hesperine ability to cast magical concealments that hide their presence and activities from humans or fellow immortals.

Verruc: guard in service to Lord Tyran known for picking fights with Lord Hadrian's men.

Vulgus *or* **the vulgar tongue**: common language of all non-mages in Tenebra and Cordium.

war mage: person with an affinity for fire, lightning, or other type of magic that can be weaponized. The Order of Anthros requires them to dedicate their lives to the Aithourian Circle.

warder: a mage with an affinity for warding, which gives them the power to create magical shields and protection spells that can block spells or physical attacks.

Will: free will, willpower. *Or* Hesperine sacred tenet, the principle of guarding the sanctity of each person's freedom of choice.

Xandra: Hesperine youngblood and initiate sericulturalist, Lio's former sweetheart in Orthros.

youngblood: young adult Hesperine who has recently reached their majority by passing the Trial of Initiation.

BLOOD SOLACE

BLOOD GRACE BOOK II

Will their Grace bond be his salvation or end his eternal life?

Lio is keeping a fatal secret. His Craving for Cassia has pushed him to the brink of death, but he can't tell anyone she's his Grace. If the Hesperines bring her to Orthros to save his life, they'll destroy the fragile peace in Tenebra she's fighting to protect.

Cassia's enemies are closing in. The king knows there's a Hesperine sympathizer at court, and the war mages are bent on unmasking her. When her father's political game forces her into a betrothal, will an arranged marriage be his weapon of choice for her murder?

Discover how fated mates Lio and Cassia reunite in this steamy romance. Lose yourself in their fantasy world and root for their forbidden love all the way to their guaranteed series HEA.

Learn more:
vroth.co/solace

BLOOD RUSE

A BLOOD ERRANT *Adventure*

Saving damsels is all in a night's work for these four chivalrous Hesperines. Too bad the gutsy women believe they're the enemy.

The Blood Errant are famous heroes. Or infamous monsters, depending on who you ask. When they set out to save a roadside inn from bandits, they can't show their fangs to the charming locals.

In a daring trick, they pose as human guests with the help of Apollon's mortal lover. Alas, Methu cannot woo the vivacious innkeeper while impersonating a cleric. Or can he? Nike pretends to be a lady, but spars with a handsome soldier. Rudhira plays the role of holy knight even as the lovely barmaid stirs his forbidden desires.

If anyone sees through their disguises, their allies will be more dangerous than their enemies.

In this romantic fantasy, join the Blood Errant on their past adventures in battle and misadventures in love.

Get this book for free when you
sign up for my newsletter!
vroth.co/ruse

ACKNOWLEDGEMENTS

SINCE I wrote the first words of Cassia and Lio's story over eight years ago, I've formed many bonds of gratitude that I'd like to honor now.

None of this would have been possible without my dad, who tells me, "This is your time. Be a writer." Words can't express how important you are to me.

Heartfelt thanks to everyone on the FaRo Authors' Discord server for professional advice and friendship. It's a joy to have found our writerly home in the "coven"!

Harriet, I'm so grateful you founded FaRoFeb and brought us all together. Colleen, thank you for first inviting me and for all your help since. Special thanks to Elsie, for boundless empathy and my beautiful logo; Steph, for being a badass carebear who champions these books; Lisette, for all your support, including the truly thoughtful hand-drawn map; Dani, for your invaluable feedback, energy, and enthusiasm; Erin, for such generous and insightful editing; Kristina and Jen, for bringing fresh eyes to the story; and Amber for knowledgeable input on my Inkarnate map.

To my reader team, I'm continually humbled by your support and friendship. Thank you for being Ambassadors for Orthros. I appreciate each of your contributions, whether reviews, beta reading, or shout outs on social. I love spending time with you via email or in the Ambassadors' group (especially if it involves chocolate cake recipes)!

Special thanks to these Ambassadors for your support during this project: Angela, Nadine, Kristen, Nancy, Tammy, Nat, Samantha, Kadie, Tia, Sharon, Melissa, Sherri, Alex, and Cheyenne.

Extra special thanks to Brittany for being not only an Ambassador, but my researcher, editor, and dear friend. You go above and beyond for me and my books every day.

Patricia, thank you for rescuing my covers when disaster struck and for bringing my characters to life so beautifully in your artwork.

Thank you to every reader who has written me to tell me my books matter. I never take you for granted.

Heartfelt thanks to you, the reader holding this book in your hands. You're the reason I keep writing.

Each and every one of you has my gratitude!

ABOUT THE AUTHOR

VELA ROTH grew up with female-driven fantasy books and classic epics, then grew into romance novels. She set out to write stories that blend the rich worlds of fantasy with the passion of romance.

She has pursued a career in academia, worked as a web designer and book formatter, and stayed home as a full-time caregiver for her loved ones with severe illnesses. Writing through her own grief and trauma, she created the Blood Grace series, which now offers comfort to readers around the world.

She lives in a solar-powered writer's garret in the Southwestern United States, finding inspiration in the mountains and growing roses in the desert. Her feline familiar is a rescue cat named Milly with a missing fang and a big heart.

Vela loves hearing from readers and hopes you'll visit her at velaroth.com.